OSTRACIZED

Olivia Majors

ISBN:

Printed in the United States of America

This book is dedicated to all those who believed in me from the start.
I love you guys.
This book wouldn't have been possible without you.

Ostracize

To exclude or banish (a person) from a particular group, society, etc.

PART ONE

Kelba

Chapter I

I follow my father down the winding streets of the capitol city of Kelba. We would have taken our carriage, but Father had not expected to be walking home after dusk so he neglected to bring it. Hugging my cape close around my shoulders to guard against the chilly breeze singing through the street I attempt to ignore the blinking eyes of the rats from the gutters and alleyways. My new boots make clip-clopping noises on the stone walk, echoing in the barren silence.

"Papa . . ."

"Hush, Kyla! I'm trying to think!" His outburst shatters the silence and freezes me in place.

Father is a well-tempered man, accustomed to hours of petty argument and rivalry in a court of High Lords like himself, and I rarely ever see him in such a foul mood. Especially at half-past midnight when he's usually relieved to be returning home. Unless he's had a strenuous fight. And the only one he's been in contact with over the last few hours has been Kelba's ruler, the Celectate.

A shiver tickles my spine. Fighting with the Celectate can be dangerous. Even I, at fourteen, know better than to argue with the man who rules Kelba and has been reported to deal harshly with those who oppose him.

"I'm sorry, Papa." I hurry to catch up with him. My toes ache badly, but I hesitate to question him about the distance home.

He keeps walking for a moment longer, suddenly turns around, and pulls me close into a comforting hug. Taken aback by his abrupt show of affection I awkwardly return the gesture and he kisses the top of my head fondly.

"No, I'm sorry, Kyla. I didn't mean to be so gruff with you or stay so late. We should have been home two hours ago."

Yes, we should have, I want to agree, but dare not say so. I chose to go with him and there was no one to blame for my aching toes but myself. The night had not been such a waste anyway – I'd had enough time to explore the Celectate's endless library.

I only worry that Mother will fret over our dalliance. She had not been happy at my Father's suggestion to leave our transport and had seemed especially displeased when I had volunteered to accompany him.

"I'm glad you came with me," Father continues and drops to his knees in front of me. "I want to tell you a big secret." He looks up and down the darkening streets before returning his attention to me, a finger on his lips.

I kneel in front of him, taking note of the deep-black alley behind him. Its darkness sends a chill across my shoulders. I struggle to keep my attention fixed solely on Father's face.

"The Celectate is going to take all criminals from the vast dungeons and place them in the Wilds. He's already working on ways to get the law passed."

"The Wilds?" I gasp. Father reaches out to cover my mouth and I stop his hand gently, nodding my head in a silent promise that I won't recoil so loudly again.

The Wilds are the land that surrounds Kelba, my kingdom. They are full of what have become known as monsters and . . . the mutants. Long ago, the Wilds were once inhabitable by my kind. In fact, they were part of Kelba. Nevertheless, a great destruction of poison and fire came upon them and turned all occupants who did not escape its poisonous fangs into ravenous beasts and sickening cannibals. There are many myths surrounding the aftermath of the devastation – some too simple to believe and others so horrifying that one hopes they do not exist. One such myth surrounding the Wilds is that all its inhabitants have one other defining trait – aside from the cannibalism – and that is deep black rims around their pupils. However, all of it is only speculation. Some say they've become demons. Terrible, frightening demons!

And the Celectate is going to send criminals to such a frightening place?

"Does he even have the right to do that?" I ask.

My father hesitates before speaking, which he should not do. The Celectate's word is the law. To question his choices is to question him personally. An action like that is oftentimes foreseen as treason.

"Yes," Father answers at last, but drops his voice a small octave. "And no."

Confusion stirs inside of me. "What kind of answer is that? You are one of the lords of the Community. Why can't you point out the horrible consequences of such an act?"

Father's lips pinch together. "That's the problem, Kyla. We can find very few consequences."

"What?" I hardly believe what I'm hearing. No consequences? What about death or just the plain barbarity of being banished from humankind?

"Don't look at me like that, Kyla. Please? If there were anything I could do to stop such an act, I would do so. I would not wish such a punishment on anyone. Death would be kinder. But that's exactly the point the Celectate is trying to make. He predicts this law will cut down crime, decrease the upkeep costs on prisons, and offer the chance to use the money for strengthening an army." For the first time in my life, Father looks helpless.

Struggling to pull in a decent breath, I clench my fists atop my knees. The cutting of costs will probably tether more than half the High Lords of the Community on the Celectate's side and then their influence will gradually sway the others. The ones on the outskirts, like Father, will be left with a simple choice. Openly defy the law to the end – or save their skins and agree.

The Community is a court of High Lords that the Celectate has gathered around him for advice and support. There were once twenty-two High Lords altogether, but two recently passed away without heirs, leaving only twenty occupants. With such numbers, it would be easy for the Celectate to pass the new act.

"How long will it take him?" I ask.

"Sometime within the coming week, when he has laid out his structure of the act in its entirety before the Community, they will vote. The act will pass under proper statistics of the vote and then the proclamation will be sent throughout Kelba that those convicted of a crime will no longer be sentenced to a dungeon."

But if the Community sends criminals to the Wilds – what is considered a crime?

"Will there be some crimes worthy of forgiveness?" I ask, my chest growing tight with panic. If I do something wrong – if I accidentally screw up – will I receive such punishment? My tongue often runs away with me before I form proper words. What if that becomes a crime?

Once again, Father hesitates before speaking. My pulse quickens at his reluctance.

"Who knows, Kyla. Who knows," he finally answers, shaking his head. "It didn't used to be this way. I remember the stories my grandfather would tell of the Wilds before the poison and the fires. It was the the 'heart' of Kelba. A land of beauty. He even told me it harbored the kingdom's deepest lake – twenty-two thousand feet. Can you believe it, Kyla?"

I shiver. I almost drowned once while playing with the Celectate's son, Aspen, in the monarch's private forest. I have never approached a pool of water more than five feet deep since. Father's description of the Wilds before the destruction is not sounding any better to me than it currently does.

My father frowns at my silence and stands. "We should be getting back home, Kyla. Remember . . . not a word, you hear? I don't want to . . . ."

I stand and draw my cloak around my shoulders again, only half-listening to him. But when I no longer hear his voice, I turn to raise questioning brows at him.

The scream on my lips dies a tragic death as panic blocks my airway. Father hangs suspended in midair, a snaky black curling thing wrapped around his neck. His legs kick furiously as he struggles to loose himself. The alley to his back is alive with swirling darkness that slowly pours from its depths. The shadows leap towards me.

They're living things!

One of them lashes out with a black tangled wisp that resembles a dying vine and smacks Father across the face. He gasps, the snaky black thing releases him, and he falls to the ground, bone colliding with stone as he lands on his back. He goes still.

"No!" I scream.

One of the shadows grabs me hard around the shoulders and presses its black vine-like wisp to my mouth. *A hand!* It smells like piss and blood, and it drags me back against a rough body. Terror courses through my veins as I struggle to free myself. To scream. To even cry.

No tears come.

Father doesn't move.

The shadows settle into a distinct form: shadowy capes and dark hoods. Nothing else.

Gods, what the hell are they?

The voice that speaks is like something from another dimension: raspy and resembling a man drunk on too much alcohol. "*Kill him . . . and the girl. Then leave them.*"

The shadow that spoke, the tallest one, turns back into the darkness from which it came. When I no longer hear its swirling cape, I know it has gone.

The harsh scraping of a sword on a metal scabbard, a sound I know well from practice with my elder brother, grates on my nerves. The sword that will kill my father. The sword that will crunch into his bones without any resistance. I try to scream, but my throat is too dry.

My cape and hood are tossed aside. I hear them hit the ground. A black leathery hand pulls aside the sheen of hair over my neck. Warm breath skates over the delicate skin. Is it going to bite me?

"*He said 'kill her' not . . .*" one of the shadows rasps irritably.

"*What he doesn't know won't kill him,*" my captor hisses back, its voice sizzling in my ear.

I try to scream again, but find it useless when the creature squeezes the side of my neck. The warm breath on my ear turns an icy cold, and I watch it shift through the air before me.

Father still doesn't move. Somehow, I am more afraid knowing that he is limp and cannot help me, than I did when he was awake and held captive in midair.

The sharp prick of teeth in the side of my neck rouses my senses, and I try to twist away, but my captor is too strong.

For a moment, I see my body lying cold, pale, and lifeless on the pavement, body twisted at morbid angles, eyes wide and frightened. I hear the screams as we are discovered and the tears glistening in people's eyes as they grieve the loss of High Lord Bone and his young daughter. Or will they? I imagine my body resting on the flat surface of a priest's embalming table as they prepare me for a burial befitting a child of nobility.

As the teeth sink deeper into my neck, I close my eyes, ignoring the prickling sensation rippling up my spine.

Is this what it feels like to die?

A harsh cry shatters the silence of the night. It comes from above my head. Something hard lands to my right. Hard enough to make the stones in the street rattle beneath me. The shadowy creature that holds me lets out a piercing shriek that is much different from the raspy voice of its leader. It skates along the nerves in my body and tingles through my ears.

"Duck!" is all I have time to hear before the sound of a sword swishing through the air reaches my ears. I obey, and a blade skims over my head and strikes the shadow. Another shriek fills the air, so loud and so horrible that I have to cover my ears, but the pain rips through the thin layer of protection and echoes inside my head.

The shadow flutters into the night sky, breaking into clumps of black smoke. Chills cling to my insides with prickly fingers as I watch the creatures who had terrorized me moments before drift away in the air like clouds.

Another raspy cry hammers against my eardrums, followed by more foggy clumps appearing and flitting away. I wait for one more. There were three shadows. If my unknown rescuer holds true to his sword there should be one more shriek, one more dissipation, and they will be gone!

But I don't hear it.

Cautiously, I tear my hands from my ears and stand. Father lies near the edge of the alley, a dark pool forming around his head.

"No!" I rush for the body.

"Come here!" The harsh, albeit human, voice of my savior reaches my ears. A hard arm wraps around my waist and abruptly stops me.

"Let me go! Let me go!" Tears soak my face in grief. "I can help him. Let go! He's bleeding! Let me go to him!" I try desperately to kick or scratch him.

He pulls me back against him, squeezing the air from my lungs in a crushing hold that forces a gasp between my lips. His voice, as cool and calm as if he were attending a ceremony, answers, "That's what it wants."

It?

I notice his stance. He holds me protectively against him while he palms the sword in his left hand. Its blade glints in the moonlight like nothing I have ever seen. Whatever the unearthly glow is, it is unnatural.

"What are you?" I ask him.

I sneak a glance over my shoulder for a decent view of his face, but all I see are dark eyes. Eyes like the shade of night. Eyes that capture mine with the intensity in which he's looking at me. Eyes with black rings around the pupils!

Holy gods, I am staring at a creature from the Wilds!

Terror seethes into my chest. I scream and try to jump away, but he is strong and keeps me captive beside him, his hand bruising my hip. His voice, now foreign and dark, answers my fear with, "It will kill you if I let you go!"

He releases my waist and grabs my chin before I can run. Nausea curdles in my stomach when his hand grates along my skin.

He turns my face towards Father's body. "Look."

All I see is the body and darkness. But darkness doesn't move like this deep black does. Around Father's body, I spot the familiar form of pitch blackness that takes shape in only one thing.

A shadow.

Good gods, it is still there! Waiting for me to come to the body. Waiting so it could . . . *kill me.*

"Come away from the Kelban, you hell-cursed creature. He won't do you any good." The Wild boy's voice now holds a tone of something dark and twisted. A voice just as evil as the groveling shadow before us.

"*Don't speak that way to me, boy,*" the shadow answers. Only it's voice isn't raspy anymore. It echoes off the walls in a steamy tone that tortures my hearing and makes every nerve in my body shake.

The shadow rises to a standing position, and I thoroughly detail its massive form. The cape-like body is all I see. Maybe that's all it is. A cape that lies on nothing but smoky fog.

The Wild boy's arm tightens around my waist, and his hand slowly squeezes the hilt of his mysterious sword. Other than that small sign of discomfort, he doesn't shake or turn a hair. I wish I were as calm as this boy from the Wilds.

"*The girl. Give her to me. I want the girl.*" The shadow's hooded head turns slightly to glance at me, and shadowy wisps of smoke from underneath its cape flutter in my direction. The boy raises his moonlit sword. The light forces the advancing darkness to stop a few inches from both of us.

Light scares this creature of the dark, but not the Wild boy.

He can't be half as bad as the shadowy demon, I decide.

"Don't listen to it. Please, don't listen. Don't let it take me," I plead, grasping his arm tight just in case he releases me.

The boy stiffens beneath my hold, the first real emotion he's shown all night. "You can understand it?" he asks, his voice layered with something akin to shock.

I tighten my hold on him. "It wants me. Don't let it take me!"

"You can understand it?" he repeats.

Even the shadow takes a hesitant step backwards.

"Yes, I can hear it. It's asking for me. Don't let it take me!"

The boy lowers his "moon sword" to glance into my face. Once more his dark eyes – rimmed in black – capture mine.

The movement of the shadow redirects my attention. It comes straight for us at a speed I didn't know was possible. Black smoke envelopes my face before I can blink. My scream fills the air, followed by the shriek of the shadow above me. Black foggy smoke billows around my body – corrupting my vision and filling my nose with the acrid scent of bile.

A blinding white light flashes across my vision. I fall to the ground and my hands scrape across the stones of the street. Needles of pain shoot through my wrists.

The boy stands above me, bathed in the beaming light from his sword as it shatters the last bits of the Darkness that remain. The last shadow is gone. He sheathes the sword in the leather scabbard at his side and the light disappears, leaving me once more in the yellow candlelight of the street lamps.

I crawl to Father, leaving a trail of blood from my wounded hands along the pavement, and press trembling fingers to his pulse. It beats gently.

He's alive!

I look over my shoulder. The boy is gone. At least, I thought he was until I look at the stone wall of the house on my right and see him scaling up the side, quick as a cat.

"Wait!" I cry and run to the wall. I put my hands to the stones he is using to climb, but my bleeding hands protest. Climbing is not an option. I look up again until my neck hurts with the strain. He is almost at the top. He will be gone. This . . . *person* from the Wilds.

"Wait!"

Maybe it's the desperation in my voice that makes him stop. I'll never know. All I know is that he turns and his eyes flash the same darkness that he'd saved me from a moment ago. I swallow my fear. He saved my life. He won't hurt me.

"Thank you."

And he is gone.

Chapter II

If I ever die, I'm quite certain I know how it's going to be. I am going to die struggling to steady myself atop a rickety ladder in the Kirath's dusty, unused library. It doesn't help that my arms are full of books and are practically useless in helping me disembark one rung after another. I count to three repeatedly in my head as I descend and the air becomes less of a prison. My fear of heights has never waned. Even though the ladder is but a mere twenty feet off the ground, my heart hammers whenever I look to the hard oak floor below me and imagine my spine giving it a kind embrace.

"Your return journey might be a lot easier, my lady, if you would hold less books on your descent," Master Rolfe quips from a corner where he is dusting the unused volumes of the shelves. It's a shame that so many books in his grand establishment go unused.

"I know," I grunt as the last rung falls away from my feet. I set my load atop one of his fine cedar tables and get to work, opening the largest of the volumes and flipping through its pages for my much-needed information.

"Your homework gets more and more tedious as time goes by, Sir Kyla," Master Rolfe comments with a smirk.

I flush beneath the scholar head covering adorned atop my mass of curly, midnight black hair. It is the epitome of fashion for a young scholar in service to the temple. However, I am not a scholar nor am I in service to the temple. No, I am simply Lady Kyla Bone, daughter of Lord Gavin Bone and Lady Elinor Bone, respectively, and if I'm discovered in my current masquerade it's a flogging I'll get for such a ruse. Master Rolfe knows it well and he has remained quiet in the last three years I have been visiting his abode.

My first few visits had been after the horrible attack in the streets. I had not bothered to disguise myself because I was running errands with my brother since he was to retrieve two books for his training at the castle. However, when the library had become an interest for me, such frequent visits could not be explained as "errands" any longer. Therefore, I had donned my disguise. Master Rolfe had not been fooled but he'd been lonely inside the four walls and, thus, welcomed me warmly.

"Yes, it does," I agree with him, hefting the volume in my arms with a grunt. I bestow an impish smile in his direction. "But if anyone finds out you've been welcoming my rebellious behavior I won't be the only one who receives a flogging."

"Threatening me, are you?"

"Simply reminding you that you are in over your head as much as I."

He glares in my direction and returns to dusting, but neglects to hide the quick smirk on his face. He enjoys my slightly mean sarcasm as much as I enjoy giving it. He's one of the few people who allows me to be so rude.

The pages of the volume contain all information possibly gathered after the "Great Calamity." It describes observations of what the poison may have been, where it might have come from, what might have caused the fires. Most of the observations blame it on gods battling for supremacy in the heavens and somehow it caused havoc on land. However, belief in such foolishness is hardly my strong point. No, I search for the information *after* the "Great Calamity."

The volume is fairly new, published by a man with the odd name of "Goldbrow." It's recent pages might contain new information – new insight – into the land that has become a mystery. It traces the historical moments of the Kelban nation up until the "Great Calamity" and then spends at least twenty pages discussing the Celectate's largest venture – the building of a Wall to separate Kelba from the decimated wasteland. It had been one of his finest achievements upon completion. The Wall had stretched for ten thousand miles through the border between the Wilds and Kelba.

I don't know what it was like when the poisons came, but the volume contains real-life descriptions from survivors who observed the terrifying moment that changed the nation forever. No one knows how it started, but rumor has it that anyone who breathed the air immediately transformed into a sort of monster. Of course, they still looked human, but their rimmed eyes would tell you what they really were. Myths abound that the infected tribes of the Wilds survive by cannibalism since all animals and plants are poisoned. Again, the rumors are unclassified. But . . .

I have seen an inhabitant of the Wilds.

Growling with frustration, I slam the book shut as it continues about the history of Kelba after the Wall's building – about political games between the Celectate and the Community. No more information on the Wilds. Nothing but myths, legends, rumors, and unclassified hogwash that does nothing to settle my mind.

"I would think you'd treat my precious documents with respect, my lady. Or have you forgotten such niceties?" Master Rolfe leans over my shoulder and takes the volume from me with caring hands, inspecting the leather cover as if it's his child – of which he has none.

"Sorry," I mutter, not really sorry at all. Goldbrow is just another foolish man seeking a fortune by writing a book that would appease the minds of his fellow citizens. But it doesn't appease me.

The questions I want to know are endless. Why did the boy not capture and eat me? Why did he save me? What were the deadly fiends that attacked my father and I? Why did the boy's sword glow like the moon? Why did it kill the shadows?

Every time my mind returns to the events of that long-ago night my skin buzzes with electrified tension. My nightmares are intense and relentless when they torment me. Every one of them contains something from that moment, be it the shadowy monsters themselves or the cold feeling of their teeth in my neck. I still bear the markings of that night – two small scars – on the delicate skin directly behind my ear along my hairline. They have remained hidden and no one has even suspected their presence. Every time the nightmares strike, they pulse with sickening accuracy and turn my brain into a hive of nauseating terror.

I pull a lone manuscript from the satchel at my side. It was a gift to me upon my fourteenth birthday, three months prior to the attack. Its first few pages are sketches of simple things a girl would take an interest in. Flowers. Birds. Trees. The Celectate's emblem. But the remaining pages are full of darkness and botched notes so close together only I can read their contents. The pages hold horrors no person should see. Every time I awoke from a nightmare, I would sketch what details I could remember onto the pages of my clean paper. Blood. War. Death. Battle. Shadows. The Wild boy. The wasteland of the Wilds. To others they might be violent – to me they are a reminder. A reminder of what the Wilds are supposed to hold.

Until I look at the pages containing my memory of the Wild boy. I had never gotten a clear view of his face, but his eyes are the most vivid of my drawings, dark and brooding, with just a hint of the evil glint he'd emanated that long-ago night.

"My lady," Master Rolfe's voice breaks my solitude and I slam my personal book shut lest he see the horrors I have documented for three years. "It is nearly dusk."

It can't be. Nevertheless, the pale light shining through the arched windows of the library atrium says different. If I am not home before nightfall and out of my boyish attire, I shall receive the whipping of my life, followed by a lecture, a grounding, and a promise to never see daylight again.

I grab the remaining books I've retrieved – including my personal one – from the shelves and shove them into my satchel. Once it's over my shoulder, the weight nearly takes me sideways, but I heft the burden to my back and straighten.

Master Rolfe shows me to the door, pats my shoulder in a gentle farewell, then closes and latches it from within. I smile to myself when the six locks slide into place. Master Rolfe is always paranoid that his precious collection will be stolen. I've assured him many times that the majority of people in Kelba's capitol city are illiterate and of the minority that can read, they could care less about his collection.

The streets of Kirath are being lit by the town torch-lighters. They hardly spare me a glance as I saunter by them, hefting the bag once – twice – from shoulder to shoulder. Perhaps I should have left some books behind.

I smooth the lapels of my scholar's overcoat with care. I retrieved the clothes from a deserted bin in the storage room of my home and managed to have my personal seamstress mend the entire outfit, all the while deceiving her with stories of a poor "scholar boy" needing decent attire for his temple visits. The head covering I had fashioned myself, tailoring it to fit my head perfectly so as I hide the mass of hair beneath. When set free my hair falls to the middle of my back in a curly mess. The strings of the head covering tied beneath my chin prevent the revelation of my true gender.

The winding streets of Kirath are practically deserted. Not that it doesn't please me, of course. Fewer people on the streets mean fewer people will take closer looks at a lowly scholar. I will get home with my disguise intact yet again.

I turn a corner and collide with several young boys running down the street. They are filthy and smell strongly of dust.

"Watch it!" I snap, struggling to maintain a deep tone.

"Apologies, scholar!" one boy says without even pausing.

Another boy, a tall, lanky fellow, has the decency to stop and bow his head before continuing. "Lord Telman's ostracizement is today."

Hell. I had forgotten about it. I had purposely come up with excuses so I would not have to attend the public punishment. It was custom for all High Lords of the Community to attend the ostracizement as a sign of loyalty to the Celectate. Well, I was not a High Lord and I was stuck in bed with a "headache."

The first ostracizement had taken place a month after the nightmarish attack in the alleyway and the Celectate had forced all High Lords and lower nobility to attend. Mother had dressed me in a dress of blood red and pinned our family seal to my shoulder. Since father was the High Lord of the white diamond mines he had a front row seat – and so did I. Fifty people were ostracized that day alone – and the city had made a spectacle of it: offering food, tokens, and spectacles to enjoy the event. Like it was a celebration or something. People had cheered and clapped whenever the screams of the damned echoed over the square. I had cried.

For a whole week, I had to attend the event while the dungeons emptied and hundreds of guilty convicts were branded and thrust behind the Wall of Kelba into the dark abyss of the unknown. Until, finally, I could not take it any longer and had shoved my way through the crowd and run home as fast as I could. I had locked the door of my room and refused to see anyone – even Father. At last, Mother found a key and entered. I expected her to be very cross with me for abandoning the Celectate's order, but she didn't say a word to me. Instead, she sat on the bed beside me and let me lay my head on her shoulder. I refused to cry. Our silence was sad enough.

I have seen what comes from the Wilds. I have been attacked by demons.

I have never told anyone.

What happened that night went down as a simple mugging. When Father woke up he could remember nothing – only that he had been talking to me and lost consciousness when something touched his neck. I had been too terrified for days to say anything. When I finally did speak I went along with the general knowledge – *Yes, it was a mugging. No, I was not hurt. Yes, they got away. No, I cannot remember their faces. They were shadows.*

That last part, at least, was no lie.

I reach the main streets of Kirath. People hurry in the same direction – towards the Main Square. Towards the ostracize platform. Towards another poor fool's banishment.

Nausea rips at my stomach and the scars on my neck begin to pulse as I sense the heady aroma of the crowd. Excitement practically drips from them and their eyes shine.

Bastards!

My head pounds furiously, echoing in my ears, buzzing along my spine, and wreaking havoc inside of me. Hesitantly, I glance behind me. The mob is gathering. Already I can hear the cheers as a wagon makes its way through the grasping hands.

I had heard the rumors around town about the unfortunate High Lord Telman of Escar, a city in the East of Kelba. A city with one function – the breeding of an army for the Celectate. Only Lord Telman had not been building an army for the Celectate. No. Rumors started months ago that he was planning to overthrow the Celectate and place a new ruler on the throne. *A ruler, who,* he said, *would respect the Community instead of trying to make them his lap dogs. A ruler who would understand the people instead of trying to silence them. A ruler who would value strength instead of craving it.* His words had not been wasted. Many people were whispering his name in back-alleys and on street corners. But that was all they were. Whispers.

As I grow further away from the crowd, the pain in my head grows. Invisible talons tear at my skin. I know what they want. They want me to turn around. They want me to join the crowd.

They want me to see.

Grinding my teeth viciously, I swivel around and join the mass. It is a slow process. Commoners are used to the crowded throngs of the streets. I am not. I do not have the educated ability to slip through arms and legs, especially with a thirty-pound book-bag hanging off one shoulder. I use my height and my false scholar attire to weave in and out of the packed bodies.

The noise of the crowd grows and somewhere in front of me, wagon wheels creak laboriously. I am close. One more shove of my arm, one more elbow in someone's gut, and I am at the forefront of the crowd, standing barely six inches away from the square of Celect Knights that surround the public platform. They block the crowd from slipping through with their spears and look exceedingly powerful in their ebony black armor.

The creaky wagon emerges from the crowd and stops beside the platform. Two Celect Knights remove the lone occupant, a man clothed in a tunic that was once pure white, but has succumbed to the filth of two days in a dungeon, and set him on his feet. The man was once clean-shaven, but now has speckled brown and white hair on his strong jaw. His hair is infested with dirt. His hands tremble as a leather tie is wrapped around his wrists, cinching them together. The knights pull him roughly by the shoulders, and he stumbles forward.

I have met all the High Lords of the Community during the many events, festivals, and special parties hosted throughout the city for them. Lord Telman was one I knew a bit more than all the rest. He did not make much effort to engage me in conversation because I was a rather quiet, sullen child after the night of the "mugging" but he always smiled. Always nodded when I showed respect. Always raised a brow when I'd purse my lips after Father would mention the "esteemed" Celectate. I knew Lord Telman as a brave man with a potency for speech making that could rouse or dissuade a crowd. If he had succeeded in producing an army, he would have been successful in overthrowing Kelba's current leader.

The guards bind Lord Telman to the tall, metal pole in the middle of the ominous platform and the knights return to their respective places.

Another cheer rises in the crowd. I recognize that cheer. A cheer of loyalty. A cheer of recognition.

Celectate Wood has arrived.

As Kelba's ruler makes his way up the steps of the platform, his bejeweled hands modestly accepting the praise, his eyes rest briefly on Lord Telman. The two exchange a look I rarely see – a look of pure hatred for each other. Celectate Wood masks his true emotions with an immaculate smile. Lord Telman makes no such efforts.

Behind me, someone elbows me in the spine – hard! I turn around; ready to give the person a good tongue-lashing, and stop short. The man is so tall – so ugly – I shut my mouth. He has a patch over one eye and a cruel scar running the length of his face, over his lip, and underneath his chin. I shiver and he looks down his nose at me, his thick eyebrows drawing close together. A glint of something dark shines in his eyes and I realize I've taken a hesitant step backward.

"What are you looking at, boy?" the man snaps, his voice so deep, so terrifying, my throat curls in knots.

"I . . . I . . ."

He grabs me roughly by the front of my tunic and drags me against him. My hands flail to his chest, pressing against rock-hard muscle, and I gasp. His eyes scan the crowd before looking back at me. "This is no place for you, scholar. You belong with books and useless writings that will support our glorious Celectate in his fine reign. Get back to the temple!" He thrusts me away and it takes every thread of balance inside of me to regain it.

I peer over my shoulder. Celectate Wood has finished his round of gratitude to the crowd. Now he has taken a small sheet from his pocket: the announcement of the accused and his crime. A small white package, dyed a blood-red color, is in his other hand. He palms it gently. For some reason, I shiver.

"Did you not hear me, whore-born? Get to the temple!" The giant grabs me by the wrist – and stops short. His thumb strokes the length of my pulse – the width of my wrist – and when he raises eyes to me, they are startled.

Hellfire! He knows. Oh, gods, he knows!

He jerks me towards him again, this time molding my face to his chest. I smell sweat and dirt and horses – *and metal.* My hands stroke a familiar shape beneath the rough fabric of his tunic. A dagger.

"Listen to me, little one, and listen close," he whispers. He doesn't look at me, and his eyes are scanning the crowd again with a slow ease I do not like. He speaks out of the side of his mouth. "Things are going to happen fast. Things are going to take a turn for the worse. Unless you want to watch your innards spilled out on the ground before you, get back to wherever you live and stay there."

His hand lingers on my shoulder and he leans down to stare me full in the face. He shows no recognition of who I am. Why would he? He is a street urchin. I am nobility.

"Hell's breaking chains today," he says.

He walks away, pushing through the crowd, drawing closer to the Celect Knights surrounding the platform. Surrounding Lord Telman.

Getting home sounds like a good idea. But as I turn – as I try to shove my way through the dense crowd – I sense it again. The hair on my neck rises. The two scars on my neck pulse with the sudden danger, and my vision grows hazy for a moment as it digests the motions within the crowd.

Not now. Please, not now.

Ever since that night, things have been so strange. My body senses things I cannot even acknowledge and weakens me. It makes my head hurt. My body ache. My skin buzz.

And the scars pulse.

Throughout the smiling faces of some within the crowd, there are others. Caped figures. They push closer and closer. Closer to me. Closer to the Celect Knights. Closer to Lord Telman.

Hell's breaking chains today.

"Lord Telman has been found guilty of high treason and intent to bring destruction upon Kelba. He has attempted an atrocious act, not only against me, but also against you, the good citizens of this fine nation. He has stepped out of his boundaries as a man meant to protect you, to protect me, and must receive punishment for it. He robbed you of your money to build his army. He robbed you of your sons to fuel his goals. He robbed you of your trust. Such a man is not worthy to sit in my company, much less yours. He is to be ostracized this day – and his foolish errand will be banished with him." Celectate Wood's voice rings with passion. With power.

I know why he hates Lord Telman. I have heard both of them speak. They are eloquent and open, possessing a strength with their words one can only wish for. Their abilities rival one another – and that is why they loathe each other.

"I know you would expect such a man to defend himself at this point." Celectate Wood peers over his shoulder in Lord Telman's direction. The hateful gaze has not left the High Lord's face and he struggles with his bonds, his face turning a violent purple. But he says nothing.

"Of course, he never was one to use his tongue wisely." The Celectate smiles when Lord Telman makes an enraged sound from his throat. He strokes his thumb along the tiny white package in his hand.

My stomach drops.

"So I had it removed."

The Celectate tosses the blood-red package at Lord Telman's feet and it unfurls. I stare at the bloody lump within and nausea strikes my gut.

People in the crowd cheer – but not all of them. I sense the tension, the rise of suppressed fury, in the bodies packed close around me.

Celectate Wood turns. "Brand him."

The tension snaps!

From somewhere in the crowd a man screams, "*Lothalar leran de revalan.*"

Ancient Kelban.

"*Long live the rebellion!*"

Rotten garbage assails the air – assaults the Celect Knights surrounding the platform. They try to take cover behind their hands, their shields, or the bodies packed close around them, but they are stained in moments. Some wipe the debris from their eyes while other gag on the diluted waste in their mouths.

"Control!" Celectate Wood screams.

From a canopied platform near the Square a squadron of Celect Knights rush forward, swords drawn and shields up, as new assailants batter the guards. I spot the tall giant leading the procession, his dagger out and ready. It shatters the breastplate of a man in front of him, spraying blood across the stones.

From behind me, a hand shoves me aside, and another attacker sweeps by me, sword raised. He smashes into the guards and breaks through, violently charging the podium steps and lurching onto the platform with an expert somersault. He slashes his sword in Celectate Wood's direction but a flying blade embeds itself in his side, stopping his attack. Blood spurts onto the wood and he falls, clutching at the offending dagger.

The Celectate reaches down and plucks the dagger from the man's side. He gets on his knees before the man and his lips move. I do not hear what he says. I am too far away. He slits the man's throat.

The surprise attack slowly settles into the minds of those who were cheering moments ago and then everything goes crazy. People scatter, for cover or for weapons, and join the fray. A fist slams into my shoulder. Another into my ankle.

I have to get out.

From close by a woman screams and falls to the ground, blood dribbling from her mouth. I step over her. A man to my right grunts in pain as a fist cracks into his knee. I hear the sleeve of my tunic tear. Feel the grope of hands around me. Sense the heavy presence close behind me.

An arm loops around my middle.

"Look here! I have one of them damned temple scholars. Are the gods gonna help you, little prick?" The man's hand rips the head covering away. My hair tumbles down about my shoulders.

"Stars! A girl!" I recognize the tone in his voice. It is the tone used by drunken men in taverns when they're overcome with violent passion.

A hand slides beneath the tunic, up my leg, to the waist of my pants, and . . .

I hear the crack of bone – the scream of pain.

I am released. Someone grabs me by the wrist and jerks me forward. I flash past sprawled bodies, wrestling, half-crazed people, and into the streets where other, saner folk are fleeing the riot. My rescuer turns a corner into an alley and practically throws me into the wall.

"I told you!" It is the giant from before. Blood is splattered in diverse patterns across his tunic and face. "Did I not tell you, girl, that hell was breaking chains?"

"You did." I shoulder my book bag again, surprised it's still intact. Moreover, a bit relieved as well. Three years of hard work would have been lost.

The giant man slams a fist to the wall, the scar on his face crinkling up horribly. He groans in exasperation before looking back in the direction we came from. The screams are starting to fade and the noise of battle is dying. The cold glitter disappears from his eyes, replaced with something else. "Fools! All of them. We try to liberate them – and they walk into the chains willingly."

"Were you not trying to start a riot?" I ask.

"Of course not. We meant for the people to rally behind us. For the people to demand Lord Telman's release. Not for them to become little children and attack the Celect Knights themselves. Or the Celectate."

"But you were attacking them too."

"When I had no choice. I would not watch my comrades die when I . . ." He stops and looks at me, his brow creasing. He looks me over, from the mass of hair to the tips of my misplaced boots.

"You are nobility!" he snaps and turns to go.

I grab at his wrist. "Lord Telman was nobility. You did not mind helping him."

"Twas not for him I did it!" the giant roars and shakes me off. His eyes dilate with fury. "I did it for those fools out there. Lord Telman risked his neck for them. I admired that. But it was all for those fools. They do not understand what they have done. We have lost our cause this night. We have lost our fire. We have lost . . ." He cuts himself off and shakes his head. The spark of rage disappears.

"We have lost our symbol."

He starts to go. I don't grab him again. I shouldn't ask him what he means. I should let him walk away, out of my life, and pretend that this day – that the riot – never happened.

But I ask anyway. "What does that mean?"

He doesn't turn around.

"It means cowards have returned to chains."

Chapter III

It is long-past the setting of the sun when I reach the gate of my home. The Bone mansion is one of the largest, considering Father is one of the richest High Lords, and rises on a small hill of the street that allows a brief view of Kirath from the second-story window of my room. I sneak through the half-open gate, which our kindly guard has left unlocked for me tonight and around the edge of the house to the kitchen door. The cook will be in bed. The kitchen maid asleep. I will go undiscovered. Mother and Father would have been watching the ostracizement from a platform nearby and their carriage will be stuck for hours in the traffic of the riot's aftermath.

I step into the dark kitchen. The dull light emanating from the fireplace embers gives the room a slightly eerie presence. I watch the shadows dance on the walls. My skin prickles. They look too familiar. Too horrifying. Too real. I expect them to jump out at me from the darkness and grab hold of me. I wait for my blood to stain the floor. But, like always, nothing happens. I grip the edge of the table while the nightmarish imaginations subside.

The heavy book-bag falls to the ground with a thud.

"Home at last, Kyla?"

I spin around, startled by the voice. Mother stands in the opposite doorway, her form cloaked in a half-torn black dress. One of her sleeves is missing. However, she is whole. She is safe. And she is frowning. She brings the lantern closer and it reveals my disheveled form. Not only my disheveled appearance but also the way in which

I wear that appearance. Out of the many excuses I've abused in the past, I don't think "playing dress-up" is going to wave this one by. Not when I've got remnants of strange blood splattered in meandering splotches across the fabric.

She gasps.

"It's not mine," I assure her.

The silence that follows is deafening. I wait for an explosion. A tirade. A scolding. A flogging. Instead, Mother steps forward and fingers the torn sleeve of my tunic – of a boy's tunic.

"Was it rough in the crowd?" she asks.

"Excuse me?"

"When the riot started, I mean. You weren't hurt too badly, were you? Oh, your lip's bleeding. And your neck is bruised." The soft chastisement sounds like a caress. Her hands stroke the bruise, and I wince.

"I got out better than some people did." How I wish to say more. I wish to call the Celectate by a hundred vile names. I wish to stomp on his face. To tear out his own damned tongue. To watch his blood stain my fingers. He started the riot. He ignited the crowd. He ruined it all. But I can never say any of that. My father is a High Lord. And a High Lord whose daughter has treasonous opinions will not reflect well on his position. I cannot shame him. I cannot betray him.

I cannot endanger him.

"What about you?" I ask.

"Your Father and I were feeling tired. Therefore, we left with his Excellency's permission. He could see I was feeling faint." Mother smiles temptingly and runs a hand across the bottom of her jaw with a smooth sweeping gesture. Flirtation. Every woman of nobility knew how to use it to her advantage – every woman but me. The thought of my mother looking that odious man in the eye and flattering him with pretty words makes me sick. But I don't say it.

If they left that means Mother didn't see the tongue. Nor did Father. They do not know the truth. By tomorrow, the gossip will provide a dozen different scenarios. And the nobility will pick the one that least implicates the Celectate. I will be unable to tell the truth of what happened. I was not there. I was not there.

But I was there.

"You were at Master Rolfe's again, weren't you?" Mother asks.

Again?

"You know?" I ask. No wonder she wasn't shocked by my apparel. "How?"

"Do you think me blind? I've seen the books in your room, Kyla. The amounts of studying you do. Where would you get such education. Certainly not that odious teacher you had last year. And your brother's more of the troubadour than the scholar. And I just happened to discover your head covering on your desk just days ago." She smiles wisely. "Why else would you need to hide such luxurious locks, darling?"

Mother had scolded me for years whenever I would return from one of my mischievous romps with my brother and his friends. She had hired etiquette teachers and organized feminine parties and daily visits to neighboring nobility in an effort to cleanse me of what the temple priests called "inner demons." And now she discovers me sneaking through the kitchen, dressed as a boy, torn and bloodied, and she has no lectures for me?

"You aren't mad?" I ask.

Something snaps in Mother's eyes and she looks at me. "I was mad when you pranked Lady Eloise with a roach in her teacup. I was mad when you joined your brother on a journey for lost gold that sprained your leg and lost you two teeth. I was mad when you climbed the roof of this very house looking for the stars your brother insisted would come into your hands. I was mad when you climbed the vine outside your bedroom window to see the new-born foal come into this world."

She leans close and taps my forehead. "I have never been mad at you for wishing to improve this. Foolish pranks are one thing. Knowledge is quite another. I want my daughter to be one of the finest, greatest, strongest, *smartest* girls Kelba has ever seen. And if she has to sneak out of this house, dressed as a boy, so she won't stain the family name, I would call that 'honorable.' Not 'unseemly.'"

I don't know what to say. I haven't the words to describe what I wish to convey.

Mother pats my shoulder. Her eyes dart to the bruise she said was on my neck. "We will have to do something about that," she says solemnly. "The First Moon Festival in honor of Celectate Wood's twenty-five year reign is two days away and we don't want you under too many suspicions."

"He's still having it?"

After everything that happened today – all the lives lost, all the bloodshed, all the havoc created – Celectate Wood would continue with the celebration. As if one of his High Lords had not been ostracized – *again*. Lord Telman was the third one this year! The Community was supposed to have twenty High Lords. Now it was down to twelve because of "high treason" edicts.

Mother nods but says nothing else. She cannot. She would disapprove the Celectate. That could be considered a sign of displeasure. And displeasure, in the Celectate's opinion, was a stepping-stone to high treason.

I took that step long ago.

I haul Master Rolfe's books onto my bed and lay them on the coverlet until they span the eight foot width. One of them *has* to contain new information.

I believe deeply in the tales I've been raised on – I believe there are nightmares and terrors beyond the Wall. I believe there are monsters unheard of lurking in the wasteland known as the Wilds. I believe there are cannibals that will tear my flesh from my body and eat it raw between their rotting teeth.

However, I do not believe that everything is as I've been told. Everything has lies when you look close enough.

One of the books contains a map of Kelba before the Great Calamity and I stare at its wondrous expanse of land. A land now divided by a Wall that protects us. We were once the greatest nation of its time until the dreadful poison ate half the kingdom. Before the Celectate took the rule with promises for a stronger, better empire twenty-five years ago. It was long before my time but historians write of the Celectate's empowering speeches and his ascendance to the reign as if he were a god. He saved Kelba from ruin – but I smell lies beneath that phrase wherever I go.

History books only tell half of the truth.

I want the other half.

Chapter IV

Learning to observe the best moments to slip out of the spotlight is a skill one does not easily acquire – especially if you're a High Lord's daughter. I have been the "star" of the spotlight since I turned seventeen years old last fall and every eligible young – or old – man has made it his priority to gain my attention. I am not the only High Lord's daughter who has come of age, but I am one of the richest. I will inherit forty percent of my father's diamond mines upon marriage. And what belongs to the wife belongs to the husband so, in truth, my husband will gain more than I will.

I have to wait until some of the other well-known eligible doves enter the room before planning my get-away. First, I must wait for the proper change in tide. When no eyes stare at me and the magnificent, sparkling white dress robbing precious breath from my lungs. Then I must wait for a distraction. Usually at gatherings like this a servant will trip over his own feet, a young nobleman will overstep his boundaries, or a servant will drop his entire tray of delicate pastries on the ground. I opt for the third distraction and nonchalantly stick the tip of my toe out from beneath my gown, apologizing under my breath for the havoc I'm about to cause. But I cannot stay here any longer!

The poor servant falls flat on his knees and silver-white delicacies roll in all different directions. Lords try to step out of the way. Women lift their skirts to avoid the mess. Other servants approach to help clean up.

I dash out the back door and only when I am thirty feet down the hall do I feel at ease to slow my pace to a fancy trot. I run my fingers over my left cheek. Mother used her best efforts to disguise the bruise blossoming on my skin but it retains an odd color that doesn't suit the rest of my complexion. The scab on my lip could not be helped.

It has been nearly three years since I've walked the palace of the Celectate but I remember every hallway, every intricately carved door, and every staircase adeptly. Exploring Celectate Wood's massive home had been one of my many pastimes when I was younger. When I was innocent. When I didn't care what kind of man he was.

The library door is not locked, as I knew it wouldn't be, and I slip inside, cautiously making sure I do not interrupt a lover's meeting. The room is empty save for the books lining the shelves on the wall. Hundreds of them – too many for me to count. Master Rolfe's collection could never compare to this wondrous supply.

Let the nobility gossip when I cannot be found on the dance-floor. Let them call me names and ruin my reputation. With all this leather – all this knowledge – at my fingertips, nothing could shatter my spirits.

Hefting my skirts up past my calves, I master the small ladder on the side of the shelves and pluck the first book that catches my attention. It is a book of tales. Another one describing the altercation of Gasan and Calaisar. I remember Celectate Wood's son, Aspen, saying how much his father loved the tale of Gasan and Calaisar. How he would tell him stories of the two warriors – even making up his own adventures so Aspen could dream about becoming a warrior just like them. A warrior who defeated the gods.

Imagining the blood-splattered man upon the podium tucking his son in bed with stories of heroism doesn't elevate my respect.

I search desperately among the manuscripts for something out of the ordinary. Nothing stands out. When mother had told me of the First Moon Festival, I had thought I'd be able to finally find something to answer – if not ease – the things I wanted to know so badly.

"Hell's breaking chains today."

"Lothalar leran de revelan."

Perhaps I could find something among the ancient Kelban texts. The idea is a slim chance. Not many copies of ancient texts are found in readable condition. If there are any they usually go to the temple, where Calaisar's priests copy the phrases and store the artifacts for the gods. However, Celectate Wood is so influential, *so important,* I'm sure he must have a small copy – even a page – of ancient Kelban writings.

Sure enough, Celectate Wood does possess a small shelf with neatly written pamphlets, all containing the centuries old dialogue. My adeptness at translating the olden tongue is somewhat lacking – I spent more time engulfing myself in old tales of Kelban folklore than I did studying with my mono-toned instructor.

The words are more jumbled together than I remember – more poetry sounding too. I try to make sense of the swirling lines and delicate strokes but can discern none of it. I catch a few words here and there: "light," "star", "saviors," and a couple references to holiness.

"I thought you'd be in here. Hiding again?" The voice is so soft, yet so piercing, that my skin shudders. I don't have to turn around when I catch the sweet scent of lily perfume that the newcomer wears. I know who it is.

"If I want to hide, it's best not to seek me out." I add an edge to my tone and return the pamphlet to its proper place on the shelf.

"Don't need to be so touchy, Kyla. Remember . . . I'm a lord's daughter too." Selena Griff reminds me as she comes to stand beside one of the Celectate's soft lounge-sofas. Her hands, delicately manicured, with nails painted black as midnight, stroke the soft silken furnish. Everything about her is black, from the dress that hugs her slim body to the jet-black hair that skates nearly to her waist in straight, smooth streaks. Even her eyes are lined with deep, thick eyeliner that gives her the appearance of a feline creature stalking prey.

"Shouldn't you be dancing?" I ask. Selena is near as popular as I am on the dance-floor. Maybe it's her gracefully thin figure that possesses the agility of a cat or her mesmerizing seduction, but she certainly has been my rival since our first acquaintance five years ago.

"Perhaps, but I find the atmosphere in here so much better," Selena comments. She rests her hip against the arm of the sofa and lets one of her nails scrape along the fabric. "So . . ." Her voice is honey sweet – and prodding.

"What have you been doing with yourself, Kyla? It's been ages since we spoke."

I smile. "I've been busy, of course. There's so many lovely young gentleman coming to call that I'm afraid my time has been spent in complete boredom."

Selena smirks – not a becoming look at all for her hunter's nature. "I see. Then I suppose the rumors I heard were just frightful gossip."

"Excuse me?"

"Oh. You didn't hear." She laughs and presses a hand to her heart with a mock gesture of surprise. "There's a rumor going around that a High Lord's daughter was caught gallivanting around the sultry parts of the city dressed as a boy. A scholar, no less! There's all sorts of foolish stories running around about the predicament. Some say she was in a tryst. Can you imagine? Such scandal! Not only does such behavior displease the gods, but it also gives the people a bad impression of their hierarchy. After all, if the people they're supposed to serve start behaving like vagabonds that's one step away from barbarity. And Kelba can't afford such behavior."

Someone must have seen me returning home last night. My hair had been a dead giveaway. Hell! I was being so careful. But they are only rumors. There is no verification behind them. And no one but Selena would dare insult High Lord Gavin Bone's daughter by asking if she would even entertain the idea of such scandalous frivolity.

"What would you know of Kelban behavior?" I ask, my own claws unsheathing for the fight. "Don't think I haven't heard the rumors about you, Selena. Trust me . . . they're scandalous."

Selena reddens but her claws don't retract. "More so than disguising as a boy and sneaking into the sultriest parts of the city to drink and romp and sully your reputation?"

"Sully my reputation?" I laugh. "I wouldn't dream of it. Believe me, Selena; nothing concerns me more than my family's honor." I'll swear that one to the gods.

"Well, consider this a word of advice from someone who values both reputation and honor." Selena leans close with a devilish grin and her cat-like eyes bore into mine. "If you value those things you'll attend the next ostracizement like a good member of nobility and openly clarify your support for the Celectate."

"I was in bed with a headache," I say.

Selena narrows her eyes and stares directly at my left cheek, her gaze boring into my skin. I turn my head away from her prying gaze and purse my lips in an annoyance.

"Ah, yes," she muses and pulls back, her legs outlined beneath the silken folds of her gown. "A headache. Dreadful things, those." She crosses her arms. "And convenient too. I dare say your health would not have improved after the showing. It turned into a rather bloody mess before Lord Telman could be ostracized properly. They had to brand him quick and drag him away. Not at all the sort of examples we've had in the past. A shame too." She eyes me again. "Lord Telman was such a fool to believe he could outsmart our illustrious ruler. A big mistake on his part. The poor man. I rather liked him. Even his tongue was a pleasant sight."

Bitch. Rotten, diseased bitch.

My fingers curl into fists at my sides.

"Rumors can be dreadful things, you know?" Selena runs her hand along the arm of the couch, her nails raking the satin into creased folds. Her eyes glitter. "They can spark a fire, start a war, kill someone . . . and ruin another."

I feel a headache pressing close to my skull. The migraine approaching is an entirely different physical ailment than what assails normal human beings. This headache is one of the aftermaths of the *mugging*.

"Once you've finished, Selena, I'm sure you'll be off to create more rumors for yourself, so get on with it." Hardly wise words to say to such a creature, but if she is in here when the pain arrives the situation will turn ugly.

Her face turns white and her lips press into thin lines on her face. "There are rumors concerning certain members of your family? For instance, your brother's wayward ways."

"Yes, everyone knows how men in the Celectate's service are known for their righteousness," I quip. My brother, Landor, is a Celect Knight, personally guarding the palace walls five days out of the week. He is one of the youngest Celect Knight's – only twenty-one – and has been honored on many occasions for his aptitude and adept swordsmanship. Of course, he also has a heap of gossip surrounding his accomplishments. One cannot be the son of a High Lord like father and go unnoticed.

Selena sneers contemptibly and crosses her legs. "There are also rumors about your father."

The breath I catch fans the talons gripping my skull and searing pain flames my body.

Having fueled her need for attention, Selena continues in cold calculation. "Well . . . there's talk of rebellion going around. You know the type that can overthrow a monarchy? Lord Essan. Lord Drave. Lord Telman. People are saying your father has, shall we say, forgotten his loyalty to the Celectate like those men. Isn't that interesting? What's even more interesting is that it's also affectionately called . . . Oh, what was the word? Ah. Yes. Treason!" Her eyes, which had been scanning the ceiling as she spoke, turn on me. "Isn't that the most absurd thing you've ever heard off the streets? I mean . . . your father is a lord. A member of the Community, for gods' sakes. He doesn't question any of the Celectate's decisions. It can only be a useless rumor. I'm sorry for even bringing it up. What a horrid thought."

My breathing feels heavy, and I'm sure it's not the dress this time.

Treason, treason, treason!

It rings in my ears. I see Lord Telman's tongue. Hear the flesh melting beneath hot iron. Smell the searing skin. I know what happens to those the Celectate believes in opposition to him.

Images of my father, bleeding and gasping for breath, flash across my mind. He's walking across a barren wasteland. Shadows claw at him, until he finally falls. Cannibals appear and he screams at them to stop as they tear at his flesh, stuffing it in their mouths hungrily. Until nothing but bones remains.

The throbbing begins, spreading down my face from my temples, spanning my neck, pulsing against the fang scars. They burn. Every part of me seems to be shaking as the world shivers around me in weird colors and vibrations. I struggle to retain my balance but the hard wood of the shelf gouges my spine when I tip backwards. I blink. Dark spots blur my vision.

"Kyla! Kyla, someone's come looking for you. Good evening, Sir Landor. My don't you look stunning!" Selena's voice has taken a seductively smooth twist.

I suck in a deep breath and try to stand straight again.

"What's wrong with her?" Lan asks. His arms wrap around my shoulders to support me and my knees give way.

Lan gasps with the sudden weight and presses his palm against my burning forehead. It feels so cool. I gently push his hand away. Selena cannot see me like this. She mustn't.

Breathe, Kyla. Just breathe. Breathe.

"Well, I'll leave you two in peace. See you later, Kyla." Selena strolls off with a confident sway in her hips.

Slowly the dizziness fades. The spasms in my neck cease and my limbs stop shaking. My brother's arms remain tight around my shoulders.

"I'm fine, Lan. You can let go of me now," I promise.

Reluctantly, he steps away. I press my hair back into place, smoothing it against my neck. I feel so sticky and a chill skates down my spine.

"You don't have to carry it alone, you know?" Lan says.

"I beg your pardon?"

"The nightmares – the terrors that make you scream in the night – the horrors you ask about . . . you don't have to carry them alone." He offers me a gentle pat on the shoulder and smiles at my surprise. "You honestly didn't think I knew? I've known something was different for a long time. You changed. A mugging doesn't do that to someone. There's something you're not telling me, isn't there?"

Though our relationship is one of the strongest bonds, the secrets I keep from him, and the secrets I'm sure he keeps from me, are better kept in the dark. I do not ask what things he's done for the Celectate, atrocious or not, and he doesn't ask what nonsense I fill my head with in Master Rolfe's abode or why I continue to return there.

"Lan, I . . . I . . ."

"Spare me the excuses, sister. You don't have to tell me anything. In time, maybe I'll understand why you persist in sticking your nose into mythological tales and the ancient woes that shattered this kingdom. But I don't understand your interest with those silly legends." He shakes his head vigorously.

Silence presses between us.

"But that's just the problem," I say.

He eyes me with curiosity. "What do you mean?"

"They're just legends." I make a fist in irritation. "There are no truths in any of it! Not one bit of solid evidence. Only nightmarish ramblings and terrifying tales. It makes me furious."

Landor sighs. "Nightmares," he snorts. "They still bother you, don't they?"

I shake my head, but it's no use lying to him. He grasps my hand in his and squeezes comfortingly. "They'll pass, Kyla," he says. "I promise you, they'll pass."

I know he's lying. I can see it in his face. Feel it in the way his skin turns a deadly cold. Watch it in the flickering memories he shields behind his eyes. I don't believe his words for one moment. The repercussions from that night have never faded. I don't think they ever will. They've only gotten worse. Grown stronger. Scarier.

"I'm better now, Lan. You should go back to the party. It's not often that you get the Celectate's personal approval to enjoy such a celebration." He usually has to guard the palace wall, but the Celectate allowed him the night off since he was the son of a High Lord.

"You should come back too," Landor urges me. He grips my hand. "People will start to wonder where you've gone. There's already too much danger to your reputation."

I raise a brow at him. "So you heard about yesterday then, eh?"

He scrunches up his face. "I heard about an 'untidy, unpresentable' scholar returning from a late night at the temple who may or may not have been a female in disguise. I was actually referring to the reputation that you can never be found three hours into a party and that you have not attended any special gatherings in honor of the Celectate for some time." His words, though said in jest, hit the mark he expertly intended.

I release my wrist from his hand and gently nudge him towards the large doors. "Just a few more minutes. Don't waste the evening on me."

When he still hesitates, I push him playfully from behind. "I want to . . . gather my senses." Gods know, I'll need them.

My answer suits him. He nods absently and disappears through the doorway, closing it gently behind him. I turn back to stare at the bookshelves, surveying the vast amount of leather and paper that, a few moments ago, had been my whole world. Now it all burns away before my eyes.

"People are saying your father has, shall we say, forgotten his loyalty to the Celectate."

The Wilds appear before me again.

"What's even more interesting is that it's affectionately called . . . Treason!"

My father is on blackened ground, clawing at dirt, while savage humans with sharp teeth tear his body to pieces.

My head throbs once more. I press fingertips to my temples but it doesn't go away. If father is against the Celectate – will he be ostracized?

Three years ago, I wouldn't have had to think of such a thing. And, to be honest, I shouldn't even be thinking about it now. My father is loyal to the Celectate. Granted, he doesn't always favor the Celectate's ideas, but he still supports him and gets the laws passed. He'd never think about starting a rebellion or a riot or anything that would harm his ruler, no matter what he thought about the man himself. He is not a violent man. He is not a Lord Telman or any of the previous seven High Lords who have met such a horrendous fate.

He won't be ostracized. He can't be.

"Lady Kyla?"

"For gods' sakes, I don't want a damned tart or a cursed glass of spirits or . . ." I bite back my words when the newcomer steps out of the shadows beside the door. I take a shocked step back – right into the wooden shelf.

"Forgive me, my lady. I didn't mean to startle you so badly." Painstakingly formal and polite, the newcomer bows elegantly in the shadows, his features a dark blur. I'm awestruck by how attractive his silhouette looks in the ill light.

"T-that's alright." My back screams its disapproval.

He steps out of the shadows and my stomach does a quick loop to the floor. A good look at his face – at his eyes – and all good feelings fade away.

It's Aspen Wood.

I have not seen him this close since three years ago – since the night of the horrible "mugging." I had left his father's library a laughing, carefree human being who didn't understand the viciousness that ran in his blood. Occasionally, I saw him at public parties or at executions and ostracizements – particularly those of the High Lords – but always kept my distance.

Struggling to find a way to insert my getting-out-of-the-spotlight skill, I curtsy as gracefully as I can. It's a clumsy attempt since my whole body feels as unmoving as stone. I take a step forward and nearly trip over the delicate hem of my dress.

Curse this thing! Curse it!

"Odd place to find you, my lady, if I may so. You do know that this is our personal library?" He quirks a brow at me, hands folded behind his back casually.

"Y-yes. Yes, of course." My tongue is in knots. I can't think of words fast enough – words smooth enough to excuse my presence in his personal quarters. I know the anger his father possesses with those who overstep their boundaries. I know the wrath that runs in his blood. It slit a man's throat just the other day. "My apologies, your highness. I . . . er . . . was getting some air . . . no, I mean, I needed to walk . . ."

Fool! Think of something to say, you ass!

"The gardens are that way," Aspen says. He points out the door and crooks his finger to the right – from the direction I had come. His lips are quirked at an odd angle. He knows I'm lying.

It is then that I recall the ill-bred language that flew from my lips at his arrival. Note to self: make sure you're addressing a servant before you proceed with a verbal lashing.

The silence is hell itself. I welcome the heat on my cheeks.

Aspen steps closer and casually lifts his chin to stare at the massive walls. "It is magnificent, isn't it? I could see why it would interest you. You haven't changed at all, Kyla. Every time you came here, you went straight to this room. My tutor despised you." He chuckles at the memory. I can barely recall it. I flush when I realize he has dropped all formality by calling me by my given name.

"What were you so interested in tonight that you had to sneak away from my father's celebration?" he asks.

None of your damned business, I want to say. The words die on my tongue.

"I . . . I heard he'd acquired numerous books on . . . on Kelban folklore, and wanted to see if it was true. Just goes to show what rumors can make a person do. But you're right. I have been away from the party far too long. I should get back."

I attempt to sweep by him, but he blocks my way by placing a hand against the sofa. He tips his head to the side and a wisp of dark brown hair crosses his eyes. Eyes I used to call temptingly sweet when I was a modest ten years of age – until I realized how strikingly similar they are to Celectate Wood's. A soft scent of wine and mint lingers on him.

"Your highness . . ."

"Aspen."

"I beg your pardon?"

"Call me Aspen," he says.

It's an order, not a request, and I swallow nervously. "Very well,

Aspen. If you'll excuse me . . ." Once more, I try to step by him.

His hand closes around my wrist and stops my departure, his thumb running over my pulse with a gentle stroke. The control I've used to stabilize my emotions begins to crumble. The last man who touched me without permission got an elbow between his ribs. But, in all fairness, I had been dressed as a scholar, with ample room to move my legs. Here, in this enclosed space, wearing a dress ill suited for my romping character, I must behave the lady. And ladies don't head-butt rude young men.

"I missed you the other day at the ostracizement. Your mother said you had a headache."

He spoke with my mother? I knew she wasn't telling me something. Knowing that Celectate Wood's son had been craving my company might have prepared me for this little altercation. Might have forced me to memorize a conversation-starter or two. Now I must blunder through like a complete idiot.

"Y-yes."

"I hope you are feeling much better."

I grasp at the chance he's just handed me. "Actually, music has always made me feel a bit ill. I couldn't listen to it any longer, and I remember the library was always so quiet – and unused."

"Indeed. You and I were the only ones who found it a pleasant place." The way he says it makes our previous relationship seem much more important than it actually was.

I pull my wrist from his. "I really have to go."

He bars my way, a mass of muscle against my petite frame. I long to cuss him out. To drive a fist into his gut and clear the obstruction from my exit. But he's the Celectate's son. I cannot endanger myself by physically attacking him.

However, I've never been one for lack of words. "You know," I say, and lean back against the shelf, "on the streets this behavior would be called harassing."

"Really?" He leans close. So close his nose brushes mine. I gasp softly and pull back, my head pressing hard into the shelf. There's nowhere to go as he gets closer – until less than an inch remains between our faces. His warm breath teases my neck. "And what would you know about the streets, if I may be so bold, Kyla? Are the rumors, perhaps, true?" He flashes a knowing grin.

"I don't know what you're talking about!" I snap.

"No?" he asks. "I was sure you'd heard the rumors. And that language – did you pick it up from your brother? It sounds familiar on your tongue. You've had plenty of practice cussing unruly vagabonds, haven't you?" He leans forward, past my cheek, and his lips hover over my ear. "Did you, perhaps, excuse yourself from Lord Telman's banishment to play the gentleman? Such scandalous behavior, my lady, needs to be punished, don't you think?" He pulls back and his gaze settles on my lips. He dips his head towards them.

I press a hand over my mouth. "What do you think you're doing, highness?"

He winks. "Waiting for you to push me away."

Which I do, with more force than he bargained for. He nearly falls over the backside of the sofa and regains his balance. He starts laughing. I recognize that laugh. His teasing laugh. The pounding in my chest calms. He was only teasing.

But it felt so real.

"Took you long enough," he chuckles and smooths the lapels of his black tunic. I am disgusted with the color. Black is the Celectate's color. The devil's color. "You've become patient. The Kyla I knew would have slapped me the moment I barred her way."

"The Kyla you knew would also have excused your behavior as childish. But we are not children anymore, are we, Aspen?"

He stops smiling. "No, we are not."

The silence is almost as unbearable as the hell moments prior to it. At this point, a bolt of lightning in the middle of the room would be a welcome distraction. I see no servants in sight to trip, and vandalizing Celectate Wood's library would certainly overstep the boundaries I'm already pressing.

"Are you well?"

I widen my eyes. "Pardon?"

"Are you recovered from the . . . the mugging?" He says the word delicately, looking flustered at his attempts to restore the conversation. "I tried to call on you when you were abed with the fever but your mother wouldn't let me in the house. She said you were delusional and didn't recognize any faces. That my presence would only terrify you. She said you would wake screaming and thrashing like an insane person. Everyone was afraid you were going to die. It was weeks before I could sleep."

I had been very sick after the "mugging." The doctors had called it an infection. The priests had called it demons. Mother and Father had never left my bedside. When I finally regained my senses a week later and pointed out their faces, sleepless nights faded from their eyes. They had looked so relieved – especially Father. He blamed himself for what happened to me, even if he couldn't remember what had truly passed on that street.

"Yes. I am recovered," I say. The words sound terse and lack emotion. I've said them so many times, to so many people, they hardly mean anything anymore. What I really want to say is "No, I am not fine. I feel cursed. Demons visit me every night. I want them to go away. I want to slaughter their existence."

"Did I do something to offend you?"

I blink in astonishment. "I'm not sure what you mean."

"You never came back, Kyla." His voice softens and cracks slightly. "I waited for you to return. To join me in the library. To meet me in the meadow. To fly through a door one day talking about the latest tale of heroism you'd picked up from your brother. But you never came. And when I went to see you . . ." He bites his lip.

I remember when he came to see me. I had been hiding in the arbor beside the house, wishing him to be gone. Wishing I didn't see the hundreds of ostracized lives shining in his eyes. In eyes that resembled his father's. Wishing I could empty the contents of my stomach so I could rid the disgust inside of me. Hoping I never saw him again. And up until now, I'd kept that oath. Mother had told him I'd gone with Father to a distant city for business purposes. Aspen had left.

"I think your mother didn't want me to see you." The pain in his tone changes to bitterness.

Slowly I release the breath I was holding. Let him think Mother tried to end our relationship. He can do nothing to Mother about such a trivial thing. All mothers meddle with their children's relationships – *especially* noble mothers.

"She's a strange person," I say. At least that's no lie.

The silence returns, and I awkwardly pluck at the sparkling beads sewn on my bodice. Aspen amuses himself by slowly walking around the room, dusting off an occasional hardback, and reading the labels on their delicate spines. I observe him carefully through narrowed eyes.

He's gotten taller. I guess six foot one. I remember him as a skinny, lanky, awkward child who looked more like a young tree than a boy. That sapling body had transformed into one of sleek muscle and agile limbs. He had sported a freckled face, which developed into a pockmarked face, which has now transformed into a clear complexion of glowing skin.

"Has my appearance silenced your tongue?"

Heat, burning and nauseating, crawls up my neck as I realize he's noticed my perusal. "N-no, High . . . Aspen."

His robes swish around him, silk chaffing against his boots, as he stomps forward. The hardback in his hand shines with newly polished leather and I can't help but notice the delicate etchings of the title. It is a familiar volume. I have read it hundreds of times over in Master Rolfe's study, contemplating its tales, teachings, and legends. It supposedly contains every single myth or story ever told in Kelban history – but it contains nothing of the Wilds. Therefore, it contained nothing useful for me.

Aspen holds the book out towards me. "We used to read it together," he says. "Do you remember?"

My stomach does a whirl. I remember. I remember lying stomach-flat on the floor of this library, shoulder-to-shoulder with Aspen, chuckling over the many mystified stories brushed onto the pages by an artist's hand. I had been such a child then – such a little, foolish child – to carelessly laugh like that.

I nod in answer to his question. "Yes."

He flips the book open. The pages smell familiar – of cider, and smoke, and wood chips on an autumn day. They rustle with age and the spine makes a sullen, aching noise – almost as if it's been disturbed from sleep. Aspen's fingers tentatively explore the well-worn page located in the middle of the giant book – a tale of the destruction of the other half of Kelba, now the Wilds.

"We had such aspirations then," he mutters.

I don't like where this is going. If I stay in this room, with him, with the building memories, everything I've struggled to keep inside, to bury, will unleash itself. I'll launch myself at him, rake my nails across his face, and ask why he doesn't see the horrors in front of his eyes. Why he can watch people – like Lord Telman – brutally destroyed by the man who sired him.

"I don't focus on the past anymore," I mumble. His head jerks up at my outburst and the dull ache disappears from his eyes. He nods and returns the book to the shelf. I breathe a sigh of relief. "We should return to the party."

He nods and we both exit the room. I wait for him to walk away. To rejoin the comrades he surely has or offer his company to some other blinded fool. Instead, his arm wraps around my back, and his fingers splay out along my hip. I feel those fingers burning their warmth all the way through my clothing to the skin beneath. I see his father holding a bloody knife and a man gagging and ripping at his torn throat for survival. Next to him lies a severed tongue. My stomach drops.

Relief slides through me when we enter the Circle and come face-to-face with my parents – Father looking very pale and tired. The sagging skin beneath his eyes makes him look like an old man. Mother looks radiant as ever, not a hair out of place or a pallor of color absent from her cheeks. They both make their appropriate greetings to the lone heir, and Aspen returns them graciously.

"Are you having a good evening, your excellency?" Mother asks, her eyes flickering from Aspen to me, and his hand on my hip. I want to sink into the floor when an understanding smile crosses her features. She knows. She knows that I don't wish for his company.

"Yes, Lady Elinor. I am having a splendid evening." Aspen smiles at me, his fingers tightening on my hip.

I smile back and look at my mother. *Help me, please.*

However, it is Father who lays a hand on Aspen's free arm. "I'm afraid we are going to have to take our leave, your grace. Your father requested an audience with me that I could not refuse and I'm afraid it has left me rather fatigued. It is a wonderful festival. All thanks to your father. May his reign be long and fruitful."

The smile never fades from Father's face. But it's a smile that opens the jaws of horror in my body. His "Art of the Mask" smile.

"*People are saying your father has, shall we say, forgotten his loyalty to the Celectate.*"

"I would very much appreciate it if Lady Kyla could accompany me for the remainder of the evening," Aspen says. He smiles at me. Those strange prickles flutter down my spine again as I imagine those eyes on a different face – his father's face.

No. No! I look at my mother.

This time she doesn't abandon me. She flashes a charming smile and places a hand on my shoulder. "I'm afraid Kyla is not used to such exertion. She gets unusually flustered as the evening wears on. It is best to let her get her rest so she doesn't succumb to bouts of fainting."

Aspen regards her with a tight, pinched expression but Mother doesn't flinch beneath his gaze. He believes she's interfering – but there's nothing he can do about it.

"Then I shall leave her to her rest." He moves his hand from my hip and takes my hand, pressing a quick kiss to my knuckles. It burns my skin with a reminder of whose son he is. "Are you sure she does not require a physician?"

"Just rest," Mother assures him. "Your excellency," she adds hastily. She wraps an arm around my shoulders and pulls me against her. Welcoming the embrace, I rest my head on her shoulder.

I really do feel tired.

"I wish you a safe journey home, Lord Bone," Aspen says to Father. He holds out his hand, which Father takes, and they give one another a hearty shake, smiles never fading from their faces. "My father has told me of your accumulated wealth with your new ventures in the white diamond mines."

Beneath the hearty facade, my father's jaw stiffens. "Yes. I have acquired great wealth. It is my luck and I thank the gods – and Calaisar – for everything. I often marvel that a humble lord like me should be blessed with such treasure and can only attribute it to my family . . ." He smiles at Mother and I. "And my attentiveness to the holy doctrines. What was that phrase? From the ancient chronicles of Kelba, I believe, it was. Ah, yes. 'Poverty wants money, money wants power, power wants supremacy, and supremacy breeds evil.' It is truly a wise text. I keep it close to my heart."

The silence could murder if it had weapons. Father does not flinch beneath the flash of darkness that glints in Aspen's eyes and it is gone moments later, replaced by a bright grin.

"Calaisar be with you, Lord Bone. Good evening, Lady Elinor."

He pauses when the time comes to wish me on my way and I wonder if he's going to drop my title and speak to me on informal levels in front of the entire crowd behind us. "Until the next time, Lady Kyla. I hope your nightmares cease."

He walks away.

The servants help me slip, or rather peel, the dress off my body. I wave them away when they try to dress me for bed. Though most high-class girls prefer their servants to dress them, I feel awkward not knowing how to put on my own clothes. I choose a simple white gown and tie a silken string around my waist to cinch it close.

The ride home had been one of the quietest of my life. Never had my parents been so sullen or smiles so absent. I hadn't helped much either. Father had attempted to ask questions about how I'd come into Aspen's company that evening – and I'd answered all in simple, one syllable phrases. Father had said he'd been in the Celectate's company for a good portion of the evening – and I had sensed the radiating tongues of emotion stirring inside his body. The carriage had been steaming with it. My stomach curdles just thinking about it.

The pounding in my ears grows deafening. Not again. Not again. However, try as I might, I cannot push back the wall of nausea and pain that envelopes my neck, buzzing along my skin, tearing at my skull. My fingers search my desk wildly for some sort of deliverance from the pain. But my carafe is gone. I entertain the notion of calling a servant for aid – and quickly shove it aside. No. No gossip will be spread about the daughter of an esteemed high lord suffering "perverse, demonic attacks."

Father has a carafe of his best wine downstairs on the table of our solar – the finest room in the whole manor. If I can make it down the stairs and just have a small sip this feeling, – this attack – will fade. My lungs burn in my chest as I open the door of my bedroom and slide out into the hall. My knuckles crack with strain as I grip the stair railing and take one shaky step after another to the main floor. The entire floor spins in front of my eyes as I meander dangerously across the open space between the stairwell and the "solar" doorway. At last, my fingers touch the knob.

The carafe glints in the pale candlelight flickering around the room. I pour some of its contents into a decanter and swallow the alcohol within. It slides down my throat, numbing my senses, and warming my insides. The buzzing in my ears fades and my limbs begin to regain control. As soon as I stop shaking, I'll return to my rooms.

I swallow another glass of the beverage.

"Hail, Sir Landor!"

I nearly choke on the frothing foam in my mouth. The servants always stand at attention and salute my brother when he returns home. It's so comical that he never contradicts them.

"Not now, Evan!" Lan's voice is as sharp as a knife and his boots stomp out a ferocious pace as they come closer – towards the "solar."

I look around for a place to hide myself but the boots pass by the slightly cracked doorway, and I catch a glimpse of his face. Its white and sagging – like he's lost his youth. The door of Father's study clicks open. Silence follows. Until . . .

"He did what?" Father asks. His voice is so loud, so startled, that I nearly drop the decanter.

I should return to my rooms. I shouldn't eavesdrop. I step out of the "solar" and face the empty hall. I glance at the stairwell and its shiny steps. I need to get some rest. But the light shining in the crack of my father's study, the hushed voices behind it, beckon me closer – until I'm pressed against the doorframe, listening as if my life depends on it.

"Celectate Wood is seizing Lord Telman's property and all of his assets . . . including Escar. He says the breeding of an army is very important to him and shall be one of his top priorities. No other High Lord can take such a matter as seriously as he does – so he's going to do it himself." There's a slight tinge of mockery in Lan's tone.

"The property of a High Lord must pass to a High Lord. There is no other way around it!" Father snaps. "Escar is a High Lord's city. A High Lord's heritage."

"But that's just the thing . . . Lord Telman had no heirs. His wife passed without the blessing of children. If he was low enough to take a mistress, his bastards cannot be found. The fight for his lands would create a rift between the Community as High Lords – like yourself, Father – bickered over who would acquire the lands."

"Do you see me as a small man?" Father growls. I imagine the angry flash in his eyes at the insult. "I am not capable of breeding an army – the funds alone would cripple us. Lord Singh would be a suitable inheritor of Escar. Not only is he the High Lord of the Treasury, but he also knows how to frugally divide wealth – the creation of an army would be a small task for a man like him."

I knew Lord Singh. He was a well-esteemed High Lord of the Community – a man with a harsh view on politics and a reputation for partaking in swordplay as well as treasury duties. I had met him twice, once at the young age of eight, and a second time when I had made my first appearance after "the mugging" at a party in High Lord Griff's home. He had found me sitting quietly in the garden with my pens and parchment, drawing the horrors of darkness from my visions. I still remember the feel of his hand on my cheek when he sat down and asked what I was drawing. "Hell," I had answered. He hadn't batted an eye. Hadn't gasped or lectured me on the qualities of a lady. Hadn't asked why I was drawing it. He'd only looked at the drawing, pursed his lips, and then nodded. "Yes, indeed, it does look like I imagined it. Perhaps our hells are one and the same." He had smiled, stood, and walked away. He'd never told my secret.

"Oh, perfect," Lan groans. "You do know that Lord Telman and Lord Singh were the closest of friends, right?"

"So?"

"So by referencing him, you announce a traitor's friend should rear an army. A traitor who had his greatest weapon – his tongue – brutally removed."

"Lord Singh has the greatest aptitude for a task like Escar."

"But Celectate Wood doesn't care about that, does he? No. He cares about keeping his ass on that throne, his claws in your throats, and seducing the citizens. He cares about power. Supremacy. He wants Kelba to himself. You're blind if you don't see it, Father!" Lan has never sounded so furious.

"And he can't do that with the Community breathing down his neck. We keep him in line. It's impossible for him to act without our consent." Father sounds so sure – but his words tremble slightly. Like the faintest breeze could decimate them.

"It wouldn't be impossible – if there was no Community!"

Father gasps and I stifle my own. No Community? Such an idea was preposterous. There had always been a Community. They kept Kelba prospering.

"He wouldn't dare!" Father snaps. "The Community gave him that throne. The Community gave him his power. And we can take it away!"

Even as he says the words – as the silence settles after them – the life fades from the conversation. Lord Drave. Lord Essan. Lord Telman. Five more names dotted that list. Five other High Lords. Once, the Community had been strong. It had held the final say in political matters. It had gripped Celectate Wood's leash. Now the collar was retracting – and the Community had lost its former strength. The people were as enraged with the High Lord as they were with the Celectate. One pretty speech from Celectate Wood and they could cease to exist.

"Celectate Wood lacks the funds to abolish the Community," Father fumbles, struggling – no, grappling – for a lifeline in the terrifying truth.

"But he doesn't lack the power." Lan's voice is full of logic and lacks emotion. He's only telling as he sees it. "He can ostracize every Community member if he has to until not one of you remains. Given a choice between the Wilds or proclaiming him a supreme monarchy, which do you think the Community lords will choose?"

They would choose life. It was the same for the people of Kelba. Rather than be ostracized, they stopped rebelling. Lord stopped refusing the Celectate. Citizens stopped refusing the lords. And fewer people were banished. Those who were became examples that we never forgot. Like Lord Telman. The Community would not want to become that example.

"It won't happen," Father declares firmly.

I hear him stand and duck back into the "solar." I watch him exit the study and start up the steps towards his room. Mother must have been waiting so long for him. I'm sure he has much to tell her before they will actually sleep. I wait for Landor to turn off the study light, for his boots to stop clicking on the floor, before slipping into the hall. It is lit purely by candles and shadows dance in the walls before me. A tingling vine wraps around my insides. Those shadows look so familiar . . . look so . . .

"You heard it all, didn't you?"

His voice startles me as he steps out of the shadows, arms crossed in displeasure. I try not to let him intimidate me. I have done nothing to be chastised for. He repeats the question and I nod.

He groans tiredly and rubs the back of his neck with his hand. "You really shouldn't poke your nose into things that aren't for your ears, Kyla. You have enough things to worry about without bothering yourself over father's matters."

Selena's cruel words harass my mind. I have to know. I have to have the rumors clarified.

Landor's body stiffens. He knows I'm getting ready to ask something that will surely change the simple "don't ask" relationship we have.

"Father doesn't support the Celectate, does he?" I blurt. I feel as if I've swallowed on of my physician's horrid concoctions when I ask it.

Landor's expression is response enough.

I know. Father doesn't support the Celectate. Father, by Celectate Wood's definitions, is a traitor. And traitors are . . .

Ostracized!

"Go to bed, Kyla." Lan wraps his arms around me, and I realize I've started shaking again. "It will be alright. Father's hidden it for years and shown no definite proof. The Celectate still needs him. Father possesses a fortune in white diamonds, the rarest gems in all of Kelba. He won't throw that away for such a mere trifle as 'disagreement.'"

He gently nudges me towards the stairs. The steps vibrate beneath my feet.

Nothing will be all right. Lord Telman hid his tyranny well. Lord Essan hadn't even shown the slightest hint of disloyalty when he attempted to poison Celectate Wood. Lord Drave had become Celectate Wood's right-hand when he attempted to bury a knife in his side.

Father's words, misplaced or misunderstood, could destroy him.

My room has grown smaller, and I feel cramped. My head pounds with frightening accuracy against the parts of my skull that are the most sensitive. I self-consciously touch the scars beneath my hairline, running fingers lightly over the indents. They pulse against my fingertips, creating their own melody in my ears.

Your father's a traitor. A traitor! He can be ostracized. Ostracized!

If the Celectate did, indeed, abolish the Community and declare himself an official monarchy that would mean he could make all the rules, laws, and decisions for Kelba. Though the "Ostracized Act" had been quite efficient in handing him more control, it hadn't completely given him everything he wanted. I had seen the hungry look in his gaze – that animal desire inside of him whenever he opened his mouth, or looked at a crowd during a "banishment." The Community still held him at bay from what he truly wanted – complete power.

If he did gain such power and found out that father disagreed with his policies, would he dare ostracize him?

He won't find out.

Father was a careful man. He had been playing this dangerous game between life and death before I was born.

I crawl into bed. The covers warm my skin and sleep brings its canopy that much closer. My memories play out before me as they do every night. The festival. Selena's torturing accusations. The numbing attack. The words exchanged between Landor and I in the silence of the library. Aspen's silent appearance from the shadows. Our conversations. Our goodbyes.

I sit up straight.

"*Until next time, Lady Kyla. I hope your nightmares cease.*"

Cold claws grip my throat. The only one who had mentioned my nightmares that night had been Landor when he'd rescued me from Selena's presence. Right after Selena had mentioned the rumors about my father.

Aspen had heard *everything.*

Chapter V

I am different from most people. When I have pressing matters on my mind, I find a way to energize myself. It is unladylike to wrestle. It is unbecoming to run extensively.

So I throw knives.

When Landor first began his training, he came home every day with some new sort of weapon. He made himself his own personal corner near the stable walls. It was bare of grass or statues that decorated our lawn and occupied a twenty by twenty square foot space. He'd position himself in that square and practice every day, for hours. He was determined, he told me, not to bring shame on his father by failing his duty. He said he'd become adept with each weapon – and he did.

Eventually, I came out to watch him practice with the fellow trainees he would bring. They'd each try to have their own matches with different weapons: swords, daggers, lashes, and even their bare hands. They would also try to scale the barn wall, which had a height of twenty feet. Very few of them ever made it without scrapes or misplaced feet. None of them could get up in under ten seconds. The Wild boy scaled a forty foot high building within seconds, and with an ease I hadn't seen in anyone else since.

I remember the day I made myself the laughingstock of Landor's group. I was two days shy of my fifteenth birthday and still recovering from the attack four months prior. I'd watched my brother's ease with the dagger. How swiftly he could aim and how fluidly the blade left his hand to find its mark. I immediately fell in love with the sight and tried to work up the courage to ask for his training.

At last, I readied myself for the task, walked up directly behind him at the water trough where he was washing the grime from his body along with his companions, and waited quietly for him to turn around.

Eventually one of Landor's friends made a grunting in his throat and gestured at me. Landor had turned around, wiping water from his nose. I still remember how intimidating he looked, all sleek muscle and incredible height. But I wanted his help too bad to back down so soon.

"Teach me the dagger, please, Lan?" I had pleaded, taking his hand in mine, and looking up at him with earnest eyes.

For a moment, silence settled over the area. All the boys stopped splashing and turned to stare at me. Then they started laughing so uproariously my eardrums thumped with the strain.

"Hey, Lan, your little brother wants you to teach him how to fight!"

"Hey, Landor, she's a regular tom-cat."

"Landor's little brother Ky!"

I remember my face burning hot with shame and tears welling up in my eyes. I looked away from Landor's face as a red rash crept up his neck and into his face. Embarrassment. I'd embarrassed him. Something I'd promised myself I'd never do to him.

I had turned and wanted to run, but Landor didn't release my hand. Instead, he pulled me back and his arm settled over my shoulders. He'd turned to face his companions. "Who said that?" he asked. I still remember the coldness in his tone. The fire in his eyes as he spoke. Everyone went silent again.

"Who called her a boy?" Landor asked. No one answered.

Landor had looked around at all the faces and picked one out of the crowd. "It was you, wasn't it, Craig? You called her my little brother."

Craig had gone white as a sheet and taken a step back. "I- I meant no harm by it!"

Landor hadn't hesitated a second. He'd pulled me over to the square, placed a small knife in my hand, telling me to begin with something small, and work my way up to larger objects, like daggers. None of the other boys dared to leave while Landor taught me all the basics and had me throw it for the first time.

My attempt was very poor and didn't even reach the wall. One boy laughed. A look from Landor silenced him forever. I threw again. Again. Again. Each result was poorer than the last, until my ears were burning with shame at my incompetence.

Landor observed my frustration and leaned close in my ear. "You're failing because you think you're going to. Don't think. *Aim.* Direct your eye towards the place you want to hit, command your wrist as you throw, and judge the weight. It's as easy as throwing a ball once you set your mind to it." The last phrase was a lie, and we both knew it. But it didn't matter. I did as he said.

The knife didn't stick in the target but it did reach its mark – the hilt where the blade should have been. I had to learn how to balance it so the blade entered the target, not the hilt.

From then on, Landor made time after his practice for me. I was there waiting for him. His fellow trainees no longer laughed at me. Some even offered to help, handing me different knives, collecting the ones I threw, and sharpening the ones I made dull with all my practice. Eventually, my knives made it onto the target – the very edge. Slowly they started having more accuracy. More precision. Until I could successfully throw a knife at the circle in the middle of the target. The resounding shuck as it embedded itself in the canvas was the most pleasing sound that ever reached my ears.

When my mother finally wandered outside to see what I was doing during the afternoon hours, I expected to be scolded and taken back inside to stitch my own clothes. Instead, she had given me a smile that warmed my insides. Behind the smile was an aura of pride. She had been proud of me. Whether it was because I was trying to protect myself from future "attacks," or because I was very stubborn about honing my skills, I've never known.

I'd once asked Landor why he'd taught me when all his friends had made fun of me for asking to do so. Why he had stood up for me when it was within his rights as an elder brother to scold me for even thinking to ask such a question. He had answered simply that I was his sister and that I had as much right to choose as he did. If I chose something that he could tutor me in, he felt it his duty to teach me. Because he loved me. The fact that my tough older brother, who had many important matters to deal with and was so much older than I, had told me he loved me chased away my nightmares for almost a week.

Pulling back my arm, I aim for a destination on the target and throw, moving my wrist fluidly forward. The blade flies through the air and lands right where I wanted it: the outer rim of the circular dot.

My heart pounds with the momentum of my exercise. Energy flows into my brain, buzzing along my spine. Any dreary thoughts distance themselves from my central focus, and I pick up another dagger, six inches in length. Its weight is greater than a minuscule knife, but its blade is thin and can surge through the air faster.

I breathe in deeply, grasp the hilt, and fling it forwards, releasing the breath. I hear it singing through the air and then the satisfying sound as it connects with the target. Directly in the middle.

I didn't even have to look anymore!

Behind me, I hear clapping. Landor walks up to the target and pulls the dagger and the knife from their places. He tosses the knife at me, hilt first, and I grasp it before it can hit the ground. He nods, approving the move, and walks straight up to me, placing the dagger back into the sheath at my waist.

"You've gotten better, Ky," he teases me, tweaking my chin playfully between thumb and finger. Though he didn't approve of his friends calling me his "little brother" that long time ago, he did adopt the nickname they'd given me.

Ky.

He was the only one who used it. He didn't allow anyone else to call me such a name. Moreover, mother and father wouldn't dream of calling me by such an unceremonious title.

"You could test my skills, Lan," I challenge with a lift of my eyebrows. I place the knife back in his hands.

"No thanks, Ky. I'm good. Craig and Asher completely spent all my energy on themselves already," Lan sighs, and stretches his arms.

"Who won?" I'd often participated as a bystander in one of the many brawls that the three boys liked to call "wrestling."

"I'd feel less of a man if it wasn't me," Lan says with a wounded look on his face. "Has your confidence in me begun to wane?"

"Not at all. My confidence in you is the same. But since Asher's lost all that 'paunch' he used to possess, he's been giving you a harder time. Do I need to make up another batch of butter-nut bread for him?"

Landor groans and flexes his shoulder. "You'd be saving my life."

I laugh.

All at once, the footman comes running around the corner of the stable wall, tugging his formal coat up his long arms. He's red in the face and panting for breath as he jogs towards the courtyard around the corner of the house.

"What's he in such a hurry for?" I ask, glancing at Landor for an explanation.

He only shrugs.

Curiosity getting the better of me, I skip towards the edge of the house and hear carriage wheels turning in the courtyard. Horses neigh and a whip hisses in the air. The wheels creak to a halt and I hear our footman yank open the door and say, "Your esteemed excellency. Your presence is welcomed!"

When I peer around the corner, I see the Celectate's carriage, with his four magnificent black horses drawing it. Our footman kneels down low to the ground as the occupant disembarks with sweeping robes that catch the edge of the door much like my dress did last night. With an irritated jerk, they are pulled free and the Celectate starts up the steps of my home. He disregards the servants who bow low to the ground with a tilt of his chin in the air. His dark eyes – eyes devoid of any emotion – stare straight ahead. The black ring on his left hand catches the light of the sun above and flashes in my face.

I blink to regain focus only to find him gone when my vision clears.

Landor has come up behind me and recognizes the carriage with a startled, "What in hell's blazes!" that Mother would surely remove from his vocabulary if she heard.

I ignore his outburst. "What's he here for?"

Did he find out about my father and come to confront him? Did Aspen squeal and tell his father what Selena and I had discussed? Was Father going to be ostracized?

I suddenly feel sick to my stomach and lean over, clutching my middle.

"Kyla! Kyla, don't!" Landor gasps and jerks me by the elbow so hard that I stand straight again. My vision grows hazy and every part of me goes numb at the same time. Landor catches me before I fall flat on the ground and sits down on a nearby bench beneath the shade of a bush. It offers a cool covering over my burning face. He rubs circles over my back until I start to breathe correctly again. "Honestly, Kyla, you've got to stop these spells you have! What are you going to do if I'm not there to catch you?" Worry stains his face.

"But father . . ." I start to say.

"Can take care of himself," Landor interrupts. He must see the horrendous images flashing in my brain written on my face because he palms my cheek and kisses my forehead comfortingly. "Father's a careful, smart man, Kyla. He can handle the Celectate. Meanwhile, worry about yourself first. This is getting serious." He presses a palm to my forehead. "Seriously, you'll kill yourself!"

I can't hold it back anymore. I grab him around the waist and lean close. "I'm afraid! I'm so, so afraid, Lan!"

Lord Telman's severed tongue. Watching Celectate Wood slit his attacker's throat. Blood splattering his robes. That man had just entered my home. That man was meeting my father.

Landor seems startled by my words before collecting himself and hugging me back. "It's okay, Kyla. The Celectate probably had some urgent matter to discuss with father, that's all. It's nothing, okay? It's nothing."

He doesn't sound one bit sincere. Uncertainty flows in his voice like poison.

It seems like hours before I hear the servants shuffling to a stand. It can mean only one thing.

Releasing myself from Landor's arms, I hurry towards the edge of the house again, just in time to see the Celectate's footman open the door of his carriage. The Celectate seems in no hurry to get inside, straightens his robes, and takes a lazy look around. I'm so awed by the complete lack of emotion in his eyes that by the time they connect with mine, it's too late to hide. His eyes draw me in and he observes my face, for a few moments, with cold calculation. Every nerve in my body jolts to attention at that gaze. It seems to look right through me.

Not wanting to be seen as a coward, I tilt my chin up proudly and walk around the corner so that he can fully see me. His eyes squint into tiny slits at my appearance and he seems to be calculating whether to approach me or get into his carriage.

It's been a good two years since I've stood this close to the Celectate. After that fateful night, my father did not bring me to any more of his meetings with the Community. I only saw the palace at festivities like the First Moon Festival last night. The Celectate rarely presented himself at such festivals unless it was absolutely necessary. However, two years has done nothing to diminish my memory. I haven't forgotten his eyes nor the youthful look he possesses, despite the truth that he is nearing sixty years of age. Not a gray hair decorates his neatly combed black hair. Not a wrinkle mars his face. The unnatural look in his eyes sends more shivers down my spine.

I refuse to flinch beneath them.

Apparently, the Celectate's seen all he needs to. He steps inside his carriage, pausing only once to turn around and give me a strange smile. It spikes every bad feeling I've ever had into my gut, twisting a knot of anxiety deep within. The carriage door closes behind him, blocking his face from view. Shielding me from his hideous smile.

His visit was not about anything good.

The carriage rolls to life, slowly departing from the courtyard, and out the gates of my home. Only when they close behind it do I get a chance to breathe.

From inside the house, glass shatters and a cry of rage reaches my ears.

Father!

Finding the correct room is not a problem. My mother would have welcomed the Celectate into the Sanction, the family quarters where we spend our time together. It's the loveliest room in the house, complete with lavish couches that the Celectate could sit upon. And there's enough glass fixtures in that room to fill the fountain in the middle of our courtyard.

The moment I enter the room, Mother shrieks, "Kyla, stop!"

If it had been anyone but Mother, I wouldn't have listened. Instead, my feet halt – right before they would have plunged into the broken glass vase shattered on the ground. Close by lies another, shards decorating the immaculate carpet that cost a fortune.

Father stands in the middle of the room, fists white with strain, his eyes ready to bulge from a reddened face. I've never seen him so angry. He's always been the most controlled man I've ever known. Now his eyes are wide and maniacal, looking around the room for something to throw.

"I swear to you I won't do it! I won't! He can hang me from the highest wall in all of Kelba and I'd still say no. This is all his wickedness. His greed for my diamond mines!" Father screeches. "That bastard!"

Realizing the servants are probably hearing every word of his rant, I turn around to close the door. Landor is already there, shutting them securely and sliding the lock into place. When he turns to face me, curiosity creases his brow. I offer a confused shrug.

"Gavin, lower your voice, for all our sakes. If the servants report what you've just said . . ." Mother tries to put a smooth polish to her voice but we can all detect how strained it is. She's slowly losing control too.

Her hand rests on Father's arm. He shakes it off.

"To hell with the servants. That bastard can have 'em! I'll be dead before I let him bind that spawn of his with my daughter!" Father lets out another roar of rage and kicks ferociously at the couch before him. The sound of splintering wood and cracking bone snaps my senses and Father falls onto the cushions, clutching his leg in one hand.

The room suddenly feels like a prison closing in around my swirling head. Everything floats insecurely before me. The buzzing starts in my ears and slithers down the rest of my body until I am light as a feather.

"What did you say?"

Father stops moaning. Mother looks up from his feet, where she's inspecting his newly broken toe. They both look first at Landor and then at me.

My vision clears, and I can finally breathe again. "The Celectate . . . what did he say?"

It's as if I haven't said anything. They just stare at me, mute and dumb.

Feeling as if I'm the only one who hasn't completely clarified the situation adds irritation to shock. The scars on my neck palpitate with my pulse, curdling nausea in my stomach.

Still they don't speak.

Grasping a white figurine from the delicately carved mahogany table, I fling it across the room. It shatters against the wall in a thousand pieces and joins the glass Father deposited moments earlier. My action rouses everyone from their silent reveries.

"What . . . did . . . HE SAY!" I scream, my throat cracking with the strain.

Father looks at me helplessly. Slowly he clears his throat. Licks his lips. Rubs his slick palms over his knees. "The Celectate said . . . ordered . . . you to be bound to his son a month hence."

I didn't hear wrong. My mind didn't register his outburst incorrectly. The Celectate came to order my bonding. To Aspen.

I can't breathe. I can't see. I can't think. There's only one question swirling around in my mind. *Why? Why? Why?*

"I won't have it! He can ostracize me for all I care! I won't have it! I'm going after that bastard and strangling every last drop of blood from his wretched body. He can't treat my daughter like filth! Like gold to be tossed around to beggars!" Father's voice grows higher and higher. With each new word, my heart pounds faster and faster. It pounds out a familiar phrase.

Ostracized. Ostracized. Your father will be ostracized!

I can't think. Not in this room. Not with my father so upset and determined to commit an act of treason. With my mother crying and begging him not to do it. With my brother standing helplessly by the doors.

I need to get out.

"Kyla, don't!" Landor cries as I dash for the door, snap the lock free, and rush out into the atrium. He makes a grab at me and misses.

Servants dodge out of my way as I fly up the stairs and down the hall towards my room. Below me in the atrium, Landor calls after me to stop and Mother pleads with Father not to yell so loudly. The door of my room opens so easily I wonder if I even touched the knob. It slams behind me just as easily. The lock is in place.

I am alone.

Curling up on the bed, my knees under my chin, I contemplate what has just happened. Everything from the Celectate's arrival to my Father's outburst that I am to be bound to Aspen.

I knew my "bonding" ceremony would come one day. I have prepared myself for it. However, I had hoped, wished actually, to be able to pick my own spouse. Father had all but guaranteed that he would trust my instincts when it came to my choosing a companion for life.

"*The Celectate ordered for you to be bound to his son a month hence.*"

From downstairs, I hear Father raging once more and Mother trying to quiet him down. Her fears are my own. If Father goes after the Celectate and refuses the order, he's defied him. By law, Celectate Wood can sentence him to his fate. Father will be ostracized! Sent behind the Wall of Kelba into the Wilds. Images of poison drifting up beneath Father's feet, eating away at his flesh until not even bones remain, makes me sit up straight in bed.

From behind my door, Landor's voice drifts in, pleading softly with me. "Kyla? Kyla, open the door. Kyla?" He tries to twist the knob. The lock holds true. "Kyla, please."

Father can't be ostracized. Father can't refuse the Celectate.

Wiping away the tears that have unconsciously stained my cheeks, I march to the door.

Father *won't* be ostracized.

When I open it, Landor's fist almost cracks against my skull. He pulls it back just in time. He stares at me long and hard, waiting for me to say something before finally clearing his throat. "Do you . . . Can I do anything?" he asks.

When I look into his face, I see it. He knows.

He knows what I'm going to do.

When I gently squeeze his hand, a shiver runs through me. It is ice cold. Releasing it, I walk to the top of the stairs. Below, Father stands, his own hands clasped together impatiently. His foot taps on the tiles, drumming out a rhyme in my head.

He won't be ostracized. He won't be ostracized. He won't be ostracized.

I take a deep breath, ready to completely abandon myself, wishing I could disappear. Mother's tender gaze catches my eye. One look and steel hardens my nerves. She knows too.

Everyone seems to know except the one I'm determined to shield.

"I . . ." The words stick in my throat. I try again. "I . . ."

Don't. You can't back down now. You have to say it. You have to.

"I will bond with Aspen Wood."

Surprisingly, Father doesn't say anything. Only stands there in shock. Then, without a word, he turns and walks inside his solar, closing the door tightly behind him. I hear no sounds from within. No chair. No desk being opened. Whatever he's doing inside, it's something that doesn't require movement.

Tears blur my vision. I shake them away.

I *will* bond with Aspen Wood.

I will.

Why can't I convince myself?

Chapter VI

I never knew how much knowledge – how much planning – would be needed for the ceremony.

In Kelba, the "bonding" ceremony is symbolic. The couple being bound comes before the holy altar. The High Priest then takes a knife from a golden dish on the altar and slits first the woman's left wrist and then the man's. Producing a diamond studded thread he then ties the wrists together, binding them, blood and all, into one. It is a blood covenant. Blood, once mixed, can never be separated. The diamond studded thread is supposed to mean the bond is unbreakable since diamond is the hardest mineral in Kelba. Finally, once the ceremony is complete, the newly bonded couple departs to private quarters where they complete the last part of the ceremony: the "consummation act." Two weeks after the bonding ceremony, a celebration is held in which the public can fully join in wishing the new couple on in life. It is held two weeks after the ceremony so the couple can present a picture of being happy together in public, indicating their bond is holy and love abounds. The wounds on the wrists will heal, leaving a scar that indicates the person is married.

My betrothed visited the house three days after I sent the acceptance envelope and properly acknowledged my parents. I could see the disgust both of them tried to hide when Aspen spoke. After that, we had met twice a week in a per-determined place for chaperoned visits with one another. Each time, Aspen found time to slip his hand into mine or to whisper his affections in my ears. Each time I nodded and inwardly retched.

Celectate Wood personally hired an instructor to school me in all the ways a proper Celecta should behave – if he dies Aspen assumes the reign. I would be wife of the ruler of all Kelba!

The instructor, Master Ragar, informed me of what I might expect in a marriage with one of the strongest, bravest, most-powerful men in Kelba – beneath the Celectate himself, of course. He talked and talked until my stomach was in knots. I pitied the long-deceased Celecta Erina. She must have been relieved when death took her.

The future Celecta was to know all about the fittings, traditions, and expectations of Kelban propriety. She should be calm and steady in times of political upheaval. A pillar of strength in wartime. A confident to her husband when he needed to empty his mind – or his loins. An approving mind if he chose to take a mistress. I often wondered if I should just make a statue of this perfect, complacent, timid, quiet creature they wanted and ask the gods to breathe life into the fixture.

Now, I am where I want to be. Master Rolfe's.

It is only two days until the "bonding" ceremony. Tomorrow night I will go to the temple for cleansing. The High Priest of Calaisar will bless my way and ask the gods to be kind to me – probably be requesting I reward my new husband with a child by the end of the year. A boy, if possible. I will pray all night long while the holy place cleanses me of whatever sinful manifestations I have thought in the past. Then I will continue to the palace, proceed with the ceremony, follow my new bond to our private quarters, and . . .

No. I can't think about any of it.

All of Master Ragar's carnal teachings slip from my mind and I lose myself in the pages of the legendary tale of "Gasan." Gasan was supposed to be a common sailor on the The Vast Sea between Kelba and Landor, the island my brother had been named for. While upon the sea, he was said to have discovered the crypt of the gods and they had agreed to grant him one wish for his great observance. He had requested immortality. However, as time went by and Gasan lived past the normal ages of men, he began to change. He watched twelve wives die and hundreds upon hundreds of offspring pass away in a world that saw them as miniscule. Therefore, he determined to make them a world where they would have power as well. He took dominion over the world and ruled it with an iron hand. As time went by, he lost sight of his original purpose and fell into ways of perversion so frightful that storybooks failed to describe its horrors. In those times, a young citizen heard rumors of Gasan's acquired immortality and went in search of the crypt of the gods. For eight years, he searched until his determination was rewarded. The gods offered him a gift too. They offered to make him even more powerful than Gasan so he could overthrow him and return the world to its former ways. However, the young lad had already made his choice a long time ago. He requested a weapon capable of destroying an immortal. A weapon like the sun. The gods provided him with the weapon. No sooner had they placed it in his hands then the boy slew them all. He returned to mainland and stabbed Gasan to death atop the roof of his palace for the entire world to see. Then he turned to the remaining gods. Wanting to live, the gods made a deal with the young warrior – they would leave for the heavens and never interfere with humankind again. However, the boy had different ideas. He ordered them to grant him immortality. With impending death, awaiting them the gods did as he asked and were allowed to live. The boy became the "high-god."

The very high-god that Kelba worships to this day. Calaisar. God of the Sun.

The story leaves me feeling empty inside. Even the gods make mistakes. I cannot count on them for help.

"You are too gloomy for one who is to be bonded in a mere two days," Master Rolfe chides. He sits down beside me.

I close the book with a sigh. "I am tired of the planning."

"Yes. The planning is the hardest part. But once you have that first lover's caress it will all flit away." I glare at him and he coughs uncomfortably. "Er . . . so I'm told."

"What would a virgin like you know about a lover's caress, Master Rolfe?" I ask.

"Well, I'm . . . uh . . . Virgin, indeed!" he snaps and reaches out to swat the top of my head.

I evade his hand and return the book to its proper shelf. "Don't be a tease today, master. I'm in no mood."

"I must offer my congratulations to you, Kyla. If I may say so, it is a wonderful match. You seem to suit one another well. And just think . . . you will be our future Celecta should our esteemed Excellency's death come soon, gods forbid." He bows politely. "If I have been mean to you in the past, please forgive those offenses."

Tingles linger on my spine. This is what I do not want. Fear. As soon as that scar stains my wrist, as soon as the bond is consummated, as soon as the gods plant a seed in my womb, I will be holding the future heir of Kelba. People will fear me. I will have power. I will have anything I want. Like Gasan. Like Calaisar. But I don't want to be them.

I just want to be Kyla Bone – occasionally Sir Ky – with my nose stuck in a book, and daydreams about the Wilds.

"I will ask one favor of you, Master Rolfe."

"Anything, dear girl."

I harden my gaze. "Don't ever call me 'Celecta' or 'excellency' or 'highness' or any of those foolish names. If I hear you call me anything but my current titles than you will be in deep danger. Understand?"

He nods with a smile. "Of course." He doesn't think I'm serious.

I've never been more serious in my life.

The door atop the library rings, and I turn my back quickly. I am still disguised as a boy, but my face has become the talk of the town since the announcement of my bonding. Everyone wants to get a look at the "seductive beauty" who stole the heart of the Celectate's heir.

"Are you too good for us now, Kyla, that you have to turn your back on us?"

"Yeah. I thought we were good friends."

I split a smile. I should have known.

Landor, Craig Hale, and Asher Rave shield the entire doorway. Through the atrium, windows the pale dusk light makes them resemble ghosts.

"We figured you'd be too busy with plans for your bonding to even consider wasting time away with warriors like us. But seeing as you're hardly the lady tonight, we wondered if you're up for one more night on the town with some old friends." Craig gives a smile so wide I think he'll split a lip. Ever since that long ago day when he'd bestowed my "nickname" he had been one of the most earnest supporters of my pranks – and eventually escapades.

I raise a brow at my brother. "A night on the town?"

"We're going by the inn and it's the end of the month . . ."

"I'm in."

The end of the month means that all the sailors return from out of sea and bring the fresh smell of saltwater and overseas news with them. Landor has always loved the tales they tell and he had a fondness for the sea that has not dissipated all these years. Though I am deathly afraid of water, Landor could live on it.

Wishing Master Rolfe a "goodnight" I grab my cloak and wrap it around my shoulders.

Asher wrinkles his nose at the head covering.

"Is it on backwards?" I ask.

"No. I just think it's a little large."

"Are you dissing my craftsmanship?"

"No." His eyes are gently honest. "But it makes your face look very thin. Have you lost weight?"

I ignore his comment. In truth, I haven't been able to eat for days. Every time I force something down my throat, Master Ragar's constant reminders of my "carnal abilities" brings it back up.

"I'd lose weight too if I had that old hound breathing down my neck twenty-four hours a day for as long as you have," Landor says. "I can't wait until the bastard leaves."

"Maybe we should send him to Asher's house," Craig jokes and pats his companion's belly playfully.

We all laugh.

However, Landor's eyes never leave me as we walk the streets towards the inn.

The inn is swarming with bodies; tall and short, fat and lean, odious and pleasant. Landor manages to secure a table for us by flirting with one of the well-proportioned serving girls. She flushes pink and quickly scoots four lads still "wet behind the ears" over to the fireplace and gives us their spot.

"What'll ye have?" the girl asks when she returns, looking at Landor first.

"Your finest ale," he says.

Craig and Asher ask for the same.

The girl looks at me, humbly lowering her eyes to the paper. Scholars rarely enter "questionable" places like inns. If they do, they usually order water or cider. And I have – until now. Master Ragar's voice croaks in my head: *"When he leans into you, spread those hips wide and . . ."*

"Ale. Your strongest," I mutter.

The girl's brows lift high but she doesn't question my choice. She disappears with a swing of her hips to collect the orders.

"Ky . . . can you handle it?" Landor asks.

I glare at him. "Ask Master Ragar to give you a lesson in 'child-making' and then see which beverage you prefer."

Landor flushes to the roots of his hair. "Another one? Gods-curses, how many lessons must he give you. It's really very simple."

"He makes it sound like a skill!" I snap.

"Oh, it is. But one not taught with words," he mutters. My insides flop.

The girl returns with the drinks before I can add my own disapproval to his statement and plops them down in front of us. I lift the cup to my lips and take my first large gulp. It burns a trail down my throat, but I don't dare cough it back up. The heat it leaves behind numbs the disgust inside of me. I can't wait until it numbs everything.

"You do remember that Aspen, the son of the man you serve, is going to be the one who isn't teaching me with *words*, right, dear brother?"

Landor chokes on his ale. Craig pounds him furiously on the back.

"Take it easy on the guy, Kyla," Asher reprimands solemnly.

Landor waves them both off and turns on me, eyes blazing furiously. "You realize I hate this as much as you, right? That if I had my way with things, I'd drive a good five-knuckled fist into that hell-cursed, whore-born . . ."

I cut him off before he can continue with what would be a traitorous sentence, even if it were conducted under the influence of alcohol. "Allow me to do the honors." It will be a good fight I'll put up before I let Aspen spread my legs – and I'll guarantee there will be blood and bruises.

But at the same time – as the liquor numbs my senses – I feel a different kind of pain. *Father.* We have not spoken much since I sent my acceptance letter. There is not much to say. I am saving his life, even though he doesn't know it. If he is ostracized, Celectate Wood gets more power, more control – and I lose my Father!

I *won't* let it happen.

The girl returns to refill our drinks, and I finish mine off before the boys do.

"A toast!" Craig says. We lift our third mugs. "To Kyla's future." He says it in a low voice so we don't rouse the attention of the crowd around us.

We down the drinks.

"Even if it is an injustice," Asher mutters under his breath.

I smile slightly. I knew Asher and Craig long before Landor was sworn in as a Celect Knight. They had been a trio of bad luck throughout Kirath, causing mischief everywhere they went. Those had been the good days: when we played, laughed, loved, and lived. The days before everything changed. Before I changed. Both boys had known me from the age of twelve and on. They had teased me every chance they got. They had helped me learn to throw daggers.

They had taught me to climb a tree properly. They had encouraged me to peruse my frequent visits with Master Rolfe just so they could tease Landor about his "little brother Ky." They had been the closest thing I had to friends – even if they were Landor's companions.

The music of pipes and fiddles in the large room drones on and on. People begin to gather around the fire – around the sailors – for the news and wild tales. I wait for Landor to join them. But he doesn't. Instead, he stares into the empty space of his mug. I nudge him and he looks up.

"Not tonight," he says dejectedly at my questioning look and stares back into his mug. I wonder briefly if he's drunk. No. A little numb, like me, but not drunk.

Craig and Asher appear just as sullen. The silence grows unbearable.

"Are you three being bonded as well? Because I see no reason for your ill-amused faces."

Landor smiles sadly, and I bite my lip. I know that smile. It's his regretful smile. His helpless smile. He looks at me and guilt shines behind his eyes. "Did you know I wanted to be a sailor?"

Okay, maybe he is drunk.

I laugh lightly. "Really? I want to be a bird."

However, when neither of the boys laughs, I stop. "What happened, then?"

Landor sneers and pulls the dagger from his side. He slams it to the table. Its modest leather sheath masks a keen, shiny blade I've seen him practice with a million times. Etched into the pommel of the sword is the Celectate's symbol – a half-lion, half-dragon head. It symbolizes strength and power. By wearing it, Landor proclaims that he is in the Celectate's service and protector of the ruler of Kelba. He is a Celect Knight.

Landor flips his finger at the weapon.

"I already had the plans drawn up. I had made a deal with a ship's captain and we were going to set sail for Landor in a week. Then father came home and informed me that Celectate Wood had requested an audience – a private audience – with me. When I arrived the man stamped me with his seal right there, and swore me in for training. I had no choice. No voice in the matter. I could see the underlying threat behind his eyes. He would punish me if I refused. He hadn't made the 'ostracized act' at that point, but he still had the power to hurt me." He laughs derisively. "And do you know what I did? Do you know what your brave brother did, Kyla? I took the coward's way out. I refused to speak my mind. I refused to refuse. I let my dreams go because I was afraid of being hurt. Of suffering. I'm a coward. Your brother is a coward."

"You are not a coward . . ."

"I am!" he snaps and drains the remaining contents of his mug in one swallow. "We all are. It was the same with that riot the other day. I was there, Kyla! I stabbed a man when he rushed for the Celectate. I killed a man – not for Kelba, not for citizens – for that odious man!"

He is breaking our agreement. He is talking about his secrets. He is shattering every last barrier between us because I'm about to do the same thing he did. I am going to throw my life away – my dreams, my choice, my voice.

"We have all killed and murdered and connived for him," Landor snaps. Craig and Asher watch him sullenly, not even attempting to interrupt. Their faces are crossed with guilt and regret. They look aged beyond their years.

Landor calls the girl again and she fills the mugs.

"So drink up, Ky," Landor mutters and thumps the mug down in front of me.

I stare at the watery brim.

"If you could go back . . . would you do anything differently?" I ask.

Lan sighs. "That's just the thing. That's what makes my skin crawl and my headache at night when I try to imagine what happened. Why I didn't speak up for myself. Why I didn't say "no" and take whatever came afterward. It's a simple answer too. I would have done everything the same. Because I'm the same person I was then as I am today. I'm afraid of that man." He slams his mug down, empty. "I'm so afraid of him that my skin comes alive around him and my thoughts are no longer my own."

Craig and Asher drain their mugs.

I do too. The burning liquid numbs my brain. I wish it would numb the fear growing inside of me too. I have more to fear than anyone else ever has.

I am going to be that man's daughter-in-law.

"What the hell have you done to her, Landor?" Mother stares at me with her mouth pressed into a thin line, eyes roaming the length of me. She wrinkles her nose. "Bringing her home past midnight – and like this! You boys ought to be ashamed!" She pokes Landor hard in the shoulder.

Landor grunts but doesn't relinquish his steady hold beneath my arms. I don't remember when he started carrying me – perhaps when we were past the third street. Or the fourth. Or the fifth. I don't remember. All I know is I had a damned fine time and everything feels so blissfully empty.

"And you two . . ." Mother spins on Craig and Asher.

"D-don't be mad at 'em, 'other. I a-am frine," I say.

Mother points a shaky finger at the boys. "I swear, if you ever do this again you'll be . . ." And then she stops. Her lips move, but no sound comes out of them. She doesn't have to say anything else. It's as if she's been struck by a bolt of lightning with how white her face has gone. Why are there tears in Landor's eyes?

"They 'on't do it agin. Will ya, 'oys?" I ask, searching their faces. Why are they so blurry?

Both boys look at me. I swear they look as pale as ghosts.

"N-no. We won't do it again," Craig says. Why does he sound like his world is ending?

Asher doesn't even have the heart to look at me.

Mother gently prods both boys with her hands towards the door. "It's late and she's going to be up all night tomorrow praying in the temple. Leave her to her rest." She pats their shoulders. "Yes. I'll wish her good luck for you when she's sober. Have a safe journey home."

She shuts the door behind them and returns to us.

Landor hefts me up in his arms again and follows her towards the stairs. Everything is so light. I could fly like a bird, I swear.

"I didn't make her do anything, mother," Landor says as we ascend to the second floor. "She made this decision on her own – it was her last one. Let her have that."

"Foolish boy. I'm not going to scold her. She wouldn't remember anything I say, anyway," Mother chastises. She leans close and whispers in his ear. I hear every word. "Do you think I've never danced with a bottle before? Honestly, son, I wasn't always such a *lady*."

Landor looks stricken but doesn't say anything. He deposits me on the floor of my room. The ground lurches beneath my feet, and I meander unsteadily in a half-circle towards my bed. I grab at one of the four posts and hold myself upright.

"Goodnight, Mother," Landor says and shuts the door behind him.

"Okay. Out of these clothes." She helps me remove the boy garments from my body, gently setting them aside on a chair. "Careful." She steadies me and slips my nightgown over my head, pulling my hair out of its neck for me. It feels wavy soft against my face, and Mother gently rubs a tendril of it beneath her fingers. "So pretty," she whispers and helps me lay back. "You rest now and I'll wake you in the morning."

She turns to go.

"I'm tired," I say.

"I know."

Everything comes rushing back. Master Ragar's lectures. Master Rolfe's fleeting moment of fear. Aspen's hand stroking my wrist. Celectate Wood's eyes boring into mine with cold calculation. Landor's aggrieved confession. Craig and Asher's sullen goodbyes. The burn of liquor down my throat. The empty abyss. The endless pains and questions and fears and doubts.

"No." I shake my head. Everything jumbles together until I don't know what I'm feeling or what I'm trying to say. My cheeks are so wet. My body feels so limp. So helpless. "I'm tired."

Why do I sound like a wailing child?

Mother returns and sits down beside me. Her cool, gentle hand strokes my forehead soothingly. "Let it out," she croons. Her hands drops to my neck – to where the scars pulse – and her fingers trace the ridges lovingly. "Let it all out, Kyla."

"I'm tired of . . . tradition." My words don't slur. They are too important to be ruined. "I don't . . . want this!"

Her hand stills and her lips press tight together as a flash ignites in her eyes. It disappears.

"I know."

Chapter VII

The journey to Kirath's Temple of Calaisar is so much longer than I remember it being. It is customary for the bonding bride to go to the temple the night before the ceremony to pray so she will be holy the next morning. She will enter the solar of the temple, where the altar is, and pray for Calaisar to calm her unrest and accept her fate that will come at sunrise.

For some reason the tales of the "sacred night" had always sounded distant and untouchable to my ears. I'd never imagined myself having to enter the solar alone, in the dark, and pray all night. Now, here I am, standing in front of the tall, marble pillars.

A long row of white clad priests stands beside the temple entrance, waiting for me to go inside. They will follow me to the solar and lock the door behind me. The idea of these creepy, tattooed men trailing my every move sends shivers down my spine.

Beside me Mother walks straight and proud, her neck gracefully poised, her chin tipped, and a neat sack slung across her arms. In the sack is the "bonding" dress the servants spent the last month preparing from blood red cloth. Though some girls have used blue or green for their "bonding" days, red is most appropriate, considering the "bonding" is symbolic of a blood covenant. In addition, the servants were in no hurry to disgrace the Celectate by not making the appropriate color for a successful bond. I haven't seen it yet. It is said that a curse awaits the girl who sees her dress before the sunrise of her bonding day.

However, being wed into Celectate Wood's family is a curse in itself.

Behind my Mother walks Father, dressed in his finest. Though we had every right to take a carriage, being part of the high-class, very few girls ever get such royal treatment when they go to their bonding days. I decided I wanted no royal treatment, considering I'd be receiving it tomorrow and every day after that.

The cobblestones rattle beneath my feet as we walk, shaking the teeth in my head. It helps to calm the nerves inside of me.

Ahead of me, two other girls are walking up the temple steps. Behind them, I observe their parents, siblings, and other relatives who have come to see them enter the temple to be cleansed. The thought of having company in the solar quells some of the shaking in my bones. I immediately notice that neither of the girls is high-class. They are smiling and look eager to enter the temple. They *want* their bonding day.

I envy them.

Standing at the bottom of the temple steps, I look up at the huge pillars that support the main ceiling of the building. The sky above the temple is turning a soft pink, giving the entire image a blissful appeal. I wish I felt as free as it did.

I prepare to bid farewell to my family. They will not see me in the morning. I will be prepared by the priestesses, and the Celectate's carriage will come to get me for the ceremony. When I do see them again, it will be in the crowd of those who gather to watch my bonding. Today is my last day with them. It is fading fast.

Landor's face remains blank as a sheet of paper when I hug him. But his arms squeeze me so tight and hold onto me so long that I know what he's really feeling and what he's trying so hard to hide. He won't cry. He won't say any nonsense. But he's falling apart.

"Good luck, Ky," he whispers in my ear. "Next time you get drunk don't tell anyone your most embarrassing memories."

It is only with the utmost control that I don't start crying.

Father isn't as strong as Landor. The moment I wrap my arms around his shoulders and hold him close to me, his comforting warmth calming my nerves, he breaks down into silent sobs that barely reach my ears. His hand pats anxiously at my hair, smoothing it, rumpling it, tangling it. I don't stop him and hold him closer.

"I almost lost you that night," he whispers brokenly. "And now I'm losing you again . . . for real."

Don't cry. Don't cry, Kyla.

I shake my head. "Never. You'll never lose me, Papa."

At last, we part. And it feels like my soul has left when we do so.

Turning away from him so I won't break down completely, I place my arms around Mother's waist. She clutches me close. I rest my head on her shoulder. It's the last time I'll be able to do so and it feels so comforting. She rubs my back calmly.

"Last quarter! Last quarter!" one of the creepy, tattooed priests says in a gravelly, high-pitched voice that grates like sand across my spine.

Fifteen minutes.

The two other girls quickly pull away from their families with happy smiles. I watch over Mother's shoulder as they ascend the steps of the temple, chattering like gossiping geese. One of them looks at me. Curiosity flashes across her face. She rejoins her friends.

Time flies fast.

Mother slowly peels my arms away from her waist and presses them to my sides. She leans down in front of me, eye-to-eye, and in a low voice, she whispers, "It's not wrong to make your own choices. No one can tell you different."

Her hands clutch my wrists tightly. Earnestly. She wants – needs – me to understand. I nod slowly, not sure, if I should take them to heart or not. "Not even a priest," she adds, flicking her eyes in the direction of the creepy temple guardians.

A twinkle glints in her eye, quickly disappearing. But it was there, just the same.

I pull away, glancing at Landor, at Father, and finally at Mother. They all smile distantly. They're not ready.

I'm not either.

A priest grunts impatiently. I turn my back and dart up the steps before real fear will force me to run away. I dash past the priests at the temple entrance and straight towards the solar. It's not hard to find. Above the solar is a carving of the fire symbol. The symbol for Calaisar, the High God. The doors are still open. Forcing myself to walk slowly is one of the hardest feats of my life. But I do it.

Finally, I pass the oak doorway and step inside the solar. It's a simple circular room with an alter placed against the curve of the wall in front of the door. Above it, Calaisar's symbol is carved in the roof, letting in moonlight that makes the silver altar gleam in gray magnificence. The floor is nothing but stone tiles, and they are cold beneath my bare feet. The entire room is chilly, and I rub hands over the goose bumps rising on my arms.

Behind me, the priests mumble something and then the heavy doors close behind me with a clang. The bar slams into place. I'm locked in.

"Who are you?"

Having gotten used to the silence, the chirpy voice makes me jump. When I glance in the proper direction, I finally see the two girls huddled together.

Only one of them is looking at me. The one who glanced my way outside the temple. Freckles dot her nose and cheeks in a peppery spray. In the cold room, they stand out like pimples on her pale white face, framed by scraggly brown hair. A modest brown gown adorns her slim body, out of which pierce long, bony arms. She regards me with curiosity.

Another girl in the circle, wearing a simple gray tunic that barely reaches her knees, snorts. She doesn't look up and she certainly doesn't glance in my direction. "Isn't it obvious, Helena? She's one of *them*. A high-class Kelban." There's ferocity in her tone. It paints me as something less than garbage.

"Are you frightened?" Helena asks innocently. Her voice is small as a child's. I inwardly question if she's being bonded.

"Don't talk to her!" snaps the fierce girl, raising a threatening hand.

Helena goes silent, but looks at me. She mouths "sorry" and

shrugs. I shrug back, offering a small smile of my own. I walk to the alter and kneel down before it. The silver light floats over my fingertips and it reminds me of the light that gleamed all those long years ago from the Wild boy's sword.

Bending low to the ground, until my forehead touches the cold stone floor, I breathe in. Then out. I repeat the process slowly, sharpening my nerves, calming my tremulous thoughts. I need to pray. I need to pray that by morning I have accepted my fate.

Father *will* be safe.

Somehow, in the silent, dark room, my senses seem so much sharper. My head feels so much more relaxed in the dark. It's as if darkness gives a comforting hug to me. I finally have the quiet I need to really think about Aspen, my bonding day, and Father.

"Father's hidden it for years. He's shown no definite proof. The Celectate still needs him." Landor's words float back into my memory. *"Father possesses a fortune in white diamonds, the rarest gems in Kelba."*

Celectate Wood needs my father's support in order to keep his tight hold on the Community. Father owns most of the investments. He owns the largest amount of white diamond mines in Kelba. With such a large quantity of wealth, Celectate Wood has two options: be pleased with the thirty percent profit he already has – or accumulate forty percent more by bonding his son with one of High Lord Gavin Bone's offspring. I am his stepping-stone to more power! I am a pawn! Which means . . .

"The Celectate stills needs Father." It's only when I hear a sudden halt in the prayers behind me that I realize I spoke aloud.

"What was that?" asked the fierce girl, irritated that I just interrupted her prayers to the gods.

"I heard her say 'Celectate'," Helena informs her companion. I hold my breath. "She must be praying to the gods for blessings on the Celectate's reign. Oh, we should too. We shouldn't leave him out."

"High-class witch can pray to that spineless bastard all she wants. I won't waste my words on him," the irritable girl retorts. When I look at her over my shoulder in surprise, her eyes glare back at me with loathing. "And if someone finds out what I just said and the officials come for me . . ." A finger across her throat is all the indication I need of what revenge she'll have upon me.

I turn my back to her.

"High-class bitch!" she snaps.

The silent prayers behind me continue.

"It's not wrong to make your own choices. No one can tell you different."

Whether I marry Aspen is entirely my decision and mine alone. No one else's.

Why does that scare me more?

Chapter VIII

When I awake, I'm prostrate on the damp floor of the temple, staring at a pair of brown, untidy feet. There's a stench in my nostrils so bad that it widens it my eyes. A stench of blood, urine, and dirt that ignites previous memories to mind. I jump up in fright, and two bony hands grasp my shoulders.

"Falling asleep on your holy night – very rude to the gods, my lady," one of the brown-skinned priestesses mutters. She presses a tattooed finger to her lips. "Don't worry, I won't tell." Her teeth are black.

Across the circular room, Helena and her companion have already risen, no sleep evident in their faces. If they did happen to drift off in the night, they were awake before the priestesses came in. The fact that they didn't bother to wake me when they certainly had enough time to do so, reimburses the idea that they despise me. Helena gives me a sympathetic smile.

The priestesses have already dragged three warm tubs of water into the room and order us into them, clothes and all. They practically rip the dress over my head and their fingers claw at my scalp as they attempt to style my hair in the ancient art of "Freya," the goddess of purity." It is nothing more than a pile of curls pulled to the top of my head and leaving the rest to glide down my back, but priestesses do not adorn themselves in frivolous fashions. Their hair – if they have any – is pulled into a tight bun on top of their heads.

At last, the torture is over and my dress is brought to me. But we will not put them on yet. Instead, they lie in front of us as we kneel on the ground. Naked knees on the cold floor. Naked body to the cold air. We are not afforded the luxury of a towel. Naked we came into this world – naked we would be blessed – naked we would leave. Oh, and according to Master Rolfe – naked would I become a woman.

The dress is a beautiful red, shimmering with dark and light. My left shoulder will have a single strap for a sleeve. My right will have no sleeve at all. Instead, a shimmering robe will clip onto the bodice of my gown and fall behind my back in a graceful train. It is a masterpiece – and Mother made it herself. I remember the blood-shot eyes, the angry barks at any servants who dared offer their help, and the most unladylike curses that fell from her mouth when the Celectate sent his best tailors. She refused to let anyone make the bonding dress for her daughter.

The priestesses leave, slamming the heavy doors behind them. I am left alone with my nightly companions, each as equally bare as I.

I struggle to keep my eyes on Helena's face but it's hard not to look at the fragile body she possesses. She hardly looks able to stand a strong breeze, much less a pregnancy.

The firebrand has no trouble staring at me eye-to-eye – or elsewhere. "Will your daddy's carriage come to pick you up?" she asks, her nose twitching. Her hand curls at her side.

"Daria!" Helena gasps and grabs her friend's arm earnestly. "You shouldn't . . ."

"What . . . offend a noble? Or I'll get lashed?" Daria stands up, her long, bare legs gleaming with muscle I hadn't noticed until now. She fixes me with a cold stare. "Did I hurt your feelings, noble? Are you gonna tell?" Both her fists ball at her sides. She slams them together, cracking knuckles. I flinch at the sound and she takes a threatening step forward, observing my reaction and mistaking it for fear. She throws Helena's restraining grip from her elbow.

I stand too. Not because I want to. But because she's come so close, I can't look her in the eye anymore. And if you don't look an opponent in the eye, you are dirt.

Daria stops just a foot in front of me, staring at me relentlessly. "Your daddy's best friends with the Celectate, isn't he? I bet he's a High Lord. One of the Celectate's little lap dogs who likes to run circles and bark on command. A prick who bows to everything that high-and-mighty bastard says. That's your daddy?"

My fist flies.

Daria falls flat on the ground and cries out when her ass connects with the stone.

Helena and the other girl move to offer their assistance, but Daria shoves them away and jumps to he feet, rage in her eyes. Her hands, however, are no longer in fists and she makes no move to strike me back. The red blotch on her cheek shines.

"Insult me all you want!" I snap, my voice low and horribly inhuman. "But if you ever say anything against my father again I will, I swear, ride you of that gorgeous nose that you possess!" I hold up a fist for definition.

The lock snaps on the doors behind us and we shuffle to our appropriate places, kneeling upon the ground once more. It is forbidden to stand until the priest has entered the solar and given the blessing – but I doubt we are the first to break such a rule.

The High Priest shuffles between Helena and I, his ivory robes chaffing against the flesh of my shoulder before he stops before Calaisar's altar. The sun is shining through the hole in radiant streaks upon the golden decorum. His bottomless eyes shift from Daria to me and I wonder if he senses the rage radiating in the room as much as I do.

The High Priest clears his throat and begins his declaration. "You go to a new pathway of your lives, my young doves. You are innocent, pure, holy virgins who will discover your womanhood and purpose in this blessing that has been bestowed upon you. The gods have filled you. Now I will beg them to overwhelm you, body and soul, and make you a spirit of their excellence."

Sounds like a curse to me.

"Tonight, each of you will experience a new turn on your life's path. You will shine Calaisar's light by being a beaming example of his holiness, his virtue, his justice, his wisdom, and his honor."

Calaisar's honor went so far it slaughtered half the gods. I wish I had that honor.

The High Priest doesn't notice his mistake – or chooses to ignore it. "Receive this blessing."

I lower my head, prepared to listen to the endless dialect of the ancient Kelban rites – rites that only Calaisar's temple servants had the right to learn or understand. I have been told the rites bless me – but the weight on my shoulders feels so much heavier as the words are spoken. They jumble inside my head, and I try to make sense of them from my endless education in the language. I want to know what is being said over me.

"*Di nai nalus vare ti sevre yan tivrana. Di nai nalus vare ti mara yan izranis.*"

My head snaps up. I know that phrase. Out of all the never-ending pages and pages of ancient Kelban my tutor dumped upon my poor brain, those words remained forever etched. They were pure poetry, but so much more.

"*Do not allow fear to cloud your judgment. Do not allow fear to make your choices.*"

Those words had meant the world to me when I'd gone through darkness and hell. And they mean the world to me now.

"*It's not wrong to make your own choices.*"

No. It isn't.

When we exit the temple, priestesses and priests returning to their daily temple chores, a crowd of people waits at the foot of the angled steps. A crowd waiting for my companions – I do not spot one familiar face among them. The crowd awaiting me will be at the palace.

"Are you walking to your ceremony?" Helena asks from behind. Her voice is fragile and timid. I sense the pity within the shallow facade she uses to hide it.

"Of course she's not walking. Her papa will probably send his carriage to the bitch!" she snaps. "She's not low enough to walk to her own ceremony like us."

Some part of me whispers I should bare it. Another part of me wants to slap her again. Still another part of me can't find a reason why I should.

Screams assault the air – and not from the crowd. I watch the Celectate's carriage come barreling around the street corner, its colors flashing boldly. Soldiers surround it on fine stallions and their armor is gleaming brightly with polish. Their spears stick violently in the air ready for any interference. There will be none. People leap out of the way, as the conveyance relentlessly plods forward.

"What the hell . . .?" Daria mutters.

Helena blanches white. "Why's it coming this way?"

Their fear increases, radiating over my skin, as the carriage comes to a halt before the temple. They take trembling steps backward and the crowd gasps in horror. They think the Celectate has come for their daughters.

A soldier dismounts and starts up the steps. The girls tremble and edge away, back towards the temple doors. As if those blessed men of the gods will actually let them back in.

I am forced to stay where I am. The dress will not allow me an easy escape if I tried and I will not be dragged, kicking and screaming, to my bonding. I will be dignity, pride, honor, and civility like the High Priest cautioned. The soldier stops before me.

"The Celectate sent us to escort you, Lady Kyla." He gestures at the carriage. "Please enter."

Daria and Helena gasp behind me. Now they know who I am. Who my bond is.

"Was it necessary to send so many guards to collect me? Or is the Celectate trying so desperately to safe-guard my value that he needs to send half a squadron?"

The soldier, a captain by the colors on his shoulder, flushes to the roots of his hair. His lips curl up in a hard line.

A tingling warms my fingers and glides up my arms into my neck, pulsing against my ears. My scars. However, it does not make me sick. I feel alive. Like I just drank a dozen mugs of ale.

"The Celectate was concerned about your safety. There are questionable individuals who might seek to make a profit by abducting his new daughter-in-law," the captain says a bit too tightly.

He's a piss-poor liar. The extra guard is meant to ensure I do not flee. The Celectate must think me a complete fool – and a bit reckless – if I would disobey his direct order by abandoning my bond. The realization raises my courage.

I chuckle. "Concern for my safety? If he's concerned for my safety, perhaps he may let you guard the bedside, since I hear his lineage is very 'violent.'"

The captain reddens at the insult I've just layered on the man he serves and his hand rests on the hilt of his sword. Were I anyone but the ruler's impending daughter-in-law – and a pawn in his political game – I'd be bleeding through a chasm in my throat.

I step towards the carriage. "Let us not keep Wood waiting."

The captain bristles at the lack of title I bestow but follows me anyway, assisting me firmly into the carriage. I glance over my shoulder at Helena. She bows respectfully and a sliver of pain stabs my insides.

Helena's honoring me. She believes I'll be the next Celecta, should Aspen assume the throne.

Daria only glares at me. I don't blame her. However, she's got everything wrong.

I wink at her. She blinks, startled.

I let the door shut behind me and the carriage rumbles to life.

Helena's timid respect burns inside me. In her eyes, I will be the next Celecta.

Like hell I will.

A crowd has gathered outside the palace walls. These are the rabble that will be barred from attending the ceremony – the solar can hold only nobles. Celectate Wood has had great consideration for the new "bride" and has been praised by Calaisar's temple and several softhearted High Lords of the Community. I am a shy, frightened, little girl about to brave a very big assignment – the role of the future Celecta. Celectate Wood has made the streets rumble with stories of my great loyalty to him and his son. He's made me a goddess of purity. *Freya.*

And before an hour has passed, he'll regret it.

However, as I peer at the faces of the crowd through my prison window, I don't see amazement on their faces. I see jawlines made primal with hunger. Eyes sunken in hollowed faces. Lips turned downwards with disapproval. I am to be their Celecta. Another noble to hold the leash around their necks. Another ruler to break their backs to feed my hungers. They despise me.

I don't blame them.

The guards use their long lances to keep the crowd back as the palace gates open and the carriage rumbles inside. It halts before the grand oaken door of Celectate Wood's abode – my abode. The harsh-faced captain opens the door for me and allows me to disembark.

The crowd murmurs at my appearance, several faces aglow in the pale morning light just beginning to spread over the earth. One head stands taller than any of the others. The giant from the riot. The giant who'd wanted to break hell's chains.

He sees me at the same time I see him, and his eyes widen a tiny bit. He hadn't expected the Celectate's knew daughter-in-law to be the female scholar from the crowd. If my entire body wasn't ripe with nausea, I might have smiled at his shock. But I don't.

I remain stone-faced, staring at the crowd, at his face, until the gates shut over them. He mouths something to me. Something I can't understand. My brain tries to make sense of his lips formation – but I don't unravel it.

It must have been a curse. A long overdue insult.

Inside, the palace is decorated in immaculate colors of white, red, and black. Red for the blood covenant. White for the purity. Black for the Celectate's color. Black, a devil's color. Red, the color of blood. White, my innocence about to be spoiled.

"Spread your legs wide and grind your hips . . . Moan in pleasure when he rides you . . . Don't show disgust towards his passion . . . Tis the noble duty of the Celecta."

I'm going to be sick. Damn Master Ragar!

My escort gives me just enough space to allow my flowing robes to flutter around me. Their gilded helmets are painted with black and red for the occasion and their eyes are the only things visible to me through the shiny armor. They stare straight ahead, respectfully. Only the captain has the nerve to look me full in the face – or gaze up and down my body – like a cur. I glare at him.

We stop before the great oaken doors of the Solar. The Celectate's Solar is a very special room, made completely of glass. A glass floor in immaculate colors, a glass roof, and glass walls to emanate the beauty of the Kelban mountain region around it. It is said that Celectate Wood made love to his beautiful wife Erina beneath the stars in that very room as a covenant before the gods. I have been in its greatness but once in my entire life – the long ago night when creatures from hell ended my childhood.

The captain raps his knuckles against the doors and an answering tap follows. They are almost ready.

I am not.

The captain steps into the space between the guards and myself, so close I can smell the harsh soap and hay on him. I wrinkle my nose at the stench. It does not become him.

"I have been ordered to instruct you on how to behave. You are to . . ."

"Walk straight and don't slouch. Stand firm and don't react to the blade sliding across my wrist. Smile beautifully when the diamond binds us. Offer my arm to my bond with a show of submission. Bow gracefully and exit the room. Correct?" I search his eyes for the anger I hope to awaken and see a spark.

"Watch that mouth, lovely, or . . ."

"And bide your tongue, captain!" I retort.

He leans close, fists forming at his sides. "You are not his wife yet! Do you really think being his whore will change a thing? You are as miniscule a piece in this giant game as I am. Another means to an end for his highness. He'll use you, flesh and all, and when that's gone, he'll use whatever else you have. Your family. Your money. Until you're truly gone." He steps closer. Grabs my wrist. Twists it ruthlessly. I wince but don't cry out. "You go ahead and kiss his Excellency's ass and whatever else he wishes your mouth on. You please him as best you can. Because that's what we're supposed to do. This is the message Celectate Wood wanted to give you . . ." He jerks my head towards him, his fingers digging brutally into my spine. "You are his." He lets me go and stalks to the doors.

Breathe. Breathe.

I am not given a chance to.

The doors swing open. "Lady Kyla Bone, esteemed daughter of High Lord Gavin Bone and his lady, Elinor Bone."

Heir to the diamond mines of her father, I want to add.

The captain thrusts me through the doors. I struggle not to stumble and regain my balance. The open room stares back at me. Five hundred feet to the large glass podium before me. On the podium stands a gleaming, golden altar – Calaisar's altar. Upon it sits a bowl, a gleaming knife, and a diamond-studded twine. A High Priest stands in his regal robes of blood red waiting. Waiting for me. For my bond. For my doom.

Deep breath, Kyla. Deep breath. It will all be over soon.

As I walk further into the room, the sun above gleams through the glass upon me, warming my skin. It spikes a sudden urgency in the daily tremors of my skin, and it buzzes with life.

Twelve men stand, six on each side, making a small pathway to the podium. The remaining High Lords. As I regally step by each one history lessons of old flash by. Lord Avrok, lord of the coal mines. Lord Singh, Head of the Treasury (and the most capable lord of improving Escar).

When I pause before my father, his robes, the "Bone" legacy, gleaming in our family colors of white and blue upon him, I can't continue. He stares at me too.

I know I should say something. But my throat is in knots. I clutch the sides of my dress in fists and blink back tears. His face turns white and his lips tremble. He knows the message I want him to receive. The words I can't convey. The hug I can't give him.

I've never been a graceful person – gods know. I'm a scandalous excuse for a High Lord's daughter. But I will get this right. With all the inner femininity inside of me, I curtsy. I don't let my knees shake. Don't let my body tremble as it lowers. This curtsy is to honor my father for all he has done for me. Tears spot my vision. I blink them away.

Father bows, arms trembling at his sides. He raises his head to look at me and his mouth forms words. I try to make them out.

At the podium, Celectate Wood's personal High Priest has grown impatient, evident by the tick in his jaw.

"His highness, his excellency, his grace, Aspen Wood."

I ascend the glass podium, my shoes feeling slippery against its sleek exterior. Guards form tight rows and use their lances to hold the crowd back. Everyone is scrambling to get a look at their ruler's son.

My betrothed approaches with smooth strides, new boots and faded red apparel looking quite dashing on his well-built frame. He is handsome. He is charming. He is regal.

He's the devil's son.

He ascends the steps and takes his place on my right, his hands trembling at his sides in anticipation. His ashen hair is smoothed back and his triumphant smirk has returned. He's getting what he wants. Like he always does.

The Celectate's entrance is met with applauds from both the High Lords and the audience. However, as he passes a choice few of the Community High lords, Lord Singh, especially, stand straight and keep their hands in fists by their sides. My father claps relentlessly and bows nearly in half when Celectate Wood brushes past him with barely a recognizing glance. He's worried. Worried that if he doesn't clap, I'll be hurt. That I'll suffer for his actions.

It's like a blow to the face. I recognize the words he mouthed to me. *"I love you."*

It was his way of telling me he was going to try to protect me from whatever Celectate Wood intended for my fate. Even as the future Celecta, I was not safe. The Celectate could use me to make my father do whatever he wanted him to do. I am a puppet. A pawn in the turmoil for Kelba's rule.

And Celectate Wood doesn't even look at the grieving father.

Fresh with rage, I fist hands at my side, forcing the rising storm down. He is taking a man's daughter away – and he has the balls to ignore him. Has the audacity to push the poor man's suffering into a corner.

Bastard.

Celectate Wood joins his son. He does not wear red. Not a hint of it adorns his apparel. He wears black. Everything, from his slick hair, to his shiny eyes, to his shoes, is dark.

When he finally looks me straight in the face with those monstrous eyes, his lips tilt up unbecomingly. Hot rage boils inside me. The black is meant for my Father – to remind him that he's losing his daughter and should be mourning. To remind him that he's going to become a puppet or watch me suffer. The black is meant for me too – to remind me that I'm going to be his tool and there's nothing I can do about it.

Fools fall for their own snares.

"*You are his.*"

I approach the High Priest and the altar. Aspen stands beside me, his hand millimeters away. Tensions cascades from that hand. He wants to touch me.

The High Priest begins speaking the bonding rites in ancient Kelban. The words jumble in my head. He finishes the rites and starts on the blessing. Sweat trickles down my spine as he drones and on. As Aspen's hand inches closer to mine. As his knuckles gently press into my wrist.

"*Do not allow fear to cloud your judgment. Do not allow fear to make your choices.*"

That same phrase. That same reminder.

The High Priest finishes the blessing. My skin burns. I have waited patiently for this moment. I have planned this to reap destruction on the devil.

"It's not wrong to make your own choices."

The High Priest picks up the silver knife and orders Aspen and I to hold out our wrists.

"I don't want this."

He draws close to me.

"I know."

The blade slides across my wrist, opening skin. Blood rolls over my reddened flesh and drips onto the floor. I stare at the droplets.

Suddenly, I remember the giant man's words. What he had mouthed to me beyond the gates. What he had told me. He had not cursed me. He had not insulted me.

"Break hell's chains."

The High Priest cuts Aspen's wrist. Returns to the table. Picks up the diamond-studded twine. Steps towards us.

"Give us a cause. Give us a fire."

The High Priest mutters something in ancient Kelban.

I reform the phrase: *"Break the devil's chains."*

"In the name of Calaisar . . ." The High Priest presses the diamond thread beneath our wrists, ready to bind them together. To seal our blood. Our bond.

The Celectate sneers. In his eyes . . . ***You are mine.*** And I swear I hear his words loud and clear inside me.

Like hell I am.

He gets every word. I've waited for this moment. His eyes flash with shock before I jerk away from the High Priest and rip the sash from my waist, binding my wrist with speed. The bleeding stops. Warm liquid soaks the cloth. I grimace at its coppery stench.

"I refuse!"

One look in his eyes. One flash from within them. One ugly twist of that mouth and all the pain and relentless torture of the last month fades away. My chains are broken. The devil no longer holds the leash. I am free. I have my own mind, my own heart – my own will!

The Celectate stammers for words. "What . . . . did you say?" His tone is layered with ice, and his eyes bore into mine, their murky depths unnerving me.

"Do you know the punishment for such outbursts?" he asks.

The punishment? My gut clenches. People dance before me. However, they aren't just ordinary people. No. They're skin is melted at the shoulder, etched with the horrible "ostracized scar." Their backs shine blood red from whips. Their skin falls from their bones as they stalk through the poisons of the Wilds. Shadows rip at their clothing and hair from the darkness. Yes, I know the punishment. I nod.

"I order you to marry my son!" His voice is deadly calm. No tremor rocks his words. Only his eyes speak volumes as they sizzle within their dark depths, glazing my face with heat. He's giving me one more chance. One last chance to obey and become the simple pawn. To become his.

But behind that threat, I see fear. He has spent the past month painting me as a simple "weakling" with no ability to think for herself. He has told of my devout loyalty to him and his son. Of my steadfast honor. Of my unbreachable innocence. Lady Kyla Bone. But I am not just Lady Kyla Bone. No. I am also Ky Bone – scholar by day, soldier companion by night.

I turn away from those eyes and look over my shoulder. Father is on his feet, as are a few other High Lords. Fear glazes his eyes in a sheen of tears and his lips tremble. He shakes his head at me. From the crowd, two people stretch over the lances, beckoning for my attention. One is Mother. The other is Landor. Landor shakes his shoulders at me in a what-are-you-doing sort of way.

But Mother only stares at me. In her face, I see no fear. No pain. She's smiling in that mysterious way she's looked at me of late. In her eyes flashes the same fire that burns within me – the same spirit.

My hands tremble, and I fist them at my sides. I won't allow myself to be afraid to make my own choices. It is my life.

My life!

I face Celectate Wood squarely. Something dark glints in his eyes and then it is gone. He tries to put all his hate, all his anger, all his threats, into one, long stare. I am his. He wants me to be afraid. He wants me to cower.

"I refuse!"

The back of his knuckles sweep across my cheek with break-neck speed and throws me sideways, off balance. My skirts wrap around my legs, cinching them close, and I can't recover myself fast enough. My hip cracks against one of the steps as I fall sideways. My right side connects with the floor. Numbing sparks hover in my neck. The podium steps swirl in my vision. A trail of blood mars their marble magnificence. My blood! It drips down my face from a gash in my temple.

It is in a time like this that my vision would blur, my neck would start pulsing, memories would flash, and I'd faint dead away. But I don't. My neck doesn't pulse. My vision doesn't blur. In fact, my thoughts have never been clearer.

"Take her away!"

Everything happens fast. Guards flank me from all sides, grabbing at my arms, pulling me to my feet, forcing them behind me back. Shackles slap my wrists with cold accuracy. The clanking chains rattle my ears and make me want to retch.

My captors turn me towards the doors that will be my exit – and my departure from life – I hear Father's screams. They chill my blood. I've never heard him scream before. Even on that long ago night on the street he had not screamed.

The guards don't pay any notice and shove me forwards. One of them cries out in pain and I see him fall. Father's hands dart towards me. I catch a glimpse of his reddened face as he tries to force his way between the security around me. Tears flow on his cheeks. One of the soldiers kicks him in the chest and he falls out of my sight.

I stop and look behind me. Celectate Wood has not left the podium. He meets my gaze – and it is my turn to present him with a message of my own. I know he receives it the moment his eyes turn so dark there's no humanity left in them.

I am no Freya, dear fool. I am no goddess of purity.

I am a fire – and I will burn you.

The guards lead me out the door. Out of the chaos. Down the steps of the palace. An iron door opens up through the maze of corners and rooms we enter. Intimidating stone steps glare up at me.

Down, down, down we go, deeper beneath the palace. To the dungeons. Now my neck should start pulsing. Memories and nightmares should start flashing. My breathing should falter.

Instead, my feet pound out a rhythm on the stone floor.

I made my own choice. I made my own choice.

I made a choice.

Chapter IX

The dungeon is what I expected. The heavy scent of human excrement, blood, and foulness corrupts the stone walls. I'm afraid to touch the bars of my cell. They are icy cold and covered in some sort of black grime I only hope is rust. A chill hangs over the room, latching onto my skin, making my whole body ache, but I don't sit. In the darkness, the ground squelches beneath my shoes when I walk. Bile rises in my throat, burning. I swallow it.

I try to draw my thoughts elsewhere. But all I can focus on is my cell or the impending trial tomorrow. The High Lords will cast their votes, guilty or not guilty. Once, when there were twenty lords instead of twelve, I might have had better chances. Now, with Celectate Wood's claws sunk into more than half of the Community elders, I can see my future flashing before my eyes. Every ghastly story, every monstrous tale, every horrific legend swirls before me in bright colors of death. I see swirling shadowy hands reaching for me, clawing at my skin. Smoky fog rises from the cell floor and engulfs me in vapor and heat. Fire latches at my ankles. Poison eats my skin.

My neck throbs. Pulses. Pounds against my throat. I should scream. I should cry out. But I don't. I won't.

Lifting heavy arms to my head, I stroke fingertips over my temples. Rub the wildly beating scars on my neck embedded in my flesh so long ago. The dizziness and nausea slowly fades.

But they will return. They always return.

I lean against the wall. The hard stone gouges my backside. I pay no mind to the pain as the rock cuts my flesh.

Father's screams echo in my head. I wish I had been able to hold his hand. To say "goodbye" in a less shocking manner.

I spare a glance for the red dress, now turning an ugly brown and black color from the grime in the cell. The skirt is in tatters, baring occasional views of my thighs, legs, and reddened knees. The bodice is ripped, showing cleavage in a far greater amount than I prefer.

Mother worked so hard creating this gown. To see it defamed in such a way is almost more than I can bare. Her efforts seem so wasted.

Nevertheless, she'd smiled at me on that balcony. She'd known what I was going to do – somehow. I remember her gentle hands on my forehead a full month ago when I'd been so tipsy I'd lost the reins to my emotions. I'd told her I was tired. That I didn't want it.

"*I know.*" She knew and she let me decide what I would do about it.

The echoing sound of heavy feet on the endless halls of the dungeons ring in my ears. The guard is making another round. I have counted his footsteps twenty times throughout the night – each one followed by the screams of some unfortunate prisoner as he deals out his "justice." So far, I have evaded such treatment. Perhaps I am to be unlucky. But there are two sets of footsteps – one heavy, the other light and graceful to my ears. The steps stop before the prison door.

The sweet scent of lily perfume in my nose and – oh, gods, why does it have to be her?

Selena peers through the bars, her eyes slanting as she tries to pick out my shadowy form in the darkness. When they find me, she purses her lips in a pleased little smile and waves the guard away. He bows and disappears.

"Well . . ." She calmly plucks at one of her delicate fingernails. "It's a bit damp down here, don't you think?"

"I've no time for your games."

"On the contrary, you have all the time in the world. For now. I mean, after tomorrow, we'll never see one another again. It won't be much of a blow to you; I'm sure, but me . . ." She rests a hand over her heart in a mocking gesture of pain. "You were always one of my favorite pastimes. I'm afraid I'm going to be a bit bored with no sullied rumors to listen to. I rather enjoyed the beautiful tales of your wild escapades."

I push off the wall and step into the middle of my cell so she can see the full, reviled form I've taken. Her nose twitches the slightest bit and I see a small spark of surprise in her eyes. She masks it quickly, but it was there just the same.

"You know what he wanted, Selena." My tone is brittle.

"I'm not sure what you . . ."

"Oh, save your damned lies! You know what he would have done to my family . . . to me . . . to Kelba!" I take a step closer, hot rage balling my hands into fists. "So you listen well, Selena Griff, whose father is in the same precarious position as mine . . . what would you have done? Would you have wed a man you don't love, don't respect – in fact, despise and loathe – because of what Celectate Wood would do to you if you didn't? Would you have allowed yourself to become a pawn and kiss his ass? Would you have allowed him to take the intelligent man you know as a father and turn him into a sniveling, groveling pup to run circles before his excellence and slave his life away? If you would have . . . if you could endure such torment, such slavery . . . then you're nothing more than a cowardly, spiteful, uncaring bitch who would rather live and let Kelba suffer for it than die and save a thousand lives!" My chest rises and falls furiously and I can't breathe fast enough.

Selena's hands are white. Her eyes are wide. Her mouth – a mouth bred for insults – stutters uselessly. She manages to squeak: "Just what are you inferring by such a statement?"

"Celectate Wood . . ." I take a step forward. She is educated. She will know my meaning. She will understand, despite the brat she is. "Ve si Gasan. Ve si Calaisar. Ve si e dravar."

She blinks. "W-what . . . How dare you, Kyla?"

"How dare I?"

"He is our ruler. He is your ruler. He is Kelba's ruler."

"Ve civi ravar ti."

Selena's breath comes in ragged bursts of emotion – of fear, wonder, or rage I cannot tell. But my words have struck their mark. "Celectate Wood is the ruler of Kelba. He has made us strong. He will continue to make us strong. He will continue to strengthen us."

"And what do you think his understanding of 'strength' means?"

"I beg your pardon?"

"What does Celectate Wood observe as strength?" I answer for her. "Power."

She shakes her head – but her eyes are no longer full of spite. Instead, there's a new glint in her eye. A glint of fear. Of realization.

I repeat myself. "Ve si Gasan. Ve si Calaisar. Ve si e dravar. Ve civi ravar Kelba."

He is Gasan. He is Calaisar. He is a devil. He will destroy Kelba.

"Go back to your home – to your family, Selena. I will not be the last to fall to his never-ending thirst. Eventually, you – and your father – will face the flames. And when they come . . . then we'll see if your are Freya or fire. If you protect or bow. If you rebel or cower." I grip the bars, ignoring the grime that crumbles beneath my fingers and stare her full in the face, fire facing fire. "And being completely honest, Selena, you may be a bitch but you're no coward."

I call for the guard. Selena remains silent as he approaches. I speak for her. "We're done here."

The guard looks at Selena, questions in his gaze.

Selena turns and starts to walk away, but she pauses, her shoulders tensing. When her eyes find mine for the last time, the battle is warring deep. She's deciding if she should say something or not. She licks her lips, losing the stern, commanding facade she keeps around herself. For a moment, we're just two girls – two innocent, harmless girls without worry, fear, or duty.

"You won't die," she says.

She leaves, and I ponder the lie.

The guard approaches my cell again. Footsteps chime with his. Another visitor. I'm popular tonight. This time the guard unlocks the door of my cell and it creaks open on hinges long overdue for oiling. I cringe at the sound.

"You have five minutes!" the guard snaps. He walks away.

I run to Landor, throwing my arms around him. He is warm and hard – his heat cascades over me and relieves the aching chill in my bones.

"Lan. Lan." I say his name repeatedly, hardly believing he is standing there. It must have cost him a pretty penny to visit me. Seeing relatives before a trial is forbidden – for fear they will offer escape. Landor is not so foolish.

He speaks first. "Drink! Drink quickly. They won't give you anything to quench your thirst and if they do, it's most likely been pissed in." He removes a leather pouch from his belt, half-hidden by his cape.

I swallow the contents, the faint hint of spice and lemon mingling in the water.

When I hand the pouch back he takes it without a word and runs his eyes over my apparel, lips pursed tightly when they fall upon the torn holes. He grabs me by the shoulders earnestly, hands shaking. "I'd get you out, Kyla. I swear by the gods, I'd get you out . . . I'd help you escape from this. But Celectate Wood came to me . . . he . . . he . . ." Landor stops and tears glisten in his eyes.

"Go on," I whisper, my voice firm.

He hesitates, lips trembling. Hands shaking so bad he has to release me. "He said he'd do something to Mother . . . to Craig and Asher . . . to you if he even caught wind that I'd entertained the notion of assisting a prisoner." His words stumble over each other. "The things he told me he'd do . . . the thoughts he put in my head . . ." His teeth grind together. "I wanted to rip his damn throat out!"

"I understand, Landor. Honest, I do."

"You don't understand, Kyla!" He walks to the back of the cell and slams a fist against the stone. I hear bone crack. Blood drip. However, I don't dare stop him. "Do you know how many High Lords tremble right now? Do you know how many Celectate Wood spoke with after he ordered you to the dungeons? Do you know I could feel the fear outside the doors of the Court? You don't stand a chance. They will all vote against you. They will all condemn you." He looks at me. "You'll be ostracized."

My stomach churns, but I don't stay silent. "I know."

He spins around and his hand catches the faint light of the torch in the dungeon hall. His knuckles are bloody and gouged. "You know? Do you? Do you really know, Kyla? You spent years in that library, in those books, searching for something. Searching those legends. Those myths. You know? I don't think you've ever known – every really known what you were looking for. For peace? Hope? Answers?"

All of them. Because I have seen the monsters of that land – but I had also seen more. I had seen a small spark of humanity that may remain in the Wilds. Cannibal or no, the boy had saved my life. The Wilds are not completely horrible.

I can't think of anything to say. My refusal is going to be so much more than mere words. Father and Mother will be scarred. Landor will be alone and under the Celectate's thumb once more, his dreams of being a sailor forever stolen.

"I'm sorry, Landor." It sounds weak and pathetic and my heart aches as I say it. I blink back tears.

His hands grip my shoulders and his eyes are ablaze. "No!" he snaps. He jerks my chin up so we are eye-to-eye. "You don't need to be sorry, Kyla. You hear me? Never, ever, ever be sorry! We . . . Kelbans . . . should all be sorry for allowing that bastard to put a leash on us – to use us – to command our lives. We are fools! Cowardly fools! All of us! If any of us had the slightest bit of courage we'd slit that bastard's throat!"

He speaks treason. I don't warn him. Don't stop him. He's been aching to say those words for years. Ever since he was robbed of his choice – of his decision. Ever since he let his cowardice become his master.

"Maybe one of us will gain that courage someday," I say, a smile curling over my lips.

Landor doesn't say anything but he squeezes my hand in

agreement. A silent pact – a promise for the future.

We both hear the guard approaching. Landor pulls me in for one more tight hug, and I clutch him like a lifeline.

He dips his head low to my ear and whispers, "I can't give you a weapon now. They'll surely find it on you before your departure to the Wall. But . . . I'll try to get you a knife before . . . before you're ostracized."

I smile. He will make sure I have a way to defend myself. He would never allow me to walk to my death without some means of protection at my disposal.

The jailer grunts impatiently from the prison door, his belt jingling with the weight of keys.

Landor leans closer, looking at me earnestly. "If you could go back . . . would you do anything differently?"

His eyes search mine, looking for the slightest bit of hesitance – fear – regret. He let Celectate Wood frighten him. Let him enslave him. Let him rule him.

I press my forehead to his. "No. I would not."

And I mean it.

The jailer unlocks the cell door. Landor exits and lets the rusty iron swing shut.

"Keep father out of trouble, Lan," I whisper.

He nods. "I'll try. And you don't get eaten."

"I'll try."

He smiles, looking every bit the brother I've always known. Strong. Protective. Determined. He's not completely broken. If there's anyone who possesses the fire to protect the Bone heritage, it's him. "Good luck, Ky." He winks.

He backs away, following the guard, but does not turn. He will not show me his back. He will not turn his back on family, traitor or no. The guard frowns disapprovingly but ignores the outright favoritism.

I struggle to hold back the tears once he's gone. I've come this far without allowing myself to break apart. I can't now – not when I've yet to face the devil himself.

An hour later footsteps approach my cell yet again. Instinctively, I crouch into a corner, willing whatever hell the jailer wishes to unleash far away. The door grates open. Closes. Someone walks back down the hall – the jailer.

The heavy rhythm of someone's low, controlled breathing joins with mine. Someone's in the cell with me!

I raise my eyes, balled fists prepared to crunch into flesh and bone if need be.

The face – the form – is not that of whom I expected. He should be up in the palace, reveling like his father, drinking wine and threatening lords over the decimation of another of his father's enemies. Aspen Wood stares at me, still dressed in his bonding apparel, excepting three buttons torn off the top of his shirt as if he'd been struggling for breath.

I lurch to my feet, nearly slipping on the tattered scraps of my skirts. Aspen doesn't move. Every feature of him is cold and distant, like he's carved from marble instead of flesh. Maybe he is. His father certainly is.

"Your highness," I manage to say firmly. I've never cowered before this boy. This boy I used to dance and chase and hunt alongside. The boy I now despise.

"So now you respect me?" His voice is cold.

There is no right answer to his question.

"Why did you refuse?" His tone changes from bitterness to complete anger. He fixates me with a dreadful stare. "Am I really so unattractive?"

The question is so absurd I nearly laugh aloud. Unattractive? Of all the things I could have refused to bond with him for he thinks it's his looks? The vain bastard! "It is not that, your highness. I concur it is not that."

"What? What then?" He throws his hands out at his sides, eyes boggled.

"I just don't want to."

There's a silence that can be felt.

"Who said you had a choice in the matter?"

Pure rage runs the river of my body. Because it's the very thing I asked myself when I'd been preparing for the damn thing. Why was I doing it? Did I have a choice? Foolish, stupid questions! Because I was a fool. A cowardly fool!

"It's my life. I make my own choices." I don't bother to hide the pride in my voice as I look him straight in the eye. "And you weren't one of them."

"The Celectate makes your choices!" he snaps, eyes ablaze.

"Not this time," I whisper, determined to keep the rage bottled up inside of me.

For a moment, he says nothing and stares me. And stares. Like he can never look away.

"You'd really rather be dead than marry me?"

Rather be dead than marry the son of the devil . . . yes. But I can't say it like that.

He takes my hesitation for fear. "I could change his mind, you know? He is my father. He'd grant me a request. Just recant, Kyla. Please?" He steps close and presses his hands on either side of my face, palming it gently. It's a lover's touch. One I can't – won't – return. I keep my hands at my sides. His eyes yearn for me.

"Please, Kyla? I love you. You'd make a good Celecta. When I played with you as a child . . . when we read in the libraries together . . . when you taught me to dance . . . I loved you. You are the only companion I've ever wanted. Kyla." He says my name with passion. With ache. "Kyla. I love you."

If I recant, not only will I be bonded to a man I don't love, don't even respect, but I will be his father's tool. A weapon meant to use against my father. My father would be a pawn. A shell of a man meant to do great things for Kelba. I won't have that. Celectate Wood will have won if I repent and ask for his forgiveness. I will not let the devil win!

"I've made my choice, your highness."

His hands move – one slides down my neck and rests there, the other tightens at the back of my head. He tilts my chin up. "Allow me to change your mind."

His lips cover mine. Whatever I'd been expecting him to do – punch, hit, kick me – this was not it! His mouth is warm and frightfully slow. Teasing me. Caressing me. Loving me. And it feels wrong.

Something inside me jolts at the connection. A line of fire blazes its way through my spine and down my toes. I'm burning from the inside! A pulse pounds in my neck and the scars sting painfully. He pulls me in tighter, molding himself against me, sweeping an arm down my backside to press me closer. My hands grab at his shoulders, fumbling with the red lapels of his tunic. He deepens the kiss, igniting another stream of hell-fire inside of me.

This is wrong. This is wrong. Wrong. Wrong!

The pain is too great. Summoning every ounce of strength, I shove Aspen away from me. His warmth disappears. Immediately, my neck stops beating. Like a reflex. But it leaves me weak. By something short of a miracle, I manage to stay standing. To look Aspen in the eye.

"I said, 'I've made my choice, your highness'," I repeat, not bothering to quell the anger in my voice.

The tether on Aspen's rage snaps. He grabs me by the elbows and shoves me up against the wall of the cell. A vein stands out on his forehead, alive and ugly. His lips smash against one another, and I know he is grinding his teeth. His touch hurts. Burns.

"Let go of me, bastard!" I snap.

He does. Storms to the cell door. Calls the jailer. Curses when the nervous man fumbles with the keys. The cell door slams shut after he exits. I wait for him to leave.

Aspen spares me one look. His eyes stir the fear inside me. They are inhuman. Shiny. Glowing with a fierce, unreadable hunger. A hunger for my blood.

"Go to hell, Kyla," he whispers and leaves as quietly as he came.

Chapter X

The jailer comes to my cell early in the morning and finds me awake and leaning against the wall, my dress almost completely torn away by fearless rodents in the night.

"'Big as a demon god, aren't they?'" he laughs and tosses me a sack. I catch it before it can join the filth on the cell floor.

"'I wouldn't know.'"

"'You will soon.'" And he leaves me with the chilling reminder that the Wilds are hell.

The sack holds a simple tunic of a blackish gray color with a strip of rawhide to tie around its waist. The cold night – and the rodents – having stripped me of all modesty during the night, I strip and pull on the tunic. It is comforting to have something over my chest, even if the tunic doesn't cover my shoulders and rests an inch or so above the knee. A pair of brown sandals lies at the bottom. The sack holds nothing else and when the guards came to tie me, they take it. My hands are bound tightly with rawhide, and I am escorted from my cell.

The solar is not empty any longer. The podium is still there – still stained in my blood. I'm certain Celectate Wood left it there as a reminder. The High Lords remain in their chairs upon my entrance. The crowd murmurs softly and then grows louder. Their voices are hollow and rough with rage. The guards draw closer for my protection. However, they cannot protect me from the onslaught of words – words that cut deeper than anything.

"High-class bitch!"

"Getting what she deserves."

"Going to hell, she is."

"Noble swine. Serves her right."

Atop the podium, a stake has been raised instead of Calaisar's altar. It is a piece of metal six feet high and stands like a menacing pillar of pain. The steps clank underneath my feet as I ascend the platform and face the giant glass window that looks out over the vast northern region of Kelba. The top of the trees is lit by the rising sun.

The guards back away from me and surround the podium, their lances raised in the air warningly.

Celectate Wood enters and the crowd welcomes his arrival. High Lords bow as he passes. Even Lord Singh. My Father remains standing upright, his eyes on the floor, his lips trembling. Kelba's ruler pays him no mind.

The Celectate is dressed in flowing, blood red robes. Aspen is dressed in black and follows his father with his head down, looking mournful and sullen. The Celectate mounts the podium and doesn't even look at me, before turning to the crowd.

"We have proceeded with the proper way of things. Kyla Bone's case has been judged adeptly through the Community elders. Their votes are being tallied. She is being accused of high treason." His voice is like death's knell.

The crowd stirs.

A boy approaches with a glass bowl. Slips of paper rest inside it. I count twelve. Twelve High Lord. Twelve votes. How many want my death? How many hated my father enough to sentence me?

One by one, Celectate Wood reaches inside the bowl. The first two want my death. My throat closes in on itself as Celectate Wood smiles victoriously. He's got every High Lord in his palm. I will be convicted.

The next three wish for my release. My heart skips a beat. One is my father's. Celectate Wood frowns, looking surprised and angry at once.

The next three ask for my death. Darkness blurs my vision.

Three more want me released. Celectate Wood's displeasure has grown and he turns seething eyes to the High Lords. None of them flinches beneath his gaze. If he will have revenge on those who wish my release, they will not make it easy on him.

One slip remains in the jar. I lick my dry lips. If it wishes my release, I can be set free. The Community will abolish my crime. I can go home. But if it wishes my death – the Celectate can determine my fate.

Celectate Wood pulls the slip from the jar. Slowly opens it. Reads the word.

The crowd explodes into chaos as people begin to shout, chant, or speak all at once.

I gasp for air.

Guilty. *Guilty,* the slip says.

Celectate Wood wastes no time and raises his hands. The crowd immediately goes silent. He's like a puppeteer who holds all the strings. He gifts a look towards me. I stare back. He can show mercy if he has it inside that hell-cursed heart. He can order me to be released in order to win the hearts of the Kelbans. But when I see his eyes – those demonic, black, cursed eyes – I shove the notion aside. He will not show me mercy.

He smiles languidly. "Such a burdening decision. I do not relish the weight of crushing such a beautiful youth. Such a choice should not be left up to an aging leader like myself. One who has yet to show his strength should determine such a pressing matter. His power. His rule." My eyes burn. He wouldn't . . .

"Aspen, my son?"

Aspen ascends the podium, sullen and cold. "Yes, father."

"I shall leave this choice to you. Her fate is yours to decide." Celectate Wood steps aside with a mysterious smile, his eyes never leaving my face. He wants to see everything.

Aspen draws close to me. His eyes don't look at me and stay on the ground as he approaches. Until he's so close, I could lean forward and brush my head against his chin. His hands are trembling.

Curse the devil. Damn his soul. I long to drive a fist against Celectate Wood's gleaming white teeth. Only a devil could come up with such a thing. To force his son to decide the fate of the girl he's loved since childhood . . . to force him to choose between power and me. Aspen knows I won't have him. Knows I don't love him. Knows I won't choose him if the end of the world was near.

"Aspen," I whisper. "Aspen, don't . . ." Don't what? Don't murder me? Don't join the devil?

He still won't look at me.

"Aspen?"

Tears sting my eyes. Because despite how much he disgusts me, despite how I hate his touch, despite the fact that he's a devil's son – I don't want him to be a devil too.

"She defied you, didn't she, father?" he asks without raising his eyes.

Celectate Wood doesn't hesitate. "Yes."

"People have defied you before, haven't they, father?"

"Yes."

"How did you answer such treatment?"

Celectate Wood's eyes flash. "I would not tolerate it."

Aspen raises his eyes and looks at me. They are empty and bottomless – deep pools of darkness. He truly looks like his father. "Why should I?" he says.

I lose the ability to breathe.

"I pronounce Kyla Bone . . . guilty," Aspen says in a loud, certain voice throughout the entire room. His eyes never leave my face. I don't bother to hide the shock or the hurt that rages within me.

"Aspen . . ."

He grabs my face in his hands and pulls me close, cracking our foreheads together. His skin welds against mine and his eyes – his eyes! Gods, it's like staring into the abyss of hell itself. Ice numbs my senses. His touch vaporizes me. Not even the branding iron could be so hot.

"I want you to remember this!" he growls in a low voice only I can hear. "Remember what you threw away because of your arrogance. You made me love you. Made me want you. You made me need you – and then you ripped me to shreds. You wanted me to bleed. You wanted to hurt me. I loved you. Hear me? I loved you!" His fingers gouge my skin, nails cutting my flesh. "But you are selfish. You are blind to love. You can't take it. You can only rip it apart."

"Whatever he's told you . . ." I gasp, looking between the devil and his son, ". . . whatever he said about me it's not . . ."

"True?" Aspen asks. He laughs mirthlessly. "That you didn't want me to hurt? Bleed? Love? Oh, you wanted it. You hated my father so much you thought hurting the son would make up for it. Well, Kyla, you were very, very wrong."

I can only stare at him. Did I truly want to hurt him? I was disgusted by him . . . but did I want to hurt him? Tear him apart just to anger the Celectate? Was that what I had done?

"You awakened the beast, Kyla!" Aspen snaps, his teeth very close to my lips. Heat radiates from his nostrils. "You'll pay for it!" He releases me and retreats.

Celectate Wood returns to stand before me. That darkness in his gaze dances with suppressed fury but I see a deeper emotion, one that far belies the dangerous facade he hides behind. He's afraid. Afraid of what punishing me can do. We both sense the tension in the crowd – in the Community. Punishing me will put complete power farther from his grasp.

Good.

"But I'm a generous man," he says. "I hate to shed blood and duel out such nasty punishments for those who are too young to see things properly." He eyes me with intent.

Oh, I understand things properly.

"I will release Kyla Bone." He smiles. "She will not have to marry my son. She will not need to be ostracized. I only ask for her to apologize, on her knees, and swear loyalty and fealty to me, like a good citizen once more."

The crowd nods approvingly – the offer is reasonable.

The intelligent bastard. He no longer worries about the dowry I will inherit – the forty percent of white diamond mines I receive upon marriage. Now he worries about something much larger than increasing his wealth and power. The tension in the crowd is more pressing, more dangerous by the minute. It threatens him. *I* have created a threat against him.

Slowly, I step forward, staring at the hand he extends. I will kneel. I will kiss it. I will swear loyalty and fealty to him. I will return home and avoid impending death.

I will become a slave.

I pause before him, mere inches of space between us. I lower my eyes. I sense him smile. I raise my head and that smile turns into a twisted frown.

"Yer od nar gavran mi."

You do not govern me.

I spit on his extended hand.

The crowd gasps. Most of them have no idea what I quoted or understand its significance. But Celectate Wood knows. He – who has hundreds of collections devoted to the tales of old – knows.

You do not govern me. Calaisar had said those words to Gasan. Right before he killed him.

Celectate Wood slides his defiled hand down the side of his robes with a frown of disgust. "Guards!" he yells.

Four Celect Knights ascend the stage, their helmets shielding their faces from view. They come close to me – I can smell the acidic metal of their armor.

"Tie her to the pole!"

Two of the Celect Knights hesitate, their hands stiffening at their sides as they stare at me. The other two jerk me towards the pole and force my hands into the shackles on top, stretching me onto my tiptoes. The hard metal cuts into the soft flesh of my wrist and opens the thin scab on the "marriage" scar. A line of blood slithers down my arm.

"For acts of high treason and national endangerment of the well-being of Kelban society, I pronounce Kyla Bone guilty. Her punishment shall be carried out immediately – ten lashes for defamation of her ruler and the ostracized scar for defamation of her country." Celectate Wood doesn't even blink as he speaks but his hands are behind his back in a vise-like grip as he scans the crowd, eyes piercing the faces that have grown terse. "It is my duty to protect the citizens of this nation from those who would seek to destroy us. To belittle us. To undermine everything we've done to stay alive. Years ago, this nation suffered the loss of half its population and geography. We were weak. We were lost. We were reckless and wild and fools. We did what we wanted to do and only what we thought we should – such ideas destroy a nation. Destroy our strength. Our capability. This is what Kyla Bone would do to us – because she is selfish, reckless, and foolish. Though I shudder at the notion of destroying such a bold youth, Kelba cannot afford to cater to her wishful fantasies. *You* cannot afford it. Enticing she may be – enticing her character is, indeed – but she will drag us under just as that poison dragged our sister nation to its knees. We must not become weak again – we must not crumble because of one youth's ambition."

"You chose me to rule you for a reason. I have protected Kelba. I will continue to protect it. Traitors such as this . . ." He points at me. "They are a fire roaring for kindling. Help me eradicate them . . . no matter how young . . ." He looks at me.

"Or old." He spots Lord Singh.

"Or loyal. Unite with me and we are strong. Go against me . . . we crumble!"

The crowd rumbles its approval, the tension slowly fading from the room. I only watch in horror as Celectate Wood's nervous hands unclench from behind his back and he bows his head sorrowfully before him as if he regrets the destruction he must wreak upon me.

I remember the giant man in the crowd at the Square. He had said the citizens were fools who took their own slavery willingly. I stare at the fools around me now and a gnawing sense of pity growls inside. They do not know what demon has made them such idiots – what devilry has been played upon them. The monster who removed a man's tongue because he had the ability to maneuver the crowd – has maneuvered this crowd.

Celectate Wood greets the black-masked man who ascends the

podium with a long, curling whip in hand. He pries the handle from the gloved fingers and strides across the glass floor. I can see the reflection of his robes behind me in the large window of the Solar. I watch as he cups the whip lovingly in his bare fist and slides the entire ten-foot length through it. He doesn't even break skin. I shudder. He's skilled with it.

"Since I am the one she defiled, should I not administer the punishment?" He looks to the crowd for confirmation, shrugging his shoulders innocently.

The crowd gives its agreement.

I turn my eyes from the window and stare at the metal pole in front of me. I focus on its height – its cold exterior – its rugged edges. I hear the whip raise behind me. I loosen my shoulders for the impact – the more I fight it the more it will hurt. My back aches to prepare for the blow and the bones in my spine tingle. I force a breath between my lips – then another. Landor was whipped once – he'd described the feeling. He'd said it felt like a herd of flesh-eating ants moving up your backside. The whip hisses through the air behind me. I close my eyes.

It slams into the middle of my back and sticks between the folds of broken flesh. As cruelly, as hard, as hatefully as he can, Celectate Wood slides the whip sideways, pulling every inch of the ten-foot long lash over the deep wound until the little tip falls away. The pain ripples up my backside, through my upraised arms, into my hands, which open in spastic jerks. My legs give way beneath me as the force of the blow rocks my body sideways. The shackles cut into my wrists and blood runs down my arms.

Hot blood slides down my back. The lash strikes the back of my shoulder and slashes a line from shoulder to waist in one long sideways line. I seize up, tightening my hands on the metal chains above my head.

Snap!

I want to whimper.

Crack! Bone in my back echoes with pain.

I rest my cheek against the cool metal of the pillar and it slides against my skin – my tears wet its surface. I close my eyes.

Crack!

"That's five," I whisper to myself.

I open my eyes and search the crowd for a familiar face – any face. I recognize many pillars of nobility – some lower than others. They are the ones who wait for me to scream – to beg for mercy – to cower.

Crack! I blink back the tears but they come anyway, dripping off my cheeks onto the podium. They join the blood pooling around my feet.

Someone in the crowd moves closer and the hood falls away from her face – Helena. She hasn't lost the delicate fragility she showed in the temple or the pale pink cheeks. Her eyes rest on my countenance gently and she sees me watching her. She smiles. A smile full of pity and sorrow. Inwardly, I tremble with outrage. I am not to be pitied! I chose this. It is nothing to pity.

Behind her, another girl joins her, a gleaming black braid intertwined with a black sash stretching down her back. The black sash is richly embroidered with tiny black birds and a curved dagger. The signs of mourning and death. The girl turns.

Daria.

Crack! I hardly recognize the sting of the lash.

When Daria meets my eyes, there's no pity in them. No spark of hate. No anger. There's also no emotional pain. No signs of tears or mourning about her. She looks just as fierce and strong as she did back in the temple, a beautiful, jeweled dagger hanging at her side. She smiles at me, a barely perceptible lift of her lips. It chills my blood. That smile – there's nothing human about it. It is gone as quickly as it came. Her mouth forms words in my direction. I struggle to make them out.

Crack!

The lash hardly stings. Daria's words click into place.

We're the same.

She smooths a hand down the side of her skirt and her thumb fondles the pommel of her dagger lovingly.

Oh, gods of hellfire!

Her brooding anger in the temple that night – her bitchy attitude towards my illustrious background – her disrespect for the the priests and their blessing – she hadn't wanted her bonding either. Perhaps, had detested it more than I. Her fingers edge along the dagger's length and I picture her standing over the body of a lust-crazed fiend, the blade dripping red. She killed him.

Crack!

She winks at me.

Crack! Crack!

It's over.

But it's not.

The two guards move forward again, unshackling my hands, only to force me to my knees and twist them behind my back. My back sizzles with serrated bones and torn flesh, blood leaving a trail behind me as the guards drag me towards a burning cauldron of coals deposited on the edge of the podium. Flurries of sparks flutter into the air. The strap of my tunic is pulled aside, exposing the bare flesh of my left shoulder.

Celectate Wood takes his time pulling a brown leather glove onto his arm. He jerks the iron brand from the cauldron, its end blazing orange with heat and the symbol of banished: the ostracized symbol. He comes towards me.

Memories of watching others being branded assail me. I close my eyes. I don't want to see the brand. I imagine a similar moment – when I was fifteen and ostracizing had been at the height of its acceptance.

Everything around me swirls and pressurizes. I struggle to push the feeling away, recognizing its familiar embrace as it edges against my skin, poking the scars on my neck to life. The pressure explodes inside my head, stabbing my ears with needles. I open my eyes at the sensation.

I don't see the crowd. The brand. Celectate Wood. Instead, I'm watching a different punishment. I'm standing at the bottom of the platform in the city Square, watching a different person receive the scar. He screams in pain as the brand is placed against his skin. Searing flesh makes a crackling sound beneath the heat of the dreadful iron. Sizzling flesh burns my nostrils. I turn my face away and hide it in the familiar leather shoulder of my brother. His arm wraps around me. My neck pulses and everything cracks – loudly!

All is white – white and gray – white and black in front of my eyes. I open them again when the vibrating closeness of heat kisses my cheeks. The brand floats before my eyes – the curved symbol of "ostracizement" grinning at me. Celectate Wood smiles with it, the tilt of his lips masked by the tendrils of hair around his face.

Now I know fear.

The brand presses against my shoulder. It sizzles, burning a layer of skin, before pressing against flesh. Then bone.

Celectate Wood grins from ear-to-ear.

And I scream – and scream – and scream.

I blink in the darkness that I awake in – broken only by the small tendrils of light through the barred window on my right. The carriage lurches beneath me on creaky wheels. Outside, horses neigh and a whip snaps. The flesh of my back prickles, recognizing the sound, and pain numbs my sense. The carriage hits a rut and I slam into the wall, shoulder first.

I see my shoulder – my perfect, beautiful shoulder that had been a graceful picture of elegance and softness – and horror slithers through me. Skin has withered back into disgusting folds, dry and crusty, and the blackened markings over the reddened flesh glare up at me in the perfect shape of the ostracized symbol. There isn't even any blood, so hot was the iron, so swift the plunge, so hard the application. Celectate Wood made sure to push it strong and deep – this scar will not heal well.

I lift a finger to touch it – it can't be my shoulder. It has to be a horrible dream. The skin burns beneath my touch. I cry out and remove the touch. It is real. Everything is real.

"Lower the gates!" a hoarse voice cries from outside.

I stumble to the window, grabbing the bars for support, and struggle to see. All I see is stone: crags of deep rock, full of weeds and hardened plants. I tremble. I know where we are.

The Gorge, built deep into the rut of the mountains, is the gateway to the Wall surrounding Kelba. It is a narrow, thirty foot-wide channel between the otherwise two hundred foot high rocks: a major geographical point in all noble history books.

The creak of old iron rings in my ears. We are at the gates. Which means . . .

The Wall.

Darkness swallows me up. We are in the Tunnel: the thin chasm inside the Wall – the only way to get to the other side of it. There are no outer stairwells or ladders. No ropes or pulleys. No one, in their right mind, wishes to go into the Wilds.

The carriage stops and the doors of the prison carriage open. Light blinds me temporarily and by the time I've regained my bearings, two Celect Knights are hauling me towards the end of the Tunnel . . . to the ledge overlooking the Wilds. They are not gentle and my shoulder suffers their ill-use.

My first look at the Wilds was always in my imaginations or from books. I pictured it as a green mist lying atop a barren swampland. However, that's not what I see before me. Instead, there's a drop-off from the ledge. A fifteen hundred foot slope that dips downwards into a meadow of yellow, swaying grass. Beyond it, about a mile from the slope's bottom, a black forest dots my vision. No green. No brown branches. Just black jagged trees, the color of smoking death. The remains of a deadly poison which life could not challenge.

Celectate Wood and Aspen stand off to the side of the ledge, a good distance from me. Though I am in a weakened state and an attack would be childish, they are not foolishly optimistic that I will feign from physical violence. They do not say a word to me. Nevertheless, they stare patronizingly, gazes stiff as marble.

Aspen glares back at me. *You'll pay for it.*

I shiver but don't flinch beneath his gaze.

Behind me, the Community is present to watch the final display of my punishment. Lord Singh wipes fresh blood from his lip and looks at me.

Father and Mother are beside him, held back by the Celect Knights barring their path. Father's eyes still shine with the replaying of my whipping. My branding. He looks aged beyond his years and so tired. He seems weak and unable to stand on his own feet. Mother offers him her arm, which he takes.

She appears calm, but when our eyes meet, a spark of fire ignites in them. If I didn't recognize it, I might not have noticed, but that spark lights a flame in my heart. She turns her frigid stare, the one that used to freeze Landor and me in place when we got into mischief, on Celectate Wood. He pretends not to notice, tilting his nose in the other direction. However, his eyes flutter at the corners. Mother smiles and flips him the finger. Every fear for the family safety disappears. Mother is strong. Mother will help Father. She will not let him fall.

She looks at me again. She places a hand over her heart and pats it gently several times with her fingers, her lips tilting up in a smug expression. There's so much pride in the way she squares her shoulders – the way she lifts her head – the way she glares at the Community elders beside her. I've a feeling she knows who asserted me guilty.

"I want my daughter to be one of the finest, greatest, strongest, smartest girls Kelba has ever seen."

Slowly, she turns that pride-filled gaze on me, the spark glistening in the corners of her eyes. She looks radiant – beautiful – the strong woman I can never match. She curls her thumb and forefinger together and splays another finger beside them, pressing it to her heart. It's a symbol I've never seen – not the Bone family vigil or the Kelban vigil of strength. She nods at me with that mysterious smile I've never understood.

I don't understand.

And there's no time.

"I love you both!" It comes out a harsh whisper, but I know they hear it.

The guards jerk me towards the edge of the slope. The tallest one steps close. He hands me a pouch. It's heavy and swishes when I move it to my right shoulder. Water. The pouch holds at least two gallons, barely enough to last two days in this heat. One if I tend my wounds properly to prevent infection. He presses a glass vial into my hand too. A white pill rests inside.

"To ease your suffering," he explains, not even looking at me.

Hot anger beckons me to throw it in Celectate Wood's face and spit on it. I don't need such a gift. I won't be so weak as to take my own life. I won't be such a coward! Yet . . . I squeeze the vial close.

I step to the edge, my feet teetering on the corner between Kelba and hell. The fifteen hundred foot slope stares up at me menacingly. There are rocks and jagged underbrush dotting its surface.

"Either you go down yourself . . . or we push you," the protocol man says matter-of-factly and looks at the sun. "It's getting late. Five seconds, or I shove you."

"Five . . ."

I try to find Landor in the crowd. I don't see him.

"Four . . ."

Father and Mother stare at me, their eyes refusing to look away.

"Three . . ."

Father mouths something. *"I love you."*

"Two . . ."

Mother spreads her thumb and fingers over her chest in that strange little symbol I don't recognize. Whispers something I can't piece together.

"One . . ."

I jump.

Air gives me the freedom of weightlessness, and then gravity regains and I begin to fall. My feet meet with the slope first, buckling my knees on impact. I roll. My black slices against the rock of the slope. Underbrush scratches along my arms. My legs. I tuck my body around the pouch of water, protecting it. If it breaks – I will die! The vial remains clutches in my palm. Everything around me spins and spins and spins.

Soft grass brushes against my face. The world stops spinning and my body slows to a stop. Dirt crumbles beneath my hands. I jump up quickly, regretting it the moment I do. Pain spreads all over my body. Bruises will dot my skin before the hour is through. Scratches line my arms and legs and my hair is wrapped around my neck, thick with knots and underbrush particles. I stare at the dirt on my hands, expecting it to eat away at my hands until only bone remains. But nothing happens. If the poison is here, it's not effective immediately.

Above me, people are shouting. Loudly. Angrily. I hear Celectate Wood bark orders at someone. A woman screams. A man roars.

"KYLA!" I look up. The sun glares at me. I shield it with a hand.

"KYLA!" It's Landor. His head peeks over the edge of the ledge, trying to search for me. I wave an arm at him. His eyes flood with relief. Someone grabs him from behind. He grunts and punches whatever – no, whoever – it is. Then . . .

"HERE!" He lets something drop from his hand and disappears from sight. It catches the glint of the sun a million times, as it twists and turns on its descent, getting closer. I see its sharpness. I gasp and jump away. It falls directly where I would have been standing.

A dagger!

He stayed true to his word.

I pick up the blade and examine the sheath he threw it in. It's a simple brown affair. Sturdy. Shock rolls through me when I see the hilt. It's his blade. Lan threw me his blade!

Celectate Wood publicly presented the honed dagger to him on the day of his knighthood – on the day of his graduation as a Celect Knight. By wearing it, Landor proclaimed to Kelba that he served its ruler. That he protected him. By giving this blade, this symbol of loyalty, to me, he has done the unspeakable. He has publicly resigned from knighthood.

Above me, the gates creak. They are closing. I will be alone.

Ahead of me, a mile away, the blackened trees glare at me. The Burnt Forest, my knowledge of Kelban folklore recollects. Beyond those black trees and this plain, no one knows what awaits me. All I have to guide me are the myths and legends surrounding this strange land. I know not what monsters lurk in the shadows. What men grovel to taste my flesh. What death I will meet.

Breathing deeply, shoulder stinging and raw from the brand that now adorns my skin; I leave the slope behind. I leave the Wall behind. I leave everything behind.

I face my nightmares.

I face the myths.

I face the Wilds.

PART TWO

The Wilds

Chapter XI

My body is so stiff it takes me nearly an hour to reach the jagged trees dotting the meadow's end. My sandals crunch into the ground: a combination of scattered black roots, earth – and bones! Looking closer, the bones are of the animal category. At least, that's what I tell myself as the trees surround me – and darkness. I peer over my shoulder but the meadow is gone. In its place are black branches, stumps, and roots striking out of the ground like mangled claws. The forest is thick – so thick I might as well have been swallowed.

The Burnt Forest has no leaves, I recall from textbooks, but I hadn't quite believed such stories. How could a forest have no leaves? Now as I look around me, I can't see a single one. Just brambles, overgrown roots, and vines. They knot along the floor, so close together, I feel skin peeling from my legs as I struggle to avoid their presence.

And though there are no leaves, I cannot see the sky. There's only a thick mass of curling tree branches and vines towering thirty – fifty – feet above my head. Like a maze. A web. The trees grow so close together I have to squeeze between them. Their roots cannot find enough soil, and their fight for supremacy leaves decaying roots and bark to the darkness. My feet bleed as the underbrush snags them. I don't cry out. Too well do I remember all the tales written by the great authors, like "Goldbrow." I do not want a "mythical" creature feasting on my flesh.

Something scurries in front of me, and I lean back against the tree, my burning backside connecting with rotten bark and gnarled wood. I bite my lip so hard I taste blood. The scurrying flees, followed by a small chipping noise.

Just a small animal. Just a small animal.

I edge away from the tree.

I walk straight into a a bush and thorns pierce my flesh and snag my hair. I tear away from them, only to fall to my knees against a rotten stump. My skin explodes in pain. My screams sound foreign to my ears.

Something else scampers near my head. When I look up, it's gone. I hear numerous other scampers and scramble to my feet, running for all I'm worth. All around the noises increase; in the trees above my head, on the ground beneath my feet, in the trees to my right, my left! My lungs scream for air, but I don't dare pause long enough to quell their spastic complaint. I cannot even see four feet in front of me – and I think these creatures know it.

Faster! Faster! Run!

A branch whips me across the face – blood, warm and thick, runs down my skin. I wipe desperately at it. These creatures feast on flesh – there is no greenery in the woods to sustain them – and the smell of my blood will only fuel their ravaging hunger.

Indeed, the noises around me grow harsher – more guttural. They smell the blood. They smell me!

A set of harsh nails lash out and snag the skin on my neck, ripping it into tiny, shredded gashes. I propel a fist in its direction, bone cracks, a creature wails, and I trip backwards over a rotten stump. The ground bites into my spine and I'm rolling again. Down, down, down until I stop fighting the drop and roll my body protectively around my water pouch. Above me, the scampers fade, the guttural growls cease, and blessed silence falls over me. The ground comes to a smooth halt – I see the slope that caused my escape and it goes up, up, up so high I don't believe I'll see the top.

My eyes have adjusted to the dark! It's as if a ghostly light shines before me, illuminating everything in different colors of gray and black. The creatures that hurry away from me are no bigger than my hand, with scaly tails, claws, and long snouts. They hide beneath brambles – beneath trees – beneath vines – and stare at me with beady, black eyes. At least they fear me.

My shoulder burns like wildfire as I stand and struggle with the heavy water pouch. My lips taste like blood and sweat and dry skin. I rub the pouch longingly beneath my hand, forcing the claws of dehydration back down my throat. I must save the water. No one – not even famed historians – know how vast the Burnt Forest is. Perhaps it is all the Wilds is. Perhaps I am doomed to eternal darkness.

The creatures slither backwards as I draw closer, pulling so deep into their hiding places that I lose sight of their eyes. They chip to one another quietly between their lairs. I entertain the notion that they are either laughing at my demise or wondering how long it will be before they can taste me too. They must be starving and –

Water! These creatures have to have some source of fluid to quench their thirst. That would mean this place had to have a stream of some sort.

My energy rises. Yes. There has to be water nearby.

I press on.

I find what I'm looking for – the stones of a dry creek bed – and lurch forward, already tasting the fresh water in my mouth, the cool liquid on my skin.

My relief is short-lived. The bed is dry – and has been for ages, so it seems. A disgusting, gooey substance coats the bottom of it, squelching beneath my feet. Sticking between my toes. Thrusting my disappointment into the farthest part of my mind, I shoulder the pouch again, eager to get to the other side. This forest cannot go on forever. The creatures must have some source of life-giving substance somewhere, be it in or outside this hell.

Something sharp cuts into the bottom of my sandal. I scream and trip over a large, mud-covered rock and fall on my knees. My hands sink elbow deep into the dirt. Hardened sticks encased beneath the filth grind against my fingers.

My stomach rolls with nausea and bile. It feels wrong. It looks wrong. It *smells* wrong. The creek doesn't smell like decaying dirt or animal feces.

I pick out one of the sticks beneath my hand, holding it close to my face. The dirt covering it is hard, but pliable. I scrape it away with my fingernails. In hazy gray vision, I recognize the pale white color. It's a bone! I toss it away, watching it twist through the air and thud into the dry dirt of the creek twenty feet away. My vision adjusts again, this time in blurring conversions of white, gray, and black. As far as the eye can see, down the trench, bones jut into the air, sink into the ground, claw at the sides of the creek-bed, as if struggling for their last breaths. Human bodies. All of them. All suffering. All struggling. All dead.

Bile rises in my throat and a sickening realization rolls over me. I shift my attention to the mud-covered rock I tripped over. It lies there, six feet long and half-buried. Ignoring the instinct to leave this place – to put it behind me – I lean down and scrape at the dirt. It peels away beneath my fingers and the stench of decaying flesh fills my nose. I convulse at the smell but press on. I have to know. Have to be sure before I let this moment torture my nightmares. The dirt crumbles easily beneath my hands, revealing the body of a man, the flesh black and receding. Flesh peels from the skull, but I lean closer. Closer. Look inside the open jaws of the unfortunate victim – I draw back, screaming.

The victim has no tongue!

Half-screaming, half-sobbing, I claw desperately at the side of the creek-bed, pulling myself over its sticky slope. The smell engulfs me. I lean over and retch. My stomach twists and turns, but there is nothing left to choke up. Cramps immobilize my legs, and I fall helplessly against a tree, clutching the rough bark beneath my hands. Hands that have decades of humanity coating them. Decades of pain and decay.

Human components stick to my legs. I unscrew the cap of the water pouch and pour a stream of the liquid down my thighs. The filth descends down my legs onto the ground. My skin feels clean – yet dirty. I look at the thousands of lives in the creek-bed – the thousands of lives that Celectate Wood took – and my nails dig into the tree bark again. Damn him! Damn the devil!

How many of those people were innocent? How many of them fought to stay alive in this wretched place? How many gave up and died? How many took the poison pill that Celectate Wood gave them?

I stare at the vial slid into the rawhide around my waist. It gleams up at me, the only beacon of hope in this dismal place. If things come to worst – would I be able to take it?

No! No! I mentally slap myself. Then strike my own cheek with a knuckled hand until I see stars. I must remain strong. I must think positively. But no matter how hard I try to imagine the sun shining above the blackened trees, the lands that surely rest beyond this forest, I find myself looking at the creek – and it's the only thing that looks peaceful and comforting. No more pain. No more suffering. Will I be one of those decomposing bodies?

"*You won't die.*" Well, it was easy for Selena to say.

But . . . I press aching palms to my temples. I know more about the Wilds than any person in Kirath. I studied – for years. I have seen a demon – a cannibal – from the Wilds and lived to tell the tale. I have made it farther than even Lord Telman. I am not dead. I am not in pieces. I am not beaten yet.

Celectate Wood had been smiling – smiling – when I'd jumped over the slope's edge. He'd been so sure of himself. So sure that I'd grovel and cry and plead for mercy. So sure that I'd fall to the same fate as Lord Telman and a thousand others.

But Landor had thrown me a dagger – his dagger. His symbol of loyalty and his one tie to the Celectate. He believes in me. He believes I can make it. Mother hadn't shed a single tear. She'd smiled and praised me – she *knows* I can make it.

Picking myself up takes every last ounce of strength I possess. The scar on my shoulder burns hot. I haven't had much time to look at it. Now, as I walk, I trace its form. Trace the lines. The skin it burned away. I feel like dirt. Like one of those decomposing bodies.

"*Go to hell,*" Aspen had said.

I have.

When I finally stop, I cannot tell if it is night or day. All I know is it feels like I've been in this darkness for an eternity. My feet are wet and sticky with what I know is blood, staining the brown sandals a permanent copper color.

I have to sit. And sit I do. On a black tree root as thick as two men. The rough bark scratches the skirt of my tunic. Scrapes the back of my thighs. I pull the skirt down to my knees but it snaps back up and flutters at mid-thigh.

No longer do I feel a humid heat lingering about my face. Instead, a cool breeze blows. Not from east or west. The trees are too thick. From above my head, swirling down into pockets of damp and dismal underbrush. There is no escape from it.

It is night. The chill has joined it, and I have no sleeves, no blanket, and no fire to keep me warm.

There are no leaves to pile around myself for comfort or protection from the cold and wildlife. I unsheathe my knife and lay it beside my head atop the tree trunk, inches from my hands. If worst comes to worse, thank the gods I know how to throw it. I rarely miss anymore.

My body begins to shake as icy prickles tingle along my body. I struggle to keep my hands warm against my mouth. Hands that hold the vial of death. A death with no cold or pain or suffering. The ice has done nothing for my backside. The wounds, which have yet to be cleaned, crackle and bleed as the scabs open up against the harsh bark of the tree, my only shelter against the wind. Everything in this forest defies nature.

I stare at the vial in my hand, eyelashes heavy with the ice beginning to form upon them. Everything within me says to throw it away. To cast it into the forest. Figures dance before me. Figures of horror. Their limbs hang in strange shapes around their body.

Their faces are in different states of decomposition. Their eyes are hollow and lifeless. They hold out gnarled arms, flesh peeling from their finger-bones, and beckon me to join them. To ease my pain and suffering. To be free of it. I am outnumbered. And yet, my heart – which pumps the blood that calls for my defeat – pounds a living rhythm in my chest.

Death is my choice.

My shoulder joins the spirits of the outcast ghosts before me by screaming for peace. With the scar I, too, am an outcast. Never again can I cross the Wall and enter Kelba. I will be found. I will be killed. Or will be placed in a cage and sent back here. Several people tried to do so when they were ostracized. They were dismembered, piece by piece, and hung in cages along the Wall, facing the Wilds. Some were whipped through the streets. And others were returned to the Wilds and never seen again.

Around me, the horrifying figures of death laugh at me. Call me "foolish." They tell me to take the pill. To end it. To not hope for something that will never come. I will die eventually. They remind me of the horrible tales surrounding the wasteland. The tales of cannibals and monsters too horrifying to comprehend. I must take the pill – I am nothing now. Death would be the best place for me.

"Death wants you," one of the figures whispers, the bony hand halting inches from my own.

I close my eyes, blotting out their faces, their taunts, their seductive whispers. A smooth brush across my cheek fills my insides with tranquil quiet. All the turmoil in my mind eases away into nothingness. My hand tightens around the vial – the pill. It would be a painless death as the poison shut down all my senses, then my heart. I would be at peace. No more suffering. No more worrying about the damned devil in Kelba or the fate of my family. I could leave it all behind.

"You can rest," the sultry voice whispers, bare meters from my ear. I can feel the cold – but also the warmth – from whatever creature lurks near me. "Join us."

The rebellion curls inside of me – but its claws are missing. I can't fight the wave of soft heat that bristles across my skin. I don't have to open my eyes to know that the deceased have drawn closer.

My body lightens and sleep weighs heavily against my eyes. Arms encircle me – warm, loving, friendly. Memories flash in my mind: Mother holding me as a child, laughing joyfully at my first steps, my first dance, my first drawing. Father teaching me to dance, his arm firm around my waist, his smile full of pride, and Landor's firm stance behind me as he directed my daggers, my mind, my focus. I wish I could see them. I struggle to picture their faces. Mother's beautiful blue eyes, which I did not inherit. Father's dimples. Landor's smug smile.

A white flash ignites against my eyes, blinding me, cracking me full in the forehead, spreading talons over the back of my head. I scream, but it doesn't stop. Everything spins and swirls around me, as if my body is flying through a maze, a whirlwind. A portal of bright light somewhere at the end of the swirling mass fills my vision. I cannot stand the brightness any longer.

I open my eyes.

I don't see the forest. I don't see the pill. I don't see the deceased. Instead I am in my house. In the foyer of my home!

It is night. The beautiful, ornate candles are lit along the stairwell and there's a light beneath the door of my Father's study. A shadow moves inside. I reach out to touch the candle nearest me, but my fingers grab nothing but air. It is not real. I am not really there. The corners of my vision are blurry and frayed, like an old picture. Like I'm looking through a lens. But I am there. I smell, I taste, I sense the room. The lilac flowers on the table nearest the door. The towering chandelier above my head. The familiar scent of Father's strongest wine.

The study door opens and Father, pale as a ghost, steps into the foyer.

"Papa!"

He shows no sign that he's heard me, his eyes staring straight at me – but not at me. They are listless and dry, like he hasn't slept in decades. His hair is uncombed and wild around his head and his clothes – I wrinkle my nose. He smells strongly – too strongly – of wine. He stumbles against the frame of the door.

"Elinor!"

She comes down the stairs, elegance in her walk. Her usually pink cheeks are colorless and dry. The remains of a tissue are crumpled in her hand. She did cry for me. She did!

"Where is our son?" Father doesn't even argue as she pulls the empty carafe from his hand and sets it on a nearby table. "He's not back yet! That bastard sent for him and he's not back yet! What's he done with our son? Where's our son, Elinor? Our son . . ." He loses his breath and stumbles forward.

Mother puts an arm to his chest and pushes him back. I see the twitch in her eyes as she struggles to remain calm – to hold that facade of strength around her, for Father's sake. It nearly kills me to see her lips go deathly white. "He's fine, Gavin. I swear, he's fine." The lie brings tears to both their eyes.

My heart pounds heavily as I watch Mother half-drag, half-carry Father into the solar and spread him over a sofa, calling for some "strong coffee." Then . . .

"Hail, Sir Landor!"

My brother doesn't even glance my direction – he can't see me no matter how loud I scream at him – and barrels into the solar. My parents look up at his entrance, but don't say a word. His back is to me so I can't see his face, but it must be ghastly because Mother looks like someone struck her. Landor stands stiffly for a moment – then grabs the nearest glittering figurine from a table and hurls it across the room. Glass shatters.

"Do you know, Father? Do you know . . . ?" Landor kicks a three-leg mahogany table and it sails through the air. Wood cracks. He stares at father, back muscles tensing. "Do you know what that son of a bitch has just done?"

"Son . . ." Father attempts to speak.

"No!" Landor slams a fist against the arm of the sofa. "I say, 'no!' You hear me? No! He called me in there . . . and do you know what he said? He said that Kyla's inheritance, the forty percent of the diamond mines that she would receive upon marriage, solely belongs to him because of her treachery. That he has the right to claim all the belongings of any traitors to him and his rule."

"It is the law," Father stammers.

"Damn the law! What law? He made the law, Father. He crafted it perfectly to make sure he profited from it. Him and only him! With Kyla's inheritance, do you realize what he can do? He won't need the Community. He won't need us. He won't need you. He already has the people hanging on his every word by whatever evil he secrets away from us. If he doesn't need you, Father . . . if he doesn't need the Community . . ." Landor cuts himself off and punches the arm of the sofa so hard the wood beneath creaks in protest. He shows no sign of pain as he stares relentlessly at Father. "Do something!"

Father practically flies from his reclined state and grabs my brother by the collar. I scream and so does Mother as he thrusts Landor up against the wall, knuckles white with strain, eyes dilated from too much alcohol. The anger fades from my brother's face.

"What would you have me do!" Father screams. He tightens his hold until Landor chokes. Mother pulls at his shoulder but he doesn't budge. "What can I do, son! I have struggled for years to keep that man from attaining his dreams. I have fought and bled until there is so much weight on my back I can barely stand. But in that fight I've learned something . . . and you might as well know it now before you get any reckless ideas in your head. I have done all I can – I have held my head high as a Community elder and struggled to keep this nation – my family – safe! I have fought . . ."

Slowly, his hands release Landor and he backs away. Landor sucks in a sharp breath and Mother gives a decent amount of space between them. Tears sting Father's eyes.

"And it was not enough," Father says. "I had to watch that man force his enemies into a wasteland left to hell . . . I had to watch one of my closest friends suffer beneath Celectate Wood's thumb . . ." His lip quivers. "I had to watch my daughter bleed and suffer and take the stand I should have taken long ago. I had to watch your sister fight a fight that was too great for her to win . . . too big for a small warrior like her to stand victorious. And through every hour, every minute, I stood there I told myself to say something. To stop it all. To stand with her. Die with her. And I couldn't. I didn't move. I didn't say anything. I left her to suffer on her own. I left my own daughter! I

turned my back on her . . . to save my own life!"

He falls to the ground, sobs racking his body. Mother and Landor stare at him – I stare at him. My lungs feel so constricted. I want to run to him – put my arms around his neck and tell him it's alright. I want to scream at him to get up – to stay strong. To fight. To wage a war against the Celectate that I could not.

"So that's it?" Landor's voice is angry again – and entwined with a bit of cynical cruelty I'd seldom seen in our growing up years. He looks at my father like one would a groveling beggar. "That's all you've got in you? You feel guilty. You are guilty. I understand. So am I. I should have put a knife in that bastard's back years ago . . . should have refused to cut up that merchant who didn't buy the Celectate's 'tax' papers. Should have refused to personally sack the village that didn't send his highness a 'fealty gift.' Should have refused to hunt down the simple pheasants attempting to craft a rebellion against him. I am responsible for hundreds of lives lost – behind the Wall and inside Kelba itself. For thousands of weeping children. For spreading the evil I served.

"But I won't do it anymore. Kyla took a stand where we would not. She said 'no' to his tyranny. To his dominion over us. To his power. She stood strong. She didn't flinch or beg or grovel like a beaten pup. Do you know what I heard Celectate Wood say tonight when he thought I had gone? He swore he'd hunt down every last lord who dared vote for Kyla's release . . . and he'd make them pay. I won't let him. He already took my sister from me. He can't have Kelba.

"So get up, Father. Behave in a manner deserving of Kyla's sacrifice. Because she didn't stand up there on that podium and refuse because of herself – No! She'd have gladly married Aspen if she knew it would protect us. She'd of allowed herself to be defiled and shamed if only to keep us safe. No! She refused on that podium because of us – because she had faith that her sacrifice would be revenged. She did it for you! And if you are too blind to see that, then you're not the man I thought you were. Get up, Father!" He grabs Father's arm roughly and jerks him to his feet, slamming a palm to his chest in the process. A palm to his heart. "If you loved her, Father . . . if your heart beats for that bastard's blood as much as mine – vow to have it!"

That coldness in Landor's eyes – the hate and the wrath and the lust curling within them – chills me to the bone.

"He will dispose of the Community," Father says, his voice no longer quivering. Instead, his eyes are glinting too. "That we cannot stop."

"No, we cannot," Landor agrees with a careless shrug. He ignores Father's startled gaze and picks up a shard of glass from the floor with such grace it doesn't even break skin. He holds it in front of him. "But the Community stopped being useful years ago. We don't need that to make him bleed."

"What do you mean?"

But I know what he means. I saw it in the Celectate's face when I stood on that podium. When he offered me leniency. A pardon for an apology.

Landor merely folds the glass in his palm and squeezes. Blood drips onto the floor. "Lothalar leran de revelan."

Father looks confused.

"Celectate Wood wants total supremacy. When people begin to rise against his tyranny, he's easily managed to deflate the rioting and return to his position of grace. But if you give the people a hero they will start to grow stronger – it's why he sentenced Lord Telman. Took his tongue. His weapon. And then he made the biggest mistake a damned fool could make." Landor smiles maniacally, eyes dancing with joviality "He relied too much on his pride – his certainty that he could frighten a girl into marrying his son for political power. He painted her as this endearing, sweet, little thing with no fire, no brains, no importance. But when she refused him it defied everything he'd painted her as. The pup had become a fox. If he proceeded with the punishment, if the girl who was "weak" but still rebelled against him could go through with it, what kind of message would that send to his subjects? That even the weakest can fight. He turned Kyla into a 'martyr' and then tried to correct the mistake. She refused again – and insulted him. Publicly. She went from 'martyr' to 'heroine' in the blink of an eye."

"What are you saying?" Father asks, understanding beginning to show in his eyes.

"I am saying that Celectate Wood underestimates us – all of us, lords

and beggars alike. He sees us as spoil for the taking. But when we fight back, when we begin to undermine his authority over Kelba, he is frightened. We can rip him apart – we can take Kelba back. We can restore the Community when he crumbles it." Landor drops the glass onto the floor, blood shimmering around its crystal corners. "And all we have to do is bleed a little bit."

The silence in the room is deafening.

"It won't be easy," Father says. "If we're caught . . ."

"If we're caught, we'll add fuel to the fire with our deaths. We'll go down fighting. We won't let him claim even the victory of our demise. That's how we beat him. It'll take hundreds of lives – maybe thousands – to do it. But we'll do it."

Mother draws close again, slipping her hand into Father's. They share a warm, pressurized squeeze, before Mother looks at Landor. "You're a little mad, son."

Landor cocks a solemn smirk in her direction. "Kyla was my anchor. As long as she was there, I could endure it all. I could do anything just to make sure she didn't fall into Celectate Wood's hands. It ripped me apart to see her as a miniscule pawn in that bastard's game. And it gave me wings when she defied him. He took her from me – sent her to a place I can no longer protect her – and he'll live to regret it." He smiles at the bloody glass around his feet. "Oh, he'll live to really, really regret it."

Father and Mother nod in unison. "He'll pay," Mother whispers, her hands bunching into fists at her sides, that kindred fire burning in her eyes.

"Kyla's death will be avenged," Father agrees, his lip quivering as he says my name.

Landor smirks and leans against the door with a reckless swagger. "Death? I'm surprised at your lack of faith in the Bone heritage, father."

"You think she'll survive? That she'll live in that wasteland?" Father asks. "Trust me, son. I have dreamed of such a thing . . . I have prayed and swore and screamed that such a thing could be true. But you know the stories as well as I."

Landor nods in agreement. "And no one knew those stories more than Kyla. She's been prepared for this for a long time . . . she won't die."

Mother steps forward. "We'll see her again."

The edges of the vision before me begin to close in on themselves. Darkness dances in blotted spots, stealing their faces from me one-by-one. No! Not yet. I have to stay in this dream. Have to memorize this goodness to chase away the horrors.

The darkness recedes for an instant – only a mottled circle large enough to see Mother's face. She crosses her fingers and thumb in that curious little symbol over her chest once more. "I know we will see her again," she whispers.

A white light cracks against my skull and my head snaps back, connecting against the sharp bark of a familiar tree. I open my eyes.

I will not die yet!

The deceased dance before me, all around me, their smell assaulting my senses.

"Join us, wanderer," that sultry voice whispers in my ear once more.

My groping hands find my objective – the dagger! The mangled figure screams, a sound that vibrates down my throat and into my legs with a force faster than light, when the blade cuts across it. There is no flesh – nothing but empty air. The deceased begin to fade, one by one, until only one remains – the one I cut. It stands before me, a hand pressed against the diagonal line across its foggy chest. Then, it too, disappears.

I clutch the dagger close, eyes scanning the forest for demons. For shadows. For creatures not of this world. This forest is not natural. This forest is cursed. I recognize the panic in my limbs and will myself to calm down. To ignore the curdling veins beneath my skin.

This forest is torturing me. It makes me see my family. Makes me see the dead. Makes me see my death, sweet and serene, with no worries.

I have to get out. But I can't move.

My eyes close.

A strange prickling sensation crawls up my back and something sharp sticks me in the side. I hear a small chipping noise – like bark being cracked – and then flesh is torn from between the whip lashes on my back. When I open my eyes, a scaly creature is straddled atop me, its tail flipping in my face, studded with tiny prongs. I scream and jump, all grogginess dissipating immediately.

The creature falls off of me, a piece of skin from my back dangling in its mouth, and scampers off into the trees with its new prize. I picture the smell of flesh drawing something larger, more horrifying, in my direction and grab the pouch of water and my dagger and run. I hurl over underbrush, avoiding thorns, and feel more alive then yesterday as my heart beats in my chest. The darkness doesn't scare me anymore. I can see into its foggy gray colors. No thorns rip my dress. No brambles trip me. As I run, I remember the vision from last night – the faces of my family determined to avenge me.

It's just a dream. But it felt so real!

The chill in the morning slowly recedes, replaced with a humid heat that traps air in my lungs and halts my breath. My legs come to a slow halt, and I lean heavily against a tree, dashing a hand across my soaked forehead. The water pouch sags at my side, its rubbery surface sliding against my thigh. I run a hand over the cap longingly – from somewhere inside my throat a low growl of hunger releases itself. My stomach responds in kind, so I press firm palms to the center of my abdomen, against the rawhide belt, against . . .

The vial! I frantically search the ties of rawhide. The bodice of my tunic. Even the torn gaps in my garment. It's gone.

The thin strand of control I've been struggling to maintain snaps. The one object that promised me a safe haven – a reprieve – an escape from this hell . . . I've lost it.

The forest seems to have loomed closer – its claw-like branches reaching for me in ravenous positions, the brambles growing higher to obstruct my path, the thorns thickening with deadly sharpness.

I must go back. I must find the vial.

Before this darkness eats me alive.

This is one battle I will not win. The tree branches jostle me in all directions, thickening, groping, pulling. I will not be able to find my way back. Every clearing looks like the next. Every large tree stump is the wrong one. Every tree is black and fearsome.

The heat has grown unbearable, sweltering around me in patches of warm vapor that assault me from all corners. I cannot breathe. I cannot think. I can only feel. Feel the fire coursing through my veins from hundreds upon hundreds of cuts and sores and bruises. Feel the buzzing in my backside and shoulder were the lash and the iron did their work. Feel the pounding in my head from lack of oxygen. Feel the merciless talons ripping at my stomach with hunger.

I must wash my wounds. The idea of using even a morsel of the precious water for anything other than quenching my thirst is unbearable. But common sense warns me of the consequences of such an action. If the wounds get infected there is no solution to the slow, agonizing death that will overtake me.

Peeling the damp, shredded dress off my chilled skin takes longer than I thought it would. Blood had caked through the shreds on the back of my tunic, drying the fabric to my wounds. Rivulets of blood tickle my tailbone and drip onto the ground. I must hurry before the smell attracts larger predators.

Using the tunic as a rag, I soak it generously wipe my arms from the shoulder downward. The crusty layer of blood and dirt and skin peels away, leaving a prickling sensation that, despite the pain, brings a sigh of relief from my mouth. I do the same to my torso, my legs, my feet, taking note of each cut, each bruise, each blister that mars my body and reminding myself that Lan – that Father – will avenge each and every one of them. My backside is the most difficult to endure. The open wounds on my back scream their disapproval as the filth is removed. By the time I've finished, I'm on me knees, fingers digging into the dirt and blood running across my lip as I struggle not to scream – not to wail in distress.

A stick snaps in the darkness. Instinctively, I crouch low to the ground, naked limbs sprawled beneath me on the brambles. I scan the tree-line but nothing catches my attention. The bark bristles against my bare skin.

Another stick snaps. Closer this time. Five feet from where I lie.

Tentatively, I peek over the edge of the tree root.

Two glowing red eyes stare back at me.

With a shriek, I fall backwards, hands flailing wildly to soften my fall. One of them strikes the lip of the water pouch resting against the tree root. Horrified, I watch the pouch fumble on its side and liquid shoots out the open cap. Pooling on the ground. Sinking into the dirt.

Forgetting all about those beady eyes, I lunge for it, belly scraping the thorny ground, and tip it upwards. Panting heavily, I cradle the bag against my chest – and it depletes into a sunken shell of leather. For a moment all I can do is stare. I tip the opening downwards towards my mouth and a few stray drops wet my lips before the pouch becomes barren.

I allow the pouch to fall to the ground, body shaking uncontrollably. I pull the dagger and turn around, fully intending to gut whatever creature so cruelly robbed me. I imagine twisting the knife between those beady red eyes. Listening to it whimper in pain for the death it has hammered upon me.

The creature is gone.

The dagger fumbles in my hand before joining the water pouch on the ground. My stomach screams for a reprieve from the endless torment and the very bones of my body cry out their protest. Fresh tears sting my eyes. Soak my cheeks. Wet my dry lips. The shield I've tried so hard to maintain around me falls away. I allow myself to feel everything. The whip on my back. The brand on my shoulder. The pain of Aspen's kiss. Landor's goodbye. Mother's pride. Father's grief. The hunger. The blood. The endless nightmare. I try to cup a hand over my mouth, but the sobs come anyway, racking my body with spasms of gagging breaths and chest pain.

"Why?" I slam my fists against the ground, hardly recognizing the pain that shoots into my limbs at the connection. "Why?" I stare at the trees that refuse to show me blue sky. To show me the life I know exists outside this nightmare. "Why! Why! Why!" My wrists protests in pain, but I punch the dirt. It squelches in my hands. Forms a circle of compacted earth.

I sprawl out on the ground, the humidity hugging my naked body, and stare up at the jagged black limbs, energy completely spent and eyes heavy with fatigue.

"Why won't you let me die?"

I don't receive an answer.

I open my eyes to darkness. To the never ending night of my nightmares. The chill has returned so it must be night. The bones of my throat vibrate with tension, pleading for water. My mouth is so dry, even saliva is paste. It clots in my throat and chokes me.

Above me, the tree branches point their fingers at me; taunting, laughing, judging. Their thick forms draw close together, like a group of bullies preparing an assault.

I search the ground for my tunic and find it carelessly tossed against the brambles. Pulling it free, I press it to my cheek. It is still wet and the dampness cools my cheeks and dissipates the heat, the fever, the headache hammering in my skull. It smells of blood and dirt – and water. That low growl erupts from my mouth again, so I press the dress against my lips and suck. My senses protest, but I force the ill-tasting liquid down my throat anyway. Another. Another. Until my stomach rolls with warning.

I slip the dress over my shivering shoulders and cinch it around my waist again. Above me, the trees creak and groan as a sharp breeze twists down through the wooded prison and circles around me, whipping my filthy hair around my face.

The trees!

I hurry to the nearest black monstrosity and jump for the lowest branch. Whether the desperation of my condition or the loss of weight, I'll never know, but my fingers latch onto it. My arms fall weakly at my sides by the time I pull myself onto the thick, elongated throne of bark. But I won't need them. The branches are so thick, so close together, so perfectly criss-crossed, the journey upwards will be easy. Then I will know my bearings. Perhaps I'll even see the end of the forest. The edge of my nightmares.

And if you see only forest? I force the horrible thought down.

My heart pumps madly at the hope that re-surges in my breast. I feel alive again. Feel the oxygen, the blood, in my body. I kick loose bark from my path whenever I can, relishing the sound as it hits the forest floor beneath me. I cannot see five feet into the darkness below me, do not know how high I have gone – and my chest tightens at the thought.

I shove the memories into the depths of my mind but it's too late. Whatever nightmares this forest feeds on have located my fears. I feel the tug at the back of my mind. The swirling memory returning to the forefront of my thoughts. It opens before me like the opening of a dark cave and no matter how hard I struggle, fight, scream I enter it.

I am a child of nine, scampering through the halls of a palace – the Celectate's palace. The golden oak walls, the exquisite paintings, the glassy light pale against the deep black of my midnight hair. Against the dark of my eyes. Eyes lit up with mischief. Behind me, voices assail me – children's voices. They ask me to reveal myself. To come out of hiding.

I search around frantically, cheeks red with the thrill of the chase, and spot an elegant, oaken staircase. I grab the rail and dash up the soft, carpeted steps. The candles lit against the walls illuminate the staircase in a dim, eerie light that mystifies my child-like examination. I remind myself to paint the staircase – to draw its luster – when I return home. A door comes into view at the top of the steps – a single, white door. I open it without a care and slam it behind me, turning to survey my hiding place.

It is the roof of the palace – not a usual roof though. A glass roof. I stare in fascination beneath me at the outline of Calaisar's sun in the gigantic room beneath. It is magnificent and beautiful and good. I spread arms wide against the expanse of blue sky and begin to prance upon the glass, watching my reflection in its mirrored exterior. I don't notice the looming shadow approaching from behind me. The soft swish of robes against the wind. The heady scent of "Barron" for the royal line.

"What are you doing up here, little one?"

I startle at the voice and turn around. Celectate Wood stares back at me, clothed in his usual dark colors, but his regal robes gone. He wears a simple tunic, tied at the front. As a young child, my eyes marvel over the gleaming muscles of his arms beneath the silken fabric and the handsome chisel of his jaw.

"Kyla Bone," he mutters.

I smile innocently.

His eyes darken. "What are you doing?"

I launch immediately into a child-like explanation. "Selena and Aspen are trying to find me and I . . ."

He steps forward, and I stop speaking, instinct hitting me full in the gut. His eyes have no mirth. No light. And they stare at me mercilessly. He continues forward, until he's standing inches from me, and I have to tilt my head up to look him in the face. The sun settles behind his head and rays encircle his skull. I marvel over his resemblance to Calaisar's symbol.

"Have you not been taught to bow in my presence, child?" he asks with a smile that doesn't look like a smile at all.

"I . . . I . . ."

"Perhaps your manners have been dimmed of late by the constant interaction in my heir's presence, but you cannot forget your place, child. Do you understand?" He glares down at me.

"I . . ." My tongue is in my throat, and I can't speak. Young I might be, but I could recognize a threat to my existence - and it frightened me.

Celectate Wood's frown deepens. He puts a hand on my shoulder. "Walk with me, child."

And walk we do. To the edge of the glass roof.

"Look down, child."

I do. I see cliffs and meadows and forests and mountains. I see a lake. A bird soaring just above its peaceful water. A deer grazing off sweet, yellow grass.

"This is something you must learn, child, and your parents have been fools not to open your eyes earlier. There are two types of people in this world: ruler and ruled. Argue it. Debate it. Fight it. A simpler truth cannot be spoken. It is the only truth. An endless cycle of who will conquer, who will rule, who will fall, and who will rule instead." His

fingers tighten on my shoulder-bone. "Who is your ruler, child?"

For some reason, I falter. I try to think of words to say. The right words. But I don't say them. I only stare at that lone deer. That soaring bird. That peaceful lake.

"Rulers stand up here," Celectate Wood continues, his voice light and soothing, as if he were speaking to a newborn. "Do you know where you stand, Kyla Bone?"

Slowly, slowly he pushes me forward – towards the mountains, towards the forests, towards the deer and the soaring bird. Towards the edge! His hand moves to my neck. Bends me over. Everything sways around me in colors of yellow, green, and blue. The hazy focus of the trees, hundreds of feet below, beckon with tangled branches.

"Down there," he whispers, low and menacing in my ear. "You, your parents, the Community, Kelba . . . all down there. The ruled always try to climb up to the highest position . . . they battle each other for it. But eventually . . . they slip." One of my feet loses touch with the edge and dangles in the air above the forest below. I whimper but don't scream.

"They fall." My remaining foot teeters on the edge as his fingers apply more pressure, more leverage. My body sways between gravity and solidity.

"They die!" He releases me.

I catapult forward, sun and trees and meadow coming to meet me face-to-face for a windy kiss, hands flailing wildly for an escape. Someone grabs my shoulder and pulls me backwards. I land solidly on the glass roof.

"Do be careful, Kyla Bone. You don't want to fall." He pats me gently on the head and exits through the door, leaving if open for me to follow at will.

I shiver. I shake. I stare. I shiver again. I look through the glass at Calaisar's sun once more and the contents of my stomach slowly rise as I stare at the fifty foot drop between the glass and me.

Ears buzzing, I crawl across the glass, praying it does not crack beneath my weight. I leave the glass roof behind and flee down the staircase. The last of the steps fall away from my feet, and I'm in the hall again.

Celectate Wood stands to my right, arms placidly locked behind his back. "Well, Kyla Bone, did you learn the dangers of journeying so high?"

I lower my gaze. My head. My pride. "Y-yes, Your Excellence."

He smiles.

I look down at my feet, past them, to the forest floor beneath me. I can see it clearly now, dangling vastly beneath me, and my stomach clenches. I recognize the weightless air around me, the gravity pushing me in the gut, the ache in my temple. I am up too high. If I fall I will die. If I fall I will die! Slowly the tree branches enclose around me, tangling with one another, imprisoning me. The wood beneath my feet begins to dissipate, leaving me open to the air – and the ground beneath.

I will die!

Grasping the nearest branch, I begin my descent.

No. Go back. Climb.

But when I look beneath me and see the thorns lengthening to spear me – imagining the pain lancing through me as they connect with my flesh – I cannot.

Go back. Climb.

I reach the forest floor and the trees spread out again, branches lifting out of my reach.

The pockets of vapor warm my face as I come to a steep drop-off and another dried river-bed. No bodies dot its landscape. No human bones.

No one has made it this far. The thought is not a comforting one.

Hunger pains roar within my abdomen, pulling flesh and bone in anger at their condition. I double over, clutching at the skin sunken against my bones. My teeth ache. My head spins. My lips crack. The wounds on my back, my shoulder, my feet burn with a heat bordering on boil. They are infected. They will weaken me.

I will die.

The darkness draws closer. Forms step out of its black folds. Gray. Desperate. Bony. The death-collectors from before. The largest draws close, nothing but bone and white shreds of stubborn flesh. It looks more like a tattered garment than skin. She holds out a wreathed arm, finger-joints clicking.

"Come, sweet one. You've fought long enough. You need to rest. Rest with us."

"You frighten me," I say, voice strained as I fight the pain in my gut.

"We frighten many. We give peace to all," she says.

I close my eyes. Think of Landor. Of Mother. Of Father.

I see Master Ragar. Celectate Wood. Aspen. Aspen leading me into his room. A fire crackling. Aspen brushing the sleeve of my dress aside. The dress falling to the floor. Aspen's lips . . .

My hand reaches for the bones.

Landor hugging me close. Landor giving me his dagger.

Mother's voice, proud and lovely, *"I want my daughter to be the finest, greatest, strongest, smartest girls."*

Father's guilty sobs. *"I turned my back on her . . . I left my own daughter."*

"Let them go," the soothing tone skates over my skin, weighing the sweet memories down. "Give it up. Let yourself fall into this emptiness, dear one. Fall. Fall."

"Do you know where you stand, Kyla Bone."

"You are mine, sweet one." A bone brushes my finger.

I'm back at the palace. I'm back in that dress. I'm back at that moment. I'm staring at Celectate Wood. Hearing his words. *You are mine.*

You are mine.

You are mine.

I open my eyes. The bony creature of darkness – of death – smiles, her jawbone waggling.

"You're right. I do need to let it go. I need to let it all go."

She nods. The other forms around her do the same. "Yes, sweet one. Yes."

I straighten, shoulders arched painfully. I grit my teeth.

"Poor dear thing. Yes. Come to me. Yes. Just a little bit more." Her hand – the bones – brush my shoulder in a cold caress.

"I have come very far," I whisper languidly, eyes heavy with fatigue.

"Yes. You have. Very far, sweet one. You are at the end." Her voice falters. "At the end of your pain," she adds.

I step into her embrace. Let her arms fold me in a comforting hold that slowly pulls the air from my lungs. The skin on my body trembles as I return death's hug. She croons softly.

I plunge the dagger's blade into her back.

She screams. A scream not human. Not earthly.

For a moment, the darkness around me wavers. Sinks in on itself as death struggles with the pain. Over the bony shoulder, a wink of light – a tiny pocket of gleaming yellow – shines at me.

"*You are at the end.*"

I pull the dagger free and run. Run towards that gleaming pocket of light. Behind me, the screams turn feral. Beastly. Branches crack. Trees stir. Thorns and brambles stretch from the black depths.

Another pocket of light joins the first. Then another. Another.

I hear it. The cascading. The rushing. The roaring.

Water!

Gray forms swirl through the trees around me. To my right. My left. Above my head. They screech. They scream. They roar. My ears tingle.

Thorns grab at my legs. Brambles roll into my path. Tree branches sweep towards my head. My arms. My legs. I slash the dagger before my face and bark cracks. A root snags my ankle and my hip connects with the ground. Muscles repositioning, I sprint from my knees, catapulting onto my feet. I ignore the pain. The screams. The trees.

I focus on the light. An opening appears between the dark branches. Behind those jutting barriers, the rush of water rings in my ears.

The light blinds me as I close the distance and make one last jump to clear the blackened trees forever. They snag my tunic, my hair, my arms in a last, desperate effort to capture me. My dress rips. The branches snap.

I fall flat on my belly and the sun blinds me. My eyes sting at its brilliance. My skin trembles beneath the rays.

Dirt crumbles beneath my cheeks. I open my eyes and see the yellow ground. The dust circling up around the soft breeze. The ground is dry and desolate. Yellow from age. Black from poison in some places. But one flickering color of blue captures my attention.

A river. A river of cold, foaming, crystal water. Thirty feet wide and bursting with sustenance. A breeze blows the freshness straight into my face.

I crawl towards the edge. Towards the lip of water rippling inches from my hand. I reach out towards it, already feeling the cool liquid enclosing my hand, quenching my thirst, washing my body.

Another low breeze disturbs the dust beneath me and wisps of light brown flutter into the air in soft puffs. The dust swirls over the river. Hovers over the water. Settles against the smooth surface.

And turns a venomous black!

I pull back my hand. The water continues to flow. To bubble. To roar with life. But that dust . . . that water . . .

Poison.. Poison ate things. Poison tricked kings and fools and wildlife. Poison turned things black

My tongue swells – so close to water and unable to taste – to touch – it. Tremors shake my fingers. My body. My lungs. I'd drink my tears if I were able to produce them.

Behind me, a long, low wail raises the hairs along my spine. It's a woman's mournful tune. A deadly tune.

I toss a handful of dirt into the river, and watch it turn black as coal and sink into the water, leaving no sign of its true origins.

The wail sounds again: longer, harsher, deadlier.

My legs tremble when I stand, muscles exhausted. They want to remain. To sit. To rest. But if I stay I'll fail. My body will betray me. My mind will trick me. I will fall prey to the poison – the beautiful, blue, tempting poison.

Across the river, a luscious, deep green forest rests, its branches darting into the sky with royal pride. In that forest is life. I can see it. Smell it. Sense it. If I can find a way across the river – I'll live. I know it.

The dust gathers beneath my feet and dries the skin into painful, hard lines. I trip on the deep cracks left in the ground by long-ago decimation. The yellow grass that manages to grow is sharp and leaves shallow slices along my calves.

Against the backdrop of the river, something dark and familiar stands out against the lurid surface. Squinting against the sharp rays of the sun, I peer closer. Step cautiously along the ground, expecting it to open up and swallow me.

It's a bridge!

I wait for it to disappear. Wait for the trick to subside. For the hunger pains in my stomach to reveal their deceit. But it doesn't disappear.

It's real!

I never knew I could run under such duress, but even my burning muscles and swollen feet can't slow me down. The bridge is rickety – a flimsy contraption made of young tree limbs and bark. It could collapse beneath the slightest change in weight.

But I've lost enough to calculate the difference.

I step towards the first rung, feet testing the wood. It bends and creaks beneath my skin. The entire bridge sways. I lurch back.

Behind me, the low wail changes to a delighted hiss.

My ire sparks. I will do this. I will enter that green forest.

I will live!

I step onto the rung again.

"On the wrong side of the Wall, aren't you, Kelban?"

The voice – so close, so harsh, so distinctly human – sends my heart into my throat. I stumble back. Away from the bridge. Away from the river. Away from the large form that rises up from the ledge concealed beneath the questionable way to freedom.

"I asked you a question, outsider!" he says in a tone bordering on violent.

His very presence sends warning messages to my hands, and I long to rest a hand on my dagger. To draw it for certainty. Protection. But I decide against it.

He already has a knife and is cleaning it in slow, casual strokes. But the tick in his jaw, the slight tremor of a muscle in his arm, betrays him.

"N-no. I'm on the right side."

He looks up.

I stiffen when our eyes meet.

I lurch into the past. The three year-old memory burns vividly in my mind. The moonlight, bright, piercing, and deathly. The eyes, dark and ringed and different. The body, agile, adept, and focused.

The Wild boy.

Chapter XII

I had thought about this moment for years. About what I'd say. What I'd do. How I'd do it. But now, staring at those eyes – eyes dark and dangerous and violent – I can't.

"You're a long way from home, Kelban," he says.

"I won't argue that," I retort. My voice sounds foreign: dry, stunned, and edgy. I wish I could recover the bite Landor praised. The sting that put people in their place.

He frowns, and the knife straightens in his hands. "This bridge is forbidden to your kind – as is the forest beyond."

Your kind? The words sting, but the meaning doesn't escape me.

"You will have to swim," he mutters and steps aside, blocking the bridge's opening. He sheathes the knife at his side, but the look he casts in my direction assures me he can easily retrieve it.

I shake my head, and he cocks his to the side. The trait is so unnatural – such an incredible familiar animal trait – I almost go for my dagger again!

"What's the matter, Kelban? Is such a feat beneath you? Should I personally escort you?" Warning bells sound in my head at his mockery.

"I'm certain you – nor I – favor that manner of passage," I tell him.

The corners of his mouth wrinkle. "And why's that?" he asks sharply, arms still crossed, eyes still dark. However, his posture has stiffened.

"I'm fairly certain you know *exactly* why," I counter, lifting a brow.

His lips curl into a sneer. "Very good, Kelban. You don't have shit for brains at least."

I bite back a retort – one that would surely have me flying headfirst into the foaming river. "Let me cross," I say instead.

"I can't do that," he says, stepping in my way. He blocks the sun's rays and for the first time I see the hardened muscle of his torso and the sword hilts located at each shoulder. I recognize the intricate designs on the hilt – ivy and ancient symbols. I'd seen one years ago, glowing with dull white vibrancy, its deadliness hidden beneath deceptive beauty. The moon sword.

He has two now.

He notices my gaze and sneers again, brow knitted together in effortless disgust. "I cannot let a Kelban across this river without a reason."

"Life and human nature aren't good enough reasons?"

"You'd be surprised how deadly human nature is, Kelban. But I shouldn't have to teach you that. Your kind offers sufficient lessons on the matter." He reaches out and jerks the strap of my tunic off my shoulder, revealing the ugly black symbol beneath. "Don't you think?"

I shift his hand aside and cover the mark with my palm. It burns raw beneath the heat of my hand, and I bite my lip to hide the contortion of pain on my features. I don't think it works.

"What were you ostracized for, Kelban?"

Defiance. Truth. Heroism.

"It's complicated," I whisper, not daring to look up. The turmoil in my eyes would surely give away far too much of myself than I'd like. There are parts of me strangers have no right to see or know.

"I've got time," he says and leans back against a rail of the bridge. It creaks beneath the weight but doesn't break.

"A difference of opinions." I look up, masking the truth behind years of practice.

He narrows his eyes and scans me from head, to foot, to head again. I try not to flinch beneath that feral gaze, but my palms and brow grow damp with sweat. He chuckles, and it's filled with disgust.

"You're a noble," he grunts, every bit of loathing crammed into that one word.

I nod. To deny would be foolish. Every single trait about me speaks "noble." The way I hold myself. The way I speak. Even the way I answer his questions.

"You must also know the tales." He steps towards me.

I resist the urge to retreat.

He stops mere inches from my torso. In noble society such a distance is inappropriate, and borders on scandalous. Any decent girl should put the offender in his place. A good tongue-lashing usually worked. A sound slap was the extremist measure. But I don't feel such measures apply to moments like these.

He smells strongly of smoke and forest – and blood.

I want to pull my dagger. My gut insists such an action would be my end.

Instead, I tilt my chin upwards. Past the muscles peeking between the opening of his dark vest. Past the bulging vein in his neck. Past the ever-present smirk on his lips.

I meet his gaze. Stare at the dark rings around his pupils. At the dark gray color of his eyes. At the lack of emotion betrayed through those eyes. There is no anger. No hunger for my blood or my flesh. No recognition of who I am or how I know him or if he knows I know him. Just emptiness and – a wall behind them. I've seen those eyes hundreds upon hundreds of times in the faces of nobility.

I am not the only one using a mask.

He breaks the connection first and stares past my shoulder. At the Burnt Forest.

The long, low wail sends ice up my spine. It's still there. Still waiting and mourning and haunting.

"*Siratha*," he mutters with disgust.

Siratha? I had heard tales of such monsters who lurked in the darkness. They discovered your deepest fears and forced them upon you. They played with your mind and your soul until you gave up.

Then they seduced you – tricked you – into accepting death and sucked the life from you. They were not one being. Every time they took a life, that life became part of them – another shadow to their endless form. The *siratha* in the forest had to be very powerful to acquire so many gray shadows around her. Or just cunning.

The idea of that monster following me through the forest – watching me sleep, watching me climb for freedom – turns my stomach.

The Wild boy turns away from me and ducks beneath the bridge. I hear him rummaging against the stones and dirt of the river-bank. He emerges a moment later, a sack slung across his shoulder and a familiar bag in his other hand.

A water-skin!

"Here!" He tosses it in my direction and it nearly sends me backwards when it lands in my arms. It lurches uneasily in my hands.

I twist the cap from the skin and cautiously sniff the opening.

"I would like to drink too, Kelban, without your nasal particles in mouth."

There's a strange smell from within – something sweet, yet savory and strong.

"If you think you can make it eight miles before nightfall without sustenance, then by all means, go ahead, Kelban. I will warn you that I'm not going to stop because you feel the sudden urge to rest or faint like *your kind* are partial to doing."

He waits for me to drink, but I let that strange smell linger on my senses. I cannot recognize it. All the ancient tales whisper their knowledge in my ears. Cannibalism. Torture. Living death.

Do not allow fear to cloud your judgment. Do not allow fear to make your choices.

I raise the opening to my lips and pour a stream of the liquid into my mouth. It slides easily down my throat and tastes like wine and tea and water all in one. My tongue sizzles, and I gag reflexively, waiting for my mouth to start foaming and my body to shut down. But it doesn't. Instead, my muscles relax. I drink until the boy grunts and snatches the skin from my hands.

"That's enough!" he snaps.

"What is that?" I ask, ignoring his shocked gaze as he stares at the half-empty skin.

"Hunter's brew," he mutters and closes the cap tightly. "Ten times stronger than water and created with the intention to restore energy to you with one mouthful."

My body throbs with renewed strength.

"How long were you in that forest?" he asks. His eyes scan my body, singling out every bruise, cut, or scar.

I mentally count off the hours I remember and shake my head. "I don't know. But it was long enough."

He shifts the skin to his free shoulder. "Follow me."

I stiffen, those warning bells sounding in my head once again.

He looks over his shoulder and frowns. "Are you deaf, Kelban?"

I pull the dagger free, the ache in my side tightening. I've seen his skills before. The uncommon dexterity he possesses. The ability to fight darkness itself. I can't beat him, but I have to make sure he's not making a fool of me.

He doesn't show any surprise at the blade thrust in front of his face. He makes no movement towards his own weapons. He smirks instead. "I can see you're not easily manipulated," he mutters.

"How can I trust you?" I plant my feet firmly in the ground, knees bent slightly to allow for quick movement.

His mouth twists into an ugly smirk and his eyes flash.

Does he think I won't use my weapon? That I don't know how?

He swings his arm in a wide arc across the landscape. "Can you trust them? The wildlife? The sky? Or yourself? I'll tell you this . . ." He steps close, his nose inches from mine, ". . . the stories you've heard about us . . ." His eyes flash. "They're not all true."

The hell they aren't! I guard my tongue and relax at the feel of cold metal in my palm.

"How can I *trust* you?" I repeat.

He growls, low and vicious. "I just let you live, Kelban."

That he holds my life in his hands – that he controls whether I live or die – infuriates me. But I ponder his words. I barely escaped the *siratha*. I am not prepared, physically or mentally, for the other horrors that surely await in this wasteland.

"I can make this decision real easy for you, Kelban, since you seem to have difficulty determining myth from reality. I've got one question for you." Maybe its his change in tone, the sudden ferocity that possesses him, but I meet his gaze, allowing my anger and unrest to deplete. "Do you want to live?"

Do I? I came close to swallowing Celectate Wood's pill. I struggled to decide if real hell was worse than this . . . banishment. I wanted to join the *siratha*. Wanted to have peace. Rest. Selfish escape. But I hadn't taken the offer. I hadn't fallen. I hadn't given up.

I was still alive. No, I don't want to die.

I tip my chin in agreement.

He doesn't smile. Doesn't frown. Just nods slowly. "Alright then. Follow me."

He doesn't say anything else. Doesn't offer an explanation. Just steps onto the first rung and starts moving across with agile speed. The rungs bend and lurch beneath his weight but he move too quickly for much harm to come.

I sheath the dagger at my side and approach the flimsy excuse of a bridge. I press the sole of my sandal against the first rung and put full weight on it, prepared to shift to the next one. It snaps and I lose balance, leg slicing straight through the bridge, towards the foaming river beneath. I barely manage to pull myself onto the bank again.

The sandals are too rough. Too heavy on my feet. The idea of taking off the one protection between pain and my feet makes my stomach clench, but slowly I remove the sandals. The Wild boy is already halfway across the bridge, dancing from rung to rung. I notice, for the first time, that he is barefoot.

Asshole! He didn't deign to inform me about such a precaution. I'm quite sure he wants me dead.

I stick the mangled sandals into my belt and put a foot to the next wooden rung. It bends beneath my weight and before I can lose courage, I push off from the bank and shift towards the next rung. The wood splinters slightly beneath my foot and I dance to the next once – the next. The next! The bridge sways slightly at the clumsy crossing, but holds.

The water rushes beneath the bridge and it dips closer to the deadly surface, inches from the poisoned fangs of water spurting around stones. I falter as a spurt of water slices into the air, drops flailing my direction on a soft breeze. One of the wooden rungs snaps beneath my feet. I manage to shift to the next one and continue on.

Don't look at the water. Don't look at the water. Don't look . . .

Everything fades to nothing around me. There's only me and the rungs and the water beneath.

I am not fast enough, and a splinter of wood pierces the sole of my foot. I cry out and falter again. A drop of blood dribbles off the broken rung and sizzles upon contact with the water.

The scars on my neck slowly burn, their ridges raised against my skin, turning the blood in my veins to fire. The rung strengthens beneath my feet and the hard surface propels me forward. The wood no longer bends beneath my weight. Snaps at the strain. Even the water in the foaming river beneath calms. The low buzz in the tips of my fingers is heavy and lingering. The moment my feet touch solid ground, it stops, leaving my body heavy with a new feeling – fatigue. My temple throbs like I just endured a mental assault.

The Wild boy leans against the tree-line of the welcoming forest, arms crossed in casual indifference. I want to scream at him. Curse him. But he's my one remaining chain to survival. Angering him could be disastrous

"Seeing as you're more than able to handle yourself in dire circumstances, I can be persuaded to suffer your presence."

Persuaded? I'm not begging him for my life. I haven't sunk that low.

I communicate that opinion by crossing my arms.

His jaw tightens. "I have a couple of rules. Rule one: you do as I say! No objections. No arguments." He pauses, allowing the words to sink in.

"Rule two? Leave if you don't do what I say. Or I'll leave *you*. Got it?" He waits for my answer.

I believe him. I nod.

"Okay. Then follow me like a good little girl and don't irk me so." He turns and steps inside the dense greenery.

I don't even have the desire to snap at him for calling me a "little" girl. Swallowing my anger, I follow him. I want to kick his arrogant ass, but he *will* leave me. I'll be dead then.

Common sense before justification is, unfortunately, my new motto.

When the foliage hides the river from my sight, I have the freedom to look around. It is like any other forest, except thicker and wilder in appearance. Vines and leaves of unknown origin brush against my skin. I entertain the idea that they, too, might be poison and keep a weary distance.

A rabbit darts out of the Wild boy's path. He makes a move towards his sword, then suddenly remembers I'm there, and returns his hands to pushing shrubbery aside.

I rub ordinary green leaves between my fingers. Smell the dirt, the wood, the life in the air. Relish the realization that it is leaves and not bones that crunch beneath my feet. In my relief, I make a misstep and topple straight into a tree. My right shoulder snags it brutally and skin rips. I stifle a scream and limp forward.

Straight into the Wild boy.

His eyes dart over my face . . . and the new wound on my shoulder. I cover it with a hand. He lifts a brow at me.

"I didn't irk," I say quickly.

He stares at me for another moment before turning and continuing to walk. He practically steps over a whole fallen tree trunk with no problem. I have to pause and use my hands to lift myself over it. The trunk scrapes against my knee.

The Wild boy's lack of talking begins to scare me. I see him thinking. Watching. Observing how many times I stumble. How often I pause to catch a breath. How many times I wince. The cold calculation in his gaze chills me to the bone.

Internally, I debate whether I should keep following him.

Instinct tells me, no.

Common sense tells me, yes. He seems to know where he's going.

It could be a trap, instinct snaps.

But it could not be.

Damn common sense. It always wins!

Somewhere through the dense smell of wood and ash and greenery, a new smell dampens the life. It is a smell I have grown accustomed to. A smell that burns my nostrils. Chills my blood. Puts my nerves on edge. A tinge of copper so strong that bile rises in my throat.

The Wild boy smells it too. His back has gone stiff and his shoulders are thrown back, prepared for the danger. The hilt of one of his swords quivers the slightest bit. I try not to compare the way the boy sticks his nose in the air to that of a wild animal. The similarity is frightening.

The smell comes from behind a rumpled patch of ivy and vines. I can see scuff marks in the forest floor. Red lines and swirls mar the ground as if an artist recently spread his greatest masterpiece with bold skill.

Unconsciously, I step towards the vines.

"Don't . . ." The Wild boy's hand skims mine but he's not fast enough. I've already turned the corner.

I grab the tree to hold myself steady, but I don't look away. I can't. Not from this. Never have I seen such butchery. The animal – or what's left of it – is only four feet long, with fragile bones and soft, brown skin. I cannot tell how many legs it possessed, how many eyes it had, how it moved, or wailed upon death. Pieces of it lie scattered around the area. Tossed into brambles. Hanging from tree branches. Soaking the ground with red stain. Puncture wounds line the brown hide that remains in one piece.

"What the hell . . .?" I manage to choke out.

The Wild boy's not listening. He's crouched low to the ground and his fingers sweep over the blood. It clots on his fingers. He sniffs it and that sickening feeling in my gut claws again. He prods the hide with gentle fingers and raises the hand to his nose again. He sniffs once and lets out a breath. Sniffs again. Frowns. Looks towards the trees in front of us, a deep tangle of branches and vines and thorns. Mutters something under his breath.

"What?" I ask.

A slight tremor shakes him and he turns around. For a moment, his eyes are blank – as if he's forgotten I exist. The mask returns, returning his eyes to the predatory gaze that turns my stomach once more.

"Shouldn't you be hurling your guts up, Kelban? Or is this type of violence a daily entertainment for you? You probably enjoy watching such spectacles. Too bad you didn't get to see this one."

The urge to hit him – to watch his blood join the other animal's – is strong. I hide the fist I've made behind my back but too late. He's seen it and understands its motivation. Slowly he stands, muscles rippling like some powerful beast of the forest. Those eyes – eyes full of nothing but black emptiness – lock on my own.

"You forget," I say with unchecked coldness, "I *was* such a spectacle."

His eyes dart to my shoulder, searching for the scar hidden behind my strap. A small spark of something ignites in his eyes – but it dies as quick as it came. The arrogant smirk is back. "I didn't forget."

He stands, wiping the blood on his fingers across his pants. I try desperately hard not to stare at the stain. He stomps through the leaves and blood and brushes past me without a word. I spare one last glance at the poor creature before following at a fast pace.

"Shouldn't we bury it?"

His step falters. "What?"

"Bury it. The . . . remains, I mean."

He turns around, brow raised high. His head's cocked to the side in that animal way again. The cold observance returns to his face. "Leave it. Some starving scavengers too weak to find their own food will stumble upon it." He continues walking.

"What killed it?"

He doesn't answer me.

But his shoulders tighten.

The light begins to fade, casting the forest in deep shadows, some so dark I wonder if they're alive. The Wild boy continues walking, leaves crunching beneath his boots. He stops before a tangle of vines and pushes them aside. I spot a clearing before he steps through the ivy and disappears from sight. When I join him a moment later he's already leaning over a stone circle, wood piled high to make a fire.

His camp, I realize.

I don't know what to do or where to sit or what to touch so I stand like a useless fool and watch him. Sparks fly and a flame forges the dry wood into a towering tongue of orange and white.

Once the fire is burning brightly, he turns around and pulls something from the tree branches. A large sack.

I flinch when he removes a rusty knife, with the thinnest of edges, and sets it on the ground nearest the fire. It is well worn with use and still bears signs of slaughter.

He tosses a well-worn bundle behind him at the foot of a tree. I stare languidly at its form. Wool. Soft, warm wool.

"Kelban!" he snaps. I swivel to face him. Something smacks me hard in the chest. I barely manage to maintain balance. He snorts disapprovingly and returns his attention to the fire.

I stare at the blanket in my hands. It's wrapped like his and bears signs of ill-use. But is is soft and fair protection against the cold.

"T-thank you."

He growls something in his throat and doesn't look up.

I search out a tree farthest from him, but close to the fire, and decide on a large cedar with overgrown roots launching out of the ground to make a protective rail around me. Should any beasts wander into camp between now and morning, I will not be the first source of a feast they find. I stretch the blanket across the ground and sit down. The fleece brushes the underside of my legs with a gentle caress. I remember the tangled thorns of the Burnt Forest. The creatures that tore my flesh. The cold that rattled my bones.

"I really mean it," I say over my shoulder. "Thank you."

No sound comes from behind me. No breathing. No movement. I turn around, confused, and my heart skips a beat. He's gone. I scan the clearing. The trees. The darkness.

Something glows a faint white near the fire. I edge closer to get a better look and sigh with relief. His swords. The twin moon swords are still there. He wouldn't have left them if he were deserting me. Assured that he's gone off into the woods, probably to take a piss, I kneel down before the swords. In the darkness, the intricate ivy patterns on the sheaths glow a faint silver light, mingling with the dark gray on the remainder of the sheath.

Slowly, I pick one up, my conscience rebelling with curiosity. It's extremely heavy. I know I shouldn't. I know I should set it down. But this is the sword that saved my life. The sword I've wondered and researched and dreamed about for three long years. The sword that cut darkness in two and destroyed it. I block out the conscience that orders against it and pull the sword from the sheath.

The melodic sound it makes as it's pulled from confinement is nothing like anything I've ever heard. It should grate against my ears or sting or sound like nails on a chalkboard. But it's something soft and lazy, like a gentle hiss of steam.

The blade is miraculous – like a sheet of glass molded to a hilt. My face reflects in the slim surface of the sword. The sword illuminates the clearing in soft rays. It is so light that my wrist feels as relaxed and swift as it does with a dagger. Instead of the fierceness of an average sword, it possesses a unique beauty and balance. I swing it in front of me and nearly topple sideways, so swiftly does it cut through the air. The edges glint razor sharp, thinner than any blade's edge I've ever seen. Landor once said that the best swords are those that cut at a single touch and that few possess such a deadliness. I wonder . . .

Ever so slightly, I lay the pad of my thumb against the paper-thin side – and my skin breaks!

Blood pours from the new wound and and drips to the ground. A thin line of red runs down the white blade and drops to the ground. I press tight fingers to the new wound. It hurts much more than a normal cut. A sizzling, burning feeling that eats at my thumb like death itself.

"Sharp, eh?"

His sudden reappearance sends me scurrying backwards as he emerges from the woods, a leathery creature slung over his shoulder. He pays the fallen sword no mind and throws the creature on the ground at my feet. The dead thing is covered in scaly skin from head to tail. It's upside down, revealing a soft belly of fat where a clean puncture oozes fat and blood. It's two feet long, complete with three claws on each limply hanging paw.

I swallow. "Is that . . ."

"Dinner? Yes," he interrupts. "Why? Not appealing to your delicate appetite, little girl?" He turns it onto its belly with a prod of his boot. Two black beady eyes stare up at me, empty and lifeless.

"That's not what I said." I try to quell the turning in my stomach. It actually looks appetizing, I'm struggling to control myself from snatching the whole thing and eating it raw. Disgusted at the depravity of my hunger, I turn away from the sight.

The Wild boy retrieves his sword, inspecting the blood that stains the otherwise silver blade – my blood – before licking his thumb and wiping the stains away. The edge doesn't cut him. A small twinge of envy hits me low in the gut until he smirks at me. A flush of heat warms my neck at the realization that he did it on purpose to show how foolishly inapt I am to touch it. He tucks it safely inside the heavy sheath and drops it beside its companion again.

"That ought to teach you never to touch one of these again."

Like hell it would. *Only next time I won't cut myself,* I ponder with a reproachful glance at my thumb. The open skin pukes an ugly dark red.

"Let me see it." His voice is so close I jump back several paces. He grabs my hand. I wince at the roughness of his skin and try to pull away.

"Hold still, Kelban!" he snaps. He presses a finger over the wound, sealing skin back together, and sizzling pain shoots up my arm. I bite my lip. The blood ceases to drip between our hands. He removes his hand from the wound and pulls my thumb towards his face – into his mouth.

"What are you doing?" I shriek and jerk back.

He loops an arm around my waist and pulls me close. He removes my thumb from his mouth and spits a glob of blood and saliva onto the ground between us. "You cannot possibly fathom, Kelban, what evil has stained that sword, no matter how brightly it shines. I would assume you're eager to remain alive and breathing."

"Use the hunter's brew," I argue, struggling to keep him from continuing.

"It is a liquid intended for energy, not healing." He pops my thumb back into his mouth, tongue circling around the tip.

I count. *One, two, three* . . . Endless seconds. Slowly, the burning fades from my arm – my thumb – until all I feel is his tongue against my skin. He knows at the same time I do and allows me to pull away.

The wound still bleeds, but not as deeply as before. I press it against the bodice of my tunic and ponder how long it will take to scab over.

The Wild boy returns to the fire and kneels down before the scaly creature. He grips it by the scales around its neck, peeling them from the flesh in one quick jerk of his arm. I watch in stunned silence as he grabs the rusty knife by the fire and inserts it between neck and scales, gives a terrifying thrust of his hand, and the shell I had mistaken for scales, pops off with a sickening crack. The shiny red flesh beneath ripples at the touch of the aging knife. Blood dots the ground. He pays it no mind as he digs the knife into the base of the skull, slicing a clean line straight across the torso. Slipping hands inside, he pulls white intestines from the oozing middle.

I sit down on the woolen blanket and tuck knees beneath my chin until I hear fat sizzling over the fire. He's speared the creature and has it roasting over the fire.

The heavy silence that follows is like death. Hugging my legs closer, I press my nose against them and stare at the boy. His appearance has always been sketched in my memory – a vague but burning presence. Now that he's this close it's hard not to look at him. He's grown so much taller since the last time we met. His hair is a dark brown and rumpled in uncombed strands around his face.

His nose is straight, but a small scar at the top lays claim to the fact that it's been broken, at least once. His jaw is firm and angled. Clean-shaven too. He wears no shirt. Only a black vest with strings to tie it shut. They are unbound, opening his chest to the night air. I can see scars lining his torso, some disappearing beneath the pants loosely belted around his waist.

A dagger is stuck in his waistband, partially hidden by the corner of his vest. The same intricate carvings of his moon swords mar its hilt. Strange little gashes adorn the golden pommel and stare back at me. Marks for how many he's killed? I shiver just thinking about it, for there are many.

As if suddenly aware of my keen observance of him, the Wild boy lifts his head to look in my direction.

"What's your name?" I ask.

I know I've spoken wrongly when a strange dark sheet passes over his face. He returns his eyes to the fire. "Keep the hell out of my business, Kelban!"

I don't say anything else.

When the Wild boy handed me a chunk of meat from the creature, the smell was enough to drive me crazy. I waited a decent amount of time – maybe, ten seconds – before devouring the roasted flesh and retrieving another. Though he made an effort to appear nonchalant, I saw the way his eyes darted to me. Saw the wince he tried to hide whenever I licked the fat from my fingers or choked because I was eating too fast. If I hadn't already admitted to bearing noble blood, he'd never guess from the lack of feminine delicacy I portrayed now.

The night has lengthened and the chill arrived. My skin shivers to life at the familiar feeling.

The Wild boy rests on his blanket and leans back against the tree casually. A small flask rests beside him and he raises it to his lips. I don't have to ask what's inside it when the color in his cheeks deepens with each sip.

For a while all we do is stare across the fire at one another. I count the sparks that the flames release.

"The *siratha* . . ." He coughs violently. When he recovers, his voice sounds almost normal again – if not for the ever-present lull between his words. "How did you defeat it?"

"I outran it."

"You lie, Kelban," he sneers, shaking his head lazily. He takes another drink from the flask. A long, slow drink. It drips down the sides of his mouth. He wipes it away with the back of his hand. "Your kind always lies."

"A feat *every* human is capable of, I promise you," I retort.

"Human," he snorts. "My deepest gratitude for the compliment, Kelban. Oh, don't look at me like that. I know all the tales your kind spreads about this land – about us. Cannibals?" He laughs so dryly my insides knot. "The knowledge your kind possesses is so foolish. Don't you ever look beyond your cowardice for the answers that hide?"

"If you're going to insult me, I've nothing more to say to you. You're drunk and . . ."

"Drunk?" His eyes widen and he raises the flask. "On this fool's brew? Hardly. I'm merely relaxed . . . at ease. You've made me tense all day, Kelban."

"Likewise."

He frowns. "How the hell your husband put up with you I've no cursed clue!"

His outburst shatters the frigid stare I intended to level on him and, instead, draws my eyes to the scar on my wrist. It has healed over. No one could tell it was made only seven days ago.

"I'm not . . ." I stop myself. Seven days! How the hell did it heal so quickly?

"You're not what, Kelban?" His eyes darken.

That niggling, warm, uncomfortable feeling inside of me throbs like a second heartbeat. That scar protects me from my past. My true identity. My true story. If I tell him I've no husband, he will ask questions. That part of me – who I am, who I was, who I wanted to be – belongs to me and me alone!

"I'm not ready to talk about that," I answer.

He shrugs. "Then answer me this one question. How did you defeat the *siratha*?"

"I don't know." It's the truth.

His eyes lower into slits. "I'm going to tell you something, little girl. You listen good. A *siratha* feeds off of your fear. Your memories. Your nightmares. It takes and distorts and forms and destroys whatever joyful or happy moment you ever possess until you long for the sweet abyss of death. Those with the least memories go first. Others hold out a little longer. Fight it. Battle with themselves. Until every memory is a curse. It turns everything around you dark and forbidding. Hopeless. You can not outrun it because it is everywhere."

"I know what a *siratha* is!" I snap.

"Like hell you do!" he snaps. "If you knew what a *siratha* was you would know you'd never survive it. Never!"

"But I did." He leans back against the tree, balancing the flask languidly on his knee with an unsteady hand.

"All I want to know is how. How a little girl – a Kelban – like you defeated such a creature. Remember? I asked you why you were ostracized. You wouldn't tell me." The bite in his words is savage. "You've given me no reason to trust you, Kelban. No reason to allow you to survive this place. No reason to lead you to the others."

"Others?"

He knows he's made a mistake, and I see the anger that crosses his face – anger at himself. He slams the flask to the ground and it shatters on the bent half of a tree stump. "Yes. *Others.* Did you think I was the only one? That I alone occupy this land you've invaded? But until I'm satisfied that you pose no threat to us – to my *kind* – you will never see them. And if I decide that you are a threat . . ." He pauses long enough to give me one long stare, his head cocked in that inhuman way. "You will never *see* again."

I count the sparks again, trying desperately hard to ignore his stare from across the flames. He says nothing. Only leans and stares and occasionally glances at the moon swords resting at his side, inches from his fingers.

So he's been testing me. Deciding if I'm a threat – a danger – to his *kind.* I try to stir the rage inside of me, but can't find it. If I were in his position – if he were in Kelba – I'd do the exact same thing. I've given him no reason to trust me. No reason to consider leaving me alive.

He could go to hell for all I cared. But my family . . . they were counting on me. They believed in me. I wouldn't let them down. Not when they were risking their lives – for me! For Kelba.

"I tricked it." He doesn't move, but his eyes refocus. "I've been around nobility – around blood-sucking, lying leeches – my entire life. Enough to recognize a desperate attempt when I saw it. When things are at an end . . . when the victim is about to slip from their grasp . . . they get clingy. Get earnest. The siratha made that mistake." He still hasn't moved. "I let it pull me in. Let it grasp my memories and take me into its arms." I shiver at the recollection of her bony grasp around me.

"And then I drove my dagger into its back."

He doesn't say anything and his features are unidentifiable in the darkness. Slowly, he lies flat on his blanket and grows still. His breathing steadies but he's not asleep.

I roll to my side and face the fire. The rhythmic sparks and flames raise a heavy curtain behind my eyes I didn't know existed. I curl into the wool of the blanket and tuck my dagger beneath my right hand. Should the Wild boy determine me a threat before morning light, I will not be without a weapon.

I'm in a dark tunnel and there's a spot of light ahead of me. I am moving towards it. Faster, faster, faster. The darkness shatters with blinding yellow light that rolls a nauseating crack throughout my skull. It collides against the back of my eyelids, forcing them open.

I am not in the clearing. I am not in the wood. I am not even in the Wilds. No. I am back in Kelba. In Kirath. In the inn I know so well I could taste and smell the spice of apple cider, the bitter-sweet of ale, the fat of stew. It is packed. Merchants and miners and pirates and fishermen of all kinds mingle in the crowd. They brawl over tables. Chairs. Ale. Women.

But one table remains at peace. No one dares bother the three men sitting at that table. I move closer.

A girl flutters by, carrying a platter of mugs, and I prepare for the pain in my jaw as the platter heads straight for me. It doesn't come.

Once again, I am not in this reality. I am watching through unseen eyes. The experience is enough to raise the hairs on the arms I cannot see.

The three men are dressed in Celect Knight garb, their swords gleaming viciously alongside the edge of their cloaks purposefully. One of them turns his head to signal the girl again.

Lan.

He looks right at me. I call his name and hold out a hand, but he turns away. The action tightens my chest even though I know he cannot see me.

The girl fills their mugs again and moves away, her steps undeniably eager. I notice the white pallor on her cheeks. She's afraid of them.

The other two Knights lift their heads. Craig and Asher. Asher has lost considerable weight since I last saw him. His face is thin and pale, and decked with several new bruises and cuts. Craig's eyes – eyes that used to sparkle with playfulness – are dull and slanted.

None of them are smiling.

Landor drains his mug in moments and that sisterly concern rises in my gut. The red flush in his cheeks is too bright and the hardness in his eyes chills my blood. His jaw is lined with stubble and his clothes are rumpled. He looks like a vagabond.

"It's unbelievable how much life a girl added to this sorry outfit," Asher says. He glances nervously from Craig to Lan. "Never thought I'd say those words of course. She always was a little inquisitive and made us act like fools. But . . ."

"Would you shut the hell up?" Craig snaps.

"Hey!" Lan barks. Craig's shoulders jerk. "Don't ever . . ." He doesn't finish but the look in his eyes is threat enough.

"I don't want to hear about her anymore." Craig waits for Lan to contradict him. When he doesn't, he continues. "Everywhere we go, it's Kyla this, Kyla that. I want to put it behind us. I want to let it go. I want to forget it ever happened. To move on. There's nothing but pain and

rage and ache if we wallow in this."

"And vengeance," Lan adds.

Craig turns an icy glare on him. "I know she was your sister. I understand. She was my friend. Our companion. But it's over. This happens every day – we have to let it go."

"First thing's first, Craig, she is – not was – my sister. Second, it is not over. Yes, this happens every day. Innocent people banished to a wasteland for crimes they did not commit. It has to stop. And it has to stop now!" He slams a fist to the table and behind those eyes I see a pain to deep and dark to describe.

"A little late for such ferocity, don't you think? She's dead!"

"She's not."

Craig sighs. "Lan, I know you loved – love her, but . . ."

"She's not dead," Lan growls, so viciously that Craig pales. He looks up intently. "Kyla knew things – things important enough to survive in that wasteland. She spent years researching all the myths, legends, and folklore about the Wilds. She is the bravest, fiercest, smartest girl I know. She is not dead!"

"You're entertaining a fantasy, Landor Bone," Craig says sadly. "And I'm sorry it's going to destroy you."

"I believe him," Asher whispers.

"What?"

"I believe him," he repeats, looking up from his half-empty mug. "Kyla had the balls to defy Wood. Nothing in the Wilds could destroy her if he couldn't."

Craig huffs in disbelief and drains his mug.

Lan and Asher share a long look, and Asher is the first to turn from it, and stare nervously at his hands. Lan doesn't pressure him and waits quietly, eyes never leaving the young soldier's face.

"I loved her," Asher whispers.

"I know," Lan replies.

"Do you think she knew?"

I had.

Craig slams a palm onto the table. "She didn't love you, you doe-eyed bastard," he snaps.

"I know that!" Asher says with equal violence. "And I didn't mind." He bites his lip and blinks rapidly for a moment. "But I wish I'd had the guts to tell her openly how I felt before all this happened. I wish I'd had the courage to visit her cell. To give her a weapon. But I was a sniveling little coward afraid of displeasing Wood, so I didn't. I'm glad she didn't like me. I am not worthy of her. She deserves someone with equal courage. Equal fire. Equal passion."

"You should have been a poet," Craig jests.

"What the hell is wrong with you, Craig!" Lan cuts in. "We are your friends. There is no reason to treat us like shit."

"Are you? The friends I knew were two completely different people. I want Sir Landor Bone and Sir Asher Rave to return. Chubby Asher with a knack for jokes. Boisterous Landor with his head held high. I want you both back." He stares at each of them long and hard. They don't say a word. He shakes his head sadly. "But I can see that's not going to happen."

"What are you saying, Craig?" Asher asks.

Lan's gaze pierces Craig like a dagger. He knows. I know. I'd always known Craig was on opposite sides of our little group. I knew if ever there came a crossroads which path he would take. He loved his sword. Loved that Celect vigil on his shoulder. Adored the position he held in the palace.

Craig doesn't even pause. "I am saying this . . . Kyla broke the law. She defied our ruler. That crime is known as treason. Treason is punishable by ostracizement. She had to be punished."

Asher blinks in shock, mouth open uselessly.

Lan is not so hesitant and straightens his shoulders. "You're a fool if you believe that." Craig bristles at the insult. But Lan's not done. "And an ass if you don't."

Craig stands. I can see the bridge between them breaking. "You know the law, Landor Bone. You are a Celect Knight and you serve Celectate Wood of Kelba. Pray remember that before I must forget our friendship completely." He brushes past Asher without so much as a look, but pauses in front of my brother. For a brief moment, his face softens. "Please, Lan," he whispers. "Put it behind you."

He exits the tavern.

Lan's posture breaks and he puts his head in his hands, letting the mask of strength fall. I see the heavy effect of alcohol on his senses and the deep frustration in the wrinkles of his forehead

Asher looks equally aghast. "He won't do it, will he?" An unspoken message passes between them.

Lan signals the girl again for more ale. She opens her mouth to protest, but decides against it and meanders through the crowd towards him.

Darkness eats at the corners of the vision, curling in on the image like a burning piece of paper. I am losing it. I reach out a hand for my brother again but only snatch air.

"Everything's going to change," Lan whispers.

And through the silence someone cries out in fear.

I open my eyes. The fire crackles. The trees shudder with the push of a strong breeze. That pitiful wail that roused me from my dreams echoes again. It is very close. I search for an animal, the dagger firmly in hand, and find the source. I lower my weapon. It is the Wild boy.

And he's asleep.

I watch him turn violently onto his side, then twist onto the opposite. Back and forth. Back and forth. He moans. Growls ferociously. Whimpers once. Then sits bolt upright with a cry of fear so guttural it chills my blood. He opens his eyes.

I slam my head to the ground and lie still, slitting my eyes gently and taming my breaths.

He looks anxiously around the clearing, eyes large and dilated in the dim light as he adjusts to his surroundings and regains focus. His skin is pasty white and shines with sweat. The vest has fallen back across his arms and my breath catches. Cutting across the sleek muscle of his upper chest rests a long, zig-zag shaped scar, so deep, so white, so deadly that I shiver. No battle could have given him such a blemish. A wound like that had to have been done purposefully. Intentionally. Painfully. I shudder at all the possibilities running through my head, but none of them fit right.

The Wild boy looks towards me. I shut my eyes and focus on breathing.

It is a long time before I hear him lie back on his blanket and an even longer time before I think it prudent to open my eyes. When I do, the Wild boy's eyes are closed again.

And his vest is too.

Something cracks.

My eyes fly open and immediately adjust to the darkness around me, forming gray and black images again. Moonlight dances over the clearing, flickering between leaves. The fire has decreased to small, glistening flames. Sparks dance.

The Wild boy is curled in a heap on his blanket. His shoulders rise and fall with the rhythm of sleep. It's not he who made the noise.

Shadows?

Rousing my senses, I press my back against the gnarled bark of the oak tree and shift upward against its trunk slowly, disguising myself with the tree.

I clutch the dagger against my chest and close my eyes to listen. Directly to my right something rustles.

I turn my head in the direction and open my eyes. A dark shadow stands right beside me, and my hair swishes with its sudden presence. It doesn't see me. It looks straight at the Wild boy and starts slowly towards him.

It will kill him. It will kill the only one who can keep me safe!

The shadow draws closer, sweeping past me. I step after it. It halts, sensing the danger, and starts to turn around.

I sweep the dagger in front of me, and its tip connects with flesh.

Chapter XIII

The wounded cry is human.

The Wild boy is on his feet, a moon sword in hand, and looks in my direction. I prepare to dodge out of the way and let him finish the would-be-attacker with a thrill of anticipation. I have not forgotten the unknown style with which he fought nor the skill in which he protected me all those years ago. To see his improvement would be worth the days in the Burnt Forest.

The Wild boy lowers his sword. “Well, you dumb shit, that ought to teach you to sneak up on me,” he growls in frustration.

Shocked, I stare at the shadow illuminated in the glare of dim light from the Wild boy’s sword as a fully human boy – a boy with rings around his pupils. He is pressing a hand against his side. Blood flows between his fingers.

“I was unaware you were entertaining a guest,” the new boy hisses between clenched teeth. He looks in my direction and stumbles before turning wide eyes to his comrade. “A Kelban, eh?” His voice is calm but the tinge of surprise is unmistakable.

The Wild boy shrugs and sits back down on his blanket.

The other turns away from me and joins him, slamming the sack slung over his shoulder to the ground. He has one moon sword strapped to his back and removes it too. He sits and growls in annoyance when he sees the blood coating his hand. Instinctively, I edge up against the tree and tighten my hold on the blade. Against one Wild boy I had hopes for my survival. Against two I already hear the hammer on my coffin.

Calaisar, help me.

"If you haven't noticed, asshole, I'm bleeding!" the new boy snaps.

The Wild boy pulls a packet from the leg of his boot and tosses it to his comrade. I watch the wounded one squeeze a dab of gooey ointment onto his finger and spread it over the gash on his side. He winces but makes no other gestures to the pain.

Anger, precise and hard, slams me in the gut. He had healing ointment the whole time. He could have put it on my finger. He wanted to make me uncomfortable. Wanted to degrade and insult me. Though the Wild boy doesn't glance in my direction I know he senses the violent glare I deposit.

"You're a fool," the new boy continues. He hands the packet back. "I told you to stop going to the Burnt Forest. You'll never kill it."

Despite my irritation, I grasp the new information with surprise. The Wild boy has been trying to kill the *siratha.* That's why he won't believe me.

The Wild boy hisses between his teeth. The new boy realizes his mistake and glances in my direction for the first time. He wrinkles his nose.

"Much as I appreciate the sudden change of your cold heart, friend, you should have left her behind. Things are bad enough without adding an outsider to the lot. You'll really get your ass kicked for this little stunt."

"*Sav gar*, Axle!"

I try to control the sudden surge of shock that rumbles through me and maintain a nonchalant position. Neither boy notices my discomfort. But those words . . . that tongue . . . that accent . . .

"Le vranar e jakar."

She found the bridge.

I am not mistaken. It is ancient Kelban.

Axle blinks. "No shit?" He looks at me, and I try to look perplexed and frightened at the same time. "She survived that place? Alone?"

The Wild boy cocks his head. "I never asked if she was alone."

Both of them look at me, and I turn from the prying eyes.

Axle snorts. "Navra brav. Igra fravlor ver nara sorv van tavranas es."

Noble breed. Always figure they know more than anyone else.

Hell, he had no idea! No clue how damned much I knew.

Axle's eyes narrow, and I realize I let the mask fall. I disguise my sudden facial change for that of pain and rub tentatively at the small of my back. He looks away but his shoulders have stiffened.

"I'll offer more information once I've had sleep." He glowers at me. "And once the wound has healed."

The Wild boy grunts an agreement and lies on his back again.

Axle, however, waits until I sit down. He watches me clean his blood from my dagger and sheath the weapon at my side. Watches me stretch across the blanket. Watches me tuck my legs up beneath my chin. I pretend to suddenly notice his gaze and flinch.

He smirks and lies across his own blanket, our gaze never breaking.

"Yes?" I ask, battling to keep the annoyance from my voice.

He chuckles softly and rolls his back to me. I do the same and stare at the base of the oak tree in front of me. The chill that spreads a canopy over my body is not entirely from the night air.

I don't think I fooled Axle one bit.

The Wild boy is gone when I wake up. In his place, Axle leans casually against a tree, watching me with his ringed eyes. They are much lighter than his companion's. A glassy blue color that could be friendly if he weren't intentionally icing me with malicious ferocity. I scramble to my feet, dusting leaves off the shredded skirt of my tunic. I will be picking them out of my hair for hours.

"Where did he go?" I ask.

Axle kicks some dust onto the last embers of the fire and uncrosses his arms. "My bosom companion is tracking at the moment . . . so you must suffer my presence as an escort." He seems strangely pleased at the idea.

I shrug. "I'm used to boring, arrogant sops following me around. Be my guest."

His eyes narrow. "Careful, Kelban. My restraint is on a short tether today."

"Likewise."

We don't speak again as we break up camp.

I wear the rolled up blanket across my good shoulder with a rawhide strap and follow Axle through the maze of trees. They grow so close together that its hard to define a pathway between them, but he seems to know where he's going so I step where he does. The silence is broken by occasional birds or foreign animal noises and crunching leaves.

We finally pause and he hands me the sack of hunter's brew. It takes only a few mouthfuls to replenish my energy. He doesn't drink any of it and swings it back over his shoulder. I wait for him to continue walking but he doesn't.

"Ostracized, correct?" he asks.

I flinch. It would be hard to miss the swollen red skin around the strap of my right shoulder. Any fool could have guessed why I'd be in this gods-forsaken wilderness.

"You are a noble. Everything, from your posture to your features, betrays it," he surmises. "But you possess muscle and mannerisms not suited to your rank. If I'm not mistaken, you've had considerable practice in the arts of self-defense – especially with a dagger. You've also had experience with hand-to-hand combat. This suggests you're either the member of a family prone to maintaining their rank through violence – or – you're interested in the knowledge denied to you. Considering the hints of foolery and stubbornness I've detected, I would opt for the latter. However, I hardly think society would have approved of such scandalous practices so you've done it in secret – which means you are rather conniving and intelligent. But who could you trust to teach you such skills without the danger of being betrayed or caught. You couldn't possibly train on your own. A family member? Brother, perhaps? Ah, it is a brother. An only sibling too for you to trust him with such a dangerous pastime. He must also be older than you – at least three years – and in the habit of acting as your guardian."

"How the hell do you . . .?" I cut myself off.

He chuckles. "His involvement has also somewhat effected your character as well. Don't take offense to that, darling. I like brash young women."

"I've had enough of you and your . . ." I spin around and stomp through the trees.

"You're seventeen years old," he calls out. I keep walking.

"You weigh approximately one-hundred fifteen pounds, but you'll put on a little more weight after you've recovered from your time in the Burnt Forest and weigh one-hundred twenty-two pounds again in no time."

I stop and turn around.

"You are tall for a girl – especially for nobility. Five foot six inches."

"How do you . . .?"

"Most noble Kelban girls are married by the time their seventeen years of age and you possess that same scar – the 'marriage scar' I believe you call it – on your right wrist. Probably a man much older than you and unpleasant to the eye, but with good heritage and substantial wealth. Your weight and height are easy to guess if you've an eye for observance." He smirks in arrogant pride.

"Since you discovered him, my companion has informed me that you've been surprisingly calm despite the circumstances. This means you either know very little of the tales your kind spreads about us – which, if we're being honest, I highly doubt – or you've decided there are greater threats than 'cannibals' in this land." He steps towards me and his brow furrows as he scrutinizes my features.

"Very observant," I praise in a berating tone. "Or it could be I don't consider you a threat."

He shakes his head. "I don't think you're that stupid. You understand when the circumstances are dire. That's why you crossed that bridge. You know how to manipulate. It's how you defeated the *siratha*. You are very observant of your surroundings. It's why you didn't drink from that river. You know we're a threat. You just haven't decided on how to defeat us yet."

"You're a madman!" I snap.

"I prefer highly intelligent creature from your kind, darling," he says, "but the human reference is equally satisfying." He stops directly before me, leaving a decent foot of space between us.

I study him too. He is very thin. I can see his ribs through tanned muscle. A rash of ugly burns long since healed deform one side of his abdomen. Three lines across his upper chest closely resemble the marks of some predatory beast. Another scar runs across the bicep of his right arm. His hair is blonde and very dirty and unkept. It hangs in wild strands halfway to his shoulders and shields most of his face from view. But his eyes – piercing blue ice – are hard to miss. So is the three inch scar above his left eyebrow. He, too, has seen battle. He is intelligent, but naturally so. His knowledge had not stemmed from hours upon hours of study but from a natural gift.

I try to discern from his features, his posture, his attitude where he comes from, how he has lived, what he enjoys. But I cannot.

"How do you do it?" I ask at last.

He smiles. "I am one of the best trackers in this land and an equally dangerous hunter." He closes the gap between us and backs me against one of the trees. "I am very intuitive and crave a deeper understanding of everything I see." He boxes me in with his arms and his breath warms my jaw as he comes closer. "I am interested in new species: why they live and love and die the same as us, but are completely different. Why the separation between our worlds is a barrier that can't be crossed." Despite his earlier disgust towards me, despite his obvious disdain for my kind, his close proximity, his breath in my face, unfurls a deep blanket of cold in my stomach. I swallow nervously and press my wounded back against the tree until I feel blood.

Behind the icy stare, a tiny spark of something akin to shock, causes Axle's unbreakable gaze to flinch. Slowly, he pulls back. I don't hide the relief that cascades through me.

Axle looks like he's going to say something to me. He opens his mouth. "I am one of the best huntsmen this land has ever seen, girl. Isn't that right, pal?" He looks over his shoulder.

From the shadows of the trees, the Wild boy appears. I cringe as he draws closer. Everything, from his eyes to the curled fists, speaks danger. Axle notices his friend's change of mood as much as I do and gives him a wide berth.

"Unsuccessful, eh?" he asks.

"Piss off, mud-crawler!" the boy growls and elbows past him.

Axle straightens his vest. "Thanks a lot, asshole. I was making an impression." He winks at me.

I brush past him, making sure my elbow gouges his arm properly.

I hear it before I smell it. Water. When I step out of the trees a small river – at least thirty feet across – cascades before me. I stumble towards it and fall at the edge. The hunter's brew is sufficient enough for energy but nothing will quench my thirst like cold water. Life sprouts up around the river but I watch for different signs. I wait for the tell-tale splash of fish in the water. The overhead buzz of a dragonfly. The croak of a frog.

A harmless green snake slithers near my hand and enters the water. I watch it twist on the surface of the water before diving into the depths.

Tiny minnows play beneath the surface of the water. They meander away when the sun casts my shadow over their playground.

The water is safe.

I cup it in my hands and drink. Water soaks the front of my tunic and drenches my skin. I slurp at the water so fast I inhale some of it and choke.

"I think we're having an improper effect on her manners, don't you think?" Axle asks as he steps right past me into the water. After two strides, he's up to his knees.

The Wild boy growls in frustration and spares me a quick glance. He hasn't said a word to me the entire day but his gaze softens when he sees me. I recognize the pitying stare and immediately hate it.

Axle tosses his vest onto the shore and reaches for the belt buckled low around his bony hips.

Heat blasts my face, and I scramble to my feet, looking around helplessly. I spot a canopy of trees upstream among the rocks. Shallow water has to be up there. I won't let them see another of my weaknesses.

"I'm going to . . . to bathe . . ." I don't dare look at the Wild boy as I speak, afraid that he's stripping as well.

Axle's pants slop onto the ground. Behind me, he chuckles. "I will say, she has the modesty of a Kelban."

The Wild boy glares in his direction and then breaks his silence. "It would be practical to remain within eyesight of one another."

I stroke a finger over the hilt of the dagger at my waist. "I'll be careful."

He frowns at the dagger, most likely doubtful of my expertise, but nods vaguely. "Suit yourself. But we won't be able to hear your screams over the roar of the river."

"I don't scream."

I turn my back before he can say anything else and hurry upstream. The rocks soon shield me from view, but I hear Axle's laughter as he splashes in the water and a growl of frustration in answer to his playfulness.

I search for a shallow bed of water and eventually find a small bay of water no larger than two men branching off of the river. I can see the stones glittering from the bottom and yank the worn tunic over my head. I remove the dagger and set it gently on the ground.

The water turns an ugly mud-brown and red color as my legs enter the cool liquid. When I am completely submerged I can no longer see the bottom. My skin prickles to life as the water laps at the wounds adorning my body. I waste no time grabbing my tunic and scrubbing my arms, my chest, what I can reach of my back, and my legs clean. The water is so red I might as well be bathing in blood.

Holding my breath, I submerge myself and grapple at my hair. Dirt cakes between my fingers and the water thickens. My lungs beat with panic, and I come up for air. I submerge again. And again. Again. Until the water around me turns clean again as the river washes away the grime. Until I can see my naked limbs through the water, clean and beautiful once more.

I lift a hand from the water to admire it. It is a hand I recognize. Tough from practice with unladylike excursions but still graceful.

I take a chance to search myself for wounds but can find none excepting the ostracized scar on my shoulder and the lash-marks across my back that burn at a single touch. Even the marks from the *siratha* are gone.

I comb fingers through my hair until not a tangle remains before exiting the water. I pull my tunic over my head and tie the string of rawhide around my waist again. The dagger I strap to my leg and pull the tattered folds of my skirt over it. The tip of the sheath is still visible but the location is practical.

All at once, the scars on my neck sting painfully, like claws have suddenly dug into my neck and choked me. I flinch and place a hand over them. They pulse beneath my fingertips and my body throbs with heat. Voices assail my ears. Guttural voices. Raspy voices. Unearthly voices.

Voices I heard three years ago and haven't forgotten.

I draw the dagger and spin around towards the tree-line, scanning it viciously. I see nothing, but a shadow would be hard to see within the darkened trees. The scars tighten, pinching skin. I hear a raspy chuckle and turn towards the noise. Nothing is there.

"*Kelban*," a voice rasps behind me.

I spin with the dagger, but slash empty air.

"*Kelban*," it rasps again. "*You don't belong here.*"

"Show yourself!" I cry.

"*You don't belong here.*" The voice is closer this time.

I turn and run. A raspy chuckle follows me. Air swishes around me. A tree branch snags my hair, but I tear free. The pulse in my scars beats rapidly as the air draws closer around me.

"*Kelban . . . you're not one of them!*"

I break out of the trees and slam straight into the Wild boy. He cries out as his back connects with the ground and my cheek slams into the hard muscle of his chest. Behind us, Axle swears. The pulsing in my neck instantly stops and the chill around my shoulders dissolves.

The Wild boy groans beneath me. I push myself up on shaky arms so I'm not crushing his chest and he splutters as my hair dangles over his face.

"Get the hell off of me, you . . ." He looks up at me and blinks in astonishment. That ferocious, animal gleam in his eyes disappears and leaves bewilderment, real and human, instead. Once again, that faint aroma of smoke and trees teases my senses. I become completely aware of the angles of his hips against mine, the muscles of his thighs against mine, and the hardness between my legs . . .

Shit!

I scramble to my feet, face hot as fire, and move locks of my hair away from my face.

He jumps to his feet, and a red rash stains his neck. He doesn't look at me and presses a hand to the small of his back. I briefly wonder how hard he landed before shoving the thought away.

"You look more like your kind when you're cleaned up. What the hell scared you this time, Kelban?" Axle asks. "'Cause it sure as hell wasn't me?" He glances at the wound on his side, compliments from my dagger, and I frown. My wounds have healed, but his remains?

"I heard things. Raspy voices. They . . ." I stop. Their shoulders have tensed up and their eyes scan the tree-line, alert and vicious. They know what it was. The animal glitter in the Wild boy's eyes chills my blood.

"They what?" Axle whispers. That keen observance that he possesses is directed at me in full force.

I remember three years ago. I had told the Wild boy the shadows had spoken to me. The look in his face – the shock – had been undeniable. To admit that they had spoken again would reveal my identity. And if I reveal my identity I reveal that I've known all along who he is and that this place is not as it seems. He will have no reason to trust me for such deceit. And also, something else keeps my tongue at bay. I don't know why, but I know in my bones I should not reveal I heard their words. For some reason, I feel it would be the death of me.

"I couldn't see the thing. But everything was cold. It hissed like a snake." Not lies. Only half-truths.

Axle frowns but says no more. He turns to the Wild boy. "*Re gav ot mov.*"

The Wild boy nods in agreement, but glances at the forest with a darkened longing. They shoulder their packs and weapons and step towards the water's edge. They are up to their necks in a matter of moments. I watch while a niggling feeling of panic slithers in my gut. There has to be a bridge or a shallow crossing somewhere. But they start swimming, pumping water with their arms in powerful strokes.

Axle is the first to notice my hesitance and glance over his shoulder. "What's the matter, Kelban? Too cold for your taste?"

I walk in up to my waist. My stomach lurches as I take one more step and the water teases my neck.

The Wild boy has reached the other side and stands soaking wet on the bank. He glares disapprovingly at me across the thirty feet distance. "If you don't hurry up, Kelban," he grumbles," we're going to leave you behind."

Axle surges towards the bank. I watch the way he circles his arms above the water and the way it spreads apart for him.

It can't be hard. I push my toes against the ground and extend my arms into the water. My throat tightens as my legs find nothing but the heavy weight of water around them. I struggle to remain above the surface and for a moment I hold the Wild boy's gaze across the water. He snorts and turns away.

A wall of water slams me full in the side and darkness is all around me. I try to scream but water rushes into my mouth. My nose. My eyes. My lungs gasp for air. I beat at the water around me but nothing happens.

The darkness deepens and the pressure builds in my head. A spot of white light spins in the water before me. It moves towards me. I beat at the water again and rise. My head breaks the surface and a gargled whimper wets my lips.

"Shit!" a voice – Axle's – cries. "Shade, she's . . ."

I hear a splash.

The water takes me.

The white light hits me full in the face as soon as I'm submerged.

Everything around me swirls and a blast of cold air smacks my forehead, forcing my eyes open.

I am in a forest of swirling green and brown. There is laughter nearby. Children's laughter. I see a girl with hair black as midnight and eyes even darker running around the tree trunks. A boy with hair the color of ash and limbs as gangly as a young sapling runs after her. His polished boot snags a tree root. He falls to his knees. The girl stops and turns around. Her face pales and she hurries towards him.

"Your highness!" she gasps and falls down beside him, hands tugging at the collar of his burgundy tunic.

"Are you attempting to strangle Kelba's heir?" he gasps and jerks free.

"My apologies, highness," the girl says.

"I've told you time and again to call me 'Aspen'," he grumbles. "Will you disobey me again, Kyla?"

The girl – me – shakes her head. "No, your high . . . Aspen. I apologize for hurting you. You've torn your trousers." My hand fingers the rip near the top of his boot.

Aspen's face furrows up in boyish amusement. "Aye. You've accosted me greatly. How shall I punish you?" He closes the distance between our faces. Our noses touch. "Shall I . . . kiss you?"

I frown. "That would be very ungentlemanly of you."

"Are you criticizing me? Many a girl would be happy to kiss me." He smiles. "You might like it."

I stand abruptly and glower down at him like a ruffled hen. "Shame on you," I whisper, but my cheeks are blossoms of red.

He stands too and dusts off his legs. "I'm going to kiss you, Kyla Bone, and you're going to like it." He steps towards me.

I hike my skirts up around my knees and skip a few steps out of his reach. "You can't kiss me if you can't catch me!"

We run. I use the trees for cover but he hears the leaves that rustle beneath my feet and follows close behind. I crash through thick underbrush and smack a branch of yellow flowers out of my way. Sun-kissed petals rain down on me.

I reach the pond. The Celectate's Wood was abundant in rivers, streams, lakes, and ponds for his enjoyment. Water lilies dotted the pond's surface, so thick I believe I could walk on them. Aspen's footsteps draw nearer.

"You can't hide, Kyla!" he chuckles.

The hell I couldn't.

I brace my fists and step onto the first water-lily. My foot doesn't even sink into the water, and I stare in child-like wonder and take another step to be sure. Water doesn't even lap at my shoe. Giggling I step onto the next water-lily. And the next. And the next. Until I'm in the middle of the pond. I focus on the sights. The smells. The sounds. A dragonfly buzzes near my ear and beneath me a bright orange fish stares up at me. The heady aroma of lilies and water and flower petals lulls a gentle peace in my soul. And then . . .

"Kyla!" His voice. So near. So loud. So startling.

I look up and all the sounds fade around me. I fall. I'm in the water. I'm choking on water. I'm surrounded by darkness. I'm dying. My skirts drag me under, imprisoning my legs.

"Kyla!" a muffled voice above my head screams.

A great blast of bubbles hits me full in the face and arms grip me firmly about the waist. I feel us ascend. Feel the air hit my cheeks. Aspen's face blurs above me into darkness.

A white light cracks across my eyes and forces them open.

The Wild boy stares down at me, his hand on my neck. Air rushes down my throat and collides with a wall of water. My lungs constrict and then fluid fills my mouth. The Wild boy turns my head to the side and water pours from my lips. I choke and cough violently until my lungs are no longer heavy and roll to my side, hugging the ground beneath my fingers. It is warm and cold and hard.

The Wild boy – Shade, Axle had called him – leans back. He takes long, deep, controlled breaths.

Axle rubs a spot between my shoulder-blades and pain ignites along my spine. Immediately, he pulls back. His hand is wet with blood.

"You fool! You gods-cursed fool!" Shade swears. He leans forward and rolls me over. "Why didn't you say you couldn't swim? Why the hell didn't you say something, you damned fool!"

Tears sting the back of my eyes. Rage burns my throat. I lift myself up on shaky elbows. "And why the hell should I have said something? Would you have given a piss if I'd told you, you hypocritical bastard?"

Shade blinks. "What did you just call me? What did you say?"

"Easy," Axle whispers calmly, but his voice is strained.

I rise into a sitting position and level an icy stare straight into those ringed eyes. "I'm a Kelban. A manipulative, cold-hearted, stubborn, malicious noble Kelban! You didn't give a shit whether I crossed that bridge or not. Why would you give a shit if I didn't know how to swim?"

Shade's hand balls into a fist, but he makes no threatening move towards me. "You'd better consider yourself damned lucky, Kelban, that I'm too exhausted to slit your delicate throat."

I see red. I'm on my feet and don't know how. I stare down at Shade, fists balled, lip curling spastically. "If you call me that again I'll cut your tongue out! My name is not 'Kelban.' It is Kyla! Kyla! Do you hear?"

He stands too and towers above me. But my rage is too strong to cave to fear.

"Shade . . ." Axle whispers from behind me. "Calm . . ."

"If you say one more word, little girl, you can continue on by yourself," he hisses between clenched teeth.

I shove him hard in the shoulders, and he flinches at my touch. "I don't give a shit anymore!" I brush past him.

They are strangely silent behind me.

"Oh, and *Shade*," I say without turning around, "I'm not a 'little girl.'" I hold up my arm for reference and reveal the scar swept across my right wrist. "I'm married, remember?"

I kick a rotting branch out of my way. Behind me, someone explodes in laughter. Axle. He says something in ancient Kelban, and his answer is a vicious snarl. I smile anyway as I inwardly translate Axle's words.

"*The beast just got his ass whipped by a little girl.*"

They catch up with me an hour later and Axle vaguely suggests I'm heading the wrong way. Reluctantly, I retrace my steps and follow him once more. Shade lags behind, claiming guard duty, and stays just out of sight from me. I catch glimpses of his shoulder here and there through a tree or an occasional flash of his black vest but that is all.

Night falls faster than I bargained for and Axle finds a clearing, half the size of the previous one, and builds a fire. Shade does not make an immediate appearance, but I hear leaves rustling in the trees. Axle says he's making sure the area's secure. I have a feeling he's sulking. I haven't missed the twitching corners of Axle's mouth. He's trying so hard not to laugh.

"It's the first time, you know, darling?" he says once the fire's crackling.

"The first time he was wrong?" I ask.

"The first time someone's dared to cuss him out like that." He coughs theatrically. "Except for me, of course."

Shade appears a couple hours later with a furry creature as long as my arm. He skins it quickly and cuts it into pieces. Axle spears each piece and hands me a sizable portion. I roast it over the fire until fat drips off in a heavy rain before eating it.

My back burns like fire again, and I struggle to maintain a nonchalant expression to no avail. I have suffered infected wounds before. They chill and warm and bite and burn like hell. This infection is no different. The swelling on my shoulder is puffy and itches terribly.

A shadow blocks the firelight, and I shift my gaze up two very long legs into the blurred face above me. It is Shade. He kneels down until we are eye-to-eye. "Turn around, Kel – girl."

I'm in too much pain to call him out for not using my name. "Why?"

He pulls a packet from his boot – the healing ointment. "If you don't want to, that's fine with me." He starts to stand, and I turn my back to him. The fabric tears easily in his hands as he opens a hole to get to my scars. The night air caresses my wounds. I hiss uncomfortably.

He swears.

"Bad?" I ask.

"What hell-born bastard did this savagery? You're cut clean to the bone!"

"The devil," I whisper.

The first brush of his fingers is poison. The second is death. The third is hell. Tears run down my face, but I don't whimper. The ointment seeps into my wounds like a beast with claws and eats at my flesh. He does my shoulder next and the pain is at the point of unbearable.

"The infection will be gone by morning," he says and strolls back to the fire.

Axle gazes at me across the fire. His lips are pressed tight together. He saw them too.

I curl into a ball and hide my face behind my knees. They've seen the wounds. The broken parts of me I don't want to remember. I feel exposed and insulted and manipulated all over again. A raw nakedness that depletes my strength.

I have no trouble falling asleep.

I don't know why I've woken up. It is still night. Beside the fire, Axle and Shade are stretched out in odd positions that would normally make me chuckle in amusement. But the tingle in the base of my spine is pressing. I search around the forest for the slightest hint of something wrong. All is silent.

But that's what wrong. Forests are not silent – even at night. There should be crickets. Crunching leaves. Chipping squirrels. Hooting owls. But none of those things erupt from the silence.

I rise and slowly walk across the clearing. It only takes six strides before I'm in the trees. The darkness separates into colors of light, dark, and even darker gray as my vision adjusts for the difference in light. The wind has shifted and blows directly towards me. Leaves rustle above my head.

Up ahead, I hear a soft flapping similar to that of a fluttering cape.

Another Wilds inhabitant? Perhaps a comrade of Axle and Shade's?

I am silent as I meander through the trees and underbrush towards the noise, hand poised above the dagger's hilt in case I'm wrong. Through the gray outline of the darkened forest a caped figure flutters across the floor, silent as silent gets. Something about it is unearthly. Inhuman. I can't understand what it is but I know just the same. The caped figure is shrouded in black, ethereal mist that spreads tongues of swirling dark clouds in all directions.

The scars on my neck stiffen and spread claws through the veins in my neck, tightening my breaths. My spine tingles. Every nightmare, every vision, every horrible, terrifying memory of that night comes roaring back, and I know what the caped figure is. The caped figure is the mist. The fog.

A shadow.

The soft sound of pressure on the earth behind me has the dagger in my hands within moments. I am slammed softly against an aged, but wide, tree and pinned. I open my mouth to cry out for help and warm pressure covers my lips. I struggle.

Two eyes – dark and ringed – stare into mine. I breathe a sigh of relief.

Shade.

Axle crouches low to the ground beside us, blending into the dark texture of the forest floor. Only his blonde hair is out of place and he quickly rubs dirt into its light strands.

Neither of them have their swords.

I shift my head in silent promise not to make a sound, and Shade removes his hand. I crane my head over my shoulder.

The black fog is moving away and the caped figure's back is to us. I watch the fingers of darkness at the corners of the fog move tree branches the size of a grown man aside. Leaves float away from the shadow's presence.

My shoulder is pressed hard against Shade's chest and the rhythmic beat of his heart pounds against my skin. It is very fast. His hand claws into the tree bark beside me like a beast, and a feral glitter stains his dark eyes. I shiver at the hidden meaning of that gaze. He had slaughtered the three shadows that attacked me in Kirath all those years ago. Such ferocity – such savagery – had a deeper, darker story behind it. No one hunted monsters without a reason.

The caped figure turns suddenly and through the black opening of its hood I see nothing but darkness. No face. No eyes. Just deep, empty black.

Shade presses against me hard, every muscle tensed, every movement guarded. I don't dare breathe. He's pressed so tightly against me I couldn't if I tried. I feel the heat of his body on my face even though his vest is closed and the smell of smoke and trees is so strong I am dizzy with it. It is not the smoky smell of cigars that father brought from Kelbain or the smell of the smoking branding iron. It is sweet and natural, like the dying embers of an evening fire in the chill of winter.

The shadow moves off through the woods, but it is a long time before Shade's muscles relax, and I know it is gone.

Axle rises on all fours, scanning the trees, and gives the "all clear" in ancient Kelban to Shade. He nods in recognition, and I feign perplexity at their language.

"I'd think you'd have learned not to walk off in the dead of night alone," Axle says in wonder.

I ignore him. "What was that?" I ask Shade.

He tenses against my body and blinks when he looks down and our noses brush. He shoves me away and it is Axle who stops me from losing my balance completely. He stomps towards camp without a word to either of us.

I look to Axle for an explanation.

He shrugs simply. "Ve si nar vey travanisas."

I blink rapidly. "I beg your pardon?"

"*Ve si nar vey travanisas*," he says, each syllable lingering on his tongue.

I huff irritably and turn my back on him. "Fine. Speak in riddles if you want."

"You understood me, Kyla," he says firmly.

"I don't know what you're talking about."

When he returns to camp a few minutes after me, he casts a knowing glance in my direction. I pretend not to notice him and pull the blanket over my head. Inwardly, though, I agree with him.

Shade is not very talkative.

Shade leaves camp quietly when Axle falls asleep, but I am watching him through slitted eyes. His blanket remains on the ground and his knapsack beside it. He takes only his moon swords with him. I count the seconds, but he does not return. He has not gone to take a piss.

Somewhere between one thousand-two and one thousand-six I fall asleep.

My eyelids flutter gently at the annoying crunch of leaves nearby. I peer through the murky blurs of sleep, and watch Axle draw his glowing sword as a shadowy figure steps into the clearing.

"You scared the hell out of me!" he growls.

Shade practically falls beside the fire and red streaks are painted across the lower part of his chest. The stench in the air turns coppery. Blood. He's wounded.

Axle swears foully under his breath and searches through his knapsack wildly. He tosses a slab of thin stone at his comrade. Shade sets it on the heated embers of the fire. When the corners glow red, he lifts it out. I watch in horror as he presses the slab against the wound and it hisses. He snarls in pain but doesn't remove the stone until Axle's counted to fifteen. When he slams it to the earth, the wound is blackened and blood-less.

"You did it again, didn't you?" Axle asks. He shoves his wounded companion in the shoulder. "Damn it, Shade!"

"It had to be done," Shade says. His voice is soft, and aside from the guttural accent in his words, he sounds as human as any Kelban. "You know it had to be done, Axle, so don't give me that look."

Axle curses at him before flicking the wound. Shade sets a hand on the knife at his waist.

"I know how much it hurts. Hell, no one knows more than I. But these impulses . . . this addiction . . . you must learn to control it better. It will destroy you. Eventually, it will kill you. I speak as a friend . . . if you want to live . . . please control it." Axle blinks rapidly and runs a hand through his hair.

Shade pops the cap off a flask he's retrieved from his knapsack and takes one long gulp. The hunter's brew runs down the sides of his mouth and the shimmering darkness in his eyes disappears. "In case you hadn't noticed, Axle," he whispers, "I was destroyed a long time ago. Torn to pieces. Ripped to shreds." He drinks again, deep and long.

"In other words," he rasps, "I'm a walking dead man."

Axle stares at him before rising and turning his back. "Fine. Piss off for all I care, you slovenly bastard." He stomps into the woods.

Shade stares into the fire, the flask balanced gracefully on one of his knees. "*Flagrana vori,*" he grumbles and clumsily falls onto his back.

I close my eyes and try to wipe the image of his bloody wound from my mind. I'd seen the scar on his chest again. It stuck out in a ridge of torn flesh that hadn't healed properly. I knew from experience that old wounds could still burn painful reminders. Did his wounds burn too?

Tentatively, I brush the scars beneath my hairline. Neither of them has noticed them – or they pretend they haven't. I cling to the belief that they have not.

Axle returns, kicking leaves and sticks and whatever nature he can find, before settling onto his blanket. He glares daggers in Shade's direction. "*Flagrana vori? Flagrana vori?*" he asks angrily.

If Shade is awake he doesn't show it.

Axle crosses his arms and lies back, eyes fixed on the sky above him. "Useless poet, my ass. If my brain were a sword, you drunken sop, I'd have your bloody guts on the ground. *Flagrana vori, mi vai.*"

Choking on my laughter, I concentrate on counting again. I don't even make it to one hundred.

Neither of the boys are in camp when I wake up, but their knapsacks and blankets are. Presuming they've gone to check the traps I heard them speaking about or to hunt for breakfast I fold my simple blanket and linger patiently in the clearing. But as the morning drags on, and throwing stones at tree branches gets boring, I become impatient.

And thirsty.

The woods are alive with noise. Birds. Squirrels. Bees.

I even see a brightly colored lizard that camouflages in the blink of an eye. It is a strange little reptile, with rows of tiny needles around its throat and ears. I long for my sketchbook. Now, when I finally have a chance to do something useful with it, I am separated from it. There are so many notes I should be taking. So many things to draw.

I find a creek. It is small and very shallow, barely reaching to my knees. But it is cold, clear, and fresh. The surface reflects my face back at me, and I gape at how bony my face has become. The cheeks I used to flaunt are sunken and my eyes are too large in my face. The only feature I recognize is my hair, still black as midnight and unruly as scattered hay.

True to Shade's words, the lashes on my back are scabbed over and healing fast. The reflection in the water reveals that one of the shallower gaps is already a faint scar on my skin. I marvel at the healing production my body possesses and tremble a little. It's not natural.

Nor are the dreams that torture me. I cannot possibly be seeing my brother or the memories of my past so vividly. But they are so alive. So colorful. So *real.*

I look up from my reflection. The birds have stopped chirping.

An arrow sweeps past my ear, lodging into a tree directly to my back. Leaves crunch in front of me. I have the dagger's hilt in my hand but something strikes me hard across the face and it's too late. I'm flat on my back and above me an arrow is poised, its tip directed at my throat.

The Wild youth is no older than I am with short blonde hair pulled back in a knot behind his head. His eyes are a piercing light green and sharp as a knife. He blinks when our gazes meet. A voice from across the creek calls to him in ancient Kelban.

"*Vi's na Kelban*!" He hollers back before returning his attention to me. The arrow moves closer, and I press back against the ground as hard as I dare.

"Good morning, lovely," the boy says. His voice is smooth. "What brings you into uncharted territory? A little far from the meadows of Kelba, aren't we?"

That arrow catches the glint of the sun. I don't break my stare but inside me is a war of turmoil. Where is Shade? Axle? Do they know I'm gone? Are they looking for me?

The boy lifts my chin with his arrow. "I asked you a question, lovely."

My jaw stings with the force of his strike, no doubt from the butt of his bow. I grind my teeth against the pain and he mistakes it for refusal.

"*Vugra*," he mutters, and I tremble at the insult. "Where were you going, lovely, on your merry little stroll? East? West? North? Perhaps I can offer you a destination."

I know very well, from the look in his eye, which destination he means. That arrow makes it *very* clear.

"Are you going to kill me?" I ask.

He chuckles and those eyes glitter. "You get right to the point, lovely. I like that. What do you think I should do?"

He doesn't really want my opinion.

"I know what I should do," he says. Behind him, leaves rustle again. He steps closer, the arrow claiming most of my attention so I don't see his foot until it's too late. He presses it between my legs.

In the corner of my vision, another Wild boy appears. "What the hell . . .?"

"I know," my captor says delightedly. "A lovely little outsider." He adds pressure, and I twist uselessly in an attempt to free myself. "Quite a rare piece of beautiful filth." He gouges me in just the right place with the heel of his boot. I bite back a scream.

"She couldn't have come this far without being spotted."

"Which makes her all the more interesting." He luridly rakes me from head to foot. "The little fox."

"She has to be with someone," the boy insists. He comes closer and peers at me beneath thick eyebrows. "She is . . ."

"Ours," a voice growls.

The one boy jumps back at the guttural interruption but my captor merely chuckles with amusement and faces the newcomer. "Shade," he says in a voice that reeks of false friendliness. "Do you usually allow your captives to wander at will?"

Axle steps towards me but Shade grabs his elbow before he gets very far and pulls him back. His face is stone.

My captor frowns but lets the line of his bow go slack. The arrow sags. "I thought you were warned already, Shade, that this behavior would not be tolerated."

"*You'll really get your ass kicked for this little stunt,*" Axle had told Shade that first night.

"Let her up, Keegan!" Shade snaps.

Keegan presses the tip of his bow against the side of my cheek and slowly sweeps it downwards, across the curve of my neck, the ridge of my collarbone. "Not that I'm questioning your sudden change of character, mind you. I can see where she would be . . ." the bow's end circles lazily around my breast, ". . . tempting."

Axle's eyes flash, but Shade's face remains blank.

"You *were* warned," Keegan continues without raising an octave. "I'll put an arrow through her lovelies unless you stop me. And if you stop me, *Shade* . . ." His voice turns feral. "Then it's your throat at risk. Are you willing to take that chance?"

"Let her up, you ball-less bast . . ." Axle storms past his friend like a battering ram.

Keegan pulls the bow-line taut and lets the arrow's tip tease the base of my throat. Axle stops.

Shade remains still, eyes lazily shifting from Keegan to me. They are empty, but I am not blind to the turmoil inside his head. He doesn't trust me. I have not proved myself. I have not passed his tests. I have not earned his trust. And that is my doom.

I will not die here. I survived the Burnt Forest. I survived the *siratha*. I survived the Poison River. I can survive this. I will not die like this.

A single spark glitters in Shade's eye and is quickly gone. But I saw it.

"Let her up," he says quietly.

Keegan stares at him and frowns. "You did hear me, didn't you, Shade? I'm warning you if you try to turn this back on me and drag me under I'll . . ."

Shade raises his head and that animal anger is clearly painted on his face. "I said 'let her up,' damn it!"

Keegan shrugs and draws back, foot and all. He positions the bow across his shoulder. "Your throat, not mine," he says smoothly.

Axle moves forward and offers me a hand, which I take. My lower region stings painfully, and I think of a hundred different ways to cut Keegan into pieces.

"*Gav's mov*!" Keegan says and strolls upstream.

I rub the sore spot on my throat and look at Shade. He returns the stare.

He still doesn't trust me.

And now there's more than my neck at stake.

The other boy's name is Hayden and, by appearances, he and Keegan are bosom companions. Both possess moon swords slung across their backs in similar fashion to Shade's . . . but neither of them carries a second one. I stare at the two hilts protruding above Shade's shoulders, wondering at their significance.

Hayden is shorter than any of the boys – close to my height – with auburn hair that glints every so often like fire beneath the sun's rays. His hair is tied tightly behind his neck with a string and forms a clump of frayed edges. Unlike Keegan, he seems on edge around Axle and Shade.

"Mave, fi le savranas, le nac frin mi dei," Keegan laughs luridly.

Hayden chuckles nervously but glances cautiously at the warriors behind him. Shade remains silent. Axle's eyes flash, but he looks at me. I flinch beneath his gaze, feigning innocence to the words, but behind my mask I imagine a dozen ways to make sure Keegan stays silent forever. Or screams in pain. He'll be in hell before I'd ever warm his bed for him.

Axle winks at me. "Sograna nels mi le covra pavran ot gat ivran."

"Hor sav le gad ot eb?"

"*Something tells me she isn't partial to that idea.*"

"*Who said she had to be?*"

I want to shout for his vulgar ears to hear that I am no downtrodden slut for him to insult. I am a lord's – High Lord's – daughter. I am from the finest lineage in Kelba. I am Kyla Bone. But to do so would betray my deceit. Shade and Axle might protect me now, but if they knew how well I could lie beneath their prying eyes they'd consider themselves lucky to be rid of me.

Everything between my legs is sore. I struggle not to stumble or show my weakness – to ignore the smug crease in the corner of Keegan's mouth when he turns to look at me. Every so slightly, he wiggles his middle finger at me beside his leg as he walks and winks predatorily. A threat. A promise.

Go ahead, you bastard. Lay a hand . . . or a foot on me again . . . and I'll cut your balls off.

The dagger shifts beneath my torn (no, shredded) skirt, and I pause to cinch it tighter.

Axle slows beside me. "You alright?" I know he isn't talking about the loose halter.

I nod. "I dealt with bastards like him all the time back in Kirath." Only they'd had the good sense to piss off.

Shade stops abruptly, leaves crunching violently beneath his feet. "Talk like that, Kelban, and you might end up regretting that Keegan didn't do you a kindness and put an arrow through that useless brain of yours."

"Shade," Axle warns, voice low.

Keegan and Hayden haven't noticed our halt and continue walking and whispering.

Shade's eyes flit in the direction of my leg and notice the tip of the sheath. I let my skirt hide it from view and glare at him. He ascends a hand. "Give it here, Kelban."

"Like hell I will," I snap.

His eyes glitter and he balls the accentuated hand into a fist, so tightly that his knuckles turn white. His voice remains calm. And it scares me more than anything. "I *can* take it from you, girl. You don't want me to have to do that, do you?"

"I *won't* let you do that," I whisper, my voice as dangerous as his. Axle turns white and glances shiftily between the two of us. "My brother risked his life to give me this weapon. He threw away his honor, his title, and his vows. If I give it to you – if I allow myself to throw away his sacrifice – I might as well spit in his face!"

Shade's resolve cracks – I see it on his face.

"Do you intend to hide such a weapon when we set you before the council?" Axle's voice is amused. "Oh, the elders would laugh at that. An armed outsider – a treasonous Kelban – right beneath their noses. Are you mad, girl? Do you know Shade and I can be whipped raw for such an atrocity?"

"Ah . . . so you'd spare your back a lashing rather than save a human life. Selfish bastard," I quip.

"We only ask for your weapon . . . not your life," Axle reasons.

"You put me before that council of drooling hounds that no doubt shares that one's sentiments," I point ahead at Keegan, "without proper means of defense and you'll be sending me to my death. You said as much that first night, Axle. That Shade would suffer such a decision. Do you remember? I'm no fool."

"You are. A great fool if you think they'll allow you to abide within the village after pulling a weapon – even in defense," Axle argues, his eyes flashing violently. Gone is the devil-may-care attitude he possesses. He's pure Wilds savagery now, lips curling over his teeth. "Those stories you've heard about us . . . exaggerated they may be . . . but there is some truth to our barbarity. We are guardians of the village. We observe. We protect. We defend. That is our vow. Much as I've come to acknowledge your existence as a positive interest of mine, that vow comes first, above all."

"I have taken no such vow," Shade says, voice so low it could be a whisper if not for the deadly calm in his words.

Axle turns on him and gapes at his friend. "Shade!"

"I have sworn no vows as guardian. I have sworn no blood to be lost on those villagers. There is one vow I hold and it shall be the only one," Shade says. "Let the little girl keep her weapon."

"Dirk shall have you flogged for it," Axle says, earnestly.

"I've never let any man flog me."

"They will have you banished for this."

"I like being on my own."

"Dirk will take your swords."

Shade sneers. "Let him try."

Axle looks helplessly from me to him before raising his arms in an angry gesture and stalking in Keegan and Hayden's direction.

"Well," Shade sighs. "He's pissed."

"About time," I mutter. "His charm was beginning to annoy me."

He grabs my elbow before I can step past him and holds tight. "Talk like that, Kelban . . . open your mouth for something other than 'yes' or 'no' before the council . . . and that dagger will not save you."

"Are you helping me?" I add poison to the words and jerk my elbow free. "So you'll act like a complete ass in front of everyone and try to suckle up to me in private? Do you want to put your foot on my 'lovelies' too?"

He flinches at the words, but his eyes are a mask. "If I'd had the slightest interest in you, little girl, you'd have known that first night. I promise you." I can't tell if his words are meant to insult or appease.

"I am merely pointing out that unless you want that tongue ripped out from its roots you think before you speak," he whispers. "If my back were not at stake I'd let you dig your own damned grave."

I lift a brow at him. "I thought you don't let anyone flog you?"

The corner of his mouth jerks up – then back down as quickly as it arose. My heart does a little twist. He almost smiled. I almost made him smile!

He notices my interest and steps back, gaze darkening once more into the familiar, predatory leer. "Fine. Let them have your tongue! A flogging would be worth the peace and quiet."

He turns on his heel and continues walking.

I follow, smiling softly. He's not completely made of stone.

Or I cracked it.

The forest begins to clear up before me. Gone are brambles. Ivy. Bushes. Clear, man-made pathways jostle against one another beneath thick trees. I see nut trees to my left. Berry bushes peeking between trees on my right. Compressed earth beneath my feet; the signs of heavy traffic. Of people.

The forest vanishes and the breath leaves my lungs. They had spoken of a village. Of their people. I had imagined huts fit for animals and people dressed in rags, eating raw plants and nuts like savages. I was wrong.

The stories are wrong.

Kelba is wrong.

For, before my very eyes, men, women, and children meander around one another in a display of harmony. Dust flies up from the ground as a group of young boys and girls toss a leather ball back and forth. Two women laugh at them from their perch against the oaken wall.

There is a Wall. Not like the wall dividing Kelba from wasteland. No. A wall made of oaken trees pummeled deep into the ground, stretching thirty feet high with iron gates and two watchtowers in each corner. The gates are open. Through them I can see modest homes of thatch and wood and stone.

The years of tension, strife, curiosity, and endless research arise from their dark pit and burn a sweet fire in my chest.

I have found the hidden half of history.

Chapter XIV

It takes three seconds – maybe a bit less – for my presence to be noticed. Slowly, like a wind gently killing a candle's flame, the noise dies around me. I thought I knew silence when I was in the dungeons. I thought I knew tension when I entered a party. I thought I knew hate among the nobility of Kirath. But I know nothing to rival the cool rage of death hanging over my head.

It is impossible for the people not to notice me – ragged, scarred, bloodied. They watch me as I follow my guards to the iron gates.

They follow.

Inside the gates is a large square encompassed between the wall and watchtowers. Men in iron helmets and leather armor patrol the walkways hammered into the top of the wall. All of them turn and look downwards upon my entrance. The square smells of iron, sweat, and hay – familiar smells that burn an ache inside me. Shirtless men, ranging from fourteen to nigh on fifty, turn from their duties.

The whispers begin. They trickle like a tiny river of water down my spine and raise hairs on my arms. The scars near my neck begin to pulse. Throb. Burn. The ground spins beneath my feet and everything seems too fast, too long, too heavy.

The calm shatters.

"It's a Kelban!" screams a woman's voice. "Wretches. Get it out of here before you bring a curse upon us! Get it out!"

"How could you bring her here?" A man's voice. Frightened.

"Mama, she looked right at me. Will she curse me?" The child is hidden to my eyes but apparently he can see me.

Soft, wet slime splatters my torso and neck. I choke on the salty taste of mud and attempt to clear the filth from my face.

"We have brought her to stand before the council," Axle says, his voice calm and controlled over the riotous crowd.

"Fools! You should have left her. Or better yet . . . killed her with your own hands! How could you do this to us? Have we not suffered enough!" The woman's voice is shrill like a morning bird.

I am relieved my dagger is hidden. Were I wearing it openly, this outraged mob could become murderous.

"Yes," a smooth voice croons from the crowd.

As if moved by an unseen hand, the crowd parts and makes way for a man. He is not much taller than I and obviously not a warrior like most of the men who surround me. His belly has been left to waste for far too long. But his voice commands the crowd and demands attention with its soft, yet powerful, tone. He reminds me of the Celectate. And his eyes . . . light green . . . I frown at their familiarity.

Keegan steps forward, brandishing his bow in a twirling motion of expertise that raises a few sounds of awe from the crowd – foolish girls. He steps up beside the man, towering with his height.

The man looks up at him with piercing eyes. "Do not tell me that my son is involved in this blasphemy?"

Keegan smirks and makes a theatrical gesture of shock so absurd that a few in the crowd laugh at his features. "Nay, Father, not I. Shade has taken the full weight of responsibility on his shoulders." He makes a sweeping bow in Shade's direction. Shade's features remain impassive.

"Did he now?" The man folds hands behind his back – a trait so familiar of Celectate Wood that I cringe. "I would have thought we gave him sufficient warning last time."

"You know how he is," Keegan remarks smugly, purposely avoiding eye contact with Shade.

The man makes a clucking noise with his teeth. "Such a pity. I hate having to repeat a student's lessons time and again. Endlessly quoting our laws gets rather tedious."

"Don't our laws state that we are to bear no grudges against Kelba, Dirk? That we are to regard them with cool indifference?" Axle asks, voice tight. He is smiling amiably but anyone could see the weapons in his eyes.

Dirk sweeps a hand at me. "This . . . is cool indifference?"

"Don't worry. We ignored her half the time," Axle says. "So we didn't break any laws." A choice few in the crowd chuckle at his wit.

Not all of the crowd is on Dirk's side.

"Charm will get you nowhere," Keegan sneers.

Axle grins. "That's what your mother told me last night."

Keegan bolts forward, bow projected like a staff. Axle's hand casually reaches for the moon blade's hilt behind his shoulder. He doesn't even hide the anticipation in his eyes. The crowd's rage changes to one of sport and men begin to laugh. Shade merely steps off to the sidelines beside Hayden and intentionally ignores Dirk's piercing gaze.

"Enough!" The mere blast of the one word stops everyone – Keegan mid-strike, Axle mid-draw, and me mid-breath.

Another man walks through the crowd. He is gigantic, molded from muscle, tanned from the sun, and possesses thick black hair tied in a tail behind his back. He steps up alongside Dirk and the man shrinks beneath the fiery gaze leveled on him. The newcomer shifts that gaze to Shade.

"Guardian?" he asks, brows raised and ready for an explanation.

"I have brought this Kelban for the council," Shade says.

"Why?"

Shade shrugs. "She wanted to live."

"I see." The man looks between the squabbling warriors and finally stares directly at me. The moment his crackling eyes meet mine, I straighten. That gaze – it's not cruel or heartless or hateful. Just curious. He frowns. "Bring her."

Axle is by my side before Keegan can assert the position. Slowly we leave the crowd behind and walk down a barren street against the seemingly endless wall.

"We're going to the council now," he whispers.

I roll my eyes. *As if I didn't know that.*

Immediately, I regret the mistake. I had become so used to the small difference in pronunciation, the constant deciphering, the incessant foreign mockery, and the assault of childhood language lessons that I no longer noticed the unique poetry of the ancient vocabulary. They had been speaking in ancient Kelban the whole time.

"Good," I whisper back.

The corners of his mouth twitch with amusement, but he says nothing.

The council house is a modest, dome-shaped building situated near the secluded part of the wall. Several men have already gathered outside it, no doubt summoned by quick-footed messengers. Gossip spreads like wildfire even in this dreadful place. They are dressed commonly in tunics, boots, and a few possess an outer robe.

I am shoved inside without a word. It is dark and smells of damp hay and mortar. A rusty hinge creaks and a trapdoor in the dome-shaped roof falls, allowing a beam of sunlight to strike the center of the floor. I am thrust beneath the light.

"I am Otis, girl, the Keeper of this city. I am responsible for the safety and security which these people entrust me to maintain." The leader's voice is no less rough than it was in the square. "I will answer my questions, girl. Oh, don't shiver so. Our interrogation is more refined than that of your Kelban society. We do not use whips or tools to loosen your tongue. We depend upon your honesty and, quite frankly, your common sense. Pray that you have a lot of it."

My eyes adjust to the blended frays of light and darkness. The council members have pressed themselves against the walls in all manner of statures. They're guarded attempts to maintain a casual attitude are not lost on me.

"What is your name?" Otis asks.

"Kyla."

"Your full name," a council member corrects.

"Lady Kyla Kelonia Bone," I whisper, curling my fingers into fists.

The barrage of insults I have waited for erupts.

"Lady?" scoffs another member. "Lady indeed. Must you rub 'nobility' in our faces now, too, outsider? Lady? Put me in a room alone with your for two minutes and we'll see how much of a lady you are."

I struggle to keep my voice from trembling when I speak. "Repeat that."

A long, low chuckle pervades the room. Dirk cranes his head so I can see his taunting eyes in the dim light. "I said, Kelban, that your skills in the art of seduction and leg-spreading are well known. Everyone knows all you highborn bastards are nothing but common whores."

In Kelba I could have had his tongue for that. I could have him flogged publicly in the streets for defamation of my honor. But here, I do not have the voice – the power – I possessed back home and must endure their taunts. Their insults.

One of the council members turns his attention to Otis, who has remained silent, and speaks in low Kelban dialect. "We have no good use to put her to and you know it. She would be a nuisance, and quite frankly, a curse upon us."

"Yes, exactly!" Dirk jumps at the chance to despoil me further. "A curse! Her kind have caused trouble for us in the past. You have not forgotten the last bastard we allowed to remain within these walls, have you, Otis?"

"I have forgotten nothing!" Otis glares pointedly at Dirk. "And I have definitely not forgotten the role you played in that little foray, Dirk of Brunt. I am a patient man. A modest man. An understanding man. But you push every single one of those virtues to the limit."

"Piss on virtue!" Dirk snaps. He points accusingly at me. "You allow that bitch to mingle within these walls and there will be hell to pay. Their kind have always been a curse to us. They trample us. They lie about us. They put us behind a wall. She deserves to hang. To rot. To die."

"The girl is a child," another council member argues softly. "My daughter is no older than her. I will not condemn her." He sits down sullenly.

"Your daughter is of this land," Dirk says to him. "This invader is a curse to us. Her kind would bleed us before we even reached their Wall. Why should we not do the same to her? You should have killed her, Shade of Smoke. You should have done your duty as a guardian and killed her, for all our sakes."

Shade steps out of the darkness, but it clings to him like a second skin, emanating in the color of his eyes, and the muscles of his chest. "First, I am no guardian, Dirk of Brunt. I have made no such vow to protect useless, cowardly bastards like yourself. I have made no such vow to defend this city which is not my home. Second, whoever I kill is my business, not yours. And you'd better thank the gods I stand by that opinion because there have been many propositions for *your* life."

"You still should have killed her. Common sense. Knowledge. Duty. Honor. Do none of these things command such a simple solution within you?"

"I possess plenty of those virtues, Dirk. But, in your words, I 'piss on virtue' too. Honor and duty have gained me nothing but pain and suffering. Common sense is rather uncommon. And knowledge . . . well . . . if my knowledge commanded me you'd make a lovely pelt for my bed." Shade steps towards the much smaller man. "Do not criticize me for finding a small portion of humanity inside of me. You'd better pray I possess that same humanity the next time we are in the same room together."

"You're a monster!" Dirk hisses through clenched teeth. He increases the distance between them.

Shade smiles and tilts his head to the side. "You'd do well to remember it."

"When you women have finished bickering we can continue this interrogation," Otis says with an impatient gesture. Shade and Dirk remain silent.

"I see you are married, Kyla," Otis says, eyes cascading over the scar on my wrist. "To whom?"

To Aspen Wood, heir to Kelba. Oh, to see the sweet shock on their faces would more than make up for the brutal insults they have thrown my way. But it would also spell my doom even if I argue that I had been ostracized for refusing to marry. For taking a stand against Celectate Wood. I am not ready for them to know that part of me. That part of me – that rebellious, conniving girl with fire for her clothing – must remain hidden. Or it will destroy me.

So I lie.

"A common, low-born bastard heir. Lord Rugen of Glothan." I add a violent bite to my words.

"An unhappy marriage, I take it," Otis queries

I stifle a chuckle and look straight in his eyes. There is no anger. No malice. No judgment. Just a man searching for answers. A man determined to protect his city and his people. For that I respect him. For that I will convince him I am no threat. I want what he wants. Safety and survival.

"Unfortunately, though nobility are wealthy in life, they suffer in love. Unhappy?" I shake my head. "Happiness is never taken into consideration among well-bred bonds."

I think of poor Asher. A lowly Celect Knight in love with his best friend's sister. I had known, and for keeping him at arm's length, I was sorry. But nothing could have grown from such a match even if I shared his feelings. He knew it too, and that was the real reason he hadn't said anything.

"You have been . . . 'bonded' is the word your kind uses, I believe . . . to this man for how long?"

"Eleven months."

"Have you born any children for this bastard lord?"

I frown. "No."

"Have you born any bastards for other lords?" Dirk asks from the shadows.

"No!"

"The displeasure in your marriage . . . what fueled it?" Otis's question is simple but deep.

I will give him a simple answer. "He was 36 years of age. Delicate.

Soft. Hardly a man to pick up a sword and fight – much less inclined to gather the courage to speak up for himself. Or his wife. Such a man . . ." I cut myself off and shake my head. They are transfixed. As I knew they would be. The man I've spoken of is the perfect example of what they consider Kelban nobility to be. By expressing my distaste for the man they assume is my husband, I have struck at their idea of what a Kelban girl is.

"What were you ostracized for, girl?" Otis asks. "Don't look shocked. Your sleeve does nothing to hide that ugly red welt growing on your shoulder. Treason? Murder?"

"Adultery," Dirk grumbles.

"The Celectate visited. His son and I had once been very close friends until I discovered what kind of man Kelba's ruler was. I distanced myself from him. He propositioned me when my husband and Celectate Wood were admiring the estate. I refused. Told him to go to hell. Told him that Rugen would hear of it." I wipe a tear from my eye, remembering Aspen's blazing eyes as he sentenced me to die. Remembering his kiss that burned and violated me. "He didn't listen. Rugen found me in his arms." Dirk sneers.

"Kissing," I add forcefully. "My word against the son – the heir – of the Celectate. Who would a man like Lord Rugen believe?"

"So you were ostracized for adultery? Prostitution." Dirk sounds ecstatic.

"I was ostracized for refusing to let a man use his title to bed me. That is all!" I snap.

"You say you're a High Lord's daughter? Forgive me, but I know a little of Kelban nobility," a council member says. "Pray, tell me, why a High Lord's daughter must marry a low-born bastard nobody? Were you sullied by this bastard lord? Was that why you had to marry him?"

I glare at him. "He had an army. Not that he used it for much good, but he had one. My father thought wedding me to a man with title, wealth, *and* an army would be a safe match for me. He also lived out of the city and away from the nobility's corruption."

"It seems you've had your fair share of trials," Otis mutters thoughtfully. He taps a finger against his cheek in silent debate.

Dirk struggles to regain control of the situation. "Her own people threw her out. Her own people lashed and branded her. If they have abandoned her she must be cursed. Defiled. Dangerous. We cannot allow her to be within these walls."

Someone laughs near my ear. I flinch at the warm breath that tickles my neck.

"On first sight, I did find her a very interesting specimen," Keegan says. He feathers my ear gently with his finger. I jerk away from the touch. "But there was one part of her I found the most interesting – the most eye-catching. It was something that not all of those smooth bastards possess." He dips his hands downwards. I remember his arrow tracing my breast. His foot between my legs. His hand pauses on the sleeve of my worn tunic.

I try to grab his hand, suddenly understanding the little game he's unfolding. The part of me he means to put on display. Too late. He rips my sleeve off, tearing shreds of clothing from my back and front. Cold air rushes over my skin. Over my shoulder. Over the scar – now exposed in its complete hideousness to the entire room.

Men gasp and lean close for a better look. Others wrinkle their noses in disgust and turn their eyes away. Otis remains blank-faced. Watching. Quiet.

Keegan grips my arm and pulls me close to his side. "Does it hurt, Kelban?" He extends his hand towards the black-and-red symbol, anticipation for cruelty shining in his eyes.

I think I'm as shocked as everyone else in the room when my gleaming dagger is an inch from Keegan's eyes. I don't remember reaching for it. Don't remember the band of my restraint wavering.

"Don't you ever . . . ever touch me again!"

Keegan stares at the toned blade with cross-eyes. His lip turns up at a corner in an undecided sneer. He doubts my honesty. My skill. My intent. That tether on my rage snaps.

He shouldn't.

"I won't miss!" I say, voice so low it raises the hairs on my own skin. "I swear by the gods, I won't miss!"

He backs away, the sneer disappearing from his face and replaced with a dead white color that normally would give me intense pleasure were the awfulness of the lashings on my back and scar not evident to the entire room. Vainly I try to cover myself, to shield against the air and the attentive stares.

Dirk doesn't pass up my moment of weakness. "She is cursed. If she was not good enough for them then she is not good enough for us. Banished was bad enough . . . but ostracized? She will eat at the soul of this city. At the soul of our hearts. We will be cursed by her presence. Her words. She will bring death just like the last one."

A presence close behind me sends shivers down my spine. A hand, rough as sandpaper, rests on my wrist and slowly creeps towards my fingers. Fingers that still hold the dagger in a crushing grip. Gently, the foreign fingers press against my knuckles. That touch . . . it's gentle, soft, and . . . understanding. I release the knife.

"Good job," he whispers in my ear.

Shade steps in front of me, his body blocking my exposed half.

"If you really fear her . . . tormenting is not the brightest idea you pricks have come up with!" he snaps.

"And you," Dirk growls, rising up to the challenge. He comes close, so close I have the urge to warn him that Shade doesn't like his personal space invaded. "I warned you last time. You, with your demons and your gods-cursed secret vow and your pride. I've warned you to keep away from that forsaken land – to keep your stories the hell away from us. But do you listen – no." He raises a finger near Shade's eyes. "You are a reckless, unlawful, arrogant bastard brat and you are the reason we're this deep in shit."

"If I were you, I'd get that finger out of his face," Axle says, stepping up next to his companion with a twinkle in his eyes. He winks at me. There's no amusement in his gaze, though.

Dirk sneers, but he removes his finger. "And you, guardian of the city. You're supposed to be his leash. You're supposed to quell his animal behavior since he is unable to do so himself. Answer me, guardian. Wasn't that your duty as his companion?"

Axle shrugs. "I did try a leash."

Dirk rolls his eyes. "And then what?"

"I took a piss on the leash. Naturally, Shade wouldn't want to wear it after that so I threw it away." Axle says the words with such sincerity that everyone laughs. Even Otis's mouth turns up at the corners.

"We are getting nowhere," Shade says pointedly. He looks at Otis. "Question her. Make your decision. I'd prefer to wash my ass and get it in some clean clothes, if you don't mind."

Otis rubs his chin. "From what I've seen I see no outright danger to her presence."

Dirk and Keegan look stunned.

"She drew a knife on me!" Keegan protests.

"Rip my tunic down the front and I'd have it in your guts, boy!" Otis snaps, his calm demeanor shattering. "Grab my arm and I'd remove them for you, too."

Keegan becomes silent.

"She is ostracized," Dirk offers.

"Doesn't mean a damn to me," Otis says with a half-hearted shrug. "Ostracized . . . banished . . . they only made it more meaningful with an ugly brand and some odd symbol. And don't spew any of that nonsense about demons and curses, Dirk. To be honest, that talk is making me rather irritable. To hell with the gods. To hell with the demons. To hell with the curses. That's where they belong. She's an innocent girl, Dirk of Brunt. A mere child, married or no. I've never had a daughter, and the gods be praised you haven't either, Dirk. But the rest of you . . . if your girls were put on the other side of the Wall with the Kelbans, would you want them stripped, body and soul, before a tribunal of men?"

The silence is answer enough.

"That's it?" asks Dirk. "You're going to allow this outsider . . . this defiled trash . . . to stay within our walls. Gods knows the turmoil she can reap. The woe she can bring upon us. You are making a dangerous, foolish decision, Otis. Think about this city. The people."

Otis slams palms to the chair arms and rises so fast that Dirk takes several steps backwards. "Do not use my vow against me, Dirk of

Brunt! I've had it with your filthy games, little man. I am no fool and I will put no lives at risk for an outsider."

"We should let the King decide," Axle says from behind me.

Multiple council members mumble their agreement.

"Tis the law," assents a reluctant elderly man. "And as good citizens we must not ignore the law."

"Send the law to hell!" Dirk snaps. He points a trembling finger at me. "She's a danger to us. A curse! Get rid of her or face the wrath of the gods!"

"And what power do you possess over the gods, Dirk, I'd like to know, please?" Sarcasm from Shade sounds foreign. He turns around to glare at the man who seeks my death. "And if you prefer, I can tell the King what your opinion of his law is?"

The threat carries clear. Dirk grows silent.

"The girl stays . . . until the King says different," Otis says. "This council is adjourned. You may return to your homes and your families."

The council members file out. A few glare openly at me as they exit. They are the ones to watch out for. I memorize their eyes. Their faces. Their steps.

When the last member has filed out, Axle turns to me and elbows Shade aside. "Damn him, did he have to rip the whole damn thing in half!" He struggles to pull off his vest but it catches around his elbows, locking them behind his back. He curses violently.

"Don't bother, lad," Otis says. He removes the cape around his shoulders and tosses it at me. I hold it tenderly across my front, relishing the warmth it brings, and cover the scar on my shoulder. It has gotten uglier.

"Do not hate your scars, girl," Otis says, noticing my discomfort. "They make you stronger."

"Says the wise old sage," Axle jests.

Shade says nothing but his back has gone stiff. That long, white scar on his chest had been horrifying, and he had tried to hide it from me. He must abhor his scars too.

"Where will she reside for the time being?" Axle asks as he tugs his vest back into place. I note the scars along his abdomen. They don't seem to bother him.

Otis shakes his head and faces Axle. "I sent for her." He sighs irritably. "Where is that woman?"

"That *woman*," says a shrill voice, "is standing right behind you!" The sound of skin slapping skin startles me. Otis gasps. "And that's 'Mama Opal' to you, you big ogre!"

I turn around and lock eyes with a woman exactly my height. She is plump, with rosy cheeks, and hair tied around the top of her head in a simple, but graceful, knot. Her nose is a bit crooked, like it's been broken, and her smile shows nearly all of her teeth. Her eyes narrow when she sees me. She turns around and slaps Axle and Shade on the back of their heads. Axle screeches.

"Mama . . .!" Axle whimpers.

"What did you boys do to the poor girl? Drag her through a bramble field? Look at her face. Her clothes. And her feet! Did you pay any mind to the poor girl's feet? They're practically shredded. Are these the two gentlemen I raised? Huh? Did I raise you to be abhorrent little bastards, is that it?" She raises her hand to strike again.

I like this woman.

Axle scampers away and uses Otis as a human shield. Shade remains stiff and silent. Mama Opal lowers her hand and glowers at him. He remains unphased. Her face softens and she turns to me.

"Come, honey. Let's get you cleaned up. A hot bath . . . some new clothes . . . you'll be good as new," she whispers and propels me towards the door, her arm firmly latched in mine.

"I'm going to write to the King about her, Opal," Otis calls after her.

"Do that," she retorts. "And that's *Mama* Opal, you rude vagabond!"

Axle and Otis chuckle at her response. I do not hear anything from Shade.

Chapter XV

Mama Opal takes me down a winding street not far from the gate's entrance. The houses surrounding me are made of stone and mud, covered with snaking vines, and crumbling at the corners. She notices my critical gaze and laughs lightly.

"I dare say it's not what you're used to, honey." She pats me gently on my good shoulder. "Don't worry, though. Bad shit they may be, but the roofs are strong."

I nod.

Mama Opal turns abruptly and stops before a solid oak door belonging to a two-story, windowless house. She opens the door and steps aside to let me pass.

It takes my eyes a moment to adjust to the different lighting. There are truly no windows. The entire room is a bit damp, but smells of herbs, smoke, and dirt. Four lamps hang from the ceiling, all lit brightly. The fireplace is so large it takes up nearly the entire left side of the wall. The entire area is just one giant room. There is a modest table before the fire with sturdy-looking stools. A large wardrobe stands directly across from the door. Two cots rest against the right side of the room. Aside from that, there is no other furniture.

Mama Opal steps past me and leans over the fireplace. She pulls a large kettle from the flames and sets it on the wooden table before looking at me with a sheepish smile. "I'm sure it's not what you're used to, honey," she says again. Her cheeks are flushed with embarrassment I hadn't expected to see. "It is very miniscule compared to the wealthy decorum of your Kelban home."

I shake my head at her and speak for the first time, "Compared to the Burnt Forest, ma'am, and a blanket stretched across leaves in Shade's camp, I assure you this is more than enough. My people have a nasty habit of collecting useless things anyway. Your home is much better without such petty decorum."

She beams brightly. "Oh, my dear, its so good to hear your voicel. I was afraid those boys had frightened you too much to talk. They have a nasty habit of taunting that is impossible to leash. And your eyes, my dear. Beautiful. It's like staring at the night sky. Once we get you cleaned up . . ." she gestures at the kettle which I now see is full of water, ". . . you'll look less . . ."

"Like a demon," I finish.

She frowns. "Dirk's a bastard if ever there was one. Don't you let him get to you. Behind all that bluster and brawn is a sniveling little coward. Come. Let's get you a bath and show him how wrong he can be."

She leads me to the corner farthest from the door and draws a curtain across it. An iron tub big enough for me to sit in is full of steaming hot water. The final kettle pushes the water to the brim.

"Now lets get you out of these." She unwraps Otis's robe from around my shoulder and, instinctively, I cross my arms over my chest. She doesn't stop me, and turns me around so she can slide the remaining shreds of my tunic over my back. She gasps. "Gods of mercy!" Her hand touches my back. Surprisingly, it doesn't hurt. "Gods of mercy . . ."

"Bad?" I ask.

She doesn't answer and leads me towards the tub. I sink in up to my chest and let her pull at the knots in my hair. The water becomes an ugly brown. A few twigs and leaves float on the surface. The black crusty skin surrounding my ostracized scar breaks away, leaving red, healed flesh. Only the ugly symbol carved black against my skin remains.

Healed. I trace it with my fingers. Already healed?

Mama Opal slides a wet rag across my back. It stings but it doesn't blast pain up my back like it had the previous nights.

"The lashes . . . are they healed?" I ask.

"There's a really deep one that is still scabbed over," she answers. "But the others have closed up completely. They've left markings, dear. Horrible markings." She realizes how much her words hurt and pats my shoulder gently. "They aren't that bad, dear. You're beautiful. You're still beautiful."

She's a horrible liar.

I hold my breath and lower my head beneath the surface. Once. Twice. Three times. Until Mama Opal says she can't find anymore blood or dirt. She holds a roughly woven blanket for me and wraps it around my shoulders once my feet are on the floor again.

She leads me to the sturdiest cot and motions me to sit. The mattress is hard – most likely packed with straw – and the wood is carved with delicate designs and ancient symbols much like the ones on Shade's swords. I determine that it must be his.

Mama Opal fumbles through the wardrobe. She swats oversized tunics and aprons out of her way in her frantic search. I imagine trying to cinch a tunic meant for her ample frame around my half-starved hips. She sighs in satisfaction and hurries towards me.

She slams a black tunic, just my size, and a dark, woven belt on top of it. "There you are," she says and wipes a drop of sweat from her brow. "How in the hell I found those I've no idea. Well, try them on before you freeze, girl."

I do. The tunic fits perfectly once the belt latches it around my waist. I stand up and do a little spin so she can see. She nods approvingly.

"Once you've eaten a few fine meals you'll fill those gaps out quite nicely, honey," she praises. "What did those boys do? Starve you too?"

I don't comment and follow her to the fire. She has a strange creature roasting over the flames. It looks like a fish, but it has two arms where fish normally have fins. Its tail has five awkward rudder-like angles at the tip.

"It's a *blugartha*," she explains. "Its bite is very poisonous, but their meat is harmless." She pulls a small vial from one of the many tinkling on the ceiling. A blue substance moves inside, thick and pasty. "We use the poison for painkillers. Mixed with the correct herbs, the venom becomes a tonic." She returns the vial to is proper place.

"So you're a doctor?" I ask. "An alchemist?"

She shakes her head. "No. Just a woman who knows her herbs and medicines. In this country, girl, you survive with brains. Brawn helps but brains . . . they can drag you out of deep shit when muscle can't. Remember that, darling." She flicks her eyes over my face and smiles. "But I don't think I have to tell you that, do I? You've done a marvelous job surviving this country so far."

"I think I'm running out of luck," I whisper and glance at the door, half expecting an angry mob to burst through at any moment and drag me out to a tree.

"Don't let Dirk or any of his fellow bastards scare you, honey. They're a bunch of big-mouth cowards. You're safe here with me. I'll take care of you just like I did the last . . ." She cuts herself off abruptly and turns to the fire again.

"The last what?" I ask. "Kelban?"

Her shoulders tighten, but she doesn't say anything, confirming my guess.

"What happened?" I remember Dirk's argument about the last "one" they let inside the wall. I am not the first Kelban to enter this village. I am definitely not the first Kelban to make it out of the Burnt Forest and across the river.

"It would do you no good to know, child," she whispers. When she turns around her face has lost its light. "Needless to say, it was horrible and wrong. Nothing will happen to you, though, honey. No one can touch you until the King has a say in the matter and that's that. Whoever dares will face not only his wrath, but also the wrath of every noble citizen of Agron."

I had been so intent on spinning my deceptive back-story I hadn't taken the mention of their king to heart. Now, it beats wildly in my breast. Not only are the stories about their cannibalism, their complete savagery, exaggerated rubbish, but they are a functioning society as well, with a hierarchy and ruler. Once again, I wish for my journal. There are so many things to take note of. So many things to draw. To piece together. My fingers ache for a pencil but I don't see a sign of any literature in Mama Opal's home. I haven't seen a book or piece of paper since I entered the Wilds. In the area of knowledge, they are still savage.

Mama Opal proceeds to cut up vegetables. I recognize a carrot but the others are foreign to me. She looks up and notices my restlessness. "My shawl is hanging by the door, honey. Wrap it around yourself and get some fresh air."

I hesitate.

"Oh, I don't mean go walking all about the town. That would be foolish. I mean stand outside the door. Breathe. Let the air dry your hair. I'll come get you when supper is ready. That door is so thick you wouldn't hear me if I hollered."

I do as she says. The shawl is woolen homespun: just like the blanket Shade lent to me that first night. She made them. I peek at her over my shoulder. She's cutting vegetables at a frightening speed and humming a strange tune to herself. I see no resemblance of any kind to Shade in her face so she cannot be his mother. Aunt? Distant relation?

I pull the door open and walk outside. Dusk has begun. Over the stone roofs and the wall trees jab sixty to a hundred feet in the air. I watch a bright blue bird flutter back and forth between the leaves, chirping a low, sweet tune. A night-bird. I lean against the wall and watch it preen its feathers. A few fall out and flutter towards the ground, out of my sight. Maybe tomorrow I can find them.

"*Mave, le nac frin mi dei naw.*" I know that voice. I know those words.

Keegan and Hayden stand directly behind me.

"Enjoying the solitude, Kelban?" Keegan asks in my language.

I stare at him, feigning nonchalance at his arrival.

"*Le drafe?*" Hayden asks Keegan, and they both chuckle.

"What do you want?" I ask, resisting the urge to tell him that I am not deaf.

Keegan moves forward, arms behind his back casually, but his gaze is anything but friendly. "You know, not many women pull knives on me. Particularly Kelban bitches." Rage dances in his eyes. He smiles. "I was right. I should have taken a tumble up your skirts – to search for weapons of course. A minor bridge of forgetfulness on my part." Our noses brush as he leans close. "The next time I won't be so careless."

"Be careful," I whisper. "I might put a curse on your head."

Keegan snarls and grabs me by the neck. "You've a dirty mouth, bitch."

I spit in his face. He lets go of me and wipes at the glob of saliva dangling from his lips and chin. He stares at his hand in disgust.

"Mind what you touch, savage!" I snap. "Where I come from they'd have removed your hand."

He raises that hand to strike at me. I don't flinch. Don't move.

"Keegan!" Axle steps between us and thrusts his upraised hand away. I hadn't even noticed his arrival.

"Nice to see you again so soon, poet," Keegan growls. He dips his head to the silent presence behind me. "Shade."

"Shouldn't you be with your father, Keegan, filling your guts with brew?" Axle asks. He sticks his hands in his pockets. "I think you'd find that far more entertaining than being trashed by some shit-talking Kelban."

"One would think so," Keegan smiles. He glares at me over Axle's shoulder.

"Why don't you head in that direction then?" Axle tilts his neck down the street.

Hayden guides Keegan forward, cautiously eying the sword strapped to Axle's back. He fails to mask the fear in his eyes.

Shade steps out of their way.

Keegan turns at the corner of the street, flips a finger at me, and winks.

I flip a finger back at him.

He sneers and disappears around the corner.

"You coming, Kelban?" Shade asks irritably.

When I turn around, they've already entered the house and he's waiting with the door open. Tripping over my own feet, I step inside and it slams shut behind me. Shade takes a seat at one of the stools situated around the table, without so much as a look in my direction.

"I'm not 'Kelban'," I remind him.

He grunts.

Mama Opal looks up. "What is your name, honey? I forgot to ask."

"No need to give her the entire thing," Axle adds.

"Kyla Kelonia Bone," I say, ignoring him.

She lets the name roll over her tongue a few times before smiling at me. "It's a beautiful name, dear. It suits you."

"It sure does. She almost was a bone when we found her." Axle laughs at his jest.

The door flies open, banging against the wall so hard, that I leap backwards.

"Axle!" a girl rushes into the room and tosses a wicker basket far into a corner. "Axle, you're back." She launches into his arms and grabs him around the neck with such momentum he spins in a half-circle and has to grab the table to prevent himself from falling. He gags and his face turns purple.

"River, you're choking your brother," Mama Opal reprimands.

The girl lets go of Axle and wraps her arms around Shade's shoulders. "I'm not choking you, am I, Shade?"

He growls.

She laughs and kisses his cheek. He shrugs her off and reaches for the flagon Mama Opal placed in the center of the table.

River turns around and looks at me. Her eyebrows rise and her forehead creases. "You . . ." She looks towards my shoulder and then nods to herself. "This explains all the commotion in the village. I wondered why everyone was whispering so much. And Dirk . . ." She chuckles. "I haven't seen him that mad since Axle pissed on his favorite sword."

"A minor miscalculation," Axle argues. "I thought it was Keegan's."

She waves him off and stares intently at me. "What's your name?"

Shade turns around, mouth half-open.

"Before he tells you I'm 'Kelban' or 'little girl' let me introduce myself." I curtsy. "Lady Kyla Kelonia Bone. Nice to meet you, River."

She stares at me in awe, eyes sparkling delightedly. "Oh, you're so graceful. Could you show me how to do that? I've never seen anything like it. None of the women in the village know anything about such etiquette. Only court ladies in the king's house know how to behave so. Please, show me? You must. You simply have to. It's so beautiful." She attempts to curtsy, and her knees buckle awkwardly.

"She's a high-class Kelban," Shade mutters and pours a mug of strong-smelling brew. "Every single one of them knows how to make a decent curtsy. It's nothing special."

I cross my arms and glare at him. "I'd like to see you try it, Shade."

Mama Opal coughs ceremoniously and turns her back to grab a boiling kettle of broth from the fire. Axle's lips turn up at the corners, and he struggles not to smile.

River laughs.

"River, really," Axle reprimands and sits down beside Shade.

She ignores him and leans close. "I like you," she whispers. "We're going to get along splendidly." She pulls me around the table and sits down next to me.

I stare across the table at Shade. He ignores me and drains his mug in one drought. By the gleam in his eyes I know it is not the "hunter's brew" from the forest.

Mama Opal sets the broth on the table along with the simmering mound of crusty *blugartha.* River heaps my plate with boiled veggies and sets a decent portion of meat on top. She sprinkles a green herb over the meat and fills my mug with the a sweet-smelling liquid.

"*Kelonia,*" she whispers several times. She looks perplexed. "What does that name mean? I've never heard of it."

I shrug, mouth full of *blugartha.* It melts on my tongue. I swallow before replying. "My mother gave it to me. She told me the first half stood for Kelba. K-E-L."

"And the last part?" River asks.

I shrug again. "Don't know. Perhaps half of an ancient family name. Who knows?"

"Odd," she remarks.

The sweet-smelling liquid tastes like a mixture of apple and spice. I like it.

River tries to pay attention to her food, but curiosity radiates from her body. She reminds me of the innocent little pigeons that would sit on my window-sill in the morning and peck at the glass between them and me like they couldn't understand what it was. Perhaps its the innocence that envelopes her – the happiness – that makes me feel so small. So different. Whenever she looks at me I want to curl into a ball and hide the deformity . . . the ugliness . . . that pervades me.

"Do you have any sisters or brothers, Kyla?" she asks. She gazes fondly across the table at Axle.

"I have a brother."

"No sisters?" she asks. I shake my head. "A pity. I always wanted a sister. Brothers are nice but they can be annoying." She glares across the table at Axle, but not in a mean way. He sticks out his tongue. "See?"

I chuckle. In truth, I'd never noticed the lack of female companionship. Landor had been good enough company.

"And you're married, too," she says looking at my wrist. "How wonderful. I always wanted to be married at a young age. Axle says there's no hope for me. What's your husband like? Was it love at first sight? Do you have any children?"

"River, your food's getting cold," Mama Opal interrupts.

River rolls her eyes and returns attention to her plate. I pass a quiet "thank you" with my eyes to Mama Opal. She nods and pops a carrot in her mouth.

Shade stares at me across the table. When I turn to question his sudden interest, he looks away quickly and drains another mug of brew.

"Easy," Axle whispers to him.

Shade ignores him and pours a third cup.

I pick at my food, appetite suddenly lost. To distract from Shade's loud guzzling, I turn my attention to River.

Her hair hangs nearly to her waist in one long, dark brown braid. She has chocolate brown eyes and they are so large that I hardly notice the black rim around her eyes. It's beginning to become such a common sight to me that I don't even see the difference between a Wild person's eyes and mine. Except for Shade's. How someone can mask so much anger behind cool indifference amazes me. River is almost as thin and bony as her brother, with cheekbones that could cut glass, and fingers that could stab someone. Her jaw seems too delicate for someone who lives in the Wilds and freckles dot her nose and bare arms. Her tunic is blue and reaches her ankles. However, despite the abundance of scars I have seen on her brother, the only blemish on her skin is a dark splotch of brown on the tissue of her forearm – a birthmark. She is not a warrior.

Mama Opal stands, ending the supper. The inside of the room has grown darker than before, and Mama Opal lights two more lanterns that hang from the stone ceiling. The fire crackles.

"Anything I can do, Mama Opal?" Axle asks, rising.

"There is something I'd like to discuss with you, Axle." She turns to look at me and River, where the girl has been whispering in my ear about her brother's intelligence. "River, you . . ."

She jumps up. "I know. Water from the well to wash the dishes. Water from the well to wash the dishes, water from the well . . ." She collects a bucket sitting by the side of the door, and skips outside, singing her foolish phrase.

"That girl . . ." Mama Opal doesn't finish and laughs instead. She pulls Axle to a side of the room and begins to make all sorts of motions against the wall with her hands. I hear the words "foundation" and "mortar" a couple of times. The wall must be needing repair.

Axle nods as if he understands, and I feel alone in the room again, finding myself wishing I knew anything that would matter to these people. I can throw a dagger. I can read. I can write. I can speak moderately proficient Kelban. I can curtsy. I can dance. But these things would either outcast me farther or get me killed.

Constantly wearing a mask is getting rather tiring. My nerves ache. My head aches. Two hours at a party, surrounded by Kelban nobility, was a walk in the woods compared to this endless disguise.

Maybe that's why Shade's so taciturn?

When I turn to locate him, he's not there. The empty room glares back at me. I stare at the door. Did he already walk out?

"Mama Opal, where did Shade go?"

Axle shakes his head warningly. "You leave him be."

"Outside by himself," Mama Opal says.

"Thanks." I stand and start for the door.

"Kyla . . ."

"Let the girl be. Now, Axle, the mortar . . ."

I shut the door behind me.

Stars are twinkling above my head. I pause a moment to stare at their twinkling forms. So many of them. I never got a chance to see so many when I lived in Kirath. The street lamps always masked the miniscule light of the weaker stars. Landor had woken me at midnight once, when I was about fifteen years old, and taken me up on the rooftops to see the "diamonds in the sky." Asher and Craig had been with us. We'd been so happy. So content. So innocent. I look away from sky, no longer able to see its beauty.

A long sigh draws my attention to the middle of the street. Shade is standing there, staring up at the sky too. The stars reflect in his eyes perfectly, and he looks calm. Relaxed. A completely different person. I shouldn't disturb him.

But there is something I have to ask him. I walk up behind him, being careful not to make any noise, lest I "irk" him.

I wait, but he doesn't turn around.

"What happened to the last Kelban?"

His body jerks and he grunts deeply in his throat, spinning around, a hand already going for the sword atop his back. He stops himself just in time. So much for not "irking" him.

"You know you have the ability to sneak up on a person so lightly, Kel – Kyla. Don't do that to me again!" He takes a deep breath.

Did I really startle him so badly?

He starts towards the door. *No, you can't leave yet,* I want to shout. But that would just fuel his intention to do so.

"You didn't answer me. What happened to the last Kelban?"

Silence thickens in the air. I don't dare breathe. It has grown so dark that all I can see is his silhouette against the stone wall. Slowly, my eyes adjust.

"Are you really certain you want to know?" he finally says, his voice a husky whisper.

"I walked into a hornet's nest because you didn't believe I *needed* to know," I say, struggling to keep the rage out of my voice.

"I told you everything you need to know."

"Now tell me everything I don't."

"You have no right to make demands of me. I . . ." The vague, white light glowing from his sword reflects over his face for a brief moment. I blink in shock. The mask isn't there. In the darkness, he's forgotten to leash his emotions, thinking no one can see them. But I can see them. I can see the pain. The hurt. The bitter ache. I recognize that look all too well.

Landor. Landor looked like that when he spoke of me in my visions.

Lost.

This Wild boy lost something – or someone. Perhaps more. So much more.

It is only a moment. The mask is back. I struggle to keep mine intact too. He cannot know that I know his pain. That, to a certain extent, I understand it, even if I don't understand what fuels that pain.

His gaze softens when I fiddle with the hem of my gown. "She gave you those clothes?" he asks.

I nod. "Are they River's?" But I know they cannot be. River is too skinny.

The corners of his mouth crinkle slightly – twenty percent of a smile. A very sad, twenty percent smile. "I haven't seen those for two years."

"Two years!" I gasp. "But they're in fine condition. There's no tears. No worn edges. How . . .?"

"She likes you," Shade interrupts softly. "She likes you a lot, Kelban. Don't disappoint her. People like her – they're too good to be disappointed."

"And what about you?" I ask.

He blinks. Startled. "What?"

I step closer. Let the faded light from his sword illuminate my face so he can see the honesty – the sincerity – shining there. "What if I disappoint you?"

That flash crosses his eyes again that I cannot understand. He chuckles softly, but it is not an amused noise.

"I am a monster. What do you think?" He turns his back on me and grips the door handle.

"Wait . . ."

My ears explode when the noise of a clanging bell and a horn loud enough to wake the gods shatters the stillness of the night. I cover my ears. Shouts along the wall raise the hairs on my neck.

The door flies open.

"Shit!" Axle snaps. "Shade . . ."

But Shade's already drawn his swords. Mama Opal rushes out of the house carrying an unlit lamp. Her face is white, and her eyes bulge from their sockets as she looks around frantically. She grabs my hand, and I wince. Her hand is cold as ice.

Axle draws his own sword and pulls the ties of his vest, cinching the open ends together.

"Stay quiet. Don't come up until you hear someone knock three times. You hear?" Shade shakes Mama Opal's thick shoulder. "Hear me?!"

She nods and tugs me towards the corner of the house. I struggle to pull loose, but she won't let me.

"Shade . . ." I plead.

"Stay and keep quiet!" he snaps.

He and Axle race down the street.

Mama Opal pulls on a mound of grass near the wall of her home and a hidden door flies open. A wooden staircase stares up at me, and she gently shoves me downwards.

I descend into the earth. Dampness clings to my neck. The strong smell of dirt wrinkles my nose. Mama Opal shuts the trapdoor above our heads, plunging us into total darkness. My feet touch solid ground.

Mama Opal lights the lamp.

Shivers cascade up my back. The lamp glows a silver-white light into every corner of the room, dousing my skin in radiant rays. It shines and shimmers innocently, but it rears deadly memories from deep within the catacombs of my past. I have seen that light once before.

Shit.

The shadows are here. The shadows have come.

The scars beat against my neck, recognizing their origins. I place a hand over them, lest Mama Opal see. A thousand lies will be unraveled if my deception is discovered.

"River?" Mama Opal looks around.

My stomach drops. Gods, please no.

"River?" Her voice trembles.

I grip the staircase for support.

"River!" Mama Opal screams desperately. She falls on the ground, fingers clawing at the dirt. Tears run down her face. "River!" But she makes no move towards the stairs.

Sweet, innocent River.

"It's my fault. It's my fault." Mama Opal rocks back and forth, hands clutching her chest like she's dying. "River!"

I look up the dark stairs. Imagine snaky black vines wrapping around River's fragile wrists. Imagine venomous fangs sinking into her delicate skin. Imagine her screaming, alone and terrified, with no one to save her. Innocent. Too afraid to move. Like me all those years ago.

"River!" Mama Opal wails. She gropes at her chest, smearing red dirt over her tunic. "Gods, please! Gods, please! Not again."

The steps feel like clouds beneath my feet as I hurry upwards and slam palms to the trapdoor. It doesn't budge.

I push again. My hands tremble, but the door cracks open and the night air rushes through to cool my burning face. Behind me, Mama Opal calls out, asking me what I'm doing, ordering me to come back. With all my strength I push, grinding my branded shoulder into the wood. It flies open.

It's dark. The air is cold. The bell no longer rings. The moon is hidden behind clouds of deep black – darkness that seems unending. The moon will not shine until it has passed. The creatures will continue to attack whilst it remains veiled.

Up ahead the sound of battle breaks the silence: swords, war cries, pain. They come from the square before the gates. There was a well in the center of that square. River will be there.

My feet throb as I run.

To my right, a man falls to the ground, the rip of a blade slicing his body. I look into the darkness, but I see nothing.

Something shrieks from the dark beside the man's suddenly still form, sending the hairs on the back of my neck straight. I would recognize that ear-piercing cry if it had been a hundred years since that living nightmare.

The sounds of hell mingle with those of battle: screeches, wind, violence.

The square is full of men. All of them possess moon swords. All of them battle with the darkness swirling before them in clouds of black and gray. Only the light from their swords reveals the true form of what they fight.

Dark capes skate between the swords – between the light – and whoosh through the empty air. Shrieks of beings not belonging to the human race fill the emptiness hovering over the square. To my left, a man screams and a blur of something dark and unearthly flutters away with the speed of lightning.

They're everywhere!

The hair atop my head shivers slightly, as something soft passes over it. I bite back a scream and remain perfectly still. Nothing happens. It passed me by.

"Don't let them leave the square!" a towering man up near the border of the wall screams, brandishing a fierce, double-edged moon sword. It's Otis.

Men rally around his order. Warriors try to form a blockade around the area. If I don't hurry, I'll be trapped inside.

The well is not hard to spot. It's the only thing that is frozen stiff in this battlefield. A hem of blue peeks out from behind stone formation. When I circle it, my heart slows just a bit. River is curled up around the bucket, head bowed, hands trembling with fright. When I say her name she doesn't answer me.

Leaning closer, I put a hand on her shoulder. She screams and strikes upward with a shaking palm. I manage to dodge the blow and grip her wrist. She screams again and begins to wail. I say her name again, louder, and her head snaps up. Her large eyes that I'd admired less than an hour before are now red and puffy.

No, she is not a warrior.

"Come on! Hurry!" I pull her to her feet. She's shaking so bad I don't know if she'll be able to run. Her knees are trembling. "Quickly!"

A wave of pain shoots up my right arm before I've even turned around, and burns a line across the muscle. My scream slices through the air, and I fall backwards with the force of the unexpected blow. River screams too, and curls up against the well again, her eyes wide and hysterical.

Blood flows down my arm from the new gash in my skin. A gravelly laugh in front of me commands my attention. When I look up, it's only with the firmest resolve that I don't start screaming like a crazy person.

A shadow stands above me, cloaked in the darkness of a ghost-like cape, a black dagger clutched tightly in its dark hand. Every single memory from that long ago night floats in front of my eyes like I'm reliving it all over again. Except there is no Shade. No light. No one to come to my rescue. No one to block the strike.

The shadow's black dagger rises above my head.

Roll.

And I do.

The dagger scrapes across the stone behind me. I bump into River and she jerks, closing arms over her head.

The shadow screeches in rage at my trickery, and sweeps towards me, its cape fluttering. I search the ground for a weapon. A stone. A stick. Anything to distract it. Anything to give us time to run. My fingers find the edge of the bucket.

The shadow raises the black dagger again. The bucket is heavy, and my wounded arm burns like fire, but I throw the water at the creature. The monster's scream reaches deep down into my ears, tingling, popping, burning. I scream along with it, but grab River's hand and pull her up. She shivers beneath my touch.

"Run!"

The shadow flails around like a dripping wet rag, and now I clearly see the outline of its body. It no longer looks like a looming monster. Instead, I see midnight black hands and a dark ebony mask that glitters beneath the hood of its cape.

River sees it too, and hesitates, staring at the shiny reflection of metal underneath the hood. The shadow starts towards her. I slam the bucket into its shoulder, toppling it to its knees – or where it should have knees – and smash the bucket, bottoms up, over its head, blinding it.

"RUN!"

This time River obeys, her skirts lifted halfway up her legs, feet flying across the dusty square. She breaks through the barricade the warriors have successfully formed, and continues running.

I attempt to follow, but I stumble. Behind me, the shadow roars in rage, its fury rising above the noise of its fellow monsters.

Run, Kyla.

But it's too late. The shadow cuts off my path, bucket spinning through the air with such force that it shatters upon landing, sending shards of wood across the stone square.

I don't see the movement. Only recognize the hard kick to my ribs that sends me flailing backwards.

Pain, like a hammer, batters my skull. My head is against the stone well. The village square tips back and forth unsteadily before me.

The shadow draws closer, and I try to stand. Something wet and sticky runs down the side of my face. Its stench fills my noise. Blood!

The shadow cages me against the well, its dagger gleaming.

Everything begins to shiver. The ground. The sky. The houses.

"Hellion!" the shadow mutters in a raspy voice and raises the dagger.

Get up. Get up! I try to rise. My arms shiver. My head pounds against my skull and a strange surge of energy pulses in my neck, against those hell-cursed scars won so long ago.

The dagger descends.

I'm going to die.

Chapter XVI

Ignoring all the drums roaring in my ears, I shove my arms against the well. I roll sideways, arms flailing helplessly. The shadow's black dagger cracks against the stone ledge of the well. Orange sparks fly in all directions.

I leap to my feet, knees weak and shaky. If I can run just a little ways towards the border of the square, maybe one of those warriors will rid me of this attacker. If only I had my knife. If only I . . .

I'm wasting time.

"*This one's got life.*" The rough phrase sinks deep into my bones.

It spoke. The shadow spoke!

The shadow surges up around me, its black cloak spreading out wide around it, dark wisps of what I had once compared to fog, sweeping towards me. The smell that converges around me is familiar. I dash out a hand, attempting to push the fog away as it draws nearer, and watch in horror as it slowly presses over my hand with a velvety touch. It skates up my wrist and my lower arm, its wispy tongues tickling my skin, pressing against veins. Nausea curdles in my belly. I try to pull away, but the fog, now strong like iron, imprisons me. The fog draws close to my face, dancing in front of my vision. Teasing me. Playing with me. The raspy chuckle of the shadow raises the hairs on my neck.

The fog, now a thick, dark goo, glides up my arm, towards the fresh cut in my skin; the wound made by this dastardly creature's blade. Its black, gooey edges reach the tip of the cut. The shadow hisses a delighted rumble from deep within its throat (if it has one), restoring a memory.

"*Drain the girl.*"

Screaming, I pull away. The shadow startles at my sudden movement, and the dark hold it retained on my limb breaks away. The goo returns to its foggy appearance and weaves through the air.

"Stay away from me!" I scream. I back up against the well, and my fingers brush a hard object resting on its ledge. It shatters upon contact with the ground into five large shards. Glass.

The shadow pauses, its black vine-like wisps jerking back into its heavy cloak.

"*A Kelban,*" it mutters. It's black hand removes a different dagger from its belt. Unlike the previous weapon, its blade shimmers with the presence of an evil I can't describe.

"Stay away from me!" I repeat, but the well prevents me from backing away any further.

"*You don't belong here anyway, Kelban. I'm doing you a favor, ungrateful bitch,*" it says.

The words are familiar. I remember the raspy voice near the river telling me I didn't belong. That I was not one of them. That I was nothing.

I was right. It had been a shadow.

I gently touch the scars on my neck. They aren't pulsing like they usually do. Instead, they are warm and relaxed beneath my touch. They have always responded to my fear with pain – why now do they falter?

"*Kelbans,*" it hisses. The dagger cuts across the already opened flesh on my arm. The shimmering, unknown evil on its blade presses against my wound like a living thing, its black form clinging like a second skin. A prickling pain of warmth slides up my shoulder into my neck. "*Now you'll die.*"

The black form over the wound drops off like a burnt leaf and disintegrates upon contact with the ground. Beneath the shadow's hooded cape I hear something similar to a gasp – if it weren't so raspy and inhuman.

"Surprised?" I ask it.

The shadow jerks back and foggy tendrils rip from its cloak. "*You understand?*"

I stare at it.

"*That's impossible,*" it rasps.

Moonlight – white and faded, but moonlight just the same – washes over the square. The shadow's foggy particles disappear inside its cloak once again, but one is not fast enough. I search the ground and my fingers find one of the glass shards. It reflects the light perfectly over its gleaming surface.

"*No*!" the shadow gasps as I rotate the shard in its direction – catching the light with it.

"*No!*" it screeches as the light disintegrates its remaining foggy wisp. The black dagger drops from its hand and, the shadow slithers into the air. I rotate the glass shard again, and light bounces after it. It isn't fast enough. The shadow disappears in the night.

The battle has ended. Shadows have disappeared – or disintegrated – in the courtyard. The square becomes a different kind of battlefield as a new enemy begins to spread its claws. Death.

Women, shouldering bags of what I believe to be medicines, swarm towards the wounded being lined up against a wall. Some let out horrified wails as they discover a relative or friend among the bleeding warriors. The remaining warriors, the ones who haven't even shed blood, begin to rally at the far corner of the square, whispering among themselves, pointing towards the woods. Do they think to follow the monsters? Hunt them?

The sick feeling in my stomach returns as the wounded cries fill the air. They are not of death, but of pain. Limbs crack as they are removed. The splash of blood on dirt makes bile stick to the sides of my throat. I have to get out of here. I can't . . .

"Kyla!" Shade dashes around the corner of the well and looks down at me. "What the hell are you doing here? Get your ass back to the cellar!" He reaches down and grabs my arm, pulling me to my feet with a violent grip.

I scream. He pulls back his hand and blinks at the blood coating it. "Shit," he mutters.

"Shade!" Axle runs up, face white. "The wounded . . . there's a lot."

I peer over Shade's shoulder at Mama Opal as she enters the square, a bag slung over her plump shoulder, and a roll of white sheets bundled under her other arm. She doesn't even see us and hurries towards the wall where the wounded are screaming.

"Axle." The voice is so quiet – so timid – I almost don't hear it. But he does.

River stands at the entrance to the square, gripping the stone wall of a hut for support. Her face is white and there's blood on her feet. She must have torn them badly in her flight.

Axle hurries towards her and wraps his arms around her. She holds him tightly and begins to sob, tucking her face to his chest like a little child. She is saying something, but I can't hear a word because of the distance.

A pang, sharp as an arrow, hits me in the chest. If Landor were here, that's where I'd be. If Landor were here, he'd have fought with me. He'd of protected me. He'd of . . .

But he's not here.

"Kyla!" It's Mama Opal's voice. She beckons me with a pudgy arm.

I approach the wounded, my insides curling as a man just opposite of Mama Opal vomits blood onto the ground. He writhes as another woman attempts to keep him lying flat.

Mama Opal ignores my horrified look and hands me a towel, white as snow. "Press this against his arm . . . right here." She points to a bulging vein within a man – her patient's – arm that is moving up and down beneath his skin. It's an unnatural phenomenon. Every time the vein moves, the man groans. I press the towel over the area and immediately regret it. The vein beneath lets out a crushing sound that it shouldn't – like a nut-shell being pulled open. The poor victim screams, his body writhing so hard that it knocks me backwards.

"Hold him!" Mama Opal shouts, desperation commanding her voice. She grabs his arm and forces it back down.

I attempt to help her, but the back of the man's hand strikes me across the cheek. I bite my lip and try harder, muscles aching as I force his arm to the hard, wooden cot. Someone grips my shoulder and shoves me aside.

Shade presses his fingers so tightly into the man's arm that his knuckles go white with the strain. Mama Opal grabs a tube of some green powder and pours its contents over the large gash just above the wounded man's shoulder. The man screams again and his pupils turn dark black.

Shade's hands begin to shake with the victim's writhing.

The green powder turns black as all the veins around the ugly gash begin to jump up and down. I put my hands over my mouth to quell the screams that want to be released. The man begins to choke as his neck begins to shrink in on itself, his skin turning a deathly white around his face, floating down his neck, across his chest.

"No, no, no . . ." Mama Opal cries and searches desperately for another tube. I realize she's not sure what to look for. She's helpless.

Slowly the writhing stops. The veins don't jump anymore. Shade hesitantly pulls back his hands.

When I look, I wish I hadn't. The man is no longer a human. His skin is pure white and his eyes are black. His skin has welded to his bones. He stares up at the endless sky, mouth open and shrunk.

Shade turns on me. "What the hell were you doing, Kelban? Are your hands weak? Have you no strength?"

"Shade, that's enough," Mama Opal interjects tiredly, pulling a white sheet over the man's face. "It's the first time she's probably seen anyone die so . . . gruesomely. Let her be."

"If she held on tighter, if she'd kept the towel over the wound, he could have . . ."

"He would have died!" Mama Opal's eyes flash fire. She slaps a hand on top of the sheet – on top of the body. "They all die! We have no cure. No cure, you understand, Shade?" Tears pour out of her eyes. "We . . . are . . . powerless."

"What cure?" I ask. "Why did he need a cure? He only got wounded. He . . ."

"It was a shadow blade," Shade interrupts. "Shadow blades are a unique specimen. Where we possess these . . ." He points to the swords crossed on his back. "Shadows possess a murderous weapon of their own. A blade that works with the effect of poison in one's bloodstream. Once you are cut with it, you die within minutes, veins popping and turning black, skin turning white, eyes dilating."

He steps closer to me, until he's towering over me. I have to lift my chin and look at him. The underside of his jaw is coated in blood where he wiped his hand. "Understand this, girl. There are many strange things you have yet to see. This place you call 'the Wilds'. . ." he leans close, until his breath skates over my neck, ". . . is a frightening place."

I pull away from him, heart pumping madly. I'd seen nightmares too horrifying to describe and never had I seen anything like that man's death. It couldn't be real. But I stare at the hand still protruding from beneath the sheet. White. Dead. Black veins. It is real. It is all very, *very* real.

Mama Opal notices my gaze and pulls the sheet over the man's hand. She gently wraps her arms around my shoulders. "Don't look, honey. It won't do you any good."

How could I not look?

Shade grabs my elbow. "Come here." He shoves me against the table and wildly searches through Mama Opal's medicine bag. He pulls a vial from its folds. A white powder is inside. He takes my arm and opens the vial, pouring the contents over the gash. The powder seeps into the wound. Blood bubbles out of the gash in thick gooey formation. I gag at the sight. Shade pays it no mind and wipes it away with the edge of a towel from Mama Opal's collection.

"Did it ever bother you?" I ask. "The sight of blood?"

He rips the towel into shreds. "No." He begins to bind my wound tightly.

"What about pain? Does it bother you?" I search his face earnestly.

His jaw tightens. "No."

I let the matter rest. For now.

"What does a shadow blade look like?"

I think he won't answer me for a moment, so intent is he on tying an intricate – but stable – knot on my bandage. "It's black, but sometimes gray. It has a sleek blade that could cut glass. It's edges are as thin as paper and it sings like hell's opening gates when it slices through the air. When you look at it closely, it seems to possess life of its own when it shines. Very few shadows seem to use them, preferring their simpler swords, as if they know the danger of the weapon they carry." His eyes have taken on a faraway look. It makes me tremble. There's something about him – I can't put my finger on it – but he knows a lot more than he's telling.

I try to restore an image of the black dagger the shadow unsheathed. It had gleamed. There had been a glossy, iridescent appearance to it that I cannot explain. As if it was – alive?

"I think . . . it was a shadow blade."

Shade's chin snaps up. "How long ago where you cut?"

"Half an hour ago . . ."

"Then it wasn't a shadow blade," he interrupts and starts to leave.

I grab his arm, hands closing around sleek muscle. Shade glares at me, the look sending chills up my spine, but I don't let go. Instead, I step closer to him, until I can look him straight in the eye.

"It had to be. It moved like nothing I had ever seen. It . . ." He tosses my hand off his arm and steps back.

"First of all, Kelban, don't ever touch me again with your filthy hands. Second, it wasn't a shadow blade. Or . . ." He takes a threatening step in my direction, forcing me to back up against the well. "You'd be dead." He backs off and wipes at his arm where I touched him with a disgusted frown.

All around the square, the sound of weeping replaces the screams of death. The wounded are carted off on strong arms for their beds. The dead are lined up against the wall nearest the gate. Six feet of dirt will be their blanket. I count four sheet-covered figures.

A cry of rage turns me around. Dirk breaks out of a group of common village men and heads straight for me. His fists are balled at his sides and shaking dangerously. Keegan makes a grab for his father and misses.

"Dirk!" Otis appears out of nowhere, stepping between us, his sword drawn. "Return to your ranks!"

"It's all because of her. All of this!" Dirk swings an angry arc around the square. He points an accusing finger at me. "Her! She brought this on us. She called them here. It's been weeks since their last attack. Why would they come here if it weren't for her?"

Around him, the echo of agreement rises.

"It's just like the last one. You're bringing death on us all, Otis, and you know it. We should do away with her!"

"It shall be up to the king. You know the law as well as I," Dirk says firmly.

"The law is killing us. Sometimes tis necessary to take the law into your own hands." Dirk casts a hateful glance at me. "If one of you doesn't do it, I'll slit her throat myself. Just wait!"

The sound of steel being drawn distracts Dirk's attention from me, to Shade, who steps up alongside me. His moon sword, the designs glowing dangerously on its form, casually rests at his side in a graceful, downward swipe. "No one is slitting anyone's throat until the king has a say in this. Or have you forgotten about the Kelbans who you don't want to be like? What happened when the Celectate saw fit to overrule the Community and ostracize his own people? Or do you want to become like him and those Kelbans?"

Dirk smirks. "I think you've been visiting Kelba for far too long. I'm beginning to wonder where you loyalties really lie, my boy."

The crowd's muffled agreement dies a tragic death. The silence could kill. Everyone (or everyone that I can see) stares at Shade – no, at his swords – and their faces tighten. Fear. Hate. Anger. Other emotions too deep to describe. But their motivation is clear.

They dislike him.

And he doesn't look like he gives a damn. "My loyalty does not belong to those who do not deserve it," he answers. "And as far as my visits to our sister nation are concerned, I have decided not to be afraid of that stagnant piece of shit they call a wall."

Dirk sputters uselessly for a crushing reply, but he comes up empty. He turns to Otis instead, voice softening respectfully. "I beg you, Keeper. I beg you to hang the bitch and be done with this matter. This curse. Before they come again. Before they destroy us all."

I stare at my arm. Beneath the bandage I can still feel the gooey touch of the shadowy hold. The hard evil that tried to press into my wound the way it had entered the poor dead man by the wall. The voice of the horrible creature – a voice I can translate and understand and speak to. I can converse with evil. I can speak with demons.

What does that make me?

My silence is noticed.

Shade's hand tightens on his sword as the crowd takes a step forward as one. I do not think he will use it on them. I see the lines in his forehead, the crease of a frown at the corner of his lips. He does not want to kill them. Does not want to defend me. He is not willing to kill an angry mob that might be right about me.

"Stop." The command is a quiet one. Like a child's voice, smooth and delicate.

River elbows her way through the crowd, Axle not far behind her. She pauses in front of Dirk and rewards him with a glare. On her fragile, kindly face it does not carry the effect I think she hoped it would. She ignores his answering sneer and looks at me. I see the silent "thank you" behind her large, red-rimmed eyes.

"You will not harm her," River says simply.

Dirk chuckles.

River turns on him. "She saved my life."

The silence breaks. The crowd starts murmuring again.

"What do you mean?" Dirk and Otis ask at the same time.

"She saved my life. She fought off the shadow." She smiles softly. "With a bucket."

Dirk shakes his head in pure shock. Otis doesn't say anything.

"It's true." Mama Opal joins the circle, laying a convincing hand to Otis's arm. "She flew out of that cellar like a guardian angel. I couldn't catch her. The girl's no threat!" The last part was for the crowd.

"She saved your life?" Shade stares at River in disbelief.

She nods.

The crowd mumbles among once more. Slowly, people turn and walk back into the village. Others move towards the wall where the dead will be buried.

Dirk looks around. He's been left on his own. Even Keegan is not in sight. He stares at Shade with rage-filled eyes. At River with cool indifference. At Otis with shocked despair.

He flings up his hands in furious surrender. "You'll all see," he snaps, turning his back. "She'll be the destruction of us all!"

Otis gently shakes Mama Opal's hand from his arm. "The King will know about this." He looks at me. "*Everything* about her."

Axle doesn't step towards me, but his eyes are searching my face frantically. Somewhere inside the catacombs of his knowledge he messed something up. I see him struggling to correct it.

Shade merely steps past me without a second look and follows River back towards Mama Opal's.

I turn towards the well. The shadow dropped its blade. I remember it clattering to the ground. If I show him the unique weapon he will surely believe me.

But the dagger is gone.

Chapter XVII

I am in darkness. The darkness surrounds me. The darkness is me. I open my eyes.

The darkness is a mountain. A mountain of black and night and fog and evil. Shadows dance among it, around campfires of ruthless light. I walk among them, but they do not see me. I watch them twist and turn and form themselves. Watch them enter the many caves dotting the mountain. Follow them. Weave in and out of the darkened tunnels carved deep into the belly of earth. Into a large, open room in the center of the mountain.

A lone, dark figure stands there, cloaked in shadow and night.

"My lord." A shadow rasps to my right. I don't breathe. "Agron stands."

The silhouette moves, a cape rippling along the glossy, black floor. "And?"

"My lord?" The shadow is confused.

"Don't play fool with me. There is something else. Something else you are hiding from me. Something important. What is it?" The voice is evil itself – dark and twisted.

The shadow bows its hooded head and hesitates. His master grunts impatiently. "A Kelban is among them – a girl. She wounded Mel-ki. He claims she spoke to him. That she understood him. I know, my lord, that such a feat is impossible unless . . ."

The evil turns. I cannot see his face. Only his form. Powerful. Giant. Demonic in the dim light.

"Should we tell him?" the shadow asks. It sounds nervous. "He . . ."

"No!" The evil force snaps. "I will handle this situation. He is busy with other matters."

"But he would want to know of this."

The gigantic shadow moves closer, towering in the entire room, spreading black talons in wide, thorny branches through the spacious court. "I will handle this situation!" he repeats.

The shadow bows. At least it's smart enough to know when to crawl. "What of Mel-ki, my lord?"

The larger, darker shadow growls. "What do you think?"

A blinding dark flash snaps in the space between us. A pathway of some sort between it and me. Evil and twisted and . . . wrong. The wound burns. The scars on my neck ache. Our connection is more than one of flesh and wounds. Deep down inside me, that darkness pulls and stabs and claws.

"Understood." The shadow bows again and retreats from the room.

The taloned branches retreat inside the giant's cloak in a matter of seconds. A feat of power and unspeakable horror. It turns and the glint of metal beneath that heavy hood blinks at me. "Where are you, Ilevanra*?"*

I bolt upright.

A dream. Just a dream. A horrible, frightening dream.

I put my hands over my eyes, damp palms cool on my eyelids. I am wet all over. My nightshirt (an old tunic belonging to Mama Opal's deceased husband Cedric) is plastered to my body.

River murmurs softly beside me in sleep and rolls onto her side, facing me. Her lips are puckered oddly, and her fingers are spread apart carelessly. She is at peace.

I don't think I've had a peaceful sleep since I was fourteen.

I kick my legs over the side of the bed. Mama Opal left some hot tea downstairs. It calmed my nerves after the shadow attack two nights ago. It can calm them again now.

The stairs feel awkward beneath my feet. Like they're built on air, instead of stone and nails.

The fireplace still burns brightly.

Mama Opal has drawn a curtain over her corner of the room. I hear her snoring.

I tip the edge of the iron canister over the mug River found for me. A stream of the thick, black tea pours out. It reminds me of the black substance on the shadow's dagger. Of the blood that coated Shade's hand when he pulled away from my arm. Of the evil in my nightmare. I step away from the table, no longer feeling thirsty.

Funerals for the deceased had been held the morning after the attack. Mama Opal had kept me locked in the house while the mourning and weeping processions passed by the door every hour, asking for donations to the widows and orphans left behind by the destruction. She had slipped a packet of her best herbs under the door, but hadn't dared open it.

The day after was no better. Several drunk "friends" of one of the deceased gave the door a good bludgeoning before Axle showed up and dispersed them.

Today, River tells me, was much smoother. People were angry, yes. But others had rediscovered reason and were adjusting to the loss.

Deep down, I don't believe her. How could an innocent, sweet, trusting girl like her know anything of the sordid thoughts that hateful people could mask?

I sit down by the fire. The ashes are warm beneath my hand. I sink fingernails deep into the soot, hoping it removes the distasteful remnants of the shadow's hold on me.

The floorboards creak, and, instinctively, I swivel on the dark silhouette standing by the table.

Shade looks down at me, eyes groggy with sleep. He clutches a kitchen knife in his hand. "Kel – Kyla." Apparently he's not sleepy enough to forget my threat to remove his tongue. "What are you . . . why are you up?"

Because I'm frightened. Because I think there's something wrong with me. Because I don't know what's wrong with me.

"I was thirsty," I mutter. I jump to my feet and drain the mug of cold, thick tea. It sticks to the sides of my throat on its way down. I have the greatest urge to force it back up. Instead, I head for the stairs again.

"Kyla," he calls after me.

I turn around. "Yes?"

His vest is half-open and the firelight dances off the muscles peeking through. The edge of that fierce scar pokes above the cinched edges of his vest. He follows my gaze there and jerks the edges of his vest together. "Nothing," he mutters.

I walk upstairs and lie back down beside River.

The second level of Mama Opal's home is sanctioned in half by a large, thick curtain, so heavy that I can't pull it aside. Maybe if I had the use of both my arms but my right arm is considerably weakened from the wound. Sometimes I can't move it at all and sicken with fright at the idea of losing the mobility.

I ask Mama Opal about the room four days after the funerals when I've exhausted my attempts to remain attentive to her constant medicine making. She says it's rather "frightful" and that the curtain separates the sleeping area from what was once her deceased husband's study. She calls him a "strange, little man" and tells me I might be sick at the sight.

She only seals my interest.

River pulls aside the curtain for me. Her face turns purple before she's even tugged it five feet. I step through, and she walks back downstairs. Apparently, she doesn't relish the study any more than Mama Opal does.

I set the lamp Mama Opal provided on the nearby table. The abandoned study is full of strange things. Creatures in glass jars. Eyeballs. Preserved animal fetuses. Toxins that haven't been opened in years. Ancient, cracked kitchenware from before Kelba's hundred year history. I even find a bit of writing within the mess that looks very similar to ancient Kelban. The writing is worn and faded. I can only make out two words: "devote" and "hope." At the bottom of the parchment, written in the clear, definable, present Kelban language, is a simple signature.

Cedric.

I presume he's Mama Opal's husband and explore the strange artifacts he left behind. None of them turn my stomach. Not even the preserved fetuses and eyeballs. Instead, I regard them with renewed interest. They do not resemble anything I'd ever seen in Kelba – but I'd been in the city ninety-five percent of my life. Perhaps they roamed the mountains or poorer plains of my homeland.

The fragments of ancient house-ware are, perhaps, the most interesting. They are delicately carved with ancient symbols (probably to ward off the gods) and in fine condition, despite their shattered state. The tales of ancient Kelba, when there had been no division, no wall, had never been a subject of interest for me. But now, holding pieces of broken pottery in my hands, I curse myself for being small-minded. If I had researched – even for a month or two – I might know which century the pottery was from. Which Kelban group it might have belonged to. Which city.

"Busy?" River asks. She stands outside the curtain and quickly looks away from two white eyeballs staring at her through the clear liquid of their glass home. "You've been up here for three hours already, Kyla."

Had it really been that long? I stand and dust off my hands on the waist of my tunic. I wish I had my notebook. There are so many things I want to write down. Eventually I might get desperate enough to climb back into Kelba just to retrieve the book.

River helps me tug the curtain back into place. She shakes her head at me ruefully. "I can't believe you aren't even pale. That study gives me the shivers." Her shoulders shake as she says it. "Doesn't it scare you?"

"A lot of things scare me," I answer as we descend the stairs. "But not a pair of dead eyeballs."

"That's not fair," she gripes. "They're an extremely creepy pair of dead eyeballs."

"Just imagine them as someone whom you love," I advice. "Then they won't seem so scary."

She makes a face like she's going to be sick. "Kyla . . . that's morbid and awful and . . ."

"It works, doesn't it?" I ask with a sly grin.

She elbows me in the shoulder, but doesn't hide her smile fast enough. She hooks me by the arm and halts our downward journey. "You're going to help me with something today, and . . ."

"If you are going to make me try and sew a stitch again, forget it. I'm not interested in bloody fingertips for the third time in a row."

River laughs. "I thought your handiwork was quite good. I've never seen that strange thing you were sewing. It was pure art."

The small handkerchief I had been busying myself with over the last few days lies discarded by the bed upstairs. The image is embroidered completely from black thread, but of many intricate shapes and patterns. However, it possesses no form, so River should be confused.

"It's a shadow blade," I say.

River grows quiet. Despite me saving her life and fighting off the shadow, she does not believe me. I don't blame her. Anyone cut with the blade has died, and I can't find the dagger that cut me to prove its legitimacy. I had River search for it in the square the day after the attack. She hadn't found it.

"We're gathering nuts and herbs today," River says. She sees my confused expression and smiles kindly. "Don't worry. You're getting the nuts. I'm collecting the herbs. If you accidentally brought back poison, Dirk won't let you go this time."

I shudder at the idea.

Downstairs, Mama Opal hands River a leather pouch. "Make sure to eat it," she reminds. "I packed an extra side of bread and tea." She casts a reproving look at the waist of my dress. A faraway look comes into her eyes, and she brushes a curly strand of hair out of my face with gentle fingers. "Eat it all."

I swear, she's like my mother in that moment.

River looks uncomfortable and edges the door open with her knee. She tosses a wicker basket from the ceiling in my direction, and I catch it. Mama Opal recovers her usual, firm appearance and waves us off, reminding River to get the "red" ones this time and not the "orange."

Outside, the sun is already high in the sky. Heat sticks to my neck. Warms my face. Glazes my scar. Self-consciously, I pull the strap of my tunic over the ghastly emblem. Even I'm sick of looking at it. I don't want any more unnecessary attention.

I have shoes now. River gave them to me as a present, in reward for saving her life, though she wouldn't admit it. They are like sandals, but represent a boot's form since they twist and tie all the way up my shin. They feel secure and are just my size. At least River and I are similar in that aspect.

The villagers hardly pay us any mind as we walk towards the square. The only people I can see are men building more homes. Everyone is outside the wall, collecting, farming, and playing. That is where I will meet the most attention.

When River and I step beyond the gate, the guards reminding us of "curfew," I discover I'm correct. Anyone standing beyond the gate immediately looks up when I step out.

Thousands of eyes upon me are nothing new, I tell myself. I was always stared at wherever I was. And, being honest, I didn't like it then either. Nausea curdles in my stomach as several woman with pitchforks tighten their grips around the tool. They want to kill me, I know it.

When the greenery of the trees swallows me up, I finally breathe and look around. The tree trunks are an assortment of colors. Dark brown. Black. Ash gray. The leaves likewise. Green. Emerald. Yellow. White. Even a couple of red. River points at my basket, and turns towards an area that is full of thick trees, so close together their trunks are practically hugging one another.

"Those are the nut trees. Fill the basket and then come find me. It'll be time to eat by then." She walks off towards the other side of the trees.

A steep embankment, six feet high, dips down into a clearing the trees circle around, their branches hanging low like canopies. I shift my legs sideways to parallel the slope, and my ankle twists. Wincing and cursing myself for such stupidity, I jump. I land easily on my feet, heart pumping from the excursion, and smile to myself. It felt good.

I set the basket in the middle of the clearing, and proceed to pull nuts from the trees. It is harder work than it sounded. Some stick stubbornly in their places. Others scratch me. Some pop out of my hands. This will definitely not be done within an hour, and River knew it.

Chuckling at her trickery, I toss one of the nuts at the basket, barely missing it. I try again, pretending I hold a dagger in my hands. The last time I practiced had been that horrible day I'd learned of my bonding. I had felt so constricted, so immobile – a prisoner – that I hadn't had the heart to continue training. Now – as my wrist warms at the familiar memory, as my muscles remember their former positions, as my body twists and turns to rediscover its rhythm – a part of me that I thought was gone returns. I feel happy. I feel whole.

I *feel.*

I imagine the basket is Celectate Wood. A shadow. A demon.

I flip one of the nuts at the wicker encasing. It lands neatly in the middle, cracking against the hard encasing of several others.

Smiling triumphantly, I turn to grasp another nut and come face-to-face with a little girl. She regards me with wide eyes and a thumb in her mouth. She can't be older than three. Her legs are still pudgy and her cheeks still round like a toddler's.

"Hello there," I greet. Her eyes widen. I soften my voice and step towards her. "Do you want to help me? It's fun."

The girl whimpers and steps back. I remember where I am. Who I am. What the little girl must think I am.

Crouching low so that I look her straight in the eyes, I hold out my hand. She backs away. "I won't hurt you." I reach out to touch her arm.

She shakes her head madly and turns to run. In her haste, she trips over her own feet. I gently grip her elbow to assist. Her pudgy hand pushes me away, and, with a frightened shriek, she disappears into the woods. Watching her run from me, like I'm a wild animal, or worse, makes some part of my chest hurt.

I return to the nuts. That elation inside of me has disappeared. Back in Kirath, I was despised. Loathed. Feared. Hated. But I had people who enjoyed my company. People who loved and knew me. Here, in their eyes, I have become a thorn. Something that can make them bleed.

Over the noise of birds and chattering wildlife, I hear voices. One is sarcastic and cheery, despite the early hours of the morning. The other speaks only in muffled growls and grunts. I grab the basket and duck into the foliage.

Axle is the first to leap down the ledge with swift, smooth strides. Curse his long legs! He readjusts the moon blade on his back and straightens his vest. He has left it open, revealing scars and all.

Shade descends the hill with less swiftness, but with such intent, such slow expertise, my stomach tightens just watching him. He's fast. He's adept. He knows what the hell he's doing. At least, in that aspect, he hasn't changed since three years ago.

His vest is closed.

"What are we doing today?" Axle asks.

Shade shrugs.

"I read eyes, not shoulders, asshole," Axle reminds him.

"Read my eyes then." Shade turns around. He widens his pupils, but they remain masked and empty.

"*Avraga!*" Axle snarls and steps past him.

"*Flagrana vori*," Shade throws back.

"Call me a 'useless poet' one more time and I'll write a beautiful eulogy for you," Axle threatens.

"What you even hope to do with such nonsense is beyond me," Shade mutters. He leans casually against one of the nut trees and picks at one of his fingernails. The trait is so human, so relaxed, my heartbeat slows just a little bit.

"Well, at the very least, I'd like to ensnare a female one of these days," Axle answers. "But you interfere with any plans like that, thank you very much, you ill-bred devil."

Shade's mouth tightens. "If you speak of the other day, then I've nothing to apologize for. What did you hope to gain by sidling up to her anyway?"

Axle rolls his eyes. "Oh, what do you think, you blind fool! A kiss. Maybe a little bit more. Do you realize how many girls don't find me attractive now that I've thrown in my tether with you?"

Shade says nothing, so Axle continues. "Honestly, must you be so frighteningly intense all the time? Lighten up a little. Relax. Enjoy yourself. You're young. You've got vigor, strength, and – I mean this in the most comfortable way possible without sounding awkward – very attractive. So what if you've gone through hell and back? So what if you've been pissed on a couple of times. I have to. You don't see me whining and complaining and feeling sorry for myself. I . . ."

"*Sav gar!*" Shade snaps, and Axle's mouth snaps closed immediately. "If I frighten the sniveling cowards, that's their fault, not mine! And I have never begged for sympathy about what happened to us? Have I? Look at me, Axle! Have I?"

Axle looks sullen and lowers his head. "I didn't mean it like that, Shade. You know that's not what I meant."

Shade's chest heaves with sudden anger. "No! You've been wanting to say that for a long time. I've noticed it. I've felt it. After all we went through together, you still can't understand. Any of it! You just can't. Don't look so apologetic. *I* understand. You have River. You have a beautiful piece of life left."

"So do you," Axle says softly.

Shade laughs but it leaves a bitter taste in my mouth. "Don't lie. I hate that more than anything. If you consider yourself my friend, don't lie. I have these . . ." he gestures to the swords crossed on his back, ". . . and that's it."

"I've never lied to you!" Axle snaps, eyes blazing furiously. "Ever! There *are* people who care about you . . ."

"There are people who pity me!" Shade pushes himself away from the tree and stomps across the clearing in my direction. I pull my knees up under my chin and hope the foliage hides me from view. This is a conversation I am not meant to hear. If he finds me eavesdropping, even on accident, I don't think he'll be as lenient as he has been. "There are people who fear me. There is *no one* who understands me."

"Because you won't let them," Axle argues. Shade glares at him so violently I expect the conversation to end. But Axle looks right back at him. Like he can see through the rough exterior. The mask.

Shade turns his back on his friend and stares at the tree. If he glances downward – even for a moment – he will see me. No foliage could hide the midnight black hair I possess. But he doesn't. Instead he looks up and sighs. Long and slow. He turns back around. His voice is not as rough – not as violent – as before, but traces of his anger still remain. "There's a great difference between you and I, Axle. You know it's true. You've known it since we first met. Since the first time we fought, bled, and made our pact of brotherhood. I don't need anyone. Write a poem about that."

Axle shakes his head sadly. "You're wrong. It will tear you apart. Kill you eventually. Can't you feel it, Shade. You're dying on the inside. You may not die until you're a man with gray hairs on his head, but you'll be dead inside long before then."

Shade's tone changes to mockery. "Seems you're already well on your way with my eulogy."

Axle growls in frustration and reaches for the sword on his back. Shade doesn't blink and rests a hand at his vest – no – on a dagger's hilt! Axle lets go of the sword and exhales a blast of steam into the air.

"Bastard," he mutters.

"*Vori,*" Shade retorts and walks into the trees.

Axle waits until the leaves stop crunching before grabbing a nut from the ground and throwing it at the nearest tree. It's rock-hard shell shatters and bark pieces scatter onto the ground. He swipes his hands through his hair, grasping at the strands, and breathes in through his nose, out through his mouth. His cheeks are very red.

Quietly, I back up into the trees, inch by inch, until I can't see the top of his head. I press the basket against my side, stand up, and start walking into the clearing again.

Axle looks up at my approach and immediately straightens, eyes blinking rapidly to clear away the emotions swirling inside them. "Kyla . . . what are you . . . where were you . . .?" He cuts himself off and stares at me. The muscles near his eyes twitch, like he sees something he doesn't like.

He suspects.

I clear my throat awkwardly and fumble with my tunic. With the belt. My hair. "I . . .uh . . . had to . . . um . . . well, it was more private up there and I . . ."

Axle flushes and looks away too. "Oh. I see."

The silence between us becomes nearly unbearable. I turn away and begin plucking nuts again. My wrist aches. I want to throw them. Practice. Let the steam inside of me escape before I burst.

"I didn't 'thank you.'" Axle's feet stir the leaves on the forest floor as he steps closer to me. "For saving River, I mean."

"There's no need," I say. My body tenses as he stops right behind me. "Anyone would have done such a thing."

His hands rest on my shoulders. "No. They wouldn't have." He turns me around. One of his arms circles my waist and pulls my closer. His hips press against mine and my stomach drops.

He laughs. "Why so pale?"

I look away, but he grips my chin and makes me meet his eyes. They are full of amusement. "Perhaps . . . are you . . .?" He leans closer and our noses brush. I jerk back at the contact. He smiles. "How did you and your husband fare?"

My neck tightens. "He . . . we . . . convenient," I manage to say.

His hand traces my face from chin to ear in such a soft, lazy stroke the blood in my neck burns hot. He plays with a curl of hair near my earlobe. "There's this observation I've noticed about you, darling. It's quite intriguing." His finger feathers my ear. The liberties he's taking remind me of the day I met Aspen in the library.

"You're so innocent," Axle continues. He grips the back of my head, fingers sliding through my hair. He leans close. His breath brushes against my cheek and the heat escaping his mouth warms my lips. "Is it possible you're still a virgin?"

Shit!

He grins like a looting bastard who's just found a piece of treasure. I shove him backwards. There is no wall to stop him like there had been with Aspen. No couch to stop me. We both fall flat on our asses.

I push myself into a sitting position with my arms, biting my lip against the pain in my rear.

Axle laughs. And continues laughing. He barely manages to rise with shaking arms and walk over to me. He offers me a hand, which I take, and pulls me in one swift jerk to my feet. I sway slightly and he grips me around the waist again.

"You sure you aren't lying to me again, Kelban?" he asks.

This time I don't look away like some innocent virgin. I weld our gazes together by sheer will and ball my fists up so tightly that the muscles on my arms tighten too. "If we shared saliva would that dispel your doubts?"

He screws up his face in a pinched expression. "When you say it like that it sounds extremely distasteful."

I pick up the nut-basket and insert it between us. "I've got chores to finish. Unless you *want* River to tan your hide when I tell her that you hindered my duties?"

Axle smirks. "Using the 'sister' play to get rid of a dashing rogue. So clever, darling. So clever." He readjusts his vest, which has been slightly ruffled by his unexpected fall, and pats my shoulder.

"Get," I warn and shrug away from his touch. "Or I'll knock you on your ass again."

He grins slyly. "I really, really like *brash* young women." He swats me on the rear and struts off casually.

I grab one of the nuts from the basket and throw it. It strikes the back of his head with a sharp crack. He yelps and turns around, eyes aflame.

"Such a bad joke is hardly worthy of an intelligent wit like you," I reprimand with a click of my teeth. "Next time come up with a better one or I'll throw it harder!"

He rubs the back of his head and contemplates my words. "You're right. Once my head adjusts to the goose egg blooming on its rear I'll come up with a better joke." He hisses between his teeth when his fingers press the wound a little too hard. "Damn! Nice shot!" He walks off, a little less cocky than before.

I start picking nuts again and ponder their conversation. Shade had mentioned something about what they'd gone through. That everyone pitied him. Feared him. Didn't understand him. What had happened to him and Axle? Did it have something to do with the anger that never left him? The pain and fear he tries to hard to mask?

He doesn't think I see it, but I do. His scars – my scars – they still hurt. They still torment and torture and burn.

He'd been ready to fight Axle. Pull a dagger on him for . . .

Dagger!

The emblem had been partially covered by his hand, but it was red and black. The Celectate's colors.

My dagger. He hadn't given it back.

But he is going to.

River misunderstands my silence for anger about her trickery when I join her for our meal (it took three hours to fill the basket). I assure her it has nothing to do with her at all, but she doesn't believe me.

As we eat in silence I observe the herbs in River's basket. She has neatly piled four different varieties in corners of the basket. One is long and has thin, blade-like leaves similar to grass on its skeleton. Another looks like a weed, if not for the tiny yellow dot right in the center of its spreading arms. The last herb is white and red in color, delicate as a child. A strong breeze could blow it apart.

River places a rag over the top of the basket and calls attention to the sun above us. It's past midday. I follow River back to the gate where we each grab one more basket.

I return to my nuts; River to herb hunting.

I fill the basket quicker this time, tossing nuts here and there. Some miss. Some don't. By the time I'm finished, I'm so exhausted I have to lie down on the ground. In my imagination Shade has a lot of bumps and bruises on him.

Now, finally at rest, I let my thoughts wander. Past these woods. Past the Wilds. It must be near dinnertime. Mother would be ordering the servants about, telling me to stay out of the way. Father would be coming home from his daily bout with the Community leaders, exhausted, but greeting me with a smile. Landor might surprise us with a visit from the barracks, bringing with him a tale that mother would find most "improper", but one that I would question him on later for further details.

My head starts to hurt again. Hidden claws punch the sides of my skull. Rip at the base of my throat. Rotate my stomach. All is white. All is black. All is gray. And then all is nothing. A black dot blasts from that nothing and grows and grows into an endless darkness. It strikes me in the face, snapping my head back. I scream as the deep black shatters into tiny pieces, like shards of a mirror. In each of the fragments, I see movement. Color. Life.

Memories. They are memories. My memories. But not all of them. Others. Not mine. I see blood. I see death. I see a battle in the streets of Kirath. More blood. More death. Screams. Rage. Death again. An endless cycle.

The fragments circle one another but never touch. One of the fragmented memories draws closer to me than all the rest. I feel its tug on my mind. The empty spot it means to fill. As it draws closer I hear sounds. Laughter. Strong wind. A soft melody in the air.

Father, I remember. *Father laughed like that.*

The shard blasts towards me.

And disappears in a flash of white that blinds me.

I fall backwards.

I open my eyes.

I am in the clearing.

"Kyla. Kyla? You okay?" It's River. She quickly scales the slope with ease and sets her basket aside. She kneels down beside me. "Kyla?" She waves a hand in front of my eyes. It's a blur!

"I'm . . . fine." I force myself to stand, knees wobbling beneath me. My neck is so stiff.

"Kyla, you . . ."

"I said 'I'm fine'." The finality in my voice convinces her – I think – because she doesn't say anything as we walk back to the village together.

Inside, I try to find that darkness again. Locate its presence. Its form. But there is nothing.

I push down the wave of nausea that rises in my chest.

What the hell is wrong with me?

~

I get more attention walking back into the village, then I did leaving it. Everyone coming back from the fields, the woods, the hunting, is staring at me – or trying to get a good look. Even groups of children cluster together, hoping to catch the eye of the "cursed girl." A great burden slides off my shoulders when Mama Opal's door slams shut behind me.

"Gossiping fiends!" the elderly woman hisses and returns to the fireplace.

Axle looks up from a strange metal object clutched in his hands. He grins wolfishly and produces a mug of strong-smelling brew in fine flourish. "You're the talk of the town. I'm hearing all about how your tongue slithered ten feet out of your mouth. Or how your eyes glow like black coals in a fire. Or how you speak sorcery." He returns his attention to the device in his hands, which I recognize as a protractor. How on earth did he get one of those here? I decide not to ask.

Shade gives me the cold shoulder and continues cleaning his sword, swiping a damp rag up and down the slim blade. I wish he'd cut his finger or something. My dagger is still tucked at his waist, its Kelban hilt looking foreign at his side.

Mama Opal sets a roasted bird on the table. It looks similar to the colorful bird that Celectate Wood liked to present to his guests on special occasions. He had said it was a rare species. I guess in this wild place they aren't so rare.

River pulls me down beside her again and pours me a mug of Mama Opal's light tea.

"Shade, you should eat," Mama Opal chides, slapping one of the stumps with her chubby palm. "Come."

Shade stands, returning his sword to its sheath on his back.

"Can't," he mutters, strapping leather wrist guards onto his arms. "I have extra guard duty. They've doubled the watch and even made extra lamps. Otis'll kill me if I'm late."

"You mean you'll kill you. You're such a stoic, boring person, Shade. How are you and I friends?" Axle sucks some roasted fat from his finger.

For a moment, the glimmer of something akin to a smile starts to appear on Shade's face. He sees me watching, and it vanishes. He opens the door. "I'll be back . . . late!" He slams it for definition.

"Pure slice of heaven, ain't he?" Axle mutters.

"I . . . I . . ." I don't know what to say about him.

"You'll get used to him. I did. Back when I first met him he did nothing but glare and cuss and hate. But I warmed him up to me. You may have to work extra hard, considering your heritage, but he'll eventually ease up – if your someone who's worth his time." Though the last part was not meant to sound like an insult, it reminds me once more "what" I am.

I don't even know *what* I am.

"Heritage," Mama Opal grumbles and takes a large bite out of her meat. "Just another word for 'family tree'. We actually don't know your heritage, darling. Your ethnicity perhaps, but your heritage . . . Who are you parents, child? We all know you're nobility. Shade certainly seemed to think so."

"Wonder what gave him that idea," Axle mumbles into his cup.

I glare at him before replying, "My father is a High Lord, yes. A member of the Community. But his position – his title – is nothing. Everyone is nothing beneath that one man – the man who believes he's the gods gift to Kelba. The man who would seek to make a graveyard of it, given the chance, just to fulfill his own desires."

"Celectate Wood, I take it?" Axle solemnly nods to himself. "You must hate him very much."

Once upon a time, in Kelba, I would have denied such an accusation.

"Yes, I hate him." My hand tightens on the handkerchief. "I hate him so much that one day, if I get the chance, I might kill him."

Mama Opal changes the subject quickly. "Otis is trying to get you a meeting with the King. He's already sent messengers and a spokesperson to present your case. I'll feel safer when this matter is settled and the King decides to let you stay. Dirk and his lackeys are causing too much trouble. Why, today, in town, at that questionable establishment, they even dared to hint that you're the cause for Agron's misfortune. That the shadows will return again, because you're some kind of witch or supernatural pull that draws them here. It stirs my blood, it does! Honestly, you're a 'child'."

Axle leans forward, eyes dancing with mirth. "And just what were you doing at such a questionable establishment to hear such news, Mama?" He grins.

Mama Opal's face grows red. She sputters anxiously for a few seconds. "I was looking for you, you fool!" She smacks the back of his head with her palm. Axle groans. "You and Shade, always hanging out at that place. I've a good mind to . . ."

My mind wanders from their argument. Shade has my dagger. My only weapon in this place full of self-proclaimed patriots lurking to cut my throat.

"Where does Shade keep watch?"

"I wouldn't go there at this time of night, honey," Mama Opal whispers. She pats my arm. "It's dark and . . ."

"And Dirk's on the loose," Axle chimes in. "Now, if that wolf weren't prowling the area I'd let you go. But under the circumstances . . ."

"I'll be careful."

Axle refused like I knew he would. River gave excuses like I knew she would. And Mama Opal advised speaking to him tomorrow like I knew she would. A good thing they didn't know what I would do.

River went upstairs to get her embroidery, and Mama Opal sent Axle to the cellar for fresher herbs. The moment she turned her back, I slipped out the door, and hurried down the street, wrapping the dark shawl she lent to me around my shoulders.

Though I have no directions, Shade had said he was on guard duty. The only guards I see are the watchmen scattered throughout the city streets and the senitals on the wall. Considering Shade's predatory instincts, I'm certain they would position him somewhere along the wall. Perhaps at the gate itself. So that's where I go.

The square is lit by more than twenty Moon Lamps situated in every corner, every doorway, every spot along the wall that could hide even a trace of shadows. Blood stains still mark the dirt.

There is a stairwell hammered into the wall beside the gates. There is no railing. Just thick, flat boards, two feet wide and four feet long, angled up along the stones. None of the guards in the square notice me as I ascend the first step. The next. And the next.

Shade is the first watchman I find. He stands directly above the iron gates, on the four foot wide plank that serves as a crosswalk, and stares at the wood-line. His back is stiff and straight. I should approach him and get what I came for but, instead, I stare at him. He doesn't blink, his eyes too focused on the clearing and wood-line.

"*There is no one who understands me.*"

I wish he'd give me the chance to try. The chance to ask him questions. I wouldn't need many. Just three or four to know exactly what I wanted to know about him. What makes him angry? Why does it make him angry? What is the vow he speaks of? Where did he get his scar? Such simple questions. But I doubt he'll ever let me ask them.

"When you finally decide to speak, Kelban, I'll be getting off my watch," he says without turning around.

"Kyla," I correct and move forward, feet carefully treading the dark pathway towards him. One wrong move, one misstep, and I'll be an unrecognizable pile of bone and flesh at the base of the wall.

"To hell with the name," he mutters. "I thought I told you to stay away from me. Get back to the house and stay there before someone sees you. I'm in enough trouble."

I place a foot on the plank he guards and step onto it, grasping the wall so tightly that my fingers sting. The air spins around my head, but I steady my legs and it fans out again. I shuffle towards him.

"Go back," he mutters. "If you fall it's not going to be my fault, understand?"

I leave a foot of space between us and hold out my hand. "I came for my dagger."

He turns to look at me. "Oh?" The amusement disappears from his face. "Alright, girl, why don't I just do that and have them bury my ass while I'm at it?"

"They don't have to know," I insist.

"Doesn't mean they wouldn't." He leans against the wall and crosses his arms. "What assurances can you give me that they wouldn't know about your concealed weapon? I let you keep it before and you nearly got yourself killed. In my opinion, you're a lot safer without it."

I look him straight in the eye. "You don't really believe that."

"I do." He turns his gaze towards the wood-line.

"No, you don't." His shoulders tighten as I draw closer, but I don't touch him. I fold my hands gently atop the wall and gaze towards the wood-line. "What are you looking at? I don't see anything."

"And you won't see anything, girl, unless you're looking," he says. His hand fondles the hilt of my dagger at his waist.

"What are you looking at?" I repeat.

His lips quirk. "I watched the shadow of a squirrel jump from tree to tree so it could return to its nest. I watched a wind blow several leaves onto the ground. I watched a rabbit dodge into its burrow as a predator passed its home. I can see no better than you in the darkness. But I was looking for them, so I saw them. If you're looking for something – even in the darkness – you will find it eventually."

I shake my head. "What I'm looking for can't be found like that."

He cocks his head at me in that animal way, only it no longer sends shivers down my spine. "And what are you looking for?"

"A home," I answer honestly. "Where I belong. Where all of me belongs. Scars and all. Secrets and all. Kelban and all." I touch the ostracized scar beneath my sleeve, and his eyes flutter there. "I think that, maybe, it is here. If I am given the proper chance, this place can become my home. I'm not meant to die. The *siratha* would have claimed me if that were my purpose. So why am I still alive?"

"Don't ask me," Shade says. "I would have killed you, Kel – Kyla, if you hadn't shown an amazing amount of ingenuity that your kind severely lacks."

"'*Your kind*,'" I repeat. "'Your kind.' You seem to have a ton of shit about my 'kind' but what do you really know about them? Do you know the families that exist among my 'kind?' Do you know the sacrifices they make? The blood they spill? The lives that are taken? Who are you to tell me what they lack?"

He sneers, teeth showing. "I know enough about your kind. I have been over that pathetic pile of rubble you call a 'wall.' I have seen your city. I have seen your ruler. I have seen your pathetic common-folk and your pathetic nobility and your pathetic Community. I have seen your pathetic world, Kelban."

I feign shock at his revelation. "You've . . . been over the wall?"

He smacks a finger against his forehead. "Hell, yeah, I've been over your wall. Do you think such a poorly guarded contraption could keep us out forever? Do you think stones and mortar could scare a man of flesh and blood?"

"Fine," I snap. "So you've been over the wall. So you've seen us and we've amused you. Why come over the wall at all?"

"Don't flatter yourself, Kelban. My visits into your precious homeland had nothing to do with such boorish skeletons. And you should thank me, little girl. I keep the darkness in this land far away from your bedside. You've no idea what I've tracked into that land. How easily you would fall into savagery like we have. You should be thanking me for the nightmares I've saved you from."

I already had. He just doesn't remember.

But it explains why he'd been in Kirath that night. He was tracking those monsters. If those three came across the wall, how many others were entering Kelba?

"Why worry about it? If you hate us so much, why not turn your back like everyone else in this gods-forsaken country has done and let it be. Let us kill each other. Let the darkness take us." I say the words casually, but they burn coming out of my mouth.

"Because, if the darkness takes Kelba, where do you think it will turn to next?" Shade asks. He doesn't wait for my answer. "Despite my dislike of Kelba, they are a good diversion."

"And where does that leave you?" I ask.

"Pardon?"

"The villagers," I whisper. "I've seen the way they look at you. They don't seem to like you very much."

They loathe him. Despise him. I see it in their faces whenever they glance his way. Whenever he has his back turned. And behind the disgust and loathing is a stronger emotion – fear. They are frightened of him. And, frankly, I can't blame them.

"No one likes me," he says casually.

"Why?"

"Because I can do what they can't."

"And what's that?"

He looks up. "Survive."

Somehow, by the way he stares at me, the way his eyes roam my face, my shoulder, I've a feeling he's not just talking about himself.

He pulls the dagger from his waistband and stares at the hilt. At the red and black of the Celectate. He stretches it out towards me, flipping it in his hand so the hilt faces me. "Take it," he says.

I grasp the hilt and flip the weapon a couple times in my own hand. He watches me. I lift my skirt and slide the dagger into the sheath around my leg. He raises a brow at me.

"Where did you learn to do that?" he asks.

Landor's face enters my mind. His arm guiding mine. His cocky grin as he flipped his dagger over and over like a juggler at a festival. His laughter when I constantly dropped the damned thing on the ground. His worry whenever the blade landed in my hand instead of the hilt and my blood stained the ground.

This time I see the white flash coming at my face. But I cannot stop it from cracking against the front of my skull like a battering ram. I cannot stop the shock wave that ripples through me like waves in a storm. I cannot stop the deep blackness that circles towards me and pulls me into its embrace.

I am going somewhere again. There is air around me. Swirls of gray and black. A white light ahead. I fly into that white light and it floods my body in such chilling cold that my eyes flutter open.

I am in the streets of Kirath, in a dirty, rat-infested alley, watching a throng of people pass in the street beside me. I am not alone. A caped figure is to my right, a gray cloak and hood shielding their features from view. The figure is bent down behind a dilapidated box like a beggar, their hand extended on one knee. Rising. Tapping impatiently.

Another dark figure rushes into the alley with casual, albeit hurried, steps and kicks a rat against the far wall with disgusted growl. I recognize that voice. Beneath the cape the newcomer is wearing I can see a firm jaw and thin lips. It's Landor.

I say his name but – like all the other times I've entered these visions – he doesn't hear me.

"What have you found?" he asks the caped figure slumped against the wall.

"Coin, good sir?" the bent form – a man with a gravelly voice – asks and raises his hand. "Coin for my troubles."

Landor grumbles a curse under his breath and produces a pouch that clinks with the sound of money. He drops it into the expectant man's hand.

"There's another group on the streets now," the beggar says in a smooth, amused voice. "One that they call the 'Vale of Death.' This group's got a leader too. A fine, young upstart just a few years shy of your age, good sir, if I'm judging your years correctly in our brief visits. She's a fighter but, more accurately, she's a bitch."

"The leader's a female?" Landor doesn't hide the shock in his voice.

"Aye. A female, sir. She stormed the southern wall last week in that skirmish that took a dozen Celect Knights and four of the rebels. Made off with a vast supply of weapons and some new followers. Apparently, the new followers made her their leader and she's done quite well for herself."

"What's her name?"

"They call her the 'Bitch of Braggard.' But she's also called 'the Vale' and, occasionally, the 'Bitch of the Vale.' Makes her sound like bad shit, don't it?"

Landor steps closer. "Where can I find her?"

"You can't."

"I beg your pardon?"

"You can't find her. No one can. No once knows her real identity. Her real face. Even her favo rite hideouts. She's a ghost. That's why they call her 'the Vale.' Because you can only find her if you're seeking death."

"But you say you know she's young. How is that unless you've met her, old man?"

The beggar laughs. "I assume she's young, little pisser, because the rumors say she is. But you're right. I shouldn't assume. She could be a slagging crone for all I know. Sorry for giving false information."

Landor growls and the beggar edges back against the wall.

"Find out more," Landor says. "Anything you can. Anything of importance. Anything you don't think could be important. I want to know everything."

"That's going to cost you, sir," the beggar remarks slyly.

"I've got plenty of coin." Landor turns on his heel and stomps into the streets.

I walk after him. People surround me. I walk through them like I'm a ghost. Landor shoves a merchant attempting to stop him beneath his purple canopied booth and dodges a passel of alley brats playing marbles. His footsteps have changed. He is more precise. More certain.

Deadlier.

I don't like it.

He reaches the fenced stables belonging to the finest inn in all of Kirath, meant for the richest merchants and well-known ship captains. Another caped figure leans casually on the rails surrounding the giant stone dome which can shelter a hundred and twenty horses. Though the thick, dark cloak hides his features, his hands are huge. He is a giant.

Landor approaches the pump behind him and flushes some of the water into his hands.

"I hear you've been looking for us, young noble," the giant whispers.

Landor's hands stop moving, but he doesn't turn around. He knows better. "That depends. Why would I be looking for a man who sounds so fearsome?"

"I've asked myself the same question," the giant agrees. "That's why

I've had my own men watching you. You're a hard one to find, despite your reputation as a Celect Knight and a High Lord's only son. The sword of the Celectate. The brother of a traitor. The stories are unending"

Landor's hands tighten. "Traitor, eh?"

"Careful, lad," the man whispers. "You've a fire. But without kindling it quickly disappears. The best of you learn to stoke that fire. For the cause. For their lives. For their dreams."

"I don't have any of those," Landor hisses.

The giant chuckles. "Of course not." He turns around and leans over the trough with my brother. They don't look at each other. "Why would you? You're a man of the sword. A man of blood and Bone. You don't need your fire stoked. You need your fire fanned. But the ones in the forest you wish to destroy beneath all those flames are not easy prey. They have wings. You need to clip the wings so they can't escape. Then you can set them on fire. You can watch them burn. But only if you know how to play their game first."

"I don't want to play their game!" Landor snaps.

"Do any of us want to play the game?" The man's hands fold tightly. "Nay. I would burn the game, too, if it didn't work. But it does."

"I will not be a pawn for him to move around at his leisure."

"Pawns are funny pieces," the man remarks. "They are small and insignificant and easily discarded. But if they play the game right, if they use other pieces as a shield, if they outlast all the other players, they become a queen. Of course, that part goes largely unnoticed. Unless you're an avid chess player like myself."

Landor stares at the water in the trough, silently.

"You are not meant to be a pawn, Landor Bone. Your sister was not meant to be a pawn. But you are different pieces in this game. Just as I am." He leans towards Landor's ear. "Break hell's chains," he whispers. He steps back and begins to walk away.

"Lothalar leran de revelan." Landor doesn't look up from the water. His words are slow. Like he's saying them for the first time and is stunned by their meaning. Their power.

"Lothalar leran de revelan," he repeats, firmer this time. Stronger.

The giant nods. "Lothalar leran de revelan," he chimes in. "Do you know the star?"

The star?

"I do," Landor says.

The giant says nothing and walks off down the street. Landor doesn't turn around once to see him. He closes his eyes and listens. I know he's remembering the man's footsteps. Pondering his gait. His weaknesses. His smell. His presence. Everything that a man needs to stay alive in case of an assailant.

"Here you are." Craig steps out of the stables. Landor calmly washes the dirt from his hands. "Any luck?"

"Nothing much," Landor says. "Another band with another leader whose got something to prove."

Craig chuckles between his teeth. "This rebellion is full of condescending little pricks with ideas about glory and riches. Perhaps, when the Celectate gives me a golden sword, I can fulfill their wishes for a taste of wealth before their deaths, the poor bastards."

Landor leans back against the fence. "That's a beautiful plan. But this new leader has no prick."

Craig swivels in a fast half-circle to face his comrade. "A woman? They made a woman leader? They are foolish bastards!"

"Yes. Fools," Landor sighs. "I've made my report, sir. May I wash up and return to my rooms until you've further use of me, captain?"

Captain? Craig has been made a captain? It had always been an ongoing joke between the four of us that Asher would have better luck getting married in the next decade than Craig had of moving up in the ranks of Celect Knights.

Craig nods and gestures wildly with his hand. "Yes. Go. Go and rest well." He laughs again and slaps his knee in amusement. "A woman? Shit, that was a waste of two weeks."

A flash of darkness glides over Landor's face. He swivels back around. "Captain." Craig looks up. "She has a name."

Craig waits patiently.

"They call her 'the Bitch of the Vale,'" Landor says. "My informant told me that no one's seen her unless they saw death next."

Craig's lips curl up in amusement. "Well, perhaps I'll give the bitch a new name. She can be bitch of the Celectate's prison before her execution, for all I care. Hell, she could be my bitch. Will capturing this whore be worthwhile?"

Landor shrugs. "You're the captain. I'll follow your orders." He turns towards the stables again.

"Lan, wait." Craig is quick to drop the formality between them. "I was thinking drinks would be nice at the old place. We haven't been there since that last time when we . . ." He doesn't finish. "Anyway, we've so much to talk about, after my promotion and all. I really want to set things straight between us. Asher agreed to come if you would."

"That sounds nice, captain," Landor replies, "but I'm eating dinner with my family tonight. Lady Bone's preparing the meal herself."

"Oh." Craig looks crestfallen. "Some other time then, perhaps?"

"Perhaps." Landor shuts the stable doors behind him and leans heavily against one of the stable poles.

The image begins to curl in on itself. I grab at the wood. A nearby horse. A saddle on the wall. They slip through my fingers as I'm pulled black into nothing by an unseen hand.

"Whoa!" Shade's arms latch around my waist as I careen backwards. My neck snaps with the strain. A vein throbs at his temple as he attempts to keep me upright. He pulls me closer, away from the edge of the plank, and my chest burns from the heat radiating from his body. "What the . . .?"

Vaguely aware of the faint aroma of smoke and trees that plays so heavily with my senses, I grab his shoulders and straighten myself. We fumble together awkwardly while we rearrange our positions, but he doesn't take his arms away from me.

"I'm . . . I'm alright," I whisper.

He presses the back of his hand to my forehead and frowns. "You're very warm. Go back to the house. Mama Opal has medicine that can cure anything from headaches to worms in your stomach. You could have some nasty side effects from that wound." He gestures at my arm.

"I thought you said it was only a shadow blade?" I ask, tilting my eyebrows. "Nothing to worry about."

"I meant what I said," he insists and lets go of me. "But every wound has a side effect. My first wound gave me chills for three nights. My second gave me a fever for four. My third . . . Well, the list is unending." He shoves me towards the plank stairs, but not roughly.

I don't argue with him and descend the steps. I feel very dizzy and spots swim in the corners of my vision like blinking lights. The vision had been so strong – so enticing – my eyes feel heavy.

I stop beneath the crosswalk and glance up. Shade's head and the top of his shoulders are the only visible features of his body.

"Hey!" I call up.

He turns around and looks down.

I hold up the dagger. "Thank you."

I don't wait for a reply and walk into the streets.

Chapter XVIII

River and I are up with the sun the next day and in the forest with a dozen other women from the village hunting for matured herbs. The dew has not dried and my clothes are damp in moments. I thank River for reminding me to bring a shawl. It keeps the droplets that fall from the burdened trees off of my skin, and covers the frightful symbol on my shoulder that looks more horrifying than it ever did while it was healing. Permanent black marks etched deep into my skin that I trace every so often with tender care.

Ugly. Unwanted. Unloved.

I shake away the words but, alone, among the gnarled trees, they pursue their malicious intentions with fierce accuracy.

Ugly.

Blood running down my back, my arm, my face, as I stood on that podium.

Unwanted.

Aspen telling me to go to hell. Craig wishing me into nothing.

Unloved.

Everyone I love watching my pain – watching – but never coming to my aid.

I feel that chasm in my chest widen. Feel the chilling cold rushing over my spine. The pulse that radiates from my neck to my fingertips in warm tingles of flame and sparks. The pulse lingers over my palm, becoming heavy. Heavier. Until . . .

"Kyla!" River's cheery voice breaks into my thoughts. "I've filled my basket. Are you ready?"

"Coming." I join her at the edge of the grove.

We walk in silence.

River had made no comment when I'd returned to the house at half past midnight and crawled into bed. And I didn't believe for one moment that the snores Mama Opal and Axle produced upon my entrance through the unbarred door were genuine. They knew where I had gone. They knew what I had retrieved.

And now they were curious *how* I retrieved it.

The gates are bustling with activity as usual, but when River halts abruptly, I do the same. Horses – no, not horses – donkeys, are lined up along the wall. Children run between them with overflowing water buckets and feed. I do not remember seeing any creatures of burden within Agron's walls.

We have visitors.

River is pale.

Panic spreads wings in my chest. "What?"

"How did they come here?" River musses to herself. Despite the fear, there is a hint of annoyance, a barely perceptible drop of anger, in her words. "We sent no invitation." She steadies the wicker basket on her hip.

I move towards the gates. A massive warrior leans casually against one of them. I have never seen him before and his attire is not reminiscent of Agron's standards. His chest is bare save for the leather straps crossing his abs in an X formation. A fearsome, double-edged sword rests atop his back, but despite its thick edges, it lacks the unwavering strength of Shade's moon blades. The warrior also has a long beard braided beneath his chin that falls nearly to his waistband in a deep black coil. Three black rings circle his eyes and give him the appearance of a monster.

"Kyla . . ." River warns me from behind, but I step into the square.

Otis stands there, facing a group of more six-packed imposters. None of them are shorter than six foot four except a single man planted between the warriors and Otis. He is my height and a red cape does nothing to hide the bony shoulders he possesses. There is not a single hair upon his head or face. Not even eyebrows. All over the smooth skin of his skull, the curve of his neck, black tattoos bedeck his flesh. There are tattoos of birds. Strange creatures. Symbols. Phrases. Men.

The hideous man turns beady eyes in my direction. I stare in horror at his marked face. His thin lips stretch into a pleased smile. "Ah. This is she."

I plant myself at Otis's side.

The man's gaze is hawkish. "I am one of the Unnamed. I have heard of your foreign newcomer. Of the darkness that haunts your abode because of her presence. I have come to clarify whether she be demonic or not."

So he's a priest. A shaman. Inside, I'd already known it before the words left his mouth. No sane person pierced every inch of bare skin and stalked into a city with a brutally armed force of hounds at his back.

"I did not summon you," Otis says. Though his face is stern, the twitch at the corner of his eyes is unmistakable. He's nervous.

"No," the priest agrees. "Why would you? A proud, arrogant, unschooled fool like yourself wouldn't know the wiles of darkness. Demons are quite famous for their deceptive antiques – especially those of the female variety."

Otis hadn't sent for the priest. I search the crowd. Dirk is not hard to spot. He stands closest to the burly warriors, a pleased expression on his face. Beside him, Keegan tilts his chin towards me. A silent message. I knew it was suspicious when Keegan did not seek me out over the last few days to torment me. He's the one who fetched the scarred holy man.

"I am fatigued from the vicious journey so do not test my patience," the priest continues. "I would appreciate a private conference with the accused in question."

"You do not decide her fate!" Otis interjects angrily. "The King is the hierarchy here, *raavgrar*, not you!"

The priest spreads his hands innocently, revealing a bony, equally tattooed chest. "We will not determine her fate. Merely her true origins." He clicks his tongue against the roof of his mouth and one of the massive warriors curls fingers around my elbow. He jerks me in the direction of the council house.

"This is blasphemy," Otis protests. "You have no authority here, *raavgrar*!"

"Silence that man!" the priest says calmly.

One of the warriors rams the hilt of his sword into Otis's skull. River screams. People whisper but make no attempt to come to his aid. A pang of understanding tightens in my chest. I know exactly what that feels like.

The council house looks smaller than it did on my first occasion within its walls, but perhaps it is the massive warriors that struggle to line its walls without knocking their heads against the low supporting beams that make its interior so primitive. The doors close behind me and the priest brushes past, his red cape snagging my wrist for a brief moment. I don't think it was accidental.

The priest lights the fire with a flick of his hand. I know he intends for me to be frightened by such a bold action, but I see the object in his hand. It's a sliver of common orb but it radiates enough power to create flames when struck against iron. The rims around the firewood are made of iron.

"Do you know why you are here, outsider?" he asks in my language. The tattoos on his head distract me from his facial features.

"No," I lie.

"Do you know why we are here?"

"No."

The priest smiles, the tattoos on his cheeks forming strange oval shapes. "We are the connection between light and dark – the Unnamed. We root out the evil and death that seeks to take hold of this land. The poison. The darkness. The devils. We have purged doom from this earth for over a century – a feat that has earned us respect and acknowledgment."

"And yet Otis hardly seemed compliant to your arrival."

The priest doesn't flinch at my words. "Otis is a simpleton. A man of figures and sums and morale and laws. But he fails to understand the fears of the people. Fails to understand the dire sacrifices we must make in order to continue our existence on this brutal path of life. He is blinded by logic. He does not see the demons and the evil that weave through the cracks of this ravaged country."

"And you do?" I try to focus on the rimmed pupils hiding within the inked patterns of his face.

"We do more than see them," he says. The tattoos curl as he flashes what I think is a smirk. "We smell them. Hunt them. You see, Kelban, you are immune to the catastrophes that befell this country when you built that hardened mass of stone to forget our existence. But we – those who endured the betrayal, the abandonment, the banishment – did not forget. We remember every life lost. Every darkened being that crept out of the night and robbed an innocent soul. Every drop of blood that hit the silent ground – unheard, unmourned, unknown. We have lost much, Kelban, while you sat behind that wall and called us 'cannibals' to ease your guilty consciences. And when your own country deems you unfit for their walls they presume we're already 'monsters' so why not send their criminals to our territory for justification? Why not put more blood on our hands? Your kind is selfish, Kelban. Selfish. Destructive. It is why the darkness is attracted to you. Wants you."

I struggle to control the rapid increase of my heartbeat. To focus on the true meaning behind his solemn words. Anyone who had not suffered a loss would think he was simply passionate about his beliefs. But I know better. I have seen passion, and I have seen revenge. I have seen belief, and I have seen obsession.

"What was their name?"

The priest's tattoos shift downwards. "What?"

"Their name," I repeat. "Wife? Daughter? Parent? Perhaps a loved one not bound to you by blood. Close friend? What darkened being crept out of the night and robbed you? Whose blood hit the ground that you heard and mourned and knew?"

The priest's calm demeanor shatters. "You . . ." His facial features quiver. Rage. "You have no right. No right!"

"You call yourself 'unnamed' but I guarantee you had a name once."

"Enough!"

"What are you really here for?" I dare a step towards him, struggling to control the building weight in my gut. "You don't give a damn about the people of Agron. About their welfare. Their souls. And you certainly do not command the respect and acknowledgment you've laid claim to. What have you come for?"

His tattoos spread out again and curve upwards. A smile. That heavy feeling in my gut doubles in intensity. He steps closer and his fingers brush my arm. It is a gentle touch, but the scrape of his nail stabs deeper than skin. Like a knife poised on the point of attack. Like the slow hiss of a viper before it strikes.

He leans close – close enough for me to see his eyes. He wears no mask to hide the emotions swirling inside of them. "We have been summoned to determine whether your soul has been compromised," he says into my ear, "but I . . ." His fingers disappear inside his cloak. "Have come for blood."

The black blade he retrieve shivers with undefined evil.

The shadow blade.

Two massive warriors grab me by the arms before I've the chance to retreat and drag me before the fire. I stare at the flames licking up into the darkness, their sparks snapping wildly, and struggle to free myself.

"We only need to see your blood. Any demon's blood is a fluid, white color. Only your blood," the priest whispers, running his finger along the edge of the blade. It hisses beneath his touch like a living creature.

"You're not bringing that thing near me!" I protest.

He smiles again.

"You're assassins, not holy men!" I lash out at the warriors' ankles but they are too quick. One immobilizes my neck with a firm grip. My muscles weaken. My throat constricts. I can't scream. I can't speak. I can't even whimper.

The priest brushes a strand of hair from my forehead. Smooths it over my ear. His nail scrapes along my lobe with delicate intention. My eyes water at the touch. The closeness. The stench of his hand.

He smells like decades of filth. He traces the vein throbbing at my neck to the wing of my collarbone.

"We are not assassins," he whispers and feathers rough fingers over my throat. He cups the side of my neck and hardens his grip. The delicate bones beneath my fragile skin protest in painful cries. My mouth is open, but I'm unable to scream.

"I am the Unnamed. We protect the blood of this land – and avenge it when necessary. You have poisoned this village." He palms the dagger in his hand. One of the warriors extends my arm over the fire. The flames warm my fingers.

"We are doing you a favor, Kelban. You do not belong here among the righteous, and a much more agonizing fate will await you should we allow you to continue your existence in this place. You are alone, *ostracized*." His eyes flicker over the branded symbol. "The ground will be your home. That has always been your fate."

He finds a vein throbbing at my arm and tightens his grip on the dagger. One cut – the poison will enter me – I will die.

The sparks snap around my fingers.

You do not govern me.

Heat gathers in my palm.

They *do not govern me.*

Pressure builds at the front of my skull, but for once, I don't try to fight it. The warm tingling that vibrates from my neck to the tips of my fingers flows like a river of certainty.

The sparks snap from the fire in a great burst of orange light.

One of the warriors steps back.

You do not belong here . . .

The flames flutter higher into the air, mere inches from my hand, but they don't burn me.

You are alone . . .

The pressure at my temple thumps madly. There are three pulses. One in my head. One in my neck. One in my hand. They beat as one. Call to each other. Grow closer. I feel their ends tie together. The pulse becomes one. The weight in my hand hardens.

The flames flutter with my pulse like a second heartbeat.

The priest's hand stills on the vein of my arm, and his eyes widen. Among the tattoos, his skin pales. The shadow blade stops above my skin. The deadly darkness that clings to its blade brushes the hairs on my arm. I feel its caress. Its soft, but evil presence. My skin warms beneath the touch.

The warriors' hands tighten. Bruise my skin. Hold me captive.

I am not their slave. They do not decide whether I've the right to live or die. They have no right to treat me like this. They have no right to put their hands on me. They have no right to speak to me of my fate. They have no damned idea what the hell I've gone through!

I am not a vagabond.

I am not trash.

The fire sparks. The embers beneath the flames begin to jump. Dance. Swirl.

The weight in my palm tightens above the heat. Beckons it. Commands it. The flames surge up towards my balled fist. I close my eyes. I can see the fire.

No! I do more than see it. I sense it. Control it. I open my eyes.

I am the fire.

I open my hand.

The flaming embers explode from the iron ring and strike the warriors with an assault of sparks and flames. Screams fill the air. Fire licks at the edges of their clothing. A warrior's cloak bursts into orange tongues of fury. The flames spread to their skin. The screams echo off the ceiling as the muscled giants dash around madly in an attempt to deliver themselves from the fiery monster that clings to their flesh.

The flames strike at the priest. He screams too. Backs away. Runs for the doors, but his bodyguards are in the way. He drops the shadow blade.

The fire molds itself to the darkness on the dagger.

My chest tightens.

The flames lick at the black, trembling sheet that clings to the demonic blade.

The muscles in my chest clench. Air leaves my lungs. I fall to my knees.

The sheet on the blade begins to shrivel up. Its ends curl over and over like claws retracting into a cat's paw. A hiss screams from its retreating form. My heart skips a beat. Then another. *Another.* I gasp for air, but there is none.

The heavy weight in my palm is like a mountain now. Crushing me. Killing me. The pressure in my skull is growing. Threatening to explode from my head. To overpower me. I hear the bones inside my skull bending with tension.

The flames reach the hilt of the blade – the last of the darkness.

The grip on my lungs retracts. I suck in a sharp breath. The weight in my palm is gone.

Smoke curls off of the shadow blade. It is no longer swimming with the presence of a ghastly evil. It looks like a normal weapon, and its surface is a beautiful, black, crystal color.

The pulse in my skull spreads fingers into the corners of my mind. I feel its gentle touch against the soft strands of control I attempt to cling to. The strands begin to rip apart.

Behind me, the door crashes open.

The smoke in the room clears as a breeze brushes it away.

"Get the hell out of here!" a calm voice whispers.

Shade.

A hand touches my shoulder. His hand. He leans down by me. His moon blade clatters to the ground.

"Kyla . . ." he whispers.

The last strand snaps.

The council room disappears. I am floating in darkness.

There is a light ahead of me. I flutter towards it. The light is reminiscent of a glass wall. From behind it, I hear things. Screams. Blades. I try to drag myself back but there is nothing to grab. The connection between the wall and myself collides in a blinding white flash.

I open my eyes.

I am in Kirath. In streets I don't recognize. People run madly around me. They run through me as if I don't exist. They trip over one another. Fall to the ground. Are trampled beneath maddened feet. Through the chaotic crowd, I catch blurs of red and black emblems. Flashes of steel. Screams of pain.

Celect Knights.

Blood seeps between the cobblestones. Pools around stagnant bodies stretched across their surface. Lifeless eyes stare up at me. My stomach clenches.

Ahead of me, the noise is deafening. The screams of pain are replaced by battle cries. The clang of weapon on weapon. The fight of death against survival.

I move like a ghost through the mob.

The bloody street opens up into the City Square. I recognize the podium upon which Lord Telman was so cruelly mistreated. A hangman's scaffold bedecks its surface now. Five bodies dangle from thick ropes. Their ankles are swollen and their eyes bulge at the sockets.

One of the faces is familiar. Though the skin has become swollen and bloated and the eyes unbecoming, it is the youngest High Lord of the Community – Lord Brand. And carved into the middle of his forehead, with blood-soaked lines, rests the ostracized symbol.

The four remaining bodies are his family!

He was one of the High Lords who must have voted for my release.

Celectate Wood found him.

Celect Knights crowd the City Square, weapons drawn, and armor covered in blood. But the common-folk are not running in this place. They, too, have weapons. And they, too, are fighting.

A Celect Knight screams in pain as a man drives a six-inch bolt through the armor covering his neck with a common hammer. He falls to the ground, blood spurting like a fountain from his wound. The man grabs his sword. Raises it above his head. Hacks the blade against the Celect Knight's neck again and again. I turn my eyes away, but the Celect Knight's head rolls in front of my gaze.

Not Landor's. Not Landor's.

The Celect Knights surround the podium, spears elongated.

The people want their High Lord returned.

A familiar face appears among the thousands of tanned, angry common-folk. It has grown thinner, the cheekbones are more pronounced, and the jaw is sharper. But the eyes are the same. Sharp. Fiery. Dark.

Daria.

Her tunic is torn. Her torso splattered with dark red blood. Her eyes are directed over my shoulder. Past dozens of fearsome Celect Knights. She screams a name over the roar of the chaos, but I only see her lips moving. I see the desperation on her face. The fear in her eyes. I hadn't believed a calm, collected person like her was capable of such emotions.

She screams the name again. Raises her sword. Hacks a canyon across the chest of the Celect Knight who blocks her path. Dashes through the fray like a rabbit among wolves. A sword misses her shoulder by a hairsbreadth. An enemy's dagger slices downwards. She grabs the Celect Knight's arm and twists him sideways. The unexpected action lands him on his back. She uses his own dagger to puncture his heart and doesn't spare him a glance.

She continues her mad rush towards me, always looking over my shoulder. Always screaming that name. She kicks a Celect Knight hard in the groin when he blocks her approach. He falls at my feet. His blood splatters the ground when she cuts him across the belly. She runs past me, screaming that name again, never seeing me, as no one sees me in these nightmares.

I hear the name.

"HELENA!"

I turn around.

Just in time to watch a Celect Knight slide his blade across the girl's fragile neck. Sweet, blonde, innocent Helena falls to the ground, eyes wide in fright, and lips trembling. She grows still.

Daria pauses. Her back muscles tighten. The sword lowers in her hand. She stares at the body. At the chasm gushing blood in her friend's throat. At the red pool that forms around Helena's head. At the blond curls that turn copper against the gray stones of the street.

The murderous Celect Knight moves towards Daria, and punches her across the face with a steel-covered hand. The force of the blow twists her around and she falls flat on her stomach, face angled towards me. A red blotch, marred with little red gashes from his iron knuckles, imprints the side of her cheek. He leans over her and places a hand on the back of her thigh.

For a moment those fiery eyes flash with fear. Her lips tremble. Her skin pales.

His hand shifts upwards, beneath her skirts.

That fear explodes into rage.

Her ankles lock around his throat. She flips him on his back. Before he can stand, she turns around and rams the pommel of her sword into his nose. His head snaps back, and she allows him to fall on his backside again. She straddles him, her knees pinning his hands to the ground. She punches him. Bone shatters. He screams. She pulls a thin blade from her side. It is ten inches long and half an inch thick. She pries open his mouth. He groans helplessly as blood from his decimated nose flows between his lips. It chokes him.

"Ve das inasanas!" she screams. **She was innocent.** *She hovers the blade over his open mouth. I watch, horrified, but unable to look away. She rocks onto her knees and the bones of his wrists shatter beneath her weight. He screams again, blood bubbling out of his mouth. It stains the tip of the blade as she lowers it downwards.*

"Ve das gard." **She was good.** *The tip disappears inside his mouth. Halts as it connects with bone. She twists it sideways and something pops. The man's eyes bulge from his sockets and he screams. It sounds like a noise someone would make underwater. He's drowning in his own blood.*

"Ve das mi vrenar!" **She was my friend.** *She twists the blade one more time. I hear the tip connect with the cobblestones as it shatters through the back of his neck. He screams again. She stands up above him. Blood bubbles out of his mouth and his eyes grow blood-clotted. The slim hilt protrudes from his mouth and he struggles to move his hands and pull it out, but they remain at his sides, broken.*

Daria smiles at him, and that smile turns my blood cold. "Lothalar leran de revelan, you bastard!"

She walks past him and falls beside Helena's body. Gently, she places the girl's head in her lap and strokes fingers along the yellow, blood-soaked hair. Helena stirs.

"Helena . . ." Daria whispers, her voice low and deep. Heavy with the weight of tears that pour from her eyes. "Helena . . ."

Helena grips her friend's hand and places it over her belly.

Daria's eyes widen as her fingers splay across the barely perceptible rise of her friend's abdomen.

Helena smiles distantly. "You w-were right. I shouldn't . . . h-have been scared . . . to fight!"

Daria freezes.

Helena forces something into her hand. Slowly, her own hand drops away. Her head sags to the side. Her eyes become empty.

Daria stares in shock. Grips her friend's head gently. Says her name softly. Then louder. Until it's a scream. But Helena doesn't get up.

Daria gently lays her friend back on the ground. She stares at the object Helena gifted her with. It's a carved, wooden symbol. At first glance, it looks like the ostracized symbol, but some of the edges have been cut away.

It forms a star.

Daria closes her fingers around it and stands. She looks towards the podium. At the bodies that dangle from its scaffold. She raises her weapon and cries out in rage. From around the square, heads turn to locate her, common-folk and Celect Knight alike. She dashes towards the podium.

Two men grab her arms before she gets a few steps and drag her back towards the streets. She screams and kicks against them, but they don't let go.

The square empties as the mob draws back, leaving the Celect Knights bloodied and shocked. Leaving the five examples to rot in the sun as a reminder to them in the future. Leaving the fragile, innocent girl and her unborn child to the roasting cobblestones and the absence of a proper burial.

Slowly the darkness surrounds me. Sucks me back into the abyss of nothing. The weight in my head grows larger and larger and larger until . . .

It explodes. I explode.

I open my eyes.

"Kyla!" Shade forces me to stand and look at him. There is blood on his chin. Blood on his hands. Blood on the moon sword at his feet. He takes one look at my face and turns around. He retrieves his blade.

The priest has time for a startled cry before Shade presses the silver tip to the Adam's apple bobbing at his tattooed throat. "Stand up . . . slowly!" Shade commands. The priest does. "Now step – backwards – through that door or you'll get the point of this . . ." he nicks the man's skin and a drop of blood glides downward, ". . . through your neck."

The priest does as he's told. His warriors follow. Their skin is blackened and ugly, red welts dot their flesh where the fire burned them. Their eyes are downcast, and they don't even look at the slightly smaller warrior commanding their every movement.

Outside, Otis blocks their exit. His men – now suddenly eager to obey his command – aim weapons of all entities at the unwanted guests.

"You will leave us now, *raavgar*," Otis says, "and if I catch even a whiff of you around Agron again I will personally escort you to the King's threshold and delight in removing your head from those ancient shoulders."

"Why not kill the arrogant son of a bitch right now?" Shade steps forward and the Unnamed backs up, eyes widening in fright. The blade cuts his neck.

Otis raises a hand. "Retreat."

Shade looks at him. "The bastard marched in here and deemed it his personal duty to take the life of an outsider under the King's jurisdiction. As I see it, that's direct defiance against his highness. Against the law. And 'defiance of the law' is a paraphrase of a very simple word. Treason! How do we punish treason?" He scans the faces of the crowd until he finds just who he's looking for. "Ah, Dirk. You've been very helpful in educating me on the subject. Would you care to provide the answer?"

Dirk glares but stays silent.

"No? Surely a man of your intelligence does not lack the answer to such a simple question?"

"Shade, that's enough," Otis warns.

Shade sneers and that animal eagerness appears in his face again. His fingers tighten on the moon blade's silver hilt.

"Shade . . ." Otis's voice softens.

"Well, if it ain't our good old friend, the Unnamed prick who so beautifully welcomed us ages ago." Axle steps in front of the priest, forcing Shade to remove his sword or cut his own friend's neck.

Shade growls at the intrusion, but Axle ignores him.

"You've grown thinner, my friend. Perhaps, has your health been endangered?" Axle pats the man's tattooed cheek. His gaze hardens. His voice lowers. "Get out of this village, you bastard, before I change my mind and let my bosom companion carve a new tattoo on your flesh." He smiles and shoves the man forward. "Nice seeing you again."

Slowly, slowly the procession moves towards the gates. Axle prods the priest with the sole of his boot teasingly, muttering words of "friendship" to the stooped crone. The Unnamed glances over his shoulder and finds my face. His eyes are bright. Shining. He smiles, those tattoos curling up on his cheeks.

My stomach drops.

I am going to break. Shatter. Fall.

I have to get away.

I turn and run.

"Kyla!" Shade calls.

I don't stop.

"Kyla!"

I find one of the hidden doors built into the wooden wall and thrust it open. The woods, their trees offering a cave to hide within, are mere yards away.

I let them swallow me.

I run until the trees all look the same and the ground trembles beneath my feet. Until my lungs are burning, and I can't breathe. Until I finally fall to my knees and vomit. I struggle to stand, but my knees are weak.

I fight to hold back the stone that blocks my throat, but it is no use.

Alone, I sob.

The visions aren't true. They cannot be true. I could not have witnessed what I saw. They were nightmares. Dreams meant to weaken – to frighten – me. The *siratha* must have cursed me. I have to be cursed.

If the visions are true – people have died because of me. High Lord Brand would not be dead if it weren't for me. Helena would not have died in that foolish assault. Her child would live to see the world. Their blood stains my hands.

I slam a fist to the ground. Again. Again. But the pain is not enough.

The visions aren't true.

But if the visions are true – if I can witness events in another time and place – what am I?

I am not who I was.

You do not belong . . .

I am not what I thought I am.

You're not one of them.

I don't know who I am.

You are alone.

Leaves crunch softly behind me. I know, without turning around, who it is, and swallow my sobs.

I wait for Shade's chastisement. His disgusted remarks about my "kind" and their weakness. His sarcastic lectures meant to taunt and degrade me. But he says nothing.

He walks around me and wrinkles his nose at the puddle of vomit. Slowly, he sits down beside me and rests his back against the tree. The tension in my shoulders dissipates. He remains quiet.

The silence spreads out for what seems like ages.

I wonder what to say to him. What bravado to force from my mouth. What lies I must make up to explain my behavior. The lump in my throat tightens.

But I'm tired of lying.

So I whisper, "I'm afraid," and look up at him.

He is already looking at me. His eyes narrow thoughtfully as they flutter over my face.

I grab the dirt beneath my hands, struggling to control the chasm that is calling my name inside my chest. The chasm that houses all my fears and nightmares and doubts. The chasm that is draining me away bit by bit.

"I'm so tired of being afraid."

Afraid of Wood. Afraid of the Wilds. Of the villagers. Of myself.

I used to know who I was. What I wanted. Where I was going. But that me was burned away with the first touch of that branding iron on my skin.

I want to know who I am and where I belong. Without fear. Without doubt.

Shade stands. He grips my elbow, pulling me to my feet. His hand slides down to grasp mine. It is a warm, firm grip. The grip of someone who knows and understands.

"Follow me," he whispers and pulls me deeper into the forest.

Chapter XIX

Shade leads me forward for what seems like hours. The forest changes around me. The trees become more spread out. The colors brighten. The vines become thicker. This part of the forest wasn't always a forest. It is young. Less than a century old.

Shade leads me around the corner of a massive overhanging rock wall. Young saplings sprout up among the stone. He pauses at the base of the rock wall. A set of stone steps crawl up the steep hill, perfectly shaped, despite the ancient cracks on their surfaces. Moss and little flowers border their rough edges.

He lets go of my hand and ascends the hill. I follow him to the very top. He steps aside, making room for me to see where he has taken me.

I peer into the thick forest that we entered. Among the long oaken trunks of the giant trees, stone ruins pervade the landscape. Many of the walls are still standing even if the ceilings caved in centuries ago. Vines and flowers slink along the ruined architecture. The ground is covered in leaves and moss. Once, a long time ago, this place would have been a city.

"It was once a great pinnacle of Kelban society – a city at the heart of Kelba," Shade says as if reading my thoughts. "A representation of Kelban unification. When we were one nation. Undivided. Unbroken. Unbreakable." He looks at me. "It was called *Lithean*."

My chest tightens. *Lithean*. The birthplace of Gasan; Kelba's evil, immortal ruler. It was said Calaisar cursed its existence long before the poison ate Kelba away. Priests said those who wandered into its interior would be cursed in return. I hesitate.

Shade frowns. "Surely you don't believe those prudish tales made up by wet nurses?" He jumps off the steps into the middle of the ruins. The edge of one of the ancient buildings crumbles with the force of his landing. He spins around to look at me. "I thought you said you're tired of being afraid."

I land so lightly the leaves hardly rustle beneath my feet. "I am."

He walks deeper among the ruins. Until they spread out and make a clearing that must have once been a grand street. The crumbling remains of four stagnant pillars atop a marble base glare at me. A skeleton of a temple.

Shade ignores it and approaches a marble, dome-shaped building hardly bigger than a shed. It is the only structure that remains in one piece. He opens the crudely fashioned, wooden door to reveal a collection of weapons.

The weapons are not ancient.

There are swords. Axes. Spears. Javelins. All shapes, sizes, make, and model. Even a crossbow, one of the newest forms of weapon technology, hangs within.

"What is this place?" I ask and draw closer.

He doesn't answer me and retrieves two wooden swords carelessly discarded on the floor of the shed. He tosses one at me.

I catch it with both hands. It is heavy and the balance is off-setting. I nearly topple sideways, but manage to stay standing. When my feet are spread apart and my knees locked in place, the weight is more manageable.

"You've held one before." It's not a question. He closes the door of the shed and steps towards me. He lets the moon blades fall from his shoulders. They hit the ground. Without them crossed X-ways on his back he looks less intimidating. And a hell of a lot shorter.

Shade holds his wooden sword with only one hand. Aware that he is mocking my weakness, I try to stifle my rising pride. He eyes my grasp on the sword. "You've used one before?" he asks.

"My brother taught me."

Shade steps closer, sword slack at his side. His arm swings at me out of nowhere. I have no time to deflect it, and Shade stops the wooden edge of the weapon an inch short of my throat.

"Not well enough." He steps back and toes the dirt. "Your brother's lessons seem pretty damn useless to me."

Anger commands me, and I rush at him, sword poised to strike. He swerves to the side and swivels behind me. I try to correct my mistake, but I'm not fast enough. He locks a foot around the base of my knee, and I fall flat on my back.

He stands over me and shakes his head, a mocking sneer on his face.

An enraged growl vibrates along my throat. He can't insult me – or my brother – like that.

I launch to my feet and slice my sword out in front of me in a two-handed arc. He sidesteps it and counters the weapon when I lash at him again. The wood grinds together. He pushes against my weapon. I push back. We lock eyes. He steps close. His leg wraps around mine from behind and welds us together – but only for a moment. He pulls my leg out from under me. I fall on my back again.

He stares down at me. "Your nostrils are flaring."

Heat flames my face as I struggle to bite back a retort. I fail.

"I suppose *now* you're going to tell me that swordsmanship is all about keeping your emotions under *control*?"

"Damn control," Shade says. "It's a useless idea made up by valiant pricks who believe in the honesty and goodness of every living thing."

The base of my spine aches when I stand. "What are you going to teach me, if not control?"

He straightens my blade between us, like an upright arrow, and looks straight into my eyes. His gaze deepens. He is not fooling around. This is not another one of his cruel pranks to flare my irritation.

"I'm going to teach you to fight, Kyla Bone. Not like a *knight*. Not like your *brother*." He sneers. "Like a warrior."

"You're going t-to . . . train me?" I try to wrap my head around his words.

He steps away from me. "That fear you possess – that fear that rules you. Turn it to rage." He notices my confusion. "It's easier than you think. Imagine all those moments you felt insignificant and weak. Imagine all those moments you were lower than dirt. Imagine all those people who frightened you. Angered you. Mocked you. What do you want to do to them?"

An endless list of names assaults my mind, and my grip on the sword tightens.

"You do realize that *you* are one of those people, right?"

He doesn't show any sign of surprise. Instead, he smiles. The breath leaves my lungs. He never smiles. There's a dimple at the corner of his lips. I didn't know he had a dimple. "Then this should be very interesting. Don't you think?"

I grip the sword with both hands, readying for another attack from him, but he leads me towards a thick oak tree.

He places himself at my back and pries one of my hands from the sword's hilt. The weight twists my wrist to the side. I wince. He slides a hand down my arm to steady my grip, igniting prickles of heat along my skin.

"What are you doing?" I ask, trying to ignore the tension of his muscles against the sensitive skin of my back.

"You need to strengthen your arms," he says in my ear. His breath feathers over my shoulder. For a moment, I welcome the embrace he's unknowingly locked me in. If he were anyone else but the solemn, pain-in-the-ass of my life I might shelter this memory – the feel of him – away in my mind.

He lets go of me. The warm feeling dissolves, but the trail of his hand down my arm remains.

"Strike at the sides of the tree with your sword. Do it."

I land two sharp blows against the bark.

He nods approvingly.

He returns to the shed and straps his blades onto his back. "Continue. Swing. Strike. Hammer. But never let your arm down or let it fall until I return."

He doesn't return at all.

When there are needles in my arms and a thousand anvils in my head, I finally relinquish the blade and return to Agron. Shade is standing dutifully at the gate, shoulders straight and chin uplifted. I avoid looking at him.

"Do you feel that rage now?" he whispers as I sweep past him into the village.

I say nothing.

But tomorrow – he'll wish he'd never handed me a sword.

Shade makes me pummel the tree again the next day.

And the following day he does the same. Calluses rise on my palms and raw blisters ooze their unappealing slipperiness to my grip. The muscles in my arms burn and tighten every night.

It is only on the third day that I notice a difference. Though the weight is still awkward, my arm does not protest its presence.

By the fourth day, the wooden weapon has become a second limb.

"A very flippant second limb," Shade deigns to remark.

On the fifth day, I insist that I am ready for the next task. I entertain the idea of knocking his ass to the ground with my newfound strength, but he leads me further into the ruins, to the crumbled remains of what must have been a lord's manor. The walls are taller and thicker than any of the other crumbling architecture.

"Stand on this." He gestures to a part of the wall that seems sturdier than the rest.

I crawl up its mossy side and position myself on top. It is only two inches long, and I rock unsteadily on the balls of my feet. The plain of the wall, though sturdy, is uneven. Like a seesaw.

My arms flap wildly as I struggle not to topple backwards. It is only with the greatest dedication that I don't release the wooden sword that adds an offsetting balance to my attempts. My stomach muscles burn from my efforts.

At last, I discover by bending one foot sideways across the top of the wall, that I can maintain both the sword's balance and mine.

"Now swing your sword in front of you. Imagine an invisible tree you're trying to hack. That's right." Shade masters a teacher's soft monotone. He paces at a casual distance from the edge of the wall, looking up at me. Watching me. Testing me. He tosses an oval pebble between his hands.

It takes me a few near-collapse attempts to swing the sword properly. But, at last, I execute a perfect chop from side-to-side without shaking. I smile, proud of my success.

Shade smiles too – and pitches the pebble straight towards my stomach.

I attempt to block it abruptly with my sword and my feet miscalculate their positions. The pebble strikes me hard in the stomach. I double over, and that's all it takes. I pitch forward and meet the ground ten feet below. Luckily, the moss eases what would have been a painful fall. Just the same, I taste blood where I bit my tongue.

"What the hell was that?" I snarl.

Shade shrugs and his lips widen into a grin. "Just wanted to remind you that even the most graceful birds can be brought down by a single stone."

I grab the wooden sword from its mossy bed and rush at him. This time he doesn't back away but meets my attack head-on. I am unprepared for the force upon which our weapons clash and narrowly miss a ricochet of my own sword as it snaps back towards my nose. I teeter backwards and attempt to right myself. Shade lashes at my sword again and gives it a light prod. My fragile hold on balance shatters. I land on my ass for what seems the eight millionth time this week.

"Your new-found strength will be useless if you lack the ability to remain on your feet." He looks down his nose at me. "The last lesson was not just about gaining strength. What do you think it was about, my fumbling apprentice?"

I glare at him. But I know the answer.

Perseverance.

He offers me a hand.

I don't take it.

I force myself to stand, and move towards the wall again. "How long must I do this?"

"Until you can strike one of my harmless pebbles without toppling on your ass, *aventra.*"

Apprentice.

He offers me a hand to hoist myself onto the wall again. I shove it away. He smiles, but doesn't persist. He returns to his own position.

The wall feels less sturdy on my second trial. My stomach tightens as I stare at the ten-foot distance between the ground and me. A chasm widens in my stomach. If I fall again, will the moss spare my bones? Or will they shatter on impact?

"You seem unsteady, Kelban!" Shade says. A stone pummels my shoulder. I grit my teeth against the prickling pain.

"Kyla," I growl.

Another pebble strikes my kneecap. I resist the urge to double over.

"Focus, Kelban!" Shade snaps.

I look at my feet, watching how they shift unsteadily on the wall.

A stone strikes my thigh.

"On me, Kelban!" A pebble clips my hip. "How do you expect to survive an assault if you aren't looking at the opponent? Look at me, *flagrana Kelban*! At me, damn it!"

I look at him. The moment I do my feet roll, and I fall – backwards this time. Shade casually turns the corner of the wall to find me flat on another mossy cushion. He leans against it and shakes his head.

"You're useless, you know that? Completely useless. Maybe Dirk was right. Maybe you are only good for what's between your legs. Is that the only activity you're fluent in, Kelban?"

My temples throb with hot anger. I scale the wall again and wait for him to return to his proper place. He palms another pebble. Throws it. I manage to dodge its strike but it costs me my balance once more.

"If you fall one more time, I'm finished with you. You can go back to sobbing, alone and helpless, in the woods," he warns me.

Angered that he's using my moment of weakness against me, I climb the wall again.

I palm the sword and look at Shade. My feet teeter unsteadily. I breathe slowly. In through my mouth. Out through my nose. Once. Twice. Three times. I focus my attention on the three pebbles in Shade's hands, but a part of me also maintains a soft awareness of my feet. It's like dancing, which I now wish I'd taken more interest in learning. I had always been scolded for looking at my feet while dancing.

The dance master, a boorish man with a hawk-like nose, had told me that balance was not located in the foot, but the ear. In muscle and understanding. I prod that memory to the forefront of my mind. I imagine the two-inch wall is a dance floor. One I must ascend.

The sword is my partner. My sole weight. My leader. My body must follow its command.

The first pebble hits my shin.

I steady my delicate existence.

The second pebble misses me when I curve out of its way. I very nearly misplace my foot. Bits of stone crumble beneath my boots.

"Careful. You don't want to fall, Kyla," Shade mocks me.

He didn't – couldn't – have known the memory that surged to the front of my mind at his taunting words. Me dangling, helpless, over the edge of a sheer, glass roof. Me, wide-eyed and frightened, at the plains rolling beneath me. Me, weakened and frightened, by the man who so placidly threatened my very existence. The man who rules my every waking and receding thought.

My fear grows a voice.

You are mine.

I grip the wooden hilt.

Like hell I am.

The angry throb in my temple intensifies, until its a pulse in my forehead.

Shade releases the third stone.

Tension collects around me like a magnet.

I am the magnet.

I swing the sword as the stone approaches.

The pulse ripples along my arm, down my hand, and lashes out.

The stone flies back in Shade's direction. He catches it in a swift, fluid motion and stares at the rough-shewn surface. He nods approvingly.

What should have been a proud moment hammers a weight in my chest.

The sword never touched the stone!

Later that night, I stare at my hands. White. Scarred. Stronger. I clench my fingers. They are not tense. Just sore. I do not feel a pulse. I don't feel a flicker of heat. I don't feel a ball of energy in my palm.

But there had been a pulse. There had been heat. There had been energy.

I know it.

I resist the urge to run downstairs and into the night, frightened and alone once more. I am stronger than this. I won't let this place mar my sanity. I won't let this fear rip me to pieces.

But I am a puzzle – and the pieces are missing.

By the eighth day of my training, balance has become a miniscule dilemma in my slovenly practices. Shade regards my final attempt upon the curved wall with a slightly-tipped-upward chin and nods when I pummel four of his approaching stones into the dirt.

"Fair," he remarks in regards to my deflections.

"I was aiming for your head."

He doesn't comment.

I scratch my elbow against the stones on my descent. Shade notices it the moment he strides around the corner. He crosses his arms and leans against the decaying stones.

"Perhaps I should teach you to climb next?"

My stomach flips. Climb? As in heights? If I didn't feel extremely close to vomiting, I might laugh at his suggestion. That's twice in a matter of days that he's reminded me of my greatest fears.

"I doubt I'll surpass your expertise in that area," I nervously chuckle instead.

His lips curve downward – confused. "You've seen me climb?"

My lungs freeze. *Stupid! Stupid fool! How can I be so gods-cursed stupid!*

"I – I . . ."

He cocks his head to the side and it sends shivers down my spine. His brow furrows. He's thinking. No – he's trying to remember.

"I meant, to scale our Wall, you have to be a decent climber."

His brow unfurls, but his head remains cocked to the side. Damn!

"After all, I have considerable faith in the architecture of *my kind.* You may consider them beneath you, but their construction abilities are far-advanced."

My well-aimed remark turns his head right-side up. "Don't push it, Kelban," he growls and turns his back on me.

I resist the urge to remind him of my name.

He tosses my sword at me when I turn the corner. "Now we'll see how fluently you've applied your new-found capabilities to memory."

Shade was unmerciful.

River makes no comment when I wash the dirt and blood caked onto my hands before supper. She sits with her legs propped beneath her chin, watching me.

I gently soothe the blisters on my hands with Mama Opal's medicine. Strangely enough, they don't bother me. I look at their ugly, puffed forms and can't explain the pride that fills me. All my life, I had delicate, beautiful, soft hands. Hands that told everyone I was wealthy. Proud. Lazy. Now they are raw, red, and cracked. They show everyone I fight. Struggle. Work.

I spread my hand palm flat before me. It's a habit I've forced myself to entertain lately. And, as usual, there is no pulse. No tingling nerves. Just the air on my fingertips.

"What are you doing?" River asks.

"Nothing," I reply hastily and bury my hands in the towel she laid near the basin.

"No, I mean what are you doing? As in, where do you go every day? Why do you return so . . . so mysteriously?"

Shade and I manage to keep our sessions a secret. He leaves early in the morning, hours before the sun will paint the sky. I leave at the first rays of sunrise. He returns an hour before dusk to take his place at the walls, always offering up an excuse as to why he has returned empty-handed from his hunts. I return directly at dusk, usually carrying firewood or some herbs I managed to pluck hurriedly. Eight days and we've managed to continue our charade without detection.

"I find it difficult on the return route and get helplessly lost."

"I could come with you and . . ."

"No!"

My interruption causes lines to crease on River's forehead when she squints at me. "Why not? It would save you a lot of time. The woods is a frightening place to be. Especially at dusk. What if you can't find your way home after dusk has fallen? You've seen the shadows once – you don't want to meet them again. Alone. Do you?"

I blink. "What did you just say?"

"I said you don't want to be attacked by shadows, alone, in the middle of a darkened forest. That is their territory. They would . . ."

"No, before that. *Home.* You said 'home.'" My voice sounds raspy.

River smiles. "Yes. I said home. This is your home, Kyla. Me. Mama Opal. Axle. Shade. We're your home." Her smile turns upside down. "Aren't we?"

"I . . . I have to . . . get some air."

"Kyla!" River calls after me.

"Mercy . . .!" Mama Opal cries as I dodge past her and out the door. "Kyla, it's dangerous outsi . . ."

I turn the corner of her house – the house River had just said was mine – and lean against the rough stones. I curl into the shadows when River runs by my hiding place, calling my name, distraught.

Home. Home. Home. This is your home. We're your home.

My throat aches, but I won't cry. I won't cry.

A tear manages to drip from my flooded eyes. *Hell!*

River returns a few minutes later. She peruses the corner of the house and sees me. I wipe the wet streak from beneath my eye and stiffen. She leaves a descent amount of space between us and rubs her arms nervously.

"I didn't mean to . . . to upset you," she whispers. "I only thought . . . well, you've been here a while and we all . . . all of us care for you. I thought maybe you'd think about us as . . . as something, I guess. I'm sorry. I didn't mean to scare you."

"I know you didn't." But how can she understand? I have a home. It's behind a five hundred foot Wall in the heart of Kelba. My home – father, mother, brother – they are my home.

River gently takes my hand. "You saved my life. No matter what anyone says you belong here." She taps her chest. "In here. No matter what. Haven't you ever had friends?"

Craig. Selena. Aspen. They were my friends once. Before I defied their expectations of me. Before I disappointed them. Before I became something that endangered them.

I shake my head.

River smiles. "I'm your first then? That's good. I like that."

She leads me back inside and makes up an excuse for my quick exit. Mama Opal swallows the lie.

I sneak a peek at River during our meal. She slips one of her round vegetables into Axle's brew, which he hacks up a few moments later, resulting in chaotic laughter around the table. Even Shade smiles – that dimple at the corner of his mouth winking with amusement.

River meets my gaze when I manage to prod her foot beneath the table.

I mouth: *"I like it too."*

She smiles.

I smile back.

Ninth day – parrying.

Tenth day – lunging.

Eleventh day – countering.

Twelfth day – all of it.

I finally hold up a hand between our thirty-second match, gagging on mouthfuls of air that never quite fill my screaming lungs. "Respite," I gasp.

Shade frowns, but lowers his sword and steps back. He toes the dirt in front of him while I claw at my chest for oxygen. No matter how many times I attack him – how many tricks I use – he's too fast. Too observant.

And to make matters worse, he doesn't even break a sweat during our lessons. If I could bring one perfect, round bead of perspiration to his brow I would count myself a victor.

"Do I need to remind you?" he asks.

I try to remember all the poetic quotes he's heaped upon my brain in the past three days, but they jumble together in strings of incoherent nonsense.

"Do not play fair," he chides when I remain silent. "Forget the rules. Forget honor. Forget all your righteous Kelban monologues about the 'proper way to fight.' This is not about your ability to duel or retain your reputation. This is about your life, Kyla. Your flesh and blood! Survival."

"I know that!"

"You don't know shit. You war too much with your inner thoughts."

I stumble to my feet.

Shade bounces his sword from right hand to left tauntingly. He finally grips it firmly in his right and points it at me. "Decide: right or left. Forward or backward. Back or front. Fast or . . ."

"I get it!"

He sneers. "Imagine ridding the world of something vile. Evil. Wretched. Monstrous. Wouldn't it make you feel good? Fight for that. Fight to rid the world of creatures like that."

He would have me fight for the pleasure of it. For the thrill of watching something bleed and die.

Bile claws at my throat. "What ill-bred madman taught you to fight?" I ask.

He halts his approach in my direction. A brief shadow quivers at the corner of his eyes and is gone. "I taught myself."

I don't stop the laugh that erupts from my mouth. "That's impossible. Everyone needs a trainer in these matters."

His grip hardens on the sword, whitening his knuckles. He lunges at me. I block the strike but he lashes out with his foot and hooks it behind my ankles. I fall flat and air leaves my lungs. This is where he usually steps back and waits for me to get up, taunting me all the while. But not now. Above me, in blurry motions of arms and wood, he cuts his sword downwards. I block the strike. Splinters of wood rain down over my face. He chops again. My wrists explode in pain.

His next blow sends my weapon clattering against the trees, out of my reach.

I stare up at him, waiting for him to retreat and allow me to stand. The rough surface of his sword strikes my cheek. Fiery pain explodes over the side of my face. I touch the hot exterior of my skin and prickly splinters stab my fingertips.

"That was my training," Shade says softly. "Are you going to let me do that to you again?"

I retrieve my sword and face him. "No way in hell."

This time, *I* lunge at *him*.

He tried for the rest of the day to put me back on the ground. To lower my guard. To destroy me.

I didn't let him.

Day fourteen. Two weeks of endless training. Two weeks of muscled effort and Shade gives me a real sword. It's an older blade – maybe thirty years – but its a sword and it's sharp. I spend several hours adjusting to the difference in weight, size, and capability. The sword is lighter than the wooden blade by a good eight pounds. I hardly notice its presence in my hand. The hilt is wrapped in rawhide to prevent against perspiration on my hands. Slippery hands are a fighter's doom!

Shade waits two minutes after our first match before speaking. "Your movements are graceful!" He hacks my sword away violently. "Piss on grace."

I retrieve it and we start again. I watch his movements. He usually steps to the right when he's ready to attack. I wait and watch. He steps to the right. I lunge and he quickly dodges to the left and flips my sword from my grasp, once again leaving me at his mercy.

"You rely on your brain to counter your opponent." He sneers. "Piss on knowledge."

Once more, I retrieve my sword, irritation spiraling in my gut, and we begin again. Two minutes. Four minutes. I lunge at him too hard, and he avoids my attack easily. He takes advantage of my slow recovery and strikes at my back, stopping the blade against the ridges of my spine.

"You depend upon the virtue of your attacker," he chides. Placing a hand on my shoulder, he thrusts me away from him. "Piss on virtue."

Anger curls inside of me in harsh protest to his words. "There is more to a fight than pure brutality. There is honor."

"Sure." He tilts the point of his sword in my direction. "Honor is why poor fools, like you, die." He retrieves the water pouch near the tree and takes long, relaxed gulps before handing it to me.

"My brother has honor. He's alive," I counter.

Shade sneers. His shoulders rise in a casual shrug. "Your brother's alive because he's a selfish bastard. Piss on him."

Rage urges a growl of protest in my throat. I lunge at him with all my strength. He raises his blade, expecting the blow, and our swords grind into a firm lock. I smell and taste the metal intensity in the air. I struggle to pull my blade free. I want to strike at him again. I want to force him to the ground. I want to make him take back his words. But I can't. The hilts of our weapons are entangled.

I look at him – and wish I hadn't. There is anger in his gaze, but it's not at me. It's the kind of anger Father had when he'd rant about Celectate Wood. The kind Landor would get when he complained about the Community. It's the kind of anger that grows from a sense of injustice and ill-treatment.

"Your brother's a bastard. Do you want to know why, Kyla?"

No, I don't. I want you to shut up. I want you to piss off. I want you to take back your words.

Shade continues, pretending he has no idea about the wretched turmoil inside my head. "Because if a real man lost his family – lost someone he loved – he'd do anything. No! He'd do everything to make sure the ones responsible wished they were in hell. He'd send them to hell. And he'd enjoy doing it. If your brother remains a steadfast, honorable man after what happened to you, then he did not love you. And he was not worthy of your affections either."

With our blades – and our bodies – locked so close, there is no way to avoid his eyes as they search my face. His forehead is creased in lines, and the corners of his mouth tremble slightly. Control. He's trying to control himself.

"Is that what happened to you?" I ask.

Our blades snap apart when he steps back. He lets his fall to the ground. "Lesson's over for the day."

He turns and walks towards the steep, descending steps to the common forest below.

"Shade," I call after him but he doesn't stop. I hurry to the top of the steps, in time to see him striding away through the branches towards Agron. "Shade! You're wrong about him!"

He doesn't respond but I can imagine his retort. How the hell would I know?

I am in the Wilds. Landor is in Kelba. There is no possible way for me to know whether he's continued on with his life. Whether he's become Celectate Wood's personal lapdog. Shade could be right.

My visions are not true. Merely wishes of what I hope everyone is doing without me. My hope that they have not forgotten about me. My hope that they did – and still – love me. There is no possible way for the visions to be true. But if they are . . .

Hairs raise on my arms as a chill settles over me.

Shade is not among the ruins when I enter them the next day. Not wanting to waste the long journey through the misty morning, I stretch and do some warm-up exercises in the circle he created for our duels. Two hours pass, but the forest still appears shrouded in darkness. It is a drizzly morning and my clothes are damp.

Four hours. I finally realize he's not coming. A vague sense of relief settles over me. There will be no one to laugh at my mistakes. No one to taunt and insult me on my lack of skills.

I lay aside my sword and retrieve my dagger from its sheath beneath my skirt. It has been a long time since I've practiced and the object feels miniscule and tiny compared to the weight of a sword. My heart starts to pound as it once did when I held the weapon in my hand. It was small. It was easily overlooked. It was deadly. The dagger and I were the same, I had liked to think.

I switch the blade to my left hand. The feeling changes. My stomach knots.

I line my body up, twenty feet from a tree one foot across. A perfect target. I adjust the dagger in my hand, perfect for throwing. It feels all wrong. I prepare my wrist for the toss.

Wrong!

The scars on my neck constrict. I haven't felt their presence in a while. Slowly, they begin their familiar pulsing. Pulsing that used to make me sick to my stomach. My veins burn from my neck, down my arm, to my fingertips. The cool metal hilt of my dagger against the burning flesh of my palm jolts my skin. I let go of the blade.

It doesn't fall to the ground. Bile rises in my throat and nausea replaces the pounding in my skull. The blade hovers just beneath my hand, a mere inch of air between my palm and its hilt. I am not touching it.

My hand is a magnet – the dagger the recipient.

Impossible, my brain screams.

The invisible, magnetic force in my hands fades.

The blade falls to the ground.

Shade is absent from dinner that evening. He is not waiting for me at the ruins the next morning either. I spend the day familiarizing myself with the many weapons in his makeshift shed, and practicing, left-handed, with my dagger. There was one lesson he didn't have to teach me: limitations could be my doom.

The dagger behaves like a normal dagger. No flying unless I am the initiator No hovering in midair beneath my hand. I excuse the previous day's action as another of my many mystified visions. Lack of sleep. Inattentiveness. A mirage.

I even took the time to listen for signs of a *siratha* in the forest, but quickly dispelled such an idea. If a *siratha* were in the forest I wouldn't be the only one fearing their sanity. No one in the village had complained of irregular happenings. Except for my presence, of course. In all honesty, I think the villagers are relieved I spend my days outside their wall.

When I return to the gates before they close for dusk, Otis is waiting for me, arms crossed firmly. I try to ignore the gaze he fixes on me. He wants an explanation. I fear I may have to give him one.

"What do you do in the forest, girl, for so many hours?" he asks, surveying the mud splattering every inch of me. Training got especially messy today.

"I go stuck in a ditch," I lie. "The basket was lost." Indeed, that part was half-true. I had forgotten to retrieve the basket full of mint leaves for Mama Opal. They were still settled next to the shed door.

"Hmm," Otis murmurs. "Seems to me . . ."

"Kyla! We've been waiting for you. Mama Opal has supper on the table," River exclaims from behind him. Her braid rocks from side-to-side as she approaches me and wipes some of the mud from my arm. "Although you may need a bath first."

I let her lead me forward.

"Kyla," Otis calls after me. I glance at him over my shoulder. "The King's reply will be here soon. I sent the information off today."

I nod to show I've understood. He turns his back, and I let out the breath I was holding.

"How long do I have?" I ask as we – Mama Opal, River, and I – sit at the dinner table.

"Two weeks. Maybe a little longer. The king has a lot of other matters besides you to deal with, honey," Mama Opal assures me. "For instance, the frequent attacks in other villages. The growing ranks of the shadows. Trust me, a Kelban is the least of his worries. And Otis is an intelligent man. He won't make you out to be a demon that you aren't. Trust me. He's a good man, when he's sober."

"And when he's not sober?" River asks, her eyes twinkling mischievously

Mama Opal shifts uncomfortably. "Then he's rather manageable. Like a baby. Or the enemy with their hands tied." She stands abruptly and mutters an excuse about needing to stoke the fire.

River struggles to hold in her laughter.

"What's so funny?" I ask.

"Nothing much. It's just, last year, when I was coming home late from the gate, I found Otis and Mama Opal in here and they were . . ."

"Having an emotional conversation," Mama Opal interjects.

"Otis had his arms around her and she was patting his back. He smelled awful, but she didn't seem to mind. And he leaned in like this . . ." She leans across the table towards me, her lips puckering up, her eyes fluttering closed. "And . . . whoosh . . . I say their names, and they snap apart!" She points at the wall. "Otis hit his head on the wall. Mama Opal set her skirts on fire because she stepped too close to the flames. It was hilarious!"

Mama Opal's cheeks flush pink.

I smile inwardly. Otis and Mama Opal. How interesting.

Upstairs, River lends me her comb to brush the dirt that the bathwater didn't reach out of my hair.

"Where are Axle and Shade?" I ask.

"Scouting." River's lips tilt upwards into a pout. "And they didn't even say goodbye to anyone. Mama Opal said Shade just stomped into the house and told Axle to get his gear and follow him. Otis says they left right after dusk without anything but their weapons and a couple day's supply of food." She doesn't do a good job of keeping the worry from her voice.

"They'll be alright," I tell her.

"I wish I believed that," River says. She props her legs beneath her chin. "But I've lost my brother once. I don't want to lose him again."

"What are you talking about?"

Her face pales. "Nothing."

"Did he leave you?"

Her eyes widen. "Gods, Kyla, how could you think such a thing? He's my brother. My brother! He wouldn't leave me."

"How did you lose him then?"

She bows her head. "It's not my story to tell. Please, Kyla, you have to understand why I can't say anything. He's barely told me much about those years when we were separated. If I breach that trust between us – it's like I don't deserve to be his sister. Please understand that."

Certain that she's going to cry herself into a frenzy, I take her hand and agree to stop asking. But my nerves tense up. River tells me anything. Asks me anything. For her to be unable to tell me something, it must be serious.

It must be horrible.

Shade and Axle remain absent. I try not to worry. River says they've been gone a whole month before and returned with enough food to feed the village through the winter. She says Shade even brought sugar in a neat package for Mama Opal. I sneak a peek at the three year-old bag that Mama Opal keeps in the pantry for special occasions. It's a Kelban item.

For three days, I withstand the loneliness of training. I commit Shade's short words to memory. I practice moving my body the way he does. Not the way he showed me. Not the way he's taught me. The way I remember him moving all those years ago, on a darkened night, with a moon blade in hand. He had been all violent grace and destructive speed. He had been smoke and forest smells against the piss and blood of the foul creatures before me.

On the fourth day, I decide not to go to the ruins. More and more people have noticed my absences, and I have fewer excuses now that Shade and Axle are away. I let myself sleep in and River shakes me awake.

"Come on. I'm going swimming. You should come and meet some of the others." The minutes she says it we both know what a mess that situation would become.

Besides . . . I can't swim.

"I . . . I think I'd rather stay here."

River doesn't hide her disappointment. "Kyla, you have to make them see you are not a threat. You have to make them like you."

I am pretty sure screaming and pleading for help as I drown in seven feet of water is not the best way to begin a friendship. They would stand on the bank and watch me die anyway. I do not want their pity. I do not want their friendship.

"I will clean Cedric's study." I point to the heavy curtain. "My arm is healed now and it's a mess in there."

River looks at my shoulder, where the ostracized symbol winks at her from beneath my sleeve. "Okay," she says hesitantly and grabs a worn towel from our cot. "If you change your mind . . ."

"I won't," I assure her.

She leaves.

I spend an hour among Cedric's items before Mama Opal calls me downstairs to the wardrobe on the far side of the room. Her hair is messed up and stringy. Behind her is a pile of over-sized garments that smell of dust and age.

"Yes?"

She looks up and blinks, as if suddenly realizing I'm there. "Oh, there you are, child. I was thinking . . . you can't always wear that tunic." She gestures at the already stained garment. "I know I used to have some clothes just your size. Suitable clothes." She regards my waist. "You're not a skeleton anymore."

No. Thanks to Shade, I've recovered my former health. Healthier, actually.

She heaves a wooden box from the bottom of the wardrobe onto the kitchen table. It is a fine piece of craftsmanship. The wood is tinted red and sandpapered into smooth, glass-like texture. I observe the brass padlock. Mama Opal pulls a chain hidden beneath the collar of her tunic. I had always thought it was a necklace. A key dangles at the end of it. She inserts it into the ancient lock and the lid cracks open. She lets it fly back.

I expected a damp, musty smell to emanate from it, but I smell flowers. Roses. Lavender. Tulips. Daffodils. Flower petals are strewn across the objects within the box. I see bright colors. A hint of lace. A small book.

"If you live under my roof, you're going to be taken care of," Mama Opal says. She blinks rapidly, but it doesn't hide the tremor in her voice. The pain in her features. She removes a neatly folded black tunic with a glossy sheen to its folds and places it in my arms. "Try it on."

I do. It fits perfectly. When I return, she produces a vest that cuts off mid-bodice and laces it shut for me. It leaves me feeling protected and stylish at the same time.

"The final touch," she says and removes two objects from inside the box. I blink when I recognize what they are. Wrist-guards Two black, leather wrist-guards She helps me put them on. They stop an inch short of my elbow, allowing me freedom of movement, but offering protection to the rest of my arm.

I feel like a warrior ready for battle when I slip my dagger into the sheath beneath my skirts.

"The clothes . . . they suit you better than they do the box," Mama Opal remarks. She smiles and stares at me.

I reassess my attire. "It's . . . it fits perfectly."

"They were my daughter's," Mama Opal remarks fondly. My chest tightens. Her daughter? "It was her favorite outfit. She told me it made her feel strong. Capable. She'd loved going into the woods. She'd be gone for hours. Days, sometimes, with her father whenever he went on what of his little expeditions. She had her father's spirit. Adventure. Travel. Creativity."

I want to ask what happened. I want to ask where her daughter is. Where her husband is. But that tight feeling in my chest demands my silence. Deep down, I know the answers to those questions.

"I . . . I think I will go see River," I say. I stop at the door and turn around. "Mama Opal?"

"Yes, honey?" She looks up too quickly. Her eyes are wet. I see my mother's face and the courage it takes to hide the pain.

"Thank you."

Her lips stretch into a smile. "You remind me of her. My

daughter, I mean. Same spirit. Same personality." Her eyes twinkle. "Same habits. Don't let Shade give you any of his shit, you hear me?"

"W-what?"

"You didn't think I knew where you went everyday? What you are doing? Who you are doing it with? Honestly, honey, give me some credit. I was young once. I had a daughter who was young. Neither of you, elusive and secretive as you two have been, could hide it from these weathered eyes." She stares at the wrist-guards on my arms. "Those might help you considerably. I don't want to see any more ugly red marks on your arms, child. You have enough as it is." She winks.

Mother and Mama Opal could be twins.

"Who else k-knows?"

She shrugs. "Axle has an idea. River's getting closer to the truth. Otis might have some suspicions. They are nothing to worry about, honey."

I believe her.

"Go on now," she urges. "You'll miss River!"

Everyone I passed took a second look as I walked by. Hell, most took three or four looks. Indeed, in my new attire, I hardly gave the appearance of the downtrodden foreigner that had been dragged into the village a few weeks prior. Otis nodded approvingly as I passed him at the gate, but behind his admiration, I saw a tinge of memory. He knows whose clothes I wear.

I am half a mile from Agron's gates when the sound of chaotic laughter pulls me in the right direction. A group of dripping wet boys runs past me, slapping one another with towels, and yelling threats. Behind them, groups of girls walk placidly, by threes or twos. River immediately breaks away from one of them and approaches me, wiping water from her eyes. Her hair is undone from its braid and fans out around her thin face.

"I tore my dress," she mumbles, mid-laugh, and points at the tear on her sleeve.

A tall boy with close-cut brown hair passes the two of us. He and River share a quick glance and a smile, before he hurries after a couple of his friends. River giggles as soon as he's gone, and my suspicions are deemed correct.

I know how she tore her dress.

River takes my hand and pulls me towards the forest, away from Agron. "I want to dry off before we go back." I'm in no hurry to return so I follow her.

The forest opens up into a meadow. It's small and surrounded by trees, but I can see the sky and the meadow is full of yellow-green grass and flowers. River makes herself comfortable in the middle of the swaying wildlife, combing fingers through her long hair. I plop down beside her.

"Don't say a word about Rod to Axle. Please?"

I nod. That is one conversation I don't anticipate having. I doubt Axle would be thrilled to know someone was sticking his tongue down River's throat. And I doubt "Rod" would be eager for an altercation with one of the village's esteemed "guardians" for such reasons.

River's voice is soft and faraway. She rolls onto her back and stares up at the sky. "He's just moved to the village from one of the mountain regions. Indeed, I should have known he got those muscles from hiking. Says he's an only child and that his parents will be moving down shortly. The air in the mountains is too unpleasant for them, he says. He knows a lot about wildlife, but he doesn't like to hunt. Says he prefers healing the creatures to killing them."

Sounds like a guy Shade would turn up his nose at.

"I don't know if I'm in love with him or anything," River says. "But he's so cute and . . . and I just feel so . . . so out of breath whenever I'm near him. He touched my arm, and, I swear, I could feel it for days after that."

I nod at her words. I had known that feeling – twice. Once, when I was fourteen. Once on a dark night, in an alley, surrounded by evil, but protected in my hero's arms.

That was before my hero became the exact opposite of what I'd believed him to be.

"But you would know," River sighs. "I wish I knew what it felt like. I wish everyone didn't think I was so flighty. Or that I am too young to think about such things. Look at you. You're as old as I and you've had the experience."

It takes me a moment to realize she's talking about my fake husband.

"What was your first kiss like?" she asks, sighing languidly on each word.

I try to immerse myself in that moment between Aspen and I. The smells of piss and human excrement around us. The damp air between us. The grip of his hands on my body. The fiery pressure of his lips on mine. The bile rising in my throat. The voice inside telling me that it was wrong. Horribly wrong, and that I didn't know why.

"It . . . burned."

River sits up and sighs. "Yes. It does burn. It burns me inside and out. But it enthralls me. Intensifies. Oh, Kyla, I never thought someone would kiss me like that. Kiss me like I was the only thing that mattered. That I was worth it."

Deep down, a pang of jealousy stabs at my rib-cage. Jealousy that River can experience such real admiration without worrying that the boy is after her inheritance. Jealousy that she reciprocates his feelings.

"Those are Leanna's," she says, eying the wrist-guards. The vest. The dress. "Those are hers too. Where did you get them, Kyla? I told you to stay out of Mama Opal's wardrobe."

"She gave them to me."

Her eyes widen. "She did?"

"Yes. She said if I lived under her roof I had to dress proper."

There is sadness in River's eyes. She looks away quickly, but it's too late.

"What?"

She tries to put the matter aside. "Nothing. I just don't see why . . . I mean . . . those things . . . they should have been burned . . . No! I mean they should have . . ."

"River." My voice sound stern. I don't mean it to be.

She faces me again. A tiny stream of tears pours from one eye. The other is full of water that gleams at me in the light.

"She died, didn't she?" I ask. "Leanna died."

River nods.

My chest tightens.

"It happened two years ago – a few weeks after Shade, Axle, and I arrived in Agron," River says. "We . . ."

"Wait . . . you weren't born in Agron?"

River's shoulder stiffen. Her eyes dart back and forth nervously like she's revealed a deadly secret. "No," she answers softly. "We were not. Axle and I are from Brunt, a little village in the middle of the forest between here and the capitol. Shade, however, he was born in Smoke."

Smoke. Smoke. I try to place the word.

"*You should have killed her, Shade of Smoke!*" Dirk had told him that in the council room.

"Smoke is the capitol of our land. Where the King lives. But it wasn't always the capitol. Not until a couple years ago when we finally decided to build a stronghold. When Shade lived there it was just another village – perhaps larger than most – but a village, nonetheless He never talks about it. Never mentions it except when he speaks of the King and our 'capitol.' I often wonder if he really considers it 'home.'"

Shade had never mentioned the word "home." Never mentioned a family. Never mentioned anything remotely close to ties of any sort. The only bond close enough to call "human" about him was his friendship with Axle and his quiet respect for Otis, Mama Opal, and River.

"Mama Opal's husband, Cedric, was a man who liked to travel. Or so we were told. He'd be gone for months on end. Once he was gone for a whole year and believed to be dead, by all but Mama Opal. When he returned he did not speak of his journey. He told no one what he did on his many adventures. He retrieved relics from ancient Kelban ruins. He found new herbs for Mama Opal. In a way, Leanna was a lot like him. She talked a lot more than he did, like her mother. She was kind and gentle with everyone. Innocent. Eager to help. But there was something about her that bothered me," River says. The smile on her lips wavers. "She would stare at people. Constantly. Like they were prey and she the hunter. She observed every little thing around her. And it scared me. When we arrived in the village, she didn't speak to me for three weeks, just watched me. How I ate. How I slept. How I walked. Ran. Played. Talked. It drove me crazy! Axle and Shade could leave the village. I couldn't. I was relieved when she started accompanying her father on his adventures. And then one day I saw her talking to Shade." She plucks a few strands of grass from the ground nervously.

"It scared me even more. Shade was a different person back then. Quiet. He never talked to anyone. Not even me, if he could help it. He trembled whenever someone touched him. Once he even hit Otis! He started sleeping in the cellar without blankets or light." River shivers. "Leanna and he – they talked for two hours. Two hours! And the next day, they both went hunting. They both came back with razors. She was smiling like a fool. He didn't smile, but – oh – you could tell he wanted to. Axle and Shade were on duty for patrol that night. It was also the night that Cedric and Leanna were leaving the village for a journey to Smoke. They didn't get far."

I want to tell her to stop. To not finish. I don't need to know what happened.

But I do.

"One of their guards came rushing back to Agron, screaming at the top of his lungs. Blood was running down his face. He had claw marks in his throat. He died a few minutes after they brought him to Mama Opal. Shade managed to force the information from him – I don't know how. Axle wouldn't tell me. No one would. He grabbed that glowing sword of his and went after them. He returned at dawn the next day with the bodies."

Dead.

"He never told us what happened or what he did to defeat the shadows. He just said that the shadows would not return. Cedric and Leanna were hard to bury." River turns her head away, face pale with fright.

"Their bodies were torn to pieces."

It is almost dusk. River and I stumble back to Agron through the thick trees.

River continues talking about Rod – Leanna and Cedric forgotten in her bliss. But I cannot forget. I imagine their horrified screams. Their bodies mutilated and torn to pieces. I remember the shadows from that long ago night. From Agron's square. How we'd spoke to one another. How I'd understood when no else could. The scars on my neck sting, and I rub a hand over them timidly.

"You okay?" River asks.

"Yes." I drop my hand by my side again.

"I was asking you a question."

"I'm sorry. Go ahead."

"Do you find Rod attractive?"

I force the best image of the tall, lanky, brown-haired lad into my mind. "He's . . . attractive enough, I suppose?" *Certainly not my taste, though,* I decide not to add.

"Yes, he is," River agrees, "but he can hardly compare to Shade."

I choke on the air I've sucked into my lungs. "You . . . you find Shade attractive?"

"Of course. I'm no fool. Don't you?" She winks teasingly at me before elbowing me gently in the arm. "Come now, I've seen the way you look at him. Don't tell me you haven't been admiring those sleek muscles and that insufferable frown on his lips."

I had. But for entirely different reasons then she suspects.

"Your taste in men is questionable," is all I say to her.

Chapter XX

Once again, Shade is absent when I arrive at the ruins.

I had a feeling he would be. But I had hoped he'd make his presence known to me before returning to Agron from his hunt. I chastise myself for the thought. He has no ties to me. No emotions. I wouldn't even call our altercations "friendship." Yet, I had hoped that we'd grown close enough to talk without making riddles of our conversations.

I ignore the swords. A part of me hates them. I reach for my dagger instead.

One hour.

Two hours.

A loud rustle interrupts my concentration mid-throw, embedding the dagger in the tree opposite of my target.

"Damn," I mutter and retrieve it from the rough bark.

I assess my surroundings quickly. It is a sunny day but the forest is so thick that only pockets of light seep through the leafy branches. It gives the forest an eerie look. The crumbling ruins and misshaped, jutting walls add to the disconcerting imagery.

Another rustle stirs the silence of the forest. Softer. But closer.

Hesitantly, I return to the fine line I've drawn in the dirt for my "respective distance" and pick up the sword I tossed aside. I sheathe the dagger beneath my skirt.

Leaves crumple.

I back away from the sound. I have practiced enough for the day.

It will be alright to return to Agron earlier than usual.

A soft intake of breath halts my departure mid-step. A snort.

An animal.

Leave. Flee.

I ignore the warnings and move forward instead. The sounds came from a corner of the ruins. I step through the thick foliage of low-hanging trees.

I try to sift out the danger. I have familiarized myself with the forest creatures that inhabit this part of the forest, but I can see none of them. Not the strange green birds that like to laugh at my practice. Not the fat squirrels that run up and down the trees as I collect their nuts for my returns to Agron. Not the furry, four-legged creatures that Shade and I ate on our journey to Agron for the first time.

In fact, there is no wildlife at all.

A soft rustling brushes my ears once again. I snap my attention to the crumbling wall from whence it came, but only see a giant pile of leaves blown against its form.

I turn my head to the left.

A soft breeze teases my hair. Leaves furl up from the forest floor in delicate circles. I hear rustling everywhere. I look to the wall again.

The giant pile of leaves is still there.

My heart skips a beat as I blink in horrified shock.

It's not a pile of leaves.

It's a beast.

The leaves unravel into the four-legged ferocious animal with three rows of shiny, white, blood-stained teeth smiling back at me through its gaping mouth. A long tail uncurls from around its legs, with pronged needles rising up from the surface of its brownish skin. It has a spine of spear-like horns all along its raised back and its ears. A long hiss vibrates from the back of its throat like a pissed off snake.

It launches towards me.

I drop my sword and rush for the nearest obstacle – a five foot high piece of ruined wall. My hands grapple with the edge before I successfully lift myself onto its surface. I turn around.

A collision of spiny needles slams into my arm. Flesh rips. Blood splatters the stones. The creature inhales as the smell reaches its nostrils. It glares up at me from the ground, its hind legs convulsing. I recognize that mannerism.

It launches itself towards the ledge, claws successfully catching the stones. I roll off the ledge and land on all fours, palms and knees burning. The beast hisses at my trickery. It struggles to scramble free from the ledge. I have seconds to find safety.

There is a large group of ruins directly in front of me. The remains of a lord's esteemed manor. Shade told me never to enter it because, though it was the only ruin with all of its many walls still standing, it was dangerously close to collapsing. I don't think. I don't breathe. I dash in through the large, arched doorway – and wish I hadn't.

It's a maze. I had always wondered what the skeleton of my home back in Kelba would have looked like had the fixtures and ceiling been removed. Now I know. An endless amount of jagged doorways and crumbling rooms to choose from – each one probably an entrapment. My mind, once again, tries to remember the typical geography of a lord's home, but a furious snort behind me makes fear choose for me. I dash to the left.

The room I enter must have been a study. It is small and the now open window is covered with ivy and moss resembling a spider's web, making it impossible for me to rush through for safety. I hear the creature's nails scraping on the stones in the foyer.

My silence is imperative.

It hisses angrily when it cannot hear me.

Softly, I enter the next room. A hallway.

Behind me, the beast snorts. It sees me!

I run. Try to think as the beast closes in behind me. As the hallway begins to narrow out.

In most noble homes, a hallway like this would have led to a veranda. Ahead of me, I spot a light. There's a doorway around the corner. An escape!

I smell dirt and putrid, damp skin behind me. Warm breath edges my spine. Its close. The back of my dress rips as claws rake the hem. I force my legs to pump faster. Reach the corner. I grab it and propel myself in a circle through the ivy-covered opening it presents. For a moment, I think it won't break. I'll be trapped in a spider's web of vines as a free meal for the sharpened teeth of my hunter. But the vines snap, and I crash through them onto the stones behind. I roll down the steep embankment of what used to be a graveled pathway and push myself to my knees.

The creature is not so lucky. Its claws rake the ground as it struggles to come to a stop. It slams into the wall by the door, unable to turn the corner at its furious pace. Stones crumble. The walls on either side of the hallway shake and begin to give way. The beast barely manages to escape as the remains of the lord's lovely manor crash to the ground. I choke as dirt and decay cling to my lungs.

The beast is clumsy around corners.

I ponder the new observation and search for the nearest wall. The creature looks at me. Rage burns in its eyes. Apparently, it expected me to be a much easier kill.

I see the wall it hid against only minutes before. My sword is not far behind it. If I can reach it . . .

The creature runs at me. I note its cat-like leaps.

I stumble around the corner. My ankle tightens from the movement. Twisted.

Shit!

The ledge I'd used as a safe-haven moments prior teeters unsteadily above me. I step away from the wall.

The beast turns the corner in a blur of brown and claws so fast it startles me. Its nails rake the leaves as it slides, but not as far as I had hoped. It is close enough to strike at me. I watch its tail ready for the attack. Blood stains my left arm in deep red. The wounds lashed across my skin burn.

Pump.

Pulse.

My palm is heavy again.

The creature lunges at me.

A pulse – like a massive heartbeat – shoots from my hand. The ledge launches sideways, uncharacteristically fast, and crashes onto the monster's back. It howls in pain – so loud that my ears pound. Blood flows down the monster's brown sides and pools on the ground as it struggles free from beneath the stones.

I pull my dagger free and throw it. The blade sinks into the beast's neck up to the hilt. I put twenty feet of distance between us and wait for it to fall to the ground. To breathe its last. To die.

But it doesn't. The monster howls and shakes its head from side-to-side like a dog trying to free itself from a collar. Blood spots the ground. It teeters on four legs.

Damn it! It's not dying!

It rushes at me, still fast for a wounded animal of its size.

I crouch low to the ground. I sense the sword behind me, inches from my foot. I don't dare reach for it. I don't dare take my eyes off of my attacker.

Fifteen feet.

Ten feet. The creature's mouth opens.

Five feet. Its eyes yellow with rage.

It leaps into the air above me. I roll to the side the way I remember Shade doing so many times. The creature lands heavily on all fours exactly where I would have been. Exactly where my sword rests. I reach over, grab the hilt, and slice upward with all the strength that I can possess. I hear the sword connect with flesh – breathe heavily as it hesitates slightly on the brink of skin – and then blood gushes, freed from its veined confinements.

The creature falls to the ground, a new smile carved beneath its fearsome one.

The hilt of my dagger glares up at me from its lifeless neck. I reach down and violently pull it free. The blade is stained red.

The creature looks so much larger up close. Seven feet in length, not counting the tail. Five feet tall.

And I killed it.

I killed something! I killed. I killed. I killed.

My tunic is torn. My boots are filthy with dirt and blood. My arms are bloody and scratched and scarred.

And I've never felt happier in my life.

I want to kill it again. I want to watch its horrible, monstrous form fall to the ground once more. I want to watch its raging eyes fill with shock as I outmaneuver it. I want to watch it shiver and quake beneath me when I rise above it, victorious.

And, suddenly, I am not alone. From across the ruins, I hear enthusiastic, undefinable shouting and hands clapping.

Axle is the first to appear from among the trees and ruins, excitement painted on his face. He doesn't even stop running when he reaches the monster and lands a good kick against its side. He kicks it again. "Oh, hell, yeah. It's dead! No doubt about that!"

He bends down and admires the gash in its throat. "Congratulations, Kyla. Not a bad job for a first timer."

I wait for his companion. Shade approaches, slow and sullen, as usual. But the corners of his lips twitch. He's proud. Even if he won't say it openly, he's proud of me. My face feels uncharacteristically warm.

"It's a razor," Shade tells me. He brushes a hand over one of the horns ridged on its back. "Their skin is so tough it can withstand a blade's touch – only once, though. We use it for our vests. Our armor. And their horns *they* use for charms." By "they" I assume he means Axle and all of the others. I have never seen him wear any charms but his swords.

Shade walks the full length of the creature before joining Axle in examining the killing wound in its neck. He raises a brow at the gouged wounds in its back.

"You're lucky those stones fell when they did," he remarks.

A wave of shock ripples through me. "You . . . were watching?"

Shade shrugs. "You needed a real test."

I don't know whether to attack him now or to plot his demise elsewhere. He watched the razor rip my arm. Watched me rush into the dilapidated manor. Watched me try to outmaneuver the beast. Outsmart it. Kill it. And he did nothing.

Axle ignores the tension between us. He is trembling with excitement. "Yes. It was risky. Damn crazy, actually. But . . . but you killed a razor, Kyla! Shit, you killed a razor!"

Axle shows me how to skin the beast. It is tedious work, but I enjoy it. With the skin removed, the beast looks a lot less terrifying, and a heap more appetizing. I marvel at myself. I am not sick. I am not retching. I am not even remotely remorse about the dying mourns it emitted before its quick passing.

I struggle not to look at Shade as we cut up the razor into transportable pieces.

Dusk has already fallen by the time we're ready for the return to Agron.

Axle opts to carry the meat on his shoulders since he cleverly designed a contraption for the purpose. That leaves Shade and I to carry the skin between us. We each grab a side awkwardly, taking extreme precaution not to look at one another. For a long time we walk in silence. Axle is far ahead of us, a ghostly silhouette through the darkening trees.

"You understand it too, don't you, Kelban?" Shade says softly.

I look at him then, struggling to determine his features in the dim light. To determine the meaning of his words.

"The thrill," he explains when I don't answer him. "Of ridding the world of something evil."

I do.

The enthusiastic welcome of Shade and Axle lasts a short five minutes before Otis addresses the subject of the "razor." I try to wiggle my way through the crowd, intent on letting Axle and Shade take credit for the uncommon kill.

"We didn't kill it," Shade says.

Everyone looks at me. The torn dress. The wounded arm. The bloody dagger that I haven't cleaned yet. Realization hits them soundly.

"That's a gods-cursed lie if I ever heard one," Keegan chuckles directly behind Otis. "She doesn't have the skills to ground a creature like that. Now, maybe, to ground me . . ." He winks.

"Would you like me to make a demonstration of my skills?" I slide a hand over the edge of my torn hem. The tip of my dagger's sheath is visible.

Keegan's grin widens. "You wanna roll in the dirt, *vugra*, just say the word anytime."

Bastard!

Mama Opal reaches me and immediately grips my wounded arm gently. Her fingers probe the lash marks. "Let's get you to the house and disinfect this quickly, honey. The last thing you need is an infection."

I dare a look over my shoulder at Keegan as she pulls me from the square, and he wiggles his middle finger behind his back in a grotesque gesture.

I might have been mistaken, but Shade's eyes grow dark for a moment.

One second, and I see the barest flash of a memory (a memory tainted, horrifying, and violent) in his gaze before it flies away.

Mama Opal has the meal hot and ready, but neither of the boys show. River eats in silence, occasionally glancing up at me from across the table. Her eyes frequently dart from my bandaged arm to the branded edges of my scar that peek out beneath my shoulder strap.

"Where are they?" I finally ask.

Mama Opal swallows a bite of her smoked fish before replying. "When a monster like the razor is killed, honey, the menfolk celebrate. It is cause for rejoicing. Razors hunt the children of the village and diminish the game in the forest. And their hides are prized for armor."

"What do they do for celebration?"

"They gather at the establishment in the center of Agron and tell tall tales, insult one another, and drink themselves under the table, that's what they do," River cuts in. "I once tried to sneak a peek at the ruckus, and Axle nearly tanned my hide. He told me it was a no place for his 'sister' to waste her time."

No place. I smile to myself. Despite their differences, not many of the rules here in the Wilds were different from those in Kelba. But none of those damned rules had stopped Landor from excluding me.

I have no scholar's uniform to hide beneath.

But I am done hiding.

"Where are you going?" River asks when I stand abruptly and excuse myself from the table.

"I killed the razor. By right of victory, I am entitled to participate in the celebration." I adjust the skirt of my new tunic. Until the other one is properly mended, I am wearing Leanna's white outfit. I never liked the color. It makes me stand out.

"Kyla, don't. You'll get in trouble. You'll degrade yourself. Tell her, Mama Opal!"

Mama Opal smiles. A far-off glint flickers in her eyes. She isn't looking at either of us when she speaks. "Leanna . . . she was so proud when she killed her first razor. So proud. I never saw her smile like she did that day. Never saw the strength she possessed because I never gave her the chance. I didn't let her celebrate that victory because of a few damned rules made up by pompous bastards. I'll be damned if I do it again."

"Thank you," I whisper and walk into the street.

The tavern is not hard to find. I follow the sounds of laughter and shouting until I approach the long, rectangle-shaped building with multiple windows open to the night air. Inside I see men – dozens of men – with their mugs raised high and their voices drowning in the chaos. The sounds draw me in. I glance over my shoulder, half-expecting to see Landor, Asher, and Craig hurrying towards me after they lagged behind as usual. A painful reminder of where I am gnaws at my gut when they are not there.

No one notices me enter. They are all too busy listening to a tall, rum-bellied elder speak of his dalliances with a girl in a neighboring village when he was in his prime. Years of hearing every obscene story known to humankind slam silent fists against what should be lady-like shock.

The tavern has a single counter in one far corner. Four barrels, twice as big as a grown man, rest on sturdy shelves behind it. A tall, thin man with a wispy black beard jutting from his chin refills mugs with the requested orders. The smells of smoke and alcohol tickle my nose.

I slap a hand to the counter.

The bartender swivels around and his eyes widen.

I recollect my encounter with Shade in the forest. Here, they don't call their liquor "ale."

"Brew," I order.

My voice – a voice devoid of male gruffness – cuts through the noise of the room. Everything goes silent. I am aware of the ninety-eight pairs of eyes staring a hole in the back of my head, but I don't take my eyes off of the bartender. I watch his lips move as he tries to think of something to say. Instead, he hesitantly reaches for one of the mugs.

"Wait," a voice snaps. I don't turn around, even when the owner of the voice stops a foot behind me, their hot breath tickling the hair on the back of my head. "What are you doing in here?"

Otis.

Slowly, I turn around, inching my chin up so I can meet the big man's eyes. "Celebrating my triumphant kill." I tap one finger – two – against the wooden counter-top impatiently.

The bartender fills my mug and sets it beside my hand.

"What makes you think you have the right to celebrate such a thing?"

I shrug, ignoring the twist in my stomach. "The razor's blood on my dagger. The marks on my arm." I gesture at the bandages. "The fact that I just saved Agron a fair amount of panic and suffering. Take your pick. Each of them is factual."

Otis's thick brows raise – and then straighten out. He smiles. The tension in the room dissipates. He claps me on the shoulder. "In that case, as leader of Agron, I offer a reward. *Alistair*." The bartender looks up. "Put her drinks on my tab."

Alistair nods.

Otis leans close. "Tread lightly, Kyla," he whispers. "There are no friendly faces here."

I glance over his shoulder at the enthusiastic face approaching. "I disagree . . ."

Otis follows my gaze.

Axle leans heavily against the counter-top, sucking air between his teeth in loud hisses. "Y-you . . ." He points uselessly at me and doubles over.

"Y-you are . . ." he tries again and fails.

Otis rolls his eyes. "Exiting immediately. He's all yours." He returns to a group of men chatting across the room. All of them tip their chins at me in acknowledgment, raising their mugs slightly in a show of "gratitude." I mimic the gesture and their attention focuses on their conversation once more.

Axle thrusts his mug at Alistair. "Another overflow, my good man! That's right. No. More. More. There you go."

Alistair plunks the mug back down and thick foam dribbles over the rippling brim.

Axle takes a long, slow sip before turning and elbowing my bandaged arm lightly. "*Hev's e lavras, aventra?*"

I blink, feigning confusion.

His lips form into a thin line, but he shrugs and repeats in familiar Kelban, "How's the wound?"

"Oh." I nod. "Fine. Mama Opal used some 'gavran weed' on it and the pain is gone." I twist my arm back and forth a couple of times. "There is no damage to movement or loss of feeling. She says they should be healed in a few days."

"Lucky. The last person to encounter a razor was in bed for five days. Tough luck. He couldn't even hold a mug of brew to celebrate his victory. Wasn't much of a kill, though. He got lucky when the creature was distracted by an approaching warrior." Axle's eyes roll towards a corner of the room, and I follow his obvious signal.

Keegan leans against the wall, chewing casually on a black weed. His pupils are larger than normal and his skin has darkened. I don't have to ask what he's grinding between his teeth. Everyone in Kelba knows what *frassas root* is; a drug that relaxes your body, mind, and senses.

"He went after a razor?" I ask. Somehow I couldn't imagine Keegan having the courage.

"Decided to be a damned fool and take only a bow and arrow with him. Don't get me wrong. He's a damn good shot. But an arrow is not going to pierce a razor's hide. They are too fast. Their tale is like a personal sword. The razor took its time making him bleed and then went for the killing strike when he was too weak to stand." Axle sighs heavily and swirls the contents of his cup. "Luckily, Shade saw the whole thing and started towards the fray. The razor looked in his direction and Keegan took that opportunity to shove the tip of his arrow through the soft skin underneath its chin. Straight through its brain to the top of its head. Quite a beautiful kill. Too bad his reputation was ruined. No one would let him forget how Shade had killed twelve razors with a simple strike."

"Twelve!" I gasp.

"That we know of. I daresay he's killed more."

"Where is he?" I ask looking around. I know the answer before Axle even opens his mouth.

"Shade celebrates moments like these in his own way."

"Alone," I add with a sorrowful nod.

Axle cocks his head to the side and stares at me through narrowed eyes.

"What?"

"When he told me about your training – about your forest meetings – I didn't believe him. I didn't believe he, of all people, would go out of his way to help – to protect – you, a Kelban."

"Protect?" I feel like someone's punched me in the gut.

"Well, what the hell did you think he was doing?"

"Taking an opportunity to bully me."

Axle nods. "Well, I won't let that idea fly completely out the window. Everyone knows Shade is a pain-in-the-ass and on the far side of darkened humanity. Perhaps he gets satisfaction in ruffling your feathers. I know I do." He brushes a thumb over my wrist –

over the scar situated there.

I pull my hand away and glare at him. "Are you drunk?"

Axle grins and drains his mug. "Not yet." He winks.

I drain mine as well, the contents burning my throat. It clears the confused buzzing in my ears. The brew is five times stronger than a mug of "ale" in Kelba.

Axle stares at me. "You've done this before?"

"No. I only attended tea with high-class nobility and embroidered table linen." When my sarcasm doesn't wipe the confusion from his gaze, I add with a wink, "You'd be surprised by the things I have done."

Axle has Alistair refill our mugs. "I'll drink to that one."

Axle becomes a pink-faced idiot less than two hours later. Alistair refuses to refill his mug, which results in a sarcasm match, which ensues into a full-out argument, which draws attention, etc. etc. I slip away from the counter-top towards the back door of the building, my own mug still half-full.

Behind the tavern is a fenced area with three small buildings. One smells of piss and vomit. The other two of hay and dirt. I spot a trough-full of water in the corner of the paddock-like area and head in its direction.

I plunge my hand into the water and it spills over the wooden sides.

"What the hell . . .!"

I bite back a scream as the shadowy figure rises from the ground behind the trough and toss the contents of my mug at it. A groan – completely human – erupts from the figure as he wipes at his eyes. I recognize the glowing objects strapped to his back.

"Oh, gods, I'm sorry. Shade . . ." I lurch around the trough and pull his hands away from his eyes. They are tightly shut and even in the dim moonlight I can see the foaming ale sticking to his eyelashes. "Shit, I didn't mean . . ."

"What the hell . . ." he sputters again.

I try to wipe the foam off his eyelashes. He stills beneath my touch. I lean closer, gently scraping the remaining foam from beneath his eyes with my fingertips.

"Alright, open your eyes. Slowly," I whisper.

His eyes flutter open and meet mine. "What the hell . . ." he starts to say and then trails off. He shifts his head to the side and the tip of his nose brushes mine.

I flinch, startled, and suddenly realize my hands are still palming his face, fingers brushing just beneath his eyes. The rough patches of his shaved cheeks scratch my skin. Warmth tingles down my arms. We are way too close. I start to pull back and stop. His hand is on my hip like a vise, holding me in place. The other gently closes around my wrist and slides up my arm. His fingertips brush the bandage. He blinks.

And lets go of me like one would drop a hot coal. The feel of his skin is fresh on my fingertips. Warm. Human. A knot ties in my throat.

Shade brushes past me, quickly, and heads towards the tavern, his pace unusually fast.

"Shade . . ." I say, but he disappears inside.

I kneel down and pick up my mug. Damn it! Why wasn't I more careful? Why did I startle so badly? Why did I want to continue brushing his face? I douse my face in the cool water, hoping to chase away the dizzying warmth in my stomach. It doesn't work.

"What the hell did you do now?" Axle's sarcastic voice lulls. He turns the corner and leans against it, trying to appear like he's got all his wits. He doesn't fool me. He's drunk.

"I threw brew on him."

His eyes widen, and he starts laughing. "You . . . you threw brew on him? Really? I've been wanting to do that for years!"

"It was an accident," I protest. "I tried to wipe all of it away. To help get it off his face and . . ."

"Wait!" A sober light enters Axle's eyes as he holds up a hand. He teeters forward clumsily and stops a few feet in front of me, eye-to-eye. "You touched him?"

I nod.

"And he let you?"

I nod again, slower this time. Confused.

Axle stares at me, mouth half-open.

"What?"

"Shade doesn't let anyone touch him. Ever."

I don't know what he's trying to tell me. It all sounds like drunken gibberish in my opinion.

"There you are."

Shade's voice startles us both. He ignores me and loops an arm beneath Axle's shoulders. "Time to go. Keegan and his pups found another stash of *frassas root*."

I follow him to a corner of the paddock where he tosses Axle carelessly over the top rail. The drunken boy flops onto his back like a wet rag, groaning.

"You could have lifted him over the edge carefully," I chastise and squeeze between two of the rungs.

Shade easily jumps over the five foot fence and mud splashes Axle's face when he lands. Axle laughs uncontrollably and unsuccessfully tries to wipe it off. His fingers fumble uselessly.

Shade pulls him to his feet. "Wanna help me?" he asks, gesturing at Axle's remaining arm.

I wrap Axle's arm around my shoulders, stealing half the weight. "Sure."

I arrive at the ruins, expecting another day of lonely training. Instead, I nearly take Shade's nose off when he steps out from behind some trees. He observes the dagger in the tree bark near his head and nods approvingly before pulling it free and tossing it back in my direction. I catch it easily – with my left hand. He nods again.

"Major improvement. How about your skill with the sword?" he asks.

I stare at the weapon, cursing its heavy, difficult structure.

"That's what I thought." Shade smirks.

Shade removes the moon blades from his back and sets them

gently on the ground beside our training circle. In daylight, their blades don't glow, but the intricate designs on their curved hilts are still evident.

"What are your swords called?"

He looks at me in confusion.

"They must have a name," I continue. "They aren't made from the usual substances."

"Illathonian blades," he says.

Illathonian. "Moonlight" in ancient Kelban.

I nod approvingly. "How did you get them?"

"I earned them," he says. "Illathonian blades are rare. The metal used to make them is precious and limited. They are ten times lighter than a normal sword and twice that much faster. Fifteen years ago a few scientists also discovered that they were a shadow's weakness – the only natural phenomenon capable of destroying the nightly predators on impact. Illathonian blades were high in demand considering how many daily shadow attacks occurred. The king would reward the fiercest warriors an Illathonian blade when they did something for the benefit of the land."

"What did you do?" I ask.

He picks up a common sword. "Strike your poise."

"Shade . . ."

He lunges at me, and I block his strike. "Answer me."

He twists around and tries to strike at my back. I whip my own blade behind me and block the cut again, dodging out of his way.

We face one another. The usual calm that he exhibits is gone. Instead, he's breathing heavily, a red rash plastered to the side of his neck. I recognize the marks of aggression.

"Is this how you release it?" I ask as he bludgeons my blade with three quick, in-step strikes. When he comes for the fourth, I strike at his heels and he retreats. "All that pent up anger? All the . . ."

"So what if it is?" he asks and dodges to my right. His left foot lags behind. I recognize the trick just in time and swerve away instead of towards him.

We circle each other, muscles tensed but hesitant to strike.

"You told me I should turn my fears – my memories – into rage and it would make me a better fighter." *Celectate Wood. Aspen. Craig. Selena. Father. Love. Loss. Hate. Betrayal.* So many things to fuel that one emotion. To flood my mind with painful, empty anger.

How many memories did this silent warrior have? How many wounds did he hide? How many people had he loved, lost, and hated?

"What about you?" I ask.

Our blades lock as they collide mid-strike, forcing us to stare eye-to-eye. I watch that mask behind his eyes peel back slightly at my verbal assault. He flinches, and the wall is back. But I saw behind it.

Pain.

"What did you lose?"

Shade's lips curl up into a sneer. "I would quit pondering if I were you, Kelban, and pay attention to . . ." His leg snaps out towards mine and his swords slices through the air towards my neck.

I grip my sword with both hands and slam it into his. The clash of the blades ring in my ears, and I swivel my feet around. His foot misses my ankles by inches. I spin away and recollect my balance at the edge of our training circle.

"Your focus has improved."

"Disappointed?"

He doesn't answer and strikes at me again – this time in the direction of my waist. I turn the sword downwards and block the strike, forcing the blade away from my abdomen with a quick twist of my wrist.

I strike at *him* this time, forcing power from my legs, and smile in victory when he stumbles back to regain his balance. When he squares his shoulders and looks at me, I know that won't happen again. We furiously battle in the circle. Surprisingly, I don't feel any sweat on my brow. My muscles don't ache.

My heart races. My pulse pounds. My head palpitates.

Our blades connect.

Leaves jump from the forest floor like a soft breath has stirred the ground beneath them. My feet numb at the reaction.

There is no wind.

Shade doesn't seem to notice the unnatural phenomenon and tries to attack my back. I quickly recover my focus and disrupt his plans. The leaves at our feet swivel up in a cone formation when I twist his sword away from mine.

My hand is burning. Heavy. Pulsing.

I feel its drumming rhythm Its connection with everything around me. The stones. The trees. The leaves! Anything my focus latches onto.

I strike at Shade's sword, focusing on the leaves beneath his feet with my hand instead of my eyes. They rush up around his legs, and he flinches at their interference.

My mind races.

Focus. Focus. Focus.

The leaves flutter back into place. The dark space in my mind widens. Weights me down. Forces my heart to beat faster.

Shade raises his sword high in an aggressive strike. I force mine upwards to cut off the intended assault. His confident sneer disappears, and his eyes widen when his sword twists sideways for no apparent reason. The hilts of our swords smash together and tangle.

"Shit . . ." Shade mutters and tries to pull free.

The burning sensation in my body dissipates. Terror – cold as ice – clings to my insides. Chills climb up my spine. The pulse in my hand is still there. Low. Quiet. But ever-present. I try to force it away, but it clings beneath my skin like a disease. No – like a home. Like it belongs there, and I didn't know it.

A cramp. Just a simple cramp.

"Lesson's over for the day," Shade says, disconnecting our weapons after several muscled efforts. He sheathes it at his side. "Let's wash up and return to Agron. I think your lessons in swordsmanship are complete."

What he won't say is that I "beat" him.

I flex my fingers again. The pulse is gone.

Just a cramp.

I wash up first in the tiny pool situated behind one of the ruins. It is only two feet deep and barely ten feet around. Normally I clean my weapons in it but, for good measure, I wash my face and hands, hoping the cold water will ice the burn from my flesh. It doesn't. The nauseous pit in my stomach claws angrily, and I want to vomit.

Not now. Not near here.

I walk back around the corner. Shade leans casually against the wall, patiently waiting his turn. He looks up as I brush past his shoulder.

"I'll head back first," I say.

What I don't say is "I want to be alone."

He nods.

I am halfway down the ancient stairwell when I recognize the naked feeling on my leg. My dagger! I left it at the pool.

Hiking back up the rough terrain, I reach the wall and turn the corner, intent on grabbing my dagger and getting the hell away from this place. Instead, my feet stumble to a horrified halt. I suck in a sharp breath.

Shade is bent down over the pool, washing his face, his back towards me. He's taken off the vest and shirt he habitually wears and tossed them aside. The muscles ascend around the bones of his spine, but for once it is not his muscles that draw my attention. All along his back, stretching from his sides to his neck and clean into the waistband of his pants are white zigzagging scars. Long streaks run jaggedly across the zigzags. The marks of a whip. The same that I carry on my own back. But the zigzagged scars are of a different origin. They are too detailed, too organized to be made by a skittish lash. No. They look like the work of a carving knife!

"How'd you get those?" I ask, stepping closer to get a better look. The sight chills my blood.

He turns quickly, his face dark. The zigzagged scar marring his chest glares at me, and I can fully see it's length now. It turns my blood to ice when I think about how painful it must have been.

Shade doesn't say a word. He grabs his vest and slips it back on, pulling the strings to closed. The zigzagged white line remains etched in my brain; a horrible, purposeful scar. He turns away.

"Shade, how . . .?"

He grabs a knife from the pool's edge. The muscles of his arm tighten. "Don't!" He swings around and fixates me with a dreadful glare. I back away. "Don't you ever ask me again, Kelban!"

He storms off.

I can't get them out of my mind. Whenever I close my eyes I see his back. His chest. His scars. Horrible, white, ridged scars. I twist onto my side, trying to get comfortable – to wipe the image from my mind – and River elbows me sleepily.

Someone tortured him. The realization burns that blistering weight into my palm once more. Someone took a knife and carved those marks into his back. Not for information. Not for punishment. For enjoyment. For sport. Who the hell could be so cruel?

I am so close to finding out why he is the way he is. Why he hates everything.

He's hurt. He's scarred. He's like you.

My ears prickle at the sound of someone's soft whimpering. I shift onto my side, expecting it to be River, but she's sleeping soundly. The noise comes from downstairs. Eyes groggy with sleep, I tiptoe across the floor and down the stairs, peering out into the the open room.

The curtain separating Mama Opal's half of the room from the cots Axle and Shade occupy is drawn. She is not the one whimpering.

Shade is curled up in a ball, knees tucked nearly to his chin. He shivers. But not with cold. I can see the sweat glistening on his face in the firelight. The quivering of his lips. The tremble in his jaw.

He's having a nightmare.

"Get off me!" he cries out suddenly. I flinch at the broken desperation in his voice. "Let go! Don't. Stop! Please, stop. Stop. Stop!" He begins to writhe uncontrollably, the covers falling off of him. Spasms jerk in his neck.

I start to step into the room, but Axle rises from beside him. He slams Shade's shaking arms to the cot and leans over his friend. "Shade! Shade, snap out of it! Open your eyes. You're safe. We're in Agron. We're safe!"

Shade's eyes fly open when Axle presses knuckles against his sweaty chest. I see the zigzag scar, partly obscured by the tossing blanket. He sits up quickly, the blanket falling away. He tries to jump off the cot. Axle grabs him around the shoulders and holds him still, until his breathing slows.

"You're safe, Shade," Axle says, his own arms trembling.

"It felt real," Shade whimpers. I've never heard him sound so broken. Never seen tears pour from his eyes. He bites his lip to keep from screaming again. "It felt like we were back there again. They were . . ."

"It's over, Shade. It's in the past. You're safe now. We're both safe," Axle soothes, patting him awkwardly on the shoulder. There's tension in his own shoulders, and a faraway look in his eyes.

Slowly, I back up the steps, trying not to make a sound. Back underneath the covers, it is hard to fall asleep. Shade's pitiful wails echo in my mind, horrifying me. I had thought him an invincible hero on her first meeting. I had thought him an ass upon our second. I had thought him an angry tyrant for the past few weeks. Now I find him strange. Why does he hide behind a mask? Why does he have nightmares? What was the "there" he was talking about?

I try to think. To sort through the puzzle, the intricate maze, that has become the Wild boy. But I lose myself in the complicated web.

What does he fear so much?

Chapter XXI

"Shit." I rub the new drop of blood from my leg. The thorns in this part of the forest are brutal.

My unintentional outburst has prodded my target even farther from my reach. Back arched and head down, I stealthily creep along the forest floor, nearly on my knees. The brown tail I've watched for near thirty minutes is gone, but the long line it left in the dirt is easily traceable. I slip the dagger from beneath my skirt and palm it gently, the cold hilt melting into my hand like a second skin.

Shade was pissed when I arrived late for our practice the next day. I tried explaining that I was unaware we had practice since he'd made it perfectly clear the day before that I needed no more training. He then proceeded to interrogate my observation skills by forcing me to tell him the differences in everything around me. Leaves. Twigs. Animal tracks.

Axle arrived halfway through but made no move to interrupt or challenge Shade's foul mood. He merely leaned casually against one of the bigger trees and chewed on a long blade of grass. Every once in a while he would smirk when I'd dare to argue against Shade's lesson. A look from my brooding teacher would wipe it away.

Finally, after hours of languid talking, Shade pointed somewhere in the forest and told me to bring him a "*ragrartan.*" The species of animal that was my first meal in the Wilds. I remembered its appearance very well.

"How?" I'd asked him.

"Track it. Hunt it. Pretend it's a monster. I don't care. But bring it to me before sunset or I'll give you another lesson in physical exercise you won't forget." The threat was empty and he had known it. We both knew I was perfectly capable of holding my own in a battle with him – now.

But unwilling to back down from a challenge I'd retrieved my dagger, refused the sword he offered me, and strode into the woods with head held high and shoulders straight. Now I regret the haughty foreplay. Little red bumps surround the many pin-sized red dots on my legs from the thorns.

The *ragrartan* is sneaky and makes me go in circles. *It knows it's being hunted, the ugly bastard.*

I am close. I can feel it. The animal's tail marks have grown deeper. It is moving slower. Tired? Giving up? Oh, gods, I hope so.

I stop.

Over the silence of the forest a slight wind stirs the leaves above my head. It's not the breeze that draws my attention, though. It's the smell it brings in the air.

Smoke. Rotting flesh.

Blood.

For a moment, my muscles tighten as memories assault me. *A smelly hand pressed over my mouth. Teeth in my neck. The icy breath of a nightmarish captor.* I shake them away.

Ducking low behind a cascade of leafy branches, I peer through the green shrubbery. Leaves rustle loudly. Branches snap beneath solid weight. Five men – no, six – stumble over the rocky ledge. My throat tightens.

They are not Agronites.

The smell of blood and rot is so strong bile rises in my throat. I drag a hand over my mouth to muffle any noise.

One of the men is supported on the shoulders of two of his comrades. Dried blood covers him from head to foot, and I note the jagged holes in his armor. All of the men are blood-stained and covered in black ash.

They also have weapons.

Slowly, I creep back. Whoever they are – wherever they've come from – they will not welcome my presence.

My foot connects with something hard. A loud screech – like rusty hinges, only ten times louder – shatters the silence.

The *ragrartan* shoots from my hiding place and straight past the newcomers, tail held high in fright.

"Who's there?" The tallest – and least wounded – of the six stumbles forward. Blood is clotted around a gash in his thigh, but his walk is steadier than the rest of his comrades. His eyes scan the treeline and pause over my canopied hideout. "You there . . ." he calls.

Shit!

I slowly creep backwards.

"Please . . . don't go. P-please . . ." he whimpers. His steps quicken with anxiety. "Help us."

His comrades join in. The wounded man whimpers pitifully.

My ribs hurt from the tension.

"C-come out," the initial leader pleads. He reaches my hideout and forces the leaves away.

I stand up and dart sideways, out of his reach. But, now, I am in plain view.

The leader's eyes narrow when he catches a glimpse of my face. "A Kelban!" he snarls.

Damn it!

He has his sword out – a fierce, double-edged object better suited for cutting trees than battling – and hacks at me. I step back and the tip of the weapon brushes past my torso, teasing fabric. Now I regret not taking the sword Shade offered me.

He hacks at me again, and air kisses my skin as I narrowly avoid the blade once more.

"S-stop!" I gasp, but realize suddenly that they cannot understand me. They speak strictly in a rough ancient dialect of Kelban.

"Kill the bitch, Westave!" one of the wounded men moans. "Kill h-her . . ."

"N-no, I'm . . ." I start to say in their dialect but pain on the upper part of my arm cuts me off mid-sentence. A line of blood tattoos the length of my forearm.

"I'll kill you, foreign bitch!" This time when he comes at me I ram the pommel of my dagger into his stomach, then his shoulder, forcing him backwards. He stumbles and regains his footing, brows raised in shock.

I position myself in a defensive stance, the soles of my feet raised slightly off the ground for quick movement. "Come on then!"

He does.

I don't fight him head on. I use every muscle in my body to meander away from his weapon. The sword is too strong for full contact with my simple dagger, and I can't kill him. That is out of the question.

I know Shade and Axle are tracking me. They wouldn't send me into the woods alone without wanting to keep tabs on my activity. They can't be far off. They'll come when they hear the noise.

I duck away from Westave's sword.

Behind me, a voice – faraway – says my name. "*Kyla . . . Kyla . . .*"

"Shade!" I scream at the top of my lungs, only to realize I've taken my eyes off my attacker. I swivel around, dagger ready to strike, but it's too late.

Iron strikes me across the face. My chest cracks against the ground as I land. I reach for my dagger, inches from my outstretched fingers. A boot kicks it away into the shrubbery. I flip onto my back, intending to get up, but that same boot pins me.

The side of my face pulses with pain.

Westave raises the sword above my head. I imagine its thick edges smashing the sides of my head. Cutting my neck. Slicing me in half. A tree branch looms above his head, strong and alive with color.

The pulse shoots from my face to my hand like a secret message and the branch sways above his head when my fingers tremble.

The sword begins its descent.

The branch sways with my movement . . . I jerk my wrist in a snapping motion.

The branch breaks. Falls. Lands on my attacker's shoulders, knocking him sideways to the ground. Pinning him. His sword clatters next to my leg, uselessly.

I scramble to my feet and retrieve my dagger from the leaves.

Westave's comrades move to help him.

I brace myself for another fight.

"Kyla!" the voice is louder and sharper than before.

"Here!" I call.

Shade and Axle crash through the remaining timbers, swords already drawn, and muscles tight for a battle.

"Kyla . . . your arm . . ." Shade is at my side without warning, fingers probing my skin. He locates the gash slashed just above my elbow. His eyes narrow.

"If you lick it, I'll kill you!" I whisper.

The corner of his mouth wrinkles. A smile? A frown?

He turns around, but doesn't step away. Instead, he places himself in front of me, sword fanned out at his side. One of the men crouches low to the ground and his face pales. *Good.* He has common sense, at least.

"Who the hell are you and what the hell are you doing here?" Shade snarls. If I didn't know him I would piss myself. He sounds like a demon from hell.

"Gavrone," the leader says, regaining his feet. He brushes leaves from his arms. "We need to speak with your Keeper!"

Otis.

"You will," Axle says, his voice tight. "But first you will surrender those weapons and walk in front of us like good boys. Can you do that for us?"

Westave's face reddens at the mockery. "Listen, boy, I don't know who you think you are but . . ."

"Me? None of your damn business who I am. And personally I don't give a *ragrartan*'s ass who you are either. You want to meet our Keeper? You surrender those weapons and walk in front or we'll leave your rotting carcasses here in the forest to consult with the wildlife. Understood?" Axle gestures at the ground with his sword. "Lay em down."

Reluctantly, the weapons meet the dirt.

"Now . . . walk," Axle says.

"What about her?" Westave snaps, emphatically waving at me. "That Kelban bitch is . . ."

"With us," Shade cuts in. "Move!" He prods them forward with a threatening twist of his Illathonian blade, and Westave has the good sense to discover silence.

"I will say this," Axle says as we gather the weapons to return to Agron, "you're increasingly lucky, darling." His eyes flick over the fallen tree branch.

I refrain from replying.

Because I damn well know that luck had nothing to do with it.

Gavrone is a quiet, sleepy village in the heights of the mountainous regions around the Wilds. It's main purpose is the breeding of wild goats and sheep. Three days ago, Gavrone had been under the appearance of another uneventful night when shadows had attacked from every corner. Destruction had hung heavy in the air. Westave, one of the Keeper of Gavrone's most trusted assistants, was given orders to get help. And quickly.

"It happened so fast. One minute we were standing guard, joking with one another, and then it happened. Fire. Screams. Darkness. We couldn't see anything. They were so many of them. The air was thick with them. Our Keeper told us to find Agron. To get your help. We all know the stand you make against the creatures and how you defend the gate of our kingdom. We must request your assistance in this matter." Westave finishes his appeal and steps back, away from Otis's chair, and returns to his place against the wall.

Otis taps a thoughtful finger against his chin, silent.

I sigh heavily. Shade cranes his head slightly in my direction from where he stands beside Otis's chair as a representative. I look away quickly. His gaze makes me feel uncomfortable.

The Gavronites spent nearly an hour telling Otis of their trek through the forest, how many shadows followed them before daylight forced them to retreat, and about their encounter with me. Westave insisted I be escorted from the room, but Shade whispered something to Otis that obliged him to ignore the request.

"It's like a curse descended on us," one of the wounded men says. Every head in the room looks at him. "They were screeching. Screaming. Celebrating. Like the decimation was a festival for them. A cursed ritual."

"A curse we seem to share with your unfortunate villagers," Dirk mutters. "Have you an idea what caused such an event to happen?" He speaks to the man – but he leers at me.

"Dirk . . ." Otis's voice carries warning.

"I honestly can't say. It goes beyond my level of understanding. But perhaps our Keeper can tell you more when you arrive in Gavrone. If you decide, Keeper of Agron." The man cranes his neck in submissive apology.

Otis stands. "We will send help. Eight of the best Guardians of this village. If Gavrone still stands, they will help you recover."

"Thank you." Westave bows.

"Axle. Shade." The two stiffen when Otis looks at them. "Accompany them. I expect a full report that I can administer to the King. He will want to know about this unfortunate attack. Perhaps this will open up his eyes to the dangers we are facing out here and persuade him to send more sufficient troops."

Keegan stumbles forward. "I will go too."

Axle curses silently.

Dirk smiles as if he and his son share some secret, and my blood chills. "Me too!" I blurt out. As soon as the words leave my mouth, I want to bring them back.

Dirk sneers. "Yes . . . take the Kelban bitch with you. Maybe the curse will lift from our village once she has left its gates."

Several people within the light of the fire visibly flinch.

"Wait. What curse?" Westave says.

"Dirk, that's enough! If I hear another thing about this curse business I will silence that tongue of yours once and for all. Do not think I won't do it." Otis turns his attention to Westave. "Rumors. Childish stories. Nothing more. It seems Agron has become a weakened city of superstition instead of the strong gateway to our homeland that we intended it to be. As soon as the winter season is upon us I will attempt to correct that." He glares at Dirk and looks at me. "You may go. But you will have a guard."

I nod in confirmation.

"Who would want to guard the witch?" Dirk mutters. "She might strike them dead in their sleep."

"Shade likes to watch her." Axle elbows his friend in the arm. "He'd be honored to accept the task."

Oh, I want to stab him so much!

Apparently, I'm not the only one, because Shade glares, and Axle puts six feet of distance between them. As if he thinks that will stop him from getting a proper beating later on.

"Yes." Dirk smiles. He's pleased? "Let the savage guard the witch. He's the only one capable of subduing the demon anyway."

"Then it's settled. You leave first light tomorrow." Otis begins his exit.

But not before approving Keegan's request to accompany us. The bastard's eyes leer over me a full minute before he shifts his attention to Shade and gives him a slow, sly wink.

Hell, this is going to be . . . well . . . *hell!*

I pack light. Only a blanket, a leather quart of water, a day's worth of food, and a shawl that River insists I will need for the change of air in the mountains.

The town square is bustling with people readying the Gavronites and fellow warriors for their journey. I search the crowd for Shade but don't see him. Probably hiding from the faces. I find the nearest corner and re-check my travel pouch.

"You're missing something," a slow voice says.

I quickly slip the pouch onto my back and turn around.

Keegan blocks my exit with an arm against the wall. He chews with his mouth open so I can see the green frassas root inside. Resisting the urge to gag, I cross my arms, forcing him to give me more space or let my nails clip his chest.

"I don't need that. I'm not an addict," I respond.

He palms the dark green leaves in his hands gently. "Nor am I, but they are medicinal relief from the pressures and anxiety of this barren wasteland. How are you adapting to our wild habitat?"

"We both know you don't give a shit how I'm adapting."

He chuckles. "Right to the point. You're not fond of beating around the bush, are you, lovely? At least that part of your personality hasn't changed since I met you."

"Trust me, you've no idea how much I've changed," I snap and try to elbow past him. He grab my arm and pushes me back against the wall.

"Really?" He raises a brow. "Fine, then. If you ever need some friendly advice or a second opinion, feel free to search out my confidence." He leans closer and his lips brush my ear. "Preferably outside of camp in the middle of the night, if you're feeling desperate," he whispers.

"Keegan! Come here, son. I've something to discuss with you!" Dirk calls.

Never have I felt such gratitude towards the man.

Keegan rolls his eyes and heads in his father's direction.

I'm tempted to ignore the two entirely, until the sinister glow in Dirk's eyes has me readdressing that decision. Dirk is always upset, but I've never seen that light, the dead giveaway of suppressed rage, so evident on his face. Nor the effort he takes to conceal that rage behind a false smile of affection as he loops an arm around his son's shoulders and leads him across the square.

I follow them.

Dirk pulls the lad into a dilapidated shed. The roof is caving in and the timbered sides are rotting. I slink up to the side and peer through one of the knotholes. They can't be up to anything good and that uncomfortable feeling niggles in my gut again.

"Are you going to continue to be a disappointing pile of shit, huh? Do you even want to succeed in this miserable little village? Answer me, boy!" Dirk's voice is harsher. Sharper. It makes the hairs on my neck stand on end.

"I'm doing my best and . . ."

"Your best is worthless! I want to see proof of your efforts! You hear me? Proof! Not excuses. No more damn excuses. Either you makes yourself worthy of being my son or you can crawl on the ground like their dog taking the scraps they decide to give you. Is that how I raised you? To crawl like a dog? I have sacrificed everything – everything – to make us what we are today. I have dug you out of the shit-hole I was born in. And this is how you repay me? With shitty achievements?"

"I'm trying!" Keegan screams. His voice cracks midway with strain. "I'm trying."

"What's that smell?" Dirk steps close and sniffs. "*Frassas root*?" The sound of flesh on flesh fills the air. Keegan gasps in pain. "You haven't quit that stuff? I told you to throw it out, you worthless shit. Throw it out! Hear me? If I catch you smelling like a useless, slobbering dog again I'll make you wish you hadn't been born!"

"I'm sorry . . ." Another slap ricochets through the air.

"Never apologize! I will not take such weakness from you." Dirk is screaming now. "Is that what you've become? A weak bastard? Everything you do is weak. Unsatisfactory. A Kelban girl took down a full-grown razor! And what happened to you? You let it put you in the sick-bed for two weeks. You couldn't even kill it on your own. Shade had to help you. He's winning, lad! He's making himself look better than you. If you aren't careful, he'll take everything from you. Is that what you want? To be nothing because of him. Answer me!"

"No!" Keegan screams.

"Then get your shit together and take his ass down! This is your last chance to prove your worth." Dirk elbows past his son and exits the shack, slamming the door behind him.

I creep away from the shed.

The Gavronites say it will take a day and a night to reach their village. What they do not say, I notice, is how rugged the terrain will be. Four hours after a painfully dense part of the forest, I find myself looking up a wall of unending stone. It juts above my head into the sky like a pinnacle of my nightmares. My stomach whirls.

I am not climbing that.

I'm not the only one ill at ease.

"We are not mountain ilk like you," Keegan complains. He stares at the barely perceptible trail carved into the mountain's side. It looks even less trustworthy than him.

"You lowlanders will adapt quickly," Westave assures him with a knotted brow. He shoves past the surly lad and places a foot on the rocks. They hold his weight.

"And if we don't?" asks one of the warriors.

Westave shrugs.

I hang back from the others as they begin their ascent.

"Either move or get out of my way," Shade growls from behind me.

I move out of his way.

"You coming?" he asks when I don't follow him.

Maybe I should return to Agron. But there's a part of me that wants to go. To see what has happened. For some reason, I've been thinking it will give me answers. Answers that have – up until now – been avoiding me.

"I . . . I don't know how to climb." It's a lame excuse. How can I tell him? *Oh, yeah, when I was a child Celectate Wood threatened to throw me from the highest tower in his palace. He said, eventually, one day, I would fall to my death like all peasants do.* Just thinking about it makes my stomach quiver.

If Shade notices the fear hiding behind my discomfort, he doesn't show it. "You go ahead of me. It's easy."

Hesitantly, I place my foot on the rocks.

One step.

Two steps.

Three steps.

Twenty feet.

Thirty feet.

Fifty feet.

A hundred feet . . . *and I'm going to die!*

"Don't look down, you little fool!" Shade snaps as he grabs my ankle to steady my feet. "Look up! Watch where you're going and look up. Never look down!"

How can I tell him that when I look up I see Celectate Wood's face leering down at me? Damning me. Cursing me. Letting go of me.

"Kyla? Kyla, look at me."

I do. At first, I see the trees and forest so far beneath us. Green blurs of distant images. And then I see his eyes looking straight into mine. No mask. No wall. Just a connection of something stronger than my fear.

"You're not gonna fall."

I turn away so he won't see the truth in my eyes.

I've been falling for a long time.

We don't stop when night falls. Westave says it's too dangerous to sleep on the edges of the cliffs when enemies prowl the stones. I silently agree with him.

My hands blacken from climbing and my water runs out quickly. The wind gets colder as we ascend higher into the hemisphere. I tie the shawl around my shoulders and chest in an intricate knot.

Shade hands me a water pouch of his own. When I pop the lid, the smell is definitely not water.

"Hunter's brew?" I ask.

"It won't make you lose your senses, I promise."

A sip of the fluid gives me the strength to continue for another hour. By that time, we've reached a part of the mountain that has leveled off into a dense terrain of shrubbery and stones.

The Gavronites pause before a giant statue carved into the face of the mountain's edge and whisper a few words: *Imana se, mavre draves, e gatranas se.*

Bless us, mother gods, and protect us.

Axle rolls his eyes dramatically.

"You mock your protectors, lad?" Westave scolds.

"I have never mocked my sword." He palms the hilt of his Illathonian blade.

"Do not give worship where worship is not due."

"Your knowledge of the holy scriptures is profound." Axle makes a theatrical gesture of pain. "I am touched."

"The gods will not be blasphemed and you . . ."

"*We* have come to defend you, Gavronite," Shade interjects, "*not* your gods. Show us the way and then defend your religion."

We silently continue our journey.

I know when we are close to Gavrone. The air smells of smoke. Burnt wood. Ash. Flesh. It strikes a familiar fear deep into my heart.

It smells like my vision of the streets of Kirath did.

It smells like massacre.

When we step out of the dense trees, the air is thick with gray fog and wet with morning mist. Through the density, shadows move. Human shadows.

I hear the sounds of weeping. Sobbing. Screaming.

Death is here.

A breeze blows through the curtain around us and reveals the sight we were briefly spared. Blood. Blackened flesh. Decimated homes. Burning timbers.

Westave's face is white. I watch a single tear slip down his cheek. I know the look in his eyes. It has been on Landor's face thousands of times in my visions.

Guilt.

"They've returned . . ." A woman kneeling over the blackened body of what appears to have once been a man, lifts her eyes to our group. White lines glisten beneath her eyes where tears cleaned the soot away.

A man in a giant cloak of fur – the skin of a bear – steps out of the gray curtain masking Gavrone's simmering remains. His beard is braided across his chest, his hair uncut past his shoulders, and his chest bare to the mountain air. He clutches a massive ax in one hand.

"Keeper, I have brought help but . . ." Westave observes the destruction around him. He falls to his knees and bows his head low to the ground before the mountain leader.

The leader shakes his head, long past the weight of tears and outward grief. "Do not let this weight on your conscience, Westave. You could not have stopped this or prevented the event. Rise. Go wash. Eat. Your wife and child are alive. They hid in the forest."

Westave stands. The guilt disappears with the joyous news of his family's survival. He hesitates, glancing between his leader and us.

"I will handle introductions," the leader says. "Go. All of you."

The remaining Gavronites disappear into the fog.

The mountain man introduces himself. "I am Alvar, Keeper of Gavrone."

"Our Keeper, Otis of Agron, sends his condolences and our services. We are to conduct a full survey of this unfortunate catastrophe and present it to the king." Axle sounds like a diplomat.

"There is no need for you to investigate," Alvar says, his voice harsh.

"Pardon?"

"We are attempting to root out the source of the problem. Once we have weeded our village of the curse, we will inform you. Until then, your services will be appreciated. Much needs to be rebuilt and, if any of you are skilled hunters, you will be very useful."

Axle's eyes widen. "The curse?"

Keegan smiles slyly.

"Something drew the monsters here. Something unnatural. Once we find it and rid ourselves of it, we will not suffer their attacks any longer." Alvar sounds convinced.

"You never considered the idea that the '*something*' that drew the bastards here was their longing for blood and destruction?" Shade's voice is border-line control.

Alvar shakes his head. "There is a curse among us."

"Yeah," Axle nods. He scans the edge of the mountain. The village is built on a cliff's edge. "The fact that you live only two miles from the Dark Mountains. That's a curse."

The Dark Mountains?

"Despite that we are certain . . ." Alvar cuts himself off mid-sentence and looks in my direction. Our eyes meet. He gasps. "A

Kelban! By the gods, a Kelban . . . *Mavre draves gav ressa*!"

Instinctively, I rest a hand against the side of my leg. Three seconds, and I can have the dagger in my hand. Five, and I can have it in Alvar's skull.

A hand closes over my wrist. Axle's hand.

"The Kelban is under the king's protection and is not open to your judgment, Alvar!" Axle's voice is no longer diplomatic.

Nearby, Shade observes the altercation with a glint in his eyes, but makes no comment.

"Protection? Her kind deserves our protection after what they have done to us? Done to our land?" Alvar's eyes bulge in rage. "Curses follow curses. *Mavre draves, gav ressa. Mavre draves, gae ressa*!"

Mother gods, have mercy!

"If you harm her the wrath of the King will be upon you, and his justice is harsher than the gods!" Axle warns. He tightens his grip on my hand.

"The mother gods will have their justice! Their revenge on her! The King cannot stop that. He cannot stop her fate if the mother gods judge it so! And the mother gods . . ."

"I am Shade of Smoke!" His voice cuts like a knife.

Alvar grows silent.

"Have you heard of me?"

Alvar nods, mutely.

"Then listen . . . I am responsible for the Kelban. Should any harm be attempted upon her person or any accident befall her, my wrath will know no bounds. It's decimated armies of shadows and cut men in pieces. If you wish to face it, then, by all means, carry out the will of your mother gods. However, if you're the smart man I think you are," Shade pauses in front of Alvar, eye-to-eye, and a few inches taller, "you'll make an excuse and let a braver man than yourself fall on my sword."

Alvar swallows.

"Show us what we can do to help," one of Agron's warriors interjects quickly.

Alvar is eager to lead the way, leaving Axle, Shade, and I alone.

"Was that wise?" asks Axle.

"He knows better than to battle with a monster," Shade replies.

"What about the 'curse' he was talking about?"

"Rubbish. Nursemaid tales. Nothing more."

"But . . ."

"If you would like to go hunt useless fantasies, be my guest, Axle. Don't expect me to join you."

I pull my hand from Axle's and glare at Shade. "I don't need you to protect me from the wrath of *the mother gods*!"

"The gods have an amusing way of using human hands to do their work," Shade remarks with a slight nod in the direction of Alvar's retreating back.

"I can take care of myself."

"You can't even get ten feet off the ground without turning into a shivering little girl. How do you expect to take care of yourself, Kelban? You couldn't even fight water. Water!"

"Shade!" Axle snaps.

I can't feel anything. In my head. In my hands. In my body. All I know is I'm shaking. Shaking. Shaking.

My fears. My weaknesses. My defeat. He's thrown them in my face.

"You . . . you . . ." I can't find curses harsh enough to proclaim my anger towards him. Can't slap him hard enough to release the rage. Can't stab him because he'd stab me first.

And it infuriates me.

"Asshole!" I scream and run into the fog.

I don't expect either of them to follow. I stand at the cliff's edge and let the breeze dry the tears on my face. It smells like the sea. When I look five miles below me, dark blue water meets my gaze. And across the water – across from where I stand – loom the darkest mountains I have ever seen. They are blacker than coal and gray smoke furls from their surface.

Evil. Evil. Evil!

And the invisible magnet inside of me reaches for it.

In the back of my head, I feel that dark pit open up. The dark claws spread out. The pulse in my head grow louder. Stronger. Larger. It breaks into pieces. Places. Events. Distant times. I close my eyes. Concentrate. The pieces draw closer. Like a puzzle I have to piece together. I hear noises. Trees. Laughter. Screams. Pain. Waterfalls. Chains.

"Kyla?"

I open my eyes and they are gone. Nausea fills my stomach, and I back away from the cliff's edge.

"He's a little shit, isn't he?" Axle chuckles. He stops when I don't join in and rubs the back of his head nervously. "Look, Kyla, I . . . He's . . . it's hard for him to . . ."

"To what? Act human? Entertain human emotions? Human understanding? Hard for him not to pity those weaker than him?" I flip my hair over my shoulder and glare at Axle. "Look, I'm sorry I was raised in the spotlight of society. Sorry I had food in my belly, a roof over my head, and money at my disposal. Sorry I haven't been through the shit that he has, or done the shit he has, or started the shit that he has. Sorry I am weak and stupid and useless and frightened. Sorry I am not a monster like he is!"

The mountains echo back my words.

"But you don't believe that, do you?" Axle asks softly. His eyes search mine.

I look away from him, knowing what he's doing. That he's trying to read my thoughts.

"You don't see him as a monster," Axle says. "And that scares him."

"Scares him?"

"It kind of scares me too, to be honest," he continues. "You aren't scared of him. You don't fear him. You don't give a shit if he's mad. You do everything that everyone else doesn't do to him."

"And what's that?"

"Call him out. Give him sass. Fight."

"You do it all the time."

"We wouldn't have survived any other way." Axle's eyes go far away – beyond these mountains, beyond the Wilds, beyond light and humanity – and he blinks it away.

"What do you mean?"

"Nothing." He holds up a hand to interrupt me. "Don't ask me again, Kyla, please? It's in the past and should stay there."

"Really?" I ask. "And have you put it behind you? Seems like you carry it everywhere."

"What?" He looks startled.

"Well, not you, really. *Shade.* It's always there. Always hanging over him. Hate. Anger. Pain. He won't let me see it. Tries to hide it. But it's there. He's dwelling in a dark place and it's killing him. Slowly."

Axle's eyes glisten.

"Don't think you're the only one who can judge characters, Axle. I may not have your gods-given talents or your insightful abilities, but I'm an excellent judge when it comes to people's actions. And Shade's actions were not that of a monster! Just a boy – scared and trying to be brave." I turn my back on him and start to walk away.

"Kyla," Axle calls after me, "don't stop."

I do and turn around. "What?"

"Don't stop looking at him. Don't stop calling him out. Don't stop treating him like a little shit. Don't stop kicking his ass."

"If I don't stop, I might kill his ass!"

Axle splits a grin. "No, you won't. Unfortunately, you're not *that* lucky, darling."

I flip him the finger and leave his laughter behind me.

Two days should go by fast, considering the amount of time I've spent in this wild land, but each minute, each second, drags like an eternal moment. I spend most of my time picking up pieces of ruined wood and throwing them on the giant pile of remains in the middle of the Gavrone. I attempted to help gather the bodies surrounding the village, but Alvar refused to let me touch them with my "filthy" hands. If I touched them, the mother gods would not allow their souls into the heavens, apparently.

I watch the mourning bury the dead outside Gavrone among the trees. I watch them pray and sing the dead souls to the "resting place." I listen to the gossip, the horror stories, the rumors as I scrape my hands raw among the wood and stones.

I see very little of Shade and Axle. Whether they are both attempting to hide from me, I have not decided yet, but in the evenings, around our campsite that the Gavronites have ordained for us, they sit on one side of the fire and I on the other.

The rumors spread. The gossip spreads faster.

The village folk talk of a "cursed being" who "called" the demons. They remind me of Dirk. He'd said I was a "curse" when I arrived in Agron. A few days later, the shadows arrived. The only problem? There had been no newcomers in Gavrone for a year and a half. But, of course, the traumatized villagers are not inclined to reasoning.

At night, when I lay in the glow of the fire, I stare at my hands, palms upwards towards the sky. They look normal. Feel normal. Act normal. But during the day – for no reason at all – they will pulse. Stiffen. Attach.

I catch Keegan watching me on the third night, brows raised. His green eyes glow emerald in the firelight, and I glare, hoping my unusually dark eyes look even darker in the night's light. He only stares back at me, unflinching, and wiggles his middle finger grotesquely once more. My neck grows warm with hate. A glowing ember from the fire jumps in his direction. He gasps and slaps the flames eating at his blanket. I turn my back to him and the fire, smiling. *Serves him right.*

Mornings dawns.

I wander closer to the edge of the village where the Gavronites say the "attack" started. My arms are loaded with sticks, but I continue on. I can carry more. That's when I hear it. Sniffling. I walk around the corner of a blackened wall. A lone figure hunches against it, skinny and covered in ash. I have never seen anyone with skin so pale – except for the unfortunate man killed by the shadow blade. The boy's arms are bones covered in a pasty white imitation of "flesh." And, from the looks of his position, it appears he's been here for days without anyone's notice.

Slowly, I settle down beside him and drop my load of wood. "Are you alright?" I ask.

He looks up. I try not to flinch. If his body was ghastly, his face was worse. Cheekbones arched with hunger. Eyes large in his sunken skin. A layer of soot paints him from head to foot, dirtying his fine, blonde hair. He isn't older than fourteen. Fifteen maybe?

"Are you hurt?" I try again. He stares at me dumbly. Can he speak?

The boy stares at my eyes a moment longer. Peers closer. Notices the absence of dark rings. The shawl falling from my shoulders. The scar peeking from beneath the sleeve of my tunic. I see the truth finally dawn within him, but he doesn't look frightened. He's too tired to be frightened. Too frightened of something more frightening to be frightened of me.

"*Yavre e Kelban,*" he says.

Vaguely, I understand. Up here in the mountains, ancient Kelban is spoken more often than the mixed dialects down below.

"*Rae yer valesa?*" I ask.

His eyes widen in shock, revealing deep blue color that pulls me in like the tidal waves of an ocean, shockingly different from the usual blue eyes. The rings are less defined around his pupils. Hardly noticeable, actually. Is he not completely of Wilds birth?

"*Yer avrandas?*" he asks. *You understand?*

I nod.

"Vel?" he asks. *How?*

"*Ral Kelban vasras levran sa pav fo tavre vasgaras.*" All Kelban nobility learn as part of their tutoring.

Silence again.

"*Vat dagvasas raeve?*" What happened here?

The boy's shoulders quake. A tremor shakes his thin body. I reach out to steady him and he shifts away from my touch. Maybe the stories about "my kind" aren't completely lost to him despite his trauma.

"*Cav yer tav mi vat ti vas ave?*" Can you tell me what it was like?

Suddenly, he's rocking back and forth at a frightening pace, his head in his hands, and his voice cracking with strained, broken sobs. "It was dark," he says in ancient Kelban. "Quiet. There were stars blinking the sky. I was looking at the stars. I always liked looking at them. So far. Yet so bright. So many of them. Like little candles lit on distant planets. That's what mom said. And then . . ." Pain shifts across his face. "There was screaming. Bright light. Fire. Pain. Everywhere. In my head. In my body. Hurting. Tearing. Ripping. I couldn't get away. I tried. I ran. There was too much darkness in the light. Dark. Everywhere. Dancing. Laughing. Taunting." He swallows, eyes bulging in fear. "Shadows." The muscles of his face constrict. He's terrified. He grabs my hand. Pinches skin. "They spoke to me."

I flinch.

"The shadows spoke to me." He lets go of me. Stands up. Stares at his hands. At his arms. At his body. Terror – so real, so frightening – radiates off of him. "Demons only speak to the possessed. The cursed. Only speak to their own evil. The mother gods prophesy it is so. The mother gods warn of curses. Of demons finding their own."

I shake my head.

"I'm the reason. I'm the reason we were attacked." Paranoia flickers in his eyes. "I murdered them! I . . . I murdered them all. I killed them. Oh, *mavre draves*, I killed them! *Mavre draves, gav ressa!*"

"That's not true!" I insist. I lay a hand on his arm. His skin is cold. Too cold. He needs warmth. Food. Sleep. "They've hurt you. Made you see things that aren't so. Come. I'll . . ."

He shoves me away. "No! I'm the cursed one! I killed them. They found me! They let me live! They found me and let me live because I'm a demon too! I'm a demon!" He gasps between words, short on breath. He's in hysteria now.

"It's not . . ."

"They killed my mom," he whimpers, staring at the ashes of his home. "They called her a 'whore.' A 'bitch.' They said she deserved it. I heard every word. I heard them speak. They tried to take me. Drag me away. My mother tried – tried to stop them! Tried. Tried. They killed her. They told me 'stay' if I wanted! Stay! Stay!"

"You need to calm down. Calm . . ." I step towards him.

"No!" He jerks away. Shakes his head. Wildly. Madly. "Don't come near me. I'll kill you too. I'll curse you." He steps back. One step. Two. Three. Farther from my grasp. And with each new step, the hysteria turns to something colder. Darker.

Panic.

"You're not cursed," I say.

I follow him. He backs towards the end of the village. Towards people. He cannot be within earshot in his state of mind. I have to catch him. Subdue him.

They will kill him if they hear him talking like this. The villagers, with their superstitions and misguided gods, will kill him. "You didn't do any of this. This . . ." I throw my hands out to encompass the destruction, ". . . is just them! They are monsters. All of them. Don't let them frighten you. Don't believe any of their lies. You're just tired."

"No. I did it. They came for me. They came for me because I'm one of them!" the boy screams. "A demon! A cursed demon!"

A gasp to my right assures me that my worst fears are realized.

"It's him!" a woman cries shrilly. She screams.

I hear voices nearby. Others are coming.

"The cursed one. I've found the cursed one . . . Alvar! Help! Help! Before he calls them again!"

"No . . ." I gasp.

The boy turns and runs.

Half the village follows him. I shove my way past most of them, kicking shins, elbowing sides, and pushing faces. A second heart throbs beneath my chest. I cannot let anything happen to the boy. He isn't cursed. He's like me.

The boy *is me*!

The boy reaches the cliff's edge and has no choice but to stop. The villagers surround him – keeping twenty feet of distance between themselves and the "curse."

"Knew it had to be him . . ."

"Always was quiet and strange . . ."

"His mother kept him inside all the time . . ."

"Knew his eyes weren't normal . . ."

I reach the front of the crowd.

Alvar spits in the boy's direction. "You're lower than a damned, devil-worshiper!" he screeches. "You deserve to be torn limb from limb. Mark my words, you'll pay for the lives we lost, boy. All of them! You son of a bitch!"

The boy isn't crying. He can't. There aren't any more tears to shed. He looks at the crowd, those unnaturally blue eyes flickering over the faces of people who, mere days beforehand, had been friendly neighbors. He glances over his shoulder at the edge of the cliff. At the sea beneath. The Dark Mountains beyond. He faces the crowd again. Those temptingly beautiful eyes finally look at me.

The air leaves my lungs in a sickening rush. I know that look. I've seen it on the thousands of faces of thousands of "ostracized" before me. Fear. Despair. Guilt.

Defeat.

My hand grows hot. Pulses. Pounds. But the pit in the back of my head wavers. Like I'm hovering over the edge of a cliff too. I can't connect.

"I'm sorry," the boy whispers.

I shake my head at him. *Don't. Don't do it.*

He turns and jumps.

NO!

I leap at the cliff's edge, kneeling over it, screaming after him. The pulse in my fist lashes out after his descending body. And – like an invisible rope suddenly appears between us – the boy wavers in midair. I see the surprise in his widened eyes. Something – nerves, bones, I don't know – snaps in the back of my head. Blinding pain. A white flash.

And the boy falls into the fog below. Out of sight.

Chapter XXII

I wait for the cover of darkness before slinking to the cliff's edge. The fog is thicker than ever. The distant sound of waves echoing below the rocky outcroppings invades the silence. Over the thick mist, across the sea beneath, I spot the Dark Mountains once again. They glare at me, warning me to retreat back to the warm fire and my blankets.

I look away from them, but their presence remains over me. Axle had said they were unknown territory – territory that the shadows infested. No one had entered the dark expanse of rock and returned. I have the unnerving feeling that the Dark Mountains have monsters of their own, besides the shadows.

I return my attention to the task at hand. I cannot see the bottom of the cliffs, but I know they are there. I know I am three miles from the surface of the water. I know if I fall my bones will split apart, my flesh become buoyant, and my body will drift out to sea and fall prey to sea monsters. I know my body will tense up, I will lose my grip, and I will fall.

I turn around. The fire is better. To live is better.

But everywhere I turn I see the boy's terrified eyes. His wide-open mouth. His screams. The people who laughed when he fell and turned, congratulating themselves on his demise. No tears were shed for him. No grave was dug for him.

All because of superstition. Because of the damned mother gods. Because of hate and malice and misunderstanding.

Because of fear.

Gingerly, I crawl over the cliff's edge onto the rocky outcropping beneath. Immediately, my muscles harden at the new weight – the new shift in gravity – as my toes dig into the side of the mountain. I left my sandals at the edge of the cliff since they would hinder my descent.

The air is chilly, and the mist clings to my cheeks. A breeze flutters beneath me and blows the edge of my skirt up past my waist.

I look down. Any confidence I foolishly built up blows away, and there is nothing but ice in my veins. The fog is gone, gently brushed aside by the tongues of sea breeze licking up from three miles below. I see the waves. The rocks. The dark water waiting to encase me. Welcome me. Claim me.

My grip on the mountain weakens.

I slip.

Stone scrapes along my side. My arm. My knee. I grapple at the mountainside and my fingers find a knot-hole. I hang over the steep embankment. Over the waves. I claw desperately at the rock. I cannot fall. I cannot hear my bones crack. My lungs explode. My eyes burst from my face. The heavy beating in my chest is like a wild animal struggling to escape its cage. My ribs ache.

Breathe. Breathe, Kyla. For some reason, a mixture of Landor and Shade's voices speak to me.

I close my eyes.

Concentrate. The voice has darkened.

I don't want to fall.

"*Be careful, Kyla Bone. You don't want to fall.*" Celectate Wood's voice.

"*You don't want to fall. You don't want to fall. You don't want to fall.*"

You will fall. Your kind always falls. Your kind is meant to be ruled.

I am lower than dirt and meant to be ruled. Ruled by him and ruled by my fear.

Tears sting my eyes. I open them.

For a moment I can see his face, etched in that dark smile, and his eyes shining into mine as he leaned over. As he let go of my hand. As he condemned me to death.

But I didn't die!

I snag the edge of the mountain again and dig my feet into the stone until they burn in pain. Slowly, his face disappears. His smile floats away. I am once again staring at the mountainside. At the sea beneath me. At the waves.

It is rock.

It is water.

They are nothing to fear.

He is nothing to fear.

Those were the fears of a little child. I am no longer a child. No longer a pawn.

I am no longer afraid.

It is a slow process, but the waves grow closer. The salty smell of the water fills my senses. Burns my nose. Stings my eyes. I finally settle my bleeding, aching feet at the base of the cliffs and look up. The air is too thick. I cannot see the top of the mountain.

A different smell captures my attention.

Blood.

I draw my dagger and weave through the fog. Water laps up around my heels as the waves slap against the rocks. A dark substance floats through the ripples like the fingers of a beckoning hand. I follow it and find the first piece. Throat tightening, I pick it up and continue the search until I've made a pile of the remainders. A few are missing – floating out to sea or in the belly of some scavenging sea urchin.

I cannot leave them here.

A crater in the side of the mountain looms in front of me. I gently pack the pieces inside of it and reverently border up the opening with stones. I shove. Push. Prod. But it isn't tight enough. At the coming of the tide, they will wash away.

He will wash away. Forgotten. Alone. Banished.

Like me.

Rage turns the ice in my veins to fire. He won't be left as food for vultures and monsters. He won't go unburied and forgotten like Lord Telman and a thousand others before him. I ball my fists and the angry pulsing in my head flows downward to my enclosed fingers.

I flex my fingers. They are heavy. Burdened.

The stones around the cave's opening flex with them. Move. Pulse. Reposition. Like a puzzle that I'm dictating and piecing together with a thousand hands.

I squeeze my hands into fists again. The stones compact. Grind. Shift against once another. They grow tighter and tighter into the side of the mountain. Pain shoots up and down my body, like I am pushing into the mountain myself.

"*Do you know where you stand, Kyla Bone?*"

The stones cease to move. The pulse slowly dies, leaving me weak and cold. I stare at my hands. Trace the ridges of my palm where that pulse had been at its strongest.

No, I do not know where I stand. But it sure as hell isn't where I thought I did.

The returning climb is more strenuous than the descent. It takes me three hours to reach the cliff's edge. A line of pink is just beginning to form on the horizon. In the dim light, my hands are torn, gnarled, and covered in dirt and the black muck of the mountain. My feet are equally bloodied.

I hurry to the trough of water positioned at the corner of Gavrone. The evidence must be washed away. I know the Gavronites will not take kindly to me burying a "demon." They will not like my explanation. And they will definitely not like the words I wish to call them.

Wretches. Filthy, horrible bastards. Child-killers. Murderers. I scrub at my hands – at my feet – with vengeance. *I want to hurt them. Want to open their blind eyes. Want to tell them what I can see, what I can do, and what I can hear. That I am not the cursed, weak Kelban they think I am. That I can destroy them. Hurt them. Kill them with just as little compassion as they showed that boy. I want to rip them to pieces.*

And it scares the hell out of me.

What am I thinking? What am I becoming? Gods, help me.

I finish washing, but the blood and new wounds still remain. I will find some excuse for them. No one will care, anyway. If anything, they'll be pleased that the "Kelban" is suffering.

I turn around to return to the campsite.

"Back at last?"

I flinch at the voice.

Shade steps out from behind one of the skeletal buildings. Both of his Illathonian blades are gripped in his left hand. His right rubs at black soot lodged on his vest. His eyes only look at me, though.

I stare right back, unblinking. Unflinching. Unafraid.

"Can't a Kelban relieve herself in privacy?" I step past him. I am tired. Shaken. Angry. And not in the mood to face one of the boy's killers.

"Was it done right?" he asks.

I pause.

"I don't know what you're talking about," I say over my shoulder.

Even though I don't look back once, I know his eyes follow me. I know he knows where I went. I know he knows what I did.

I also know he doesn't know why.

And if he finds out – he'll run his Illathonian blade through my body.

Chapter XXIII

"Goodness, child, you'll get dust in my bread. Then how will I explain to Otis why his meal is so clumpy. He's picky about his food, you know?" Mama Opal struggles to remove the imaginary dust specks I've scattered over her dough.

We returned to Agron last night and Keegan was more than happy to relay the dreadful Gavrone event to Otis personally. Otis disregarded the story with horrified, enraged outbursts about Alvar's foolishness and the poor boy's demise. He stood alone in that opinion. Several of the villagers followed Keegan to the inn for a drink and more of his wild tales.

I have not seen Shade. He made an effort to stay away from me on our return journey. We have not spoken since that night. He's angry with me.

At least, this time, the feeling is mutual.

"Don't you have somewhere to be, Kyla, instead of dirtying up my cooking?" Mama Opal winks at me slyly.

"I . . . not today, really. You see, Shade and I . . . we've kind of . . ." How can I tell her we're having another one of our "hate" days?

"Ah . . . I see." She bustles around the edge of the table and pats my shoulder with a pudgy hand. "Lovers' spat."

I make a face at the idea. "More like a mutual agreement not to kill one another."

"Hmm . . . that's a very generalized explanation of a rift between two equally stubborn individuals with mild attractions to one another."

"Mama Opal . . ."

"No whining. He left early this morning. We both know where he's gone."

"He won't want to see me," I argue.

"Since when did that stop you?" She pushes me towards the door. "Go find him. That boy's a problem when he's alone."

I won't go see him. I'll just take a walk. And if I accidentally happen to run into him . . . well . . . then I might broach the subject that's been tearing at my mind.

Otis approaches me as I stare at the wall surrounding the village. His face is stern. He puts his arms behind his back and looks up at the wall too. "Fine piece of craftsmanship, isn't it, Kyla?" he asks.

"Yes, sir." I don't show any sign of being disturbed. "It is magnificent." And it is. For me, who hadn't even considered anyone in the Wilds capable of basic hygiene, it is a masterpiece.

"It took years to build. Three, in fact, with a harsh winter. There hadn't been many men, thanks to the shadows. The king agreed to send us reinforcements, but they never came. 'Too preoccupied with other matters' he'd replied. I find it odd that the shadows are getting bolder. Getting closer." He looks at me. He expects an answer.

"It is odd," I agree.

"Very."

I widen my eyes. "You don't think that I . . . I am bad luck, do you?"

"No. I am not privy to Dirk's hell-cursed superstitions. I care only about the safety of this village and the people within it. And I worry. The people of this village are mine to protect. I am their Keeper. They are my children. Even Dirk and Keegan. I am charged with protecting them. That is a responsibility I cannot ignore – even if my personal beliefs challenge that role." He sighs. "Do you understand what I'm saying?"

"Yes, sir. You're saying if it comes down to a choice between the Agronites and a Kelban you won't hesitate to choose the former."

"Kyla . . ."

"Don't." I hold up a hand to stop him. "I understand. That's the way it's always been. Everything in my life has always come down to choices." Me or my father. Aspen or banishment. Agron or Kelba. And, in each circumstance, I wasn't important enough to be chosen.

"But," I add, "I hope you understand this, Otis. I lived my entire life fighting to keep the right to make my own choices. I'm not going to give that up."

Otis smiles. "I don't know why you would."

"You understand what I'm saying, don't you?"

"Yes." He claps me on the shoulder. "Yes, I do. And if that day comes when your chance to make your choices is at risk, I will be there. I will make sure you retain that right. It is the basic right of any individual, Kelban or not."

"Thank you." I know he means it.

"If I ever chance to have a daughter, I prey she has your spunk. She'll need it for this world we're living in." He looks sad and enthusiastic all at once.

"Mama Opal will come around."

It takes him a moment to register my meaning. He blushes. "I-I don't know what you mean, girl!"

"Don't you?" I raise an eyebrow.

He coughs uncomfortably and waves his hand in the gate's direction. "Continue about your business. I interrupted you. I have business to attend to at the . . . uh . . . at the . . ."

"Mama Opal has almost finished making your bread. You could go retrieve it."

He turns even redder. "That woman does make the best bread in existence, but . . ."

"But she's very impatient. If you don't pick it up on time, she'll be very cross with you, Keeper." I turn my back on him. "Go get it. She's waiting."

"Y-yes." The gravel crunches beneath his feet as he walks off. Very quickly.

I chuckle. River would be ecstatic right now.

"Making all the right friends a little quickly, eh, Kyla?" The voice is so close, so hot, against my ear that I jump with surprise. It's impossible to not know the smooth, oily tone that has become the annoyance of my life.

"My father says you're a 'witch'. Are you using your supernatural abilities on Agron's Keeper now? How shameful of you, I must say." Keegan pokes his face close to mine, his eyes darting over my features mockingly. He wrinkles his nose and draws back. "You even smell charming. No wonder Otis would be dragged into your little schemes."

His father says I'm a witch? What else is he saying? No. I won't think about that.

Drawing back, I cross my arms over my chest and give the impression of being totally unruffled. Heat floats throughout my body, fanning flames that have been left alone for far too long. "Still angry about our last encounter, I see. I must apologize, but I'm very unused to having foul-smelling vermin so close to me. After all, I was nobility." His face has reddened. I lean closer, relishing the fact that it's my turn to infuriate and mock him. "And you know what they would do to vermin like you who stick their faces, knees, and other body parts in unceremonious places?" I pause, waiting for the words to sink in. For his eyes to blink shockingly. For his jaw to harden. I land the gut-punch right where it will mean the most. "They cut their slagging balls off!"

Keegan actually has to swallow before he can speak, and only after his eyes dart towards his manhood. "Really?" He takes a step towards me. His hands shake. He wants to hit me. Wants to hurt me. I see it in his face. "And who's going to help you with that? I guarantee, it's a little difficult to do by yourself, little girl. Why don't you try? Let's see if you can even begin to attempt it. Winner takes all." He grabs at me, his hands framing my face, and pulls me in close.

I am faster, though. He stops, his face hovering inches above mine. His skin turns a white pasty color. Slowly, his eyes glance down at his crotch where I have just placed the tip of my blade. His hands tighten on my jaw unsteadily, fingers shaking.

"Winner takes all," I say quietly, allowing the dagger's tip to move forward just a fraction of an inch. It hovers just over the brink of puncture point. All it will take is one effortless push of my wrist. I look straight into Keegan's eyes. "Make your choice."

Keegan makes his decision. He lets go of me and backs away. When the tip of the blade can no longer reach him, he lets out a huge breath. Rage lights his eyes. "I'll . . . I'll get you for that, Kelban!" he snaps. "And it won't just be my boot on your lovelies when I do."

The words, though meant to frighten, only make me laugh. He widens his eyes at the reaction.

I twirl the dagger lightly between my fingers, not even looking at it as they move swiftly over the rough surface of the hilt. Instead, I watch Keegan's face. Watch his eyes trace the fluid motions of my wrist. Watch as he follows the blade all the way to the sheath on my leg where I secure it tightly. When he looks at me again, the rage has disappeared, replaced with sudden surprise.

"You . . . where did you learn to do that?" he stammers.

"Oh . . . in Kelba, where I spent my time attending parties, sipping wine, and spreading my legs for pompous lords. Later, Keegan." I turn and walk away.

I stroll through the gate and pass Axle, standing on duty, and he lifts the corner of his lips in an elated smile. From the twinkle surfacing in his rimmed eyes, I deduce he must have seen the interaction. And every so conspicuously, he gives me a thumbs up as I head into the woods.

Shade is sitting on the steps of the ruins when I arrive with his eyes closed and one of his Illathonian blades sweeping the air in front of him. He opens his eyes when I breach the distance between us and stop his blade with my dagger. For a moment, he looks startled.

Did I really surprise him?

"There's no lesson today," he growls.

"I didn't think there would be."

He frowns. "You've come to talk." It's not a question. "I don't talk."

"I noticed. But we have to talk about this," I say. "What happened to that boy was wrong and you know it."

I might as well have thrown a torch into a bucket of oil.

"The boy could consort with the devils. He could speak to the shadows. That is a crime!" he snaps.

"Why?"

He stares at me. "Doesn't that scare you, Kelban? That he could understand the fiends? Think about it. He could understand what they were saying. How? How could he understand if he wasn't one of them? He deserved what he got. Deserved worse. Those monsters – they deserve to burn for a thousand years in pain and suffering for what they did to . . ." He cuts himself off.

"So this is about fear?" I ask.

He swings out an arm to encompass the forest. The sky. The crumpling ruins. "Isn't everything in this damn place?"

"That boy did not deserve to die just because you're afraid of what you couldn't understand."

"Can't understand?" he asks. "What don't I understand? Enlighten me, Kelban. Am I missing anything? One: he could understand the devils. Two: they came to the exact village where this boy who could understand them was living. Three: they annihilated everyone they could find, *but they let him live.* Tell me . . . what I am misunderstanding."

I want to tell him everything. I want to make him remember the first time we met. I want to tell him that I hear them too. That I see them. That I have a power I don't understand. That I know who he is and not who he is pretending to be. That deep down – despite the facade – he does care about something other than fighting.

Instead, I decide to be brutal.

"You're afraid," I whisper. He flinches. He doesn't like those words. Of course he wouldn't. He thinks he's not afraid of anything. But I've seen him, coated in sweat, and screaming in his nightmares. I've seen the raw pain in his eyes whenever he thinks I am not looking. "And I know what you're afraid of."

He does what every foolish male does. He attempts to brush it off. "Do you?" he asks.

"You're afraid of people that care about you. You can't understand it." He flinches again. "You're blind to emotion. To feeling. To humanity. And everyone knows it. Everyone is afraid of you. Grown men twice your size cower when you look at them. It must make you feel big and important. Powerful. And you waste your time gallivanting around my 'kind' in Kelba where you don't belong."

"Where I belong?" He practically spits the words. "Where I belong? Who are you to tell me where I belong or not? Look at you. I found you, bleeding, abandoned, and shattered on the brink of defeat! Who doesn't belong here? It's you who doesn't belong anywhere. Not here. Not in Kelba. Not anywhere! Understand, *Ostracized*? Not *anywhere*!"

Ostracized. He called me "ostracized." Not "Kelban." Not "little girl." *Ostracized.*

He grabs my arm, pulling me against him harshly. I'm too shocked to pull away. His hand tears the thin sleeve of my tunic over my shoulder, revealing the scar behind it. The scar that says I don't belong. The scar that says I'm alone in the world.

"You don't belong here," he snaps and shoves me away.

I rub my sore shoulder, trying to think of something to throw back in his face. To make him hurt. To make him bleed beneath skin like I am. "Neither do you, Shade."

That does it. He stops. Turns around. Stares at me, sudden curiosity replacing the anger. "What do you mean by that?"

What do I mean? I mean you're just like me. You're ostracized, only without a scar. You're alone, just like me. You're a plague. A person who can't find where he belongs. Tell him, Kyla. Tell him what he is. What you meant.

We both stare at one another, waiting for answers.

Make him bleed, that sinister voice inside of me whispers.

"You don't have anyone because everyone hates you," I snap. "You hurt everything. You despise everything. You hate everything. How could anyone like you if you can't return the feeling?"

How can I?

For a brief moment, there is pain in his eyes. And then . . .

"I told you I was a monster," he sneers.

I flinch. What the hell?

"Shade! Shade! Is Kyla . . .?" Axle turns the corner and stops so fast that leaves whirl up around him. He is panting heavily and leans over to clutch his breath. "The king . . . ah, one second . . ." He coughs and tries again. "The king . . ." He pauses again.

"Damn it, Axle, spit it out!" Shade and I both say.

He looks at us, eyes wide in surprise. "Well . . . what's up with you two? I . ."

"I swear, Axle, I'll . . ." Shade takes a threatening step forward.

"The king has sent word."

"And . . ." Shade and I say in unison.

Axle looks at me. "He has sent for you."

PART THREE

Fate

Chapter XXIV

The king's answer sparks a bustle in the village; pivoting protesters against loyal citizens. Dirk and his followers are easier to spot inside the square. They openly glare, make faces, or curse me silently when I walk by.

Otis started putting a group together seconds after the king's decree was officially read in the square. It was a simple paragraph, explicitly verbalizing the king's eagerness to meet the new "outsider" and to bring the "specimen" to the capitol for his perusal. Somehow, the idea of being referenced like supplies gives me the irresistible urge to show the king just how "human" I have become in this savage land.

Mama Opal had already been working on a dress, but she pushed herself to finish it overnight. I had to have a dress, she said, that was appropriate for an excursion in the capitol. One that would make the king see how delicate and small I was, but also speak to my noble upbringing. I didn't have to mention that it should hide my ruined shoulder. She already understood my distaste for the scar I permanently carry. The dress, when finished, is a beautiful forest green color. She used leaves from a certain tree in the forest to make it an authentic vibrancy, and I am grateful for it. The dress had a V-shaped neckline, flowing sleeves that fan out around my arms, but are up to my elbows to allow freedom of movement. The skirt sweeps the floor. It is inappropriate for a woman's legs to show in front of the king, Mama Opal says.

River signs up to accompany me but her request is denied based on complaints arising from a "secret secondary party." I have a feeling it is Axle's doing and watch River sniffle dejectedly on her pallet the night before I am going to leave.

"He probably doesn't want you to overexert yourself. He is going to have to be a guard on the journey and he doesn't want to shirk his duties by . . ."

"By watching me. I understand." River wipes her nose with a bony fist. "But that isn't why he doesn't want me to come. He would be perfectly fine leaving me in your hands. It's because he's . . . he's going to be passing . . ." She doesn't finish.

I don't press her for questions. I've come to realize that anything I ask about Axle or Shade's mysteries will go unanswered.

The next morning those accompanying me to Smoke wait in the square, bags packed, weapons shouldered, ready for the long walk ahead of us. River lent me a pair of her boots and they're snug, scrunching my toes slightly. I'll have to make due, though, because sandals would have my feet aching *and* bleeding by the end of the day.

I count the guard that Otis organized around me. Fifteen men in all. I am not surprised to see two of his most trusted companions among the group. I am, however, disturbed to see Dirk, Keegan, and Hayden standing comfortably with sneers that imply their going to give me no peace. Dirk says he's speaking for *"the people"* when he stands before the king.

Who speaks for me?

River tips her nose at the troublemakers, and helps me slide into the pack she's created for me, situating the straps on my shoulders so they don't rub the scar too hard. She pats my back lightly, before stepping aside.

Otis unfurls the king's decree and holds it up for the gathering crowd to see.

"This is the word from his majesty. I and everyone in this

company," he gestures to my guard, including Dirk and his companions, "have read it thoroughly and know the punishment should his wishes be denied. You are to provide escort and protection for one ostracized Kelban, Kyla Kelonia Bone, to the capitol, Smoke, for a meeting with his majesty, King Arkran. Should any fate, accidental or otherwise, befall this person your punishment will be dealt out, according to the law. If the King hears of any failure to meet these demands from the plaintiff herself, or secondary parties, he shall punish accordingly and appropriately." Otis looks around. "Are his majesty's requests understood?"

The group nods solemnly.

"Good," Otis says, satisfied. He steps back. "Captain of the guard, my trusted comrade, Gregor, will lead the journey. His second-in-command is to be obeyed and his wishes enforced should a situation in which Gregor is unable to give orders arise. Shade, my boy, are you prepared for such a responsibility?"

My head snaps up, and I search for his face. I find it, situated next to the tall, black-haired artifact named Gregor. They are exact opposites. Gregor is old and weather-beaten. Shade is young and muscled. Maybe Otis did it on purpose, in an attempt contrast their strengths with their flaws.

"Why make him second-in-command?" a female voice in the crowd hisses. "He's no guardian of our village. He doesn't give a flying piss what happens to any of us. He'll lead them all to their deaths like he swayed that young child. Poor Opal. Poor, heartbroken Opal."

"Hush, woman," a man snaps. "That girl was bound to get into trouble sooner or later. Those things happen all the time. It wasn't his fault that she decided to accompany her father. The girl volunteered."

"Just the same, he had a hand in it. That girl wouldn't have been so wild if she'd been forbidden from indulging in his company altogether. The boy probably just wanted to screw her and shove off."

"You're just upset because he wouldn't screw your daughter when she went looking for his attention," the man retorts.

"Angus, you take that back, you hear . . ."

"Is there a problem?" Otis asks.

The bickering couple grow silent.

Shade levels an icy stare in their direction.

My hands ache and I realize I've balled them into fists. Slowly, I spread them straight at my sides again. Apparently, Mama Opal's daughter had been quite the scandal. What had she been to Shade? A friend? Something more? Not that I should care. I don't. I just wonder if their meetings in the forest had been purely innocent like Shade and I, or far more physical – and sexual.

Slowly, Shade looks up and meets my eyes. His gaze sharpens. I hadn't expected him to forget our last meeting. I had hoped we could leave it in the past, though. Because as much as I hate him for pretending, I like what he is beneath the rough exterior. I like the person he's allowed me to catch glimpses of over the past few weeks. The real face hiding beneath all that asshole and bluster.

The thought makes me feel sick, dizzy, and elated all at once.

"Tell me again, what I'm supposed to do?"

We've made camp after a long day of endless walking. The road to the capitol through the forest is overgrown. Axle says that's because very few people who travel on it ever reach Smoke. Wild animals prey at night. Wild animals prey during the day. Among other things. He doesn't have to tell me that those "other things" are shadows.

Now, I sit near the edge of the clearing we've chosen, and listen to Axle describe, in detail, how I should behave when I meet the king.

"Walk straight. Don't slouch. Make sure you look him in the eye as much as possible . . ."

"Yes, yes, yes," I wave him off. "I know that part. What I mean is . . . are there 'manners' in Smoke. Do I bow? Curtsy? Use 'royal' pronunciation? Things like that."

"I would curtsy," Axle says. He flushes red. "I mean . . . I wouldn't curtsy. You would curtsy. I . . . I would do nothing. I would glare and . . ."

"And mask your feminine behavior," I jest. I pat his arm to make sure he knows I'm kidding.

He glares at me anyway.

"Definitely curtsy," Keegan says. He sits in the middle of the clearing, his feet held up to the fire the men have created. "And if you, maybe, raise the hem of your gown high enough to reveal one of those glossy legs, the king may end up calling you 'your highness' before the night is through. Maybe you'll even get to sit on his lap like a good 'little girl.'"

"Are you mocking the king, boy!" Gregor snaps from somewhere in the dark forest. He appears a few moments later. Shade is not far behind him. I assume they were scouting the perimeter.

"No," Keegan says. He winks at me. "Just advising her to use every means at her disposal."

Gregor ignores him. "Men," he addresses the group, "there will be three guards, one at each corner of the clearing, ten feet into the trees. I don't want any shitting on this duty. We are in enemy territory, without a village for thirty miles in either direction. Do not disregard any sound. Do no disregard silence either. Be on your guard. There is not a single soul in this forest but us."

"Not anymore that is. Right, Axle?" Keegan croons.

Axle's face darkens. "Eat shit, bastard!"

"Keegan, you have first watch," Gregor says.

"What! But . . ."

"Are you defying a direct order, boy?" Gregor asks with raised eyebrows.

Dirk nudges his son in the shoulder and shakes his head warningly. No – threateningly. Keegan wags his head, a begrudging "no," and stumbles to his feet.

As he passes me, sword in hand, he whispers, "If you're lonely tonight or in need of protection, I'm open to a midnight session in the forest if Shade isn't in need."

"I'm not interested in whatever you could possible teach me."

"Oh, but, darling, you've no idea what session I've planned for us. And you . . ."

"Are you lounging on a direct order, boy!"

"No, sir!" Keegan says quickly. He disappears into the dark forest.

"Shit-head!" Axle mumbles under his breath.

Gregor chooses two more men from the group to watch the "east and west" sides. "The rest of you . . . get some sleep. Stay alert. We've got a long night." He settles down by the fire and starts warming his hands.

Shade volunteers to watch the "north" side.

"You need sleep too, idiot," Axle protests.

"I'd rather not get caught with my pants down," Shade responds.

Axle shrugs. "Alright. Alright. I won't argue with you, dumb-ass. But don't complain when I'm energetic and spry in the morning, and you're sagging behind like a little old woman."

The corner of Shade's mouth tilts up – an imitation of a half-smile. "It won't happen."

"Yeah. Yeah. I know. You're the man of wonders, the man who never sleeps, the man who never loses. Got it. Registers, man." Axle taps a finger to his temple. "Shove off and let me sleep then. I'm not as fond of midnight watches as you are. Wake me if you're lonely." He throws a blanket next to mine.

"What are you doing?" I twist sideways as he slumps down next to me.

"Sleeping. I thought I made that obvious. I rarely throw my blanket on the ground for fun."

Shade's chin snaps up. "You can't sleep there, Axle. You . . ."

"Why not?" Axle props his arms behind his head and stretches lanky legs across the blanket. They are so long that his feet rest on the hard ground. "I'm not putting myself at the mercy of Dirk and his comrades, thank you very much, pal. Believe it or not, a Kelban seems like a more idealistic partner."

Shade fumbles for words. "Yes, but . . . but Kelbans are . . . you shouldn't be sleeping next to one of them. They . . . she . . ."

Hot rage burns my cheeks. "Is nothing," I finish for him. "Don't worry, Shade. I am 'ostracized' and I'll be sure to know my place. If Axle isn't offended by my presence and wishes to keep my lonely self company, I am not adverse to it."

Shade stares at me. The corner of his jaw moves back and forth, like he's grinding his teeth. *Good.* About time I pissed him off.

Again.

"Unless, you have objections to me sleeping next to her because maybe she's . . ." Axle's mouth widens into a sly grin. "Because you think *you'd* do a better job?"

Shade's eyes blacken. "*Vagra flanver*!" he snaps and stalks into the forest. I watch him until the faint glow of his Illathonian blades disappear.

Axle chuckles softly and pulls an animal skin over his shoulders. "G'night, Kelban."

"Is that why you're sleeping next to me?" I ask. "To protect me?"

"I have ulterior motives, but yes, if you wish to think that, it's completely fine with me," Axle whispers back. He reaches out and pulls my own blanket over my shoulder, his thumb grazing my skin lightly, before pulling away. He winks.

I roll my eyes.

Axle smirks. "He's gonna be so pissed at me in the morning."

"It's nothing he should be mad over. You can decide who you socialize with, even if that person doesn't belong among you." I tuck my arms beneath my head. My feet throb beneath the blankets. River's shoes are definitely too small.

Axle laughs like I've told a joke.

"What?"

"Oh, gods, you are naive" Axle shuffles closer, until our faces our so close I can smell his breath. Hunter's brew. Murky water. Pine needles. "Is that really why you think he's mad? Damn, you were such a child even in marriage, weren't you? Didn't your husband ever get insanely jealous?"

I widen my eyes. "You think Shade is *jealous*?"

"Time will tell," Axle says. "He could just be objectifying you. After all, you two hang out all the time. He might be used to having you all to himself and doesn't want to share. It's a basic primal instinct."

"Now you sound like Keegan," I balk in disgust.

"Simply observing my bosom buddy, Kyla *Kelonia* Bone." He draws out my middle name in a soft voice. "It wouldn't be beyond him. He's objectified a lot of people. Leanna, for instance."

The breath leaves my lungs in a soft gasp. "What?"

"She was the first who didn't care if he talked to her. She'd talk anyway. She brought him food. Made him clothes. Cleaned his wounds when he came back from a hunt. She didn't push him. Didn't ask questions. Just said she'd be there and help if she could. She told him he was a 'good boy' and that he just needed 'time' to sort through it all. She never had any idea what he'd gone through or what he'd done or what he'd seen. She just let him keep it to himself. Let him stay silent. She didn't force him to face any of it." I don't miss the bitterness in Axle's voice. "In a way, it broke him. He started talking. He started treating everyone like humans. Masked his hate. His emotions. His true thoughts. Whatever he said, Leanna did. Whatever he asked her to do, she would do. Like a puppet. A perfect, compliant puppet."

He notices my startled gaze. "I didn't hate her, Kyla. Gods, she was the sweetest, strongest girl I'd ever met. Smart. Witty. Talkative. Charming. But she could never understand a person like Shade. She was not willing to breach the things he hid. She wanted him to stay the same elusive, quiet, mysterious boy he was."

The same way I'd first thought of him. The same way I'd idolized – no, objectified – him for three years into something he was not. Sadly, I learned how wrong I'd been about him.

"You're not an object to him, Kyla," Axle whispers, "but you're not nothing to him either. I haven't figured out what you are to him."

"I don't care what I am to him." I turn my back and try to sleep.

Counting doesn't work this time, though.

Shade enters camp, mid-morning, with both blades drawn. He appears so suddenly that Keegan chokes on a spoonful of porridge.

"Pack up," Shade says quickly. His entire body radiates tension.

"The forest is thick. The light won't keep these monsters away. They will congregate in the shady parts of the forest. We don't want them to realize they're not the only ones here."

"You heard him," Gregor prods.

In fifteen minutes, we're ready to walk.

Shade ignores Axle and I.

"Rough night, pal?" Axle asks him. "Was something on your mind?"

His reply is Shade's middle finger.

"Haven't seen that one in a while. Usually he's verbal." Axle frowns.

I smile.

"What?"

"Pissed-off Shade is more fun," I say loud enough for him to hear. "I don't have to listen to him be an asshole."

"Excellent point. Hear that, Shade? You're sexier when you're quiet."

I grab Axle's arm, fingers digging in. "That's not what I said!"

"No? You said he was 'fun.' Doesn't that mean . . . ow, ow! Okay, yield. Yield. Damn it, I said yield!"

I let go of his ear.

And I don't think I imagined it, but Shade's shoulders shiver as if he were laughing, quietly.

A stone gateway arches over our heads. A single name is carved on it in bold, thick engraving.

Brunt.

Everyone is solemn. Like they're walking on holy ground.

Or cursed ground.

"We'll make camp here," Gregor says.

"But it's the middle of the day!" Dirk whines. "We can keep going and be in Smoke before nightfall if we . . ."

"Your eagerness is understandable, good sir. But it is also foolish. There are no clearings. No springs. No natural substances. Brunt is the last inhabitable place on our journey. If we sleep in the middle of the forest, we will certainly decrease our chances of survival," Gregor says. He glances around sorrowfully. "And though it may be home to ghosts, they will not mind sharing. Make camp, men. We will reach Smoke tomorrow morning."

Keegan is tasked with finding a decent campsite and suggests the crumbling remains of what must have once been a tavern. The roof is caved in, leaving only the walls (which suffer from many holes) and a staircase that winds upwards into nothing but air. Hayden suggests it might be more of a prison than a camp, since we are boxed in on all sides. Dirk says it will hide the firelight from demons. Gregor ignores their bickering and sets his packs down in a corner of the building. The argument ceases. The once-upon-a-time tavern is our camp.

I set my packs in one of the other corners as far from the group as possible and search out the brook that I saw running through the middle of the village. I admire the view on the journey there. Brunt would be gorgeous if it weren't for the unfortunate ruins and the dismal light.

Axle is already bending over the water, washing the grime off his back and torso. I note the lash marks on his back. The remains of a burn on his hip. But he doesn't have the same purposeful, gouged scars like Shade. No one took a dagger to him. Why?

"The water's safe," he says as I get down on my knees next to it.

I splash some on my face and look around. "What happened here?"

"What always happens when people get too happy and secure," Axle mutters without looking up. "Things go to hell." He purposefully tries to ignore my gaze, but he isn't fast enough.

A wave of nausea curls in my stomach. That look in Axle's eyes is too dark. Too painful.

Too full of memories.

Axle stands up and looks straight ahead. He walks through the brook to the other side. Confused, I follow, wiping water from my mouth. I have to jog to catch up with his long legs.

He stops in front of a beautiful stone house. It's roof is caved in and the doors and windows are gone. In the stones are carved hundreds of images. Tales. Symbols. I had read about ancient Kelban tradition jotted down in the history books of Master Rolfe's collection. The ancient Kelbans used to mark their houses with the symbols of the old language every time something beneficial occurred. The birth of a child. A girl's first bleeding. A marriage. The death of a loved one. All of it was marked upon the surface of a home as a personal history of sorts.

Axle reaches out and touches the corner of the stones where the door should be. He draws his finger over one of the symbols carved there: a tree with tiny leaflets on it and roots sinking into the ground. A sign of beginning life.

"My father carved this when River was born," he says.

I blink. I remember River telling me where they were from. *Brunt.* It hadn't clicked until now. That's why he didn't want her to come. She would have seen this. She would have seen her home. *Their* home.

"The shadows came seven years later. Sacked the village. Massacred everyone they could find. I don't know how many escaped but it was less than twenty. My parents . . . I buried what was left when I found them." The pain in his voice makes my chest hurt.

River never told me what happened to her parents. Although, it's possible, she doesn't remember very well. Young children find it easier to forget a traumatic experience when a loving relative like Axle is there to depend on.

I nod in understanding."So you kill them. Hunt them. Make sure no one else dies."

He shrugs. "I became a guardian because I couldn't stand to see Agron suffer. But it was more than that. I cared about River. She needed a home. A place to be safe. Personally, I'd be fine wandering the countryside and hunting every last shadow I could detect, but she needs me. Needs Agron. Needs Mama Opal and Otis and everyone in that village. She doesn't know what it's like to be lonely, cold, hungry, and frightened for her life. I vowed she never would. Not after that day." He runs his fingers over another of the symbols in the stones – a boy holding a sword. No doubt, his father carved it for him.

He moves inside the house, touching symbols, smoothing the stones, and muttering under his breath.

Slowly, I leave him to his solitude. This is not the place for me.

Did the same thing happen to Shade?

I cannot return to camp. Instead, I head uphill. There are still stone steps where people must have taken morning strolls. I am sure many a lover walked the molded stones on a moonlit night, staring at the stars blinking in the openings of the trees. If it weren't for the bloodstains dried on their gray forms, they would be beautiful. The steps finally disappear into a grove of trees with red and white buds between the leaves. Several skeletons are scattered around the trunks, their bones jutting at awkward positions. Broken. Smashed. Torn apart.

My stomach sinks at the gruesome sight. They were tortured.

I turn around. I won't stay here. It's too familiar. Too painful. Too . . .

I face a lone body tied upright against one of the ashen trees. Red buds sit upon the shoulder-blades. A caterpillar rests in one of the barren eye-sockets. Patches of remaining hair, flaxen blonde, twist in the light breeze blowing around us. My throat tightens. Those empty holes that used to be eyes stare right at me. The rawhide binding the poor skeleton's arms to the tree are still tightly knotted. They didn't kill this one. They made it watch as they tore the others limb from limb.

The lead feeling returns to my hand. Heavy. Pulsing. Angry.

This was wrong. This was butchery. This was the devil's work.

The black cave in my head opens its doors, releasing a flood of light. *No!* I don't want to see. I try to force the light back. Push it from the forefront of my thoughts like I pushed those rocks into the side of the mountain. It doesn't work. The light envelopes me.

Flashes!

I open my eyes, and I am face-to-face with Axle! I step back, startled. He doesn't acknowledge my presence. He looks straight through me. He has left the dilapidated home behind him and a grove of thick, vine-covered trees surround him on all sides. He uses the tip of his Illathonian blade to cut the vines gently from his path. The ground is well-worn and still carries the imprints of a great mass of people.

"Shade?" he calls.

Axle reaches the end of the spindly trees and halts at the edge of a deep crater hollowed out in the middle of the clearing he's entered. His skin turns a pasty white and he backs away from the gaping hole.

The smell reaches my nose. Decaying flesh. Mud. Rotting wood.

It smells like the creek within the Burnt Forest. I don't even have to look to see what lies within the crater, but I do anyway. Piled high in unceremonious stacks lie the bodies of Brunt's villagers. An open burial.

"I knew you were going to come here ." Shade's voice breaks the uncanny silence. He appears from the trees like a phantom and halts next to Axle. He stares into the crater too. "You're a shitty liar."

"I . . . I had to . . ." Axle finally turns his eyes from the devastation. His lips tremble.

"Had to what? Had to make yourself remember?"

Axle puts a hand over his eyes. "Please, Shade. Not now."

Shade's brow furrows. "You did forget! You did, didn't you? You forgot to hate them. You forgot to despise them with every breath in your body because you got used to Agron's blessed silence and prosperity. You forgot to remember what they did to your home – to your parents!"

"I never forgot!" Axle screams. He spins around and nearly loses his footing. Dirt crumbles down into the gaping hole. "I remembered everything! I still remember everything!"

"Then why come here? Why make yourself look at this carnage? This barbaric savagery?" Shade gestures at the bones filling the chasm. "I'll tell you why. It's because you weren't sure why you started carrying that 'shadow-killer' on your back." He points at the Illathonian blade.

I shouldn't be here. I shouldn't be watching this.

"You were lucky, don't you know, Axle?" Shade says. "There was

nothing left of my family to bury."

"Shade . . . what happened to us was wrong . . ."

"It was more than wrong!" Shade snaps.

"And," Axle continues, "we righted those wrongs."

Shade shakes his head wildly. "No. We didn't even come close. Not yet anyway."

Axle's eyes flash fire. I have rarely seen him so angry. "You would spent the rest of your gods-damned life hunting them. That's not what you want in life. I know it isn't! Go after what you want! What you want, Shade! Hear me? Chase it. Grab it. Hold onto it. It is a shame to waste your life hunting them when they are not worth it."

"You can't understand, Axle. You've never understood. They didn't do the things to you that they did to me."

"Shade . . ."

He holds up a hand and halts Axle mid-sentence. "They never dragged you from your cell at night and shoved you into a corner full of pronged spears until you were bleeding from a thousand holes. They never unlocked your cell and woke you up with bludgeoning fists because you wouldn't succumb to them. They never pulled you from the slave ranks into a dark room and dug their knives into your back because they thought it would be fun to hear my screams. To see what emblems they could make on my back with their blades. To see if my blood really did run red." His lips are quivering and the mask is gone. My chest hurts from the pain of holding back my tears. There is nothing behind that mask. Nothing but an empty void of emotionless memories. "So don't talk to me about what I want, Axle. All I have wanted since that day is to make them suffer the way they made me suffer. Make them scream. Make them bleed. Make them feel pain."

"They did those things to break you," Axle admonishes. "Because they knew you were the strongest."

"And they'll regret it," Shade growls.

I want to fall. I want to curl up on the ground. I want to scream and cry until there isn't any breath left in me.

Axle falters. "Shade, I . . .

Shade strips off his vest and turns his back to his friend. The scars –

red, raised, zigzagged pieces of skin – snake along his flesh. "This is what they do, Axle! And they enjoy it!"

Axle turns his eyes away and stares at the crater. He tries to turn his eyes from that too and stares at the forest. A single skeleton hangs, suspended, from one of the branches. There is nowhere to turn. Nowhere to run. The shadows are everywhere. Axle shuts his eyes, but I have done the same thing too many times to believe he doesn't see the nightmares swimming in the darkness.

"What happened the first night they came to Brunt? I'm sure you were all certain it was another one of their small raids. A couple lives would be lost, you'd bury the bodies, and go back to your normal lives." Shade kicks at a clod of dirt. It rolls downhill. "You never dreamed it would turn into carnage. Your father probably told you he'd be right back. Your mother probably didn't even bother getting a weapon for herself. She was so certain everything would be alright."

"Stop," Axle whispers.

"They killed your father right outside the door. Killed your mother, too. And then they saw you . . . Oh, you expected them to kill you, but no . . . they took you with them instead and . . ."

"Stop it!" Axle screams. "Stop it, stop it, stop it!" He grabs Shade's shoulder and spins him around. "What are you trying to do to me?"

Shade eyes quiver at the physical connection and he pries Axle's hand from his shoulder. "I'm trying to make you remember. Remember your first night in captivity. The first night we met. The first time we dared to show backbone. The anger we felt when we watched them butcher another boy just like us. Remember the night we escaped! They hunted us like animals. Mercilessly. Savagely. We both swore, on the gods and on the lives of those we had lost, to slaughter them someday. To throw them in hell. Together! Do you remember?"

Axle's eyes tremble. He opens his mouth. Closes it again. He shoves Shade away from him and turns his back.

Shade flinches at Axle's unconscious show of disgust.

"I . . . I can't be like that anymore, Shade. Please try and understand that," Axle whispers at last.

Shade stares at him for a long time and, for a moment, I think he might show a hint of sorrow in his gaze. Instead, he smirks, his lips curling up against his teeth in that vicious way that used to frighten me. Now it makes me want to cry with guilt. "See? I told you, didn't I?"

Axle lifts his chin.

"I am alone in this world," Shade says. He kicks some dirt into the crater one last time and stomps off.

The edges of my vision blacken and the darkness spreads into the scene before me, swallowing Axle and the deathly crater in a black abyss of smoke and white, flashing lights.

I am blown from the vision so fast that I fall on my knees. I lower my head and vomit. The stench smells better than the rotting carcasses around me.

I lie on the ground, too weakened to get up. My head is an iron cage, and my thoughts hammer against the bars like a wild mob.

The shadows did that to Shade! Why didn't I figure it out before? His hate. His tirades. His scars. His vengeful nature. They shattered him. Pulled him apart. Took everything from him. That time he'd saved me, in Kirath, all those years ago – he'd been hunting them. Hunting them out of hatred. Out of emotional havoc. Out of vengeance.

I want to console him. I want to help him. But I don't know how.

The eyes of the bound skeleton watch me rise.

I cannot leave it like that. That person – the shadows traumatized it just like they did to Shade. The thought fills me with hot anger. I see shadows cutting into Shade's skin. I see shadows laughing at his pain. I see shadows craving his screams.

I will not let them rob this poor dead soul of a proper burial.

I find a rusty scythe and pick out a spot near the border of the grove where yellow daffodils bob in the light breeze.

I start digging.

I wander through Brunt from dilapidated building to burnt tree-lines to hanging skeletons searching for the inn. I know I am lost before I've even begun, but I don't care. Every step I take reminds me of that grove. Of that unspeakable, furious rage in Shade's eyes. Of that horrible night where one of the shadows spoke to me – twice.

"There you are!" Axle's voice startles me so badly that I pull my dagger. "Whoa. Whoa. Easy there, Kyla." He stops laughing when I don't join in. "You okay?"

Shade isn't far behind him. He looks up when he detects the concern in Axle's voice and scans my face. He frowns at what he sees.

"You look pale," Axle remarks.

Shade joins us.

"I'm fine." My throat sounds scratchy. Like I've been crying. I have. *But, gods, don't let them know that.*

Shade reaches out and touches the back of his hand to my forehead. It burns a cold chill into my veins. I push it away, quickly.

"I'm fine," I repeat, forcing some volume into my voice. Why does his touch frighten me?

Axle's eyes narrow. That gods-damned intuition of his knows I'm hiding something.

Shade's eyes suddenly darken, and he pulls both of his Illathonian blades from his back so quickly that I shift away. He's looking towards a mangled patch of ivy and branches.

My nose detects the keen scent in the air.

"Blood," I whisper.

Axle slowly pulls his blade, too.

Shade creeps towards the bushes, both swords crossed X-wise, so that if an animal jumps at him he can slash upwards and easily kill it.

I palm my dagger and start to follow him, but Axle pushes me behind him and shakes his head. I glare at him. He remains stubborn and blocks me with his wide shoulders. We creep forward together.

Shade steps through the bushes. They only rise to his waist, so we still see his reaction when he sees where the smell is coming from. A vein pulses at his neck wildly.

I duck beneath Axle's arm and rush into the bushes before he can grab me. I stop beside the pool of blood and stare at the remains. An animal. Or what's left of it. There aren't any legs, eyes, or ears. Bloody intestines hang from a branch directly above the body. They steadily drip blood onto the ground. Flies cover the carcass and relentlessly buzz through the air. I swat four or five from the same spot on my neck. A few attack the ostracized scar on my shoulder. The scar from the shadow blade on my arm. The fresh cuts on my legs.

Shade lashes out and swats a handful of the black bastards away from my face.

"Thanks," I mutter. The flies don't even touch him.

He kneels beside the pool and dips a finger into the blood. It comes back red and watery. I know what that means.

It's a fresh kill. Maybe an hour at most. Just long enough to attract buzzards and let the forest animals know that something has died.

I've seen this butchery once before on my first day in the Wilds forest.

Shade also remembers. "Do you want to bury it this time too, Kelban?"

I shake my head.

He stands, grips his swords in both hands, and walks off.

I wonder where he's going. It's almost dusk.

Axle grips my elbow and turns me away from the gruesome sight. "The others will think we've deserted them."

I follow him back to camp with one word ringing in my head.

Shadows. Shadows. Shadows.

Gregor doesn't say anything when we return an hour after dusk has fallen. He throws both of us two portions of jerky and continues to warm his hands by the fire.

"I can sleep alone tonight," I tell Axle.

He doesn't argue.

Dirk, Axle, and two other men are chosen for the first shift on night watches.

Keegan and four men sit by the fire smoking a black stub that I recognize as a "*chafrass root.*" It is not a drug, but it is flavored and very addictive. Some alchemists claim that it can be used as a life enhancer. But alchemists are known as glorified merchants unless they have a certificate from the Celectate or a priest to prove their occupation. Although, here in the Wilds, things are probably different.

Axle makes his bed fifteen feet from mine. He bites into his jerky.

I watch him as conspicuously as I can. How did he survive captivity? I wasn't even aware that the shadows left people alive, much less, took slaves for themselves. It almost sounds like they have a grasp of what a "society" is.

Almost.

"Guardian, where is the hunter?" Gregor asks Axle when two hours have passed and the brooding warrior hasn't returned.

"Ignoring his duty," Keegan mutters beneath his breath. A few of the men around the fire mumble their agreement.

Not good.

Axle shrugs. "Patrolling the perimeter. Allocating a border. How should I know? I'm not his damned nursemaid."

Gregor ignores Axle's verbal annoyance. "Do you know if he'll return before daybreak?"

Axle shrugs again. "I know he'll return. That's all."

"Well, that's good," Keegan snorts. He puffs out a breath of gray smoke. "I was afraid we'd lost him for good."

Everyone but Gregor, Axle, and I chuckles.

Raw anger eats at my insides. If they knew . . . if they only knew what had happened to him would they laugh? Would they laugh if they'd been through a damned second of what he'd endured? Would they have survived if they had? I almost want to find out and that heavy pulsing returns to my hand.

The fire near Keegan crackles and a shower of sparks snap from the flames. Several men jerk backwards. One of them trips over his own feet and falls flat.

Axle laughs so hard he doubles over.

I smile and curl my fingers into a fist. The pulse dissipates.

I don't know what wakes me. Perhaps a stick cracking. A snort from one of the slumbering men. Or even the crackling fire. But when I open my eyes, Axle is gone. He already had his first watch. He should be sleeping.

I sit up and look around. He's not in the camp.

Stumbling to my feet, still groggy from sleep, I walk to the corner of one of the crumbled walls and spot him leaning against the edge of the wall that surrounds Brunt's perimeter. His neck is stretched as he scans the forest. I know who he's looking for. I start walking towards him until a dark shadow steps up next to him. I almost scream a warning until I recognize Shade's Illathonian blades glowing on his back. But Axle didn't notice him and jerks in surprise. I slip behind some nearby trees. They are ten feet away.

Slowly, they start to walk past me, Shade in front. When he passes beneath the moonlight, I flinch. He's caked in blood. Spots dot his face. Drench his vest. Color his boots. He doesn't seem to notice it.

"Holy shit, man, what happened?" Axle asks.

Shade doesn't answer him and bends down by the creek that runs between our camp and the wall. Hopefully the rippling stream disguises my heavy breathing because if Axle or Shade turn around they will definitely see me.

"Shade, would you answer me, damn it?"

"I found it." Shade splashes some water on his face.

Axle groans. He shakes his head. "That's not gonna do you any good. You'll need to get that water all over you. And your clothes are filthy too. If the others saw you like this do you know what they'd do? They'd . . ."

"They'd call me a monster," Shade says. He wipes some blood from his lips and stares at the stain on his hands. "Or a cannibal."

"More than likely they'd ask questions. And we both know how much you hate those. So clean up, man!" Axle tosses a towel he'd been sitting on at Shade. He catches it.

"You came prepared, I see," Shade remarks.

Axle rolls his eyes. "Once you've been through this half a million damn times you learn a few things."

"About time."

Axle flips him the finger and turns his back.

Shade strips off his vest and struggles with the belt around his hips.

Heat eats at my cheeks. *Oh, gods, is he going to strip?*

He pulls the belt free.

Shit.

He turns around to lay his Illathonian blades on the ground. The single white, zigzagged scar on his chest stands out on his tanned abdomen. I stare at its lines. Now that I know it's origins, my gut clenches whenever I look at it.

I turn away as Shade finishes undressing. I hear water splashing. A few gargled curses as it laps up against a fresh wound. I count the minutes in my head. Stare at the trees. I never knew how intricate the development of tree bark and leaves were until now. When I grow bored of that I try to count the number of stones at my feet.

Water drips onto the ground. He's stepped out. He hisses with discomfort as he pulls on his pants. The belt jingles as he struggles to slip it on.

"Don't even bother getting into that," Axle says.

I turn around. Shade's trying to loop his arms through the vest but grimaces every time he twists his right arm into the arm-hole. He bends over and tries to wiggle into it. I watch the vest slide upwards farther and farther to his shoulders until finally, when he straightens out, it falls into place.

"You never listen!" Axle complains.

Shade ignores him and grabs his swords. "Just a good bone bruise. It'll heal in an hour when I get some ointment on it."

"It put up quite a fight, didn't it?" Axle asks.

Shade shrugs. "They all do."

"And there was only one?"

Shade nods.

Axle sighs with relief. He looks towards camp.

Shade notices. "What? You thought there would be more?"

"I don't know. It's hard to say. They're more difficult to track than the usual animals. Hell, even a razor is easier to hunt. I know that Brunt is dead spot, but that would make it a safe place for them to congregate.

They enjoy resting in cursed places. I expected there to be at least three or four of them. I expected a damn legion." Axle rubs a hand across the edge of his vest nervously. "It doesn't sit right with me."

Shade nods to show he understands. "Who has next watch?"

"Keegan. Averick. Lex. Croner."

"What the hell was Gregor thinking?"

"I don't know. You weren't here to help him, were you?"

Shade elbows past him. "Piss off."

"*Avraga*!" Axle mutters and follows him.

Shit, I'm supposed to be up there, asleep.

I pick up a stone and throw it as hard as I can. It smacks into one of the trees just beyond Brunt's wall. Shade and Axle spin around.

"You sure there was only one?" Axle asks.

They approach the spot.

I slip away from the trees and run as fast as the forest floor will allow me. Less than two minutes after I've crawled under the covers and half-closed my eyes, Shade and Axle return to camp.

"I'll give you the honor of waking royal lazy-ass." Axle gestures at Keegan. "Maybe tell him that you heard a few noises in the woods and that he'd better not piss himself."

Shade growls an inappropriate retort, and Axle flips him off.

I roll onto my side and try to fall back asleep.

Something hard smacks me in the back. I groan and reach behind me, searching for the offending object. When I find it and hold it up to the light, it's a stone.

"That belongs to you, I think," Axle whispers. "You left your scent all over it, darling."

"Too bad it missed you," I reply softly.

"Might want to try throwing it in my direction if you want to strike me. That's the ideal way, at least." He chokes on a laugh.

I toss it over my shoulder and smile satisfactorily when I hear his heavy intake of breath. "Like that?"

"Damn it, Kelban, why can't you throw like shit just once in your life?"

I bury my face in my blanket so he won't hear me laugh.

Taking a piss in the middle of the night, in the middle of an especially dark forest, is damn annoying. I almost wish I'd done it around the corner of one of the dilapidated buildings but it seemed like an offense to the dead souls who used to inhabit the homes. Me and my damned manners can have a little conversation the next time I have to walk nearly a mile to attend to my private business.

My eyes have adjusted to the dark so seeing isn't a problem. It's the utter silence throughout the forest that irks me. There should be birds. Squirrels. A *ragrartan*, even.

"*She's pretty.*"

The voice comes from nowhere and cuts into the silence like a blacksmith's hammer. I suck in a sharp breath and stop in my tracks.

"*She's very pretty,*" the voice repeats in a low hiss.

I recognize those tones. Those high-pitched, nasal sounds that don't belong to the normal verbal elocution.

Shadows!

I don't turn around. I don't run. I don't blink. I keep walking quietly.

"*She's alone.*" It's a different shadow. The voice is on my right.

"*There are others. They are still in the camp.*" On my left.

"*Sleeping peacefully too.*" On my right.

Four shadows.

"*Maybe we should wake them up,*" another one chuckles. Behind me.

My throat is so tight I can barely breathe.

"*They need to pay with their lives for killing Lavon.*" A darker, harsher voice than the rest of them. The leader, most likely.

That's six.

"*Grag said don't engage. He told us to watch them, but not engage until we were certain that we had the right one.*" The voice of the first shadow.

"*Grag isn't here.*"

"*It'll be easy anyway. They're sleeping. We'll make up something to tell Grag. Lavon won't die for nothing.*" The third one.

They're going to kill us all!

I force myself to walk at a casual, *faster* pace; until their voices are a good distance behind me. When I break into a run they won't be able to adjust the mileage fast enough and everybody will already be warned. I keep striding forward. I splash through the creek as loudly as I can, praying Axle or Shade awaken at the noise.

The run-down tavern is fifty feet from me.

One.

I hear the swish of a breeze behind me. Or was it a shadow?

Two.

A stick cracks beneath the heel of my boot as I prepare to lurch forward.

Three.

A hand wraps around my wrist and jerks me sideways behind the trees. Bark bites into my back as I'm shoved against the thick oak. A dark figure boxes me in, pinning my wrist.

"Evening, darlin'. Did you finally get lonely?"

Keegan!

I open my mouth to tell him that the shadows are coming. That they're getting closer. That we still have time to warn the others. He covers my mouth with his hand, pinning my lips to my teeth. I taste blood.

"Shh. No need to wake the others. I'm sure we can be more than civil to one another without them." He presses closer, until I'm welded between the tree and him. His hips grind against mine. I flinch at the heat boiling in my chest and struggle to shake my head loose. He grabs my neck so hard with his other hand that the bones shiver beneath it.

I shove at him with both hands. He's too strong. I can't kick him. He's too close. Over his shoulder, I spot the shadows sliding towards us through the trees, their foggy forms floating like cursed smoke. Slowly, they spread out. I lose sight of five of them. The sixth continues towards us.

Forty feet.

I claw at Keegan's chest. He grunts in pain and tightens his hold on my neck.

Thirty feet.

I scream so hard my neck burns with the strain, but through Keegan's hand it comes out a muffled gargle. "Stop it," he hisses.

Twenty feet. The shadow pulls a dagger from beneath its cape.

I pound my hands against Keegan's shoulders. His chest. His arms. Struggling to gesture behind him. To make him look. To make him see what's coming towards us.

"Be quiet, you little bitch!" He tries to pin my flailing arms against his chest.

Ten feet.

I pry at his hands over my mouth.

"You . . ." The ripping sound of flesh, the lap of blood, and the grind of bone shatters the silence. Keegan's mouth hangs open in silent screams. Behind him, the shadow molds into feathery white wisps and releases the dagger its embedded up to the hilt in his side. It floats back a few paces.

Keegan falls heavily at my feet, writhing in pain, but making no sound. He struggles with the dagger's handle. His hands are too slick with his own blood to pull it free.

The shadow lurches towards me.

Keegan moans as I pull the dagger from his side.

The shadow hesitates when I raise its own blade in my defense, but only for a moment. It glides forward again, the white wisps spreading out towards me in seductive, curling tendrils. One of the wisps touches my arm. It feels like a wet paintbrush.

"Get back!" I snap.

The shadow flinches. The wisps pull back slightly. It's hooded head glances anxiously towards the inn, which remains shrouded in darkened moonlight. The rest of his comrades are probably almost there.

I scream. Loud. Long. Terrified. Until my own ears burn with the volume.

"*Bitch*!" the shadow rasps and the white wisps stab towards me like tangled vines.

This time I don't even feel the presence of the magnet cascading through my body until its there, in the ball of my hand – hot, heavy, and pulsing angrily. The pressure builds around my head, like I'm gathering air and gravity into my mind. The ball of spinning control shatters. The shadow lurches backwards about twenty feet and the trees quake.

Keegan screams. I look down at him. A black, vine-like substance swirls out from his wound. It looks just like the shadow's wisps. Keegan writhes and claws at his wound as the black wisps swirl between his fingers and into the night air. After a few seconds, nothing comes from the wound except blood. The ball of fury in my palm dissipates.

Behind me, swords clash. Men cry out to one another. Shadows screech. Relief eases the tension in my chest. I wasn't too late.

A screech draws my attention back to the woods. A white cloud of fog shoots in my direction. I am not fast enough to dodge away from its path and it slams into me full force. Unlike fog, it is not transient and is similar to a brick wall. It shoves me to the ground and holds me there. Through my hazy prison, the black, caped demon glides towards me. Its cape flares out at the sides slightly, and a flash of gray from beneath its hood blinds me. A mask. A silver mask where there should be a face.

Keegan rises to his knees, startling the shadow. The white cloud pulls back. I stumble to my feet. Keegan lifts a rock twice the size of his hand and slams it into the shadow's midsection – or where it should have a midsection. There's a dreadful sucking sound. The shadow doubles over.

Keegan rises to his feet and presses a hand to his side. He turns to me. "What are you waiting for, fool? Run! Run!"

Despite his wound, he matches my furious pace. And then, suddenly, he begins to drop back. He breathes heavily behind me. I hear the thud as his body falls to the ground. My own feet shift to a halt. I look back over my shoulder. He claws at the ground, pulling himself forward frantically, but he's lost too much blood. His head sags on the ground as the strength to keep it raised drains away.

The inn is a less than a minute's run away. I can reach safety.

I turn. Keegan still struggles to move, but he's not really moving at all. A few more seconds, and he'll pass out.

Keep running, that voice inside of me whispers urgently. *Let him die. He'd do the same to you. He's not worth it.*

Simmering hate shivers along my veins. He's a vile bastard.

I can leave him. I can let the shadow have him and be rid of him. I can live.

I hear the shadow chuckle as it approaches and sees Keegan's helplessness. The sound vibrates along my skin and awakens a memory. Another chuckling shadow clutching me around the shoulders while I was helpless. My father lying unconscious and bloodied on the ground. Teeth scarring my neck. And then, a rescuer leaped into the fray and saved me – a Kelban – just because . . . because humanity demanded it.

Keegan manages to shift onto his back and look up as I step over him and shield him from the shadow's approach. He tries to speak, but only a strained gargle emanates from his lips.

The shadow's ethereal claws spread out and surround me on all sides until my vision is smothered in blurs of white and gray. I make no attempt to unsheathe my dagger. Not yet. The shadow is too far away. I have to wait. The wisps close in around me. Closer. Closer. Until they touch my skin. I feel like grass covered in a morning dew. The wispy tendrils warp around my neck and become taut as a rope. I try not to flinch even as the wisps – now like ropes – press against my flesh.

Against my scars.

The shadow jerks in surprise.

The cloud around me dissipates. I see the forest again. Two other shadows flutter nearby.

"*She's been bit before,*" my captor rasps. His voice contains a hint of nervousness.

"*Impossible,*" one of the other shadows retorts.

"*I feel them.*"

My bonds tighten again, closing off air. If I don't act now, I'll die! I retrieve my dagger, but another wisp, this one taut as iron, wraps around my wrist and prevents me from throwing it.

The shadow flinches. "*She feels unnatural . . . not at all like a human normally does.*"

"*Grag said to kill her!*" one of the shadows hisses impatiently.

"*Yes, but . . .*"

"*Do it!*"

The shadow hesitates. My lungs scream. "*But what if she's the one that . . .*"

"*Do it, damn it, or I will!*" The shadow reveals a long, black, curved blade from its interior that glitters majestically. A shadow blade!

The wisps force themselves against my skin.

No! No! I gasp for air and claw at the prison around my throat. The shadow lifts me off the ground and my neck lengthens as gravity struggles to retain its hold on me. I feel the bones stretching. The veins crumbling from loss of blood. The roaring river in my ears as messages between my brain and body fail. My legs stop kicking as my body numbs.

A white flash burns my eyes and an awful screech fills the air. It echoes along the tiny chords of my ears, burning, screaming, tearing. The wisps around my throat slowly crumble – no, burn from the inside out – and shatter when the furious light tears them apart. I fall to the ground. The shadow tries to release the white blade plunged through its chest even as it disintegrates around the gleaming weapon. The light eats up the last tendrils of smoky fog and explodes in a shower of white crystal sparks. The force of the eruption knocks me back into a tree. I fall flat on my stomach. Air rushes into my lungs too fast, and I choke on it.

"It's him!" one of the remaining demons rasps in fear. "He hunted down Lavon!"

Shade doesn't hear them, but when he turns towards the woods, he sees them. I watch his hand tighten on the blade. The shadows slowly float away into the woods. They're not going to risk attacking him.

Shade sheathes his sword and looks up quickly when Axle comes running from the campsite. Blood flows down his arm from a cut on his shoulder.

Shade doesn't even look at his friend and gestures vaguely to Keegan's unconscious body. "Check him!" he barks.

He kneels beside me and lifts my head. A searing pain shoots down my spine. I arch my back in an attempt to lighten it. It doesn't work. I cry out instead. I still can't feel my legs and my neck burns. Shade palms my neck. It burns like a branding iron. I shove his hand away.

"No . . . please," I whimper. "It hurts."

His jaw tightens, and he lays my head back onto the ground gently. I see the spark in his eyes. The unmasked hatred and fury written all over his face. He fists his hand, and I know. I know what he's going to do. He's going to hunt down the two surviving shadows. He's going to send them to hell. He stands up.

I grab his hand. "Stay."

He looks down at me.

My arm aches with strain, but I refuse to let go of him. "Please. P-please stay . . ."

The rage leaves his face. His jaw softens. He drops on his knees beside me and slips his hands underneath my back and legs. He lifts me up. My spine rotates, and I grab him around the neck for support.

My head is near his face. My hair brushes his cheek.

"I'm not going anywhere," he whispers, so faintly I think I might have imagined it.

I can't feel anything. My senses are gone. I feel like I'm falling. Falling in heavy, deep air with nothing to stop me. Nothing to save me. But through it all something is there – carrying me. Shade.

I chuckle, but it sounds like choking. I look up at Shade. "You said you'd never carry me."

And I fall into darkness.

Chapter XXV

Something cold latches onto my forehead. Wetting my skin. Startling my nerves. Making my eyes open. I see a face above me – a face with two, rimmed eyes staring back at me. I sit up with a cry and immediately regret the action. Iron clangs inside my head. A hand gently pushes me back into my former position. There are trees above me.

The Wilds. I'm in the Wilds. A boy with scraggly blonde hair tied back in a grungy tail reapplies the cool compress to my forehead again.

Axle.

I let out a breath. I'd almost forgotten where I was.

It all rushes back to me. The attack. The shadows. And . . .

"Keegan . . ." I start to sit up and Axle pushes me back, stronger this time.

"He'll live." He doesn't sound pleased with the fact. "But he'll have a decent-sized scar to show off."

I let out another relieved sigh.

"It's interesting, though," Axle continues. "I examined on his wound to determine how it was inflicted. Dirk had some wild idea that you lured his 'boy' into the woods and tried to murder him."

"He . . .*what?*" Was Dirk blind? Or just a fool?

"The wound seems to have been inflicted from behind." He stares at me. "Now, I ask you, how does Keegan, a man supposed to be on guard duty, turn his back to the enemy and remain unaware of their presence? He must have been preoccupied. And the only other person out there was you, Kyla."

I look him straight in the eyes. "I didn't stab him."

His eyes narrow. "How can I believe you?"

I'm not used to seeing this Axle. He usually understands me. Knows me from inside and out. Now he seems tense. Ill at ease. Cold.

"I . . . I . . ."

He presses a hand to my forehead. It feels like ice. "I did an exam on you too, Kyla."

His hand shifts down the side of my face. Down my neck. Stops just below my ear. His fingers press against my neck.

Against the scars made by a shadow!

I look into his eyes. He looks back at me. My stomach flips.

He knows what they are.

I grab his hand. "Don't tell him!" I gasp in as loud a whisper as I dare. I try to look over his shoulder to make sure the voices at the fire have not grown silent during our conversation.

They continue in a slow hum.

Axle stares at me, uncertainty in his gaze.

My scars pulse suddenly, and his fingers jerk in surprise at the reaction. Slowly, I pry his hand loose from the side of my neck. He hesitates, but allows me to set his hand back on the ground.

"Don't tell him," I repeat.

Someone by the fire calls to Axle. He growls a frustrated answer and stands up.

"We're not finished, Kyla," he says.

As he walks away, I lean back and cover my face with my hands.

What the hell do I do now?

Shade is mysteriously absent when nightfall arrives. The rest of the traveling group remains in a close-knit pack around the fire with weapons at the ready. I see the fear in their eyes whenever a stick snaps or a night owl cries out.

There were zero casualties from the battle, I discover, but four of the men were injured. One shadow blade was discovered. It was near the place where Keegan and I had fought the shadow.

"It has blood on it," Axle had confirmed when Gregor handed the blade to him for further analysis. "A recent kill, maybe. Or Keegan is luckier than we thought."

When they'd asked Keegan if it was the blade that had stabbed him, he admitted that he didn't know. He'd had his back turned. He'd abruptly cut himself off when he made that little slip, in which they proceeded to interrogate me. He anxiously waited for me to oust his unruly behavior, but the only thing I revealed was that we had been talking. I don't begin to explain that I knew the shadows were there because I would have to explain *how* I knew. It shall remain a secret to the grave between Keegan and I. He relaxed a little bit when I continued to hide the truth. And despite my hate for the bastard, he *did* fight.

Dirk had proceeded to remark upon Keegan's recovery and the throwbacks of the wound. Gregor struggled to assure him that Keegan's wound would heal and he'd be wiser from the event, but not permanently disabled. Relieved, Dirk had settled down by the fire without another word to his son. I watched Keegan's face visibly sink and he turned his back on everyone, including me. A pang of pity briefly wiggled in my heart.

I wait for everyone to fall asleep. It takes longer than usual because everybody is on edge from the previous night's attack. But, slowly, one by one, they lay down and close their eyes. They snore. They roll uncomfortably. Even Gregor slumps against his place at the wall.

Shade hasn't returned.

Axle is the only one who remains awake. He stares at me from his seat by the fire. I know he is tired. His eyelids sag during brief moments, and he yawns a couple times. But he watches me with relentless attention.

One of the on-duty guards returns from his shift. He moves towards one of the men snoring and murmuring "Leah" by the fire.

"Tavus," Axle says, "I'll take his watch."

"Are you sure? It's four hours."

Axle nods, and Tavus lies down by the fire. It takes him less than a minute to fall asleep.

Axle leaves.

I know he wants me to follow.

I wait ten minutes before leaving my bedroll and walking into the darkened woods. Tavus was guarding the west side. It's a secluded spot, shrouded in trees and underbrush. Convenient. I wrap a blanket around my legs to protect them from unseen brambles.

Axle is propped against a tree, his moon blade settled at his side against the rough bark for easy access. We both know he probably won't have to use it. Shadows rarely test their luck, I've noticed.

He doesn't say anything to me. Just watches with those calculating eyes, judging my movements and my silence. My heart thuds against my ribs like a hammer. I want to run. I want to flee this place. I would face a dozen shadows if it meant I wouldn't have to be under this interrogation.

"Ask your questions," I sigh.

"When?" He gets right to the point.

"I was fourteen."

"How did it happen?"

I try to picture the event in my mind. It isn't hard. I've dwelt on that brief fifteen minute altercation for three long years. "My father and I were walking home from the palace. Celectate Wood had called for a late-night meeting about something important. We hadn't taken our carriage because Father hadn't expected it to go past dusk. Still, we weren't scared. The streets of Kirath near the palace weren't nearly as crime-ridden as the lower sectors of the city. My father informed me that Celectate Wood would be initiating the Ostracized Act within the month. I turned my back, distressed."

I had only looked away for a moment. One moment that shattered the innocent, childish girl I would never be again.

Axle patiently waits for me to continue.

"I turned back around. He was hanging in midair." I'll never forget the fear that laid a cold hand on my heart.

"It dropped my father on the ground. He hit his head and didn't get back up. There were three of them. No, there were four. One grabbed me and held me close. I still remember its cold claws. Its icy breath. Its smell. One of the shadows left. And then it bit me." I remember the pain. The feeling of two fangs in my neck. The terror icing my veins, turning me to stone, trapping my voice inside my throat.

Axle's eyes widen. "How the hell are you still alive?"

Now we get to it.

"Someone saved me." He looks up. "Someone shrouded in darkness. Someone with a sword. A sword that obliterated shadows."

"Shade," he breathes. Awe thickens his voice.

I pull the blanket tighter around my shoulders. "He disappeared – like a ghost. No one would believe me when I spoke of the event. They thought I was hallucinating. I saw doctors who determined I was under a spell or a curse. Others called it 'fever talk.' I insisted I was telling the truth – until my mother finally pulled me aside and said that no one would believe me. So I buried it. It became my dark secret." I look up at him. "I was raised to believe Shade was a 'cannibal.' But what I'd seen – what he'd done – didn't make sense."

Axle's face turns a sudden shade of red, and he pushes himself away from the tree so fast that his lanky legs tangle and he nearly falls flat on his stomach. "You – he spoke of you! He returned to camp after hunting a group of four shadows beyond the Wall. I told him not to. That it was a foolish errand. But they'd killed two hunter companions of ours and you know his nature. He came back to camp. He was pissed. Like 'throw his swords on the ground and punch a tree' pissed. He said he'd shown himself. To a girl. A *Kelban* girl. But that wasn't all . . ." He trails off, his gaze deepening. Something knots in my stomach. That look – I've seen it before. He had the same look when he suspected I knew ancient Kelban.

A tingling sensation urges me to grip my dagger. I resist it.

"He said he saved a witch." Axle takes a step towards me. "He said she'd told him they spoke to her. That they wanted her. That they were going to take her." His gaze darkens. "She'd understood the shadows."

Kill him. Kill him now, my inner voice screams. Fear freezes me in place. That lead ball of pulsing power spasms in the palm of my hand, ready to lash out. To defend me. To kill.

No. I fist my hands against their presence, holding them at bay.

Axle draws closer. I wait for him to take his Illathonian blade.

End his life.

He puts a hand on my shoulder.

Cut it off.

His fingers brush the ostracized scar. Gently.

The pulse inside of me slows. Grows faint. Disappears altogether.

He's not going to hurt me.

Axle finally looks at me. His face is passive again, and there's a spark of genuine pain in his eyes. "It must have been hard having to hide all this time. Hiding what you can do. What you can hear. What you have seen. Keeping secrets isn't healthy." I know he's not completely speaking about me now. "But we keep them anyway."

I feel like I'm holding my breath. "Does that mean . . . are you . . . will you . . ."

"Your secret is safe with me." He pats a hand over his heart. "Until this turns to stone, at least. Mind you, when that day comes, I might seek a more reliable confidant who actually gives a shit."

He gasps when I wrap my arms around his neck and pull him close. "Thank you," I whisper.

"Uh, yeah sure, Kelban. No problem." His words slur uncomfortably. "You . . . saved my sister's life. Witch or not, that's a debt I'll be repaying for the rest of my life. I don't give a damn whether or not you're cursed or if demons speak to you. Hell, I wouldn't care if the gods spoke to you from the abyss of darkness itself. You saved her. You didn't have to. Witches and demons don't do that – usually."

"Thank you," I say again.

He shifts nervously. "Sure, Kelban. But would you mind letting go of me now? No offense, but it's hard to breathe when all I can smell is 'girl' mere inches in front of me."

I release him and he straightens his vest with a nervous cough.

The silence between us grows. I count the leaves in the trees. The leaves on the forest floor. The rings of my palm. He pretends to scout the perimeter, but every few minutes he looks in my direction.

"So . . ." He blows out another breath and leans back against the tree again. "That night . . . what did they say to you out of curiosity? Do you remember?"

There's no way in hell I would ever forget the first words spoken in that harsh dialect.

"The fourth one – I think he was the leader – told them to kill my father and . . ." I pause as the experience – the feelings – rush back into my mind. "And me. But it didn't. Not then, anyway. It bit me. I . . . I remember the pain of the teeth and then Shade was there – killing them. He protected me. One was still alive. It asked for me. Told Shade to give me to it."

With each new sentence, Axle's face darkens and the corner of his mouth tilts up at an odd angle. "It . . . *asked* for you?"

"Yes."

He grips my shoulders, firmly, and forces me to look him straight in the eye. "You're sure. You didn't mishear it. It asked Shade to give you to it. It said, *specifically*, that it wanted you?"

A ball of fear tangles my throat in knots, but I croak, "Yes."

He falls back, face pale. Then, he stands up and begins pacing. Back and forth. Back and forth. I wait for him to explain himself. To say anything to quell the ropes knotting and pulling at my insides.

Finally, I can't take it anymore. I grab his arm and swing him around to look at me. "What the hell is wrong . . .?"

"Shadows don't do that, Kyla!" he says. His voice cracks with strain as he struggles to hold back the panic and fails. He tangles hands in his hair. "They don't . . . they are monsters, understand? They don't exclusively hunt down people unless you're famed killers like Shade and I. They enjoy causing mayhem and creating chaos. They enjoy watching people die. But they have plenty of us to kill here in the Wilds. Very few go into Kelba. Shade's tracked maybe a dozen loafers into that country in the past three years. Only a dozen versus the millions we hunt here in this land! They don't pick out specific people to destroy. Do you understand what I'm saying, Kyla. They just don't do that!"

"Are you saying they were hunting me? That they came after me . . . on purpose?" A wave of nausea overtakes me, and I lean heavily against the tree. All this time, I'd thought it was in their nature to hunt and kill, but Axle's right. Why Kelba? Why over a wall they had to take serious endeavors to scale? Once again, I feel like a fool.

"You said your father's a High Lord. Would they have been after him?"

I ponder the idea and shove it away. "No."

He blows out a frustrated breath. "What the hell . . ." he mutters. I can see the mind behind his eyes whirling for answers. He releases another ragged breath. There are no answers. "What the hell . . ." He allows the sentence to trail off.

I shift uncomfortably, looking around at the stillness, a new terror growing in my chest. I remember shadow words.

"*Grag said to kill her.*"

"*What if she's the one . . .*"

Grag said to kill her. Kill her. Kill her.

I struggle for breath. They were hunting *me!*

That boy in Gavrone – they came for him too. What is our connection? Why do they hunt us?

Axle places a hand on my shoulder. "You alright?"

No. I'm cold. I'm afraid. I'm ripping into tiny pieces of myself that I can't recognize or put back together.

"Yeah. It's just . . . frightening." Not even the correct word for it.

He nods.

"Shade . . ." I say.

Pain crosses his features, like it grows in my chest, and he lowers his head. His grip on my shoulder tightens.

"We can't tell him, can we?"

"No."

We stand like that, his hand on my shoulder, mine on his hand, while a slight breeze blows the leaves at our feet. I wish it would blow all our secrets away too.

Axle and I return to camp, him supporting me beneath the shoulders since I am still recovering from the battle. My spine feels like a broken ladder that's missing several rungs.

We discover Shade by the fire when Axle moves me towards our pallet. He starts to walk towards us and stops. He looks from Axle to me and back to Axle again. His eyes darken and beneath my arm, Axle tenses. I wait for Shade to speak, but he doesn't. Instead, he turns his back and continues to stare at the fire.

Axle gently sets me down and returns to his own bedroll after patting my shoulder comfortingly. "Goodnight, darlin'," he whispers. Shade's shoulders visibly tighten.

I rest the dagger beneath my blanket, close enough for me to grab it if the need arises.

Shade remains by the fire.

I stare at his broad shoulders. At the white lines that disappear beneath his vest. The ache in my chest deepens, and I close my eyes, when seeing him becomes unbearable.

He'll kill me if he knows. If he knows what I can do – what I can hear – what I remind him of with his past. He hates the shadows too much to ignore what has become a part of me.

I pull my blanket over my head, shrouding myself in darkness.

And I allow myself to drift to a place where Shade smiles and laughs and the shadows of our lives don't lurk in the darkness, threatening to ruin us.

I am in darkness.

The darkness opens.

I have seen this place before, in another of my nightmarish visions. The garish carvings in the stone jump out at me with demonic claws and bulging eyes. I shuffle through the winding tunnels. Around me, shadows shuffle around me like a normal crowd, silver blinking from beneath their hoods.

The tunnel suddenly opens up into a giant room that I recognize instantly. Fires glow from cauldrons lit in the center of the floor. Torches line the walls and swirl up higher and higher revealing an unending ceiling. And, situated in a corner of the room, a giant swirl of deep black moves slowly towards the fires.

"We failed, lord. Forgive us." I recognize the shadow's voice. One of the demons that escaped last night. "We took our stealth and skills for granted and it brought us shame and ruin. We were angered, lord, at Lavon's death."

"I thought I made my orders very clear." The deep black speaks and swirls into a monstrous, caped form similar to all the other shadows, except it possesses more power. "I told you to follow them. Spy. Be stealthy. To not engage until the right moment. All of these things you fools forget so quickly."

"Please, lord, we didn't forget. We intended to do exactly as you said but . . ."

"But? But? You dare provide me with useless excuses, you pissing bastard! If you had completed half of the mission I might be merciful, but you failed wholly and entirely in every essence of each instruction I gave you!" The darkness spreads foggy talons from beneath its cape. They glitter like obsidian.

"We tried. But the girl . . . be wary, lord. She possesses unique skills. Perhaps, is she the one he's been looking for. If she is . . ." The shadow cries out as a talon wraps around its throat and disappears inside its hood, strangling its cries into silence. The shadow curls in on itself and then . . . explodes into a ball of dark light that quickly disappears.

"My lord . . .!" The talons wrap around the second escapee. Moments later he, too, is nothing.

The remaining shadows in the room draw back, terror in their movements.

One of them steps forward. It possesses more of a build than the others. "Grag," it says in a deep voice that crawls along my skin with a familiarity that makes me cringe. "Have you switched sides?"

The dark shadow – Grag – tenses. I watch his talons visibly shiver.

The deep-voiced shadow unfurls its own talons from beneath its hood. They match Grag's on each glorious branch. "What are you planning, you vile traitor?"

Grag doesn't answer and lashes out instead. Their talons connect like a thousand swords flashing their dark colors in the giant room. Shadows move out of the way. Grag is thrown across the room and into the wall, but he recovers quickly and transforms into a ball of floating fog. He moves like a strong wind has blown into him and slips through the other shadow's talons until he's close enough to strike. I gasp as Grag's talons rip into the shadow's hood. I hear crunching noises similar to bone and flesh and the talons shoot out of the tormented shadow's back. Slowly, they spread out, ripping him into tiny pieces. He explodes.

The talons disappear back inside Grag's cape. "Anyone else?" he asks.

The room remains silent.

Grag turns towards the fire again.

One shadow moves forward, visibly disturbed. "My lord, he was the only one who knew Agron . . ."

"I will handle Agron!" Grag snaps.

"And the girl?" another shadow asks, the voice softer.

Grag growls beneath his cape like a fearsome beast and the talons shoot out angrily, curling up towards the endless ceiling like vines. "She's nothing, but a bitch's bastard."

The darkness explodes around me, forcing me back down a tunnel of darkness.

I bolt upright into a cold sweat, gasping for air. I feel like I've been underwater.

Strong hands grip my shoulders. "Breathe." Axle's voice.

I am drenched in sweat.

"Nightmare?" asks Axle.

Sure, we'll go with that. I nod.

He sits with me until my breathing returns to normal. When he leaves, I feel the icy kiss of the cold.

What the hell did I just witness?

Chapter XXVI

I stare into the valley below me where the vast city of Smoke, the capitol of the Wilds, resides among the base of the mountains and the edge of the vast forest. I had pictured a civilization very similar to Agron's culture. Modest homes. Muddy roads. A stone palace of some sort. Smoke is nothing like that.

A dense cloud of smoke resides over the city, pumped through holes in the sides of the mountain. Forges. It blankets the capitol in a cold, protective hug. I can see cobblestone streets. Brick and stone homes (most of them several stories tall), and a wall around the city four times as high as Agron's thirty-foot imitation.

"Enjoy the view," Axle says from beside me. "This is the only spot which gives you a full peek at Smoke."

I search the city. "Where's the palace?"

Axle chuckles. "You're staring right at it."

Confused, I look again. I don't see anything but the mountain.

"Look closer. See that river running along the side of the mountain . . ." He leans over my shoulder and guides my hand along it. "There!" He stops my finger over a certain spot.

"I don't . . ." *Wait! No way in hell!*

It's a drawbridge. An iron drawbridge. I can barely make out its form from this distance but my eyes locate openings in the mountain that resemble windows, doors, and, occasionally porches. Damn! The mountain is the palace.

"You look stunned, Kyla. Don't be. For modest cannibals like us, that palace is only a taste of what we can accomplish." He winks at me.

I ignore him and turn to Shade, who has kept a wide berth from us since dawn. "This is your home."

"It's where I was born," he says casually.

But he doesn't call it "home."

The guards along Smoke's wall quickly inspect our group and Gregor's edict from the King Arkran. Their eyes rest longer than necessary over me and several of the wounded men.

"Have we anything to fear?" he asks and scans the edge of the woods.

"Boredom, perhaps," Shade mutters.

The guard looks at him and a sneer crosses his lips. "Haven't seen you in a while, shadow-killer. The tales about you are ripe, though. Tell me . . . did you really slaughter an army of razors on the banks of hell?"

Shade's reply is a glare.

"I hear you brought this bitch to our borders, too." Malice drips off his words. "Noble of you, I must say. Did you do it out of the kindness of your heart or did the bitch relieve the searing pain between your legs?" He slaps a hand to his knee, laughing hysterically.

Shade wants to hurt him. I see the rage turning his neck a bleeding red. But he won't. Not here. Not for comments he's been enduring his entire life.

I hate this guard. I hate the things he says. I hate him so much that . . .

His knee is near the edge of the wall. I locate the connection between the pulse in my hand and his flesh. He screams as his leg crashes into the wall. The guards behind him laugh, and several of our company add their own amusement to the fray. Blood leaks through the guard's woolen pants.

Another guard waves us through.

"Well, Shade, isn't that strange. I was hoping that would happen," Axle remarks.

Shade doesn't answer him. He's too busy watching me.

The iron gate lowers over the moat in front of the palace on strong chains that gleam like silver. The guards inside the small room beyond the moat reassess the king's edict and affirm our identities. They open two double doors on our right and wish us luck.

I expect the inside of the palace to be dark and drab, but it shines inside like day. The walls are not dull, gray stone. They are covered in bright colors of paint, glass, or shiny obsidian that reflect my appearance back at me. It's been so long since I've seen a mirror, since I've had the luxury to see all angles of my face in perfect harmony with each other, that I flinch. I am thinner. My cheeks, cheeks that I had called "unceremoniously plump," stretch over the bones of my face like a piece of hide being cured.

There is no ceiling. At least, none that I can see. The atrium we have entered stretches up as far as the eye can see, revealing hundreds of floors, railings, and stairs climbing into the air. This mountain must be a hundred stories high! There are people everywhere inside: maids, guards, servants, noblemen who walk past with flitting robes and self-righteous, uplifted chins, and ladies with pert noses in the air and dresses that gleam with beauty. It's like I'm back in Kirath. Though I never relished the chaos of noble life, the setting is familiar. It feels like home. I half expect my family to walk around the corner, bustling for attention. But, of course, they don't.

A noblewoman walks past in a flowing dress lined with fur and sharp, tinkling objects. As she passes, I see the objects are razor teeth. Axle did say they were sold as charms in the market. I don't think anyone told the woman that they make her charm fairly lessened by their presence.

A white-haired man approaches us. His hair is not naturally colored. I smell the acidic tang of dye. His bony fingers fiddle with the razor teeth sewn along the lapels of his tunic, which is dyed an outrageous blue. Even worse, his hair is pulled up around his head in a Mohawk style while half of it is grown long behind him in a tail that he has braided. Disgust rolls inside of me. He's trying too hard to be noticeable.

Gregor bows respectfully.

The man looks down his thin, crow nose and purrs in a voice that sickens me, "You're late. The King expected you yesterday and you disappointed him."

"Apologies, Lord Lucius. We were detained by unforeseen circumstances. I beg the King's apology and yours for the inconvenience." Gregor gestures for Shade to bring the King's edict forward and Lord Lucius's mouth widens with amusement.

"My second-in-command, Shade of Smoke," Gregor introduces.

"No need for that. Who doesn't know about the famed hunter of nightmares. The legend of Smoke. The tales about you, boy, are extraordinary. If I do say so myself I've spent many a night thinking about you, facing darkness, with those majestic swords crossed along your back. You've made something of yourself. The tales of your rage and your savagery are almost as famous as those of your exploits. Tell me . . . do you really bathe in the blood of the shadows?" His eyes narrow. "You weren't such a famous pisser six years ago, though. You've changed."

"And you haven't changed a bit, Lucius. You're still the same perverted son of a bitch you were back then. Although, back then, wasn't your hair brown from all the shit you love to swim in?" Shade's tone stays formal, but the corner of his mouth twitches.

Lucius sniffs and pulls the king's edict from Shade's hand. "Still the little rat, I see. Six years has done nothing to change your manners." He taps a delicate finger on Shade's shoulder. Everyone flinches. Everyone knows Shade doesn't like to be touched. "If you wish to remain in his majesty's service and good graces to gain future employment, do not try my patience, boy."

"You can shove your patience up your ass," Shade snaps. He throws Lucius's hand from his shoulder.

Lucius smiles. "I will have you shown to your rooms." He snaps his fingers and a hoard of guards and tiny maidservants appear, their heads bowed low. Lucius points at all of us. "I charge you with showing them their proper quarters. Make sure that everything has been prepared and that they have no need of you before returning to me." His voice is harsh despite the soft purr. His servants bow in response.

"The king shall send for you," he turns to me for the first time, giving me a single once-over, "so make sure you are ready when the request arrives." He wrinkles his nose in imitation of smelling something foul, and walks off, the heels on his boots making a clacking noise against the tiled floor.

Shade, Axle, and I eventually follow two of the maids and a single guard up the many stairs and walkways, until I can't even keep track of how many turns and floors we've ascended. The walls don't look like they're carved into a mountain. They are as smooth and polished as the tiles on the floor.

I fall into step beside Axle as Shade converses with the guard in front of us. "What did Lucius mean when he said 'future employment'?"

Axle snorts. "There's been talk going around that King Arkran is interested in the rumors about Shade's unique ability with an Illathonian blade. There are few who can wield a weapon with such a talent at so young an age. At least, that's what everyone says. Any of the tales that folks spread about Shade's daring exploits in the Wilds, or his questionable extended hunts into Kelba, have been magnified to almost laughable extents. They make Shade seem like some hero. Some invincible warrior when I am clearly the best of the lot." He puffs his bony arms out at his sides, grinning like a court jester. I elbow him in the side and he rubs the spot, his lips puckering up like a wounded puppy. "What? You don't think so?"

I ignore him. "Why would King Arkran be interested?"

"The king likes talent when he sees it. He likes power when he sees it. He admires abilities that he doesn't possess. Shade would be a powerful pawn for him." Axle shrugs. "Damn politics."

"To hell," I finish for him.

The room I am shown nearly takes my breath away. Compared to sleeping in a room, on a thin, bendable cot, with a bony companion my quarters is a palace. The bed that situates itself in the middle of the room is already made, complete with a coverlet, an actual under-sheet, and several pillows. The floor is white, polished tiles. A large fireplace fills the middle of the wall directly across from my bed.

There is no fourth wall. Instead, there are pillars and a long, almost transparent curtain, with an adjoining thicker curtain. When the maid swings them open by their golden ties, it reveals a porch with a stone railing. She says I can look out over the city. The opening allows the cool air to float into the room.

She draws the curtains again and says my bath is ready. Opening a door just to the right of the bed, reveals another large room carved completely out of stone. A large tub is designed into the wall and its full of hot, steaming water. The maid takes my tunic delicately between her fingers, wrinkling her nose with disgust. I can't blame her. It does smell foul. Days of sleeping in the woods next to equally foul-smelling human beings will do that to a person.

The maid drops the soap on the floor when I turn to step into the water. I don't have to ask what has frightened her. Her pupils are large in her delicate face as they roll over the base of my neck, all the way to the tip of my spine.

"Awful, isn't it?" I ask, trying to make my laugh sound care-free. "Hurt like hell when it happened, I have to admit." I sit down in the water, hiding the scars against the stone slab. Only my shoulders are visible over the steaming luxury.

She says nothing, merely coming to sit on the edge of the slab.

"I can bathe myself. Don't worry." I try to wave her off. She doesn't move.

When I turn to assure her I'm capable, she is staring at me, her own garment untied at the sleeves and drooping around the belt at her waist. She removes her chest covering and my stomach twists. Small holes mottle her bared breasts. They have healed over, but their dark surfaces make her look like a pock-marked victim of the plague. She turns and the same lash marks that adorn my back cross over her own spine. Only she has more of them. Hundreds, applied over a series of several years.

"Who?" I ask, lightly running my fingers over the raised grooves. "Who did this to you?"

She doesn't answer. Her back tightens beneath my touch like a frightened animal.

My thoughts instantly go to her master.

"It was Lucius, wasn't it?"

She nods, then pulls her clothing back on. She turns to face me.

"Why did you show me?"

"Because you're just like me. You don't belong anywhere. You're a prisoner of your fate. Your fate depends on the king. Mine depends on whether Lucius still finds me attractive." She crosses her arms across her chest and I've a sickening understanding about what those punctured holes were. "But we both hope for a time when we can make our own decisions. Our own choices. Fates change all the time – or so I'm told." She begins to lather my back. "I know how to wash these without making them hurt. I'll show you." And she does with the utmost care.

When she leaves me alone to return to her master, I ponder her words. Otis had said I belong. Shade had told me I'd never belong. Axle had accepted me. And now the strange maid has told me I'm still a prisoner and I don't belong. Would I ever truly be free?

Or will I forever be a prisoner, bound by a fate I haven't chosen?

I spend hours staring at the tapestries around my room, trying to keep my cool. To remain focused on the task at hand. To impress the King and remain alive. But now I question *why* I am forcing myself to do it. Celectate Wood's smiling face as he branded me dances in front of my mind. He'd known what he was sending me to. What hell he'd condemned upon me. He'd cursed me to forever remain alone, on the outskirts of life, but unable to participate in it. To have no place – no one – in which to seek solace. Every time I imagine those dark, gleaming eyes, I imagine what it might be like to rip them out. To hold them in my hands. To brand his flesh as he branded mine. To rip him apart piece by piece. And as my anger grows stronger and the things I want to do increase in savagery, cold claws settle in my throat, and I want to scream. Because, deep down, I know I can't.

I throw aside the curtains of my room and step onto the porch. A breeze washes over me. I see the city stretched out below me beyond the railing. The porch is quite large. Twenty feet long. Fifteen feet wide.

I startle when a shape shifts near the corner of the railing. Shade is propped up against the mountainside, dangling a leg over the side of the railing over the city. His hair is damp, like mine. He's also not wearing a shirt and among the muscles of his abdomen that white, zigzagging scar glares at me, reminding me that I'm not the only one who's got nowhere to go.

I approach him.

He doesn't look up but keeps his gaze fixed on the gray haze enveloping the capitol. "There will be no training today."

"I didn't come to train," I say and lean against the railing, purposefully putting myself in his line of sight. "I came to listen. To you."

That makes him look at me. The line of his jaw tightens, and he slips off of the railing with a graceful shift of his powerful legs. "I've got nothing to say." He stomps towards another open, pillared room adjacent to mine. His scarred back glares at me and forces courage into my throat.

"Your captivity . . ." I don't finish the sentence, but it was enough.

Shade stops. His shoulders tighten and a vein throbs at his neck. He's exerting every bit of control he possesses to lock down his emotions. I've done the same thing a million times against my nightmares. My powers. My memories.

He doesn't ask me how I know. He doesn't ask me when I found out. He doesn't even fly into a hot rage like I expected him to do. "There are things you will never learn," he says, his voice tight. "Never understand."

"Then help me understand."

"Go!" he snaps.

Anger heats my skin. I stamp my foot. "Stop hiding it!"

I move forward and grip his arm. He finches beneath my touch. "Stop masking it."

I force him to turn around. To look at me. His mask is cracking. "It is only hurting you. Making you suffer." His eyes try to shift away from me, but I jerk his arm and he looks at me again. "It is tearing you apart, Shade. You have to let it out. Unleash it. All of it. The hate. The rage. The pain. Tell me what it was like. Everything. Every horrible, vulgar, vile thing they did to you. Tell me. Let me know what it was like."

One moment we're standing close together, my hand on his arm, and his eyes trying to keep the wall upraised between us and the next, my back is against the stone mountain and he's pinned me against it, his face inches from mine.

"You want to know what it was like?" he screams. His eyes are wide open, swirling with memories I can't gauge. "It was hell! It was pure, fire-breathing, damnable hell!" His hands bite into my shoulders. My bones ache beneath the grip.

"Shade," I press my hands to his shoulders, "Shade, calm down."

"None of you understand," he continues. "None of you understand what it was like . . . to have knives in your back and darkness at your front. To be torn apart and forced to look at the pieces. To watch your entire family butchered like pigs in a slaughterhouse. To watch your captors laugh at your pain. Want it. Enjoy it."

His skin is fire beneath my touch, burning my hands. I don't like his grip on my arms. It feels dangerous. Like a viper's hiss before the bite.

"They are monsters – all of them! They destroy whatever they touch. Whatever they find. I became a monster to rid this damned world of them. I am a monster," he sneers. "You'd do well to remember it!" He thrusts me away from him.

I stumble across the porch in the direction of my quarters and manage to regain balance before I would have fallen to the stones.

I am a monster.

Suddenly, I'm enraged. There are spots of light in my vision, and I see red that curves into lightning and splinters through my body in waves of pure, unchecked anger. I'm tired of his pathetic, self-inflicted pain. Tired of his emotionally withdrawn pretenses.

I grab his arm. "You're not a monster!" I can't tether the fury cascading through me. I slam a hand to his chest. To the scar that mars his abdomen. He moans in pain.

"You . . . are . . . not . . ." I look him straight in the eye. Past the flames. Past the anger. Past the mask. To the boy beneath. "A monster." I grab both his arms.

He tears away and stalks towards his room, faster. Trying to get away. Trying to hide like he always does.

It shatters the barriers of my restraint. "You think you are some damned warrior, Shade of Smoke," I call after him, "but you know what? You're just a frightened little boy who's too afraid of admitting that he's scared shit-less. All that bravado. All that recklessness. It masks a liar. A coward. A little boy still pissing his pants because he'll never let that fear go."

When he turns around I know I've struck the mark because his face is alight with a fury that matches mine. "And you know what, *Kyla Kelonia Bone*? You're family didn't even fight to protect you. They let a single man tear you away from them. They let a single man condemn you and did nothing to stop it because, deep down, they didn't care. You are unwanted. Unloved. You don't and have never belonged – and you never will. You are cursed. Cursed to remain alone and forgotten." He says it in ancient Kelban.

My eyes burn, and I blink against the tears filling them, but they slip down my cheeks. I wipe at them. They don't stop coming.

The fury disappears from Shade's face with a single blink. I see the shock etched into his mouth. He didn't know I could understand.

I see red again, but its of a different nature. A crueler color. "Those nightmares did turn you into a monster," I acquiesce. "You let them make you. Shape you. You were clay in their hands. A perfect creation of their darkness and evil. I don't know why I ever thought of you as a hero. As someone worthy of love. Of care. Obviously, my feelings were wasted on a primitive animal like you. Humanity is wasted on things like you."

I shove past him, but he grabs my arm and forces me up against the wall. His lips crash against mine. For a moment I am too frozen with shock to react as the pressure of his lips burn my mouth. But when his tongue runs over the curved space of my mouth, I shove my hands against his chest and manage to push him far enough away to break the connection between our faces.

"What are you doing?"

He molds my body between the stone and him, pinning my wrists against the mountain. His gaze flutters over my face. "This is what you're frightened of," he growls. His breath warms my cheeks. Sweeps my face. Narrows on my lips. And then his lips are on mine. Hard. Insistent. Coaxing.

A deep black opens in my mind. A memory surfaces. Alive. Burning. Painful. Aspen holding me. Aspen kissing me. Aspen forcing me to a wall. His lips burning mine with heat and passion that none would deny him – except me. His smell – fire and cologne and nobility. Everything that smells wrong. Fire pulses on the sides of my vision. I smell burnt flesh – my flesh. A branding iron burns into my skin. Celectate Wood smiles down at me. Laughing. Laughing at my fear. At the memories I cannot let go. The memories that keep me from living the life I tell myself I cannot partake of. The life I want.

The smell of burnt flesh and fire and Aspen threatens to overpower me. To dull my senses. To drown me in fear. But, through it all, the faint scent of something different – something familiar – softly encompasses my lungs.

Smoke. Metal. Harsh soap.

I latch onto the distinct scent. I push the unwelcoming stench to the far sides of my mind. I push Aspen from my mind. His voice. His taste. His touch.

"*This is what you're frightened of.*"

No. I shove every last feeling of that dungeon memory from my mind and replace it with the here. The now. This moment. *I am not frightened anymore.*

I pull my wrists free from Shade's hold and grab him around the shoulders. I move my lips against his. Run my fingers along the back of his neck. His skin shivers beneath my hand, and I feel his body stiffen at my response. I tighten my hold. Deepen my kiss. Grab at the fine, short strands of his hair. It is coarse and wet in my hands. He remains stiff. I press myself up against him and run my tongue over his bottom lip.

He growls, and I am against the wall again, his arms around me, and our tongues welding together. My senses fill with that scent. Smoke. Metal. Hunter's brew. I am drowning in it.

His skin is hot beneath my touch. The cold inside my body responds to the heat. Craves it. Grabs at it. Our bodies fuse together. Chest-to-chest. Hips-to-hips. Core-to-core. Against every aching, wanting part. His hands move to my hair and my back. Searching. Grabbing. Caressing. I respond in kind, running my fingers down his backside. My fingers roll over the ridges – the scars – that mar his back. His own runs across my scars, and I arch against the ticklish, unnerving feeling in my spine. His hand slows on top of them. His fingers trace the scars. I do the same to him, feeling each deep, zigzagging welt.

His lips slow atop mine until our mouths no longer move. He pulls away, and the moist pressure leaves my lips. I almost follow it out of a needing, craving sense of want and desire, but hesitate when I see his face. He's pale in places where I have surely become red.

"You . . ." he whispers in a choked voice.

He pulls away entirely, releasing me. I sag against the mountain, suddenly weak, now that he no longer holds me in his arms. My body notices his retreat, and instantly grows cold.

Shade leans against the railing. He grabs at it with white-knuckled hands. His chest rises and falls in spastic waves.

I dig my fingers into the cold mountainside behind me.

"Shade, ole boy, where the hell are you?" a voice calls from behind the sheer curtain, and, seconds later, Axle steps through it. "Oh, there you are. Told you the view would be spectacular, didn't I? I . . ." He sees me.

A darkness that I've never seen falls like a curtain over his ecstatic features. He looks at his friend's pale, trembling face. "What the hell did you do?"

Shade remains silent. He clutches at his hair. Hair that I held in my hands a few moments earlier.

Axle looks at me.

I ignore him and stare pointedly at Shade. Struggling to keep calm, to conceal the tremors rocking my body, I stroll towards my room. My legs are stiff and I wonder how I maintain the power to stand. The moment I enter my room and draw the first curtain, I fall on my knees.

The cold feeling that rushes over me chills the last lie I've been telling myself into thick ice and freezes my lungs. I choke on the dawning truth.

I like Shade.

The curtains flutter wildly at Axle's violent entrance an hour later. "We need to talk," he growls.

I remain curled into a ball on my bed, my back to him. I don't want to talk about anything. I want to be left alone. I still taste Shade on my lips.

He grabs my the shoulder and flips me over. "You're not doing that, Kyla!" he snaps. "Did you enjoy playing me for a fool? Why didn't you tell me you knew about our captivity? Huh? Why? When did you . . ." He doesn't finish and runs a hand down his face with a groan. "You and your damn eavesdropping!"

"Maybe you should learn to whisper," I retort and slip off the bed. I walk to the fireplace and kick at one of the logs. Sparks flutter into the air.

The mattress quakes as Axle sits down. "What the hell happened?" he asks.

I keep my back to him and watch the fire. The flames eat at the wood, turning it a rich, black color.

Axle sighs. When he speaks again, his voice is softer, and slow. He's tired. "It took me half an hour to get him calmed down. It never takes that long. I thought I would have to wrestle him to the floor. He went crazy. Started talking about how you questioned him. Reminded him of it. Made him go back to those moments – those memories – he uses to fuel his rage. And then he said . . ." Axle pauses. He sighs again. "He said he might have hurt you."

A pang hits me in the chest.

"Kyla . . ." Axle's voice is softer. "Did he hurt you?"

He was worried he'd hurt me? After all I said – all I'd done to hurt him, to make him bleed – he was worried he'd hurt *me*? And he called himself a monster?

"No," I answer and turn around.

Axle's eyes narrow.

"No," I snap with finality. "He didn't hurt me. We . . ." I pause delicately, searching for the right words. "We discussed our differences."

He leans back against one of the thick bed-posts. "I was sure you'd already discussed your differences. You're nobility. He's a vagabond. You're a Kelban. He's a cannibal. I'm pretty sure those are the only differences you two have from one another." A smile plays at the corner of his lips.

"Is this a time to be joking right now, Axle?" I ask.

His face falls. "No. No, it isn't." He sits up straight again. "It is a time to be honest with one another. Just once. For five minutes. No lies. No deceit. Just plain, honest truth. Three questions each. Alright?"

I nod.

"Did Shade hit you?"

"No!"

"Was he rough with you?"

"A little," I admit. "But it's nothing I am not used to."

Axle frowns, but continues. "Did you really speak our tongue to him?"

I lower my head and nod. I wait for him to yell at me. To angrily accuse me of lying. Of being a deceptive, sly Kelban.

Instead, he blows out a breath and says, "Damn, I was right."

I look up.

He shakes his head, face stiff with awe. "I knew it . . . there was no way you could look so intent whenever we spoke around you. But . . . damn . . . you played that game well, Kyla. I'm impressed."

I give a mock bow.

"Your turn," he says. "Ask your questions."

I have prepared them for a long time.

"What happened the night Brunt was attacked? I want everything."

Axle stiffens, but slowly, he allows his shoulders to relax. "You want detail or just a brief description?"

"If it isn't painful, detail would be most helpful." I need to picture it. Feel it. See it.

Axle crosses his legs and inhales slowly, watching me. The fire. The curtain fluttering in the breeze. I don't rush him. Don't coax him. If what he's about to tell me is even half of what I've pictured, he'll need all the gathered courage he can muster. He releases the breath and begins like the poet Shade's always referenced him as.

"It was a night like every other one. We ate dinner. The sun went down. The guards lit the lamps along the wall. They called the times. Mother wanted us – River and I – to go to bed early but I didn't want to. So I begged my father to let me stay up. I promised to do a month's worth of chores. I promised to help him make a batch of his favorite tea – which I hated more than anything – if he'd let me stay up and keep watch with him outside the door. You see, on nights when the moon was covered by clouds, Father would sit outside and watch to make sure no animals tried to snatch the chickens we raised." He smiles at the memory. "River pleaded and cried. Her tears won Father over. A half hour past ten o'clock we were sitting on the bench outside our house on either side of Father, listening to his stories from his youth.

"The air was the first thing that alerted me. It didn't feel right. My lungs were constricted for no apparent reason. Like my senses knew that something was coming, but I hadn't picked up on it yet. We heard the first scream. Heard the gates being opened. The guards yelling. We waited for the bell. The bell that would order us – I mean, Father – to pick up arms and prepare to fight. We never heard it. And then they were there. All around us. Dark. Screeching. Angry. Mother came out of the house and threw my father his sword – an

Illathonian blade he'd made himself over a period of ten years. He'd never used it until that night. He didn't know how to wield it properly. I didn't tell him that I knew how. I knew he wouldn't let me fight. I remember debating whether I should ask him. I waited too long.

"I heard my mother scream. When I turned to look at her by the house, a shadow was cutting her open from neck to waist. You've never seen violence until you watch your own mother's insides flop onto the ground. Hear your father scream as he watches her die. Hear your little sister gasp in horror. I remember being stunned. I didn't scream. Didn't cry. I just stared. Like I was in a dream and hadn't woken up. And then they came for us."

Tears stream down his face. He tries to wipe them away with his arm, but it doesn't work. The firelight glistens on the droplets beneath his eyes. He looks at me.

"Father killed the first one with a savage lunge that blew it into a dark cloud," he continues. "I stood there, watching him, while River grabbed me around the waist, and hid her face in my tunic. Father dispatched four shadows before turning around. He saw me. 'What are you doing?' he'd asked me. He looked at River. Looked at me. 'Run. Protect your sister. Run, boy.' A shadow stabbed him from behind. I remember the shadow blade. I can never forget what the object looked like. Father hit the ground. He didn't die immediately. I didn't watch him die, either. I grabbed River, and I ran.

"I ran uphill towards the mountains. I thought we might be able to hide ourselves in one of the caves. Or a tree. But I heard the shadows following us. Fast. River was clinging to my neck, terrified. I remember feeling her shiver. I remember the whimper that escaped her. And I had a brief image of her lying on the ground, insides protruding from her stomach, and blank eyes staring at me and asking me why I didn't protect her.

"I found a small crevice between the trees and a rock where the roots had grown out of the ground. It created a little nook beneath the roots of the tree large enough for River to fit in and hide herself. I piled branches and rocks in front of it as quickly as I could and told her to be quiet. To cry when she didn't hear anything anymore. To count to a million. Anything. So long as she remained silent. I kissed her head. Patted her cheek. And I turned around and waited. The shadows came. Five of them. They surrounded me on all sides. I waited for them to kill me. And, then, they started talking to one another. I couldn't understand their language. It was raspy. Short. Harsh. A completely inhuman tongue. They swept towards me. I grabbed a stick and hacked at the first one. I expected my make-shift weapon to go straight through it like a ghost, but it connected where there should have been a shoulder. It screeched, and I was flung back into the trees. I got back up. I fought. They overpowered me. They tied me up. Flung a bag over my head. I don't know if they carried me or flew me. I'll never know. When the bag was taken from my head I was in a cave. I never saw the sun again for three long years."

He wipes at his eyes again. "And you know what?" A low chuckle vibrates from his throat. "I love the smell of that tea now."

I wrap my arms around his neck, knocking him backwards onto the bed. His arm circles my waist. "I'm sorry. I'm so sorry, Axle."

We sit like that for a few moments until he shifts beneath me. I pull away and sit down on the opposite side of the bed to face him. His shaggy hair hides his eyes now, but his cheeks are still wet.

"It's been more than five minutes," I say.

"But I still owe you two questions," he admits with a sigh. "Ask. It's only fair."

I breathe slowly. I don't want to hurt him anymore.

He breathes softly. "It's alright, Kyla. I've been alright for years now. Go ahead. Ask."

"What was captivity like?"

He shakes his head. "It would take me hours to describe everything about it. I'll shorten it for you. It was like living in hell, but never dying. Like drowning in water, but never actually drowning. Like falling from a tall building and never hitting the bottom. It was eternity.

"When they took the bag off my head I was in a cell. A ten by ten foot square of dank muck and stone walls. It smelled awful. I gagged on the smell for days until my nostrils got used to the filth. The shadows came and put shackles on my wrists. They weren't like the shackles we use here, though. They were simple iron bands around my hands that were heavy and stuck to my skin like leeches. There were no chains. They forced me to follow them. I didn't fight them. I was smart enough to know it wouldn't do any good. I found myself in thousands of tunnels. So many I couldn't keep track of all of them. I passed dark figures. My eyes weren't used to the light, but when they did adapt, I saw others like me. Children. Teens. A few adults. They were shackled like me. They were covered in dirt and filth. They were bloody. They were crying. Screaming. But most were silent. The shadow holding my shoulder rammed a pick into my hand. If I had had any hope left in me I would have killed it. I think that is the moment that it dawned on me. I was a slave. And I started digging.

"It took me months in the caves to learn what we were actually digging. A form of obsidian ore that wasn't really obsidian but something more precious to the monsters who called themselves our masters. Over time I learned to understand what they wanted me to do without really learning their language. They never spoke around us. They made noises in their throats. I think they knew I was trying to decipher their words.

"Things continued like that for almost a year. I remained passive. I never complained. I never showed any fight. I pretended to be the perfect little puppy and I lived because of it. I watched others die. I watched others beaten to death. I watched others thrown into the deep pits we dug for the enjoyment of our captors, but I was never one of them. Instead, I listened. I studied. I watched their behavior. Their mannerisms. Their habits. And then . . . one day . . . I made a mistake. I broke a piece of obsidian ore."

He shivers. "I learned then how precious the ore really was to them. They went into screeching convulsions all around me. One grabbed a knife, lifted my head by my hair, and pressed the knife to my shoulder. I was terrified. For the first time in a year, I screamed. I showed resistance. I kicked at it. It got up and came at me. And . . .

suddenly . . . like an illusion, he was there.

"Shade let the shadow wrap its wisps around him and then he kicked it too. It flew back. He grabbed a piece of their ore and threw it. Three times he did it. The shadows forgot about me. They went after him. They beat him into the ground. He covered his head. When they were tired of that, they looked at me. Pointed at my pick. I started digging. But when they left, I knelt down by Shade and helped him up. I took him to my cell and cleaned him up with the water I'd saved. For some reason, saving someone's life can make bosom companions out of the strangest, most different people in the world. I wasn't a fighter. He was. He never stopped fighting them. He broke their ore when they weren't looking. He stole extra supplies. The children in the caves loved him.

"And then – one day – I couldn't find him. A fellow prisoner managed to tell me that he'd been dragged away by a group of shadows. The next day he wasn't working with us. Nor the next. I managed to sneak away and find his cell. His back was torn open and bleeding. He was on his stomach. He had a fever. And he wasn't moving. I spent two days in that cell. No one brought food or water. I managed to get some for him. When he finally woke from the fever, I cried. I thought he'd been about to die. But when he woke up, there was a rage I'd never seen in him. A determination, I thought then. Now I know it was nothing but pure hate. That night, one of our guards disappeared. They found him later at the bottom of a mining pit with an obsidian shard in his neck. Apparently, Illathonian blades aren't the only thing that can kill them. They didn't find the killer. I knew who it was, though.

"Three years passed. We grew stronger. I taught Shade to remain silent. To stay out of their way. It didn't do much good, but sometimes it was effective. I'll never forget the morning – or, I think it was morning – when we were walking together towards the mines for another day of labor and he leans over and whispers 'we're escaping.' Not 'let's escape.' Not 'do you want to escape.' He just told me we were. No buts. No ifs. No excuses. Throughout the day, whenever we were alone, he'd tell me the plan in snatches. He'd made an obsidian blade from a piece he stole six months ago. And he said with my knowledge of the tunnels and the guard changes, we could make it out. So – for three months – we purposely took more tunnels and more mines further into our area. Until, one day, shadows stopped us at a gate. We didn't have to understand their language to know what was behind it. A way out.

"The night came. There were two other boys we knew at the time. Both strong. Both good lads. Shade refused to leave them behind. He'd grown especially close to one of them. They were like brothers. They shared a cell. My cell-mate had been killed a year earlier. The other boy was a lad in the cell next to Shade's. They were secretive and knew the consequences of letting the information slip. Shade picked his lock with the blade and we crept through the tunnels. It looked like we might make it out. Shade only had to kill one guard. It was a silent death. We reached the gate and killed the guard there too. Shade picked the lock. We opened the gate and smelled salt air. The sea! I'll never forget the cry of joy that Shade's neighboring boy let out. That was all it took. A bell clanged. We ran like our lives depended on it. But it didn't matter. We reached an opening in the caves and when we looked down we were on a mountainside, leaning over the vast sea beneath. We'd have to jump. We made the boy who gave us away go first. I forced Shade to jump next. Then I did. When I hit the water I moved out of the way so Shade's cell-mate wouldn't land on me. He never came. We heard a scream. A dreadful, long cry of horror and fright. And then everything was silent. We knew he was dead.

"The other boy crashed against the rocks within the sea. We saw his blood before the tail of a sea creature headed in his direction. I remember his screams. The fear that clogged my throat as I watched a thousand teeth tear him apart, and the water around me filled with blood. Shade grabbed me and pulled me onto a nearby rock. We hid. Until the water was blue again. Until the body was gone. And we swam. It took a day and a half. We rested on the rocks. Finally we reached land. The sun came out. It blinded us for days. We found a small village and were fed and taken care of. I went searching for

Brunt and my sister. Shade followed me. We've been together every since."

I can't say anything. I just stare at him as he stares at his hands. His shoulders visibly shake at the memories assaulting him. He looks up, though, and there is no pain on his face. No fear.

"It took me years to not see those memories at night. Years to push them away. Years to forget what they did to me," he whispers. "I found River and didn't feel the need to hold on to that hate – that anger – that drove me to become a warrior. But I felt the need to protect. To make sure River never knew what pain really was. And she hasn't. I never told her what really happened to us. Only bits and pieces. Enough to make her understand but not understand, if you know what I mean?"

He shrugs and notices my concerned gaze. "Maybe it's a bad idea, I'll admit it. You can't pull the blanket over a person's eyes forever. Sooner or later they wise up. At least, that's what I think happens. One day River will know. Perhaps I might tell her myself when the time is right. But she's happy. She's whole. She's no idea what the shadows really are. She doesn't wake up in the middle of the night, screaming from nightmares. I would like to selfishly keep it that way for another year – or two."

I shake my head.

"What?"

"Nothing," I sigh and look him straight in the face. "It's just . . . I don't think you'll ever tell her. I don't think you can."

"I told you," he says.

I nod. "Because, on some level, I've seen the nightmares you're talking about. I've faced them myself. But River . . ." I pick at the blanket beneath my hands nervously. "River is . . . is . . ."

"A child?" Axle offers. I open my mouth to protest but he waves it away with a gentle hand on my knee. "I know. Don't feel bad about it. That might be the mistake I made. Letting her grow up trusting and naive to the world's faults."

"She's a kind person."

He looks at me, lips slightly upturned in a sad smile. "Kind. Yeah.

She is. But you and I both know that kind people . . .well . . . you know?"

An image of Helena stretched lifelessly across the cobblestones, a hand over the unborn child in her stomach enters my mind. "Yes, I know."

"That's why I'm here. To make sure that kind person doesn't end up like all the other kind people in our history books," Axle says. He straightens his vest. "I've been doing a good job so far, don't you think?"

I nod. "A very good job."

His smile falters as he remembers something. "What's your third question, Kyla?"

I hesitate.

"Oh, please, Kyla. I've told you the most painful memories I have. There's literally nothing else you can ask me that would make me feel worse than I already do."

I glare at him. "Thanks for that."

He shrugs. "It's the truth, though. So ask while I'm offering the chance."

"Do you really believe I belong here? In the Wilds. With you. With Shade."

"Yes," he answers without batting an eye. "I think you do."

His answer doesn't give me the feeling I crave.

He leans closer and quirks a brow. "But it's not my opinion you really want on that question, is it, Kyla?"

I don't do anything to deny his inquiry.

He sits back. "Let me give you some friendly advice. Shade and you are of a unique species. To be honest, you don't need someone to survive. But you need someone to *live*. That's the simplest answer to your question that I can give you."

"Thank you."

He smiles and takes the hand I stretch towards him.

Loud murmurings from the next room cut into the silence. Something shatters. Squeezing my hand in a silent goodnight, Axle stands and hurries through the curtains.

I close my eyes to drown the throbbing in my temples. I imagine Shade in the next room, alone and frightened. The white flash I've become accustomed to experiencing snaps against my eyelids. This time it hurts more than the previous one, like a thousand needles stabbing me in the face, brain, and neck at the same time. I open my eyes, prepared to see a different interior.

Shade is lying in his bed, sheets wrapped tightly around him like a cocoon. His face is red and he's moaning something about "shadows" under his breath. His whole body shakes as he struggles to break free of his blanketed prison. A vein throbs at his neck dangerously.

Axle appears at the bedside, pulling the sheets away from his friend and tossing them aside. He grabs a glass of water on the nightstand and empties the contents over Shade's head. Shade sits up, sputtering.

"Sorry, pal," Axle murmurs and steps aside as Shade swings an awkward, half-asleep punch in his direction. "It's alright now. You were just dreaming again."

"She said something," Shade mutters, eyes groggy with sleep. Sweat and water plaster his hair to his head like wet paper.

"What?" Axle asks.

"I had a nightmare. Shadows were there. And a faceless girl. She said something."

The vision starts to slip away, becoming blurry with gray and black colors that dance in front of my eyes. The voices grow distant.

No! Not yet. Not yet!

I concentrate and bring up the previous images and thoughts. Pain flowers in the back of my head, spreading dangerous claws towards my temples.

It hurts too much!

I only have a few moments. The blurry image becomes clear again for a brief moment, but it is enough.

"She said 'thank you.'"

White flashes blind me and crack against my head, sending me backwards with an almost flying force. My skull cracks against the bedpost, and I fall flat on the pillows. Everything spins in hundreds of different spirals of color in front of my eyes.

Everything goes black.

Chapter XXVII

It is still dark outside when I finally come to my senses and find the sore spot on the back of my head where it struck the bed-post. It's been a while since one of my visions has thrown me from its interior so violently. I sit up.

Everything in the next room is quiet.

The maid from the previous night returns. Dark circles mar her eyes, along with a new purplish bruise on her cheekbone. She says nothing to me. She turns away for a brief second, her hair fluttering against her shoulders. A mark the size of a man's mouth, teeth included, mars the fragile skin. She flushes and tries to turn, but I have her arm. I grab the ointment River packed for any danger I might meet. The poor girl makes no argument as I sit her on the bed and slowly dab the soothing liquid over the marks.

For a long time there is silence. The girl stares at her hands. I stare at the mark, disgust curling in my gut.

"He did that to you, didn't he? Lucius."

She nods.

My hands curl into tight fists. *Bastard.*

"There's nothin' you can do, miss," the girl sighs, hands clasped tightly, her knuckles white. She looks like death itself. Truly, she must want to die. "Once you're gone, he'll do it again. And again. Again. Until I'm so marked he won't like seeing me. Then I'll be sent to a brothel, or an inn, and less kinder men than he shall have me. Tis my fate to bear."

Damn her fate!

And damn Lucius.

"Are you sure putting a couple of slices into his loathsome gut wouldn't change your fate just a little bit?" I intend for the sarcasm to hide the violence simmering on my tongue, but I fail.

The girl shakes her head. "Don't tempt either of our fates too much, miss. You'll be free before long." Something in the way she says "free" makes me feel as if I won't really be free at all.

She helps me into the dress Mama Opal made for me and combs my hair around my face in attractive, glossy locks. She dips low in a curtsy and turns around, heading for the door.

"Might I have your name?" I call after her.

She turns around. She smirks. "Celeste. I'm 'Elaine' to everyone else. But my name is Celeste. I'll be damned if they took my name too." She looks and me and smiles, mysteriously. My throat tightens. "I'm not the only one who's got secrets to hide."

"Celeste . . . ?"

"Good luck before the king, Kyla. I really, *really* hope you pass." Her eyes dart to my neck. When the door clicks shut behind her exit, cold swirls inside of me.

My scars. She saw the scars!

Shade and Axle are both waiting for me when I open the door of my room.

"Breakfast bell rang ten minutes ago," Axle says. "We'll be late."

"Which means what?" I ask.

"That we'll have an audience," Shade mutters. He doesn't look pleased by the idea.

Axle playfully elbows Shade's arm. "We'll have an audience anyway. We're the shadow-killers! Remember?"

Shade ignores him.

Axle looks at me and gives me a once-over. "Very nice. Clean. Neat. The king will have no reason to find fault with you." His eyes rest for a brief moment at the center of my skirt. "And there are no weapons allowed on the premises without the king's consent."

"I know."

He shrugs and turns down the hall. Shade and I glance cautiously at one another before following him at a slower pace.

I can taste the tension between us – not to mention his taste is still in my mouth.

Our silence continues for six more hallways, and two staircases, before his words finally interrupt our silence.

"We won't speak of the other night again."

"I'll wait," I reply.

"You'll what?" He stops.

I stop, too, and look him in the eye. "I'll wait until you're ready to talk about it again."

He releases a slow, steady breath from his nostrils and leans back against the wall. He crosses his arms. "Fine, lets talk about it then. You kissed me and liked it."

Damn him! He's trying to make me uncomfortable.

Well, two can play that game.

"Yes." He's so startled that the mask drops from face, widening his eyes in disbelief. I lean close. "And *you* kissed *me* first and liked it too. Who wouldn't respond to such an action? Tell me, Shade, in your right mind, do you believe I would have kissed you if *you* hadn't *initiated* it?"

"You weren't supposed to like it," he snaps.

"Well that's just too damn bad, isn't it? But it's not really the fact that *I* responded that's bothering you, is it, Shade?" He flinches, but I lean in closer. "It's the fact that *you* responded too, am I right?"

His face reddens.

I twist the probing knife a few inches deeper with, "Honestly, how long has it been since someone kissed you?"

He growls, the embarrassment fading. "How long has it been for you?"

"So we're going to play that game, are we? Dancing around the subject without . . ."

"It is not a subject I relish approaching, yes," he interrupts with a probing stare. "And I find it surprising that someone with traumatic experiences regarding sexual encounters would approach the conversation so lightly. Honestly, don't you . . ."

He stops when I hold up a hand. "W-what did you say?"

"You didn't let me finish. I was about to say . . ."

"No. No, the other part. The part about my . . . m-my traumatic experiences. You said . . . what do you mean?" There is heat – so much heat – inside of me. Why is it so hard to breathe?

"Did you think you could hide the fact that your husband abused you from me?"

Oh, gods! The hallway spins around me.

"*This is what you're frightened of,*" he'd said.

This. This. This. What was this? Physical affection. *Sex.*

"Kyla . . ." The feral growl in his voice is gone. His hand touches my arm. I jerk away from its unexpected warmth – a warmth that makes my stomach flutter. His eyes narrow. "Kyla, I . . ."

I shake my head. "I . . . I . . ." *I what?* I've never had a husband? I've never had intercourse? I've lied to you!

His jaw hardens. "Or . . . was it *him*?"

Aspen. The white lies I'd made up about my banishment are coming back to bite my ass in ways I hadn't expected. And now – it seems – I have to make some more.

"My husband and I . . . never consummated our marriage." The words taste like ash on my tongue. "H-he had a performance . . . issue and he just . . . he just couldn't . . . uh . . ." At least the flush of my skin is not a lie. I can't even look him in the eyes. Instead, I stare at my hands. At the hands that have started shaking.

Don't. Don't lie to him anymore.

But I have to.

"His excellence . . . used that to his advantage. Taunted me that I was missing out on the pleasures of life. That life with him would be better. That I should divorce my unworthy spouse and come to his bed instead." Anger I'd buried for so long reemerges. "He'd treated me like I was a prized possession to be bought and sold for his whims. He'd never asked my opinion. Never cared to hear it.

He'd been selfish. He was the Celectate's son so he could have everything – or so he thought. One day he tried to prove that. All I wanted to do was get away. It hurt. It burned. I knew it was wrong. I knew it was so, so wrong." I wipe at my lips. At the burn Aspen's mouth inflicted. "I refused him. And . . . you know the rest."

Lies. Lies. Lies.

I don't hear any sound, so I look up and find myself resisting the urge to back away in terror. I've never seen his face so – so angry. Icy rage chills his eyes and tightens his jaw. I'm pretty sure, behind the contained lips, he's grinding his teeth.

"He . . . he raped you?"

No. Tell him no. "I . . . don't want to . . . I can't talk about it." I stare at my feet. Fist my hands at my sides. A single tear slides down my cheek.

A firm grip lifts my chin. Forces me to stare straight ahead. To stare at him. "Don't cry." His voice is missing it's usual harshness. "Don't let that memory break you."

If only he knew what the tears were for. Half-truths. Little lies. Always lies between us.

"And what about you?" I ask him. "The things you're allowing to break you . . . what about those?" He lets go of my chin. Instantly, I miss his touch.

He runs a hand through his hair, a sigh escaping his lips. "What if I make a deal with you?" he asks, still not looking at me. "You agree to remain calm and composed and strong for the next forty-eight hours, and I'll do the same. We'll get through hell together for a change."

"Does that mean a united front?"

He nods.

"So we're friends for forty-eight hours?"

He grips my elbow and urges me forward. "We're going to miss breakfast altogether if we don't hurry."

"You didn't answer my question."

"Yes," he whispers, softer than he needs to. That voice – that new tone – it weakens my sudden resolve. "Yes, for forty-eight hours.

Gods know what we'll be after that."

The moment I walk through the towering double doors twenty-two hallways and sixteen staircases from our secret pact, I wish there was some way for me to disappear. The setting is too familiar. Thousands of eyes. Hundreds of voices. Everything silent the moment I enter.

Everyone is looking at me. At my hair. My dress. My eyes, in which the dark rings of Wild ancestry, are absent. And my shoulder – where the ostracized symbol is securely hidden. They know what I am.

A soft brush of heat lingers over my fingers for a brief moment.

I'm not alone.

Shade gives the room a single once-over, the softness disappearing from his features and replaced with the familiar dark, brooding gaze of a dangerous predator. I follow him to a far corner of the giant dining hall where he picks out an empty table. It is piled high with breads. Fruit. Meats.

Shade sits down and fills his plate. I hesitate. He gestures for me to sit opposite of him. I lower myself onto the bench, aware of all the eyes boring into the back of my skull.

"Don't look at them," Shade mumbles through a mouthful of buttered bread. "They don't deserve the satisfaction or your efforts. Use what energy you have to eat. I guarantee you you'll need it when you meet his highness."

As I spread a red-colored jam over a piece of soft bread, I realize I haven't asked him anything about the king. And, from what Lucius insinuated, it seems like Shade and the king were well-acquainted.

"What's he like?" I ask in a low voice. I'm no fool to believe people aren't listening.

"I have no opinion on the man." Shade takes a drink from his goblet. He notices my irritation and leans forward. "Honestly? The man is a drunk. He's a coward. He's useless as a ruler. And he's a bit of a dick. Is that what you want to hear? Or should I say he's the greatest ruler that our land has ever had, and he's got a big heart for the people and for outsiders like yourself. I would be lying and you would hate me for it, yes?"

I nod absently.

"King Arkran values those who have something he wants. He valued Axle for his wisdom about shadow characteristics so he tried to charm him into joining his personal court as an adviser."

"Axle didn't tell me that."

"Of course he wouldn't. He's not proud of that day."

"Why?"

Shade shakes his head. "It is not my place to tell that story. Ask him yourself. You're unusually skilled at discovering our secrets." I don't miss the vague sense of anger in his words. "My point is, you better have something that the king is interested in." He sits back and stuffs a piece of meat in his mouth, signifying the conversation is over.

"Or what?"

"Or you have no worth to him. And we both know what happens when something has no worth, don't we?" His gaze hardens. "They throw it out."

I lean back. "There really is no difference between this land and Kelba, it seems."

The corner of Shade's lips twitch. "Oh, there's a difference," he says. "At least – here – we don't banish you to Kelba."

I don't know whether to kick him beneath the table or glare at him. So I do both.

He grunts, but doesn't reach down to rub the sore spot. And I *know* it is sore.

"Nice one," he hisses between clenched teeth.

"Leave sarcasm to Axle from now on. You're bad at it." I take a sip of my water.

"I'm kind of out of practice," Shade mutters. He leans across the table on his forearms, inches from my face, and whispers, "But I'm not bad at other things, am I, Kyla?"

The pulsing heat that rises in my neck – in my face – also takes my vocal abilities. "I . . . I . . . w-what are you saying?"

The corners of his lips turn up into a half-smile. "Do I have to remind you?" His gaze flickers to my mouth.

"You do and I'll . . ."

He sits back in a normal position again. "It seems I'm recovering my former skills."

"Oh?" I raise a brow. "What other skills could you possibly have?"

"Do you really want to know?"

"Yes."

He shrugs. "Maybe I'll show you sometime."

"Don't mind him. His skills hardly compare with mine." Axle sits down next to me and I shift further down the bench to give him space. He grabs a handful of fruit off the table and begins to shove it in his mouth hungrily. "I lost sight of you guys. What took you so long?"

"I see you've forgotten your table manners," I reproach.

"Never had them," he retorts and takes a gigantic bite out of a juicy peach. He offers the oozing fruit to me. I shake my head. He shrugs and takes another large bite before he's even swallowed the first one. Orange juice dribbles through his lips.

"You're disgusting."

"A minor characteristic, I assure you. My good looks far outweigh my bad habits. Wouldn't you say, Shade?" He flips the corners of his blonde hair, which he's combed for once, and bats his eyelashes.

Shade shakes his head, but doesn't growl like he normally does. Instead, his lips twitch.

"You should smile, Shade."

He looks at me. "What?"

"Smile if you want to. Laugh if you want to. Trust me, we won't judge you even if you look positively horrible."

He recognizes my words for what they are – a silent challenge. "Are you saying I have a bad smile?"

"Well, why else would you refuse to let us see it? Are your teeth rotten?"

He narrows his eyes at me and a corner of his lips turns up into a smirk. "You know, firsthand, that my teeth aren't rotten, Kyla."

Axle stops chewing for a moment and stares at my flushed cheeks and Shade's amused eyes. "Am I missing something?"

I jump at the chance to change the subject. "No. We both know that an intelligent lad like yourself doesn't miss anything. Am I right?"

"Trying to make me admit I'm on the same level as your primitive mind. Clever, Kyla. Very clever. Fine. I yield." He winks. "For now."

"If we're talking about primitive, would you mind shoving that *ragrartan* tail back in your mouth. It's not a good accessory to your face at all," Shade pleads.

Axle stares at him. "Shade . . . did you just use sarcasm? You did. Holy shit! You do know what it is!"

Shade bursts into laughter. I burst into laughter. Axle bursts into laughter.

And, for a moment, we're perfectly normal human beings without a care in the world.

The bell, signaling breakfast is over, chimes loudly above my head.

"I suggest you go to your usual place," Axle says to Shade as we stand, "and wait for the summons. I met someone in the hallway who's very eager to see you."

"Appreciate the warning," says Shade. He rests a hand on my elbow. "Come with me." We leave Axle behind us and head for the double doors.

"Where are we going?" I ask.

"You'll see," he whispers.

"Shade! Oh, Shade!" the high-pitched, albeit feminine, voice stops us both in our tracks. Soft, clipping footsteps echo along the hallway as the girl approaches us from behind. "Shade, you're back. I was looking all over for you. People said you were in the dining hall. Then they said you were in your rooms. Then they said you were in the city. I've been rushing around all morning. I haven't even eaten. You should have seen the guard's face when I walked past him. He was like 'your majesty, can I help you' and I was like 'oh, goodness me, I must find Shade' and he was like 'who' and I said . . . *Who is this*?"

We've turned around. I swear I'm face-to-face with a portrait of the "goddess of beauty" hanging in Master Rolfe's library. The girl's cheekbones are chiseled and outlined in rosy color. Thick lips, the color of cherries, curl up as she peruses me with aqua-blue eyes outlined in thick, black eyeliner. Her blonde hair is frizzled and curled in a unique style I don't recognize.

She doesn't wait for Shade to answer her. "Oh, I know. It's the Kelban outsider everyone's been talking about. I swear, no one has talked about anything else. Are you assigned to watch it? How scandalous. They can't stick one of our land's best warriors with such a low duty. I shall talk to my father about this. Perhaps he can assign it a guard more suitable."

I hate her. I want to rake my nails across her face. And if she calls me "it" one more time I swear, to the gods, I'll do it.

Shade's hand tightens at my elbow. "*She* is Lady Kyla Kelonia Bone, and I am not guarding her. I am *accompanying* her."

That steals the words long enough from the girl's mouth for Shade to say, "Kyla, this is princess Arene, King Arkran's youngest daughter."

I stare at her.

Princess Arene shivers. "She's making me very uncomfortable."

"I have that reputation," I respond icily.

The princess's eyes widen the tiniest bit. "It talks."

"Relentlessly," Shade adds. I glare at him but he shrugs innocently.

"A feat all primitive Kelbans like myself are capable of achieving, I promise you, highness." I keep my voice silky smooth and polished, a voice I haven't harnessed since my days as a High Lord's daughter.

"Oh." Princess Arene gives me a long, slow once-over from my shoes to my hair, her eyes resting a second longer at my shoulder which, gods be thanked, is covered. "The stories about the Kelbans are quite scandalous. Has it tried to eat anyone yet, Shade?"

"I haven't found anyone in this land suitable for my appetite," I answer her question before Shade has the chance to open his mouth. I lavish a slow once-over of her too, and lick my lips. "Until you, that is."

Her face reddens and she looks at my companion. "Shade, are you going to let her talk like that to me?" she snaps. She reaches out and grips his arm with her manicured hand. I watch him flinch at the connection and a cold, dark feeling twists in my gut.

"However, now that I've thought about it, you're much too small to suit my appetites." I sneer down at her beneath dark lashes. She is shorter than I by a good six inches.

"Shade," she gasps, "punish it."

He doesn't move.

Her eyes narrow. "That's an order." Her hand tightens on his arm – nails digging in! He winces.

That cold, dark feeling inside of me spirals out of control and the princess screams in pain as, for no apparent reason at all, her hand twists away from his arm. She clutches her wrist between shaky fingers. Tears well in her eyes.

"Did you hurt yourself?" I ask.

She glares at me before returning her eyes to Shade. "When you're done with it, come see me. I've so much to tell you. I've even arranged for a . . ."

"No, thank you."

"Pardon?" Her brows raise.

"I said 'no, thank you.' I will be quite occupied with Kyla for the remainder of my stay in Smoke. We have much to discuss before *she* meets your father." He bows, turns around, and continues walking down the hall.

I follow him, leaving princess Arene, baffled and furious, behind us.

"I'm assuming that was the 'someone' Axle referred to back in the dining hall?"

"Yes."

"Did you know her well?"

"Many years ago." He grips my elbow and guides me around the corner to a stairwell carved into the wall. It winds upwards to places I cannot see in the darkness. He takes a torch from the wall.

"Were you close?" I ask.

"She certainly thought we were." The torchlight paints our flickering shadows across the stone walls in dancing images.

"So," he says, pausing on the first step and looking at me, amusement in his gaze, "too small to suit your appetite? Just how large is your appetite, Kyla?"

"It fluctuates from time to time." I glare at him, indicating that he's included on the list and glance up the stairwell. "Where are we going?"

"To my lair."

I expected a cave that smells like animal skins and rotten meat. Instead, Shade opens a hatch door above my head. I climb through and a soft, chilly breeze kisses my cheeks. When I stand up, we're on a portico, much like the one outside our personal quarters, except there are no rooms to walk into. It's just a portico built into the peninsula of the mountain. And there is no railing to protect us as we look thousands of feet beneath us to the city below.

"Watch your step," Shade warns as he joins me. "If you get too close, a light breeze could send you plummeting to your death." He sits down and dangles his legs over the edge. He pats the spot right next to him. "I'll catch you before you fall," he assures me when I hesitate.

I stare past the city below us to the forest beyond. It stretches forever, like an eternally green stripe along the hemisphere.

"What's beyond it?" I ask.

"The wasteland your kind believes our land has become. Deserts. Poison. Swamps. Sandstorms. Monsters you only hear about. All the stories that are written in your history books most likely came from tales about that cursed portion of our world." He sighs. "I've been there once."

I stiffen. "Really? When?"

"Before . . ." He pauses delicately. "Before I was taken. With my . . . my father. You see . . . that was his homeland. It's where he learned to fight like he did. Curse like he did. Survive like he did."

It's the first time he's mentioned his previous life willingly. The first time he's spoken of his family to me. The first time he's even admitted he had a family.

"He told me he was going to make me strong. I was ten years old. We made camp halfway through that cursed land. I went to sleep while he stood guard. When I woke up, he was gone." He shakes his head at the memory. "I'd never been so terrified as I was, standing there, in the foggy darkness, screaming his name. I remember imagining all the horrible things that might have happened to him – that might happen to me. It took me two days to find my way back to the forest you see before us. And when I did creep out of that living nightmare, naked and bleeding from several wounds, he was standing there. Waiting. Smiling. Arms wide open." He blinks rapidly. "I attacked him. Screamed at him. He only laughed. I punched him in the stomach. He punched right back. And when we were both exhausted he took me back home and my mother carved a symbol into our doorway. A sword."

I stare at him in awe. "That was cruel of him!"

Shade chuckles and shakes his head. "No. In his mind, it was the best thing he could have done for me. He was gone a lot when I was growing up. Always on some new journey or expedition. I stayed home and took care of my mother. Our house. Our small crop of potatoes."

"You were a farmer?"

"A very young farmer," he musses before returning to the topic at hand. "My father taught me how to survive when he wasn't there to protect me. I owe him for that. I'd still owe him if I lived a thousand lives."

He self-consciously rubs at his chest – over the scar hidden beneath the linen garment.

"You okay?"

"Not used to wearing a shirt," he mumbles.

The shirt must be rubbing his scar. That must be why he always wears a vest. It allows freedom. "My brother didn't wear a shirt when he was training either. He enjoyed it, much to my mother's chagrin. Noble ladies would always drop by at odd intervals of the day just to see if they could get a peek at them. You'd never believe how much tea they drank just waiting for him to walk in."

The corners of his mouth flicker. "Your brother . . . tell me more about him."

"He is a knight."

"I gathered that. But why do you have his dagger?"

I take a breath before speaking. "He gave me the dagger when I was ostracized. That dagger symbolized his loyalty, his kinship, with the Celectate. The Celectate's symbol is carved into the hilt." I produce the weapon from beneath my long skirt and tap the blood-red symbol carved into the pommel. "As long as my brother possessed it, he was under Celectate Wood's command. He served him. When he gave it to me, not only did he openly break the law, but he also publicly forfeited his knighthood. He said in the most base way possible that he no longer serves the ruler of Kelba."

"What's the punishment for such an act?" he asks.

I hadn't given it much thought. It had never been done before. No knight had ever dared. "I don't know."

"What was he like?"

"He was a lot like Axle. Kind. Witty. Caring. He taught me things he shouldn't have. Things that made him seem odd to his comrades. He taught me to fight as best he could. He taught me to curse when nobles weren't looking. He taught me to raise hell, drink like a sailor, and to recognize shit when I saw it. He looked out for me." There's an ache beating in my chest. Hammering at my ribs. Squeezing my heart. A single tear slips down my cheek. I don't bother wiping it away. "I miss him."

Shade nods and stares at the forest. "I had no siblings. Often, when I was lonely, I'd watch others who did." I'm certain he means Axle and River. "They seemed so close. Like they'd fight and die for each other. Sacrifice everything. I have no one, but myself to fight and die for.

"I had parents who fought and died for me. Bravely. Rashly." The hurt in his voice turns to bitterness. "I sometimes wish I'd died with them."

My chest tightens. *He wants to die?*

"All I do is hurt. I hurt those around me. I hurt myself. I hurt society. It would be better if I was merely bones in the dirt. Harmless bones that cannot endanger good people." He slams a fist on the ground, looking out over Smoke. "They don't understand. And I don't blame them. I blame myself. Everyone asks why I fight so well. What's the secret?" He laughs bitterly, talking more to himself now than to me. The faraway light in his eyes scares me. "It's a simple secret. I don't care if I die. That's why I fight so well. Simple. Easy. I could care less whether they gut me. The only thing that keeps me going is the idea that I can't let one of those filthy, bloody, hell-cursed monsters roam this area while I live." The bitterness has become fury. And I've seen what he does when he's furious.

"Shade." I draw close.

He's mumbling, still staring at the city below. "They don't know . . . They don't know the horror that they could face. The agony. The pain. They live happily. They smile. *Smile*!" He grinds the word between his teeth. "Why do they smile? They have family. Life. Love. Ignorance. They have their pious, pitying ignorance. 'Oh, you'll be alright.' 'Oh, I'm so sorry. That's awful. How awful for you.' I hate them. I hate them all for their pity. And they hate me too. For everything those damned monsters turned me into, they hate me."

I grab his shoulders, turning him to face me. "You listen to me! They didn't turn you into anything. You're not a monster! Hear me? You . . . are . . . not . . ." I draw closer, with each word, looking him straight in the eye. "Are *not* a monster," I finish. "And you are alive, whether you like it or not. And I, for one, am glad you're not dead!"

If he was dead, I would be too. I'd have been killed a long, long time ago on a darkened street, bleeding beside my father, while shadows cackled, hissed, and rasped above me.

They were monsters. He is not.

I realize how close we are, my hands on his shoulders, our faces leaned towards each other. Our breath blends in the air between us, fogging into clouds of moisture. He blinks – the fury, the tension, the self loathing – slowly vanishing from his face. He's calming himself. I start to pull back, afraid of the static rushing between us.

He grips my arms and gently pulls me back in front of him. The air becomes pressure as he leans closer, flicking his eyes over my face.

I see it beyond his head, carved into the wall of the mountain, so faint that I nearly pass it over. But it is there. Shade pulls back, noticing my shift in attention. He looks over his shoulder at the place my eyes have suddenly become fixated on.

Bordas equistia selentia vermana.

Where had I heard those ancient words before?

"How did that get there?"

Shade follows my pointed finger, his old self back again. He looks eager to change the subject. "I don't know," he says. "It must be ancient Kelban. I can't read much of it."

It didn't look like ancient Kelban on closer examination. No. The words were too strange. Too mysterious.

Someone clears his throat behind us. Shade and I turn to behold a man dressed in soldier colors, a glinting emblem on his metal shoulder pad. A captain. He looks nervous, as if he witnessed something important. How much had he heard? Or seen?

"What is it, man?" Shade asks in his stern, taciturn voice. The harshness is back. The Shade I'd spoken to – comforted – moments before is gone.

"His majesty will see her now."

Chapter XXVIII

Axle meets us at the bottom of the stairwell. His hair is plastered to his forehead with sweat and his cheeks are red as if he's been running. He sucks in a couple of breaths.

"What's wrong?" Shade asks.

"Not good. N-not good at all," Axle gasps. "Lucius is already in session with the king."

Shade shrugs. "That's nothing new. The worm never wastes any time trying to degrade us."

Axle's brow furrows. "Dirk is with him."

Shade stiffens and looks at me. The same reaction is written plainly in both of our faces.

Oh, shit!

I have to run to keep up with Shade and Axle. They stop in front of a large oaken door. The two men guarding the entrance are covered in metal, plate armor from head-to-toe. I can only see their eyes peering through the slits welded into the shiny helmets.

"We have an appointment with the king," Axle says in his diplomatic tone.

The taller of the guards speaks in a gruff voice, "His majesty is otherwise engaged at the present moment. A messenger will be sent to inform you when he is ready to entertain your company."

"A messenger was already sent," Shade grinds between his teeth.

There is no shadow of diplomacy in his voice. Only blunt power.

The guard cranes his neck – helmet – to look at the fierce warrior. "King Arkran will request your company shortly. Until then, be so kind as to wait, patiently and quietly, *shadow-killer.*"

Shade and Axle exchange a guarded look. I step back cautiously. I know that look.

"To hell with that," Shade growls, and slams the pommels of both his swords into the guard's stomach so fast I don't even see him draw the weapons. The guard slams back against the wall.

Axle trips his guard and rams the pommel of his Illathonian blade into the man's neck. The guard goes still.

Both warriors sheathe their swords and turn to me.

"Follow," Shade gestures as Axle opens the large door. There's a hallway behind it.

As I match my steps with theirs, a pit of nausea circles in my stomach. Back in Kelba, anyone who dared to dispatch the Celectate's guards would be drawn, quartered, or worse.

What barbaric punishment is meted out in this land?

The hallway turns a sharp corner. Before we've even reached it, angry, raised voices chime in my ears. Once again, Shade and Axle share a knowing look before turning the corner harshly. I follow and nearly collide into their suddenly immobile forms.

The room is very large. Fifty feet across. Fifty feet wide. The ceiling has to be at least twice that. And from its stone embodiment hangs an immaculate, iron chandelier lit with hundreds of candles. It lights up the entire room.

The room is packed with people – most of them noble. The scents of foreign cologne, animal skins, and rich dye tease my nostrils.

". . .your highness, is a threat to our city and a curse to our kind. I . . ." Dirk stops mid-sentence and gapes at us. Obviously, we were an unexpected arrival.

Everyone notices our entrance now.

"What are you doing here?" Lucius strides forward, his deep

purple robe brushing the floor. An amethyst ring glints from the middle finger of his left hand.

"Arriving at the king's summons," Axle answers and glares at the noble pointedly, "despite your best efforts."

Shade turns towards the center of the room – the part that I cannot see over his shoulder – and cranes his head slightly. "Your highness, I introduce Lady Kyla Kelonia Bone of Kelba." He steps aside, allowing me the free will to move forward.

A podium is carved into the stone wall thirty feet in front of me. On top of it, a stone throne is also set and molded into place. In the throne, King Arkran of the Wilds stares back at me through heavy-lidded brown eyes. He looks half-asleep. A long brown and gray streaked beard shields his neck, but his hair is cropped close around his head. He lifts his head straight when he sees me and those eyes widen.

I curtsy.

"Your majesty, this is the one who has caused so much trouble in our peaceful realm," Lucius stretches a hand in my direction.

"Peaceful," Gregor scoffs. "Where have you been getting such shitty information?"

"Such language, Gregor, in front of the king is most deplorable," Lucius chastises.

"We won't talk about what else is deplorable right now."

"What are you saying?"

"You, of all people, know what I'm saying."

"Your highness . . ." Lucius faces the king, ". . . your highness I move in favor of citizen Dirk's suggestion. Get rid of the Kelban."

"Before allowing her a chance to speak?" Axle asks. "That seems most unfair." But his eyes shift between Lucius and the king nervously.

"Seems to me," says a muscled young man on King Arkran's right side, "she doesn't speak at all."

"She speaks," says a clipped voice. I recognize it immediately. Princess Arene. She stands on King Arkran's left and glares at me beneath thick lashes. "Don't you, outsider?"

I stare at her, but don't respond. King Arkran's head leans forward a fraction of an inch, his eyes circling my face intently.

"Why don't you say anything?" Lucius snarls.

"I speak when I want to," I glare pointedly at him, "and only when I want to."

"See! I told you, father. She's a bitch," Princess Arene whines and pulls at King Arkran's arm. "You believe me now, don't you? That she's . . ."

"Oh, quit your bawling, Arene. Can't you see father's got enough problems to deal with? Don't add your incessant whining to his list?" the young man sighs.

"Back off, Ivan!" she snaps. "Father, you . . ."

Prince Ivan looks in my direction and spots Axle. His lips widen into a smile. No – a sneer.

Axle's reaction is a snarl between ground teeth.

Apparently, the royal children were royal pains in the ass to both of my elite friends.

"Your highness, I move that this meeting be adjourned. She is obviously invaluable to us. What possible use could there be for another outsider cursing our existence?" Lucius adds a hint of desperation to his tone. "I believe it would be better for us if she . . ."

"You believe it would be better for *you* if she was done away with," Gregor interrupts him.

"I've had enough of your insinuations!" Lucius draws himself up to his full height.

"They weren't insinuations."

"Why you . . ."

King Arkran shoots from his seat, fire in his gaze. "Enough!" he roars.

Silence fills the room.

"You . . ." He points at me. "Come here."

The stone grinds into the soles of my feet, which I had left bare earlier that morning. I had not expected to be called, so soon, into the king's presence. I stop at the bottom of the podium and try to ignore Princess Arene and Prince Ivan's eyes boring into each side of my skull.

"You are of Kelban nobility?" the king asks.

I nod.

"I take it your father was a lord?"

"Yes."

"And you are married?" So he *did* notice the scar on my wrist and its purpose.

"Bonded. To Lord Rugan of Glothan, sire."

He chooses to ignore my correction and move on. "Have you born any children for this lord?"

"Do I look like I have?"

"You ask his majesty no questions, outsider!" Lucius snarls.

King Arkran holds up a hand to halt his adviser. "Quite alright. I'm assuming from your answer, Kelban, that you have born no heirs for this lord and remain barren."

"Unyielding, sire. Not barren."

"Correct his highness one more time, outsider, and I'll lash you," Lucius threatens with an upraised hand.

"Like you lash your slaves?"

His jaw tightens in fury.

"Lady . . . Bone, was it?" At my nod, King Arkran gestures towards a side-door behind his throne. "Follow me. I think our conversation will go a lot smoother with far less supervision."

Someone snickers behind me. *Keegan.* I had forgotten he was there.

"Your highness, I find that extremely unwise and . . ."

King Arkran cuts off Lucius's warning with a wave of his hand. "Not another word, Lucius, or I confiscate half your wealth. Understood?"

The adviser remains silent.

The king beckons me again.

Don't follow.

But I do.

He closes the door behind me.

The king's solar is not what I expected. There's a crackling fireplace. A couch with a bearskin stretched across its unruly mass. A modest table and chair. A four-poster bed big enough to hold ten men. And, last of all, a giant map of the entire kingdom of Kelba – before the poisoning decimation – hanging on the wall opposite of the fire.

"Sit." King Arkran gestures to the chair and the couch.

I brace my legs. "I prefer to stand."

He turns around from where he'd been admiring the sleek, leather map and the corner of his mouth twists upwards. I don't know if he's amused or irked by my behavior. "You're a bold one, aren't you?"

I shrug.

"A girl who only speaks when she wants to and does what she wants . . ." He cuts himself off and shakes his head. "It's not a common sight."

On that, I agree with him.

He pours a glass of wine from a decanter on the nearby table and offers it to me. I shake my head. He shrugs, and downs the contents, before filling again. Beneath his regal robes, I locate the paunch of his belly. The round torso. The meaty legs. He is no Celectate Wood of muscle, power, and charm.

"It's been a while since I've entertained a Kelban visitor. And a noble Kelban at that." He peruses my garment – and the shoulder my sleeve carefully covers. He frowns when he can't see the scar. "One could simply look at you and know you had a fine upbringing. The way you walk – the confidence, the pride, the honor – it all speaks to your fine heritage. And you said your family name was . . . it was something of the human anatomy . . . gods, it slips my mind." He snaps his fingers.

"Bone."

"Yes. Bone. Good family name. Fine heritage, I assume?"

His honey-sweet words are making me uneasy. I cross my arms. "With respect, sire, are we here to discuss my lineage?"

"No. But I find it helpful to know every bit of back-story behind the outsiders I must allow within my borders. Wouldn't you, if you were in my place?"

He's caught me there, and he knows it.

"My father is a High Lord." I'd almost forgotten the importance of that part because it didn't matter.

"You're . . . you're a High Lord's daughter?" he asks, breathlessly.

That nauseous pit in my stomach tightens. "Y-yes."

Beneath shaggy eyebrows, his eyes glitter. His lips widen into a smile. He walks up to me and places a hand on my shoulder, close to my neck. I flinch beneath it. It is ice cold. He leads me towards the map. Some of the markings are incorrect. He has placed several important cities too far from their actual posts. There are also several river branches that do not exist inked onto the fine leather. Wherever he got the map, it was poorly made.

"Fine piece of work, isn't it? It's three hundred years old."

I stare at him in astonishment. Three hundred years old? Gods, that was decades before the poison decimated Kelba. The river branches might have disappeared over time since then. And the cities have been moved closer to their current positions to account for the lack of water in those areas. The map is practically worthless. And the cities of Smoke, Agron, and Brunt inked onto the leather have obviously been added within the last few years.

"It is ancient," is all I say to him. *Worthlessly ancient.*

"Aye," he agrees. "Old as the mountains, but still strong. Like us. Like the people of this land your kind deserted." He says it like a fact, without a trace of bitterness or resentment. "But it is lacking. I am hoping you might be able to help me with that."

His eyes hold mine in a steady gaze. I dare not look away. "What?"

"For instance," he whispers and grips my hand. Disgust rolls within me at his touch. His hands are too soft. I am used to Shade's callused, gnarled fingers. Axle's bony, strong hands. To feel softness, especially in one from the opposite sex, discomforts me. King Arkran guides my hand upwards. Up, up, up until it's positioned over the inked dot named "Kirath." "The fortifications around this city – are they stone? Brick? Mortar? Both?"

I stare at him in shock.

He tries again and positions my hand towards the edge of Kelba.

Over *Rag-vara* – Kelba's leading city of trade. "What kind of dealings go on here? Illicit? Legal? Who conducts trade with your land? Who . . .?"

I pull my hand away from his and step back. "You want me to betray them."

"Haven't they betrayed you?" He takes my arm gently and his coercion changes to soft understanding. "They hurt you. Branded you. Carved you up like a piece of meat. A slave. Something to be used by them. Does it not make you angry? Don't you want a little revenge on them? The way I see it, you're the same as us. You want your life back – but they took it from you, didn't they? I can give it back to you. All the wealth. The splendor. The recognition. The title. All you have to do is help me. Help me and together we can restore this land to its former glory. We won't be in the shadows any longer."

I spent my entire life around bastards like him. Around soft-spoken lords and secretive sons-of-bitches. If he thinks his smooth words and his feigned understanding of what I went through and what I lost will make me divulge all the information he desires, he picked the wrong Kelban to seduce.

Shade and Axle said the man used people for his own gain. That he desired ability when he saw it. But Shade had also said if I had no worth to King Arkran then I was useless. And useless people were thrown out.

Killed.

"Why? Why do you need this information?"

"To take back what is rightfully ours. What your kind stole from us. Humanity. Recognition. Life. We want it back. We'll take it back in the end, with or without cooperation from those like you, Kyla Bone."

"You want to unite the nations again?" Truly, such a thought had once crossed my mind. To have the separated halves of Kelba joined once more would be a dream come true.

And, unfortunately, I was smart enough – and critical enough – to know that's all it could be.

A dream.

"Unite. Divide. Destroy. It doesn't matter what our nations do. What matters is I will be the one leading my people against your pathetic wall and securing your borders and taking back our lands." His eyes are glittering with the idea of his future victories.

He's obsessed. He wants to be an undisputed king. He wants to rule. He's as bad as Celectate Wood – except Celectate Wood knew better than to admit what he truly wanted. King Arkran is as much a fool as he is a mad-man.

"I don't know anything about the Wall so I can be of no use to your plans of conquest."

"That's not important. I have other means of tackling that priority. What I need from you is facts – about Kirath. I know Celectate Wood makes his home there. I know he lives in a palace that hides great fortifications and secrets. I've been told it would take years to lay siege to it. With your father as a High Lord, I'm sure you had plenty of access to the place?"

Oh, he had no idea. Exploring the palace was a popular hobby of Aspen, Selena, and I until that frightening event on the rooftop. I could walk its interior with my eyes closed and still find my way. But fortifications? I knew little of those. Celectate Wood could hide things in plain sight – it was highly unlikely I discovered any of his secrets.

"Any of those facts would be of no use to you unless you can get over that wall. And you can never do that. It's built to keep things stronger than you away from our land. There is no possible way to breach it." I tell the lie as earnestly as I can. Nightmares came over the wall four years ago and ruined my life forever. There is no telling what else could destroy Kelba if the wall was simply an imitation of strength.

King Arkran shakes his head. "A wall it may be, but it does not keep everything out. It cannot keep us out any longer, either. I have resources that I will call in when the time is right to deal with that portion of the conquest. Until then, I need to know every inch of what is behind it."

"What resources?" But I know before I even ask the question. I see the answer written plainly on his face.

Shade.

Shade had been over the wall. He knew its weaknesses. Its strengths. Perhaps, he even knew a way to disable it. Fear. Anger. Disgust. Bitterness. They roll in my gut. All this time he'd said he wanted nothing to do with King Arkran – nothing to do with my kind or their wall – and he'd been spying on them. Plotting against them. Of course, he would want revenge on us. We were cowards to him. Monsters.

And I know exactly what he thinks of monsters.

"What is it that you want?" I ask, struggling to keep the emotion from my voice. Above all things King Arkran must not know I am troubled.

He's too ecstatic with his plans for the future to pay any attention to my sudden change in mood. "I want to be the man who takes back what was stolen from us. I put the old ways behind us once to make us stronger. It is time to redeem your nation from its strangling depths and strengthen it too. I will go down in history books as the man who reunited the kingdoms and brought a unified Kelba to peace and prosperity. I will be a hero. I will be important. And, for centuries to come, people will remember my name."

"So you want to be Calaisar?" I shake my head with a soft chuckle. "You want to be a god."

His brow furrows. "There are no gods. There is no Calaisar. That ancient religion of your ancestors is dead and buried. There are only men – and men have the willpower to make themselves gods."

"And that's what you think you'll become by doing this? A god?"

"I will be immortal on the pages of history books for millenniums to come. Is that not being a god? I will occupy a portion of people's minds for ages. Is that not being a god? I will be praised and worshiped as 'Kelba's savior?' Is that not being a god?" He pauses in his brief self-glorification to gesture fondly with his hands. "You could join me along with others – an adviser by my side."

Like he'd offered Axle. All I want to know right now is how Axle turned down the king's offer without sentencing himself to a dramatic end. Of course, the surly warrior hadn't shared that portion of his wisdom with me.

And now I had to climb out of this shit with my own technique. Technique that, for the past two months, was growing dimmer and dimmer. I try to find that piece of myself that once existed. The girl who knew how to play political games and wage and extinguish warfare with words alone.

And – in the dark recesses of my mind – I have one thing to offer him.

"Or I could give you something better."

King Arkran laughs. It sends shards of ice down to my clenched knuckles. "What could you possibly give me that is better than Kelba?"

"You like to collect things, if I'm not mistaken." I take my time scanning each object he's placed in his room. A set of manuscripts, tattered and falling apart. A fossilized sword thousands of years old. A diamond necklace that shares amazing characteristics of Kelban heritage. And – at last – a jade pendant. I knew from years of research who the jade pendant belonged to, once upon a time.

Gasan. Gasan, the ancient ruler and self-made god, wore a jade pendant.

"I do." King Arkran pauses long enough to glance over his collection with pride. His similarities with Celectate Wood both terrify and intrigue me. "I have spent thirty years gathering ancient artifices. My collection will be written in history books some day." Once again, he pays homage to his "future" accomplishments.

I know my offer will be accepted.

"You seem to be missing something, however."

King Arkran looks at me, curiosity replacing the pride in his eyes. "What is that?" he asks, not bothering to hide the irritation in his voice.

I had prepared for a moment like this – known it would come one day – but it still hurts as I retrieve the Celect dagger from beneath my skirt – Landor's dagger – and hold it, palms up, towards him.

"W-what? Where did you get that?" King Arkran's eyes shine with suppressed excitement. His fingers twitch. He wants it. He wants it badly.

"My brother gave it to me when I was ostracized. He was a Celect Knight. I offer this as a token of my good will and good faith. I will consider your offer to advise you on the conquest of Kelba. Until then, consider this a down payment on my stay here within your borders."

"Let me hold it!"

I hand it over. The moment the slim blade leaves my hands, something rips inside of me. I cage it in, like I've always done, and put a mask on my face. I know what it feels like to be Shade now. And it hurts. I am burning and can't let the fire show.

King Arkran admires the smooth craftsmanship. The red emblem in the pommel of the hilt. The reflection in the blade. "And not a scratch on it!" he muses. "Very fine condition." He looks at me.

I know I will live.

I was right. He was a fool, because only a fool would trade the valuable information I can give him for an artifact.

That's how Axle stayed alive. He offered King Arkran something better. Who else would have retrieved the jade pendant for him?

"Yes. Yes. We can put future plans aside," King Arkran agrees. He slides the blade between his fingers. It doesn't even cut him. "An absolutely splendid work of art."

He sets Landor's dagger above the fireplace, on the mantle, and gestures for me to follow him out of the solar. I spare a glance over my shoulder, one last time, and the emblem glints at me, as if saying "goodbye."

That was the last piece of my home. The one chain binding me to Kelba and to my family.

I've never felt so broken.

King Arkran steps onto the podium. Everyone in the room shifts their attention to him. Had they all really been waiting this whole time? Shade and Axle are in the same spots they occupied when I left them.

Shade's eyes search mine and he frowns. Obviously, he doesn't like what he sees.

"The Kelban . . ." King Arkran's voice resounds through the entire room, ". . . shall stay. Return to Agron. Give Otis my edict. As of this moment, she is an official citizen of our land and one of my subjects."

The hell I am, but I keep silent.

"Your highness, she . . ." Dirk isn't going to let me go that easily. His eyes are alight with flaming rage. "She is a curse to us. If you value our safety please . . ."

"Do not attack me, Dirk of Brunt!" King Arkran's voice takes on a new note – one filled with icy warning. "I did not hear the same hypocritical thinking when your mother was recognized as a citizen, did I?"

I look at Dirk, shocked. His mother was a Kelban? How could he have such hate for his own flesh and blood?

Dirk lowers his eyes and steps away.

"This meeting is adjourned!"

Shade and Axle are waiting for me at the entrance where they'd dispatched the guards. Not surprisingly, there are two different guards now. I am the last one to leave. The king kept me longer than the others because he wanted to know exactly how he should clean his new artifact and make it shine like I had. It took me a good half-hour to explain.

The cage around my rage is slowly starting to recede. And when I look at Shade – at the boy betraying my homeland – the bars start to fracture.

He moves forward to say something. I elbow past him.

He grabs my arm and stops me. I want to pull myself free, but I resist the urge. If I pull free my hand will start swinging, and I know his jaw will suffer the consequences. I've never hit him – but I know enough about him to know what his reaction would be.

"What happened?" he asks, his tone somewhere between intrusive and worried.

"You were right. He wanted to use me for his own gains."

Axle swears under his breath.

Shade doesn't say anything. He just looks at me, his eyes searching mine for the secret I'm hiding. The reason for the enraged glitter dilating my vision.

"And?" Axle prods.

"I gave him what he desired." I lower my gaze. It hurts too much to look them in the eyes. "I exchanged the last piece of my home for citizenship. For my life." I stare at my naked leg. The imprint of my dagger is still cold against my flesh.

"Kyla . . ." And when he says my name, I know he knows. He knows what I gave the king. He knows what it meant to me. He knows why it hurts.

"Everything's gone now."

"Kyla . . ."

My name on his tongue – a tongue that's been dooming my kindred to King Arkran's maniacal dreams – shatters the restraint around my anger. I rip my arm from his grasp. "And you . . ." I glare at him pointedly, ". . . can go to hell for all I care."

"What?" Axle asks, mouth agape. "Kyla, what's wrong? Why . . ."

Shade says nothing. He knows. He must know why I'm angry. His eyes narrow and he cranes his head to the side – in that wild manner that resembles an animal. "What did he tell you?"

He does know.

"You know damn well what he told me. And don't you dare deny it. Don't you dare . . ." My lips are trembling too much for me to finish the sentence.

Axle looks between the two of us in confusion. "What the hell is going on?"

"What's the matter, Shade? Can't tell your friend what a back-biting, two-faced son of a bitch you really are?"

Axle's face pales. "Shade . . ." His tone holds warning – along with a touch of fear.

Shade ignores him. His eyes are only for me. "Whatever he told you . . . are you really such a fool to believe it?"

"Yes. Yes, I am a fool. A fool to let you blind me – to trick me – into thinking you weren't a vengeful bastard under the king's drunken thumb. But I won't be again. Not after this. You . . . stay the hell away from me! I don't want to see you. Look at you. Hear you, even!" I turn my back on him.

"Kyla . . ." Axle starts to say.

I run away.

I find my room easily, having mapped it out earlier in my head. I slam the door behind me.

I sit down by the fire. All this time I'd thought he honestly didn't care. That he didn't want my kind to pay for what they'd done to this land. For the lies they'd made up about him and these people. I'd been naive.

I won't be again.

I stare at the flames, and it isn't the smoke that brings tears to my eyes. For a while, in the moments at the dining hall and up in the towers of the palace, I'd really thought he might be different. That the hero I'd once imagined him to be might exist.

Fool.

The doorknob clicks as someone opens it and steps inside. I keep my back turned. I'm in no mood to hear Axle's useless explanations about his friend's mood and character any longer.

I don't wait for him to speak first. "You can tell Shade to go to hell. I'm not listening to your little lies anymore."

"Once was good enough, but I appreciate the reminder."

Shivering, pulsing anger slides down my arm and into my fist. It's Shade.

I keep my back turned to him.

"We need to talk," he says.

How many times had I said those very words to him?

And what had he said to me?

"There's nothing to talk about."

He takes a moment to breathe. I hope it pissed him off to hear his own words thrown back in his face. Now the bastard knows what it feels like.

"You don't understand," he tries again.

"The hell I don't."

"Kyla . . ." His voice is strained – like his restraint is on the verge of snapping.

"Say my name again, and I'll carve it into your hide."

I know I've gone too far the moment the words leave my mouth, but it's too late. The silence behind me is like a sharpened dagger. I don't want to see the anger – the pain – that must be in his face. His boots clip against the floor as he steps up behind me. Every muscle in my body is tight. Something clangs onto the ground beside me. I look at it. It's silver and designed with ancient Kelban scribblings and ivy patterns.

One of his Illathonian blades.

"Outside," he snarls. "Now."

He stomps towards my curtains and throws them open, revealing the portico beyond. "I'm not going to ask twice."

I grip the Illathonian blade and follow him. The sun is hiding behind the clouds, giving the entire mountain a hazy look. He stands on one side of the portico. I take the other.

"You want to fight, we'll do it right," he says, not a trace of any emotion in his face.

"I'm going to make you regret that you ever met me," I whisper, rage curling around the words while my fingers curl around the blade's hilt. It is light. It is lethal. And I am powerful.

"You're a bit late. I already had that revelation the very first time I saw you."

The very first time he thinks he saw me.

The very first time he spied on my land.

I lunge at him.

One-two; one-two; one-two our blades sing.

He deceived me.

I knock his blade aside with my momentum.

I am sick and tired of being deceived.

I pivot around, and he narrowly avoids the tip of my blade through his eye. Instead, it sweeps over the hair at his forehead. Several black strands fall to the ground. He looks at them, and then at me. A knowing spark flashes in his eyes.

"He wanted information, didn't he? About Kelba? About your precious capitol? Don't look so shocked. He's been trying to plan an attack on that forsaken world since he took the throne a few years ago. It's his sole desire – to go down in history as the man who took back what once belonged to us." He chuckles. "It consumes him."

"Like it consumes you?" I lunge at him. He blocks my strike, welding our blades together, so we can stare eye-to-eye. I show no sign of relinquishing my stance or the strength in which I press the silver metal harder and harder against his own.

"Many things consume me, Kyla," he whispers, "but fueling that man's dreams for self-glorification is not one of them. Nor is wasting my time trying to determine the strength of a wall that hardly garners a single percent of my interest." He forces me back with a sudden twist of his muscled arm. My feet slide easily across the smooth stone floor until I use the tip of his blade to steady myself. Sparks fly up from the ground as I come to a slow halt.

"You're a liar!" I snarl.

"And so are you. I'd say we're evenly matched, yes? Or am I wrong in thinking that you – for maybe a brief moment – actually considered his offer? Didn't you? You thought about it. You wanted to know what it would be like to march back to your homeland as its conqueror. You wanted to know what it would be like to see the people who hurt you, who screamed for your death, who mutilated you, fall prey to a similar fate. You wanted to see it. You wanted to see it so bad you could almost taste the smell of destruction in the air, couldn't you? And that's why you're so pissed off, isn't it? Because, deep down, you hate them as much as I do. You hate them for the cowards that they are. You hate them for the cowardly human beings they have become. You hate that they couldn't stand up just once – just once in their miserable lives – and fight. Fight for their lives. Their freedom. Their rights. But no . . . they cowered. They cowered and you paid the price for their cowardice. And it angers you! They threw you away – and you realize you were worthless to the very place you call your home. Isn't that it?"

The rage consumes me. I hardly recognize the scream that rips from my lungs as my own. I just know I can taste the metal in the air between us as the Illathonian blades clash together again and again. I lunge, beat, strike, and swing at him with all my might. Blurs dance in front of my eyes. Blurs of light and dark and everything in between. The blurs turn into shards.

I realize what's happening, but I am powerless to stop it as one of the shards shoots towards me. A white flash cracks me hard between the eyes. When I open them, I am blind. But only for a moment before the images surrounding me become clear.

I am in Kirath. On a dirty street that I don't recognize. There is mud and gods know what else staining the cobblestones an ugly brown. The buildings are in need of fresh paint, new wood, or new structure altogether. Kelbans, all dressed in modest homespun, struggle to keep their clothes clean as they saunter down the ill-made street.

Up ahead, a sign hangs from the eaves of a two-story stone building with several windows. Scrawled in scrappy, downtown dialect are the words "Lazy Eye Shop." The door to the inside is propped open with a square of iron.

"I asked you to accompany me, Landor, because you're the only one I trust to fulfill this mission. I realize it's a strain on you – especially with the amount of reliance your father puts on you these days, but I promise, when we're done here, I'll give you the rest of the week. Deal?" Craig's voice is charming. Friendly. It makes me feel ill even before I see him standing at the corner of the little shop. My brother stands at his side, head bent, and arms at his sides in resignation.

"You are my captain," Landor replies. "I'm yours to command."

Craig bites his lip in irritation, but makes no comment. He stomps through the shop door. Landor follows him, shoulders straight. He's readying for the worst.

I follow them inside.

The room is lined with shelves full of antiques and intriguing objects of all shapes, sizes, and colors. A girl is dusting some shelves in a far corner. Landor and Craig approach her. She is very slender, and I don't miss the way in which Craig circles the shape of her sleek black skirt that leaves little to the imagination. Something about the way the girl cranes her neck to one side or gracefully flicks a mound of dust off the top of the offending shelf is familiar to me.

Landor clears his throat loudly.

The girl stops dusting but doesn't turn around. Her feet still on the edge of the stool she's standing on.

"Pardon us, ma'am, but we are looking for the owner of this fine establishment," Landor says.

The girl turns around. I am not a bit surprised to recognize the high cheekbones and flashing eyes. It's Daria. She looks down her nose at them with the haughty expression of a high-born lady rather than a lowly citizen. She releases a whisper of a chuckle – low, taunting, and meant to sting the pride of those who believe they're above mankind.

"And what would you want with the owner of this ***fine*** *establishment." She drawls out their high dialect tone without missing a single syllable.*

Craig doesn't miss a beat either. "We were told they might have some information about the rebellion that's been nipping at our heels for the past few months."

Daria gracefully steps off the stool, relinquishing her advantage of height, and stares across the counter at both of them, duster still in hand. "Well, ***I*** *am the owner and I don't seem to have any information for you."*

"This gentleman was pretty certain you do." Craig isn't giving up.

Daria smiles – her lips curl around her teeth and a gleam sparkles at the center of her eyes. "Was he now? Well, he must have been mistaken. You came all this way for nothing." She turns her back on them.

"There was an attack on a weapons supply just outside Kirath's northern wall of defense. We have reason to believe the rebels may have taken the shipments into this very vicinity. Have you seen anything suspicious lately?" Landor asks.

"No."

"Are you sure?"

Daria turns around and sneers at him. "I'm quite sure."

"You didn't see any men, perhaps wearing masks, moving anything suspicious between houses? Or the clang of weapons in the middle of the night? Maybe even a dog barking from sudden disturbance?"

"I didn't see any men in masks or hear any clanging weapons. As for the dog barking from a sudden disturbance . . ." She flickers eyes over him with disgust. ". . . you're not the first one to come in here."

"Be careful, girl!" Craig snaps.

"Or perhaps . . ." Landor leans across the counter-top, so close to Daria's face that their noses almost brush. She doesn't flinch. Doesn't retreat. She holds his gaze, her lips drawing closer and closer together into a tight line. "Are you a rebel too?"

Her lips widen into a smile. "Piss off!" she snaps.

The force of her words spreads saliva across Landor's eyes. He draws back and wipes at them, a groan of disgust surging from his throat. Part of me wants to strike her for it.

Craig draws his sword and points the gleaming tip at Daria's throat. "Try that again, bitch, and this will slice your mangy throat in half."

Daria smirks. Craig blinks in surprise.

And she has a knife directed at his throat in a matter of moments. She must have hidden it beneath the counter-top.

"Not today," she whispers.

Landor recovers from his sudden blindness and steps between the two weapons. "Cra – Captain! Now's not the time for such a skirmish. We don't need another riot on our hands. Neither does Celectate Wood."

At the mention of the man he serves, Craig sheathes his blade. "It's your honor, Landor, not mine. If you wish the diseased bitch to stain it, then so be it."

"Landor?" Daria slowly lays the knife beneath the counter-top once more. "Landor Bone?"

He turns around to look her in the eye.

"Ah, yes. I knew I recognized you. The coward who left his sister to the hands of a monster. Who could forget you? Everyone knows your name. Everyone knows what you did. How you let your sister be dragged

away while you, a knight sworn to protect people like her, did nothing."

Landor's face turns white. "Not another word, bitch . . ." he growls. His fists shake dangerously.

"I have to thank you."

Daria, knowing she has their full attention, crosses her arms and leans across the counter-top. "You . . ." she says to Landor, ". . . started a war. A war that will change this land forever."

"Rebellion," Craig corrects.

She shakes her head, that playful smile on her lips curling into a smirk of amusement. "It will be a war. And – unlike all the other countless rebellions and riots this land has endured in the past – this one will not die."

"Won't it?" Craig asks. "Who's going to keep it alive if all the rebels fighting it are dead?"

"When a rebel dies, more come alive. The more of us you kill, the more of us you create. A rebellion is a cycle of trial and error. We have to find out just what makes us stronger and what makes us weaker. What makes our enemies stronger – and what makes them weaker. A war is what happens when we learn those things. When we know what the enemy wants, needs, and lives on. And between you and I," she whispers with a seductive wink, "you're dangerously close to a war."

Craig and Landor leave the shop abruptly. Craig smashes a pane of glass on the door before following my brother down the steps and back towards the proper streets of Kirath.

"The little pisser has just ruined my day. Maybe I'll return the favor some time, the slagging crone!" Craig swipes a hand through his curly hair.

"She was a real piece of work," Landor agrees. "And what a wasted trip."

Craig shakes his head. "Not wasted at all. I learned all I needed to know. Besides, we've got something better waiting for us back at the palace."

Landor's shoulders visibly stiffen. Craig doesn't notice his unease, but I do. It strikes fear into the core of my heart. What has he done?

Craig turns around when he realizes Landor isn't following him.

"What's waiting for us?" Landor asks, trying to pretend he was fixing his shoe.

Craig claps him on the shoulder. "The way to end this rebellion," he whispers excitedly. "Lan, we caught him! We finally caught him!"

"Caught who?" Landor manages to choke out.

"The giant! We caught the giant!"

The blast of white light blows me through darkness. I register the crack of my shoulder, then my back, on hard ground, and the blood sizzling through open skin. I open my eyes and the sun blinds me. I am flat on my back.

"Kyla!" Shade slips a hand behind my shoulders and lifts me into a sitting position. His hands drift to my face, forcing me to look at him, pressing hard, callused palms into my cheeks. His eyes are wide. Panicked? "Kyla, can you see me?"

"You're four inches from my nose. Of course I see you, you ass!" I shove his hands away from my face and resume my former position – flat on my back. Air is close around me, but I can't breathe any of it.

"We caught the giant."

The man who'd saved me from the riot. The man who'd encouraged me at the gates. The man who'd approached Lan in the stables and shared secrets I couldn't unravel. He was caught? And Landor looked distraught?

What has my brother done?

"I'm sorry. I didn't mean to strike at you so hard. To hurt you like that, okay? It was just . . . you need to know, sooner or later, that in this world you cannot trust anyone. Everyone wants what they want. And everyone wants to live. So they are cowards. They will grovel, kneel, and submit just because they don't want to be buried in the dirt before their time. It's a shitty view on life, I know, but it's the only view on life that remains true." He leans towards me and places a hand on my shoulder – over the scar. "You, most of all, should know that."

I did know it.

But I also knew, like he couldn't, of those who were not cowards.

Of those who were willing to make sacrifices. Of those who had made sacrifices! Daria. Landor. The giant. Mother. There were people like them in Kelba. Thousands of voices silenced beneath a single man's reign who would not remain silent any longer. A cry in the night that would not go unheard. A voice that would not be silenced.

People had turned their backs on Shade his entire life. Mocked him. Pitied him. Judged him. No one had ever fought for him except his parents – and they'd paid dearly for it. No one had ever accepted him – scars, temper, and all – as a person. They looked at him and they saw a monster to be feared. A mutilated boy to be pitied. A raging fire that would destroy them.

"You're wrong about them." I stand up and head for my room.

He grabs my wrist before I can slip through the curtains. His touch is gentle, but insistent, forcing me to turn around and look at him. "I am not working for King Arkran, Kyla!" he breathes. "You have to believe me on that. I hunt shadows for him – that is all! I have never, once, thought about accepting his offer."

Deep down, I believe him. Why? Because I want him to be the person I'd begun to unravel. I want him to be the hero hiding beneath a monster's mask. It's a blind, biased belief, but it's the one thing I can hold onto.

"I hate Smoke," I whisper, pulling my hand free. "It is dirty."

"When we return to Agron, things will be different," he whispers back as I step into my room and close the curtains behind me.

That is what frightens me.

I shut the door securely behind me once I've entered the washroom. The clean tiled tub is full of steaming water – compliments of a dutiful maid. I stare at the wisps of heat rising above its glossy surface and try to concentrate. On the polished exterior of the water. On the marble gleam of the tiles. On the droplets of concentration sliding down the sleek, stone walls.

But I cannot re-enter my vision.

I slam my hands onto the side of the tub.

Landor's is in danger. I can feel it!

"*We caught the giant!*"

Lan has done something!

"*The way to end the rebellion.*"

"Let me in!" But the black hole inside my mind remains a black hole – it does not pull me into its depths. I try to force myself into the black hole. My skull resounds with a noise like crackling fire and splitting pain quivers down the sides of my head and out of my ears. I scream against the pain and tighten my hands on the corner of the tub – hands pulsing with fiery heat.

The water leaps from the confines of its rectangular prison and swirls into the air, a perfect ball of shimmering liquid. The iron torches in all corners of the room shake and cracks splinter down their ornate handles.

The black hole tightens, suffocating me, and then I am thrown from its interior. My skull explodes. My hands explode. The room explodes.

I am sequestered in darkness.

When I leave the room, the iron torches are shattered beyond recognition, and the bathwater is dripping from every corner of the room.

Chapter XXIX

Hours later, Shade taps gently on the door, and gestures at Axle's room when I raise questioning eyes at him. It is late. I am tired. But amends must be made.

Axle's room has no windows, but the fireplace is larger and an iron chandelier hangs from his ceiling, which is twice as high as mine. There is a big, furry rug in front of the fire. It is where Shade and I find him sitting, propped up with a book in one hand and a glass of wine in the other. The only thing he's missing, I internally realize, are Master Rolfe's spectacles. He would be a scholar in Kelba. A scholar with a killer sarcasm and killer skills.

"I thought, for a moment, you had decided to completely disregard Shade and I for good. I see now that your good sense has flown," he mutters as Shade and I sit down on the rug in front of him, forming a triangle of unspoken peace.

"I apologize for my behavior earlier."

"No big deal," Axle waves off my apology and shuts his book. The familiar sound of rustling paper makes my chest ache. "King Arkran brings out the worst shit in people. It's part of his stunning personality."

Such words, said with such careless abandon, would be severely punished in Kelba. And from Lucius and Dirk's obvious displeasure, they weren't even allowed to be said here.

"How can you make fun of him so lightly? He is the king."

"He's not my king. I didn't pick him. I didn't even know he

existed until we came back from the gates of hell itself," Axle says, bitterness in his tone. "If I'd had my choice, we wouldn't have a king at all. I like the idea of tribes so much better. Agron would be its own dominion. Gavrone would be its own dominion. Smoke would be its own dominion. On occasion, we would band together to fight a growing evil – namely, the shadows. But that is all. We would go about our business and rule ourselves how we saw fit. Otis would make a good ruler, yes?"

"Axle . . ." Shade starts to say.

"I know, I know. It's impossible. Nothing like that would ever happen. But, hell, if I can't wish and dream like any common fool, right?" He finishes the wine in his glass before throwing the polished object into the fire.

"What I meant was how are you allowed to make fun of him so lightly? Shouldn't you be punished?"

Shade stretches out onto his back and puts his arms behind his head in a relaxed position. "That, I believe, you already know the answer to, Kyla Bone. All your experience in the noble scepter of life should give you a decent-sized guess, at least."

"Or perhaps she believes he keeps us around for our stunning good looks and dazzling charm?" Axle suggests.

I glare at him.

"He endures us," Axle admits, "for now. Because, without us, the shadows would overthrow Agron. Then where would the monsters turn? Smoke."

"We're his bodyguards at the border? Without us, he's a dead man," Shade says, "and he knows it. We've been his eyes, ears, swords, assassins, and advisers since the beginning of his reign – just not the kind he wants. We do as we please, when we please, and he doesn't have a say in any damn part of it. We are our own leaders – or at least – we were once." He looks pointedly at Axle.

Axle shrugs. "Being a guardian of Agron means I owe my life to the city and its people. I will die protecting them, at all costs. My allegiances did not change, Shade, just because I actually chose to have allegiance to someone other than myself."

"They won't appreciate it," Shade muses.

"I don't expect them to."

"Selfless prick."

"Introverted asshole."

"Do you two need privacy?" I interrupt. "Because if this is going to turn into petty name-calling, I have other things to do."

Axle chuckles. "What? Comb your hair? Face it, Kyla, we're your only source of entertainment in this bleak land."

"Gods help me," I grumble.

Shade sighs, exasperated. "Axle, why did you want us here? I've had a shitty day, a shitty argument I could have done without, and I need to get some sleep."

"I heard from a servant who heard from a maid who heard from a guard that tomorrow, in your grand hometown of Smoke, they are hosting a market fair. There will be games. Food. Acts of daring. We should go." He shakes with excitement. "We could explore Smoke."

"It's a shit-hole," Shade grumbles without much enthusiasm. "Not much to see."

"Let us be the judges of that," Axle says. "You don't have to come. Kyla and I can keep each other company quite well without you, pal. What do you say, Kyla? Want to explore Smoke? Maybe have a little fun before we're stuck on a shitty return journey with a bunch of annoying pricks?"

"Hell, yeah."

"It's settled," Axle slaps his knee. "We leave, bright and early in the morning, before Keegan or one of his cronies catches wind of our plans."

"Fine. I'll go with you," Shade sighs.

"You won't be dull and ruin our fun, or I'll dump your ass in the moat," Axle warns.

"I won't," Shade promises. His voice sounds disinterested and his eyes are closed so I can't see his true thoughts. Maybe that's why he's keeping them shut.

Axle winks at me.

I ignore him.

We don't return to our proper rooms. Instead, we play some sort of game with some cards that Axle pulls from his pocket. It's a game of trickery. Two cards of the same color and shape placed on top of one another forces the person who placed the second card to answer any question the other players ask them.

Shade and Axle taunt each other back and forth about stories from their slavery days. Even within hell's gates they had memories that weren't completely painful. Apparently, Axle pissed in a cup for their jailer once, and Shade drank it instead, unaware of its contents. Also, Shade installed a trap designed to catch small prison animals and caught Axle's foot instead. Axle shows me the two-inch scar on the sole of his foot as proof.

I end up confessing about a three year crush on a neighboring lord's son ten years my senior and admitting that my first kiss was a stable lad who I swore to silence when he caught me sneaking out of the mansion to meet Landor at the tavern.

I don't know when we doze off. I think Shade went first. Then me.

All I know is when I wake up the next morning, Shade and I are curled together, his arm around my waist, mine on his arm, and his chin on my shoulder.

Axle chuckles softly from where he lays, an arm propping up his chin, and stares at me. "Warm enough?" he asks.

I disentangle myself from Shade's hold and squirm a proper distance away. Gods, how can he still be asleep?

"Trust me, he isn't," Axle answers my thoughts out loud. "Are you, pal?"

His answer is a sleepy murmur.

Axle winks at me. "He isn't." He pats the space beside him. "You're welcome to curl up here, though. I promise, you'll be more comfortable."

I swear, Shade's eyelids flutter.

"No thanks," I mutter and stand up groggily, "you're much too skinny for me."

Axle laughs.

Shade picks the perfect time to roll his back to us, a shiver running down his shoulders.

He doesn't fool me.

Strolling into Smoke, a warrior on each side of me and my leg bare of weapons, gives me a naked feeling of being at the mercy of the wild-folk who imprison me on all sides. The stench of hundreds of bodies packed close together is enough to drive my senses into a frenzy.

Merchants hawk their wares from canopied carts, and performers line the streets, each clamoring for the attention of interested passerby. One girl bends herself in half and does a flip, landing perfectly in spider formation. A young man forces a silver blade, reminiscent of an Illathonian sword, down his throat and draws it back out a minute later.

"Idiot," Shade mutters underneath his breath.

Axle follows a savory smell to a cart full of smoking meat. A girl with red curls and eyes circled in charcoal dip, offers him a taste. His eyes roll into his head as he chews on it. He begins flirting with her.

"He's desperate to get laid before we return to Agron. Here, in Smoke, he's famous," Shade mutters.

"Aren't you?" I ask, brow raised in question.

"Yes, but I am not the 'laying type.'"

"What makes you say that?"

His brow rises too. "What do you mean by that?"

"I just find it unbelievable that no girls approach you . . . at all?"

"I'm too rough."

"And you think girls don't like roughness?" The minute the words leave my mouth I want to drag them back.

"Do you?" He leans close – so close his breath teases my ear.

"I- I don't know."

He leans closer, until his lips are touching my earlobe – barely. "Or do you like it slow . . . gentle?" His fingers brush my elbow. "Hasn't anyone ever been soft with you? Touched you like you were something that could break and shatter?"

"Hasn't anyone told you there are things you're not supposed to touch?" I shield. I slip my arm from his grasp, ignoring the growing ache in my lower regions at the loss of his touch.

"All the time," he whispers, drawing close again. This time his hand rests on my shoulder, fingers tracing the scar beneath the strap of my tunic. "But no one ever *let* me touch . . . until now."

I slip back, heat rising in me at the look in his eyes. The tilt of his lips. The warmth of his hand. And the rising realization that I want to push him into an alley and ask him to show me just how gentle and slow he can be.

"I . . . I'm hungry." I glance towards the cart. Not surprisingly, a different girl, this one with a hood covering her hair, has taken the red-head's place. Axle and the girl are nowhere to be seen.

Shade notices my gaze and nods. "I'll get you some." He walks towards the girl. She smiles at him. He ignores her and focuses on the meat.

I slip away.

The constant bustle of people around me – the stench, the heat, the noises – makes my stomach constrict. At the nearest empty street, I escape. The buildings and the air changes. Clouds of smoke dull my vision. Stone houses carved out the rocky valley wink at me through the natural curtain.

I take a sharp left off the paved street. Domed formations that look like temples rise up on each side of the abandoned road I've discovered. They are not in good repair and appear to be completely abandoned. The thick vines and weeds that grow from the cracks within their stone walls give it a weak appearance, but when I put my hand to the stones, they are hard and brittle. Curious, I search for an entrance into the nearest one, finally finding a great iron door burrowed into the side of the massive stone structure.

Five pulls at its rusty handle and the door creaks open wide enough for me to slip inside. The interior is nothing but a long stairwell leading down into damp darkness. Warning bells sound in my head, but curiosity gets the better of me.

I have to see what's down there.

Bunching my hands into the fabric of my tunic I take one step – then another. There is no light, but my eyes have adjusted perfectly to the black abyss. I can see the walls and steps in faint highlights of gray.

The air, which smelled of stone and damp earth, begins to change – the remains of something dark and horrible curling into an overwhelming stench. Holy incense faintly scents the air, mixed with a familiar smell I hoped never to breathe again; blood, death, and rotting flesh. The stairwell ends.

A corner is ahead of me. I don't want to push beyond it. I shouldn't. This place – this dome – is evil. However, my body keeps moving.

I turn the corner.

The dome is indeed a temple. A rusted altar sits atop a small, three foot podium, complete with candles, incense burners, and torn scrolls surrounding its base.

But it is not the altar that makes my insides swirl. Around the rusted furnishings of holiness lie the twisted, ugly remains of people, all with their arms and legs at odd angles, necks craned violently, and skin falling off their bones. Rats scurry away at my presence, disappearing into their homes within the walls. Weapons lie, unused, against the walls. Moon Lamps, long diminished of their power, fill a corner. A bone cracks beneath my sandal and, when I look downwards, it's a child's arm. Air seizes in my lungs. I gasp.

I need to breathe! But the only stench I inhale is that of decomposing flesh.

My stomach constricts. I put a hand over my mouth. I mustn't retch in such a holy place, but I am frozen, limbs unyielding.

The grove in Brunt had been similar – but shadows had done that. This – this was something different. Something more sinister. Brutal. Evil. An evil that bit close to home. The iron door – there had been no handle on the inside.

Panic hits me low in the gut.

I'd shut the door behind me.

"You shouldn't be down here."

Shade's presence doesn't startle me. Not anymore. I hurry to his side and grip his arm. He doesn't flinch beneath my touch. He doesn't gape or wrinkle his nose at the sight around me. A sickening part of me knows why.

"Take me out," I plead. "Please."

Shade doesn't say a word and leads me back the way I came. He propped the door open with a foot-long brick. When the iron door closes over the centuries-old grave, I fall to my knees and clutch at the dirt, sucking in mouthfuls of cool, delicious air. I can't see anything but the odious, ghastly appearance beneath the ground I kneel upon.

"You shouldn't have gone down there. They close them for a reason. Did you not know of . . .?" Shade cuts himself off, realizing how little I know of Wilds history.

"I thought it was a temple." Tears sting my eyes. "W-what happened? Why were they – that way?"

"Are you sure you really want to know?" asks Shade.

I nod.

"It happened forty years ago when the temples of Calaisar still thrived. The remaining survivors of the Poison Wall were determined to return the old ways and restore the old religions and myths of their former land. So these domes were built, boring deep into the ground for safety and 'humbleness' to the gods. It was the night of the Half-Moon. A time when all believers in Calaisar would enter the temples and worship." His face darkens and his mouth twists up in a cruel smirk. "Do you know what *my* people did?"

My fists clench up. *No. Please no.*

"'*Loyal'* Wilds inhabitants said that the ways of the past were over and done with. That if we focused on the past we would be subject to ruin. The religious fanatics of the old ways were too much of a danger. Too much of a liability for progress. We needed a future – not the demise of the past." His lips tremble, and I notice his struggle to maintain a nonchalant expression. "So, on the night of the Half-Moon, when all worshipers had to gather in the temples for their holy rites, the inhabitants, lead by three *grand* leaders, surrounded the domes and barred the iron doors."

"No." I shake my head. "You're lying."

He glares at me. "Would I lie about something so sinister? They barred the doors! They cut off what remained of our past with Kelba. They started anew. And do you know who one of the leaders was?"

I know it, but I let him say it.

"It was King Arkran's father, Brock of Smoke, and Lucius's father, Lucien of Smoke. They go down in our history books as the leaders of the reformation. The restorers of a nation. But no one writes about how they reformed this shit-hole. How they made the damned kingdom. History books decline to inform us how the Wilds was built on lies, deceit, greed, and the lives of fellow countrymen." He turns, a deep fire in his eyes. "I hate such people. I hate such dishonesty. I hate the very idea that we –" He gulps in air, a vein throbbing at his neck. "That we need to sacrifice our own citizens for a nobler cause. Damn them, it was no noble cause. It was murder. It was – abominable!"

I stand, suddenly angry. "And you hate my kind? What are you – to do that to your own people? What kind of animals have you become?"

"Don't be so quick to judge, Kyla," Shade sneers, pointing an accusing finger at me. "You – your kind – are no different. Do you know how many were assassinated so Celectate Wood could maintain his position in Kelba? Do you know all those who are bribed, threatened, and tortured so Kelba can be under his thumb? Do you know how many nobles – such as yourself and your father – shiver beneath such a man because they're afraid of angering him? Afraid of ending up – like that?" He points at the dome. "You would rather live your life in fear than face it head on."

"Is that why you think I was ostracized? Because I cowered? What about you, Shade?"

"I beg your pardon?"

"Are you a coward? Do you face your fear head on?"

"If I were to face my fear head on, the entire world would suffer the repercussions," he whispers. "I would destroy every last shadow, I would raid their land, I would slaughter the monsters, I would punish all the greedy bastards sitting around King Arkran, and I would make this land – these Wilds – a true nation. A nation built on honesty, on morals, and peace."

Even as he says it I see the sparks fade in his eyes. He lingers on the word "peace" like a lover. I want to caress the word, too, and I draw closer to him. When our eyes meet, the lies inside of us become open – because we both know the truth. And the truth is always honest – as blunt as a spinal blow, as sharp as a sword, as hard as iron. The truth – no nation has ever been built on honesty, morals, or peace. Every nation in its birth had underhanded means of achieving its individuality. We both know it.

All the anger fades from Shade's eyes. "Well . . . we can have our dreams, can't we?"

I echo his bitter laugh, a single tear skating down my cheek against my will. I want a nation like that. I want to see such a dream come true.

I catch my breath when Shade's thumb gently wipes the drop from my chin and palms my jawline. He leans close, looking me in the eye, and our noses brush.

"I want a world like that," he whispers. "Where justice is served."

"I want a world like that," I whisper back, "where peace abounds."

Shade smiles and leans closer . . .

"There you are!" Shade and I tear ourselves apart, a flurry of arms and legs.

Axle stalks over from the corner of the street. "I've been looking everywhere for you two. I thought Dirk had initiated plan B and somehow managed to defeat the great 'shadow warrior' and his 'avraga.'" He slaps Shade playfully on the shoulder.

I sigh with relief. He hadn't seen anything.

"What do you want?" Shade asks, sullen once more.

"Time to return to the palace. It's nearly dusk. Didn't you

notice?" Axle asks, ignoring his friend's aloofness. He leans close and elbows him in the side playfully. "Or were you too preoccupied?"

On second thought, maybe he had seen something.

Shade growls and stalks down the street, leaving me to keep Axle company. We follow his fast gait as best as we can, but eventually Axle has to slow his pace.

"What was that I heard about dreams?" Axle asks.

"Nothing." I don't want him to know about my escapades in the domes or what Shade and I discussed.

"It sounded like more than 'nothing', wouldn't you say?"

"Are you doubting me?"

"Hey, don't get uppity. I'm just wondering why two people who are supposed to *'hate'* each other to their very cores were standing together looking *real* friendly." Axle's eyes glint with suppressed mirth. He leans close, until his nose brushes my ear. "Or could it be that I was right? Could it be that Shade doesn't hate you?"

I dodge the question. "Where did you disappear too?"

"Wouldn't you like to know?"

"Was she good?"

He coughs, suddenly, and finds interest in the stone wall that keeps his head turned away from me. "What do you think?"

"Well," I reach out and pluck a strand of yellow straw from his hair, "considering your dishevelment, I would say she either fancies wrestling or something akin to the sport."

He releases a low chuckle. "You're not far off target, Kyla. Let's just say, between you and I, I came out on top." He winks and laughs at his foul joke.

"That's disgusting," I groan.

"Really?" He cocks his head to the side. "You prefer the top?"

"Another word and you won't *wrestle* again!" I touch the side of my leg and find it empty. I drop my hand casually at my side, once more, trying to hide the pain that stabs my rib-cage.

"I'll have Otis officially gift you a new one," Axle promises. He pats my shoulder. "Upon my word of honor."

"When did you have that?" I grin up at him wryly.

He scratches the top of his head, releasing another yellow straw from his hair, and frowns at it. "Good point."

"Hey, you wanna hurry up, maybe?" Shade calls from the street corner, his black hair peeking around the stone building.

"Keep it in your pants! We're coming!" Axle shouts back. He elbows me in the arm. "But seriously, *did* he keep it in the entire time he was with you?"

I glare at him.

He grins. "I'm lucky you don't have that dagger, aren't I?"

"*Hell, yeah,*" I snarl and punch him in the ribs.

We meet in Axle's room for the second night in a row. He's prepared this time. There are three bottles of wine instead of one. We don't play games though. Instead, we try to figure what will happen when we return to Agron in two days.

"Dirk will be pissed. That's for sure," Axle affirms. "And some of the villagers will back him. But they won't say it openly. You'll have to watch your back, Kyla."

"Like I've always done?"

Axle nods. "Keep doing it. You've got more at stake now than you did as an outsider. Now you're a citizen of our realm . . . and that paints a big red target on your back."

"Am I cursed to forever be looking over my shoulder?"

Axle shrugs. "Perhaps."

"After a while, you'll get used to it," Shade mutters from his place by the fire.

"I don't want to live in constant fear," I whisper. "I want to have . . ."

"What?" Shade interrupts. "Peace? It's been centuries since that word existed. Not even the gods could bring this land peace – even if they did exist."

"You don't believe in the gods?"

"Do you?" His dark eyes flicker over my face. I look away. "I didn't think so. If you did, you'd have stayed away from the domes today."

"You went inside?" Axle's eyes widen. "Kyla, that's . . ."

"She didn't know what they were," Shade cuts in. "Don't reprimand her. Honestly, she needed to see it. She needed to know that *her kind* aren't the only doomed species."

"Shh," Axle hisses and looks around. "Walls have ears."

"And if they did, I could still find a way to cut them off, so calm yourself," Shade says. He rubs the flat of his knife along the round of his knee. He tests the edge with his thumb. "'The three saviors of Wilds' are nothing more than lies, built on lies, built on blood, built on more lies."

"'Three saviors?'"

Shade notices my confusion. "Brock of Smoke. Lucien of Smoke. Fair of Smoke. The three saviors of the Wilds. The heroes of the configuration. The leaders of this land. They lead those of the New Age against those who wanted to restore the Wilds to its former glory. They won – but they lost." He points at one of the leather-bound books next to Axle. "All the stories of our lands are written in those – sequestered away in the king's private library."

"The king has a library?" A kindling flame of warmth circles in my stomach. "With books?"

"No. A library with animals. Of course, with books," Axle chides. He props the manuscript in his lap. "Lots of them. Ancient as ancient gets, but most of them are still legible."

"Take me there!"

Axle draws back at my eagerness and shakes his head. "You can't, Kyla. I have to sneak in and sneak out with these. However, even if I am caught, they won't punish me. I'm a shadow-killer. You're a Kelban, and if you're caught in there . . . the punishment is cruel, I assure you. Just take this, and I'll get you another when I can."

In two days we are leaving. He cannot get a book fast enough for me to read. I will have to take one. I know better than to tell that to Axle, though.

"You don't understand. I have to see it. It's been so long . . . so long since I saw a place like that. Please, Axle. Please . . ." I reach out to touch his arm. He draws back. No amount of convincing will break his decision.

"I'm sorry, Kyla. I can't. It's too risky."

I shrug. "Fine. No problem."

After a few uncomfortable minutes of awkward silence, Axle launches into a topic about red-heads and how much "ginger" they possess. I feign amusement and try to act like I've forgotten about the library.

Shade stares at me from his place by the fire, never flinching, never saying anything, but he doesn't have to. He knows me better than Axle. He knows I am stubborn.

He knows I will go to the library.

And, in the middle of the night, when Axle has fallen asleep and is snoring on the rug, he tells me exactly how to find it.

Chapter XXX

King Arkan's private library is hidden behind two private lounges and four guarded doors. The guards, however, all switch at the same time, leaving five minutes for me to get into the library, which I do without any trouble. I hear the guards come back and resume their places. I have two hours before they rotate again and, if I am quiet, I will learn a good deal within that time.

King Arkran's library is, by no means, as fancy as Celectate Wood's. The shelves are carved out of the stone mountain itself and give the entire room a crude appearance, despite the fifty foot ceiling and colossal, glass window that provides a perfect view of Smoke. To make matters worse, most of the books are in ill-repair. Pages are torn. Spines disintegrating. Covers mutilated or missing. I wrinkle my nose in disgust at the smell of mold and decay.

Treasures like these should be valued and cared for like fine jewels, and King Arkran has let them shrivel into ruin.

I begin my search. Some of the newest additions include one of Goldbrow's tall tales forged about the Wilds and its inhabitants. Others resemble certain manuscripts I'd seen and read in Celectate Wood's own collections. In a far corner of the room, wooden shelves have recently been added to the room's furnishings. Scrolls, neatly rolled and tied with bits of garnished string, fill the space they provide.

I rifle through them. Most of them are letters of old between ancient diplomats, long before the destruction of Kelba. They speak of creating havoc or ruining a lord's reputation to take his place. Of back-biting and malice. At least, times were not too different before the poisons came.

But one of the letters is different. It smells of perfume – a scent unfamiliar to me. The words are written in thin, black ink and scrawled out across the page. The author wrote it in frenzy. It's a poem.

I was alone and judged among the living,
Unwanted and unclaimed among the dead.
Where in this life could I find my place?
Go to hell," my persecutors said.

What place is there for me,
In this world I've come to know
Cares nothing for the living
But for the grief and strife they sow.

I was foolish, and my eyes were blind
To the truths they hid from me.
They cursed and tore me down,
And, like a fool, I did not see.

And then my eyes were open
Lo and behold, I saw
The answers to the questions
That bled my heart raw.

The time is coming.
The hour is near.
The doors of hell will open,
Their worst fears will appear.

The grief and strife they've sown,
Will be restored tenfold.

The lies and tales they've spread
Will become whispers of old.

Hear my warning
Hold it close.

Bordas equistia selentia vermana

The poem is untitled and the author unknown.

I recognize the last few words. They'd been carved into the mountainside in Shade's secret lair. Ancient tongue. Foreign tongue.

Undefinable.

Shivers skate along my spine. I don't know why . . . but the words fill me with dread. Like the person who wrote the poem knew about something evil, but was afraid to say what it was.

The doors of hell will open . . . Their worst fears will appear.

Whose fears?

The click of the door handle behind me startles me so badly I drop the parchment onto the ground. I hear one of the guards chuckle as he greets the newcomer. I duck behind one of the shelves and press myself against the wood. I can see the door through the slits created by the scrolls. It opens halfway, revealing a tanned hand, followed by an equally tan, young man with a clean-cut jaw and light blue eyes.

Prince Ivan.

He shuts the door solidly behind him and steps towards the ornately carved table resting in front of the colossal window. I hadn't noticed the modest carafe resting on its surface, nor the small iron cups. He pours wine into two of them.

"Are you going to come out? Hide and seek is a rather dull game to play by yourself."

I hold my breath. Maybe he's talking to someone else.

He turns and stares directly at my hiding place and holds out one of the iron cups. "Well, m'lady?"

I reveal myself and take the glass he offers me. "Your highness." I incline my head.

"Please, Kyla, we're both nobility. No need to be so formal." He gulps down some of his wine, eyes staring at me over the rim of his cup. They don't leave me. "So . . ." He wipes the corner of his mouth with his thumb. "Are you going to tell me why you're so interested in my father's private library? Actually, hold on a second . . . ignore that last question. I'm more interested in how you got in."

I shrug nonchalantly. "Luck, I guess."

"Or one of your savage friends?" He regards me with a furrowed brow.

I open my mouth, and he holds up a finger. "No need to explain. I'd much rather ignore the fact that those bastards can come and go without punishment anywhere they choose merely because my father thinks they're our saviors."

I remember the look he and Axle had shared in the courtroom. "Not friends, I take it?"

He snorts at the word. "Maybe once . . . before Axle became a sarcastic asshole with no manners and no regard for nobility. Shade . . ." He shrugs off the name. "We've barely shared two words in the past five years."

He eyes me curiously, luridly raking me from head-to-toe. "I really am curious."

"What?" I cross my arms over my chest.

"Which of them is fucking you?"

Raging heat blossoms in my neck. "I should slap you for that!"

He shrugs. "Can you blame me? They never leave your side. Perhaps . . . are they both . . ."

"Finish that sentence," I growl, stepping towards him, a fist at my side. I don't have to touch him to silence him. I could wrap the invisible line of my power around his neck and strangle any following ridicule from his mind. But, of course, he doesn't know that. "I dare you."

I wish he would. I want to choke the noble arrogance from his perfect face.

He shakes his head. "I'm no fool." He bows. "My apologies. A test, m'lady, to see if you're really the spineless bitch everyone is saying you are. It seems the rumors are true."

"What rumors?"

He sits on the edge of the table and slaps a hand on his knee. "Where do I begin? You killed a razor on your own. You saved the life of an Agronite from a shadow. You discovered one of the 'cursed' in Gavrone, saving hundreds of lives." He grins at me, revealing a mouthful of straight, white teeth. Is everything about him perfect? "In short, you've become a very interesting case for me, Kyla Bone."

I ignore his attempt at charm. "So you've decided you want to try and seduce me?"

His smile widens. "Who said that?"

An amused laugh echoes from my mouth. "I lived around noble brats like yourself for nearly eighteen years. I know when boys like you want me in their bed."

"Give me a proper chance, m'lady, and I will show you I'm no longer a boy." He steps towards me.

I step away from him. "I'll have to decline your offer."

"You should learn, Kyla Bone," he whispers in a low voice as he approaches me, "that when a nobleman offers something, you take it."

Bastard.

He grabs my arm, and my knuckles clip him underneath his jaw. He stumbles back and falls against the table. Blood drips down his chin from his lip where he bit himself. He presses a finger to it and stares at the red droplets staining his hand.

"And you should learn, Prince Ivan, that when a lady says 'no', she means 'no.'"

Rage dances in his eyes. "I can have you flogged for being in here!" he snaps. "Killed, even."

I smile and approach, leaning close to his ear so I can whisper, "And the same fate awaits you if I tell a certain someone what transpired between us in this room." I draw back, giving him room to stand straight.

He chuckles. "So you *are* fucking them?"

I shake my head. "No one fucks with me. Least of all, little pricks like you."

"No one, eh? Rumor has it that your Shade's new pastime. Let me give you a word of advice . . . after you've satisfied his hunger, you'll be nothing but a piece in his endless collection." He tweaks my chin. "River. Now you. A shame."

River?

"What do you mean?"

"Two years ago, when the three of them showed up in this very palace, desolate and without a penny to their names, who do you think kept Shade's bed warm? Why wouldn't he fall prey to my sister's infatuating charms? Because he already had a whore . . . he was fucking his best friend's sister right beneath his nose. And when I called him out on it . . . when I told Axle about his friend's deception . . . do you know what they did? They beat me bloody. Stripped me naked. Threw me in a pit. And they left." He sneers. "Ask them and they'll deny it. They'll tell some shit tale about how I made it all up. But it's true. Just wait. Once they've both gotten you naked and laid you a few times, watch how they change."

I feel like he's punched me in the gut. River always did admit that Shade was attractive. She certainly showed that she cared for him. And Shade was always nice to her. Protective. Kind. Was it because she was his best friend's sister . . . or because she'd been more?

Ivan watches me intently. "It makes sense, doesn't it?"

"Shut up," I growl, trying to think. To sort through everything I can remember transpiring between River and Shade. Nothing comes to mind. All I can remember are a few moments of friendly kindness and understanding.

And the way he'd touched me – the way he'd kissed me – the way he looked at me – he never looked at River like that. He never looked at River at all, come to think of it.

I glare at the prince. "You're lying."

"Am I?"

"You don't know Shade like I do," I whisper. "He would never do that to Axle . . . for a number of reasons."

"They're both messed up bastards. You've no idea what they would do," he argues.

The palms of my hand burn with the urge to throw him halfway across the room. To smash his head against the wall. To make him trip and hit his head on the table. I curl my fingers into a fist. "We're done here. Thank you, your highness, for tolerating my presence. I'll take my leave now."

He grabs my arm as I step past him. "I'll say when you're leaving!"

"The hell you will," I snap and slam a palm to his chest. He surges backwards like a gust of wind in a sail and falls on his ass. I relish the crack of bone upon wood. He shrieks.

The door slams open. A guard in an iron helmet peers inside, "Your highness . . ." He gapes at me.

I glare down at the prince. "Tell him to leave," I snarl in a low voice. "Tell him to leave or when I leave this room, I'll go straight to your father and tell him of your behavior."

He sneers. "Go ahead. I'm his son."

"And I'm his connection to Kelba," I retort. His face falls. "Tell the guard to leave."

He gestures for the guard to return to his position. The door closes once more.

"What do I need to do to make you be quiet?" he asks.

I allow myself a triumphant smile. "Which of your books contains the history of the Wilds? I'll be relieving you of it."

I meet Axle halfway to my rooms. He's leaning against the wall, waiting for me. He sees the book in my hands. A feral growl emanates from his throat.

"Damn it, Kyla! I told you not to go there."

"You forgot to mention that the prince likes to enjoy solitude among manuscripts as much as I."

His shoulders stiffen. "What did he do?"

"Oh, he was positively charming," I say in a voice much too high-pitched. I wave my hand theatrically at the book. "He let me keep this – for nothing. Such a gentleman, wouldn't you say, Axle?" I make sure to narrow my eyes at him.

He clears his throat nervously.

"Unless, there's something you're not telling me – again!"

"What would that be?"

I shrug. "Doesn't matter."

We walk in silence for what seems to be ages. Guards stare at us as we pass, no doubt smirking behind the iron helmets.

Did everybody really think I'd taken both boys as my lovers?

"He didn't ask you to do anything for him, did he?" Axle's voice is a bit too low.

"Like what?" I stare at him pointedly as we walk.

His cheeks grow red, but he blunders into an explanation. "Like spread your legs, okay? There! I said it, damn it!"

I continue to stare at him blankly. "Whatever makes you think he'd ask such a thing?"

Axle shakes his head at me, irritation evident in the hard line of his jaw. "Because he's a prick. A noble brat who thinks he has the right to everything because his father's the king and he's charming and handsome and rich. And because he thought he had rights to my sister."

I'd waited patiently for that information to come out. I'd been fairly certain Axle and Shade had a reason for whipping and stripping him. They wouldn't have wasted time on a bastard like him unless he'd done something to warrant the ill treatment.

"Did he . . .?" I can't finish the sentence. The thought of Ivan touching – hurting – River makes my blood boil. I can only imagine what Axle felt when the situation occurred.

"He tried. She refused him. Many times. One day he cornered her in the library. Forced himself on her. Shade and I had been dispatched on patrol. We came back a week later. There was a bruise healing on her cheek and marks on her neck. Her lip was split. She'd fought him and gotten away. The king interfered in the matter and said there was no harm done. Prince Ivan had looked at me smugly. He knew he'd get away with it. But I wanted him to know – to know that he couldn't lay hands on my sister without severe consequences. So Shade and I waited for him after he went into town for easier conquests of the female variety and ambushed him on the way back. We took our time. Broke his arm. A couple of ribs. As a final wound, we stripped him and threw him in a pit near the corner of the city. When daylight came, everyone saw him. Everyone mocked him. It was a fitting justice. The king knew he had to get us out of Smoke before we clashed again. So he sent us to Agron to defend the border. We've been there ever since."

"I'm sorry. At least she was okay. It doesn't seem to have affected her."

"Why should it? A handsome man found her attractive and went a little too far. That's what it is to her. Only Shade and I know the truth. That he's a lust-crazed fanatic who would bed anything that possessed curves." He swipes a hand through his mangy hair before looking at me. "So, Kyla, I'll ask you for the last time . . . did he do anything to you?"

"No. He didn't. Honestly, Axle, I find your lack of faith in my abilities quite offensive."

His eyes narrow.

"No. He didn't," I repeat with finality.

"If you say so."

Silence again. Until we reach his room. He invites me in and pours us both a glass of wine from the decorated pitcher.

"Let's drink to tomorrow, where we will leave this shitty place forever." He downs the beverage.

I do the same.

"Now," Axle says, "let me see that book that you went through so much trouble to get."

Chapter XXXI

One moment I am breathing clean air through my nostrils, and the next, the frighteningly close stench of leather is assailing my senses. Something hard closes over my mouth. The smell envelopes me. My eyes fly open, adjusting immediately to the dark. To the faint light provided by the fireplace. And to the dark figure kneeling over my sleeping form, a dagger in one hand and the other over my mouth.

I wriggle beneath my captor, struggling to pull my arms from beneath the blanket where the person has pinned them, to no avail. If I had them free, the pulse would quickly throw the heavy person away.

"Don't," my captor whispers in a voice that sounds strangely familiar. "I'm not going to hurt you, unless you scream. Understand?"

For some insane reason, I believe her.

My captor pulls back slowly. I rip my hands from beneath the covers, and she angles her dagger at me. She is covered in black clothing from head to foot. I can only see her eyes – crystal sparkles beneath all the dark layers.

"Who are you?" I ask, ignoring the urge to thrust her in the direction of the flames.

She pulls the hood and mask from her face, allowing me a clear view of her smooth skin, marred only by a single scar on her forehead.

Celeste.

"What are you . . .?"

"Keep silent, you fool!" she hisses. The sweet demure look she'd worn is gone. Instead, there's a harsh, yet commanding, twist in her face. "I've only come to warn you."

"Warn me of what?"

"Those scars on your neck . . . I know what they are! I know what *you* are!" she says.

My veins turn to ice, but my palm remains hot and ready. I can silence her quicker than she thinks.

"I am too."

The pulse in my hand fades. "You're what?"

"I can hear them," she whispers. "I can understand them. I am a 'witch' as King Arkran and his kind call us."

I stare at her, blankly, trying to contemplate everything she is telling me.

"You must not tell anyone what you can hear. They will use you for it. Until you're of no more use. Or, they will kill you because they're frightened. Frightened because they can't contemplate how we can hear demons unless we had ties to their darkness. But I don't think you'll tell anyone. You know what they'll do already. What I really came to warn you about was telling *them*." Her voice shifts ominously.

"Them?"

"The shadows, as everybody calls them. Don't let them know what you can do when they find you. And they *will* find you, eventually. I don't know how they do, but you can't hide forever. If they do, don't ever let them know you understand them! Worse things will await you if you do!" Her eyes are wide.

"How do you know this?" I slip out of bed anxiously and face her, despite the icy cold of the floor seeping into my feet. "Tell me!"

"I had a brother," she snaps. "They came for him!"

My mouth dries up. I can't say anything.

"You know all about that, though, don't you?" she asks maliciously. "He was in Gavrone."

I stumble backwards, the weight of her words disrupting my balance.

She follows me, step for step, eyes never leaving my face. The dagger in her hand shakes unsteadily. "I sent him there because I thought he'd be safe. I thought my mother would be able to hide his unique gift, but she couldn't hide it from those that live in shadow!" she snarls. "They came, but they didn't take him. I heard they slaughtered my mother. But *they* didn't kill him. The people did. Forced him off a cliff. My brother died, not because of something he'd done wrong. But because he had something no one could understand! Because people are cowards and fools."

Holy gods!

"No one knows. I had to mourn him in silence, knowing that his body is ripped apart at the bottom of a cliff, without anyone to bury the pieces or say prayers over him." She falls on her knees, the strength fading from her eyes. The dagger falls from her hands. Tears pour silently down her cheeks as her mouth trembles. I know the feeling. I know she wants to scream.

I walk to her and let my palm rest on her shoulder. "No, he isn't."

She looks up, confused.

"I found him," I whisper, "and buried him for you."

She doesn't say anything for a long time. When she does, its etched in disbelief. "But – he fell off a cliff!"

I shrug. "He could have fallen out of the heavens themselves – I would have still gone down to bury him. He deserved that much. He didn't deserve what happened. He didn't deserve death. And he sure as hell didn't deserve to lie, cold and alone, by the sea."

Celeste's arms are around me, tight and trembling. "Thank you," she whispers, the floodgates of her sorrow finally opening. Her tears wet my neck. "Thank you, Kyla."

I hold her until she finally pulls away, wiping any signs of mourning from her face. "Stay safe, okay? I don't want to hear about how you fell off a cliff too."

"You wouldn't. There are no cliffs in Agron."

She smiles and starts to move away.

"How did you know they would come for you?" I ask her. "For your brother?"

She sighs and looks at the fire. "My brother, my mother, and I used to all live together . . . in a small house in the middle of the woods. There wasn't a village around for miles. One night I walked out into the woods to get some more wood. I was coming back. I heard voices. People normally didn't travel into our corner of the forest and the voices weren't . . . natural. But of course, you know all about that?"

I nod.

"The voices got closer, but wherever I looked I couldn't see them. They kept saying they'd 'found' us. When they did reveal themselves, I knew what they were. Everyone knows about the shadows. There were only two of them. They came after me. I fled, got my mother and brother, and we ran for our lives."

"You escaped them?"

Celeste levels a cold stare at me, and I bite my lip, chastising myself for my ignorance. "We ran into a hunting party who made short work of the shadows. But when . . . when I told the three men what I'd heard they grew frightened. Superstitious. It didn't help that my brother admitted he'd heard them too. The men talked about turning us over to the authorities in the nearest village." She looks at me, a hardness in her gaze that chills my blood. "Naturally, I couldn't let them do that."

She doesn't say anything else and I don't embarrass myself by asking another foolish question. I know what she must have done.

"I sent my mother and brother to Gavrone. I'd heard about it from a friendly goatherd who happened to stop by our house a couple weeks prior. It seemed like the proper place. And I . . ." She pauses and rubs her arms nervously. "I struck out on my own."

"To Smoke?"

"It seemed like a good idea at the time." She shrugs helplessly and it gives me a glimpse of what she once was – an innocent, naive girl who'd just discovered she was destined to die. "When I got here, there were few options for a single young woman with no penny to her name and no trade. I found work in a tavern. One of Lucius's servants found me there and offered me a job in the palace. I'd be a fool not to take it, yes?" She laughs, but it lacks any sort of gaiety. "I wish I'd stayed a fool."

I open my mouth but no words come out. What words are appropriate for something like that?

"It could be worse," she says casually. "And it's not like I was a virgin before. Lucius could be a complete barbarian."

"You mean he isn't?" I ask.

She levels a critical look in my direction. "You're an innocent in these matters, aren't you?"

I duck my head to hide the flush of my cheeks. "I know enough."

"Sure you do," she quips. She stands up and brushes a hand over my shoulder. "And I pray you never have to know more."

She glances towards the door, eyes alert as if she'd heard something. "I have to go," she mutters, retrieving her dagger and slipping it beneath the folds of her dark outfit. "I don't want to be discovered missing for the third night in a row. Lucius gets insanely jealous if he thinks I'm whoring myself to fellow palace-dwellers." She stalks towards the door.

"Celeste?" I call after her. "What was his name?"

She turns and looks at me. "Averick."

"Thank you."

She opens the door. "Farewell, Kyla Bone."

"Farewell, Celeste."

The door closes.

I hope, to the gods and the holy heavens themselves, that she was wrong and the shadows forget all about me.

I open my eyes, and I'm standing in a familiar hallway past a flight of stairs. My house. In the foyer below our butler walks back and forth at a frightening pace. His face is pale.

Dread fills my lungs.

Ahead of me, a light shines under the doorway of my parents room. I see shadows passing in front of it. Leaning against the door-frame, Landor has his eyes closed and his head tilted back against the wood. There is blood on his hands. On his face. Under his fingernails. His Celect Knight uniform is torn at the shoulder.

"Landor," I say.

Like always, he doesn't hear me. There is an invisible wall between us. A wall that cages sight and sound.

My parents door opens.

Landor jolts to attention.

Mother storms out the door and heads straight towards me. Her hair hangs wild about her face. Her eyes are stormy.

She's been crying.

"Mother!" Landor calls after her. She doesn't answer him. He follows her.

They breeze past me and down the stairs. I follow, floating on the air like a whisper.

"Mother, where are you going?" Landor asks. His voice is laced with concern.

"To get a drink!" she snaps. She throws open the doors of Father's study and walks to his desk. A carafe of his best wine glitters in the sunlight streaming through his large, colored-pane window. She pours herself a glass and downs it in one swallow. She starts to refill it.

"Mother . . ." Landor protests and grabs the carafe from her hands, spilling some of the red liquid on the sleek carpet.

"Really, son? You're a voice of reason now? Now! When your father lies upstairs, beaten to a bloody pulp because of that son of a bitch! Because that puppet of a man was too cowardly to defend your father and take a stand. What other wise words of reason will you give me, son? I guarantee I've heard them all."

"You are Lady Bone and . . ."

"Heard it," she interrupts him.

"Father would want you to be . . ."

"Don't even finish that sentence, Lan!" she snaps.

The corner of his cheek twitches. He's biting it from the inside.

They stand in silence for a moment longer. Finally, Mother breaks eye contact first and sags against the desk. She doesn't cry. She doesn't sigh. She stays silent and stares at the carpet. At the red stains dotting its surface.

"Do you know I regretted it too?" she asks.

Landor looks up.

"I regretted that I let that man take my daughter – my only daughter – and cast her out like she didn't belong. Like she was worthless trash. Just because she knew tyranny when she saw it and stood up against it. Just because she wanted a life that she chose instead of one chosen for her. That's what I want for all of you. I want you to choose a life. I want you to have the opportunity to choose a life. I wanted both of my children to be able to stand up for what they wanted and grab at it with both hands, consequences be damned. But . . ." She shakes her head. A single tear slips down her cheek. "But, in the end, I regretted ever encouraging such behavior. When he branded her – her screams – do you know they tore me apart inside? To hear her scream and watch no one go to her rescue is something I'll have to live with the rest of my life. I regret not encouraging her more. I regret not telling her everything about her strengths. I regret . . . not talking to her more."

"Mother . . ." Landor's voice is deathly quiet. "What did the doctor say?"

Her hands bite into the wooden rim of the desk so tightly that her knuckles turn white. "He'll live . . ." she whispers. "And he'll lose his leg."

Oh, gods!

"Father!" I scream but, of course, there is no answer. I cannot move. Cannot flee this scene before me.

Landor stands quietly for a moment and stares at the red stains in the carpet too. Slowly his eyes flutter closed, and he balls up his fists. He's thinking. No! He's not thinking. He's bracing himself. He's preparing to do something he knows he shouldn't do and . . .

He grasps the carafe and pours himself a glass. He drinks it quickly and slams it back onto the desk. My mother looks up as the glass smacks the wood. Landor starts towards the door.

She grabs his arm. "Where are you going?"

He looks at her, and I shiver at the darkness in his gaze.

"No!" She tightens her hold on his arm. "No, son, I can't let . . ."

He shakes loose. "You told me you wanted me to make a choice and grab onto it with both hands. I am sorry what I have chosen is not what you had in mind but it is necessary. I failed to protect my family once. I won't make the same mistake twice."

"This is not right, Lan. It's too late and . . ."

"Right? Right?" He slaps a hand to the door. "Who the hell gives a damn about what's right?"

"Landor, listen to me, please." She grasps his shoulders and turns him to face her. He avoids looking into her eyes. She notices and frowns. Gently, she palms his chin and turns his face towards hers. "It is not the right time or the right place to do such a thing."

"If it was Kyla you'd have done it!"

I know he didn't mean it, but the effect of his words knocks Mother backwards. Her eyes widen. Regret stains his face the moment the words leave his mouth.

"I . . . I'm sorry . . . I didn't mean . . ."

"If only you knew," Mother whispers, her voice so low – so sad – that it tears at my chest. It is the same voice she used to console me when I was drunk. The same voice she used so many times when I would constantly berate my existence. The same voice that urged me to break the devil's chains and free myself. "If only you knew half the story behind your sister and what happened you'd . . ." She breaks off and shakes her head. "No, you wouldn't understand, would you? No one would. No one could."

"I . . ."

"Do you know you and your father died?"

His brows rise in question.

She leans against the door. "Your father took you . . . when you were five . . . on a journey to the island of Landor. Celectate Wood had a mission for him and you wanted to see the land you were named after. I protested . . . no, I fought against the idea with every bone in my body because I knew the dangers of sailing the Argan Sea. No one listened to the 'pleas' of a woman. Two months after your departure I get word that your ship sank off the coast of Landor."

Landor's stares at her, his expression blank. He doesn't remember.

"I mourned you five months. Five months, son! Five months I had nightmares about sea creatures feeding on the flesh of my husband and son. I envisioned your screams. Your cries for help. And I couldn't help you. Do you know what that does to a mother, son? No, probably not. I

will never forget it." There's a deeper sorrow in her eyes. A part of this story she's not telling. I feel it. "You both lived. A group of scavenging merchants fished you out of the sea. Your father couldn't remember who he was. You wouldn't talk. It took them months to figure out the chaos. When you finally returned, I had nearly given up hope. I had tried to move on." Again, her eyes darken with an undisclosed sadness. "When your sister came seven months later . . . I swore I wouldn't lose her. I promised I wouldn't lose her."

"And she was sent to the Wilds!" Lan snaps.

"That wasn't losing her. That was letting her go." That mysterious smile plays at the corner of her mouth.

"What the hell are you saying?" Lan asks.

"Your sister isn't dead."

"I know that. That's the only thing stopping me from killing that son of a bitch."

"Your father isn't dead either."

He sees her point and that darkness in his eyes fades. He sags against the wall and puts his head in his hands. "His leg, mother. His leg . . ."

"Is not his soul," Mother admonishes. "He'll live."

"He'll wither. Father was not meant to be a cripple."

"Your father was not meant for these times. He was meant for times when the Community was sovereign and beasts like the Celectate were in chains. We all knew those times would pass, but not all of us were prepared for it." She leans close and pats his shoulder. "But we are. And together we can keep your father alive."

"Mother . . ." He lowers his head. "I can't do this if . . ."

"You are your father's son!" she snaps and lifts his chin. "Just as Kyla is her father's daughter. You have your gifts and she has hers. Both of you – look at me, Landor! Both of you are strong. Both of you are meant for these times. Both of you, understand?" She wraps her arms around him, pulling him close.

"If something happens to you because I'm too weak to stop it . . ."

"I am strong enough to take care of myself, thank you very much!" she snarls. "I've faced evils far greater than pompous lords trying to get on Celectate Wood's good side. And if something does happen to me, Landor,

it is not of your doing. Don't blame yourself."

"Kyla was my doing. I should have killed the man, mother, before he harmed her. I had many chances and I . . ." He shakes his head sadly. "I failed her."

"You didn't fail your sister. Kyla is where she belongs," Mother argues.

He looks up. "What do you mean? No one belongs in that savage land!"

A mysterious smile plays at the corner of her lips. "Your sister has her gifts," she says, "and you have yours. Don't ask me any more questions, Landor. Time will answer them for you. Until then . . . trust me."

The butler appears in the doorway. "My lady," he says, "Celectate Wood has sent a guard bearing his condolences and wishes to offer you whatever he can as compensation for your misfortune."

Landor and Mother share a look – an icy spear of rage and cunning – before looking at the butler.

"Has he offered to arrest Lord Belman for his attack on my father too?" Landor asks, sarcasm and hatred burning in his words.

A kindred hatred simmers inside of me. High Lord Belman, the sole owner of half the coal mines of Kelba, was known for being on the sidelines when it came to disagreements between the Community and Celectate Wood. Most of the time he sided with Celectate Wood in attempts to become his personal lapdog. If he was behind the attack on Father, then Celectate Wood was the one who orchestrated the plot.

"Thank you, Clive," Mother says ignoring Landor's outburst, "but you may tell him we have no need of his services. The Bones have had many misfortunes as of late – another shall not be too trying."

Clive hesitates, for a moment, but bows, at last, and exits the room to inform the guard of Lady Bone's answer.

"Do you really think that was a wise choice, Mother?" Landor asks, but a twitch of a smile plays at the corner of his lips as he looks at her.

The Lady of House Bone smooths her skirts and lifts her chin. "That man may be the ruler of this nation but I'll be damned if we're to become the 'rabble' he throws his condolences at. I am sick of his presumptuous offers. House Bone will do just fine without his pity."

With that, she exits the room, Landor trailing behind her, respect shining in his eyes.

Chapter XXXII

"What the hell happened to you?" Axle asks as I exit my room the next morning, packed an ready for the return to Agron. "Your face is pale as death."

"Nothing. Nightmares." How can I tell them I'm mourning my father – mourning the leg he's lost? The confidence he'll lose. The battle he'll face.

Shade regards my face curiously, but doesn't say anything.

Our group gathers outside the palace, and we are presented with horses, as a gift from his highness, for our return journey. A black, glossy stallion becomes my ride.

I fail to mount it the first time.

Keegan snickers nearby.

I glare at him and his reins fly up and smack him in the eyes. He snarls.

I mount my stallion the second time with no trouble.

With horses, it will take us only one night to reach Agron. We pass the remains of Brunt by half-day and at nightfall, we make camp in a large clearing near a rustling creek. Several of the men in the group disappear, and from the sound of laughter and splashing, I presume they're bathing. I help Gregor find enough wood for a fire while Shade and Axle discuss perimeters with the more responsible members of our group.

After a modest meal of dried meat and porridge, most of the men retire for the night. Axle takes first watch with several others, and, from the way he grins at Shade, I don't think he plans to spend it idly.

I make my bed in the farthest corner of the clearing, between two sturdy tree roots, and pull the Wilds history book from my sack. It smells strange among the trees and stench of the forest, but I open its pages and lose myself in the words. The firelight is very dull, but my eyes are good, thank the gods.

I read about the horror the Wilds inhabitants experienced after the poison came. There were monsters. There were cannibals. There was poison. But not everywhere. Eventually the deserted found a part of the Wilds that had not been destroyed by the poisons. They tried to establish connections with Kelba again, but were always killed on sight – because of the rings around their eyes. Because they spoke the "old" language. And then the wall went up and everything changed.

I am in the middle of a story about an ancient warrior named "*Cartava,*" which means "white-hair", when the presence of someone close behind me pulls me from my stupor. I stare up a muscled abdomen and find Shade's dark eyes staring at me. The shadows from the firelight dance across his features, and my heart skips a beat. He looks so handsome.

"What?" I ask.

He tosses his bedrolls down beside mine and spreads it out. He stretches across it and props his chin in his hand. "The question is . . . what are you doing?"

"Reading. It's what educated people do." I can't resist the barb.

But he doesn't frown or glare like I'm used to. Instead, he presses closer and peers over my shoulder, the tip of his chin grazing my skin. Heat catapults through my veins. His eyes narrow. "That's an old book," he whispers. "From the king's library. How did you get it?"

"The prince gave it to me . . . as a farewell gift."

There. Now he's frowning. "Really? What compelled him to do such a thing, I wonder?" He leans back again and studies me through slitted eyelids.

"I compelled him."

"How?"

I look around to make sure no one is watching us and lean close to his ear. The scent of smoke and pine drives my senses wild. Beneath my lips, his skin is hot, too. "I threatened to tell his father what a bastard he was." I pull back, but not enough to lose his comforting smell.

Shade's lips turn up, slightly. A half-smile. "Did you? He should have given you the library."

"I wish he had."

"I bet." He leans over my shoulder again, this time resting his chin atop it. His eyes scan the pages but, if he's feeling any of the emotions swirling in my belly, he's not even reading the words. Gods, I want to do so many things to him right now. What is wrong with me?

I grunt, but he doesn't move.

"Tell me some of the stories you're reading. I've never read this one before," he whispers. He shifts closer to me, until his chest is against my spine. The upraised scar on his abdomen presses into my lower back, and I realize he's taken his shirt off.

"O-ok!" I stammer and begin to read him the myth of the "*Cartava*."

According to the legend, *Cartava* was a man born during the chaos of the poisons. It, supposedly, turned his hair white at birth, and gave him the appearance of a mad-man; with his dark, ringed eyes and his snowy locks. While the horrors of the poison aftermath shook their nation, *Cartava* hardened himself by purposely putting himself in dangerous situations. He learned to survive before, at the age of twelve, he killed his first shadow with a bit of silver moon-glass he kept as a souvenir. He was the first to discover that moon-glass, hardened in forges of intense heat, could slaughter any shadow. His discovery spurred the "Age of Restoration" in which, slowly, the Wilds inhabitants took back their land, piece by piece, driving the evil that had enveloped it into farther lands. Until the conquest was over, and they had their land back.

"'After the fight for the land, *Cartava* disappeared. Some say he ventured into the far north and spent the remainder of his days learning new things about survival in the tundra wastelands. Others think he settled down with a woman, her hair red as the autumn leaves, and raised a family. Either way, history will never know what became of the warrior. We can only surmise.'" I close the history book. "What do you think, Shade?"

His cheek is against my neck and a low growl emanates from his throat. I resist the urge to chuckle. He's asleep.

I slip the book beneath the blanket I've rolled into a pillow, and slowly move away so Shade can rest his head on his own pallet. He grumbles something under his breath before looping an arm around my waist and pulling me back against him. He repositions his chin on my shoulder, the edges of his hair tickling my neck and cheek.

"Shade . . ." I whisper.

My only response is another snore.

I should push him away. I should give him a tongue-lashing. I should . . . but I don't. Instead, I relax my body against his.

His hand rests across my stomach, burning through the layers of my clothing to the skin beneath and beyond. I rest my own hand on top of his, the harsh feel of his skin scratching my palm. The rough patches of his knuckles betray his fighting past.

Gods, why? Why can't I hate him like I used to?

Or had I ever hated him? Now that I think about it, I felt things for him before I really knew him at all. He was the hero who saved my life. Then the asshole who saved my life. Then the warrior who saved my life.

I love him.

But does he feel the same about me?

Or was Prince Ivan right, and I am just a piece in his collection?

When I wake up, Shade isn't beside me. He's by the fire discussing something with Gregor and doesn't even look in my direction.

Axle does, though, and walks over, extending a bowl of porridge towards me. I take it. He grins.

"What's got you so amused?" I ask, taking a bite of the steaming mush.

"Nothing much," he says casually, hands in his pockets. He steps closer, until he's looking down at me and I am staring at his lanky legs. "Did you sleep comfortably?"

I resist the urge to choke and swallow my food before saying, "Yes."

"Unusually warm anywhere?" he asks.

"No."

"Strange."

"Why?"

"Because when I came to wake Shade in the middle of the night for his turn at the watch, he and you were . . ." He links his two pointer fingers together, a sly grin on his face. "And Shade's hand was here . . ." He presses a hand to his stomach. "And his mouth was here . . ." He puts a hand to his shoulder. "So, I'll ask again, are you warm anywhere?"

"*Avraga*!" I snap and threateningly raise the bowl of porridge. He stumbles back to the fire, chuckling.

Shade finally glances at me. His cheeks are red. He quickly looks back at Gregor.

I blush.

Keegan is staring at me from his perch near the tree-line where he's feeding his horse. One look in his eyes, and I know Axle isn't the only one amused by the previous night's events.

It is late in the afternoon when Gregor announces that we're only an hour's ride from Agron. We'll reach the city before nightfall. Our guide resumes a slower pace to allow his horse to rest, so Shade, Axle, and I roam a few miles ahead with a couple impatient Agronites, Keegan among them.

My stallion – who I've nicknamed Torch – slowly pulls ahead of the others. I don't slow him down. I want to get to Agron. I want to rest. I want to eat. I want to return to the ruins early in the morning and train again. It's amusing how much I've actually come to miss the place.

"So . . ." Keegan pulls up alongside me, cinching the reins of his horse in tight with one hand. Much as I hate to admit, he's an excellent rider. A born horseman. "How long have you and the shadow-killer been sleeping together?"

I tilt my head away from him. "You know the answer to that question. Since the journey started."

"And do you two *just* sleep?" he probes.

"I don't see how that's any of your business!"

"Don't you? You tame a horse quite well, Kyla. I wonder if that's all you've tamed." He leans across the space between us, sniffing like a bloodhound on a hunt. I pull away, and he grins. "Never fear. Just wondering if I could detect traces of your latest victim."

The sound of a horse closing in on us from behind thumps in my ears.

Keegan looks towards the noise. "Shade, my friend, we were just talking about you."

My spine tingles with a mixture of anger and embarrassment. I don't dare look at Shade as he pulls up alongside me.

He doesn't speak.

"Have you started letting Kyla use your body wash? She smells unpleasantly of smoke. It's almost overpowering." Keegan pinches his nose shut in a mock gesture.

I meet Shade's eyes. Swirls of suppressed anger swim inside them.

"Just one question, Shade, for old times sake. When you two tangle, who has more experience? Who's the dominant force? Tell me – is the little whore good at bed?"

Shade's lips go a deathly white.

"Everyone knows Kelban females are the most fickle creatures in existence. It's a rumor that they'd spread their legs for the glory of it."

Shade shocks me by smiling. "Keep in mind, Keegan of Brunt, that your grandmother was a Kelban."

Keegan turns red. "You . . .!"

The voices fade around me. The air no longer smells of trees and fresh dew. Something stronger wafts the air. It fills my nose, my mouth, my ears in dreadful, painful memories.

Everyone else smells it too. One by one the horses stop.

Shade straightens atop the saddle, his nose in the air, trying to discern its origin.

"Oh, shit, that smells awful," Keegan grumbles and pinches his nose shut.

Indeed, to him, it would smell strange. But, to me, it awakens a terror so deep and so old inside that it takes all my inner effort to control the shaking in my hands.

It is the smell of shadows.

Never has it been so powerful. It fills the air and makes Keegan and Shade choke with its stench.

It shouldn't be like this. It shouldn't be this overwhelming. Unless . . .

Oh, please Calaisar, no!

My head begins to buzz. Slowly, gray and white swirls appear in front of my eyes. I see Otis's face through the foggy tendrils of my mind. A wave of emotions crash into my skull. Pain. Guilt. Anger. Sorrow. Grief. The white wall comes from nowhere and lashes across my face, but I am prepared for it. I open my eyes, despite the pain.

I am in Agron. Smoke and fire surrounds the houses. The well is tipped sideways, its stones scattered like an ancient artifact. Everywhere, shadows of men dart between the smoky embers and attempt to dash water on the fires. But the well's destruction makes it difficult to draw water.

Wounded lie in streets, bleeding profusely. All around, women and children run with medicine and water, but their attempts are clumsy. Screams fill the air. Sheet covered bodies are carried out through the gate. Lots of them!

I glimpse a white, bloodless arm hanging from one cot.

Otis stands in the middle of the court looking around with blank, bloodshot eyes. Blood runs from a cut in his forehead. His entire body is covered in guts and stench. And he's crying. Crying as two men carry a heavy-set form towards a wooden building. Crying as he looks at the woman's face. Crying as he watches the men disappear inside with the woman.

Claws grip me by the throat.

The woman is Mama Opal!

"Hellfire!" Keegan snaps, moving his horse aside as I tip over the back of my horse and fall flat on the ground. My spine thrums painfully.

Axle reaches me before Shade, his bony arms latching beneath me and lifting me to a sitting position. His hands wander my back and shoulders, searching for broken bones. They pause over the ridges beneath my tunic.

"Damn that horse!" he hisses. "Why the hell did it do that?"

I grip Axle's hand, which he's placed on my shoulder, tightly.

Mama Opal is dead! Mama Opal is dead! Mama Opal is dead!

Gregor finally joins our group and sniffs the air. His aged eyes widen and he slaps a hand to the sword at his side. "Agron's under attack. Let's go!"

"*Was* under attack," Shade says underneath his breath.

They will find you.

Agron's attack is because of me. People are dead because of me. *Mama Opal* is dead because of me.

The shadows came for me.

Chapter XXXIII

We enter through the north gate and the destruction becomes more evident as we enter the heart of the city. The air becomes smokier. Flames lick at the corners of stone homes. Blood coats the cobblestones. The horses snicker nervously.

We reach the city square.

The well is broken and its stones scattered – just like it had been in my vision.

Otis stands in the middle of the fray, dictating to several men what to do. Bodies are lined up against the defense walls, their forms covered by white sheets stained a deep red.

We dismount.

"Otis!" Dirk calls. Agron's leader turns around. He shows no sign of surprise at seeing us.

He glances at me. "So the king decided favorably," he says in a voice that is much too soft. "Good for you, Kyla."

"What the hell happened here?" Dirk snaps, gesturing around at the destruction. Keegan hovers behind him, the flames reflecting in his green eyes. He says nothing though.

"What do you think?" Otis sighs tiredly.

Dirk growls a curse in ancient Kelban under his breath before turning around and backhanding me across the face.

"Father!" Keegan gasps, grabbing Dirk's arm and preventing him from landing another blow.

I press a hand to the sting against my cheek. Tears well in my eyes.

I don't say anything. I don't look at anyone. I look at the ground. At the blood staining the edges of my boots a crimson reminder.

I did this. I'm the reason they came here. I'm the reason everyone is dead.

I am the reason Mama Opal is dead.

"You bitch! You did this to us! Bitch! Kill her! Kill the damn bitch!" Dirk screams at me. He struggles against his son. "Let me go! Let me go, you bastard, and do me proud. Lay the bitch on the dirt!"

"That's exactly what he's wanted to do all along," Axle snarls through grinding teeth. He steps forward, a finger raised in Dirk's line of sight. "If you ever . . ."

"Touch her again, I'll slit your throat, old man!" Shade finishes, sliding one of his blades from his back. His eyes are like pits of dark flame. "*Slowly.*"

"Enough!" Otis snaps. He looks at Shade. "They came in the dead of night. Without a sound. A trace. A whisper of wind. They were in the houses – inside, for gods sakes! Watching us. Surrounding us. Mama Opal found them and sounded the alarm. The bastards stabbed her because of it! Tell me, Shade, what possessed them to do that?"

"They've . . . they've never done that before!" Axle stammers, mouth open in disbelief. "They d-don't attack like that." He looks at me. A glimmer of fear flickers across his face, and then it's gone.

They were looking for me. That's why they went into the houses. They wanted me.

I can't breathe. I can't stand. I have to lean against something. But there's nothing to lean on. Nowhere to run. To escape. To hide. I am trapped. Cornered like a beast in a cage – a frightened animal surrounded by bars of fear and anger and hate.

Shade shrugs. "The important thing is they are gone. You fought them off!"

"For now!" Dirk grinds between his teeth. "But what about next time? Then what, boy? What will you do then? Wave your little moon-induced blades around and show us a few tricks? They'll keep coming. Like they always have. Until we get rid of *her*!" He points a trembling finger at me.

"For all we know you could be the curse, Dirk!" Axle snaps. "You've been in this village far longer than Kyla has."

"A good woman gave her life – her life – for this village. She is dead because of her!"

Otis looks up. "She will be soon."

I freeze. *She's still alive?*

Everyone seems equally shocked.

"The shadow blade's poison is spreading through her body. She was conscious until five minutes ago. She told us what medicines to use. What remedies to insert so they could fight the spreading poison. She succumbed to it, though. She'll be dead soon." The leader's eyes fill with tears that he doesn't bother to wipe away. They drip down his cheeks and drown his brown beard.

She's not dead. She's not dead. She's not dead!

"Kyla!" Shade gasps and tries to grab my arm as I swerve around Otis and run towards the house I saw them carrying Mama Opal to in my vision. "Kyla, where the hell are you going?"

Inside the room is practically empty, save for five victims spread out on tables. Women run back and forth between them with buckets of water. Two men are busily attending one wounded young man. Near the back of the room, in a tight corner, another healer bends over a plump form.

Mama Opal.

The healer gasps as I appear at his side and grasp Mama Opal's hand. Her eyes are open but they stare upwards. Blind. Dark. Lost. Her dress has been cut open from neck to waist to expose the long gash carved into her belly. Around the wound, a thick, green paste has been applied.

Lanakin, I remember Mama Opal telling me. It could cure wounds and minimize the effect of ingested poisons if applied right.

But it hasn't helped. Curving upwards towards her neck, black veins pulse beneath her skin. It's like darkness curling through her bloodstream. The head of the poisonous venom has reached the skin just beneath her collarbone.

I press the back of my hand to Mama Opal's forehead. It is cold. Cold like death.

"Otis," the healer I've interrupted snaps, "who is this girl? Get her out of here!" He grabs my wrist.

I jerk it free. "No!" I snap and turn to Mama Opal again, framing her face with my hands. "Mama Opal," I whisper. "Mama Opal, can you hear me?"

Her eyes find mine.

I smile at her.

She screams and her nails scrape my shoulder – just over the ostracized scar. Blood drips down my arm.

"Kyla, be careful!" Shade snaps and pulls me away, securing me with an arm around my shoulders. A tremor shakes his body when his hand draws away from my shoulder, wet with my blood.

"It's taking her!" the healer snaps.

Mama Opal's body starts shaking. It shakes the cot. It shakes the wall behind it. Her mouth opens and her screams are savage. Brutal. Painful. The veins along her neck pop out in strain.

The healer grabs her arms and slams them to the cot. He turns to Otis, who stands just behind Shade and I.

"I've done all I can!"

No. I shake my head. *She can't die. She can't die. After all she's done for me, she can't die. Not because of me. She shouldn't die because of me.*

"It would be best if you didn't watch this, Otis," the healer whispers softly. "Wait outside. I'll come to you when it's over."

They're just going to let her die?

"You can't! She's . . ." Even as the words leave my lips, I know they'll be futile. Everyone dies from a shadow blade's sting. Everyone.

Or do they?

That night in Brunt – when Keegan was stabbed – hadn't it been a shadow blade? And he was alive.

And me – I had been cut with a shadow blade. I was alive.

Mama Opal could live too.

I pull away from Shade and dart to her side again. I press a hand atop the black head of venomous poison spreading beneath her shoulder. It rises and falls like a living, breathing breath of oxygen in her veins. What if it is alive too?

"Give me your Illathonian blade."

"What?" Shade stares at me.

"Give it to me," I repeat, stretching my arm out towards him.

He hesitates. Everyone in the room is staring at me.

The black head of the poison reaches Mama Opal's collarbone and, slowly, with deadly precision, inches over it. She screams, loud, long and clear, once more. The tremor of pain that rocks her body spurs me to action.

I stomp towards Shade and take the Illathonian blade from his hands myself. He doesn't stop me. It's like he's in a daze, watching what I'll do, but powerless to stop it.

The healer grabs my wrist as I raise the Illathonian blade over the spot near her shoulder. The black head of darkness is pulsing towards Mama Opal's neck. Towards the veins bulging at her throat.

"You'll kill her!" he snaps.

"She's dying anyway!" I try to pull my arm free, but he doesn't let go.

"I won't let you do it."

No. He'll let her die.

"Go back to the hell you came from, Kelban, and let that woman alone! You hear me? Get away from her!" Dirk screams. Keegan grabs his arm, eyes locked on me.

Mama Opal cries out again.

There is no time.

The healer screams as I switch the Illathonian blade to my left hand and bash the hilt into the side of his head. Blood leaks from his ear. He falls to the ground, moaning. I move to the other side of Mama Opal's cot where the black vein is shifting towards the curve of her plump neck.

"Shade! Axle! Hold her down!" They stare at me, shocked by what I've just done to the healer. "NOW!"

Shade stretches himself on top of her, and Axle pins her legs to the table. She thrashes beneath them, but, for some reason, I feel she's not the one fighting them. Something else is battling them – something that knows its presence has been discovered.

"Stop her!" Dirk screams. He darts towards me, knife in hand.

Otis grabs him around the shoulders.

Keegan remains in the doorway, staring at me.

I close my eyes and place my hand over the pumping black vein making haste towards Mama Opal's throat. A buzz tickles the back of my neck, vibrating throughout my entire body. I clutch the Illathonian blade tightly in my palm. The white flash I've prepared myself for doesn't crack against my skull this time. Instead, it flashes in my face like a bright light and is gone.

I open my eyes.

I am inside Mama Opal, hiding in the red flesh of her shoulder. The black gooey vein that is the darkness moves beneath me. I search for the head of the infection. It hisses and growls.

Strange.

I find the head and resist the urge to scream. It ***is*** *a head. The actual head of a grotesque little monster. Black needle-like teeth push flesh and bone aside as it seeps through the folds of its victim. From outside the encasing of skin I hear Mama Opal scream and everything shakes around me. She's writhing again.*

The poison on the shadow blade is a living thing!

I don't wait for the vision to curl in on itself. There's no time. I close my eyes and mentally push myself with all my strength from the image.

When I open my eyes, everyone is staring at me.

I can kill it!

Mama Opal thrashes beneath the Illathonian blade as I press it against her neck and wait.

And wait.

Until the head of the poison approaches the silver edge. Until the poisonous demon presses against the blade, thinking its another collarbone to dodge. Until it tips its black vein-like talons underneath the blade's edge and they are sliced off. It pulses beneath the skin, shocked and pained.

Now.

I slice.

Screeches fill the air – so loud, so horrifying – that they tear at the insides of my ears. Axle and Shade fall back, cupping hands over their ears, screaming. A black, smoky substance pours from the gash I've made in Mama Opal's neck. It floats into the air, creating a dark cloud of pure night above her cot – and between me and escape.

The cloud begins to spread out, in inky talons, all over the room. Blinding me. Disorienting me. Trapping me against the wall.

Mama Opal's bleeding a shadow!

The darkness leaves her body. She stops writhing.

I did it!

The black cloud hisses from every part of its creation. There is no mouth. No eyes. Just darkness and talons.

It knows it was me.

The fog moves towards me. I raise the Illathonian blade, and its weak light spreads out over the advancing vapor.

It is not enough. The darkness slams against the light, pressing me back farther and farther. The light fades away. The sword falls from my hands and clatters onto the ground.

I scream.

The darkness pushes up against me, slamming me against the wall with such force my spine tingles, and my legs go numb. Its wisps are like grips of iron around my arms and body. They flutter towards my mouth and nose.

The familiar attack produces an old memory – of foggy wisps fluttering towards my mouth and nose.

I cover them with my hands, as the goo slides from my ankles, up my legs, and over my entire body. The wisps push against my flesh, searching for a way to enter me.

I can't breathe.

The gooey talons reach my neck and pause against the indents beneath my hairline. The formless monster screeches. My neck burns beneath its touch.

I scream along with it and the talons retreat from my neck. Raspy cries of pain fill the air.

A light flashes from behind the darkness. The vapor begins to curl in on itself. It screams, high and shrill, into the air. Light penetrates it.

It disappears.

With the seething darkness no longer holding me against the wall, I fall. The hard ground cracks against my knees. I take my hands from my mouth and nose. Air rushes into my lungs. I violently let it back out.

I can't breathe. I can't breathe.

I cover my ears in panic as my head fills with cackling voices and angry hisses. White flashes dot my vision, swirling in odd colors of gray and black. I force my eyes to remain open. I don't want to know where the colors or dragging me. I don't want to know the vision they will show me.

I don't want to go.

They disappear.

"Holy shit!" is the first thing my throbbing ears hear. Axle is still on the ground staring at the space that the black cloud occupied just moments before. His eyes are wide with fear. "Holy shit. Holy shit!"

Shade is standing in front of me, his Illathonian blade stabbing empty air. He killed it!

He saved me.

He drops his Illathonian blade on the ground next to the one he lent me, and grabs my face, gently, in his hands. "Kyla," he breathes. "Kyla . . ." His eyes flick to my neck and widen. He sucks in a sharp breath and places a hand on the right side of my throat.

Over the scars received so long ago.

The vapor shadow must have made them swell.

And, from the look in his eyes, he knows what they are.

Why is he covering them?

"Mama Opal!" Axle gasps.

Oh, gods, is she . . .

"Easy," Shade whispers as I jolt to my feet. He presses me close, his hand still on my neck, and his arm around my waist, preventing me from approaching her cot right away. He leans close, his lips brushing my temple. "Easy."

The healer moves to her bedside and checks her pulse. When he draws back his hand it is covered in red blood.

Did I cut too deep? Did I kill her?

He turns around. "She's alive."

Axle releases a whoop of joy while everyone else in the room releases a breath all at once.

Dirk sags in Otis's arms, his eyes going blank in shock. He stares at me like he's seeing something different in my place. His eyes narrow as he observes Shade's hold on me.

"I think, Otis," Axle says sweeping Shade's discarded Illathonian blades off the floor with one hand and holding them out towards Agron's leader, "that you have a new cure for a shadow blade's bite, eh?"

Otis takes the swords without another word. There are tears in his eyes. He looks towards Mama Opal's unconscious body.

"Go to her," I urge.

He does, handing the healer the Illathonian blades. The healer stares at the swords, then at Shade.

"Use them to the best of your abilities. Return them first thing in the morning," Shade instructs. He returns his attention to me and lifts his hand slightly off my neck. He lets go of me.

Apparently, the scars are no longer visible.

"Shade. Axle. Help me," the healer pleads, approaching another unfortunate victim of the shadow blade.

The moment Shade walks away, I slip outside.

In place of the well, a trough has been set up in the middle of the city square. I bend over its edge and splash water on my face.

But no amount of water will wash away the feeling of the vapor's hold on me. Its gooey exterior latching onto my skin like a leech sends icy chills down my spine. The feel of its wet edges trying to force its way between my hand and my mouth raises bile in my throat. I bend over and retch until nothing else is left.

I lean against the hard wooden side of the trough. Parts of my mind are shattering around me as fear bludgeons them with hammers of its own evil making.

I have dark gifts that I can and cannot control.

I have strange visions that can and cannot be explained.

I have shadows that will and are hunting me down.

The next time they come, they will find me. They will take me. They will hurt me.

Should I run?

Immediately, as the thought enters my mind, I know its impossible. Where would I go? I am banned from my homeland. And, if my talents are discovered, I will be banned here as well.

I thought if I tried hard enough, worked hard enough, proved myself, I would belong in the Wilds. But, truthfully, I never have and never will. Not in the Wilds. Not in Kelba.

Not anywhere.

I splash water on my face again, staring down at my reflection in the water. I cannot recognize the girl I see in the water as the Kyla Kelonia Bone that existed just three months before.

"You okay?"

I wipe the water from my face, but don't turn around. "Yeah. Aren't you supposed to be helping with the wounded?"

"I am." Shade leans against the trough beside me and crosses his arms, tilting his head to the side in that animal way that has become somewhat attractive to me. "But, for some reason, Axle felt that you needed me more than the poor, bleeding fools in there so . . ." He spreads out his arms. "Here I am."

I chuckle half-heartedly and stare at my feet. They are so dirty. Since we'd been riding horses I hadn't bothered to put on my shoes this morning.

"You're quiet," Shade observes. "I'm not used to that."

"More than half of my personality is quiet, so I'm surprised you haven't noticed that," I whisper back.

It's dusk now. The sun has disappeared over the rim of the trees. It'll be pitch black soon. Chills skate along my spine. If the shadows come back tonight looking for me . . .

I step away from the trough. I should go. Far away. A place where no one knows. Where no one can find me.

And then he steps in front of me, and I stop. He stares down at me for a few moments, eyes flickering over my face, before whispering, "We need to talk."

My arms tighten and the lead weight in my hand returns with pulsing magnetism.

No. I force it into silence.

"But not here." He grips my arm gently. "Follow me."

He leads me towards Agron's gates. The guards are too tired to argue with the city's famed shadow-killer and let us pass.

"Where are we going?" I ask.

He doesn't answer.

Chapter XXXIV

Shade forges a trail through the forest. Leaves crunch beneath my feet. A knot tightens in the pit of my stomach, but his hand that leads me forward isn't tight or rough.

He could be leading me like a sheep to the slaughter.

But I don't think he is.

Finally, Shade pushes aside another leafy branch to reveal a clear, blue pool of water that shimmers in the moonlight. A small waterfall cascades into its rippling surface from the corner of the mountains. The water from the pool branches off to the right in a channel that must lead to a river or the sea I saw from Gavrone's cliff.

The ground surrounding the pool moves in an unearthly fashion. It isn't grass swaying or leaves fluttering. It ripples like a fur rug disturbed a slight breeze.

"What . . ."

Shade cuts me off with a shake of his head and lets go of my hand. He leans down and picks up a pebble from the strange earth and tosses it near the pool.

Millions upon millions of tiny lights rise into the air – blinking, flashing, glowing. Some are large. Others are so tiny they appear to be mere sands of sparkling gold. They illuminate the falls, the water, the trees, in a pale, golden light. It is beautiful.

Shade takes my hand in his again and leads me into the galaxy on earth. The insects flutter around my face, brushing their soft wings against my cheeks, and resting on my arms. My skin glows golden. I must look like a goddess.

I look at Shade and catch my breath. None of the little lights dare land on him, but they illuminate his ruddy complexion in a pale, unearthly glow. And I realize, with awe, that he's staring at me just as amazed.

The lights begin to dim as the insects return to their beds on the ground. A few remain on my arms, their lights going out. "Shade, I . . ."

"I'll answer your questions," Shade interrupts. He speaks fast. Too fast. "Any that you have."

I hadn't been expecting that. I'd been expecting him to ask about the scars on my neck. To question their making. The lies I've spun weight me down. And, as I stare at his silhouette against the now star-twinkling sky, I realize I can't lie to him anymore.

He's saved my life more times than I can count. I owe him the truth.

"I'm not who you think I am," I blurt out before I change my mind. "I . . ."

"I don't think it's your turn yet," Shade interrupts me, his tone sharp. "Be patient."

"Shade . . ." He must know what I'm going to tell him. That must be why he doesn't want to hear it.

"I am pissed off that you have to keep going behind my back and asking Axle everything about *both* of us. It really irks me, Kyla. And I've told you before – I don't like to be irked." He steps closer, but not close enough for me to see or define his features. "So . . . ask what you want of me. I promise, I will answer."

Once, I would have relished this chance. I would have bombarded him with all the curiosities of my soul. But now . . . I'm afraid.

"Or does this game no longer interest you?"

"It was never a game," I protest.

"No?" His voice is devoid of any emotion I might use to determine his mood. "You sure treated it like one. Didn't you want to delve deep into the mysterious shadow-killer's dirty secrets and finally know the reason why he was such a cruel, heartless bastard?"

"I never thought you were a cruel, heartless bastard!"

He cocks his head at me.

"Okay," I relent. "Maybe at first. You can't say that you were the most charming person I'd ever met."

"Like Axle?"

Now there is something else in his aggravated voice. Harsh. Critical. Painful.

"What do you mean by that?"

"I think we both know what I mean by that."

I square my shoulders. "Say it then."

He pauses, but doesn't back down from the challenge. "You find him fascinating. Attractive. He's charming and bold. He knows how to live life and he knows how to have a good time. Who doesn't like that? It's exhilarating, yes?" His voice sinks. "I can't be like that. I can't be care-free and charming. I can't hide my true feelings behind a smile and pretend to enjoy life when everything that's happened to me makes me so angry. I thought, maybe, you understood that feeling. What it feels like to be torn apart and thrown aside. What it feels like to be looked at as something not entirely human."

I stare at him, unable to speak.

"You were always a strange one, Kyla," he whispers, stepping closer, but keeping his face in the dark. "And there was always something about you that seemed familiar. When I would look at your face in the dark, there was something there that made my head ache as I tried to remember – to remember where I'd seen those large eyes before."

I resist the urge to step back and, instead, clench my fists at my sides.

"Everyone else feared the Kelbans," he finally says. "Merely because they had built a Wall. What's so fearsome about that wall? I wanted to know why they needed to build a wall. What were they hiding? What did they think of us? Why did everyone think they – *you* – were so terrible? So I visited Kelba for the first time. For such a fearsome replica of strength like your Wall it was remarkable how poorly guarded it was. When I saw your kingdom, the emptiness inside me deepened. I discovered I wanted nothing to do with Kelba either."

"Why?"

"They were selfish. They were cowardly. They were and are the exact replica of people in Agron, in Smoke, in the Wilds. And I hate them for it. I can't respect such people. I never will." Venom has crept into his tone.

He hates us. Hates me and my kind to his very core.

Run. Far away.

But I stay where I am.

"But, of course, even though I had wanted nothing to do with Kelba, the shadows had no qualms about sneaking into your land and feeding off of whatever they could find. I refused to let any of them slip through my grasp so I would follow them. Over the wall. Into Kelba. And I'd end them."

My mouth is dry.

"One night I followed four shadows all the way from the Poison River, through the Burnt Forest, into your land. They were different than the others. They were stronger. Darker. And they knew where they were going. It was difficult to track them. I lost sight of them for nearly an hour and thought, for the first time, I'd failed." He breathes in and out slowly, before continuing. "I heard someone scream. Well, more of a half-scream, half-sob. I was on the rooftops and it wasn't too far away. I found the shadows, just three of them now, and a man lying prostrate on the cobblestones, blood leaking from his head. It wasn't an uncommon sight. What was an uncommon sight was the girl one of the shadows was clutching, its teeth buried in her neck. It was very dark, but I could still see the terror in her large eyes. Rage, like I'd never felt before, filled me. I knew that terror. It was the same terror that had rattled through me for three years. And no one had come to my rescue." I catch my breath as his hand glides over my shoulder and brushes my neck. His fingers find the indents in my skin, applying gentle pressure to tiny ridges. Heat floods my face. "That girl was a High Lord's daughter who I now know was called 'Kyla Kelonia Bone'."

He knows. The revelation sends terrified shivers down my backside. I try to draw back, afraid of what he'll do. I've lied to him. He has every right to hate me.

He jerks me towards him, slamming me against his chest, his hand tightening against my neck – curling in my hair. I want to close my eyes. Want to wish everything away. I shouldn't have let him drag me out of Agron. I should have stayed. I should have pressed my hand over the scars when the vapor shadow attacked me. That is why he pulled me out here, in the middle of nowhere. I wait for his rage to unleash.

"You knew who I was. There was no way you couldn't have known," he whispers softly. It stings worse than a slap in the face. "Why didn't you tell me?"

Because I was afraid. Because I didn't trust you. Because I was a Kelban and you had every right to hate me.

But I whisper, "You would have killed me," instead.

"Is that what you really think?" he asks quietly. I don't miss the hurt in his tone. The tremor that shivers through his fingers on my neck as they brush my scars in a gentle caress. My legs shake. Several of the insects on the ground, disturbed by my sudden movement, rise into the air, illuminating Shade's face. His eyes – eyes rimmed in black rings – are so close to mine I blink and try to draw back. He doesn't let me. "Tell me, Kyla, do you think I would hurt you now that I know the truth? Now that I know *who* you are?"

"Is there a reason why you shouldn't?" Because I can't think of one.

"You thanked me," he says, "for killing them. That long night ago, when I was trying to get away as fast as I could so you wouldn't scream my presence to the entire city like I expected all Kelbans to do, you thanked me." He leans closer, until our foreheads are nearly touching. His hair brushes against mine with soft static. "No one ever did that before. No one ever . . ." he swallows, a vein standing out on his neck, ". . . thanked me for what I did."

"Do you know I spent years thinking about that girl? Years, wide awake and awestruck, by the girl who hadn't been afraid of me. Who hadn't behaved the way I'd thought all Kelbans acted." He shakes his head, his hair tickling my nose. "And now, I feel like a blind fool. I should have known who you were from the very beginning but I was so angry – so hateful – that I couldn't see it. Kyla, would you look at me?"

I do.

"No one ever took the time to know me," he whispers, sliding both of his hands upwards to caress my jaw tenderly. "Except you."

I am unprepared when he leans in and his lips find mine with gentle pressure. I start to pull away, memories of our last kiss burning in my memory – rough and wild. He glides one of his hands down to my waist and pulls me flush against him, the buckle of his pants pressing against my abdomen. His other hand continues to brush my cheek, guiding my mouth against his. Slowly the fear inside of me dissipates. Little buzzing motions spread along my arms like gentle wings. Something low and warm spirals through my body, spreading pleasant claws into the tips of my fingers. There is nothing wrong about this kiss. It is gentle and coaxing, tasting of gratitude, love, and passion. There is no anger – no pain – in this moment. Shade deepens the kiss by looping his arm around my neck with a greater force. It grows fast and furious, a desperation so wild that my head swims. I clutch him around the waist desperate for support as I am tossed into a sea of emotions I've only dreamed of. The waves begin to fade. Slowly – slowly – until he pulls his lips away, releases me, and jerks back like he's been slapped.

"I won't do it again," he says in a rush. The moonlit insects rise from the ground again and flutter around us, illuminating the flush on his cheeks. "I won't touch you. If it hurts you, I won't do it." He's staring at the scar on my wrist. At the brand on my shoulder.

My stomach sinks.

"I'm not married, Shade."

He blinks. "W-what?"

"I never have been." I hang my head in shame and rub a hand along my arm, suddenly feeling very, very cold. "I was ostracized for refusing to marry Aspen Wood."

"You were never . . .wait!" He shakes his head in disbelief. "Your bond to be . . . was Aspen Wood? The Celectate's son?" He stumbles backwards. "You . . . you could have had wealth. Power. Security. For the rest of your life. And . . ."

"Watching the Celectate use *me* to make my father, a man who can do much for Kelba, become a puppet? Watch my family suffer because I was the Celectate's pawn in one of his grand schemes to attain power? Sleep in a man's bed – a man's arms – that I had no inner feelings or respect for? Because I was too much of a coward to make my own choices? No, you were right. Kelbans are cowards. But I didn't want to live like that. I didn't want to be the girl who ruined her family because she was too afraid to stand up for what she believed."

"So you chose this?" He swings a hand in a wild gesture around the forest.

I shrug, forcing a half-smile. "It wasn't as bad as I thought it would be."

"And you . . . you weren't raped?"

I'd known the question was coming. I'd even prepared for it, but now that his words hang in the open air between us, the only remnant of my former preparation shudders out in an almost imperceptible, "N-no."

The insects have returned to their nests upon the ground. I don't see his face, but I hear the steady intake of breath through his lips. The sigh that hisses from between his teeth. "So . . ." He falters, breathing deeply. Instinctively, my shoulders tighten as he shifts his body in the direction of the glistening water. "So . . ." he tries again, once more pausing to breathe deeply, ". . . you . . . you lied."

I don't feel the need to answer him. My throat is in so many knots I couldn't even if I wanted to.

"Why? Why the hell would you tell me something like that if . . ." He turns to face me again, but it's still too dark to see his face.

"I . . . had my reasons." Even if they seemed as useless as shit now. "You can h-hate me if you want. I had my secrets. You had yours. We both made poor judgment mistakes when it came to dealing with our pasts and the lies we wove around them."

"Poor judgment . . . my secrets?" he sputters. "You made met think you were 'raped!' Raped, Kyla! Do you honestly know what that did to me? To imagine what you . . ."

"And do you know what it did to me when I had to find out that the person I've come to lo . . . care about lived in hell itself for three years? To know that you didn't trust me enough to tell me?"

His silhouetted face stares at me. "You could have said 'no.' Was it that hard? You didn't have to lie. You didn't have to protect yourself. Not from me."

If his voice were still aggravated it would be easier. Now the aggravation has changed to hurt. It hurts me too. "And you could have answered all my gods-damned questions about your captivity in a civil manner. Don't think that the way you've handled your own past is any nobler than mine. You didn't have to shield yourself. Not from me."

"You didn't have to lie."

"You didn't have to push me to the wall and kiss the daylights out of me just to prove a damn point!"

We square off against his each other, breathing heavily, our hands clenched at our sides. Our enraged voices have forced the glowing insects into the air again, illuminating both our faces. We both take advantage of the moment and look at each other.

"So . . ." He closes his eyes and breathes deeply, ". . . we're both admitting we made some shitty mistakes to cover up the lies or truths we refused to shed light on. Is that it?"

I glare at him, but nod, sullenly.

"And neither one of us is going to apologize for those mistakes, are we? Because we both did what we could to survive." His words during my training flutter through my memory and they must have reemerged in his because he growls, "Shit! I trained you to do that too!"

"I learned from the best," I mutter with a slight shrug of my shoulders.

The silence draws out between us. I rub my arms nervously and glance at the peacefully rippling surface of the moonlit water. "D-do you hate me, Shade?"

Say "no." Please say "no."

"What the hell, Kyla?" He grabs me, but his hold is gentle. He grips my chin and forces me to look at him again. There is no anger in his face. Only a rippling surface of water in his own eyes. "I thought you'd been hurt. Violated. Abused. To find out you haven't . . . that you've never had to go through something like that . . . how could I hate you, when I spent endless nights lying awake, wondering how I could make you look past it? How I could make you forget the pain that a man might have caused you and understand what a man could make you feel? I could never hate you for that. But why did you lie to me?"

"Because I was afraid if you knew, you would ask more questions. I didn't want you to know who I was. I was afraid . . ."

"That I would hurt you," he finishes for me.

"Honestly," I admit, "after a while, I don't think I was afraid of you. I think I was just afraid of the truth." Of admitting I was one of the lying, cowardly Kelbans he detests.

He must have read my silence for what it was because he says, "I never thought you were a coward, Kyla. Never! A coward would have taken one look at me at that bridge, gotten on their knees, and wailed like a babe. Or pissed their pants. A coward would have died in the Burnt Forest. A coward would have run from that razor – and been killed for their effort. A coward wouldn't have gotten up after being knocked down again and again and again and . . ." He palms my face. "And, if we're being honest right now, Kyla, I always knew you were a liar."

We both chuckle softly.

"So," he says, "those times when I would draw near – when Axle acted like a lewd asshole – you didn't draw back because of traumatic experiences, but because you had never done something like that with anyone."

My cheeks burn with embarrassment. "I . . . I've kissed before."

"Oh, yes," he whispers, his breath warming my face, "I know.

And, for the record, you do it very well."

I don't know if I should turn away or thank him.

"It makes me wonder," he says softly, leaning in towards my ear, "what else are you good at?"

"Kicking your ass," I retort.

"How about swimming?" He takes my hand and draws me towards the pool. The surface shimmers in the moonlight and reflects in his eyes like glass.

An old fear tightens in my gut. "I – I can't swim."

"I noticed," he answers wryly, no doubt remembering the time he'd pulled me from the river before we'd arrived in Agron. "I'll teach you. Of all the things to be afraid of in life, water shouldn't be one of them."

I hesitate.

"Tell you what," he says, stripping off his shirt and tossing it beside the pool, "I'll go first and show you a few tricks. You follow, okay?"

Doing my best not to stare at his bare chest, I nod, grateful for the darkness that hides my reddening cheeks.

He wades in until the water is up to his knees, which is only three steps, and dives beneath the crystal surface. I wait for him to emerge, and my heart skips a beat when several seconds pass and he remains underwater. I release a steady breath when his head and shoulders finally burst from the surface, raining droplets of water all around him as he wipes it from his eyes. He waves a hand at me, signaling for me to watch. He proceeds to sweep one arm in front of the other, swimming in a graceful circle before coming back to the edge of the pool. He holds a hand out towards me.

I glide my hand into his, relishing how smoothly my fingers slip over his skin.

We slowly walk into the water. It laps up around my ankles, then my shins, then my knees. Nausea leaves chunks of dread in my throat as the water reaches my waist. The ground leaves my feet.

I latch onto Shade, fingers clawing at his shoulders, his back, his neck. He laughs, but doesn't shove me away. His hands glide over my waist, feeling strangely heavy in the weightless effect of the water.

"Kick your legs. No, not like that. You're kicking *me.* Kick one. Now the other. Keep doing it. There you go. Give yourself a motion. It's like dancing, just without the ground." His instructions are low and calm, so different from the rough chiding I'm used to. My body begins to level itself out.

"You know," I say, "if you'd been this way during our recent training I wouldn't have been so focused on killing you and I might have focused on . . . other things."

His low chuckle ripples over my skin like a breath of steam. "In that case, avraga," he leans close and his lips feather my ear, "I'll eagerly await our next training session."

My body feels as light as my head, and Shade grips me harder as I level myself atop the water.

"Very good. Now we're going to employ the second half. I'm going to let go of you. Don't worry. There you go. I've got your waist. Now make sweeping motions with your arms. Fight the water. Pretend you're fighting me. There you go." In slow motion my arms and legs take their toll against the water, propelling the rest of my body through the cool element.

"Now I'm going to let go of you. Fight the panic and do as I told you." His hands pull away.

I grab at them in vain and go under, water enveloping my head in its cold pressuring claws. I kick upwards with my feet. Pump my arms. Nothing happens. I am sinking. The panic rises.

Slowly, Kyla. Slowly. Gently.

I try to put some effective timing into when I kick and where I place my arms. Slowly, the water around me gives way as I push it aside. My head breaks the surface again, and I gasp for air.

"You did it!" Shade says. "Now try swimming towards me."

Propelling myself on top of the water is easier than I thought. I keep my eyes on Shade's silhouette in the water. The moon casts beams of light on the rippling surface, giving his face a soft, silver glow. I wrap my arms around his shoulders and pull myself that much closer to him, until our sides weld together.

He forces me to try three, four times more. I go under every time, but manage to bring myself back to the surface. My limbs burn with exhaustion. But no water finds its way into my lungs, even when I panic. I conquer the twisting pains in my belly and break the chains of my watery prison.

"Tired already?" Shade asks when I lean heavily against him. He edges towards the rocks beneath the falls and grabs one, pulling himself onto it with a flex of rippling, shiny muscles. He grips me beneath the arms and pulls me on too.

Together we scale the many rock formations lodged between the cascades of water until we finally find a flat stone only a few feet from the falls. The gentle roar is not overpowering. I can still hear the crickets on the bank. Shade lies flat on his back across the smooth surface, so I join him, staring up at the millions of stars that wink at us from the night sky. Droplets of water rain gently down onto our faces from the nearby fall of water.

Exhaustion, pure and painful, offers a dull ache in my legs. I can barely move my arms.

"You did well," Shade says from beside me.

I open my mouth to reply and water from my wet hair glides down my throat. I cough violently.

Shade sits up on his elbows. "You okay?" He leans close.

I turn to assure him I'm alright and our noses brush. He sucks in a sharp breath, his jaw going taut. Our breath hangs in the air between us, warm and heavy. Shade reaches over and brushes wet tendrils of curling hair away from my face.

As if drawn by some magnetic, unearthly pull I lift myself up on my elbows, my lips hovering over his. I make sure to look in his eyes. He has to want this as much as I do. Has to feel the same way as I do. If he doesn't, it is all for naught. I will not – can not – waste my feelings on another person unless he cares about me. I don't want to end up like Aspen, alone and hurt after false hope. Aspen may have been an asshole, but I'm sure he really, truly felt something for me. I understand how he must have felt – how angry and hurt – when I brought all his dreams crashing down around him.

Shade stares back at me, his gaze hungry and wanting, just as much as I.

I press my lips against his, unsure about what I should do. I have no experience being the initiator of a kiss. I flush, afraid I'm doing it wrong. That the first real, honest kiss I've ever given anybody will be awkward, clumsy, and foolish. I start to draw away.

I know I'm doing it wrong.

Shade palms my face and pulls me back, taking charge where I would not. He deepens the kiss and slowly tilts me back. My body is so alive with heat that the stone against my back doesn't hurt at all. Taut muscle presses against my chest as he stretches on top of me, leaning his elbows carefully beside my head to keep his full weight off of my fragile form. I chuckle at his careful approach, remembering very well that I've felt his full weight before in many of our training exercises. His sudden gentleness – his attempt to treat me with soft dignity and care – throws any cautions I may have had to the wind. I grip his face in my hands and kiss him back, wrapping my legs around his waist. Beneath my hands, he trembles.

He pushes himself up on his elbows and stares down at me. He opens his mouth – I wait for him to say something – and he changes his mind. He lowers himself again and continues our kiss, turning it from slow and sweet, to hot and hungry in a matter of seconds.

I shift my hands down his shoulders and across his chest, finding the scar viciously carved into his abdomen. I brush a finger over it. He arches his back against my touch and a low growl vibrates over my lips. Thrilled at the sensation, I do it again. Twice. Until he reaches between us and grips my hand.

"That's not nice," he says against my lips.

"You're the one who told me to never play nice," I retort and shift my hips against his.

A low, steamy chuckle curls over my mouth. "Two can play this game, Kyla," he whispers and shifts his mouth down the side of my face towards my ear, pressing his lips against the two, tiny indents. My body burns beneath him, and my senses hone onto that one spot where his mouth roams my skin in slow, lazy circles. Now it is my turn to arch against him as ripples of ticklish vibrations drift down my spine and gather in a bundle of warmth within my core.

"D-don't," I whisper, but I don't mean it, and he knows it.

He allows his full weight to crash down on top of me, pressing hard into the center of my core and eliciting a shocked cry from my lips. He releases my hand between us and grips my hip, singing through the wet layers of my tunic. His skin is hot beneath my touch as I wrap my arms around his back to stroke the scars there and he trembles against me as I stroke them softly. Gently. Teasingly.

"Kyla . . ." but he growls before he can finish the sentence and takes my mouth again, filling me with the taste of him.

His hand moves down my leg towards my knee and slips beneath my tunic, inching upwards at a snail's pace. His scent – his taste – drives me crazy. His hand is almost there, halfway up my thigh and approaching the burning, pulsing ache between my legs when . . .

A raspy chuckle from the shore-line slices into my gut like a dagger.

I grip Shade around the shoulders and roll him sideways off the edge of the flat rock. We fall into the water, me on top of him. We both come up sputtering, the cascading falls crashing down on our heads.

"What the hell . . ." he grunts and tries to swim while wiping water from his eyes.

I put a hand over his mouth and shake my head, casting earnest eyes towards the bank. He stops moving. Even his breath stills. Slowly, I pull him back with me against the rock, out of sight from the bank.

Hopefully, the noise of the waterfall has allowed our presence to go unnoticed.

Four shadows are on the bank, their capes fluttering around them. Two of them lean down by the water and dip their ebony black hands into it. I blink. So the bastards do have hands!

"*Grag's pissed,*" says one of the shadows who stands nearest to the tree-line. "*He had hoped to finish this ordeal in one, fluid motion, but now we have to come back again.*"

"*Why can't we just leave things as they are?*" asks another shadow who is brushing a hand through the water.

"*Because,*" the one snaps, "*he didn't get what he came for. And he won't stop until he does.*"

"*I say we cut our losses,*" remarks another. "*After all, this could be another wild goose chase and . . .*"

"*And Grag seems to think it isn't. Imagine what would happen if he's right and we don't do it now. We could be facing the end of our way of life. Do you want to be the cause of that, Igor?*"

"*I don't want to be the cause of Trithar's anger!*" snaps the petulant one. "*He can be much more brutal than ten Grag's combined if he knew what we were doing – what we are going to do.*"

"*Grag will make him see reason. And Trithar doesn't have to know. He's already given up anyway.*" The leader-like one looks at the moon, which is hidden behind dark clouds. "*We had better return to Grag. He'll be wanting to know what we learned.*"

"*And what are we going to tell him, revrant?*"

"*That she's returned . . . and Agron will be his,*" the one snaps.

The four shadows converge together and disappear into the trees.

I count to sixty before releasing the breath I've been holding.

Who the hell is Trithar? Another of their leaders?

I discover Shade watching me intently, his eyes narrowing with a sudden realization. "What did they say?"

Now he remembers the other half of why I was so strange.

I grab his arm earnestly. "They're coming back. I don't know when. Tomorrow. Perhaps tonight. But they're going to come back."

"Why?"

I tell him half the truth. "They want Agron."

Shade nods and motions for the bank. We swim for shore, arms sweeping wildly in the water. I drag myself onto the pebbled ground.

He stares at me intently, blinking water out of his eyes.

"I'm not a witch," I say.

He smirks and my worries disappear. "Whoever said that?"

As we head back towards the village, all thoughts of running away disappear from my mind.

Everything that happened is because of me.

And, damn it, I'm going to make it right.

Chapter XXXV

The bell that Shade rang gathers everyone who isn't wounded into the middle of the square. The closely packed bodies add a warmth in the chill air.

A storm is approaching. Thunder claps in the sky and lightning flashes ominously as Shade details what we saw and heard. Almost as if spurred by the storm itself, Dirk turns white in the face and steps forward, hands clenched and ready for a fight. I knew this would not be easy but I'd hoped for once that Dirk could be wise enough to think first and ask questions later. Foolish me.

"She's a witch!" he roars, pointing a shaky finger at me. People draw back in fear, staring at my eyes, my arms, my lips. Do they expect me to call the demons from beneath their feet to speed them to hell?

"A witch who saved Mama Opal's life and could save us all if you'd shut the hell up and listen!" Shade snaps.

The square goes deathly quiet as the crowd shifts attention from Dirk to Otis, who's just stepped out of the sick house. He's covered in blood from helping the wounded. His eyes are bloodshot, and he hangs his head as he walks straight towards me. The mob shivers in anticipation. They expect him to pronounce my sentence. Instead, he places a hand on my shoulder and pulls me against him into a tight embrace. My shocked gasp mingles with the crowd.

"Thank you," he whispers. Then louder, so the people can hear, "T-thank you!" His voice shatters, and when he pulls back there are tears in his eyes.

"Otis, let go of her!" Dirk warns. "She'll damn your soul, she will . . ."

Otis spins on him, drawing his Illathonian blade. It flashes silver in the darkening square. "One more word, Dirk, and I'll make sure you never speak again!" Thunder claps above him.

Dirk gapes at him, tongue wagging in his open mouth.

"Do you know what a miracle has happened tonight?" Otis asks. He doesn't wait for an answer. "In there," he points at the sick house, "six wounded souls were facing a horrifying, hell-cursed death. They were being eaten from the inside out by those soulless bastards. And we could do nothing! Witch? By gods, she's no witch! Do you know all six of them are alive, lying in there and breathing. They will walk. They will rise. They will live! And you want to kill her? By gods, just you try it. Take one step in her direction, even look at her wrong, Dirk, and your attempt at attacking her will end the way it should. One more accusation, one more curse, and your blood, not hers, will stain the ground!"

"You dare . . .?" Dirk shivers with rage. The crowd is just as stunned. "You speak that way to me? Me? I am only looking out for the safety of every man, woman, and child in Agron. She'll be the destruction of us all! There's something wrong about her. She's not human! There's evil inside of her. You must get rid of her . . ."

Shade steps up alongside me, static vibrating off of him. He draws his Illathonian blades and shields me with them. "One more word, Dirk, and . . ."

"And you!" Dirk turns on him. "You . . . You're so centered on what's between your legs that you can't even see it. She's blinded you, boy."

"Everything she has done is to save your worthless hides!" Shade snaps, to Dirk and to the crowd. "For gods sakes, Dirk, she saved that thing you call a 'son.' Shouldn't you, of all people, be indebted to her?"

"I owe no debts to demons!" he snaps and spits at my feet.

Shade surges forward, but I grab his arm. "Stop it! Stop it all of you! Do you not hear what I'm saying? They're coming back!"

The crowd stops murmuring. Lightning flashes across the sky and they all quake at his brilliant light. A clap of thunder follows the illumination. They look at me, as if I might be the one commanding its ferocity.

It fills me with anger. "You hate my kind – the Kelbans. Why? Because they locked you out. They built a Wall. They lie about you and you can do nothing. The Kelbans – they are cowards!"

The mob ripples with shock as I condemn my heritage. But I'm not done.

"You hate and fear the Kelbans. In the same way we hate and fear you. How are you any different from my kind? I know you are brave. I know you can fight. I know you live and die and battle with the horrible elements you have been left to face. You are the strongest people I have ever seen. I have lived among cowards my entire life. I have played politics with sleeping lions. I have defied the monster that rules my people. I have been thrown away like a toy that lost its use.

"I am like you. I am locked out. I am frightened. I hate. I fight. I struggle to live. To be strong. To conquer and remain victorious." I point a finger at Dirk. My skin vibrates with tension. "I am no witch. No 'demon prophet.' I am merely a lost soul struggling in this empty, power-play of life to find where I belong. I don't want to be a coward. I'm sure you don't either."

Dirk glares at me.

"The shadows . . . they want to conquer you. They want you to be afraid. They are taking your lives and your land, piece by piece. Is that what you want?"

"We can't defeat them. They always keep coming," says a man from the crowd.

"That may be true," I agree, "but I know something that none of you have ever known before. Their leader is coming."

Shade stiffens. I had declined to share that information with him.

"Their what?" Otis asks.

"They have a leader. He is personally coming to destroy Agron. If we can kill him, they will be weakened. We will show them that

Agron can fight. That Agron is still strong. Like you've always wanted. And, then, they might change their minds altogether." I highly doubt my last argument, but I won't kill the enigma I've placed over the crowd.

They are pondering my words.

"You are the evil that draws them here – like that boy in Gavrone!" snaps Dirk. "We should kill you!"

I raise a finger. "But there's the tricky part. *I* draw them here. You can use that to *your* advantage."

Axle appears out of the fray, his hands red twins to Otis's. "I like what the Kelban has in mind. The element of surprise. Any warrior, guard, or soldier would tell you that's half the battle right there at our fingertips. Will you throw it away?"

"We can rid ourselves of this pestilence, once and for all. We can be free of attack. We can send the rest of those hell-cursed demons the message that you will fight, and you are not simmering cowards hiding behind your Illathonian blades," I add.

Keegan appears behind his father. "Do you have a plan?"

Dirk turns on his son. "What are you doing, you fool?" he asks. "We should do away with her."

"On the contrary, she has a point. Witch or not, I don't want my carcass lying white and bloodless in six feet of dirt." He draws his own blade and steps towards me. Shade bars his way, eyes flashing with warning. Keegan shrugs and stands beside Axle instead. "Who else wants to live?"

People, warriors and common folk, make their way through the debating mob. One by one they stand in a straight line before Otis, drawing their blades, knives, or literally anything that resembles a weapon. I spot several boys younger than I, and a few women and girls baring Illathonian blades. Fresh tears stain their eyes. The blades must have belong to deceased family members.

Dirk searches for his own army. None join him. Glaring hatefully at me, he joins the line, drawing his sword. At least he'll fight.

"What's the plan, Kyla?" Otis asks. He hands me complete leadership in that brief moment.

I am in charge.

A smile splits my face. "Let's *reflect* on that for a moment, shall we?"

It storms all night.

The next day is foggy and wet with mist. The thickening air offers a cover of white clouds over the earth. It is in this natural covering that we lay the groundwork of my plan. My head spins as I give directions, mustering all the managing skills Mother taught for running my own household. I don't suspect she knew I'd be using them to provide framework for a battle one day.

My cloak sticks to my face in moist folds. It is going to be a long day. The shadows could come tonight. Or tomorrow. None of us must sleep. The plan will not work unless everyone is where they're supposed to be. There can be no warning bell. No sign of alarm. The trap must be foolproof.

Otis appears out of the fog. He presses a tin cup of something warm into my hand. I taste it and find it to be tea. It is Mama Opal's favorite. "Is she back in her house?"

He nods. "She returned a few minutes ago. River is helping her clean up the mess the shadows made. Curious that they would ransack her home and not any of the others, though. Her husband's things are all destroyed." There's suspicion in his voice. I suspect foul play too. The shadows decimated everything on the second half of the house. Jars shattered. Shelves irreparable. Documents ripped apart.

"I'll take charge here," Otis says, giving me a gentle push towards the wall. "Go rest a bit, Kyla. They won't be coming in this weather."

I wrap my cloak tight about me and step outside the wall. Boys and men are training for battle in the misty setting. Elder, more experienced warriors show the newest recruits some tactics in fighting shadows.

I recognize the sharp orders from a square that has been drawn in the dirt. Stepping through the crowd of eager children that has formed around it, I stand at its edge and watch as Shade instructs a young girl, barely fourteen years of age, in practical defense. She wields an Illathonian blade. Not Shade's. Possibly a dead brother or father's. In her eyes shines the spirit of revenge.

She won't die.

Shade looks up, sees me, winks, and goes back to his teaching. He took me two hours to convince him to offer a few sparring lessons to the less experienced fighters we'd collected, but he finally agreed.

I smile and turn to find Axle. I'd been told he was working on the main focal point of my plan. His inventive skills far surpassed those of average Wilds folk. He and Gazel, the healer who'd tried to prevent me from saving Mama Opal, were a matched pair, both addressing the positive and negative aspects of my plan until it was foolproof.

I find Axle halfway up one side of Agron's wall, nailing part of our plan in place. He looks down and grins when he discovers me watching him. "Turn you on?" he asks.

"Keegan would be more effective than you," I retort.

"I wouldn't doubt that." He finishes and shimmies down the rope he's attached to the wall. "Believe it or not, he's very popular with the experienced ladies. I hear he has quite a few tricks up his sleeves."

"None of them catch my interest."

Axle's eyes twinkle. "Ah, yes. I heard Shade's story of how you came upon these creatures of the night. At the falls, was it? Now, what were the two of you doing all the way out there, I wonder?"

"Minding each others business!"

"Which part of Shade's business were you minding?"

He ducks as I swing at him and grabs me from behind, gripping my wrists firmly so I can't hit him. "Alright, I'll agree that was a low-blow. If I let go of you, will you promise not to hit me?"

I nod. He lets go.

I kick him in the leg.

He yelps and hops on one foot for a few moments. "I should have known better than to fall for that one," he hisses between clenched teeth.

"Shut up, and show me what you've done so far."

I return to watch Shade and find him alone, cleaning his blades.

His hair sticks to his head in a damp pile of soggy strands. Droplets of water form on his eyelids and flicker on his lashes. I stare at him. He doesn't look up. His hand glides over the shiny surface of his weapon.

"When you finally decide to speak, I'll be leaving," he says. He places the sword atop the water bucket and looks at me in complete sincerity. "What is it that you need?"

I blink, feigning shock. "Is it so bad if I wanted to see you? Or are you not used to people staring at you?"

"Usually people only search me out when they want something."

"That's a twisted point of view."

"But true, wouldn't you say?" He winks at me. "So what do you want from me?" He steps around the bucket and comes to lean against the wall in front of me, eyes darting over my face carelessly. They drift to my lips. "Did you not get enough satisfaction last night?"

I draw back, putting a hand to his chest as he advances. His vest is open and my palm presses against the warm skin over his heart. It pulses beneath my hand and the outlined ridge of the dreadful white scar scratches my flesh. I pull it back immediately, a wave of heat wafting up my neck.

"Does it hurt?" I whisper.

He smiles. "It doesn't hurt when you touch it." He takes my hand and traces it over the zigzagging white line until I can memorize its shape. "It is rather ugly, isn't it?"

I push aside my cloak to reveal the ostracized scar. "Really?"

He smiles. "We're quite a couple, eh?"

I pull back, suddenly uncomfortable, and cover the scar with my cloak again. I hate looking at it. It is too dark. To horrible. It sickens me. It must sicken him too. I remove my hand from his chest and play with my fingers.

He stares at me, but doesn't say anything. The silence draws out until I'm sure I could thread a needle with its length.

"You'll be fighting with us, I presume?" he asks, returning to his sword and gripping its hilt. He swerves it in front of him. It radiates silver light.

I nod. "I'm borrowing one of Axle's vests since he's nearly as skinny as I."

"You wish," he grunts. He glances at my waistline. "If Axle were as thin as you I'd be giving him serious criticism on his diet." He walks towards me, blade at his side. "What will you use as a weapon?"

"One of Agron's stocked swords. A blunt knife." I count off the weapons on my fingers. "Oh, and maybe a frying pan from Mama Opal's kitchen."

"Hardly sounds like a credible list for survival," he remarks. He holds up the Illathonian blade. "You should have one of these."

I catch my breath. "As I understand, Shade, you told me one must earn such a blade. They are rare."

A strange smile flickers on his lips. "I think you've more than earned it, Kyla." He pries my hand open and presses the hilt between my fingers. "A million times over."

I stare at the blade – his blade – and can't think of anything to say. It's the same one that he used to save me back in Kirath. Its designs shine up at me and the blade gleams silver, washing my face in its light.

I throw myself into his arms and kiss him. His giving me the blade means so much more than mere protection. He's given me his life – his past – his protection.

He's given me *him*.

That night, I sneak into Shade's cot and curl into his warmth. We lie there, trying to remain silent, so we won't wake River and Axle sleeping nearby.

"Are you afraid?" Shade whispers.

"I'm always afraid." I brush a hand across his chest, feeling the heartbeat beneath his skin. "But not when I'm with you."

He sighs peacefully.

"Will you have nightmares tonight?" I ask, pressing my hand across his scar. It has become my favorite part of him – its what makes him *Shade*.

He leans over and brushes my mouth with his in a gentle caress. "You'll chase them away for me," he breathes.

We fall asleep kissing softly.

Chapter XXXVI

It has been two nights. We have stood, awake, all over the streets, hidden in darkness, waiting for the nightmares to appear.

They don't.

We sleep during the day, struggling to retain our energy. Others act out a scene of everyday life for the shadows if they are watching.

And then it happens. From my hidden spot in the shadows of a dilapidated cottage, the moon disappears behind gray clouds. The square is plunged into complete darkness. Dipping into the square from the sky, like gods, shadows quickly fill the enclosure. Wisps of fog flutter into the air as more and more land.

I catch my breath.

There are at least a hundred of them.

Beside me, Axle reaches out and brushes a comforting hand over the buzzing spot on my bare shoulder. My legs cramp beneath me as I crouch so low my chin touches my knees.

Across the square, somewhere up on the wall, Shade is hiding with a group of the experienced warriors, waiting for my order.

One word from me will change this village forever.

One word from me will either save or slaughter every man, woman, and child in Agron.

One word from me will fuel or end the attacks from hell.

Beside me Axle stirs, as the shadows begin to flutter towards the peaceful homes. Homes they believe are inhabited by sleeping individuals. Homes that will fall easy prey to them tonight.

I hold out a hand when Axle starts to stand.

Not yet.

The shadows stop landing. There are no more. They are all in the square. All waiting for their master's orders. All blissfully unaware of the danger that sits atop the wall they've just scaled.

I look at the sky. The moon peeks out from behind the clouds again, bathing the square in a dim light once more. It is not powerful enough to dissipate the shadows.

But it will be.

Soon.

I scan the caped figures, struggling to listen.

A shadow leans closer to one that is slightly larger than all the rest. "*Orders, sir?*"

"*When you find her, bring her to me. Leave no one else alive.*"

I recognize that deep, dark voice as the shadowy leader from my visions.

Standing, I draw Shade's Illathonian blade – *my Illathonian blade.* "NOW!"

Up atop the wall, Shade hears my order. Suddenly the square is surrounded on all sides by such a great silver light that it hurts my own eyes. The giant oval mirrors that Axle and Gazel spent hours situating atop the wall, reflect the light of the moon straight into the square.

The air fills with evil. Shadows scream and flit about as great clumps tear away from their bodies and drift away in the night. Dark fog fills the air, choking off some of the light. The monsters hurry out of the middle of the square where the light is, straight into the warriors that surround them on all sides, Illathonian blades drawn and ready.

The moon disappears behind clouds again. The square is plunges into darkness once more. The shadows revitalize themselves and pull their own blades.

I step into the open, the Illathonian blade casting pale light across my face. I hope I look frightening, with curly hair spilling around my face, the ostracized mark glaring proudly on my shoulder, and the powerful blade clutched firmly in hand.

The shadows draw back, rallying into a circle. Their shrieks of terror are replaced with rage. They realize they've been tricked.

"Don't let any of them escape!" I scream and plunge into the shadowy circle, swinging left and right. Clumps of darkness dot the sky above me. I let out a warrior's cry of battle.

The other warriors echo the same cry, and the battle begins.

All around me, shadowy talons reach for my skin. I hack them away. Darkness pushes against me more than once, tripping me, but my blade holds true.

"Kyla, duck!" I obey and Axle slices over my head, destroying the shadow attempting to come at me from above. Sweat dots his forehead as he leans over to catch a breath.

We look around the square.

Half of the shadows were wiped out by the lights. More are slowly dissipating into the sky. Still, they fight. Their leader is still alive.

I search the area for him.

The giant shadow is finishing off two warriors, his weapons of a very different make. They are like whips but, as if by silent command, they take the shape of a sword. The deception of the weapon is unique.

This shadow is not any normal shadow. He's something much more dangerous.

And, unlike in my visions, he doesn't reveal the talons from beneath his cape.

I move in its direction. Axle notices I've walked away and sees where my attention has gone. "Kyla!" he tries to grab at me, but two shadows step in his way, demanding his attention. "Kyla! Don't."

Five other shadows see the direction of my mission and dart in front of me, their own dark blades rivaling with mine. There are too many for me. One blade scrapes across my thigh, slicing through fabric. I gasp, and watch it bleed for a few seconds. One of the shadows gets too close, too quickly, and I take advantage of the moment, slicing it around the shoulders of its cape. It screams as the light blinds it and immediately drifts away into the sky like a stream of ink on paper. The remaining four energize their attack.

One shrieks again and dissipates into a black clump of smoke. Keegan steps up beside me, pressing shoulder-to-shoulder. "Need help?" he asks.

I really want to tell him to go piss himself, but when he slams the hilt of his Illathonian blade into the shadow sneaking up behind us and laughs at its pain, I know I need him.

I press back-to-back with him.

He chuckles. "Not half bad of a plan, by the way, Kelban? Are you sure your father wasn't a general instead of a High Lord?" He kicks a shadow away, and it falls to the ground, a raspy groan emanating beneath its hood.

"Well . . ." I slice at a shadow's shoulder, catching it off-guard, ". . . there is quite a bit of warrior's blood . . . in my family tree!" Two more shadows fall to the blade. My path towards the leader – Grag – is slowly opening. A few more swings of Keegan's wild maneuvers, and I will be able to reach it.

But with each frantic strike of my blade, Grag is retreating at exactly the same pace. He lays another warrior to rest on the hard cobblestones and casts furtive glances around the square. In every corner, shadows are screaming and fluttering away, lifeless, in the night sky.

The clouds hiding the moon are almost gone.

Grag turns and disappears over the edge of the wall, skating towards the forest.

He can't get away.

Keegan sees the direction of my gaze. "Kyla, no . . ." He tries to grab at me, but I slip between the two shadows in front of me and run towards the wall. Keegan tries to follow, but the two shadows prevent him from doing so. "Kyla!"

I peer over the rail of the wall and spot Grag's cape disappearing through the trees. Without a second though, I launch myself over the rail and twist and turn on the sixty foot descent. To my shock, I land as softly as a breeze on the ground below.

Ignoring the mysterious event, I rush into the forest, enabling all the tracking skills Shade drilled into my pulsing mind.

Grag . . . You are mine.

It is difficult to follow the shadow's trail in the darkened forest, but the Illathonian blade casts a faint glow on the forest floor, revealing patches of smashed leaves and broken vines. Shadows can't float forever, it seems.

I am gazing at the ground so intently that I almost walk straight into the stone building in front of me. When I peer at it more closely, it is nothing but a ruin. I raise my blade high above my head.

I am in the ruins of *Lithean.*

The stone relics rise up through the mist, eerily, and cloud my senses. Everything looks like a shadow now.

"*You were a fool to follow me, girl!*" The voice came from behind me.

I spin around, but there is only mist.

"*Speak. I know you can hear me.*" The voice is on my right this time.

"I'd of thought a grand leader like yourself wouldn't succumb to retreat." I glance furtively around the ruins, but I am blind to Grag's presence.

His laughter rises up all around me in unearthly echoes. I swing the Illathonian blade in circles around me.

"*That damned weapon can't protect you from me!*" A black talon slices out from the mist and my Illathonian blade falls ten feet to my right. I rush towards it, but another black wisp grips my ankle and trips me. I fall flat on my stomach. I crawl to the blade anyway and grasp it, stumbling to my feet once more.

Grag finally reveals himself . . . emerging from the mist like a creature of death coming to take me away. His two whip-blades slither at his sides, but I know they can harden into a solid entity in a matter of seconds. He is smaller than he'd appeared to be in my visions. Only seven feet tall.

But seven feet or twelve feet, he is terrifying.

He strikes at me with one of the whips, trying to curl it around my leg. I slip to the side in a fluid motion that leaves the whip grasping empty air.

"Don't test me, girl. I've grown tired of hunting you down. Make this easy for both of us and just let me cut your throat." He slices the whip towards me again. I duck. It hardens into spear-like form and dips downwards towards my head. I turn and it slams into the dirt, inches from my feet. I back away from it.

"*Last chance,*" Grag snarls, "*you let me cut your throat – or I'll cut you in pieces while you're still living and breathing to hear every tendon, every muscle, every bone rip apart.*"

Images of the grove in Brunt, where bodies had been tied to trees and tortured, fuels the anger inside of me.

My fingers find a rock, and I throw it at him as hard as I can. To my surprise, it doesn't go straight through him like I'd expected, but strikes him beneath the hood. I hear a sound that is very familiar to metal.

A helmet? A mask?

"*Bitch!*" Grag snarls.

A talon lashes from the mist and crashes into my side, throwing me ten feet sideways into a brick wall. My ribs crack against the hard surface, but I don't relinquish my blade. The next talon that strikes at my legs, I hack in two with all my strength. Grag screeches and the piece of darkness I cut off starts to wither. I watch in awe. It doesn't turn into fog like a shadow's wisps should. Instead, it hardens into a block that looks like burnt wood.

"*You shouldn't have done that,* Illverna!" A wave of darkness crashes into me, slamming me against one of the ruins. Stones crumble with the force of the blow, and I scream in pain as the rocks rain down over my body. A wisp of darkness wraps around my ankle and lifts me into the air. I try to kick at it, to no avail. It throws me. I come to a rolling halt against the ground, my shoulder crunching against a tree. Blinding pain sears my entire left side.

Grag looms towards me. "*You're a foul piece of worthless filth that should never have been created,*" he says as he wraps a hard talon around my neck and lifts me into the air again. I grasp the shimmering wisp tightly, but he throws me anyway. I roll to a painful halt, my legs throbbing from the impact.

"*You are meant to die,*" he rasps, kicking me with another of his dreadful, hardened wisps. I curl protectively into a ball. My rib-cage feels too tight against my lungs. "*You will destroy Ebonia if you are discovered.*" He pauses above me and flips me onto my back, pinning me to the ground with four talons on my legs and arms. He dangles one of his whip-swords over the curve of my waist, the rise of my chest, the dip of my throat. "*Our way of life will fall apart, girl.*" His black, gloved hand tightens on the weapon's handle. "*You are our doom.*"

"Kyla!"

No.

Grag spins around at the sound of his voice. I watch him tense as both Shade and Keegan appear from the mist, their eyes wide and alarmed. Watch his cape unfurl around him. Watch a black, wispy talon shoot from inside and pierce Shade's abdomen in a sickening crunch.

My scream sounds silent in my ears as I watch Shade crumple into a heap on the ground, his limbs loosening.

Grag turns his attention to Keegan. Keegan pulls his gaze from Shade's immobile form and raises his own blade, casting a shimmering glow of light in Grag's direction. The shadow chuckles, and releases me, aiming its poised talons in his direction.

Fighting against every aching cry of my body, I force myself to my knees and scan the ground. The mist. The forest. A dull silver light emanates in the distant fog of my surroundings. My Illathonian blade.

Shade's groan reaches my ears. Even from my present spot, I can smell his blood as it drenches the ground.

I stand and stare at Grag's retreating back as he angles in on Keegan. He strikes once. Keegan chops the talon in two. Rage glows in his eyes. Grag only chuckles.

Shade groans again.

This is the last time a shadow is going to hurt him.

I step after Grag, the pulse flaring to life in the palm of my hand.

This is the last time a shadow is going to frighten me.

From the mist, the dull silver light moves towards me.

This is the last time this shadow is going to breathe.

"Grag!" I snap.

Shocked at the sound of my voice, so close, he turns around and shrieks as we come face-to-face, less than a foot of space between us. Beneath his hood, silver flashes at me. I ignore it and raise my left hand beside my body.

Behind Grag, Keegan tries to take advantage of his distraction and strike. One of Grag's talons knocks him sideways next to Shade. He groans.

"You were right about one thing," I tell Grag, opening the palm of my hand, "I am *your* doom."

My Illathonian blade cuts through the mist, flying through the air by silent command. Its hilt slams into the palm of my hand. Grag has no time to attack, and I plunge the shimmering blade deep into his chest. He screeches, long, pained, and enraged, as his body decays around the light. His cape burns away, revealing the charred remains of a body very similar to a man, except for the silver mask where his face should be. I reach up and peel the mask away. The charred body decomposes and sinks to the ground in a pile that resembles old leaves. My Illathonian blade rests on top of it, its light dimming.

I stare at the mask in my hands, my mind throbbing with questions. But I toss it aside, and rush to Shade instead. I clamp a hand over his wound, blood leaking between my fingers. He's unconscious.

"Keegan," I snap.

He stumbles to his feet.

"Help me bind his wounds."

Once we've returned Shade to Agron and Gazel has assured me that his wound is not critical, I return to the ruins in search of the silver mask.

It isn't there.

Chapter XXXVII

The victory celebration that Otis insisted on having is unlike anything I've ever seen. Wild, pumping music rocks the town square and delicious scents from the tables lining its perimeter tease my nose. But, despite the gaiety, music, and food, I can't forget about the silver mask and Grag's form. He had looked so human without that cape and those cursed talons. Or had I been seeing things?

I'd allowed Grag to toss me around like a toy. I had planned on stabbing him from behind as soon as I located my Illathonian blade. But the improvised version of my plan hadn't been so bad.

Grag had been talking. He'd been giving me answers to questions that had been brewing in my mind from the day I entered this gods-forsaken land. Now, thanks to the boy I killed for, I may never have them.

"You're not smiling." Shade's soft voice hovers near my ear. "Does it still hurt?" He slides a hand to my side, against my hip.

"No. River patched me up. You?" I pat his abdomen. A bandage hides beneath his vest. He winces. "Sorry."

"I'd never fought a shadow like that before," Shade muses. "Their wisps are too harmless and weak to penetrate human flesh. But .. ." He shakes his head. "That one was different."

He had no idea.

"In all your years among them you never saw one like that? Even once?" I'd of thought with all the time he'd spent in their land he'd know everything about their hellish existence.

He shakes his head. "If you remember," he says in a low voice, "I was their slave. I was too busy trying to survive to document their appearances."

I lean back against the rail I've staked out, biting back a yawn.

"You alright?"

"A bit tired. Oh, and not to mention scarred for life, mentally and physically. You forget that was my first time. Battling shadows, I mean."

"Trust me," he says, an amused light flickering in his eyes. "I didn't forget."

"What's that supposed to mean?" I step towards him, clenching fingers into a fist. "Are you saying I didn't look like I was kicking ass?"

A voice out of nowhere startles us. "Actually you looked scared shit-less to me." Axle stands behind us, two wooden cups of liquor in his hands.

I glare at him. "No, I think that was you. 'Kyla. Kyla, don't!'" I mimic his last words to me before I'd gone for the leader, adding a high pitch for effect.

Shade chokes and grabs one of Axle's cups.

"It's a completely normal reaction when a scrawny, little girl – no offense – turns and says to you, while we're battling an army of sadistic monsters, mind you, 'Oh, I'm taking the leader.'" He grins despite the mockery. "Which, was kind of bad-ass of you, I have to admit. Are you sure you're not meant for me instead of Shade?"

Shade chokes on his liquor. "On the contrary, you're rather gangly for her."

Axle presses a hand to his chest and mimics an injured look. "Well, thanks, asshole. Nice to know I can count on a friend in time of need. And I am not 'gangly,' for your information. Gazel says I'm just more 'skeletal' than the rest of you."

"Okay, you're skeletal," I confirm. "Is that supposed to be attractive?"

Axle looks between me and Shade a couple times. "Damn, you guys, why are you both picking on me?"

"Trust me," Shade says, elbowing his friend's arm playfully, "I'm sure you've done something to warrant it."

My stomach growls.,

"I'll be back," I mutter. They hardly pay any attention to me. They're too busy exchanging insults.

The food tables are stacked high with meats, fruits, and simmering veggies. I pluck a wing from the gorgeously prepared tray and take a bite. It melts on my tongue.

"Having a good time, honey?" Mama Opal loops an arm around my shoulders. No sooner had she woken from her deep eight-hour sleep then she'd been back on her feet. She'd been slow and pale, but refused to rest while others needed her help. With her home ransacked, she'd had to borrow supplies from other Agron women, but she'd made her special medicines and teas. The wounded had appreciated her kindnesses.

"You should be resting, Mama," I chastise.

"Enough of that. I've had Otis, Gazel, Shade, and anyone who participated in your brilliant plan telling me that I need to sit down and breathe. Well, they can take their advice with them and shove it . . ." She pauses before she says something unladylike. "You understand, honey. Of course you do. Why, you lead the charge, for gods sakes. Who knew when you came here, shivering and scraggly, that you'd be so brave. You're a miracle, honey." She pulls me into a tight, warm hug. "And," she whispers, "bless you, child. For saving me."

She releases me, wiping something she insists is a speck of dust from her eye. "Well, go have fun, Kyla. If I may be so bold there's a young gentleman somewhere in this crowd who I've never seen tapping his toes, and I'm sure he'd be the perfect partner for you. That fellow's got so many secrets I wouldn't be surprised if he could move his feet properly." She hurries off towards Otis who is standing nearby trying to appear like he wasn't watching Mama Opal's every move.

I am returning to Shade when someone grabs my arm and pulls me into the darkness of a nearby alley. My eyes adjust, almost immediately, to the darkness and locate Keegan's face.

"Let go!" I snap, tugging on my arm.

He does, throwing me into the stone wall of the alley. He leans in close and cages me in with both arms on either side of me, forcing me to stare straight at him. His eyes sparkle with grin fire. "What the hell are you?" he growls.

My chest pumps madly. "I don't . . ."

"I saw you!" he snarls. "I saw you kill it!"

Fear spreads cold claws around my throat. "Have you been eating frassas *root* again?"

He blows into my face. There is no scent of the drug on his breath. "I'm as sane as I was when I watched that blade fly through the air and land in your gods-damned palm! You better have a hell of an explanation. And, please, save me the innocent, little girl tricks that you've used to deceive everybody into believing you're Agron's savior."

I remain silent.

"I want an explanation, *vugra,*" he snaps, grabbing my throat in his big hand and forcing me to look at him, "now! You owe me that."

"I don't owe you a damn thing!"

"No?" He releases me and steps back, gesturing wildly at the alley around him. "I've kept your secret for almost twenty-four hours. Twenty-four hours, Kyla, sitting in a dark room, contemplating if I was going insane or not. If what I saw really happened. If I should tell my father and give him a reason to cut your throat, once and for all."

I should kill him. I should bash his head against the stones and make it look like an accident. But self-control stays my hand from lashing out.

"Why haven't you?"

"Because, damn it, it doesn't make sense!" he snarls. He runs a trembling hand through his blonde locks, that hang wildly around his face. "You're not what you're supposed to be! You . . ." He pauses long enough to catch a breath. "You saved my life! You weren't supposed to do that. You were supposed to let me die. You were supposed to hate me enough to watch me die with a smile on your face. That's what my father says about your kind. About demons. But you . . . you saved me. You saved Agron. You . . . Damn it, what am I supposed to think about you?" He slams a hand against the wall in a rage. "Y-you're a demon. I know it. I should kill you." He stares at me. "Shouldn't I?"

"I prefer to live."

He snorts. "Of course you would." Blood clots against his knuckles where the stone sank into his flesh. He wipes it on the edge of his tunic. "And since you saved my life, I'm going to give you a chance."

He cages me in with his arms once more, leaning over to press his lips against my ear. I don't dare move a muscle.

"I'm going to give you twenty-four hours to get out of Agron and as far away as you can before I tell Otis and my father exactly what I saw. Otis may praise your name now, but even he won't be able to stop my father and a hundred others from coming after you. If you head towards the desert wastelands you may stand a chance of survival with those cursed skills of yours." He pauses, his lips trembling against my ear. "If they do not catch you, they will send word to the king. He will hire mercenaries to hunt you down. He will not kill you. He will use you. He will force you to feed his ambition. You'll be a bird in a cage. A slave. And I may have hated you once, and I may fear you now, but you don't deserve that."

He pulls back, leaving me weak and trembling against the wall, because he's right.

I've known for some time that I could never belong in Agron. But, just once, I thought if I tried hard enough I might build a place in this land for someone like me.

I was wrong.

"Remember," Keegan whispers, "twenty-four hours."

He backs out of the alley and returns to the celebration. I watch him fade into the darkness and sink to the ground, struggling to hold back the sobs that tremble through me.

I pack a satchel of my things – two pairs of extra clothes, boots, a blanket, a week's supply of food and water, and a flask of hunter's brew – and hide it in the forest just outside Agron's wall before sneaking back towards the celebration. I will not wander into uncharted territory without a weapon to defend myself, and my Illathonian blade is still leaning against the rail where I left it.

"There you are!" Shade finds me before I can slip quietly away. He takes my hand. "I've been looking all over for you. Where did you go?"

His hand – so warm, so comfortable – in mine strikes a chord deep in my heart. I will leave – after I savor one last moment.

I let him pull me into his embrace, relinquishing my hold on the sword – on the urgency to disappear – and rest my head across his shoulder. "You don't want to know," I whisper and run a finger down the curve of his jaw playfully. His skin is rough beneath my touch. "And what could you possibly want to do with me anyway?"

He spins me around to face him, pressing me against his chest tightly. "You've no idea all the things I want to do to you . . ." He leans down to whisper in my ear. "*Alone.*" He lightly nips at my earlobe.

It takes every ounce of willpower within me to push him away instead of pull him closer, into the darkness, with me. "Swim?"

His eyes darken with thrilling intent that sends spirals of heat circling into my gut. "Swim," he agrees.

The guards let us pass, warning us to be back in two hours so they can close the gates, and we walk, hand-in-hand towards the pool.

The moon is full when we reach the pool and casts a white reflection across the base of the mountain. Stars twinkle in the water. We swim until our limbs are numb with exhaustion and finally take rest on the bank.

It has been more than two hours.

"You never intended to get back in time for the closing of the gates, did you?" I ask with a wry smile.

Shade turns to look at me. "No. I intend to spend the whole night out here, under the stars, like I should. This place is more of a home for me than Agron."

I shift onto my side and rub a hand along his arm. "Why?"

He sighs. "I spent years in a dark cell without the sun. Without the moon. Without the stars. Now that I'm free again, I could stare at them for centuries and the sight would never cease to amaze me."

I draw a lazy pattern against his side, teasing the ends of the lash marks on his back. "You know they make you look fierce, right?"

He follows my gaze to the edges of his long-ago wounds. "Fierce," he snorts contemptuously. "Or broken?"

"They never broke you!" I snap, angry at the thought. He winces when I accidentally press the fresh wound in his abdomen. "Sorry."

Shade turns onto his side, as well, and faces me. His gaze shifts to my shoulder. "You told me, once, that you thought it was ugly." He slowly brushes the lines of the scar with his fingertips. The scar tingles expectantly. "Would you believe me if I told you it makes you so beautiful . . . so strong?"

I stare at him, unable to form words. Beautiful? Such an ugly black mark . . . beautiful?

He leans in and presses his mouth against the burnt, scarred flesh in a tender kiss that stirs a wave of heat, ice, and ache inside me. His hair sweeps across my skin as he trails soft, little kisses up my collarbone to my neck and back down to the ostracized scar. I sink my fingers into the sand at my sides as the waves surge into a storm within me. His kisses become passionate. Stronger. Harder.

"S-Shade . . ." I moan and he covers my mouth with his own, devouring the passion that rises in my throat.

I run my sand-filled fingers through his hair, pulling him closer until there is no more space between us to fill. He breaks away from my lips to play with the curve of my neck.

Oh, gods, I can't do this.

"Shade," I say again, "did you really mean it when you said you felt alone in this world?"

He kisses me again – hard and insistent – and I almost forget the question I asked. "I'm not alone when you're with me," he says, breathless.

He should come with me. We could survive together – no need for people, Agron, or the Wilds – just the two of us.

"Shade . . ."

We both hear it at the same time. Metal sliding against metal. A raspy order in the darkness.

Shade dives towards his blade, which he dropped beside the pool, but two shadows grab his arms and have them bound behind his back in a matter of seconds. He lets out an enraged cry, tinted with fear, and one of his captors slams the hilt of his blade into Shade's gut. Shade doubles over, coughing for air. Blood drips onto the sand.

There are too many for me to count all at once. They surround me, their capes fluttering against the harmless moonlight and their dark blades gleaming. One of them steps towards me. I scurry to my feet, scanning the forest, but knowing full well that no help will come.

I should have run when I had the chance.

The shadow reaches out and grips my jaw with a gloved hand that is so cold it might as well be carved from ice itself. It roughly jerks my face to the side, clawing at my neck. Its fingers grind against the two little indents behind my ear. Satisfied, it releases me. I wipe at the icy sensations on my skin, resisting the urge to vomit.

"She's the one," it says in a deep voice, devoid of any rasp. If it weren't for the dark undertones, the voice might sound human.

Strong hands tug my arms behind my back and bind them before I can struggle. I am jerked back against a rough body and a bag is thrown over my head, blinding me.

I can blow them apart with a single twist of my wrist. I can destroy them with a snap of my fingers. I can free myself with a single thrust of my palm and run.

Run where? Back to Agron where, in twenty-four hours, I will be murdered because of what I can do? Run towards another wasteland where the elements will kill me, or I'll be hunted like a rabid beast? Run towards Smoke where the king will use me, or back to Kelba where my people will kill me or . . .

Or let these monsters drag me to the one place that remains a mystery to me?

I clench my fingers into tight fists.

I let them take me.

PART FOUR

Ebonia

Chapter XXXVIII

It is hours of being lead by iron hands in a strange, zigzag pattern that throws any chances of tracing our direction into oblivion. And, to make matters worse, I know they're doing it on purpose. They know who I am and there's no way in hell they don't know who Shade is. They won't risk letting one of the most fearsome hunters of their kind pinpoint our direction.

The shadows grunt harshly at one another from their throats, but they don't speak.

The terrain dips unexpectedly and the air around my arms and legs changes from moist and warm, to damp and chilly. The ground is harder beneath my feet too.

We walk for another hour before one of the shadows harshly shoves me to the ground and I hear them setting up camp. The noises they make echo before fading into nothingness. When they rip the bag from my head, I know why.

We're in a cave. A tunnel, actually.

The shadows – eight of them – gather around an iron circle hammered into the ground. A fire is burning. It imprints their shadows against the walls, making me see double their actual ranks. How can shadows have shadows?

Shade groans from behind me. I turn around.

Slowly, he uses his shoulder against the wall to rise to a sitting position, and look around. The terror that fills his eyes cuts deeper than a blade in my heart. I've never seen that cold, frightened twist in his face before.

I shift my eyes to his abdomen. His shirt is coated with dried blood. "Are you still bleeding?"

He doesn't say anything.

"Shade?"

He's staring at the shadows.

They're staring right back. Watching. Listening. Waiting.

"Shade, look at me! Look at me!" I tap his leg, gently, until his eyes flicker to mine. "Are you still bleeding?"

He shakes his head.

The shadows start conversing again – but with guttural sounds from their throats.

Shade shifts towards me at a snail's pace but finally manages to brush up alongside me.

"What are they saying?" he asks.

"Nothing," I whisper furiously. They know I can understand them so they're using a different form of communication. "Bastards!"

One of them chuckles. "*Trithar sure likes them sassy and . . .*"

Another snarls at him. He doesn't finish the sentence.

There's that name again. *Trithar. Trithar. Trithar.* I let the name roll around in my head for a few minutes. It is foreign and dark, but strangely elegant.

Shade burrows his face into my shoulder, his cheek cold against my skin. I wish I could run my fingers through his hair or wipe the blood from his face. But, with my hands tied, the only comforting action I can offer is to lay my head against his and shiver at the soft static of his hair brushing my cheek.

"They won't break us. Hear me?" I whisper, even as every nightmare I've ever had about the monsters comes crawling back into my mind.

He doesn't say anything.

Our captors pull us to our feet a few hours later and we walk. They don't put the bags over our heads. There's no need. The caves are too dark and there are too many tunnels – we would never find our way out again in time to escape.

I am shoved to the front of the line, behind a single shadow, much taller and stronger in appearance than the others. Its cape doesn't quite brush the floor and the clip-clop of shoes resounds off the walls.

Odd.

"Where are you taking me?"

No answer.

"Have you no tongue?"

Silence.

I grab the shadowy folds of its cloak and jerk it back against me. It snarls and spins on me, slamming me against the wall. From somewhere in the back of the assembly line, a feral voice growls. I claw at the black leather hand that cuffs my throat.

"*Behave,*" the male voice warns. "*Understand?*"

"Where the hell are you taking me?"

I catch faint glimmers of silver from beneath his hood. A mask – just like Grag's. What is behind it?

"*We're not going to kill you, girl,*" he says. "*Just behave.*"

He lets go of me and straightens his cloak.

Once again, I stare at the silver mask beneath his curtained helmet. "What are you?"

He doesn't give me an answer.

We continue walking.

Up ahead, a light blinks in the long tunnel, pure and bright. Our pace slows. The leader notices and turns around. The remaining shadows hesitate to approach the opening.

"*If you insist with your slagging page I will let you explain to the emperor why the journey took longer than necessary,*" the leader hisses.

Emperor?

The shadows start moving again.

We reach the opening. A wide space of dark, stormy sky and shards of yellow light greet us. We are standing on a ledge, overlooking a long, dark plain below that rises in jagged hooks, claws, and ridges that create a maze of boulders beneath me. I look at it more closely and a wave of shock rolls through me.

It *is* a city. The dark plain is split in two, revealing levels of hollow black rock beneath the surface. In the hollow black rock, buildings have been erected from stone and dark figures skate between them like ants. Shadows. And, rising above the dark city, at the edge of the steep plain and high above a stormy sea, a black, glistening mountain points a jagged fist at the sky. No, it is not a mountain.

It's a palace.

I shake my head in disbelief.

They are monsters. They're not supposed to have a city. They're not supposed to have a palace. They're not supposed to have any civilization whatsoever. They're supposed to be living nightmares that feed off of fear and thrive in their lonely existence. But . . .

What the hell?

The shadows don't lead us towards the city. Instead, we crawl down the rock outcropping of a stairwell in the side of the mountain and enter a damp tunnel once again. As we walk deeper and deeper beneath the earth, a vulgar stench taints the air. Sewage. Blood. Decomposing bodies. Vomit. Fear. *Death.*

Up ahead, a door opens as we approach. The air beyond smells even worse than the tunnel. Through the darkness, I see rows and rows of hard, gray bars.

A prison!

We stumble into the new tunnel, lined on all sides by bars and torches, through which I see emaciated shapes. They lie on their sides, against the walls, or curl into corners. As we walk further down, the shapes change into horrible forms. Some look like animals. Others are monstrous beasts that growl at the edge of the cells.

A handful of six inch talons slashes at my ankles.

I scream and leap away from the cell.

The shadow leader stomps on the monster's talons. They snap beneath the weight and the paw disappears with a pitiful moan of pain. We leave the monsters behind.

Now the shapes that hover behind the bars drool loudly, their feathery white fingers clutching at the shadows that pass them. They are shadows too. From the slobber pooling on the floor I believe they're drunk. If it's even possible for shadows to get drunk, that is.

We are forced to take a harsh turn to the right. The cells around us are empty. The horrible smell in the air fades. I still smell sewage, blood, and vomit, but it is not as overpowering as before. Or maybe I've just gotten used to it.

The leader opens one of the cell doors with a gnarled key and shoves Shade and I inside. I shiver against the damp chill hanging amidst the walls.

Several of the shadows snicker at Shade as he collapses against the farthest wall and turns his back to them. They flutter away, still chuckling.

The leader reaches through the bars and cuts the bindings on my wrists with a single slice of his gleaming, black knife. "*My name is Roke*," he whispers. "*Remember that, Ilevrana, when we meet again.*"

He walks away.

I hurry to Shade and rip the leather bindings from his wrists. He doesn't move when I place a hand on his shoulder and shake him. He doesn't answer when I say his name. I start to turn him around, afraid he's passed out from loss of blood, but he shakes free from my grip and stands up. He paces back and forth, combing fingers through his disheveled hair.

"Shade . . .?"

His answer is an irritated growl.

I stand up. "Shade . . . stop."

"Stop what?" He looks at me. His eyes are wild and maniacal. He looks more like a caged animal than a human being. "Stop thinking about what they'll do to us. Stop looking at my surroundings. Stop smelling the air around me. Gods damn it, Kyla, we're not in a damn nightmare or a forest clearing. We're in their territory! Their cage! Do you know what that means?"

"This is what they want us to do," I snap. "They want to frighten you!"

"Frightened?" He shakes his head. "No, Kyla, I'm terrified."

He peers through the bars of our cell.

From far down the tunnel, I hear screams. Horrible, human screams.

His fists clench at his sides. "They won't break me!" he snaps. "I'll kill myself before I let them torture me again!"

An hour hasn't even passed before footsteps ring far down the tunnel and raspy chuckles approach our section of the prison. I scoot into the darkest corner and pull my knees up to my chest. Shade is curled in the opposite corner, but when the shadows stop in front of our cell and look in at us, he stands up.

The shadows stare at him, their hoods pulled back just enough to reveal ebony masks and their eyes – deep black eyes. I don't like what I see in those eyes.

One of the shadows unlocks the prison door and steps inside, gesturing for his comrades – three of them – to follow him.

The ominous tingles at the base of my spine put me on edge.

They close the cell door and approach Shade. He doesn't move. Doesn't blink. He just watches them through narrowed eyes, fists clenching behind his back. Fists clenching for a fight. For survival.

The daring one – the one who'd unlocked the door – steps closer than the others. "*Eat shit,* Ilkanari!" he snarls and slams a gloved hand into Shade's abdomen. Blood coats his leather knuckles when he draws them back and a red circle blossoms over the crusted copper color of Shade's vest.

The three others kick and punch at him.

I stand up and launch myself at them, curling fingers around the daring one's cloak and tugging him backwards with such force we both fall on the ground. Searing pain splinters through my knee, but I have the shadow beneath me. Using the opportunity, I jab my fingers beneath its hood, where they meet with resistance. I claw at it with both hands. The shadow screams and, with a mighty heave of its shoulder, throws me aside. My hip explodes in a series of little shooting stars of pain up my side.

Shade screams. He's fallen to his knees, but they aren't stopping.

"Leave him alone!" I force myself to my knees, but the pain in my side prevents me from rising any further. "Stop!"

Blood spurts from Shade's mouth when a leather hand gives him a smooth uppercut and puts him against the wall. His head sags, and he falls to the ground.

Hot, pulsing waves surge into a storm inside my head.

One of the shadows screams as I lash out with my right hand and slam him against the wall with the heavy power radiating through me. The sickening crack his body makes on connection with the stone makes me smile.

The three remaining shadows come for me at once. I cross my arms in an X, locate their forms, and blast them aside when I unfurl my arms – and the power that I'd been converging.

The blast shakes the prison cell.

I hear a harsh voice. All four shadows stand to attention immediately.

Roke stands outside the cell, the door already opened, waiting for them to exit. When they do, he has them doubled over within seconds, clutching their midsections. His foggy talons creep back inside his cloak.

"*I gave you an order. I told you not to harm the* Ilkanari *in any way, didn't I?*" His head jerks in the direction of the daring shadow. "*And you dared lay hands on her too?*"

"*What's the matter with you, Roke?*" The daring shadow squares up. "*Have you gone soft all of a sudden? Don't you remember . . . remember what he did to us. All of us? He took everything from me! Everything! A little shit-eater like him doesn't deserve to live, let alone breathe our own air.*" He steps closer. "*Let me kill him.*"

"*No, Avril.*"

"*You know what he is!*" Avril snaps. "*You want him dead as much as I do. Just let me . . .*"

"*No.*"

"*Why not?*"

Roke cocks his head at me. "*Because he's hers. Can't you see that?*"

"*Who gives a shit?*" Avril jabs a finger in my direction. "*If you ask me we should kill her too. She . . .*"

One of Roke's foggy talons is around Avril's throat in less than a second. "*No one gives a shit about your opinion. No one gives a shit about you. Stop thinking that they do, and you might live a little longer.*" He releases him.

Roke turns and tips his head in my direction. "*Apologies.*" He turns back around to face the trouble-making group. "*You're still here?*"

They hurry down the tunnel, trying extremely hard not to make it obvious that they're eager to get away.

Avril flicks two shadowy wisps in my direction before disappearing into the darkness of the tunnel – a silent threat of things to come.

I hurry to Shade and roll him over. He's out cold, blood and bruises coating his face and neck. I open his vest and wince at the open wound spitting blood down his sides.

"*Does the* Ilkanari *live*?" Roke asks.

I tear the bottom of my tunic and press it against his wound. "Go away!"

When I turn around to face the silence, he is gone.

I return my attention to Shade, applying pressure to the hot pulse beneath my hands.

What had Roke said? *"He is hers."*

They had better remember that the next time they decide to touch him.

~

"*Kelban!*"

My eyes flutter open.

A different shadow watches me from behind the bars.

"*Kelban!*" it snaps again. "*Your name is Kyla Bone, is it not?*"

"Yes," I say.

The shadow sighs – low, soft and . . . relieved? "*Good. We won't have to dance around that subject,*" it says and places gloved hands against the bars. Its fingers are incredibly thin and there's something different about its voice. "*You've caused quite a lot of trouble for us, lately, girl. You've prevented us, on numerous occasions, from wiping a troublesome village like Agron off the map and your man there . . .*" She gestures at Shade, still unconscious against the wall, "*. . . has slaughtered thousands of us – recently with your help. You even defeated Grag.*" There is awe in its voice.

"Friend of yours?" The shadow's hands tighten on the bars. I can't resist smiling. "Accidents happen."

The shadow glances anxiously down the tunnel before speaking to me again. "*Actually, I'm of the opinion that he got what was coming to him. The arrogant son of a bitch had been floating on his own air for far too long. If you hadn't dispatched him, chances are I might have slit his throat within the next year anyway.*"

Now I realize why it's voice sounds different. The shadow is female.

I laugh in amusement. "I always wondered how you hell-cursed bastards reproduced. Never figured that some of you possessed the organs for such a *human* act. Do you lay eggs or birth through your legs like normal species?"

The shadow shows no sign of offense. "*You're hardly in a position to be giving me lip, girl. Do you realize that killing Grag already places your life on edge? He was Ebonia's greatest general . . . and you killed him. The people will be upset. His highness is grieved. And I . . . I regret that a little girl like you had to do it.*"

So help me gods, if someone calls me a little girl one more time . . .

"*You don't like feeling inferior, eh?*" she asks, noticing my irritation.

I lean against the bars. Within seconds I could show her inferior. I could blast her clear down the hall with one swipe of my hand.

"Go to hell!" I snarl.

"*Don't you want to know why Roke dragged you here?*" she asks, her voice taunting. She knows her words will dig deep into my skin. "*Don't you want to know why Grag was hunting you, and why he tried to 'rid you from existence?'*"

Shade stirs, and his eyelids flutter.

"I won't demean myself by talking to filth like you." I turn my back on her and approach Shade.

"*That arrogant pride is why fools like your Kelban stock, die*!" she snaps.

"And its because of heartless monsters like you that we're dying!"

The shadow shrugs. "*Someone always has to be the tale mothers tell their children at night. To protect what is theirs from those who would seek to take it. We have become monsters to protect our land.*"

"You broke the land!" I scream, the tether on my rage snapping.

"*We did not break this land!*" she screams right back, the darkness fading from her voice. Shivers skate up my skin. She sounds as human as I. "*If you want to know the truth, we hate the violence, the agony, and the fighting, as much as you. We want it to stop. We want peace. We want respect. We want justice.*" Her voice lowers, until its a soft rasp again. "*But you, of all people, know that world is nothing but a dream, don't you?*"

I don't like this. I don't like how she seems to know my innermost thoughts. My greatest desires. My worst fears.

And I don't like how, with each passing second, she becomes less of a monster and more of a . . . a . . .*a what?*

Human?

"Kyla . . ." Shade moans behind me. I hear him standing up.

The shadow glances between him and I for a few seconds. "*Take note, Kyla Bone . . . what do you think our history books say about your kind and his? As I understand, you've always tried to look for the truth hidden behind fancy words and foppish tales. Open your eyes and look for the truth behind what you've been told about us. I guarantee you, it's easier than you think.*"

"Kyla!" Shade gasps from behind me. He yanks me away from the bars. "Don't touch her, hell-cursed bastard!"

I hadn't even noticed her soft and comforting touch on my hand, until it is gone. It leaves a chill on my skin.

"Did she hurt you?" Shade asks, grabbing my hand.

I see the female's knife flash in the dim light before it strikes Shade across the shoulder. Blood runs down his arm and he gasps. She chuckles.

Hot anger pulses through my arms.

When a blast of my power strikes her full in the chest, intended to splatter her against the wall, she remains upright, her cape flaring back to reveal a solid body beneath it – two arms, two legs, and a torso. All human. All flesh and blood.

"*Interesting,*" she musses. "*Very interesting.*"

She turns and walks away.

Shade clasps his arm tightly. "What the hell . . ." he growls.

I pull his hand away and examine the wound. Relief whispers through me. It wasn't a shadow blade that cut him, thank the gods!

"What did that thing want from you?" Shade asks, suspicion in his voice.

Open your eyes.

Open your eyes and see the truth.

It's easier than you think . . . open your eyes.

"Kyla?" Shade lowers himself beside me. He puts a hand on my shoulder, over the ostracized scar, and brushes it gently. "Kyla, look at me."

I do.

"It's going to be alright," he whispers and pulls me against him, wrapping arms around my shoulders. "They're not going to hurt you, understand? They're never going to hurt you."

He thinks I'm frightened. He thinks I'm afraid for my life.

He has no idea why.

When I open my eyes, I'm not on the cold, dank floor of a prison cell, but standing in the middle of a dark, candle-lit room with a glass roof sixty feet above my head. I stumble to my feet.

Never, in a million years, would I forget this room.

Moonlight bathes the Celectate's solar in silver glory. It reveals the dark fingers of dried blood coating the marble podium and the expensive floor tiles.

Celectate Wood never wiped my blood away!

Craig, his jaw tight, is standing in front of the podium, arms clasped behind his back. "What do you say to the charges laid against you . . . Landor Bone?"

My brother stands before him, two guards flanking him, left and right.

What the hell?

"I'd call them barbaric lies, sir," Landor answers firmly.

Craig's eyes glitter in the dark room. "Would you?"

Landor doesn't flinch beneath the harsh gaze his former friend levels upon him. "Honestly, sir, I don't see why you'd be the least bit incredulous about me. I've been nothing but loyal to you through this entire ordeal."

"Loyal?" It comes out a harsh whisper. "Loyal to whom?"

Landor gasps theatrically and places a hand over his heart. "I'm deeply wounded, sir, by your lack of faith in my fortitude."

One of the guards next to him tries to hide an amused smirk.

Craig doesn't miss the action and snaps, "It is not your fortitude I find lacking, Sir Bone, but the misplacement of its efforts. You were the only one who had access to that cell, other than myself. Who else could have released the prisoner?"

There is a commotion from one of the solar's side-doors and Asher appears a few moments later, sword drawn and sweat glistening on his brow. "Craig," he gasps, "what are you doing?" His eyes flicker to Landor.

Landor's eyes lose their light instantly.

Craig notices. He turns to Asher. "Performing, with Celectate Wood's approval, an investigation of Sir Landor Bone and his involvement with a prisoner's escape."

"What prisoner's escape?" Asher stutters.

"The giant rebel, affectionately known as Scythe."

Asher's features pale.

Craig renews his attack on my brother. "I know you did it, Lan! I know!" He pulls something from his pocket and holds it up. It's a key, hanging from a blue ribbon. "Recognize it, Lan? Where do you think we found the copy I made? Come on, good man, take a guess!"

Landor's face has gone pale.

I want to scream at him, "What have you done?"

Craig's lips widen into a sadistic smile. "By the guard Scythe killed on his way out of the palace." He pulls another key from his pocket and dangles it next to its twin. They are almost identical except for the ribbons. One ribbon is dark blue. The other is light blue.

A trap!

Landor realizes it, too.

"You betrayed the Celectate and Kelba," Craig continues. "And why? For revenge? You sold your soul to the devil because you are unable to forget the past. Sadly, it is a decision you must pay for. Do you know the punishment for such an act, Lan?"

My brother just stares at him.

"Your rank and title must be stripped away as a Celect Knight," Craig says, "and your right eye plucked out as punishment for your lack of insight."

"Craig!" Asher gasps.

Landor says nothing – his jaw trembles slightly, but he doesn't flinch beneath Craig's hardened gaze.

Craig draws a knife from his side and steps towards my brother.

Asher grabs his arm.

"Let go!" Craig orders.

Asher holds on. "Don't do this, Craig. Please. He's our friend. He's ***your*** *friend."*

"He defied the Celectate."

Asher stares at him, shocked. "And since when did your loyalty to a man who cares nothing for you, become more important than your loyalty to your friends?"

"My loyalty has, and always will be, to the ruler of Kelba," Craig snaps, "and that is Celectate Wood."

"We were raised together. We fought, bled, and got drunk together. We were sworn in together. And now, because of one man who doesn't give a flying piss about your existence, you'll rip us apart?" Asher blinks back tears. "Why? Why, Craig?"

"He is my ruler. My only allegiance. My Celectate!" Craig snaps. He points a shaky finger at Asher. "And he's yours too."

"Like hell he is," Asher snarls. He steps in front of Landor.

"Have you switched sides?" Craig asks in a low, steady voice.

An icy prickle of nerves gathers at the base of my spine.

"My allegiance has never changed!"

"Asher," Landor says, "stop . . ."

"You say Landor sold his soul to the devil," Asher continues, "but you were the one who did that. And for what? For a title and rank you couldn't get through honest means? A title and rank you had to steal from Landor? Oh, don't give me that look, Craig. You and I both know you don't have the skill or the mindset to be a captain. So how did you get that emblem on your shoulder? By suckling up to his highness. By betraying your fellow countrymen. You'll always be the babe hanging on Celectate Wood's tits, dependent on him for every breath you breathe."

Craig's tone is still low and steady. "Have you finished?"

"Not quite. You've always been jealous of Landor. Jealous of his family. Jealous of his skills. And jealous because you couldn't have his sister."

"What?" Landor breathes, glancing between the two.

"Oh, did Craig never tell you?" Asher asks.

Craig's face turns red. "Don't . . ."

"He was interested in her from the day they first met. But he knew what you would say about it. He told me once, in a drunken stupor, that if he were Kyla's brother he'd be taking advantage of that authority. On the night she was imprisoned in the dungeons, awaiting trial, he went to the Celectate and asked for permission to 'fuck her'."

The air leaves my lungs in a collective gasp.

"You son of a bitch . . ." Landor snarls. The guards grab him around the shoulders and prevent him from approaching Craig. "You sick bastard!"

"Who's the real traitor now, Craig?" Asher asks angrily.

Craig sighs and blows a long, steady breath before unsheathing his sword. "I believe you are, Sir Rave."

Asher blinks. "What?"

"Well, I do think we all heard it, didn't we?" Craig asks with a wide gesture to the soldiers around him. "You insulted his highness and openly admitted you bare no allegiance whatsoever to him or that seal that rests on your shoulder. You have also interfered with an investigation's edict.

Step away from the accused, Sir Rave." He moves towards Asher.

"Like hell I will."

"Asher . . ." Landor says softly, eying Craig. "Please step away and . . ."

"And what? Let him harm you. I stood by and watched one of my friends suffer," he whispers. "I won't do it again!"

Craig stops in front of Asher. "Move aside, Sir Rave!"

"Eat shit!" Asher snaps.

I don't see it, but I hear it. The tear of flesh. The crunch of bone. The slice of metal. The whoosh of one's breath. The fall of a body.

And Landor's horrified cry.

Craig steps back, pulling his blade from Asher's abdomen, just beneath the rib-cage, and sheathes it at his side.

Asher falls flat, gasping. Blood bubbles from his mouth. Craig's strike had been intentionally painful – he punctured a lung.

Craig watches with cold, calculating eyes as Landor throws himself beside Asher and presses a hand against the wound. But the damage is too deep to fix.

Asher's hand fumbles with his tunic pocket and his fingers claw a folded piece of paper from its interior. The paper is yellow and worn with age. He slides it in Landor's direction, too weak to raise his arm.

Landor grasps it.

Asher's hand stops moving. A moment later his chest doesn't rise or fall. The only thing that moves is the blood pulsing from his mouth and the gaping hole in his torso.

My brother unfolds the paper, and his eyes darken.

Craig steps close, curiosity in his gaze.

Landor stares up at him. "Look!" He thrusts the piece of paper into Craig's face.

It is a sketch. A sketch of four people – three boys and a girl – standing side-by-side with smiles on their faces and their hands joined together. It was one of my very first drawings. Asher was the only one who would let me sketch him and when it was done, as a reward for his patience, I gave him the portrait. I didn't even know he kept it.

"This is what you've ruined, Craig Hale!" Landor snarls. He gets to

his feet. Several of the soldiers around him pull their blades.

"This is what you've lost!" He presses the paper against Craig's face, smearing blood all over his skin. Asher's blood. His friend's blood.

Craig draws back, wiping frantically at his face.

"This is what you threw away . . . for that!" My brother gestures at the emblem sewn onto the shoulder of his tunic.

"This . . ." Landor points at Asher, ". . . is what you destroyed, you fucking son of a bitch, for ambition!"

Craig kicks him hard in the groin.

Landor falls to his knees.

Craig kicks him again – this time in the head.

My brother falls flat on his back, a pained groan vibrating from his throat.

Craig jumps on top of him, pinning Landor's arms down with his legs. He rips the glove from his hand, and pins my brother's head to the floor with the other.

"Get off me, you son of a . . ."

Craig sinks his fingers into the flesh around my brother's right eye. Landor screams. There is a wet, oozing noise, followed by a sickening pop.

Craig stands up.

My brother's eye sits in the palm of his hand.

Landor grabs his face, screaming, while blood pools around his head.

Craig calmly places the eye in his pocket before returning his attention to Asher's corpse and my brother's writhing form. "Get this filth out of here!"

I lose the vision in a sea of darkness.

Shade gasps when I launch myself towards the wall and slam a fist into the stone. My knuckles crack beneath the hard surface and blinding, white pain immobilizes my arm. I scream but it could never be loud enough or furious enough.

Damn Craig! Damn him to the lowest pits of hell and beyond! Damn him! Damn him! Damn him!

With each damnation, I pound a fist against the wall.

My brother. First my father, now my brother.

And Asher . . . sweet, kind, loveable Asher.

And that son of a bitch killed him!

Damn him! Damn him! Damn him!

"Kyla!" Shade tries to pull me away from the wall. I throw him off. "Stop! Kyla, stop it!" He grabs my fists , spreading his hands over them to prevent me from punching the wall. I don't stop. He hisses in pain as I slam his own hands into the stone. "Kyla!"

Slowly, the fury fades, replaced with a heavier feeling of despair. And the memories – oh, gods, the memories. Asher, toasting to my success when I mastered the dagger. Asher, blushing whenever I patted his arm or said something kind. Asher, insisting I join them for a "night on the town" whenever I was feeling down. Asher laughing. Joking. Singing.

And my brother – his eye! Oh, gods, his eye! I think of the pain he must be in. The terror, the grief, the guilt that must be ripping him apart. I should be there with him. Gods dammit, I should be there!

I sag against Shade, heaving silently. I sink to the floor, bringing him with me.

"Shade, he's dead. He's dead!" I wail.

"Who's dead?"

I turn around and press my face against his chest, hiding the terror on my face. "He's dead!"

I don't know how long I lean against him like that.

I don't know how long I utter that single phrase.

I just know it will never be long enough to forget what happened or change it.

Chapter XXXIX

The female shadow returns the next day.

"*Come*," she says and unlocks the door. It swings open.

I stand up. Shade remains with his back against the wall, watching the shadow with critical, predatory eyes.

"Where?" I ask, equally suspicious. There's something different about her walk. Something . . . excited?

The shadow throws back her hood to reveal the ebony mask beneath and black, glossy waves of straight, sleek hair. "*To the answers that you seek.*"

I go with her – but I take Shade with me.

A door opens in front of the long, prison tunnel and the female shadow helps me ascend the cold stone steps that stretch thousands of feet in the air. There are so many different staircases around us that my head spins. How does this thing remember where to go?

The shadow opens another door at the end of our staircase.

We stand in a large hallway where the ceiling stretches so high above my head I have to crane my neck to see it. Black, glossy pillars envelop us on all sides, giving the hall a regal appearance.

And there is light. Beside the pillars to my left the ground drops away violently creating a ledge. A thin black curtain floats down from the ceiling to brush against the drop-off. The sun shines through the curtain, offering a dim example of its brilliance.

Shade gasps, and I turn to see what's astonished him. The shadows are no longer shadows. Their capes float about them as usual, but any fog that floated around them has disappeared. Beneath the hoods, their masks gleam in the faded light. Shade stares at them in horror.

Has he truly never seen them like this?

The shadows lead us through the pillared hall into another room. This room is different from the rest. The floor shines like black glass and the walls are carved with intricate shapes. The ceiling is closer to the ground; thirty feet instead of a hundred. A large stairwell, wide and shining like dark glass, ascends upwards into another pillared hallway lined with doors and stairwells leading to gods-know-where.

I tap my toes against the steps. They are stone, but I've never seen any stone like it before. It ripples as my shadow passes above it.

The hallway is long, stretching a hundred yards at least, before ending in front of intricately designed double doors, twenty feet high.

The female shadow removes her hand from my elbow, tucking it back inside her cloak.

I could run if I wanted to. *I should.* I should escape or die trying. Shade would do it if he were in my position.

To the answers that you seek.

I look at the shadow.

She looks right back.

"Where are we?" I ask.

"*You wanted the answers to your questions, yes?*" she drawls quizzically, her voice sounding every bit as human as my own. "*The emperor has them.*"

"Is your emperor a giant?" I ask and gesture at the twenty-foot doors.

The shadow chuckles and raps her knuckles sharply against the doors. "*See for yourself.*"

The doors swing open. I enter another large room. The ceiling rises a hundred – maybe two hundred – feet in the air and all along its surface are strange markings, strange symbols, and strange crystals marring its expanse. There is only one window – an oval circle carved into the roof, that allows a beam of light to brighten the middle of the room. Everything around the light, however, remains cloaked in darkness.

At the end of the room, six steps, shining like black jewels, stretch upwards onto a platform. A podium.

Shivers ripple up and down my spine.

This room – the design – is almost exactly like the Celectate Wood's Solar. The podium. The expanse. The eternal ceiling. And the oval window is exactly where the symbol of Calaisar would be if this was the Solar.

A dark figure stands on the podium, its back to us, its broad shoulders covered by a luxurious cape. The figure turns as we approach and when the cape flutters around him, I can't help but catch my breath.

If this is the Emperor, he is not what I expected. He wears no shirt beneath the cape. The muscles that line his abdomen are unnaturally tight. They look so strong I wonder if a sword could even pierce that hide. He wears dark pants that are tied around his waist with a simple, black belt. A short blade hangs from his side.

But it is his face that throws me. He is no shadow, even in the dark. His hair falls around his face, wild and untamed, gathering near his shoulders. He is clean-shaven. I admire the chiseled jaw. The straight slope of his nose. The hard press of his mouth. He looks like a human.

And his eyes – eyes of dark, untamed fire – why do they look so familiar?

The female shadow edges me into the light beneath the oval window. "*This is she.*"

The Emperor inclines his head to her – a sign of gratitude.

The female shadow turns to me. "*Kyla Kelonia Bone, this is Trithar of Darkness, Emperor of Ebonia, Slayer of the Wind-Bearers, Conqueror of Darkness, and . . .*"

"*Thank you, Trish,*" Trithar cuts in. "*I think she understands.*" His voice is every bit as deep as I expected.

So this . . . is Trithar.

And he's their damned emperor?

I flinch beneath the gaze he levels on me. He removes something from beneath his cape. "*I am told this is your work.*" He tosses the object at me. It slides to a grinding halt at my feet.

Grag's silver mask.

The sight of it fills me with pride.

I meet Trithar's gaze. "One less bastard in the world."

We stand like that, our gazes locked intensely, for a few moments, until the corner of his mouth tilts up in a half-smile and he turns to Trish. "*Did you tell her?*"

Trish shakes her head, her long straight hair gleaming. "*It wasn't my duty, sir.*" She bows, slightly, at the shoulders.

Trithar turns his attention to me again. "*Do you know why you're here, Kyla?*"

I open my mouth . . . and the sight of his eyes, once more fixated on mine, closes it. I have seen those eyes before. I know I have. The strange, dark depths . . . the starless night color . . . the sparkle of light within the pupils.

He steps towards me, each sound of his foot echoing in my head. Those eyes get closer. And with each foot of distance he leaves behind, a chasm of heavy, unyielding weight opens in my stomach. He stops at the edge of the circle of light.

"*Do you know why you're here, Kyla Kelonia Bone?*" he asks again.

Shade tenses behind me.

I squint against the light and study his face again. The strength of his jaw. The angle of his cheekbones. The slope of his forehead. And, once again, the midnight black hair that flows from his head in wild, untamed waves.

That face – those features – I've seen them before.

It hits me like the winds of a sea storm, and I can't breathe.

"Kyla!" Shade gasps as I stumble backwards and bump into him.

Trithar, noticing my distress, steps forward.

When he does, I draw back.

No! It can't be true! It can't!

Shade glares at Trithar and steps in front of me. His eyes glow furiously. "Don't come closer!"

Trithar takes another step.

Shade lunges at him.

The emperor extends an arm towards the advancing warrior.

Shade clenches a fist, preparing to smash the emperor's fine, chiseled nose into unrecognizable pieces.

Trithar flicks his wrist to the side.

As if lifted by a sudden gust of wind, Shade furls into the air like a ship's sail and lands, hard, against the wall! He sinks to the floor, dazed.

Shadows rush to restrain him.

The breath rushes from my lungs with one startled cry.

Shade lumbers to his feet, face red and etched with pain. He lunges for the emperor a second time. His feet drag uselessly against the floor as Trithar sends him skating down the room and smashes him against the wall – again – with nothing but the twist of his hand. Shade slumps to the ground, unconscious.

Trithar looks at me and sorrow taints his face. "*Elinor never told you, did she?*"

The sound of my mother's name – my mother's name so familiar on his lips – forces the breath in my throat to a shuddering halt.

Those eyes . . .

I recognize them now.

They are the eyes I see every day – in a mirror – staring back at me.

They are *my* eyes.

Chapter XL

To my credit, I don't faint.

Trish moves to Trithar's side again, pulling the hood back over her head. It ages her by centuries. "She's the one," she says. "She has your gifts and . . ."

"She knows."

They both watch me, warily.

I don't know what they're expecting me to do, but from the look in Trithar's eye, he's expecting violence.

Every blasphemous phrase in existence rests upon my tongue, aching to be unleashed, but I fight against that urge. It has become so hard to breathe. So hard to focus and think with that face – those eyes – staring back at me with shocking resemblance.

"Would you like to leave?" Trithar asks. He turns to Trish before I can even answer. "Take her to the room I prepared. See that she is fed and well-rested."

Trish grips my elbow.

"Wait!" I pull free and glance at Shade. "He comes too."

"That is out of the . . ." Trish begins.

"Of course." Trithar nods to several shadows standing throughout the room, and they carry Shade between them towards the door.

"I'll see you this evening, Kyla," Trithar says.

I don't dare look at him as I exit the room.

If I do, I'll shatter.

And I don't think anyone would ever find the pieces.

Trish leads me down many hallways, stairs, and sharp turns until we come to a beautifully carved door with an obsidian knob. She opens it and waits for me to walk inside.

Inside is more than just a room. It's an entire house on one floor. The first thing I see is a large fireplace with a sofa, a table, and a chair situated in snug decorum around it. A large, four-poster bed rests directly across from the door. Four doors take an immense amount of space along the north wall of the room.

"Bathing. Dressing. Studying. Private quarters," says Trish pointing to each one. She motions for Shade to be laid across the bed and waves the shadows out of the room. Her eyes rest longer than necessary on the shadow-killer, perusing his limbs, and particularly his hands. Hands that hold the blood of her kind.

Trish tears her gaze away from him and returns her attention to me. "My advice . . ." she says and steps towards the door, ". . . change your clothes."

The door closes.

My thoughts explode inside my head.

Everything has to be lies. Trithar of Darkness, Emperor of whatever he called this cursed land, is a fraud and a liar and . . .

And he has my powers. He has my eyes. He has my hair, for gods sakes.

Or is that backwards? Do I have his powers, his eyes, and his hair?

The fire crackles wildly as I walk past it, stripping the torn tunic from my body and throwing it on the floor. The dressing room Trish had gestured at is stuffed with clothes in all different assortments. I pluck a simple black shirt and a pair of dark pants from the collection. To my shock, they fit perfectly.

I return to the fireplace.

Trithar is a lying bastard!

Lord Gavin and Lady Elinor Bone are my parents. Sir Landor Bone is my brother. That is my lineage. That is my family. That is where I come from.

A pulse of leaden weight vibrates in the palm of my hand as if to say, *"Then where do I come from?"*

"To hell with you!" I try to force the weight from my hand. The sofa flips over on its side. "To hell . . ." The table flips. "With you!" The fire explodes, shooting sparks in every corner of the room.

The weight is still in my hand.

I close my eyes. I feel the distance I have put between the room and myself. I feel the disconnection with the physical world.

I open my eyes.

I am in the throne room.

Trithar is still there, standing on the podium, hands clutched behind his back.

Trish enters the room at that moment, her hood drawn back. The mask on her face gleams and she fixes her coal-black eyes on him.

"Trish?" Trithar says.

She stands at attention, her body gracefully straight. All around her, fog curls from beneath the cape and swirls around her hair. "Yes, Excellency?"

His brow creases up thoughtfully, and he looks Trish straight in the eye. "Will she accept it?" His lip quivers.

Trish looks perplexed and uncomfortable at the same time. "I don't know, Excellency."

"If Elinor had . . ." He cuts himself off, a far-off glitter in his eye. It is replaced almost immediately by a twinge of pain. "If she had told me I would have raised her. I would have. I swear by the gods I would have taken my child and . . ." He pauses, his eyes swirling furiously. "She wouldn't have had to live in a world she didn't belong in."

Trish nods solemnly. "She's lived her entire life among them – the Kelbans – and it won't be easy for her to adjust to the idea of being an Ebonian. She sees us the way all the others see us. Shadows. Monsters. Demons. Not a completely different race."

Trithar nods thoughtfully.

Trish steps closer. "What will you do if she turns you away and doesn't accept her lineage?" Her voice is laced with concern.

Trithar sighs, but answers without any hesitation, as if he prepared for this question. "She can refuse, but if she's my daughter she'll know . . .

she doesn't belong in any world but ours. The Kelbans and the Ilkanari will kill her when they learn what she is. She can't hide it no matter how hard she tries. Eventually her powers will grow stronger and she will be unable to harness control without proper training." *A deep, dark anger surfaces in his eyes. "They will destroy her for what she is."*

I jerk myself away from the vision. I don't want to hear anymore.

The pain hurts more than usual, like a whip slashing into the very core of my face.

From the bed, Shade moans. He's gaining consciousness again.

What will I tell him? How will I tell him?

My mother . . . why the hell did she never tell me?

Guilt? Shame?

Fear?

Had she been afraid to tell me because of how I might react . . . or had she been afraid of something else entirely?

Had she been afraid of *him*?

I look at Shade again. His vest is open and that white, zigzagging scar glares up at me.

They did that to him.

Trithar did that to him.

The shadow guard they've placed outside my door doesn't even know what hit him when I slam him against the opposite wall. He's out cold immediately. I relieve him of the black, glittering dagger at his waist and, closing my eyes, I search for Trithar.

He's walking down a dark hallway.

I follow.

Chapter XLI

Trailing the Emperor of Darkness is easier than I expected. He walks slowly, as if he's lost in thought, and this gives me time to catch up with him in the physical sense. I make sure to keep my footsteps light and my breathing natural. But as I get closer to him – as the physical traits that he and I share become more evident – that feat becomes harder. He even walks the same way I do with a firm, gliding step.

Finally, he opens a door on his left and steps inside, shutting it securely behind him.

I wait . . . One, two, three minutes before approaching the door, turning the knob gently, and stepping inside.

Even before I turn around the smell creates an ache in my chest. Paper. Ink. Old books. Firewood.

A library.

The room is a large oval area, a hundred feet in circumference, and rises into a ceiling twice that length, complete with glorious shelves full of hardbacks, scrolls, and portfolios. There is a fireplace between a couple of the shelves that gives the room a welcoming feeling. There is a couch, cushioned and soft to the touch, and a large, furry rug stretched out in front of the fire. Straight across from the door is an open walk-out leading to a beautiful porch made of the blackest stone. A black, translucent curtain has been drawn over the walk-out, blocking the sun's rays from entering.

But books . . . there's so many of them. Hundreds. Thousands. Maybe millions.

"Do you like it?"

His voice reminds me why I've come.

Trithar stands beside the fireplace, his arm poised and relaxed on top of the mantle. "Magnificent, isn't it? There is none like it in the world. It has taken centuries to build, but it was worth every one of them."

I stare at him, too startled by his sudden presence to say anything.

He smiles. "Didn't I tell you I'd see you this evening?"

Heat spreads callous fangs across my neck. He lead me here.

"I knew you would come to see me," he says.

"I've come to kill you." I reveal the dagger I've been hiding behind my back and point it directly at him.

He barely acknowledges the weapon and shrugs. "You wouldn't kill me."

"Why not?"

"Because," he says, stepping away from the fireplace, "you believe me."

There's no way. There's no possible way unless . . .

"My mother . . . you raped her?"

A feral growl rises in his throat. "Don't you dare . . ." He cuts himself off, and breathes slowly. In and out. In. Out.

Oh, gods! Everything he does reminds me of myself?

"Don't you dare make what happened between your mother and I into something evil," he says, his voice quieter – calmer – than before. "I loved her. *We* loved each other."

"Like hell she did. You're a piss-poor liar!"

"Well," he breathes, "you certainly didn't inherit grace from your mother's side."

I choose to ignore his statement. "You're a demon! A monster! There's no way in hell my mother would ever . . . ever . . . love something like you!"

"Something like me?" His tone changes. "What am I, exactly, Kyla? Do you know?"

As he speaks, his skin disappears and turns into white, shimmering mist. Beneath the mist, I can still see his body – completely human –

except for the hazy, unnatural phenomenon occurring with his flesh. The mist swirls back into his arms and torso. He is natural looking, once more.

"I . . . we . . . are as human as the Kelbans – with a few minor differences in regards to our anatomy. That is all. We are not demons. We are not monsters. We are people – flesh, blood, and bone. A race of gifted, ethereal beings that surpass the normal functions of the human species, but that doesn't make us evil." He looks at me. "If you think I'm a demon – a monster – then kill me!" He steps towards me. "Drive that blade through my heart. Pierce this flesh you say is wicked. Rid the world of another 'bastard', as you called it. Go on. Kill me!"

He is closer now. I could easily strike him without even moving. My blade would fly true. His blood would splatter the air. His eyes would lose their light. He'd fall, and I could forget any of this ever happened.

I regret not telling her everything . . .

If only you knew half the story behind your sister and what happened . . .

Kyla is where she belongs.

She hadn't cried when I'd been sent to the Wilds. She hadn't given up hope, even for a moment, that I was alive. She had been certain. Confident. How?

Kyla is where she belongs.

Everything I've known – all lies! Deceit!

My life is a lie!

"Kill me, Kyla."

I pull back my hand with a cry of rage and release the dagger. It soars past Trithar's ear and embeds itself in the ebony black wall behind him. He stares at it, confused for a moment, and turns back to look at me.

There's a commotion outside the door and Trish enters, a black blade in her hand. She glances between Trithar and I. The ebony mask hides any emotion. "Excellency . . ." She pauses when she sees the new accessory to the library wall.

"It's alright," he says.

She looks at him again.

Trithar raises his hand in an odd symbol – his thumb and forefinger fused together with another finger stretching parallel to them.

Trish mimes it back to him and slips out.

Trithar walks to the wall and examines the dagger. "I see you inherited some of your mother's talent." He pulls it free with a quick jerk of his arm.

I stare at him.

He chuckles. "She never told you that either, did she?"

"What does that mean?" I ask. I try to mimic the odd symbol Trish and he had shared. It is easier than I thought. It looks so familiar.

"It's the Imperial sign," he says. "In other words, the Ebonian sign for 'royals,' as Kelbans would call it. It symbolizes respect but it can mean other things as well. Comfort. A promise of things to come."

That sign . . . Mother had given me that sign before I'd jumped from the Wall's ledge into cursed territory. She had smiled. Smiled! Mysteriously. Confidently. She hadn't cried – she'd smiled.

What had she said to Landor when he'd talked about losing me to the Wilds?

That wasn't losing her. It was letting her go.

I know we will see her again.

You are your father's son. Just as Kyla is her father's daughter.

"*Her father.*"

Oh, gods!

She hadn't said "your father's daughter." She'd said "*her* father's daughter." My father. *Not his.* My father . . . a different man . . .

Kyla is where she belongs.

Where she belongs.

Everything is so clear and so shady all at once. "She knew you would find me," I say, watching Trithar move from his place by the wall to finally rest upon the sofa near the fireplace. I hesitate to join him.

"Do you want to know how your mother met and fell in love with a 'monster' like me?" He gestures at a chair straight across from him.

I sit down.

He stares at me for a moment, particularly at my shoulder. He must know about the ostracized scar even if I have hidden it well, but he doesn't ask me about it. "I was a wild and reckless heir," he says, "and hated the idea of being tied down. My father was weakening day by day. And a weak emperor is a curse to this land. I knew I was next in line. So I decided I would hide from my rule – just for a little while, that is. So I went to Kelba. I went to Kirath.

"All the stories I'd heard about Kelba didn't do it any justice. It was different from the life I'd known here in Ebonia. So much different. The change was good for me. But, slowly, I started feeling guilty. About leaving my father and Ebonia behind. About ignoring what I truly was and where I truly came from. And then I met your mother."

He smiles, but his eyes are full of shadows. "I was walking down a street in the high class part of town late one night. I'd been drinking at one of the taverns and listening to the latest gossip. Some mortar fell from the top of an overpass. When I looked up, a woman was standing on the top of the wall, arms spread out and toes teetering on the edge. It was Lady Elinor Bone."

I'm on my feet. "That's a lie! My mother would never think about committing suicide! You're a liar!"

He calmly motions for me to sit down. "She stepped off the edge . . . and I caught her with my powers and lowered her safely to the ground. I still remember how she'd looked at me. Shock. Confusion. Fear. Her sorrow and shame quickly replaced those first emotions. I'd tried my best to comfort her while she chastised herself for trying to take her own life. I knew of the Kelban religion and asked if she would like me to escort her to the temple and ask the gods forgiveness. Mind you, I didn't believe in such rubbish, but I didn't want to openly admit that. Do you know what the fine Lady Elinor Bone said? She'd looked me, straight in the eyes, and snapped, 'Damn the gods! I'm not fool enough to believe they'll interfere on the behalf of an insignificant human being like me.'

"Just like that," he snaps his fingers, "I fell for her."

Once, I wouldn't have been able to picture those words leaving my mother's mouth. But now, after my visions – after realizing my mother wore a mask and wore it well – I'd believe anything.

"Do you know the reason for her abrupt decision to end her life? Lord Gavin Bone and her son, Landor Bone, had recently boarded a sea vessel and sailed for the coast of Landor on some business for his eminent grace, Celectate Wood." He says the name with contempt. "Their ship sank. They were said to be dead."

Just like Mother had said in my visions – just like she'd told Landor. *If only you knew half the story behind your sister and what happened.*

This is the other half.

"I should have walked away. I should have left her. But I didn't. I came back. I attended the funeral of empty caskets, but kept to the shadows. I followed her home, in the shadows, mind you. There was no way I was going to let her see me after what I'd done. I had never revealed my powers in Kelba until that night. The fact that she knew about my unique abilities was reason enough to kill her. My father would have done it. I knew I should. I watched her approach the gates of that lonely mansion, and she'd paused. Turned around. Looked right at the spot I occupied in the darkness and asked 'Are you coming or are you going to make me stand here all night?'" He chuckles. "How she knew I was behind her – stalking her – I have no idea. She took me inside. She didn't waste time but got right to the point, immediately asking what abilities I possessed to save her. And, for some fool's reason, I told her.

"We saw each other often, after that. Secretly. She didn't want rumors spreading about a High Lord's widow consorting with a dark, shady gentleman of foreign birth. I didn't want rumors to spread anymore than she did. If word reached Ebonia of what I was doing – if word reached my father – he'd be livid and your mother would have been executed.

"We . . . our relationship didn't become one of passionate nature until a couple months later." He notices the accusations on my face. "*After* I told her everything about what I was and where I came from," he adds hastily. "And you know what? She didn't care. She told me she loved me."

I remain quiet, unsure about what to say. My mother loved him?

Trithar smiles, but there is no amusement on his face. Just a deep, dark pit of sorrow. "Only two weeks later, news arrived that a man and his son had been found in a distant trade city. Their names? Lord Gavin Bone and his son, Landor."

I don't miss the bleak feeling that takes hold of him.

"We both knew what we had to do. Despite our affair, despite our passion for one another, your mother still cared for Gavin. She cared about her son. And she knew that Gavin would never understand what had happened, and she didn't want to try and explain. We agreed it should be forgotten and we separated. I was there when the High Lord arrived home. I watched him hug her. Kiss her. And it hurt like hell." He sighs. "When word reached me by courier from Ebonia that my father was fading fast, I went without hesitation, leaving Kelba and Elinor behind.

"My father died. Two months later I became emperor. Five months after that, on a stormy night, you were born. And though I was not there in person to watch the delivery, I opened a portal between my mind and that room to watch you come into the world. I remember feeling so empty inside as I watched the midwife place Lord Gavin Bone's first daughter in his arms. You'd been so tiny. Beautiful. And your eyes – it was like the night sky came down and blessed you with their eternal glory. That should have been my first clue. But, like a fool, I believed you were Gavin Bone's daughter. The child the ancestors would never have blessed Elinor and I with. As you grew up, I would occasionally watch you and your mother. And, gods, were you a handful. Sass. Spunk. Boyish. Stubborn. But through it all, Elinor turned a blind eye. She let you grow up the way you chose. That should have been another giveaway. But your powers . . . they never showed up. If you were my child, you would definitely have them. They would have become evident by the time you reached your eighth year. I held onto that one hope. I even waited until you were ten. Nothing. I gave up. I stopped looking in. Stopped hoping. For seven years I kept the portals of my mind closed off from that portion of Kelba."

He looks at me again, tears shining in his eyes. "Word reached me that Grag, my leading general of the Ebonian forces charged with defending our borders, had been killed . . . by an ostracized Kelban girl with the mysterious ability to move objects without touching them. I opened the portal again and saw your mother. You weren't with her. I knew. I knew you had to be the one. I sent Roke to retrieve you, but I had to be sure. After all, you had slaughtered half of Grag's small force. Trish attempted to make you demonstrate your gifts – which you did perfectly."

In the dungeons she'd tried to infuriate me. She'd gone after Shade – my obvious weakness.

It had worked.

Trithar stands up. "The answer was in front of us both all along, Kyla. Elinor was a very sly woman. She hid your true origins in plain sight and neither of us was clever enough to figure it out."

I stare at him blankly.

"Your name," he says. "It's unique, yes? Say it. Say it out loud, daughter, and listen to the words."

"Kyla Kel . . ." *Oh, gods!*

Kelonia. The middle name that everyone had thought was strange. The middle name that had no meaning, whatsoever, except to sound strange. The middle name I had thought was a cursed joke.

Kelba.

Ebonia.

Kelonia.

The truth of my birth, my heritage, and my ethnicity hidden in plain sight.

A particle of two worlds, combined.

One simple word held all the answers to my existence.

Trithar laughs when I look at him. "Clearly, your mother is the smartest woman alive."

Quietly, I agree with him.

But there's something not right. Something still nagging at the back of my mind. He said he'd closed the portals between my mother and himself. He said he hadn't looked in seven years. But Grag . . . Grag had known about me. Grag had been hunting for me. Grag had tried to kill me.

How the hell had Grag known who I was?

I turn towards the man who calls himself my father and brush the hair aside. "Do you know what these are?"

I watch his face change to dark, suppressed rage when he sees the scars. "Where did you get those?"

Does he truly not know?

"Four years ago you sent your shadows or Ebonians or whatever the hell you call them to kill me and my father . . . to kill me and Lord Gavin Bone!"

The rage on his face gives way to shock. "I . . . did what?"

"Don't you dare deny it. Who else could have known, but you? There are a million reasons you could want me dead. After all, I am a half-breed. I am not truly an Ebonian like you. Perhaps that scares you."

He stares at me like I've punched him in the gut. "Do you truly believe me to be such a monster? You are part of me, Kyla. You are my own daughter, for gods sakes! I would never . . . never want to hurt you!"

"Grag tried to kill me because he knew who I was! He knew I was your daughter," I scream at him. "How could he have known? I watched him – through that thing you call a portal. I watched him as he hunted for me. As he kept the truth from . . ."

As he kept the truth from *Trithar.* I remember the one shadow who had asked if they should tell "him" about me. Grag had refused. When the shadow protested, he'd killed him. When another shadow called him a "traitor" he killed that one too. He didn't want Trithar to even know I existed. Why?

Trithar steps close, his massive shoulders tightening as his hands ball into fists. "Grag betrayed me, didn't he?"

I nod solemnly. Nothing else makes sense.

"Trish!"

She enters the room at the sound of his voice.

"Who brought Grag's mask to you?" His voice is deathly cold and hollow.

She isn't oblivious to it and her fingers tighten on the doorknob. "Pardon, Excellency?"

Trithar loses control. "Who the hell brought back Grag's mask!"

"Luthar, Grag's second-in-command after the recent death of Captain Lavon," she answers quickly. "He . . ."

"Bring him to the court room. Now!"

Trish's face hardens, and she leaves the room without bowing, her shoes making earnest clacking noises down the hall.

Trithar gestures for me to follow him.

We walk down the long hallways without saying a word. The anger and power radiating from him both frightens and amazes me. I say a brief prayer for the poor fool who will be on the receiving end of it.

The guards don't even wait for his command and open the large double doors for as he approaches, admitting us into the throne room.

The caped shadow situated beneath the oval sunlight turns around, the breath leaves my body in a harsh gasp, and I recoil in horror. If it had been centuries since that night I would still remember that shadowy form. That black hood. That raspy laugh.

"Good evening, Excellency," Luthar says.

It's the shadow that disappeared on that long ago night.

Chapter XLII

Luthar's gaze drifts languidly from Trithar to me. I know he recognizes me because he steps back, startled, and darts a wary glance at Trish. Her blade is drawn, and she's standing way too close for comfort. His shoulders tighten.

He knows why he's here.

"Excellency, let me explain . . ."

"Lie and I'll rip your fucking throat out!" Trithar growls, sounding more demon than man. He points a shaky finger at the shivering soldier. "Grag knew that the strange Kelban was my daughter. There was no way he couldn't have known. Why didn't he tell me?"

"I swear, my liege, I had nothing to do with it. He went mad. He was enraged. Violent, even. No one could get in his way. He . . ."

"If you give me one more damn excuse I'll blow you apart right now!" Trithar opens the palm of his hand for warning and Luthar's cape quivers around his shoulders, blown by the invisible power that the emperor and I share.

"How did he know about her?" Trithar continues.

I watch hundreds of different scenarios shudder across Luthar's eyes in a matter of seconds as he contemplates the situation before him. One shuddering breath later, his gaze returns to normal and he shrugs. "I don't know, Excellency. None of us did."

"He's lying."

Everyone looks at me.

"He's lying," I repeat, and look straight at Luthar. His hood is pulled back, revealing the ebony mask and the dark eyes behind it. They warn me not to continue. Threaten me to remain silent. But he can't frighten me like he did that night. Nothing like him will ever frighten me again. "Or have you forgotten me already, Luthar?"

He freezes at the sound of his name on my lips.

Trithar glances between us, confused. "What?"

"We've met before," I continue in a slow, casual voice, "about four years ago, wasn't it, Luthar? On a dark street in Kirath? Don't you remember? You told your men to kill me."

"You son of a bitch . . ." A blast of Trithar's power knocks Luthar to his knees with a loud crack.

He screams in pain, sounding very human. "Excellency, please. I didn't know she was your child. Grag thought she was Gavin Bone's." Luthar screams again as another wave of power rattles through him. "Grag found out about your affair through *her.* Empress Lilath. He wanted to punish your whore, and he thought killing her husband and child would be a good place to start."

Now it's my turn to be confused. *Empress Lilath?*

"You're married?"

Trithar's face darkens. "*Was.* She died twelve years ago."

"And that information wasn't convenient an hour ago because . . ."

He shakes his head in irritation. "My father made me marry a Darthan, one of the noble Ebonians. It just so happens that Grag was her brother. She told him everything. I always suspected she knew about Elinor. She was certainly suspicious that there was another woman. She must have learned the truth when my interest in Kelba remained long after I left that land behind."

Luthar hastily interjects, "He was enraged that you would dare betray his sister like that. Enraged at you and at the other woman. He spent years investigating the matter until he was certain he'd found the right one. He said taking her life wouldn't be punishment enough for the grief she'd caused his sister. She would have to suffer the loss of a loved one as well."

"He failed," I snap.

Luthar trembles, but I don't think it's from fear.

"When did he know she was my heir?" Trithar asks.

Luthar hesitates. The emperor's lips curl and his fingers jerk as that invisible line of power that the two of us share grips the Ebonian with painful claws that fill the room with screams. After a few seconds that seem like hours, Trithar releases a steady breath and Luthar stops screaming.

"When did he know she was my heir?" The deadly quiet in the powerful man's voice is more frightening than his rage.

"From the moment she arrived in Agron and word reached him that she could understand us.," Luthar spits out hastily, splattering the floor with specks of saliva. "Only one of Ebonian birth or heritage could understand us without knowing how to speak the language itself."

Only an Ebonian?

Holy gods! The boy from Gavrone – Avarick. Celeste. The "*cursed*" ones..

They were shadows too!

Half-breeds.

Luthar continues with his story. "The girl in Agron was a Kelban. The daughter of a High Lord. And her mother was Elinor Bone. Grag knew immediately whose child she really was. He ordered for her to be brought to him, but the force he sent failed to do so. He decided to do it himself. He attacked Agron, but she wasn't there. We came back a few days later . . . *she killed him.*" Luthar looks at me again and, even though he wears a mask, I don't miss the hatred simmering behind it. "He said she could never be found. That Trithar of Darkness's half-blood heir never existed and should remain that way."

Trithar stares down at him, lips curled in disgust. "You knew he was a traitor. You knew what he was about to do. And yet you did nothing. You did nothing while he was preparing to butcher my only daughter! I should have your head, you son of a bitch. Hear me? Your head!"

The trembling shadow has the good sense to lower that head. "I was afraid, Excellency. Grag slaughtered those who opposed him. I was afraid I was next. I brought you his mask and told her," he points at Trish, "the truth because he was dead. I have and always will be loyal, Excellency. Forgive me." He sinks onto his knees and puts his head on the ground.

Trithar stares down at him, repulsed. "You thought only of your own life and not of the crime you were committing. To murder a blood-line heir is treason. That heir is as much your master as I am. By following Grag's orders, I have to believe you were involved in the assassination plot."

"Excellency, please . . ."

"Enough!" He turns to speak with Trish.

Leaving his back exposed!

Luthar sees it too, and a distant light of hope flares in his dark eyes. From beneath his cloak he pulls a long, dark blade and slinks towards the emperor.

Trithar, unaware of the danger, continues speaking with Trish. She doesn't notice the approaching warrior either.

Luthar lunges at Trithar's back, pointing his sword arm straight out in order to push the blade deep.

There is no time to cry out a warning.

A great roar, like a wave crashing on the beach, shatters my eardrums and rolls down my arms, lashing out into the room with violent claws. Luthar's sword flies from his hands, turns, and stops in mid-air. He screams – too late – and impales himself, through the head, on his own weapon. Blood – red and thick – splatters the ground.

Trithar turns around slowly.

Luthar remains standing, held in place by my power, a sword where his face should be.

My arms tire. The pulse fades.

Luthar falls.

His blood flows in a thin, red line between Trithar and I. We look at one another.

The dawning truth strikes me sharper than a blade.

I killed a man – to protect *him*!

Trithar smiles.

He knew, I realize. *He knew Luthar would attack him. He wanted to know if I would stop him.*

Trithar holds out his hand.

And, in this moment, I have a choice.

I can cross that red line between us and take his hand, accepting who I am and embracing it. *Or* – I can turn away and return to a world that will never understand or accept me because of what I am.

"*She doesn't belong in any world but ours . . . They will destroy her for what she is.*"

I can return with Shade. I can choose to hide what I am.

But can I force myself to hide the abilities that long to be unleashed? Can I ignore the fact that I am an heir to the blood-line throne of Ebonia? That I am, in fact, a step away from ruling? A step away from having the chance to change all the mistakes and fix all the wrongs?

I am not a Kelban.

I am not an Ebonian.

I am someone for whom there is no place in this world.

But I can make a different world.

I have a chance.

I have a choice.

"*We want peace. We want respect. We want justice. But you, of all people, know that world is nothing but a dream, don't you, Kyla?*" Trish's words.

"*I want a world where justice is served.*" Shade's words.

"*I want a world where peace abounds.*" My words.

We all can have our dreams, can't we?

But what if it didn't have to be a dream? What if I could make that dream a reality?

I make my choice.

I take Trithar's hand.

Chapter XLIII

I know I should return to my rooms, and check up on Shade, but I can't bring myself to head in that direction. Maybe it makes me a coward. Maybe it makes me pathetic and weak and frightened. But every time I turn down that long hallway and stare at the door, guarded by two, armored Ebonians, my stomach twists.

A dark shadow paces behind the door.

You should go to him, that little voice inside of me whispers.

And tell him what?

Shaking my head against the hammer pounding inside, I walk in the opposite direction – towards the library which Trithar so kindly guided me. Perhaps he knows me better than most absent fathers usually knew their estranged children.

Once the library door closes behind me, I close my eyes and lean against one of the shelves, letting the moments, scenes, and scenarios of the past few days play across my mind. All the questions that have haunted me for a lifetime are finally answered. Even the questions that I had not deigned to ask.

A great weight no longer burdens my chest.

And my identity . . .

Ebonian. Heir to a throne. Heir to an empire.

An empire of killers.

That burden grows a little heavier.

I shove it away.

"Open your eyes and look for the truth behind what you've been told about us."

The stories about the Wilds had been lies. The stories about this place – this place to which half of me belongs – could very well be lies as well.

But Axle. Mama Opal. River. Otis. And Shade . . .

The thought of them brings tears to my eyes. I take deep steady breaths but it does nothing to quell the emotions rising within my throat, threatening to break free. I clamp two hands over my mouth and sink to my knees. I shouldn't be crying. I shouldn't be hiding. I shouldn't be feeling like I'm about to drown.

Slowly, slowly, I push the tears – the screams – the pain – back.

I made my choice. I chose to let go of the past. Of Kelba. Of the Wilds. If I don't let go I will never move on. I will never see what I can become. I will never see what I am meant to be – and I know I'm meant to be something. Deep down, I've always known.

The realization fills me with a new hope – a new feeling of empowerment and confidence that I haven't felt in a long time. The same feeling that flowed through me when I defied a ruler. When I defied the Burnt Forest. When I defied any sort of barrier that attempted to cage me.

I cannot spend my life in fear any longer.

I will let go – even if it means letting go of *him*.

The idea threatens to deflate the energy pulsing inside of me, but I push it from my thoughts.

I have a purpose. As an heir of this deadly empire I have a power that most people do not possess. The power to change things. The power to make a difference. The power to tell all those other powers that threaten to frighten and degrade me to go to hell.

I open my eyes, staring at the hundreds of books shrouded in the faded light of dusk, and smile.

I don't have to run anymore.

I don't know how long I remain on my knees, but the library is dark except for the fire burning loyally, when the door creaks open and a dark figure steps inside. He searches the perimeter of the room before his eyes finally meet mine. He gently closes the door and bows.

"I'm to escort you to your room," Roke explains, his deep voice no longer raspy to my ears. A trick. To frighten other races, perhaps?

I don't move.

He sees the expression on my face. "You're staying." It's not a question.

"That bother you?"

"No," he says, a little too quickly. "No. Just creates . . . tension, that's all."

I don't have to inquire about the meaning of his last sentence. We both know who waits impatiently in my room.

"What will happen to him?"

"The boy is responsible for the deaths of a hundred soldiers, several captains, a Darthan on the court of your father, not to mention many others that we don't have on file; guards, spies, slavers, and simple hunters." Roke lists of the casualties, name by name by name, as if he's studied Shade's violent history for years. He notices my surprise and adds, "All Ebonian soldiers in a high position like mine are required to know and assess threats against our ranks. But even the common Ebonian housemaids know that your lover is a great danger to anyone roaming outside our borders."

"What will happen to him?" I repeat firmly.

Roke's shoulders tense but, to his credit, he still has the balls to ask, "If you were in my place, my lady, what do you think would happen to him?"

"He would be executed."

Roke nods and that's confirmation enough. They're going to kill Shade.

"The idea doesn't sit well with you, does it?"

I glare at him, making words unnecessary.

After a couple moments of silence, I whisper, "When?"

"Tomorrow."

I gasp. "So soon."

"'The sooner the better,' one of my men said to me."

I don't miss the sudden softness in his voice and tilt my head in his direction. "But you don't think so?"

He shrugs. "He's killed Captain Lavon, a prestigious member of our ranks, and a very great loss for Ebonia. That makes his existence intolerable to a great many fellow Ebonians."

"I killed Grag. What does that make me?"

"T-that . . . that's different. Grag was a traitor. You were within your rights to kill him."

"Lavon was under Grag's command and met his death while hunting for me so Grag could *kill me.* I would call that conspiracy to murder and a good enough reason for execution, wouldn't you?" I stand up, no longer willing to look up at the Ebonian when I could look him in the eye. "So, if we're being honest, Shade did you all a favor by saving my life. If it weren't for him, I'd be dead."

Roke grimaces. "That doesn't excuse the countless others he's butchered."

"The countless others involved in attacking peaceful villages like Agron and innocent civilians? Yes, I could see how devastating their loss must be to your army, but they knew the consequences when they chose to act so foolishly. Or perhaps they thought it would be easy – conquering another race."

"We don't want to conquer anything," Roke snaps, his calm demeanor disappearing. "The Ilkanari will find our borders eventually if we don't keep them at bay. They will discover the towns, the cities, the people we fight to protect. I, and my kindred fighters, are willing to bare the stories that paint us as nightmares if only for the chance to see our loved ones live one more day in safety and happiness. It's a shitty existence, I agree. This empire has gone to hell. Pretend to be a nightmare and, sometimes, you become that nightmare. Honestly, I regret the loss of life on both sides. I wish it didn't have to be this way. I wish . . ." He stops, realizing he's said to much to someone like me.

"Go on," I prod. "What do you wish for?"

He doesn't say anything, continuing to stare at me from behind his ebony mask.

"What do you wish for?" I repeat, slowly, taking a step towards him with each word. Until we're standing so close I could put out my hand and touch the emblem on the breastplate beneath his cloak.

"I want an empire where peace exists. Where peace isn't just a word that we say, but a word that we feel. That we know. That we love. This empire . . . it doesn't know the value of such things anymore. If it did, I would fight – fight with everything I have – for it. I swear by all the damned gods and the ancestors." Beneath that mask, I think I see the glint of tears.

"Then you're in luck," I whisper, stepping close, so I can whisper in his ear. "You and I share the same dream."

He doesn't say a word as I pull back. As I smile at him. As I gently rest my hand on his shoulder and make him look me in the eye. "But so does the boy who's made himself a monster to protect what he loves." Even if what he loved died years ago at the hands of men like Roke.

I step back, leaving Roke to ponder my words and stare at the fire, crackling with brilliant sparks.

The soldier sighs. "What do you want from me?"

"His life."

"Is he worth it?" Roke holds up a passive hand when anger crosses my face. "I only mean what do you plan on doing, my lady? Do you really think that he will remain by your side when he learns what you are?" He pauses, allowing the words to sink in. "Do not misunderstand me? I know what you must feel for him. But when he learns what you are will he share those same feelings? Or will he take that blade of his and run you through, avenging his past? Think, my lady! Think about this Ilkanari warrior – will he stay or will he kill?"

"*I would destroy every last shadow, I would raid their land, I would slaughter the monsters . . .*"

He would kill.

I steel myself against the pulsing ache in my chest and meet Roke's gaze. "His life. Just his life is all I ask of you."

Roke stares at me, as if he's seeing me for the first time, and shakes his head. "It's a waste, Excellency, if you ask me. His life, I mean."

"You don't know that."

He sighs, glancing around the room, as if he's afraid the books are documenting our every word. "An hour is all I can give you, my lady. Make good use of it."

"I will."

He turns to go.

"Thank you.

He pauses, hand on the knob, and turns around. The glitter of tears are still in his eyes. "There is no need to thank me, Kyla. I owe you a debt that I was afraid I would never be able to repay."

"You owe me a debt?" I try to remember every moment with the strange Ebonian but can think of nothing remotely responsible for the favor he has offered me.

"Grag murdered my brother in cold blood. I owe you for killing him. My brother was one of the bravest young soldiers ever to enter the ranks. He had passion. Brains. And a dutiful, loyal spirit that inspired those around him. Grag blew him to oblivion because he questioned him. All because he dared to say what everyone already suspected – that Grag was a traitor."

Holy gods! Holy gods! My lungs feel too tight in my chest. My vision – the one in which Grag shattered a fellow soldier for asking if he'd switched sides – I watched it. I watched Grag slaughter Roke's brother.

"I'm sorry I couldn't have done something," I whisper.

Roke shakes his head. "He died bravely. That's all that matters, I guess. In the end, he won't be remembered for it. Another name written on the wall – another number to remove from the books."

"I'll remember him," I say fiercely.

Roke tilts his chin in the opposite direction, hiding his face from view. His hand trembles on the knob.

"What was his name?"

"Rev."

I repeat the name, committing it to memory, before saying, "I'll make sure everyone knows. Everyone will know that he died bravely."

"Thank you," Roke whispers, his voice breaking. He quickly exits the room, shutting the door securely behind him.

I glance around the room, blinking tears from my own eyes.

No, not all Ebonians are demons.

The stories about *my* people aren't true.

I have an hour to save the one boy who may never understand that truth. Frantically, I search the corner of the library that contains articulately designed maps until I find what I'm looking for. Squaring my shoulders, I head down the hall, no longer afraid of my future.

No longer afraid of anything.

I stand in front of the door, watching that black shadow move across the bottom of it with furious movement, and try to steel myself for the scene I am about to play – the act I must uphold. Only for one more hour. One more hour I must be the strange Kelban girl with a mark on her shoulder and no place in the world. I accept that commitment and step inside the room, allowing the two guards outside to pull it close behind me.

Despite my resolution, it still hurts like hell when strong arms envelop me in a comforting hold and the smell of smoke and pine needles tickles my nose. And, as hard as I try to hold them back, tears trickle down my cheeks.

"Gods be praised. Gods be praised," Shade whispers, more to himself, than me. His hand gently cups the back of my head. "Are you alright? Kyla?" He pulls back, lifting my chin with gentle fingers, despite the tremors of loose control evident on his face – his body. A body bruised and beaten for what, I promise, will be the last time. My eyes meet his and a whole new cascade of tears and feelings burst out of me. I wrap my arms around his neck, forcing him to hold me, to not look at my face as I weave lies between us once again.

"They took me to a room. It was so . . . so dark."

Shade trembles beneath me. "What did they do to you?" His voice is deadly quiet, raising hairs along the back of my spine.

"N-nothing. They asked me questions, but one of them . . . one of them tried to kill . . . tried to kill . . ." I don't finish the sentence, leaving Shade to fill in the blanks with his own idea of what must have occurred. "They didn't want me dead yet so they . . . they sent me back. Said they'd continue when I was more inclined to t-talk."

"They didn't hurt you?" I can sense the struggle in him as he tries to discern whether I'm lying to him – lying to protect him from what he thinks they must have done to me. "Tell me, Kyla. Tell me what happened. What they did to you. Don't lie to me."

Those last four words break me completely, and I let out my first sob. In an hour he'll be gone. In an hour he'll no longer be in my arms.

In an hour he'll hate me.

Gods, I can't do this.

But I have to.

I won't let them take his life when he hasn't even had the chance to decide who he wants to be or what he wants to become. When he hasn't had the chance to live a life for himself.

At least, even if it tears me apart, I can give him that chance.

I can give him that choice.

He deserves it.

"It's alright, Kyla. It's alright," he whispers softly, cradling me, protecting me, in his arms. I shed tears for his gentleness – a part of him that he wasn't afraid to show me and would become a part, within an hour's time, that he would never show me again.

Frantically, I look at the clock. Forty minutes remain. Forty minutes to get him to safety. Forty minutes to save his life.

I pull away from him, despite craving his touch, his warmth for a few more minutes.

"We have to get out of here tonight. Before they come and . . ." I don't finish, opting to grab his arm instead. He flinches at the touch – the urgency within it.

That glitter – the thrill of life – that I've missed in his eyes, reappears. "Don't be afraid, Kyla. It doesn't become you. I'm not going to let them touch you. Hear me? They're never going to touch you again." He palms my face. "Don't be frightened. Please."

He doesn't know who I'm really frightened for.

"While you were gone, I came up with an idea. There's only two guards outside. I can easily take care of that. But finding a way out of this palace is going to be . . ."

I gently place a hand over his mouth and pull up the hem of my shirt. The map I took from the library is tucked into the waistband of my pants. I hand it to him. "Will this help?"

He stares at it, then at me. "That's my Kyla."

His Kyla. He called me his Kyla.

Maybe there is hope for him and I. Maybe he won't mind about what I am. Maybe his feelings for me might push my true origins aside.

"Shade," I say.

He mumbles a quiet answer as he peruses the map's contents with quick, darting eyes.

"Do you think that, maybe, we might be wrong about them? The shadows I mean?" Despite the urge to look away when his eyes meet mine, I continue to look at him. To watch his dark eyes squint at me from beneath furrowed brows.

"Why would you think that, Kyla?"

I shrug. "They had a library. Books. Knowledge. Would monsters have that? Would monsters care about such things?"

He shakes his head. "They could have a damn temple, and I would still think they're monsters. Things like them aren't fit to breathe. To walk this earth. And someday, I'll make sure they don't."

Those words affirm my decision.

I lean over the map with him and point to the place I'd already planned as his only chance for escape. A small lift operated by a crane on the outskirts of the city, along the cliffs and the edge of the mountains. It lowers to the sea beneath. From there he'll be able to swim towards the Wilds.

I don't let myself think about how I'm going to convince him to leave me behind.

Shade's plan to bash the two Ebonian guards heads together doesn't go as planned because I smash them against the wall with my power under the guise that they jump up too quickly and slip. One of them I leave conscious long enough to let Shade slam him into the wall, but I grab his arm and rush him down the hall before he can do any serious damage. Shade, his heart pumping with the same adrenaline, doesn't protest.

The map gave a very detailed sketch of the palace, but there was no time to commit it to memory. With thirty minutes left to get Shade halfway through the city before Roke makes good on his promise to follow us, I had to be satisfied with a brief study. Three long hallways, four stairwells, and eight more hallways should lead us to a room labeled as the "Obsidian Court." That room is supposed to provide access to the city.

Our flight goes uninterrupted by any guards. I make a note to speak to Trtihar about the absence of proper security. Although, I suppose, with our powers we're hardly in need of much protection.

Shade, who is leading the way, suddenly pauses, throwing out a hand, but I've already stopped. From down the long hallway, one of the last ones towards our destination, the tramp of feet is plainly evident. Shade's muscles tense, preparing for a fight, but I know, from the sound, there are too many to fight. Grabbing his arm, I pull him into the darkness that coats the hallway, cursing the smooth walls for robbing us of proper cover. Shade shields me behind him. I ache to tell him that it's not I who cannot be caught.

A small group of Ebonian soldiers, dressed in black uniforms with glittering ebony breastplates, stomp past us, glancing neither left nor right. They follow a single Ebonian captain as he plods forward relentlessly, no emotion in the eyes peering through the slits of his mask.

Roke, if he notices my presence, doesn't show it and he and his men pass by.

I know they're heading towards my room to get Shade. To execute him.

At their pace, they'll reach my room in twenty minutes.

I grab Shade's arm and practically run the rest of the way down the hall, ignoring Shade's whispers of warning. I'll snap the neck of any Ebonian who might see us if it means getting him out of this palace in one piece.

The hallway opens up into a large room and when I step into it the beauty steals my breath away. The "Obsidian Court," as it was wisely named, might as well have been carved from one block of mass, glittering ore. It glints and gleams in the light of torches lining its walls. Large, glimmering pillars stab upwards into the air, hundreds of feet high. It is so dark, I cannot see the ceiling, but I'm sure it shines just as beautifully. This is the entrance to the palace of Ebonia. An entrance to a place of dark, unearthly beauty beyond words or knowledge.

I could stare at this room forever, but Shade, who also marvels at the sheer willpower and talent that must have been required to make this masterpiece, must escape.

We run through the room, our shadows glimmering on the shiny pillars and floor as we pass. The room is endless, stretching for what seems to be eternity, until I spot two double doors open to the night air. They are so tall I'm sure they were designed for the gods instead of mere men. When Shade and I step beyond them, the city lights, blinking at the foot of the mountain this palace occupies, steal my breath, yet again. So many of them, so close together, and so bright. A sign of life and warmth in this dark place. Were it not for the occasional white flutters of fog blotting out the lights, I could have mistaken it for a Kelban city.

There are no guards down the long slope, but when we reach the city limits, absent of gates, and step onto the paved streets, the slight fluttering sound of capes reach my ears. Shade reacts first, snatching me into a nearby alley with him and pressing me tightly against the wall. An Ebonian guard slowly floats past our hiding place, his head sagging slightly. He doesn't wear a hood and his brown hair is braided down his back. Were it not for the ebony mask on his face, there would be nothing shadowy about him. His feet don't touch the ground and white wisps flow out from within his cloak. I make a note to ask Trithar of the strange phenomenon later.

Nudging Shade away from me, I step into the street again. The lights are scarce throughout the city, despite the appearance from the palace doors, making it easy for us to keep to the shadows. But as we pass through the city, closer and closer, to the mountains that it presses up against, the pain in my head burns fiercer. It becomes increasingly difficult to keep Shade focused as more shadow guards pass us by. Our hiding places become fewer and fewer when the stone houses we use as cover become closer and closer together until there is no space left to squeeze.

I see the next guard before Shade does, but only by mere moments. Before Shade can launch himself into an attack, the guard's cape suddenly finds itself torn from his body and floating halfway down the street. Cursing, the owner of the cape hurries after it, giving us time to sneak by him and into darkness once more. Shade doesn't remark upon the strange occurrence, but his body remains tense and ready to attack.

At last, the city comes to an end and the ground becomes rocky and barren. I stumble across several gaping holes in the formation before turning a corner and finding myself staring at a large formation of rock going up, up, up one side into the mountains and the other side rising into a black marble peak. A crane of iron rests atop the peak, stretching out over the cliff's edge.

And it's snapped in two, it's broken end hovering over the sea thousands of feet beneath.

I stare at it, willing it to rise, whole and strong again, but nothing happens.

Shade shakes his head, rage and fear lighting his face. He rubs his jaw nervously.

I step up to the cliff's edge and peer over. I cannot see the sea hiding beneath the layers of fog swirling up from its surface. But I can hear the waves, crashing against the side of the Dark Mountains. Just weeks ago I had stood on a cliff on the opposite side of the sea, staring in this same direction.

"We'll have to climb down," Shade says, as if reading my thoughts.

I shake my head. It took me hours, without any experience, to climb down the cliffs from the village of Gavrone. It will take Shade just as much time, if not longer, because of his injuries. Every wince and slight intake of breath he uses to disguise his pain hasn't escaped my attention.

I shake my head.

"We can," Shade insists, that determined ire rising in him. He steps up behind me. "A few bruises won't stop me."

"You've got a broken rib, Shade!"

He blinks. He must have thought I didn't notice.

"You can get to safety," I say softly. "Just go." I point at the edge of the cliff.

He stares at me, confused.

"You can get to safety," I repeat.

He shakes his head. "No."

"Shade, please . . ."

"No!" he snaps, anger in his eyes. "There's no way in hell I'm leaving you behind. Forget it!"

"You have to,"

"No. I left you once – I won't do it again. I'm not leaving you behind to face these monsters on your own. It's not happening, Kyla, you hear me? You don't understand what they can do to you. What they will do you. I won't let that happen. I can't let them hurt you like they . . ."

"Shade," I try to interrupt. It's been over an hour.

He'll never leave me behind – unless what he leaves behind is what he despises most in the world.

"If you think for one second, Kyla, that I'm going to leave you here like some damned fool than you . . ."

"Shade!" I scream and the desperation in my voice cuts his sentence in half, leaving him stunned.

I draw a sharp breath inward, preparing to say the words that will break us into irreparable pieces.

"I am a shadow."

Chapter XLIV

Shade stares at me for a long moment before releasing a steady, slow breath. He shakes his head, that cool rage in his face shifting to something else I can't identify. "If you think a shitty lie like that is going to make me leave you behind, Kyla, you must take me for a bigger asshole than I really am."

I keep my face calm – even I'm grasping, very loosely, for restraint. "It's not a lie. In fact, it's the only thing that makes sense."

He laughs off my words, but the gleam at the corners of his eyes has dulled.

"It didn't make sense that a Kelban girl could survive a shadow blade's blow, did it? Did it make any sense when a Kelban girl could understand them when no one else could?" I see the thoughts churning behind his eyes as they remain fixated on me – on my eyes. My face. My shoulder, where the ostracized scar is hidden beneath my shirt.

"I can understand them," I continue, "because I'm one of them. Because the same blood that flows in their veins, flows in mine. I'm a shadow, Shade."

"Bullshit!" he snaps.

"Shade, please . . . I've bought you some time. In a few minutes, Roke will be coming for you. He'll . . ."

"Roke? Coming for me? What the hell are you say . . ."

"Damn it, Shade, would you just listen to me and go already!" I point at the cliff's edge, glancing behind me, afraid I'll see a squadron of soldiers marching around it coming to take him away. Coming to kill him. "Go! Now!"

Shade doesn't even look at the cliff, keeping his gaze locked on mine. And it hurts. It hurts that he's still looking at me. Still denying the truth I've laid in front of him. Still wasting time when his life is hanging by five minutes. He shakes his head at me, stubborn to the end. "Kyla, I'm not . . ."

The pulse in my hand is there without hesitation and gently lifts one of the tiny rocks, no bigger than my hand, from the ground. I let the rock hover in front of me, far from any limb that might appear to be holding it, and move it from side to side. Up and down.

Shade's eyes widen, his eyes never leaving the rock, as I bring it closer and closer to his open palm and allow it to fall into his hand, releasing my invisible hold. His thumb strokes the harsh ridges as if he needs to feel it to believe what I just did. He blinks, but the rock is still there.

I wait for him to look at me, but he doesn't.

"T-this doesn't prove . . . you're . . . it's not . . ." He stammers for the right words, but there are no words to explain what I've just done.

He wants proof. So I give him proof.

"The tree branch that mysteriously fell on the Gavronite, the stone wall that collapsed on the razor, the destruction of Grag, the fire lashing at the Unnamed . . . do those all seem like coincidences? Do you really believe that? You don't, do you? No one – *no one* – is that lucky!"

"Stop," he whispers, his eyes still fixated on the rock in his hand. A hand that has started trembling violently.

"That man who tossed you into the wall with nothing but the slice of his hand is Trithar, Emperor of Ebonia . . . of shadows . . ." I pause, allowing those words to sink in, ". . . and I'm his daughter."

Shade's chin snaps up, his eyes meeting mine.

"Remember his face," I say, "and compare it to mine. What do you see?"

He narrows his eyes, squinting at my features in the dim light. I flinch beneath his harsh, prying gaze. It resembles the looks he used to give me when we first met – when I was nothing to him. His eyes widen and I don't have to tell him anything else. He knows. He knows I'm telling the truth. He turns his back and stares over the edge of the cliff.

Climb, I want to scream at him. *Climb, you stubborn ass.*

He lifts the rock in his hand and, with a cry of rage that shatters the silence of the night, hurls it into the open air beyond the ledge. We both watch it sail like a bird until it loses its momentum and plunges into the foggy clouds beneath.

Shade keeps his back to me. I watch his muscles tighten as he squares his own shoulders and curls his hands into fists. He remains silent, staring at the distant mountains on the other side of the sea.

"Shade . . ."

"Don't," he snaps, his tone deadly cold – and full of denial.

"I'm a shadow."

"Don't." His voice breaks.

"I'm a shadow," I insist.

"You're not!"

I step towards him and, grabbing his shoulder, I spin him around. He tries to keep his head down, but not before I see the tears slithering down his cheeks. His lips quiver as he struggles to look anywhere but straight at me. Anywhere but the truth written on my face.

"I'm a shadow, Shade." I grip his chin, gently, and force him to look at me. To meet my gaze. To watch my lips as I speak. "A gods-damned shadow."

He believes me. Despite how hard I see him trying to deny it – trying to avoid it – he knows. And it's breaking him.

It's breaking me.

I palm his face in my hands, his skin warm against mine, as his tears drift over my fingers. I wait for him to pull away from my touch. To throw me aside. To deny the truth one last time.

But he doesn't.

My throat is tight, like someone is choking me, and I can't breathe. I can't think. I can't focus. All I can see are his eyes. His tears. His lips . . .

I kiss him, thumbs brushing over the tears and stubble on his face. I kiss him softly, at first, wanting to savor the moment. To memorize how his lips feel beneath mine and how his warmth starts a fire through every part of my body. I thread my fingers through his hair, grasping desperately at the thick strands, and deepen the kiss.

He doesn't make a sound. Only pulls me in close to him, until every part of him is flush against every part of me, and he's kissing me back with trembling lips.

It takes me a moment to realize I'm crying too. Trying to hold in the sobs that ache to be set free. Trying to concentrate on kissing him so I forget the pain. The loss. The burn that is groping at my heart with shredding claws.

Shade holds me so tightly, it hurts.

Don't let go. Please, don't let go of me.

But he does, tearing our lips apart, and shoving me away.

I remind myself that I was expecting his disgust, but it still hurts when he wipes furiously at his mouth.

Wipes *me* from his mouth.

I wanted that. I want him to despise me. To hate me. To leave me.

But, despite what I knew he would do, I had hoped he'd forget what I was. What blood ran through my veins. What those with that same blood in their veins had done to him.

I shake my head. *Fool.*

We stare at each other warily, neither one of us knowing what to say or what to do.

The tramp of feet just around the corner reaches my ears.

Shade hears it too and wipes the tears from his eyes.

"Go!" I plead, but the word is useless. We both know he won't climb fast enough.

"Damn it," I growl through clenched teeth, staring at the ledge. At the broken crane. At the foggy clouds that hide the sea from view. "Damn it!"

Shade merely ignores me and stares at the corner with calm determination. The glint returns to his eyes, but this time it's different. It's violent and brutal and completely devoid of any humanity. He will fight them . . . and he will die for it.

I stare at the ledge again, a vivid memory churning in my mind.

I shake my head. *No.*

It didn't work last time. It won't work this time.

But last time, I wasn't strong.

I am now.

The noise of the approaching soldiers becomes closer, until its echoing in my ears. When I turn around, there they are: ten soldiers in gleaming black armor. Standing in front of them, his legs planted firmly against the stony ground, is Roke.

He glances at me first and shrugs a silent apology for the extended time he cannot give me.

Roke turns his attention to Shade. "On your knees, Ilkanari." He motions emphatically with one hand.

Shade slowly bends towards the ground, his hand creeping along his leg, towards the rim of his boot, and . . .

There is no time to stop him. The blade leaves Shade's hand the moment he pulls it from the inside lining of his boot. It strikes Roke clear through the heart. The Ebonian stumbles for a moment, his eyes wide behind his mask, before falling to the ground in a crumpled heap. His hand remains on the blade, struggling to pull it from his chest. When his hand slows and, finally, drops away I suck in a sharp breath.

Roke's soldiers rush to his body, attempting to restore the life to his lungs, but to no avail.

The loyal Ebonian is dead.

The soldiers let out enraged, raspy cries of protest and hate. Drawing their blades, they launch themselves at Shade, revenge sparkling in their eyes.

Shade quickly backs up against the cliff's edge, but there is no way for him to escape. No way he'll be able to climb fast enough before the bastards reach the ledge and one, well aimed weapon becomes his doom.

I step between him and the advancing shadows. Our eyes lock on one another. He blinks, startled by my sudden interference, as I lean in close and brush my hands up his chest – over the scar my kind gave him.

"I'm sorry," I whisper.

I shove him off the cliff.

I watch his body flail wildly as he falls through the air, nothing to slow or stop him from crashing into the waves beneath. For a brief moment, it isn't Shade, but another boy falling through the air. A boy I couldn't save.

Not this time.

I stretch both hands towards Shade's increasingly vague form and wince at the painful pulse of power that shoots from my hands in his direction. The invisible chords of my power grasp him and, suddenly, become heavier. Harder. Sharper. As if his weight has become mine, and we are falling together. I grit my teeth against the pain as it spreads from my hands throughout my entire body. I dig my heels into the rock at my feet as it becomes harder to keep that power steady, but I don't relinquish it.

Not yet.

The burden on the other side of my power becomes lighter. He's hit the water – safely.

I release him.

A million prickles of ice numb my body as my power recedes.

The Ebonian soldiers gape at me as I turn around, the wind whipping my hair wildly around my face. They flinch beneath my gaze, recognizing the features that their emperor and I share.

Another shadowy form sails around the corner and comes to a swift halt, staring first at Roke's lifeless body and then me. I recognize the straight, black hair flowing behind her.

Trish doesn't say anything. She merely motions for the Ebonians to pick up their fallen leader and carry him away. Before they do, she pulls the blade from his chest and stalks towards me. The soldiers leave us alone together and begin their trek back through the city. A few cast glances in my direction. A majority of them are shocked, but a choice few have rage dancing in their eyes. Those looks fill me with sudden guilt.

I killed Roke as surely as if I'd thrown the blade myself. I should have known to check Shade for weapons. Should have known he wouldn't attempt an escape without the means to defend himself.

Trish stops in front of me. I struggle to keep my posture relaxed and my shoulders straight. But she still doesn't say anything. She pries my fist open and places the blade, stained in Roke's blood, against my palm.

"You should have killed him," she says quietly. Without another word, she turns and stomps after the disappearing squadron.

I stare at the weapon in my hand – its blade stained with the cost of Shade's life.

It was worth it, I tell myself.

I walk to the cliff's edge and peer down. The fog blocks my view, but I know Shade is swimming safely towards the coastline.

"I love you," I whisper.

I let the blade fall from my hands towards the sea – and the boy – beneath.

Chapter XLV

Trithar insisted I be at Roke's funeral – despite the fact that I'd made every possible excuse to avoid it. Every excuse to hide behind my guilt and the lies wrapped around the entire ordeal.

The Emperor had addressed a court of angry Darthans – a high class faction of Ebonians – and told the story he had created specifically for that moment. I had returned to my rooms to find the guards unconscious and my foreign lover gone. Knowing that he intended to escape, I had hunted him down and was in the act of securing him when Roke and his soldiers had stumbled upon us. The captive had killed Roke before I could stop him and, in my anger and shock, I'd shoved him off the cliff to his supposed death.

To make matters worse, Trithar then had to explain that I was his heir. Trish, apparently a well-respected soldier, had backed up his story and several of Roke's men – the four who'd so brutally attacked Shade and myself in the dungeons – begrudgingly confirmed her testimony.

The remainder of Grag's forces who'd stayed behind during the attack on Agron, were being called to the capitol for questioning. I knew, from the look in Trish's eye when she'd told me, that "questioning" was an understatement.

Trish arrives precisely at a quarter to midnight to escort me to the funeral pyre. She hasn't said a word to me since the incident other than the information Trithar required her to convey. When she looks at me, I'm not sure what she's thinking.

We exit the palace onto a long, ornately designed patio stretching out the tip of the mountain beyond the Ebonian palace. It drops off to the sea below in majestic stone designs that resemble wings. Placed at the edge of that drop-off is a single stone slab. Roke's body rests upon it.

As we approach, I survey those who have gathered. Trithar stands at the foot of the slab, his head bowed. He looks up as I approach. On the other side of the slab, at the head of their commander, stands Roke's legion. Twenty-three Ebonian men. All standing stiffly. All staring at me accusingly.

And all holding Illathonian blades.

I look at Trithar, a question in my gaze, but he makes no move to answer it. Instead, he motions for me to stand at his side. My curly hair is piled on top of my head in a strange, yet becoming, style but it does nothing to adjust the height difference between the emperor and I. However, despite my size, dressed in the same shimmering color of black as my birth father, and sharing the same remarkable features, I give the appearance of a powerful force.

A powerful force that didn't save the life of the commander in front of me.

A powerful force that allowed his killer to escape.

I look at Roke's soldiers, but none of them will meet my gaze. They'll never forgive me for it, and they sure as hell won't forget.

Trithar clears his throat, breaking the uncomfortable silence, and says, "Commander Roke died fulfilling his duties to Ebonia. His death will be remembered. His honor spoken about for ages to come."

One of the soldiers snorts contemptuously and dares to meet the Emperor's gaze. "Spare us the pretty words. He'll be forgotten. Like all of us are forgotten, *Excellency*." He practically spits the last word, causing Trithar's fist to convulse. The power balling in that fist tickles my spine.

"He won't." My voice, sharp and commanding, cuts the violent tension like a knife. I breathe with relief as Trithar's power recedes.

The soldier sneers at me.

"He won't," I repeat.

The soldier glares. I refuse to look away as the grief and anger in those eyes shout silent accusations at me. I refuse to look away and deny that I am responsible for Roke's death. I refuse to look away and hide the guilt and apology I offer him with my sincere gaze. Tears quickly pool in his eyes, and he looks away first. I release the breath I've been holding.

Trithar says a few words in a language I don't understand and steps away from the slab, gently pulling me with him. Roke's soldiers surround the slab on all sides but the fourth one – the one facing the cliff and the sea beneath.

A night breeze drifts over the patio, chilling my skin. The sleek black dress I'm wearing offers no protection against the cold. Slowly, Trithar slips his arm around my shoulders. I look at him, unsure if I should allow it, and see the same hesitation in the look he levels on me. I shrug and pretend to ignore it, returning my attention to Roke's slab. The soldiers have unsheathed their Illathonian blades and they glow with dull, white light in the darkness.

I flinch as they slowly angle the weapons downwards towards Roke's body.

"Ebonia has its own customs," Trithar whispers to me, "and, though they may seem strange to you, they are the pillars of this empire. They are what hold it together. Roke was an Ebonian soldier – bound since birth. In death, he also belongs to Ebonia. We do not bury those who are bound to the empire. It is a great honor to die for Ebonia – to die and keep it strong."

But I don't see any appreciation of that honor – of that strength – in the eyes of Roke's soldiers as they step close to the slab. As they raise the Illathonian blades. As they plunge them downwards into their former commander's body. Only tears and grief as they watch that body disintegrate beneath the dooming light and his ashes flutter over the edge of cliff to the sea beneath.

This empire has gone to hell, Roke had said.

I stare at my hand. At the small, angry pulse that emanates from it.

I'm going to change that.

Roke's soldiers are the first to leave the patio. None of them so much as glance at their emperor, but they do look at me. The one I'd spoken to – promised that Roke would not be forgotten – stares at me longer than any of the rest. His fists ball up at his sides, but I'm unsure whether its from anger or grief. Perhaps both.

Trish hastily excuses herself, casting another of her mysterious glances in my direction. It's hard to tell what her feelings towards me are with that silver mask over her face.

I look at the slab again. All that remains of the former commander is a silver mask resting against the smooth stone. Slowly – hesitantly – I approach and pick it up. It's cold as death, but I refuse to let go of it.

"Why?" I don't really know what I'm requesting to be answered. There are too many questions swirling in my head. Too much pain tingling down my spine. The power I used to guide Shade to safety has left me weak and drained. The strain I put on it was too much. How long will it be before I can return it to normal? Before I have enough power to never strain it again?

"Why?" I repeat, this time certain of the question I want answered. "Why the mask?"

Trithar doesn't approach me. "Monsters are not supposed to have faces. The moment a Crepuscular puts on the mask they are never to remove it again, for Ebonia's sake. They are bound to the empire. The mask becomes their identity."

"That's some real bullshit," I snarl, turning to face him.

He shrugs, ignoring the ferocity in my tone. "Perhaps, but it's kept this empire alive. Were it not for those tales where do you think we'd be?"

I stare at the mask, knowing the answer. *Nowhere.*

"We wouldn't exist," Trithar says for me. "Perhaps you don't know, since Kelba's history books are somewhat one-sided, but before there was Kelba, there were other nations. Other races. What do you think happened to them? Where do you think the dragons went? Where do you think the powerful beings you worship as gods disappeared to?" He doesn't wait for me to answer. "They were wiped from existence. Destroyed. Never spoken of again. Ebonia is alive today because we made ourselves into living nightmares. And would you like to know the irony behind Ilkanari ve se Stanos, the land you call the Wilds?"

Slowly, I nod.

"Were it not for the tales spreading about the Wilds in your homeland, where do you think they would be, as well?"

Dead. Wiped from existence. Forgotten.

Like so many other nations. So many other cultures. So many other powerful . . .

"You said the beings we *called* our gods . . . what did you mean?"

Trithar smirks. "Did you really believe they were gods, Kyla?"

I never had. Not for one moment. But Gasan . . . The crypt of the gods he went in search of. His powers. Calaisar. How did any of that make sense?

"Where do you think our powers came from, Kyla?" Trithar asks, using the force in the palm of his hand to take the mask from my grasp and hover it in midair. "We – you and I – are a gifted race. A gifted lineage. But we were not the only ones. There were other races – other unique beings. Some with the power to gift others with their supernatural abilities. Your gods – Freya, Gasan, Calaisar – were not really gods. But because of their gifts, mankind crafted them into that likeness. That image."

My entire world might as well have just been knocked out from underneath my feet. Just when I thought I had all the answers . . .

Trithar offers me a half-smile and returns Roke's mask to the slab. "There is much you have to learn. But, I've a feeling, you'll be up to the task."

I curl my hands into fists, the new information spreading a tingle along my nerves. All those stories – all those tales about Kelba's gods and history – and there's still so much more to learn behind them. So many mysteries and unanswered questions.

For some reason, it frightens me. Some unknown instinct warns me that those questions might be fatally answered.

"Kyla . . ." Trithar's hand grips mine. I flinch beneath it, and he lets go. "Are you alright?"

"Y-yes." I pull away, the night air chilling my body once again.

Part of Trithar's arm has taken on its second appearance – a foggy ethereal wisp that floats around the solidity of his human form.

"How do you do that?" I ask.

"It is part of me," Trithar explains. "It is part of you too. We call it the 'transformation' and all Ebonian children are taught how to adopt their ethereal form when they reach eight years of age." He looks at me, sympathy in his gaze. "It will be hard to master at your age, Kyla. Hard to learn the technique. Hard to develop the strength required to attempt it. But once you do . . . the effects it will have on you – on your powers – will be indescribable."

I take a deep breath, staring at my hand as I hold it up to the night. I concentrate on it, hard. Nothing happens. I try to search inside myself, pushing and prodding with the leftover claws of my power. Still nothing.

Trithar smiles. "It takes Ebonian children a solid year to master it, daughter. Give it time. Patience and time."

I remember my short encounters with Avarick and Celeste. They had shown no signs of possessing unique gifts.

"Our powers," I say, "do all Ebonians have . . ."

"No," he cuts in quickly. "Only bloodline heirs to the throne of Ebonia possess abilities like ours. We hail from the Imperial faction. Those powers you have, Kyla, have been passed down from generation to generation. They are what give us the right to rule. Only an Ebonian with powers, with supernatural proof of their strength, has the right to rule"

"But . . ." I stare at his arm, now returned to its original appearance, ". . . all Ebonians can . . . shift?"

"Yes. It's what makes us Ebonians. But, occasionally, an Ebonian will be unable to shift – to master that part of themselves," he says. I don't like the look in his eye as he says the words.

"And what happens to those who cannot master it?"

He is silent for a moment, and I know the answer before he speaks. "They are outcasts and either condemned to a life of solitude in the mountains or to the mines beneath the earth."

"And if I cannot shift? What will happen to me?"

"You are an Imperial. You have the powers capable to rule this empire. Whether you can shift or not, won't mean a damn thing. But you will shift, Kyla," he says confidently. "I know you will."

I stare at my hands – hands that have begun shaking.

"Are you afraid, Kyla?"

"No," I whisper. "I'm terrified."

He stares at me, understanding in his eyes. "Why are you terrified?"

"Terrified that, once again, I won't belong, I guess. That all I've done to reach this point – all I've given up – won't matter in the end." I regret the words the instant they leave my mouth. I thought I was done with wondering where I belong.

"You don't belong, Kyla," Trithar says. I look at him, perplexed, and the kind understanding has not left his face. "You are something that doesn't fit in this world. But that's why you need to fight. You need to fight to make a place for yourself. And we both no damn well you're capable of doing just that. Every day of your life in this empire will be a new battle. A new test. A new opportunity to prove yourself. You're heir to an empire, Kyla of Darkness, but you need to fight for it. You need to fight for your right to rule."

I stare at him, an intense feeling of power rising inside of me. "Alright," I say," but I'm warning you, I make a damn big mess when I fight."

He laughs, the sound as human and elegant as any man. "I'd expect nothing less from an Imperial heir."

We stand together, staring at the crashing waves beyond the patio ledge for a long time, before I finally look at him again. He doesn't return my prying gaze, but his shoulders visibly tense, as if he knows what I'm about to ask.

"Your Empress . . ."

"Lilath," he says. There is no emotion in the word. "You're familiar with the custom of political matches in highborn matrimony, aren't you, Kyla?"

I stare at my right hand, forever scarred by the marriage I denied, and cover the mark with my hand. "Yes."

"My father sought out a powerful Darthan whose ability to create equally powerful armies was well-known. Lilath and I never met each other until the ceremony . . . needless to say our relationship was a scheduled one. I needed her because of the armies her father possessed and her ability to provide me with heirs . . . she needed me to be empress. Not the best circumstances to fall in love and I was young – too young – to put much effort into someone I despised from the moment we met. I had argued with my father until the very hour of the ceremony, even threatening to leave the empire." He looks at me. "I was a fool in my young years, Kyla. A fool who, after four years of being confined to an empire and empress who didn't offer me anything but misery, ran away. I ran from my duty . . . and you know the rest of the story."

I shift uncomfortably. "Mother . . . did she know about Empress Lilath?"

"I told you that I told her everything."

"And she still . . .?" I shake my head, unable to contemplate the woman – the righteous, upright woman who raised me – capable of such a sin.

"Your mother didn't love Gavin when she was bound to him, you know," Trithar says. He smiles at my shocked expression. "It's true. It was as loveless a marriage as mine. But when he came back . . . your mother gave it another chance. For her son's sake. I believe she loves him now."

"She does," I whisper quietly, remembering all the times my parents – my mother and Lord Bone – locked eyes from separate corners of a room or secretly joined hands in the privacy of their home. "She truly does."

Trithar smiles, but there's pain in his features. "I'm glad. Elinor deserves happiness – more than anyone I know. I could never have given her that. Never offered her such peace. I'm happy someone else was able to give it to her."

"You really did love her," I say, unable to keep the amazement from my voice.

"Maybe." He shrugs, but a tear from rolls down his cheek at the feigned nonchalance. "Sometimes, we need to let go of the things we love in order to move on with our lives. But I don't think I have to tell you that, do I, Kyla?"

I turn my face away. I hadn't thought much about Shade since the night of his escape. Hadn't let myself think about it. The wound is still too fresh – too raw.

"Does it still hurt? Letting go of mother, I mean?"

"You learn to get over it with time. Time and determination and every other gods-damned thing you can think of to forget what you felt. To forget the dreams you built around that one significant person. Yes . . . it still hurts." He sighs. "I don't think it ever stops hurting."

"I tried looking in on her last night," I say.

Trithar's eyes widen.

"B-but . . ." My power has weakened, and I only caught a glimpse of my mother's face before everything had gone dark. I'd tried for hours to get that glimpse back. Tried until the black void had overtaken me, and I'd finally slithered into unconsciousness for my efforts.

"Would you like to see her?" Trithar asks.

I nod.

He holds out his hand. The moment I grasp it, the power in his body flows into mine and I don't even have to command the darkness before it is there and a shard of flashing color is shooting from its depths in my direction.

The room I'm standing in is cloaked in darkness. Dark flowers. Dark drapes drawn across the windows. Darkly clothed nobles with their heads bowed reverently.

Candles light the entire room, but it does nothing to change the mournful atmosphere..

People are weeping. Sobbing. Wailing.

A casket rests in the center of the room. It is closed, but the words etched into its marble lid are clear and precise:

Asher Rave, Noble warrior and Devoted friend, Rest in Peace.

My lungs constrict.

His funeral is being held in the ballroom of my house.

Standing regally near the casket, Landor accepts the condolences of the guests instead of the bereaved family members.

The Rave family – consisting of Asher's widowed mother, two little brothers, and his baby sister – sit in a corner, weeping quietly and surrounded by extended family. I can tell they aren't ready to accept other people's sorrow on top of their own. They also don't have the money for this kind of funeral. I have no doubt it is my brother's doing.

Behind Landor, stands my mother, looking strong and extremely beautiful, even if she is dressed in black. Somehow, the color suits her. My father is in a wheelchair beside her, the stub of his severed right leg extending a few inches over the rim of the chair. He grasps my mother's hand, and occasionally she glances sidelong at him, a smile on her lips.

Yes, she learned to love Gavin Bone.

Landor wears an eye patch over his right eye. However, even with one eye, he still manages to convey everything he needs to convey without saying a word. And right now, all I sense from his frigid stare is icy, unparalleled rage.

A rumble of whispers catalysts throughout the crowd of attendees.

Celectate Wood and Aspen enter the room. Seeing the savage ruler again after so many months causes that small, weakened part of my power to rumble ominously. If I had known on that day so long ago, that I could have destroyed him with the mere wisp of my abilities, things would have gone differently.

Landor and mother both stiffen at the unexpected arrival, the ice in their gazes becoming twin storms.

Celectate Wood whispers something to Aspen. The royal heir approaches the casket and stops in front of my father. His eyes rest for a brief moment on the place where my father's leg should be before he finally looks him in the face.

"Lord Gavin Bone, I am pleased to see you in good health and wish you the best in your recovery," he says, the arrogant tone of his voice lighting a small, but uncontrolled, flame of anger inside me.

"T-thank you," my father mumbles, eyes darting nervously between Aspen and Celectate Wood in the far corner of the room. I sense the fear

radiating from him – but also something else. A squaring in his shoulders. The touch of confidence in the way he holds his head. The look that passes between him and my mother.

"My father wishes to offer the grieving family members his condolences and, for the loss of their son, who was a knight in his service, he wishes to compensate them generously, so they never need suffer the affliction of poverty, as well as grief." Aspen produces the document that his father slipped into his hand and holds it out to my father – or the man who had been my father.

Don't take it! I want to scream. Don't you dare let that man make a puppet out of you again!

But I know he will take it. He can't do anything else. He is beneath Celectate Wood and beneath his own fear. He always has been, and he always will be. I chose to be ostracized so he could have the chance to strike at Celectate Wood – and he didn't take it.

Lord Bone grasps the document.

My heart sinks and, across the room, Celectate Wood smiles. I want to rake my fingers down his face.

But Gavin Bone turns and hands the document to Landor, without a word. My brother accepts it with a small bow and opens it. His eye scans the words neatly etched onto the fine white paper. He look at Aspen – and rips the paper, slowly, into tiny pieces. He tosses the torn strips on the ground.

"The Bones will protect what is theirs to protect," he says with cold firmness. "Make sure you tell your father that." He tips his chin in Celectate Wood's direction.

Aspen's eyes widen. "My lord . . ." he falters, glancing at Gavin Bone.

"As of this moment," my mother interrupts coolly, "Sir Landor speaks for House Bone."

The air leaves my lungs. My brother . . . is High Lord?

The man I'd called "father" for seventeen years adjusts his position in the condemning wheelchair so he can look up at Aspen, whose face has gone red. Everyone in the room is glancing in their direction. Everyone in the room saw Landor throw Celectate Wood's generous offer to the ground.

"I . . . I don't understand," Aspen stutters.

"Last night, under the witness of Calaisar's priests, my son Landor was officially given the title of High Lord Bone of Ianthar," the former Lord Bone says.

Aspen's shock is equal to mine. Ianthar is the ancient city of the Bone ancestry. It has lain in ruins for nearly forty years near the white diamond mines our family owns. My father – Gavin – always said it would take a leader with great strength and power to return the Bone family to its rightful roots.

The newly initiated High Lord steps forward, a powerful, foreboding force to be reckoned with. "I will be repairing the city so we might return there – along with any Kelban citizens willing to bind themselves to my House in return for land, jobs, and a place to live."

Aspen's mouth moves but no words come out.

If Ianthar is repaired, the city and the surrounding land is capable of holding ten thousand citizens. If all of them are bound to House Bone, my brother can create an army. My brother – and those who call him "lord" – will pose a great threat to Celectate Wood's reign.

And there isn't a damn thing the devil can do about it.

"What do you mean by this, my lord?" Aspen asks, failing to keep anger from his voice. He glares down at my father.

It is my mother who steps between the heir and former High Lord, her expression full of pride and arrogance that causes Aspen's hands to curl into tight fists. "My husband has done what he can for Kelba."

Now it's Landor's turn.

Aspen smirks at my mother. "Need I remind you what happened to your daughter, my lady? Surely you don't wish to tempt fate a second time."

She smiles coldly, the chill in her features spreading throughout the room and appearing on Aspen's face. He is not used to this part of my mother – the "bitch" she kept buried beneath the surface. "Don't flatter yourself. My daughter will avenge herself one day. Tell your father that."

Aspen stares at her, shocked, but quickly delivers her message.

Celectate Wood looks across the room at her, curiously. She stares back at him, shoulders straight and chin uplifted.

He frowns, eyes narrowing, and leaves with Aspen trailing in his wake.

"I can't wait to watch your sister tear him to pieces," Lady Bone snarls.

"What, mother?" Landor turns to look at her from where he'd been speaking with another distraught guest.

"Nothing, son. Nothing."

She smiles.

I smile too, as the vision disappears and I find myself, once again, standing on the dark patio overlooking a vast sea. The Bones will do just fine.

My real father removes his hand from mine. "What did you see?" he asks quietly.

"Fire," I say. "I saw the devil discover that there's other fires he neglected to bank."

Trithar stares at me, confused.

I ignore his confusion and press a hand to my burning forehead. The pain has returned, dragging its claws down the side of my neck. I grit my teeth and fight back against it. The claws recede, but I know they will return.

"Do they hurt?" Trithar asks after a moment of silence. "Your powers, I mean?"

I hesitate, not sure if I want to reveal such a weakness too soon, but perhaps he can help. "Sometimes."

"That's to be expected," he reluctantly admits. "Right now they are only part of your instincts."

Now it's my turn to stare at him in confusion. "My instincts?"

"They attack when you feel attacked. They protect when you want to protect. But when you have formulated control over them, you can attack even if you don't feel threatened. You can protect without the sudden urge to do so. You will have to sharpen them. Hone them. Strengthen the small amount of control you have on them already. But once you find that control *you*, not they, will be the real master of that power. Do you understand what I mean?"

I nod. The idea of having control over my powers, without having to force them to obey, fills me with excitement.

Trithar observes me, silently. "Kyla," he finally says, "before we begin there is something of valid importance that you must know."

"What?"

"No two Imperials have ever shared the same abilities within the bond of offspring. In other words, a father's powerful gifts would not pass to his children. Maybe one of his powers might, but not both of them."

"What are you saying?"

"You have the ability to move objects with the will of your mind. You also have the gift of telepathic entrance – the ability to see things happening in another place at the present moment. I have both of those gifts, as well. You inherited them from me. But I inherited them from ancestors hundreds of years back."

I regard him with wary eyes. "And what does that mean?"

"It makes you a very special – very different – heir, Kyla. In time, we might come to know what it will mean for this empire." He leans on the railing. "Now, we have so much to do and very little time to do it in. Every heir, once they've passed their fifteenth year, is required to make a demonstration of their powers and receive their full title. You are born my heir, Kyla, but you must participate in an acceptance ceremony in order to prove to Ebonia that you are my heir and capable of ruling the empire. When I spoke to the Darthans about your existence, they were intent on disregarding you as an heir because you are well beyond the age of fifteen. But I convinced them to allow you an acceptance ceremony when you turn eighteen years old."

"But I turn eighteen in three months!" Three months to harness control of my powers. Three months to adopt my second form. Three months before I must prove to Ebonia that I am fit to rule it.

"You will need training. Trish shall be your mentor. She will train you every day, for as long as it takes, until your gifts are perfected and you no longer need the training. It will take time. Patience. Dedication. But you're my daughter, Kyla," he says, "and you will succeed."

I let him touch the brand on my shoulder – the symbol that says I am alone and will never have a place in this world. It has become part of me. A part of me I will us to show the world that they are wrong about outcasts like myself.

"Now," Trithar says, releasing a slow, steady breath, "we must prepare you to meet them."

"Them?"

"Your brothers," he says, "the former heirs of Ebonia."

Epilogue

One day I'm going to return to that land of shadow and fog.
One day I'm going to rip their ethereal bodies to shreds and
smile as I watch them float away into the darkening sky.
One day I'm going to face the girl I loved.
The girl who deceived me.
The girl who I wanted to be the next chapter of my life – and
I'm going to have a choice.
When that day comes, I will do what should be done.
I will slaughter the hell-cursed demons.
I will destroy their gods-damned land.
And I will look at that girl – and I will have to kill her.

Acknowledgements Page

I dreamed for years about reaching this moment – having my book in print and being blessed to write an acknowledgements page to all the people in my life who made that dream a living breathing reality! There are so many people who took time, effort, and love out of their own busy lives to help me achieve this. I hope I can convey my heartfelt appreciation to everyone with mere words!

Laura Jaycox: best friend, reading buddy, first reader. You were there with me from the very beginning. You were the first person to read Ostracized and the first person to make me believe it could be a success. On the bad days, when I felt unimaginative or had a deadly case of writer's block, you would endlessly brainstorm with me until something clicked. You've been there for me when I needed a fresh set of eyes or a confidence boost. Ostracized was possible because of you! You're such a confident, smart, impressive woman who encourages me everyday to keep going and never give up no matter how hard it is. Thank you for being with me through thick and thin, girl!

To my little sister, Katie: You were my first real fan. My adventurous sidekick. My eager listener when I had a new story or book idea. From the very beginning, you were always there for me when I had ideas and needed to get them out of my system. You never allowed me to stop writing because you always needed a new story. I love you little sis and I'm so proud of the badass you've become!

To my beta readers: Nakia Steel, Summer Salmon, Bethany Doe, David Romanko, Laura Jaycox, Lily Reid, Caitlin Anderson, and my beloved sister, Katie. Words can not begin to express my appreciation for all the hard work and time you put into making my book a true masterpiece. Your honest feedback and suggestions shaped a bare manuscript into a beautiful finished edition! Thank you so much!

Thank you Paramita Bhattacharjee: you brought Ostracized to life by designing a cover that really captured the essence of this empowering tale and its character. I could not be happier with the results. Working with you was amazing. Your awesomeness made this important part of the process a complete breeze!

Thank you to the many friends and family whose presence in my life provided the ultimate source of material for quick-witted banter and embarrassing situations. I'm so grateful to have you all in my life and you've inspired me in ways you didn't even know.

To my seven amazing siblings: I give you full credit for my ability to capture relatable dialogue and irritating characters (just kidding, not all of them). I love you all so much and couldn't be more grateful for all the inspiration you gave to me, unawares.

To my parents: Your support, love, and unwavering faith in my abilities never let me give up hope. Even at a young age, you told me I had a gift and my talents would one day be recognized. You told me I could do anything I set my mind to. I owe you for not just the writer I've become – but the woman as well. I love you both so much! Thank you for always believing in me and pushing me to stand up, no matter how many times I got knocked down!

And finally, to all my readers, this story was written for you. To empower you. To give you hope. To inspire you. No matter how alone you feel or how society treats you, you can stand up and fight! You can keep going! You are only truly beaten if you allow yourself to feel that way! Do not allow fear to cloud your judgement. Do not allow fear to make your choices. I love you all! I can't wait to give you more empowering adventures.

OLIVIA MAJORS

has been an avid writer since she was four years old and devoted the entirety of her childhood and teen years into turning that skill into a career.

Olivia keeps herself busy running a successful website and YouTube channel devoted to inspiring the youth and young writers of the twenty-first century alike.

When she cannot be found writing or running her business, Olivia is exploring nature, kickboxing, drinking coffee, and working full-time as an Account & Logistics Coordinator.

Olivia currently resides in Missouri.

Website: www.oliviamajors.com

YouTube Channel: Olivia Majors

Made in the USA
Monee, IL
17 December 2023

49543627R00385